BOOKS BY ERNEST HEMINGWAY

THE HEMINGWAY READER (*Selected, with a Foreword and twelve brief prefaces, by Charles Poore*)

THE OLD MAN AND THE SEA
ACROSS THE RIVER AND INTO THE TREES
FOR WHOM THE BELL TOLLS
THE FIFTH COLUMN AND THE FIRST FORTY-NINE STORIES
TO HAVE AND HAVE NOT
GREEN HILLS OF AFRICA
WINNER TAKE NOTHING
DEATH IN THE AFTERNOON
A FAREWELL TO ARMS
MEN WITHOUT WOMEN
THE SUN ALSO RISES
THE TORRENTS OF SPRING
IN OUR TIME

CHARLES SCRIBNER'S SONS

THE HEMINGWAY READER

Ernest Hemingway

THE
HEMINGWAY
READER

SELECTED

with a Foreword and twelve Brief Prefaces

by CHARLES POORE

CHARLES SCRIBNER'S SONS

NEW YORK 1953

CONTENTS

STORIES

From ACROSS THE RIVER AND INTO THE TREES

From THE OLD MAN AND THE SEA

THE HEMINGWAY READER

FOREWORD
by Charles Poore

THE HEMINGWAY READER

FOREWORD

BY CHARLES POORE

THIS book is planned for the pleasures and rewards of reading. The selections are arranged chronologically. They were chosen mainly to give variety and balance. Other hands, I am aware, would make other choices; no doubt they duly will. The field of choice is as wide as the world the men and women who live in these stories wander over, in peace and in war.

There is the full text of a novel that set the flags for a generation, *The Sun Also Rises*, and a freely sketched satire on the eternal pomposities of unconventionality, *The Torrents of Spring*. There are complete episodes from five other novels in Hemingway's chronicle of modern chivalry: *A Farewell to Arms, To Have and Have Not, For Whom the Bell Tolls, Across the River and Into the Trees,* and *The Old Man and the Sea*. There are chapters on Spain and the art of the torero, "the only art in which the artist is in danger of death and in which the degree of brilliance in the performance is left to the fighter's honor," from *Death in the Afternoon*, and the wonderful dialogue on American writing from *Green Hills of Africa*. There are eleven short stories. These, alone, would be worth a book.

The stories and the novels together represent a body of work that has changed the course of storytelling and given new cadences to the language. They are not gathered here, though, to illustrate academic principles or to pepper elegies. They are alive, a part of experience that tells us more vividly than any casual actuality ever can, where men and women have been, and what they have done and left undone in this brightest and bloodiest of centuries.

Excellence is never as recent as its discovery. The elements of what we admire in a late story, toward the end of this book, are unmistakably present in an early one. It is the field of operations that broadens, from Michigan to the Gulf Stream, from Spain and Paris to the Hurtgen Forest, from Tanganyika to the Venetian Plain; it is the perception that deepens as all that is not essential is burned away to make a story like *The Old Man and the Sea*.

The clarity, the intensity, the humor, valor, grace and love of life in an age that happens through no particular fault of Hemingway to be much concerned with death, were always there. The rough passages of our day's hallowed and unhallowed forages, pilgrimages and crusades are rendered as scrupulously as the smooth ones along the way. These are qualities that have given him his place as the outstanding storyteller, the finest stylist, of his time.

It is idle to observe that he has written no three-generation dynastic family novels, no romances in which Napoleon wins the Civil War and marries Mary Queen of Scots. We have many eminently available novelists for those occasions; we can depend on other authors to create for us private counties and principalities of their own devising. The measure of Hemingway's stature is that he shows us what he has seen of the world as it is, with its gallantry and havoc, its dreams of fair women and hopes of peace.

The age of Hemingway is as shaken and open to adventure as the end of the Middle Ages and the Renaissance. We are all Tudors now, whether we like it very much or not. Yet these pages also remind us that we always have marked Napoleonic characters around in hot, close pursuit of destiny; wars civil and uncivil, and heroines as appealing as the Scottish Queen. He might have written his own chronicle of chivalry in the manner he used when he composed the inscription for a book of stories, *Winner Take Nothing*:

> "Unlike all other forms of lutte or combat the conditions are that the winner shall take nothing; neither his ease, nor his pleasure, nor any notions of glory; nor, if he win far enough, shall there be any reward within himself."

Instead, he created his own prose for a new time.

It is for him, I imagine, a process without ending. After service in the first World War on the Italian Front where he was severely wounded before he was 19 and won the Medaglia d'Argento al Valore Militare and three Croces al Merito di Guerra, he came back to America and then went abroad as a correspondent for Canadian and American papers, serving in Europe and the Middle East. "I was trying to write then," he said in *Death in the Afternoon*, "and I found the greatest difficulty, aside from knowing truly what you really felt, rather than what you were supposed to feel . . . was to put down what really happened in action; what the actual things were which produced the emotion that you experienced. . . . The real thing, the sequence of motion and fact which made the emotion and which would be as valid in a year or in ten years or, with luck and if you stated it purely enough, always, was beyond me and I was working very hard to try to get it."

Then there were the years when none would pay money to publish stories that now are in a hundred anthologies, the times he remembered in *Green Hills of Africa*, living in Paris: "in Notre Dame des Champs in the courtyard with the sawmill (*and the sudden whine of the saw, the smell of sawdust and the chestnut tree over the roof with a mad woman downstairs*) and the year worrying about money (*all of the stories back in the mail that came in through a slit in the sawmill door, with notes of rejection that would never call them stories, but always anecdotes, sketches, contes, etc. They did not want them, and we lived on poireaux and drank cahors and water*) and how fine the fountains were at the Place de L'Observatoire (*water sheen rippling on the bronze of horses' manes, bronze breasts and shoulders, green under thin-flowing water*) and when they put up the bust of Flaubert in the Luxembourg on the short cut through the gardens on the way to the rue Soufflot (*one that we believed in, loved without criticism, heavy now in stone as an idol should be*)."

The years of fame have not banked the fire. He will say, I think, "Aún aprendo," like Goya, "I'm still learning," in his eighties.

Ford Madox Ford pointed out in an introduction to *A Farewell to Arms* that "the aim—the achievement—of the great prose writer is to use words so that they shall seem new and alive because of their juxtaposition with other words. This gift Hemingway has supremely. . . . You cannot throw yourself into a frame of mind and just write and get that effect. Your mind has to choose each word and your ear has to test it until by long disciplining of mind and ear you can no longer go wrong. That disciplining through which you must put yourself is all the more difficult in that it must be gone through in solitude. You cannot watch the man next to you in the ranks smartly manipulating his side-arms nor do you hear any word of command by which to time yourself. On the other hand a writer holds a reader by his temperament. That is his true 'gift'—what he receives from whoever sends him into the world. It arises from how you look at things. If you look at and render things so that they appear new to the reader you will hold his attention. If what you give him appears familiar or half familiar his attention will wander."

It was Ford who defined the style many have bumbled through a volume trying to define when he said: "Hemingway's words strike you, each one, as if they were pebbles fetched fresh from a brook. They live and shine, each in its place. So one of his pages has the effect of a brook-bottom into which you look down through the flowing water. The words form a tessellation, each in order beside the other." That judgment, made early in Hemingway's career, sets Ford apart from those who cherish the simple notion that the style is all a matter of simple sentences. The simplicity is there—but few things are more complex than Hemingway's simplicity. It is about as simple as a Bach fugue or a Cézanne landscape and it is as clearly, cleanly present in this book's first story, the classic "Big Two-Hearted River" ("the river shallow ahead entering the woods, curving into the woods, shallows, light glittering, big water-smooth rocks, cedars along the bank and white birches") as it is in the 424-words-long sentence about all our yesterdays, todays and tomorrows in *Green Hills of Africa*.

It is in *Across the River and Into the Trees*, a novel of man's experience that can best be experienced by those who have known girls as lovely as Renata and worn Cantwell's armor, where dusk and dawn seem to happen on the page, somehow, as he thinks, "I could be part of the ground where the children play in the evenings, and in the mornings, maybe, they would still be training jumping horses and their hoofs would make the thudding on the turf, and trout would rise in the pool when there was a hatch of fly." And in the memory of the West in "The Snows of Kilimanjaro," ". . . the ranch and the silvered gray of the sage brush, the quick, clear water in the irrigation ditches, and the heavy green of the alfalfa. The trail went up into the hills and the cattle in the summer were shy as deer. The bawling and the steady noise and slow moving mass raising a dust as you brought them down in the fall. And behind the mountains, the clear sharpness of the peak in the evening light and, riding down along the trail in the moonlight, bright across the valley."

The observation is always miraculously precise, as in *The Sun Also Rises*, where Jake, crossing the Seine, notices "a string of barges being towed empty down the current, riding high, the bargemen at the sweeps as they came toward the bridge"; Pilar, in *For Whom the Bell Tolls* remembering Finito, "as he furled the heavy flannel cloth around the stick; the flannel hanging blood-heavy from the passes where it had swept over the bull's head and shoulders and the wet streaming shine of his withers and on down and over his back as the bull raised into the air and the banderillas clattered." That is writing, isn't it?—

the "sequence of motion and fact which made the emotion," as it is in the unforgettable opening sentence of "The Light of the World": "When he saw us come in the door the bartender looked up and then reached over and put the glass covers on the two free-lunch bowls."

I do not hold with those who are comparing Chaucer favorably to Hemingway these days. Nor do I think it is wise to expend spirit in trying to move him farther away from the Browning Automatic Rifle, closer to the circle of Robert Browning. One world at a time, please. There is still reason to wish that he had begun *The Sun Also Rises* at Chapter III, that he had left stuff about Radiguet and his band out of *Death in the Afternoon,* and that Colonel Cantwell were less touched with vainglory. But I am most certain that he will stand with Yeats and Joyce as one of the three principal men of letters of our time. And since clocks and calendars move forward, not backward, from here on out he may be the strongest influence in literature that this age will give to posterity.

The readers of this era have passed many worthy authors by to choose in Hemingway's books their emblems. He gives us grace and fortitude to face the Toynbee-paced calamities of modern history and a measure of laughter to deal with follies and pomposities. His standards of writing are severe and arduous. They are serious. But they specifically exclude solemnity, as he has said in a passage from *Death in the Afternoon* that anybody interested in writing should read once a year:

"Prose is architecture, not interior decoration, and the Baroque is over. For a writer to put his own intellectual musings, which he might sell for a low price as essays, into the mouths of artificially constructed characters which are more remunerative when issued as people in a novel is good economics, perhaps, but does not make literature. People in a novel, not skillfully constructed *characters,* must be projected from the writer's assimilated experience, from his knowledge, from his head, from his heart and from all there is of him. If he ever has luck as well as seriousness and gets them out entire they will have more than one dimension and they will last a long time. A good writer should know as near everything as possible. Naturally he will not. A great enough writer seems to be born with knowledge. But he really is not; he has only been born with the ability to learn in a quicker ratio to the passage of time than other men and without conscious application, and with an intelligence to accept or reject what is already presented as knowledge. There are some things which cannot be learned quickly and time, which is all we have, must be paid heavily for their acquiring. They are the very simplest things and because it takes a man's life to know them the little new that each man gets from life is very costly and the only heritage he has to leave. Every novel which is truly written contributes to the total of knowledge which is there at the disposal of the next writer who comes, but the next writer must pay, always, a certain nominal percentage in experience to be able to understand and assimilate what is available as his birthright and what he must, in turn, take his departure from. If a writer of prose knows enough about what he is writing about he may omit things that he knows and the reader, if the writer is writing truly enough, will have a feeling of those things as strongly as though the writer had stated them. The dignity of movement of an iceberg is due to only one-eighth of it being above water. A writer who omits things because he does not know them only makes hollow places in his writing. A writer who appreciates the seriousness of writing so little that he is anxious to make people see he is formally educated, cultured or well-bred is merely a popinjay. And this too remember; a serious writer is not to be confounded with a solemn writer. A serious writer may be a hawk or a buzzard or even a popinjay, but a solemn writer is always a bloody owl."

He is more at home in the world beyond American borders than any writer of his stature since Henry James and Stephen Crane, and he has given us aspects of that world they could not have known as contemporaries, for Crane died young and James would scarcely be the man to help Hemingway move into Rambouillet. Nor go with him on the 4th Division's run north from Paris that led to St. Quentin and Le Cateau, crossed the Ardennes, and broke the Siegfried Line in the Schnee Eifel. In the second World War he was called a war correspondent by masterly understatement. In actual fact, his activities had a somewhat longer trajectory. He began amphibious action by hunting German submarines in the Caribbean when their sinkings of our oil tankers were making those waters a sea of fire. Then he went on to fly combat missions with the Royal Air Force. Officers and enlisted men of the 4th Infantry Division, those who survived out of the more than 24,000 casualties that Division suffered, speak of him with affection and remember how he tried to be of service to that Division in any way that he was able to, in more than one hundred days of combat.

He had already seen more of war, in Italy and Spain, than some of the leading novelists of the second World War would ever see. His books were records—and prophecies. A rout, a long march in the dark

backwash of defeat, is one of the tragic commonplaces of our era. There
have been many, all over the world since Caporetto. It is not easy to
find on ordinary maps. In *A Farewell to Arms* Lieutenant Henry had
first seen it as "a little white town with a campanile in a valley. It was
a clean little town and there was a fine fountain in the square." But
the world knows Caporetto better than many more famous battles now
because it remembers Lieutenant Henry and the retreat to which it
gave the name, and the way "the whole country was moving, as well
as the army," and the battle police, the questioners who "had that
beautiful detachment and devotion to stern justice of men who are
dealing in death without being in any danger of it."

In Hemingway's books the dialogue, the famous dialogue, varies
more subtly than any hasty reading shows. The cadences change not
only from speaker to speaker, but also in the way the same person will
discuss the same subject with different people. Lieutenant Henry discussing matters of love and religion with Rinaldi, the young Italian
Army doctor he has served with for two years so that they understand
each other ribaldly and completely, changes when he speaks to Count
Greffi, the old diplomat with the beautiful manners who had been a
contemporary of Metternich and was living to be one hundred years old.

"All my life I encounter sacred subjects," Rinaldi says, "but very few
with you." And Lieutenant Henry challenges: "I can say this about
your mother and that about your sister?" They both laugh as Rinaldi
says swiftly: "And that about *your sister*." It gets rough. When
Lieutenant Henry is talking to Count Greffi, though, the difference is
like the difference between the captured enemy cognac Rinaldi pours
into what he calls "your old toothbrushing glass" and the cold dry
champagne Count Greffi serves in stemmed crystal.

Lieutenant Henry has asked the Count whether he would like to
live after death, and Count Greffi says: "This life is very pleasant. I
would like to live forever." He smiles. "I very nearly have." Count
Greffi asks Lieutenant Henry to pray for him, if he ever becomes
devout; "I am asking several of my friends to do that. I had expected
to become devout but it has not come." Like Jake Barnes and others
in Hemingway's books, Lieutenant Henry is more deeply concerned
with matters of faith than the glib salvationists who have never prayed
in true humility in the Duomo or at Santiago de Compostella. He tells
the Count that his own devotion comes and goes. "I might become
very devout. Anyway, I will pray for you." And the Count says: "Then
too you are in love. Do not forget that is a religious feeling."

Catherine gives Lieutenant Henry the faith of love, as Renata brings

the faith of love to Cantwell in *Across the River and Into the Trees.*
It is Catherine he is thinking of in a passage from *A Farewell to
Arms* that became a part of the belief of a generation: "If people bring
so much courage to this world the world has to kill them to break
them, so of course it kills them. The world breaks every one and afterward many are strong at the broken places. But those that will not
break it kills. It kills the very good and the very gentle and the very
brave impartially. If you are none of these you can be sure it will kill
you too but there will be no special hurry."

When Hemingway was writing it, he said, "the fact the book
was a tragic one did not make me unhappy since I believed that life
was a tragedy and knew it could only have one end. But finding you
were able to make something up; to create truly enough so that it
made you happy to read it; and to do this every day you worked was
something that gave a greater pleasure than any I had ever known.
Beside it nothing else mattered."

The tragic sense of life is always present in the minds of thinking
men. It is a part of existence to Harry Morgan in *To Have and Have
Not,* a novel that answered stingingly those who had said Hemingway
was not enough concerned with the state of his own country. It is in
"The Short Happy Life of Francis Macomber" and "The Snows of
Kilimanjaro" and "A Clean, Well-Lighted Place" and "Old Man at
the Bridge" and "The Capital of the World," the story of the boy who
"died, as the Spanish phrase has it, full of illusions. He had not had
time in his life to lose any of them, nor even, at the end, to complete
an act of contrition."

Yet even in the face of death the pleasures of life are remembered.
El Sordo, dying on the hill in *For Whom the Bell Tolls,* hates the idea
of death but has no fear of it: "But living was a field of grain blowing
in the wind on the side of a hill. Living was a hawk in the sky. Living
was an earthen jar of water in the dust of the threshing with the
grain flailed out and the chaff blowing. Living was a horse between
your legs and a carbine under one leg and a hill and a valley and a
stream with trees along it and the far side of the valley and the hills
beyond."

There are two inscriptions on the flyleaf of *The Sun Also Rises.*
One, naming the lost generation, ascribed to Gertrude Stein, was mind-
lessly taken up by many strange people who somehow seemed to think
it forgave them their trespasses forever. The other, the longer one, is
taken from the Book of Ecclesiastes, the words of the Preacher, the

Son of David, King of Jerusalem, who gave his heart "to seek and
search out by wisdom concerning all things that are done under
heaven," and it may well have led a few readers back to read Ecclesiastes on vanity and responsibilities. A part of the iceberg-depth of the
novel that on the surface concerns Lady Brett Ashley, who at 34 is a
little old for her generation, is to be found in her despairing efforts to
share Barnes' faith. She wants to go to church when he does. Once he
says, "I'm pretty religious," and she asks him not to start proselyting,
and at the end Jake reminds her that "Some people have God. Quite a
lot." These are not points that were emphasized when the book was
published in the Nineteen Twenties, though they may be a part of the
reason why the book is still read, just as Jake prays for the bullfighters
in the cathedral and the bullfighters pray before they go into the ring.

The dialogues give the story its incomparable vitality. A thousand
writers have tried to imitate the conversations between Jake and Bill
Gorton, Brett, Mike (who upon being offered a chance to go into the
bullring grandly said: "It wouldn't be fair to my creditors"), and
Robert, in a thousand books.

At one place Hemingway now seems to have an uncanny air of
having parodied ahead of time what vicarious moralists would say for
years about his work. "You know what's the trouble with you?" the
slightly sauced Gorton happily asks that reasonably diligent correspondent, Jake. "You're an expatriate. One of the worst type. Haven't
you heard that? Nobody that ever left their own country ever wrote
anything worth printing. . . . You've lost touch with the soil. You
get precious. Fake European standards have ruined you. You drink
yourself to death. You become obsessed by sex. You spend all your time
talking, not working. You are an expatriate, see? You hang around
cafés." "It sounds like a swell life," Jake suggests. "When do I work?"

A few decades later, the uproars over prolonged residence abroad
that once made livid the little reviews and large ones had grown hazy.
Several million Americans had since then served their years of expatriation in South Pacific former-paradises and the European Theater of
Operations, U.S. Army. The effect on the styles of those who wrote was
the least of their concerns, but they were often in very close touch with
the soil.

The Torrents of Spring, which mentions expatriation, Mencken,
rustic fertility rites and other institutions, is a satire of many devices.
It has a plot of awsome, Benchleyan complexity. The author obviously
can't quite follow it, but others may try. At one time I thought it might

be meant as an antidote to Franz Kafka's fatal allegories. Many savants have noticed that it holds in no reverence Sherwood Anderson's dairy tales; some have charged that Hemingway was trifling with Gertrude Stein's massive affections. The bedeviled existence of Scripps O'Neil is shrewdly paralleled by the bewildering fate of Yogi Johnson. Academicians who conduct scholarly safaris through Hemingway's subconscious will find a challenge here. In one place we are told that O'Neil's father was a great composer, his mother an Italian lady from Northern Italy. In another place we learn that his father was a Civil War general and that Sherman himself put the match to his mansion. Now here is the question for psychoanalytical exegetes to ponder: *What part of Northern Italy did O'Neil's mother come from?* For if it can be proved that she came from one region she may be significantly related to one aspect of the Hemingway canon; if she came from another, she may even be the great-aunt of the post-war Milanese rich in *Across the River and Into the Trees.* Who knows? Who cares?

The chair of Hemingway studies will have many far more irrelevant matters brought before it in the years ahead, and some that only seem irrelevant to those they do not interest. Somewhere, right now, I hope, a student inspired by the wonderful references to Mr. DiMaggio in *The Old Man and the Sea,* is tracing other ballplayers in other stories, such as Frankie Fritsch in *The Sun Also Rises* and Heinie Zimmerman in "The Three-Day Blow." There is an interesting study to be made of the amazingly wide range of painters mentioned throughout Hemingway's works, and I have entertained the idea that Colonel Cantwell and the Countess Renata might be considered as an allegory of Goya and the Duchess of Alba, only slightly deterred by Bernard Berenson, speaking of another book in the chronicle of chivalry.

"Hemingway's *The Old Man and the Sea,*" Berenson said, "is an idyll of the sea as sea, as un-Byronic and un-Melvillian as Homer himself, and communicated in a prose as calm and compelling as Homer's verse. No real artist symbolizes or allegorizes—and Hemingway is a real artist—but every real work of art exhales symbols and allegories."

No part of Hemingway's work, in Donne's words that stand at the beginning of *For Whom the Bell Tolls,* is only an island, entire in itself; every part is a piece of a continent, a part of a main, created in a new prose for a new world.

Alone among so many of his earliest and best contemporaries, Hemingway has never needed a revival.

from IN OUR TIME

BIG TWO-HEARTED RIVER

"BIG TWO-HEARTED RIVER" is a story about a boy who has come back from the war. The war is never mentioned. That is one of the things that give it the undertones and overtones of a timeless experience. Young men who fought at Waterloo or Gettysburg or on any D-Day have thought of coming back some day to old fishing grounds and tranquility remembered. They would understand how he savors everything, the unimportant details now tremendously important, the feeling of shadowed peace as he returns to a country that has changed in some ways yet is more true to what survived in hope than any journey with maps. He has changed as much as the country.

The story was written in Paris, probably in 1924. "I can't tell you when, exactly," Hemingway once said, "but it was before The Sun Also Rises, when we lived at Notre-Dame des Champs over the sawmill. I used to write it there and at the Closerie des Lilas mornings and at another cafe in the Place St-Michel where I didn't know anybody and would go to work." Information like that damages a theory he was an expatriate who collected franc-numbered saucers and held the scenes of his own country in disdain while worthier scriveners were building tall, deeply rooted epics in Iowa.

An anthology might be defined for our day as a volume by many hands that contains a story by Ernest Hemingway. "Big Two-Hearted River" may be one of the stories that came back through the slit in the sawmill door, before it appeared in In Our Time in 1925. It has been reprinted as often as any. There are always new things in it to be discovered.

C. P.

BIG TWO-HEARTED RIVER

I

THE train went on up the track out of sight, around one of the hills of burnt timber. Nick sat down on the bundle of canvas and bedding the baggage man had pitched out of the door of the baggage car. There was no town, nothing but the rails and the burned-over country. The thirteen saloons that had lined the one street of Seney had not left a trace. The foundations of the Mansion House hotel stuck up above the ground. The stone was chipped and split by the fire. It was all that was left of the town of Seney. Even the surface had been burned off the ground.

Nick looked at the burned-over stretch of hillside, where he had expected to find the scattered houses of the town and then walked down the railroad track to the bridge over the river. The river was there. It swirled against the log spiles of the bridge. Nick looked down into the clear, brown water, colored from the pebbly bottom, and watched the trout keeping themselves steady in the current with wavering fins. As he watched them they changed their positions by quick angles, only to hold steady in the fast water again. Nick watched them a long time.

He watched them holding themselves with their noses into the current, many trout in deep, fast moving water, slightly distorted as he watched far down through the glassy convex surface of the pool, its surface pushing and swelling smooth against the resistance of the log-driven piles of the bridge. At the bottom of the pool were the big trout. Nick did not see them at first. Then he saw them at the bottom of the pool, big trout looking to hold themselves on the gravel bottom in a varying mist of gravel and sand, raised in spurts by the current.

Nick looked down into the pool from the bridge. It was a hot day. A kingfisher flew up the stream. It was a long time since Nick had looked into a stream and seen trout. They were very satisfactory. As the shadow of the kingfisher moved up the stream, a big trout shot upstream in a long angle, only his shadow marking the angle, then lost his shadow as he came through the surface of the water, caught the sun, and then, as he went back into the stream under the surface, his shadow seemed to float down the stream with the current, unresisting, to his post under the bridge where he tightened facing up into the current.

Nick's heart tightened as the trout moved. He felt all the old feeling.

He turned and looked down the stream. It stretched away, pebbly-bottomed with shallows and big boulders and a deep pool as it curved away around the foot of a bluff.

Nick walked back up the ties to where his pack lay in the cinders beside the railway track. He was happy. He adjusted the pack harness around the bundle, pulling straps tight, slung the pack on his back, got his arms through the shoulder straps and took some of the pull off his shoulders by leaning his forehead against the wide band of the tump-line. Still, it was too heavy. It was much too heavy. He had his leather rod-case in his hand and leaning forward to keep the weight of the pack high on his shoulders he walked along the road that paralleled the railway track, leaving the burned town behind in the heat, and then turned off around a hill with a high, fire-scarred hill on either side onto a road that went back into the country. He walked along the road feeling the ache from the pull of the heavy pack. The road climbed steadily. It was hard work walking up-hill. His muscles ached and the day was hot, but Nick felt happy. He felt he had left everything behind, the need for thinking, the need to write, other needs. It was all back of him.

From the time he had gotten down off the train and the baggage man had thrown his pack out of the open car door things had been different. Seney was burned, the country was burned over and changed, but it did not matter. It could not all be burned. He knew that. He hiked along the road, sweating in the sun, climbing to cross the range of hills that separated the railway from the pine plains.

The road ran on, dipping occasionally, but always climbing. Nick went on up. Finally the road after going parallel to the burnt hillside reached the top. Nick leaned back against a stump and slipped out of the pack harness. Ahead of him, as far as he could see, was the pine plain. The burned country stopped off at the left with the range of hills. On ahead islands of dark pine trees rose out of the plain. Far off to the left was the line of the river. Nick followed it with his eye and caught glints of the water in the sun.

There was nothing but the pine ahead of him, until the far blue hills that marked the Lake Superior height of land. He could hardly see them, faint and far away in the heat-light over the plain. If he looked too steadily they were gone. But if he only half-looked they were there, the far-off hills of the height of land.

Nick sat down against the charred stump and smoked a cigarette. His pack balanced on the top of the stump, harness holding ready, a hollow molded in it from his back. Nick sat smoking, looking out over the country. He did not need to get his map out. He knew where he was from the position of the river.

As he smoked, his legs stretched out in front of him, he noticed a grasshopper walk along the ground and up onto his woolen sock. The grasshopper was black. As he had walked along the road, climbing, he had started many grasshoppers from the dust. They were all black. They were not the big grasshoppers with yellow and black or red and black wings whirring out from their black wing sheathing as they fly up. These were just ordinary hoppers, but all a sooty black in color. Nick had wondered about them as he walked, without really thinking about them. Now, as he watched the black hopper that was nibbling at the wool of his sock with its fourway lip, he realized that they had all turned black from living in the burned-over land. He realized that the fire must have come the year before, but the grasshoppers were all black now. He wondered how long they would stay that way.

Carefully he reached his hand down and took hold of the hopper by the wings. He turned him up, all his legs walking in the air, and looked at his jointed belly. Yes, it was black too, iridescent where the back and head were dusty.

"Go on, hopper," Nick said, speaking out loud for the first time. "Fly away somewhere."

He tossed the grasshopper up into the air and watched him sail away to a charcoal stump across the road.

Nick stood up. He leaned his back against the weight of his pack where it rested upright on the stump and got his arms through the shoulder straps. He stood with the pack on his back on the brow of the hill looking out across the country, toward the distant river and then struck down the hillside away from the road. Underfoot the ground was good walking. Two hundred yards down the hillside the fire line stopped. Then it was sweet fern, growing ankle high, to walk through, and clumps of jack pines; a long undulating country with frequent rises and descents, sandy underfoot and the country alive again.

Nick kept his direction by the sun. He knew where he wanted to strike the river and he kept on through the pine plain, mounting small rises to see other rises ahead of him and sometimes from the top of a rise a great solid island of pines off to his right or his left. He broke off some sprigs of the heathery sweet fern, and put them under his pack straps. The chafing crushed it and he smelled it as he walked.

He was tired and very hot, walking across the uneven, shadeless pine plain. At any time he knew he could strike the river by turning off to his left. It could not be more than a mile away. But he kept on toward the north to hit the river as far upstream as he could go in one day's walking.

For some time as he walked Nick had been in sight of one of the big islands of pine standing out above the rolling high ground he was crossing. He dipped down and then as he came slowly up to the crest of the bridge he turned and made toward the pine trees.

There was no underbrush in the island of pine trees. The trunks of the trees went straight up or slanted toward each other. The trunks were straight and brown without branches. The branches were high above. Some interlocked to make a solid shadow on the brown forest floor. Around the grove of trees was a bare space. It was brown and soft underfoot as Nick walked on it. This was the over-lapping of the pine needle floor, extending out beyond the width of the high branches. The trees had grown tall and the branches moved high, leaving in the sun this bare space they had once covered with shadow. Sharp at the edge of this extension of the forest floor commenced the sweet fern.

Nick slipped off his pack and lay down in the shade. He lay on his back and looked up into the pine trees. His neck and back and the small of his back rested as he stretched. The earth felt good against his back. He looked up at the sky, through the branches, and then shut his eyes. He opened them and looked up again. There was a wind high up in the branches. He shut his eyes again and went to sleep.

Nick woke stiff and cramped. The sun was nearly down. His pack was heavy and the straps painful as he lifted it on. He leaned over with the pack on and picked up the leather rod-case and started out from the pine trees across the sweet fern swale, toward the river. He knew it could not be more than a mile.

He came down a hillside covered with stumps into a meadow. At the edge of the meadow flowed the river. Nick was glad to get to the river. He walked upstream through the meadow. His trousers were soaked with the dew as he walked. After the hot day, the dew had come quickly and heavily. The river made no sound. It was too fast and smooth. At the edge of the meadow, before he mounted to a piece of high ground to make camp, Nick looked down the river at the trout rising. They were rising to insects come from the swamp on the other side of the stream when the sun went down. The trout jumped out of water to take them. While Nick walked through the little stretch of meadow along-side the stream, trout had jumped high out of water. Now as he looked down the river, the insects must be settling on the surface, for the trout were feeding steadily all down the stream. As far down the long stretch as he could see, the trout were rising, making circles all down the surface of the water, as though it were starting to rain.

The ground rose, wooded and sandy, to overlook the meadow, the stretch of river and the swamp. Nick dropped his pack and rod-case and looked for a level piece of ground. He was very hungry and he wanted to make his camp before he cooked. Between two jack pines, the ground was quite level. He took the ax out of the pack and chopped out two projecting roots. That leveled a piece of ground large enough to sleep on. He smoothed out the sandy soil with his hand and pulled all the sweet fern bushes by their roots. His hands smelled good from the sweet fern. He smoothed the uprooted earth. He did not want anything making lumps under the blankets. When he had the ground smooth, he spread his three blankets. One he folded double, next to the ground. The other two he spread on top.

With the ax he slit off a bright slab of pine from one of the stumps and split it into pegs for the tent. He wanted them long and solid to hold in the ground. With the tent unpacked and spread on the ground, the pack, leaning against a jackpine, looked much smaller. Nick tied the rope that served the tent for a ridge-pole to the trunk of one of the pine trees and pulled the tent up off the ground with the other end of the rope and tied it to the other pine. The tent hung on the rope like a canvas blanket on a clothesline. Nick poked a pole he had cut up under the back peak of the canvas and then made it a tent by pegging out the sides. He pegged the sides out taut and drove the pegs deep, hitting them down into the ground with the flat of the ax until the rope loops were buried and the canvas was drum tight.

Across the open mouth of the tent Nick fixed cheesecloth to keep out mosquitoes. He crawled inside under the mosquito bar with various things from the pack to put at the head of the bed under the slant of the canvas. Inside the tent the light came through the brown canvas. It smelled pleasantly of canvas. Already there was something mysterious and homelike. Nick was happy as he crawled inside the tent. He had not been unhappy all day.

This was different though. Now things were done. There had been this to do. Now it was done. It had been a hard trip. He was very tired. That was done. He had made his camp. He was settled. Nothing could touch him. It was a good place to camp. He was there, in the good place. He was in his home where he had made it. Now he was hungry.

He came out, crawling under the cheesecloth. It was quite dark outside. It was lighter in the tent.

Nick went over to the pack and found, with his fingers, a long nail in a paper sack of nails, in the bottom of the pack. He drove it into the pine tree, holding it close and hitting it gently with the flat of the ax. He hung the pack up on the nail. All his supplies were in the pack. They were off the ground and sheltered now.

Nick was hungry. He did not believe he had ever been hungrier. He opened and emptied a can of pork and beans and a can of spaghetti into the frying pan.

"I've got a right to eat this kind of stuff, if I'm willing to carry it," Nick said. His voice sounded strange in the darkening woods. He did not speak again.

He started a fire with some chunks of pine he got with the ax from a stump. Over the fire he stuck a wire grill, pushing the four legs down into the ground with his boot. Nick put the frying pan on the grill over the flames. He was hungrier. The beans and spaghetti warmed. Nick stirred them and mixed them together. They began to bubble, making little bubbles that rose with difficulty to the surface. There was a good smell. Nick got out a bottle of tomato catchup and cut four slices of bread. The little bubbles were coming faster now. Nick sat down beside the fire and lifted the frying pan off. He poured about half the contents out into the tin plate. It spread slowly on the plate. Nick knew it was too hot. He poured on some tomato catchup. He knew the beans and spaghetti were still too hot. He looked at the fire, then at the tent, he was not going to spoil it all by burning his tongue. For years he had never enjoyed fried bananas because he had never been able to wait for them to cool. His tongue was very sensitive. He was very hungry. Across the river in the swamp, in the almost dark, he saw a mist rising. He looked at the tent once more. All right. He took a full spoonful from the plate.

"Chrise," Nick said, "Geezus Chrise," he said happily.

He ate the whole plateful before he remembered the bread. Nick finished the second plateful with the bread, mopping the plate shiny. He had not eaten since a cup of coffee and a ham sandwich in the station restaurant at St. Ignace. It had been a very fine experience. He had been that hungry before, but had not been able to satisfy it. He could have made camp hours before if he had wanted to. There were plenty of good places to camp on the river. But this was good.

Nick tucked two big chips of pine under the grill. The fire flared up. He had forgotten to get water for the coffee. Out of the pack he got a folding canvas bucket and walked down the hill, across the edge of the meadow, to the stream. The other bank was in the white mist. The grass was wet and cold as he knelt on the bank and dipped the canvas bucket into the stream. It bellied and pulled hard in the current. The water was ice cold. Nick rinsed the bucket and carried it full up to the camp. Up away from the stream it was not so cold.

Nick drove another big nail and hung up the bucket full of water. He dipped the coffee pot half full, put some more chips under the grill onto the fire and put the pot on. He could not remember which way he made coffee. He could remember an argument about it with Hopkins, but not which side he had taken. He decided to bring it to a boil. He remembered now that was Hopkins's way. He had once argued about everything with Hopkins. While he waited for the coffee to boil, he opened a small can of apricots. He liked to open cans. He emptied the can of apricots out into a tin cup. While he watched the coffee on the fire, he drank the juice syrup of the apricots, carefully at first to keep from spilling, then meditatively, sucking the apricots down. They were better than fresh apricots.

The coffee boiled as he watched. The lid came up and coffee and grounds ran down the side of the pot. Nick took it off the grill. It was a triumph for Hopkins. He put sugar in the empty apricot cup and poured some of the coffee out to cool. It was too hot to pour and he used his hat to hold the handle of the coffee pot. He would not let it steep in the pot at all. Not the first cup. It should be straight Hopkins all the way. Hop deserved that. He was a very serious coffee drinker. He was the most serious man Nick had ever known. Not heavy, serious. That was a long time ago. Hopkins spoke without moving his lips. He had played polo. He made millions of dollars in Texas. He had borrowed carfare to go to Chicago, when the wire came that his first big well had come in. He could have wired for money. That would have been too slow. They called Hop's girl the Blonde Venus. Hop did not mind because she was not his real girl. Hopkins said very confidently that none of them would make fun of his real girl. He was right. Hopkins went away when the telegram came. That was on the Black River. It took eight days for the telegram to reach him. Hopkins gave away his .22 caliber Colt automatic pistol to Nick. He gave his camera to Bill. It was to remember him always by. They were all going fishing again next summer. The Hop Head was rich. He would get a yacht and they would all cruise along the north shore of Lake Superior. He was excited but serious. They said good-bye and all felt bad. It broke up the trip. They never saw Hopkins again. That was a long time ago on the Black River.

Nick drank the coffee, the coffee according to Hopkins. The coffee was bitter. Nick laughed. It made a good ending to the story. His mind was starting to work. He knew he could choke it because he was tired enough. He spilled the coffee out of the pot and shook the grounds loose into the fire. He lit a cigarette and went inside the tent. He took off his shoes and trousers, sitting on the blankets, rolled the shoes up inside the trousers for a pillow and got in between the blankets.

Out through the front of the tent he watched the glow of the fire, when the night wind blew on it. It was a quiet night. The swamp was perfectly quiet. Nick stretched under the blanket comfortably. A mosquito hummed close to his ear. Nick sat up and lit a match. The mosquito was on the canvas, over his head. Nick moved the match quickly up to it. The mosquito made a satisfactory hiss in the flame. The match went out. Nick lay down again under the blanket. He turned on his side and shut his eyes. He was sleepy. He felt sleep coming. He curled up under the blanket and went to sleep.

II

In the morning the sun was up and the tent was starting to get hot. Nick crawled out under the mosquito netting stretched across the mouth of the tent, to look at the morning. The grass was wet on his hands as he came out. He held his trousers and his shoes in his hands. The sun was just up over the hill. There was the meadow, the river and the swamp. There were birch trees in the green of the swamp on the other side of the river.

The river was clear and smoothly fast in the early morning. Down about two hundred yards were three logs all the way across the stream. They made the water smooth and deep above them. As Nick watched, a mink crossed the river on the logs and went into the swamp. Nick was excited. He was excited by the early morning and the river. He was really too hurried to eat breakfast, but he knew he must. He built a little fire and put on the coffee pot.

While the water was heating in the pot he took an empty bottle and went down over the edge of the high ground to the meadow. The meadow was wet with dew and Nick wanted to catch grass-hoppers for bait before the sun dried the grass. He found plenty of good grasshoppers. They were at the base of the grass stems. Sometimes they clung to a grass stem. They were cold and wet with the dew, and could not jump until the sun warmed them. Nick picked them up, taking only the medium-sized brown ones, and put them into the bottle. He turned over a log and just under the shelter of the edge were several hundred hoppers. It was a grasshopper lodging house. Nick put about fifty of the medium browns into the bottle. While he was picking up the hoppers the others warmed in the sun and commenced to hop away. They flew when they hopped. At first they made one flight and stayed stiff when they landed, as though they were dead.

Nick knew that by the time he was through with breakfast they would be as lively as ever. Without dew in the grass it would take him all day to catch a bottle full of good grasshoppers and he would have to crush many of them, slamming at them with his hat. He washed his hands at the stream. He was excited to be near it. Then he walked up to the tent. The hoppers were already jumping stiffly in the grass. In the bottle, warmed by the sun, they were jumping in a mass. Nick put in a pine stick as a cork. It plugged the mouth of the bottle enough, so the hoppers could not get out and left plenty of air passage.

He had rolled the log back and knew he could get grasshoppers there every morning.

Nick laid the bottle full of jumping grasshoppers against a pine trunk. Rapidly he mixed some buckwheat flour with water and stirred it smooth, one cup of flour, one cup of water. He put a handful of coffee in the pot and dipped a lump of grease out of a can and slid it sputtering across the hot skillet. On the smoking skillet he poured smoothly the buckwheat batter. It spread like lava, the grease spitting sharply. Around the edges the buckwheat cake began to firm, then brown, then crisp. The surface was bubbling slowly to porousness. Nick pushed under the browned under surface with a fresh pine chip. He shook the skillet sideways and the cake was loose on the surface. I won't try and flop it, he thought. He slid the chip of clean wood all the way under the cake, and flopped it over onto its face. It sputtered in the pan.

When it was cooked Nick regreased the skillet. He used all the batter. It made another big flapjack and one smaller one.

Nick ate a big flapjack and a smaller one, covered with apple butter. He put apple butter on the third cake, folded it over twice, wrapped it in oiled paper and put it in his shirt pocket. He put the apple butter jar back in the pack and cut bread for two sandwiches.

In the pack he found a big onion. He sliced it in two and peeled the silky outer skin. Then he cut one half into slices and made onion sandwiches. He wrapped them in oiled paper and buttoned them in the other pocket of his khaki shirt. He turned the skillet upside down on the grill, drank the coffee, sweetened and yellow brown with the condensed milk in it, and tidied up the camp. It was a good camp.

Nick took his fly rod out of the leather rod-case, jointed it, and shoved the rod-case back into the tent. He put on the reel and threaded the line through the guides. He had to hold it from hand to hand, as he threaded it, or it would slip back through its own weight. It was a heavy, double tapered fly line. Nick had paid eight dollars for it a long time ago. It was made heavy to lift back in the air and come forward flat and heavy and straight to make it possible to cast a fly which has no weight. Nick opened the aluminum leader box. The leaders were coiled between the damp flannel pads. Nick had wet the pads at the water cooler on the train up to St. Ignace. In the damp pads the gut leaders had softened and Nick unrolled one and tied it by a loop at the end to the heavy fly line. He fastened a hook on the end of the leader. It was a small hook; very thin and springy.

Nick took it from his hook book, sitting with the rod across his lap. He tested the knot and the spring of the rod by pulling the line taut. It was a good feeling. He was careful not to let the hook bite into his finger.

He started down to the stream, holding his rod, the bottle of grasshoppers hung from his neck by a thong tied in half hitches around the neck of the bottle. His landing net hung by a hook from his belt. Over his shoulder was a long flour sack tied at each corner into an ear. The cord went over his shoulder. The sack flapped against his legs.

Nick felt awkward and professionally happy with all his equipment hanging from him. The grasshopper bottle swung against his chest. In his shirt the breast pockets bulged against him with the lunch and his fly book.

He stepped into the stream. It was a shock. His trousers clung tight to his legs. His shoes felt the gravel. The water was a rising cold shock.

Rushing, the current sucked against his legs. Where he stepped in, the water was over his knees. He waded with the current. The gravel slid under his shoes. He looked down at the swirl of water below each leg and tipped up the bottle to get a grasshopper.

The first grasshopper gave a jump in the neck of the bottle and went out into the water. He was sucked under in the whirl by Nick's right leg and came to the surface a little way down stream. He floated rapidly, kicking. In a quick circle, breaking the smooth surface of the water, he disappeared. A trout had taken him.

Another hopper poked his face out of the bottle. His antennæ wavered. He was getting his front legs out of the bottle to jump. Nick took him by the head and held him while he threaded the slim hook under his chin, down through his thorax and into the last segments of his abdomen. The grasshopper took hold of the hook with his front feet, spitting tobacco juice on it. Nick dropped him into the water.

Holding the rod in his right hand he let out line against the pull of the grasshopper in the current. He stripped off line from the reel with his left hand and let it run free. He could see the hopper in the little waves of the current. It went out of sight.

There was a tug on the line. Nick pulled against the taut line. It was his first strike. Holding the now living rod across the current, he brought in the line with his left hand. The rod bent in jerks, the trout pumping against the current. Nick knew it was a small one. He lifted the rod straight up in the air. It bowed with the pull.

He saw the trout in the water jerking with his head and body against the shifting tangent of the line in the stream.

Nick took the line in his left hand and pulled the trout, thumping tiredly against the current, to the surface. His back was mottled the clear, water-over-gravel color, his side flashing in the sun. The rod under his right arm, Nick stooped, dipping his right hand into the current. He held the trout, never still, with his moist right hand, while he unhooked the barb from his mouth, then dropped him back into the stream.

He hung unsteadily in the current, then settled to the bottom beside a stone. Nick reached down his hand to touch him, his arm to the elbow under water. The trout was steady in the moving stream, resting on the gravel, beside a stone. As Nick's fingers touched him, touched his smooth, cool, underwater feeling he was gone, gone in a shadow across the bottom of the stream.

He's all right, Nick thought. He was only tired.

He had wet his hand before he touched the trout, so he would not disturb the delicate mucus that covered him. If a trout was touched with a dry hand, a white fungus attacked the unprotected spot. Years before when he had fished crowded streams, with fly fishermen ahead of him and behind him, Nick had again and again come on dead trout, furry with white fungus, drifted against a rock, or floating belly up in some pool. Nick did not like to fish with other men on the river. Unless they were of your party, they spoiled it.

He wallowed down the stream, above his knees in the current, through the fifty yards of shallow water above the pile of logs that crossed the stream. He did not rebait his hook and held it in his hand as he waded. He was certain he could catch small trout in the shallows, but he did not want them. There would be no big trout in the shallows this time of day.

Now the water deepened up his thighs sharply and coldly. Ahead was the smooth dammed-back flood of water above the logs. The water was smooth and dark; on the left, the lower edge of the meadow; on the right the swamp.

Nick leaned back against the current and took a hopper from the bottle. He threaded the hopper on the hook and spat on him for good luck. Then he pulled several yards of line from the reel and tossed the hopper out ahead onto the fast, dark water. It floated down towards the logs, then the weight of the line pulled the bait under the surface. Nick held the rod in his right hand, letting the line run out through his fingers.

There was a long tug. Nick struck and the rod came alive and dangerous, bent double, the line tightening, coming out of water, tightening, all in a heavy, dangerous, steady pull. Nick felt the moment when the leader would break if the strain increased and let the line go.

The reel ratcheted into a mechanical shriek as the line went out in a rush. Too fast. Nick could not check it, the line rushing out, the reel note rising as the line ran out.

With the core of the reel showing, his heart feeling stopped with the excitement, leaning back against the current that mounted icily his thighs, Nick thumbed the reel hard with his left hand. It was awkward getting his thumb inside the fly reel frame.

As he put on pressure the line tightened into sudden hardness and beyond the logs a huge trout went high out of water. As he jumped, Nick lowered the tip of the rod. But he felt, as he dropped the tip to ease the strain, the moment when the strain was too great; the hardness too tight. Of course, leader had broken. There was no mistaking the feeling when all spring left the line and it became dry and hard. Then it went slack.

His mouth dry, his heart down, Nick reeled in. He had never seen so big a trout. There was a heaviness, a power not to be held, and then the bulk of him, as he jumped. He looked as broad as a salmon.

Nick's hand was shaky. He reeled in slowly. The thrill had been too much. He felt, vaguely, a little sick, as though it would be better to sit down.

The leader had broken where the hook was tied to it. Nick took it in his hand. He thought of the trout somewhere on the bottom, holding himself steady over the gravel, far down below the light, under the logs, with the hook in his jaw. Nick knew the trout's teeth would cut through the snell of the hook. The hook would imbed itself in his jaw. He'd bet the trout was angry. Anything that size would be angry. That was a trout. He had been solidly hooked. Solid as a rock. He felt like a rock, too, before he started off. By God, he was a big one. By God, he was the biggest one I ever heard of.

Nick climbed out onto the meadow and stood, water running

down his trousers and out of his shoes, his shoes squlchy. He went over and sat on the logs. He did not want to rush his sensations any.

He wriggled his toes in the water, in his shoes, and got out a cigarette from his breast pocket. He lit it and tossed the match into the fast water below the logs. A tiny trout rose at the match, as it swung around in the fast current. Nick laughed. He would finish the cigarette.

He sat on the logs, smoking, drying in the sun, the sun warm on his back, the river shallow ahead entering the woods, curving into the woods, shallows, light glittering, big water-smooth rocks, cedars along the bank and white birches, the logs warm in the sun, smooth to sit on, without bark, gray to the touch; slowly the feeling of disappointment left him. It went away slowly, the feeling of disappointment that came sharply after the thrill that made his shoulders ache. It was all right now. His rod lying out on the logs, Nick tied a new hook on the leader, pulling the gut tight until it grimped into itself in a hard knot.

He baited up, then picked up the rod and walked to the far end of the logs to get into the water, where it was not too deep. Under and beyond the logs was a deep pool. Nick walked around the shallow shelf near the swamp shore until he came out on the shallow bed of the stream.

On the left, where the meadow ended and the woods began, a great elm tree was uprooted. Gone over in a storm, it lay back into the woods, its roots clotted with dirt, grass growing in them, rising a solid bank beside the stream. The river cut to the edge of the uprooted tree. From where Nick stood he could see deep channels, like ruts, cut in the shallow bed of the stream by the flow of the current. Pebbly where he stood and pebbly and full of boulders beyond; where it curved near the tree roots, the bed of the stream was marly and between the ruts of deep water green weed fronds swung in the current.

Nick swung the rod back over his shoulder and forward, and the line, curving forward, laid the grasshopper down on one of the deep channels in the weeds. A trout struck and Nick hooked him.

Holding the rod far out toward the uprooted tree and sloshing backward in the current, Nick worked the trout, plunging, the rod bending alive, out of the danger of the weeds into the open river. Holding the rod, pumping alive against the current, Nick brought the trout in. He rushed, but always came, the spring of the rod yielding to the rushes, sometimes jerking under water, but always bringing him in. Nick eased downstream with the rushes. The rod above his head he led the trout over the net, then lifted.

The trout hung heavy in the net, mottled trout back and silver sides in the meshes. Nick unhooked him; heavy sides, good to hold, big undershot jaw, and slipped him, heaving and big sliding, into the long sack that hung from his shoulders in the water.

Nick spread the mouth of the sack against the current and it filled, heavy with water. He held it up, the bottom in the stream, and the water poured out through the sides. Inside at the bottom was the big trout, alive in the water.

Nick moved downstream. The sack out ahead of him sunk heavy in the water, pulling from his shoulders.

It was getting hot, the sun hot on the back of his neck.

Nick had one good trout. He did not care about getting many trout. Now the stream was shallow and wide. There were trees along both banks. The trees of the left bank made short shadows on the current in the forenoon sun. Nick knew there were trout in each shadow. In the afternoon, after the sun had crossed toward the hills, the trout would be in the cool shadows on the other side of the stream.

The very biggest ones would lie up close to the bank. You could always pick them up there on the Black. When the sun was down they all moved out into the current. Just when the sun made the water blinding in the glare before it went down, you were liable to strike a big trout anywhere in the current. It was almost impossible to fish then, the surface of the water was blinding as a mirror in the sun. Of course, you could fish upstream, but in a stream like the Black, or this, you had to wallow against the current and in a deep place, the water piled up on you. It was no fun to fish upstream with this much current.

Nick moved along through the shallow stretch watching the banks for deep holes. A beech tree grew close beside the river, so that the branches hung down into the water. The stream went back in under the leaves. There were always trout in a place like that.

Nick did not care about fishing that hole. He was sure he would get hooked in the branches.

It looked deep though. He dropped the grasshopper so the current took it under water, back in under the overhanging branch. The line pulled hard and Nick struck. The trout threshed heavily, half out of water in the leaves and branches. The line was caught. Nick pulled hard and the trout was off. He reeled in and holding the hook in his hand, walked down the stream.

Ahead, close to the left bank, was a big log. Nick saw it was hollow; pointing up river the current entered it smoothly, only a little ripple spread each side of the log. The water was deepening. The top of the hollow log was gray and dry. It was partly in the shadow.

Nick took the cork out of the grasshopper bottle and a hopper clung to it. He picked him off, hooked him and tossed him out. He held the rod far out so that the hopper on the water moved into the current flowing into the hollow log. Nick lowered the rod and the hopper floated in. There was a heavy strike. Nick swung the rod against the pull. It felt as though he were hooked into the log itself, except for the live feeling.

He tried to force the fish out into the current. It came, heavily.

The line went slack and Nick thought the trout was gone. Then he saw him, very near, in the current, shaking his head, trying to get the hook out. His mouth was clamped shut. He was fighting the hook in the clear flowing current.

Looping in the line with his left hand, Nick swung the rod to make the line taut and tried to lead the trout toward the net, but he was gone, out of sight, the line pumping. Nick fought him against the current, letting him thump in the water against the spring of the rod. He shifted the rod to his left hand, worked the trout upstream, holding his weight, fighting on the rod, and then let him down into the net. He lifted him clear of the water, a heavy half circle in the net, the net dripping, unhooked him and slid him into the sack.

He spread the mouth of the sack and looked down in at the two big trout alive in the water.

Through the deepening water, Nick waded over to the hollow log. He took the sack off, over his head, the trout flopping as it came out of water, and hung it so the trout were deep in the water. Then he pulled himself up on the log and sat, the water from his trousers and boots running down into the stream. He laid his rod down, moved along to the shady end of the log and took the sandwiches out of his pocket. He dipped the sandwiches in the cold water. The current carried away the crumbs. He ate the sandwiches and dipped his hat full of water to drink, the water running out through his hat just ahead of his drinking.

It was cool in the shade, sitting on the log. He took a cigarette out and struck a match to light it. The match sunk into the gray wood, making a tiny furrow. Nick leaned over the side of the log, found a hard place and lit the match. He sat smoking and watching the river.

Ahead the river narrowed and went into a swamp. The river became smooth and deep and the swamp looked solid with cedar trees, their trunks close together, their branches solid. It would not be possible to walk through a swamp like that. The branches grew so low. You would have to keep almost level with the ground to move at all. You could not crash through the branches. That must be why the animals that lived in swamps were built the way they were, Nick thought.

He wished he had brought something to read. He felt like reading. He did not feel like going on into the swamp. He looked down the river. A big cedar slanted all the way across the stream. Beyond that the river went into the swamp.

Nick did not want to go in there now. He felt a reaction against deep wading with the water deepening up under his armpits, to hook big trout in places impossible to land them. In the swamp the banks were bare, the big cedars came together overhead, the sun did not come through, except in patches; in the fast deep water, in the half light, the fishing would be tragic. In the swamp fishing was a tragic adventure. Nick did not want it. He did not want to go down the stream any further today.

He took out his knife, opened it and stuck it in the log. Then he pulled up the sack, reached into it and brought out one of the trout. Holding him near the tail, hard to hold, alive, in his hand, he whacked him against the log. The trout quivered, rigid. Nick laid him on the log in the shade and broke the neck of the other fish the same way. He laid them side by side on the log. They were fine trout.

Nick cleaned them, slitting them from the vent to the tip of the jaw. All the insides and the gills and tongue came out in one piece. They were both males; long gray-white strips of milt, smooth and clean. All the insides clean and compact, coming out all together. Nick tossed the offal ashore for the minks to find.

He washed the trout in the stream. When he held them back up in the water they looked like live fish. Their color was not gone yet. He washed his hands and dried them on the log. Then he laid the trout on the sack spread out on the log, rolled them up in it, tied the bundle and put it in the landing net. His knife was still standing, blade stuck in the log. He cleaned it on the wood and put it in his pocket.

Nick stood up on the log, holding his rod, the landing net hanging heavy, then stepped into the water and splashed ashore. He climbed the bank and cut up into the woods, toward the high ground. He was going back to camp. He looked back. The river just showed through the trees. There were plenty of days coming when he could fish the swamp.

THE TORRENTS OF SPRING

A ROMANTIC NOVEL
IN HONOR OF THE PASSING OF A GREAT RACE

And perhaps there is one reason why a comic writer should of all others be the least excused for deviating from nature, since it may not be always so easy for a serious poet to meet with the great and the admirable; but life everywhere furnishes an accurate observer with the ridiculous.

—HENRY FIELDING

THE TORRENTS OF SPRING is a hilarious and disorderly masterpiece of humor with a deep center of gravity. It seems to have started as a knockabout parody of Sherwood Anderson's mechanized folkware. Particularly Dark Laughter, whose eerie chapter endings are scrupulously transposed into an aboriginal key ("there came to Scripps's ears the sound of a far-off Indian war-whoop"). But the story soon soars into a saga of prevailing gaga. And the scene at the patrician Indian club, where the varieties of human snobbery are satirized for their own sad sakes, has more bite to it than I would believe Anderson ever dreamed of writing.

An air of surrealism hangs over these pages. When celebrities such as Scott Fitzgerald and John Dos Passos turn up they appear to be characters of fiction. When richly gifted waitresses in Michigan wayside inns quote one of the Henrys (James or Mencken, as the case may be) and poetic pumpmakers yearn for Paris we feel they are wonderfully true to the higher life of the glittering, unfathomable Nineteen Twenties.

This "Romantic Novel in Honor of the Passing of a Great Race" has entertained many persons, not including Horace Liveright, Hemingway's first publisher, who was also the publisher of Sherwood Anderson. Hemingway had spent an entire week before Thanksgiving, 1925, writing it, and when Liveright declined to publish it he grieved, though only moderately. "I wrote it after I had finished the first draft of The Sun Also Rises," he has tersely and definitively explained, "to cool out."

C. P.

THE TORRENTS OF SPRING

Part I

RED AND BLACK LAUGHTER

The only source of the true Ridiculous (as it appears to me) is affectation.

HENRY FIELDING

CHAPTER I

YOGI JOHNSON stood looking out of the window of a big pump-factory in Michigan. Spring would soon be here. Could it be that what this writing fellow Hutchinson had said, "If winter comes can spring be far behind?" would be true again this year? Yogi Johnson wondered. Near Yogi at the next window but one stood Scripps O'Neil, a tall, lean man with a tall, lean face. Both stood and looked out at the empty yard of the pump-factory. Snow covered the crated pumps that would soon be shipped away. Once the spring should come and the snow melt, workmen from the factory would break out the pumps from piles where they were snowed in and haul them down to the G. R. & I. station, where they would be loaded on flat-cars and shipped away. Yogi Johnson looked out of the window at the snowed-in pumps and his breath made little fairy tracings on the cold window-pane. Yogi Johnson thought of Paris. Perhaps it was the little fairy tracings that reminded him of the gay city where he had once spent two weeks. Two weeks that were to have been the happiest weeks of his life. That was all behind him now. That and everything else.

Scripps O'Neil had two wives. As he looked out of the window, standing tall and lean and resilient with his own tenuous hard-

25

ness, he thought of both of them. One lived in Mancelona and the other lived in Petoskey. He had not seen the wife who lived in Mancelona since last spring. He looked out at the snow-covered pump-yards and thought what spring would mean. With his wife in Mancelona Scripps often got drunk. When he was drunk he and his wife were happy. They would go down together to the railway station and walk out along the tracks, and then sit together and drink and watch the trains go by. They would sit under a pine-tree on a little hill that overlooked the railway and drink. Sometimes they drank all night. Sometimes they drank for a week at a time. It did them good. It made Scripps strong.

Scripps had a daughter whom he playfully called Lousy O'Neil. Her real name was Lucy O'Neil. One night, after Scripps and his old woman had been out drinking on the railroad line for three or four days, he lost his wife. He didn't know where she was. When he came to himself everything was dark. He walked along the railroad track toward town. The ties were stiff and hard under his feet. He tried walking on the rails. He couldn't do it. He had the dope on that all right. He went back to walking along the ties. It was a long way into town. Finally he came to where he could see the lights of the switch-yard. He cut away from the tracks and passed the Mancelona High School. It was a yellow-brick building. There was nothing rococo about it, like the buildings he had seen in Paris. No, he had never been in Paris. That was not he. That was his friend Yogi Johnson.

Yogi Johnson looked out of the window. Soon it would be time to shut the pump-factory for the night. He opened the window carefully, just a crack. Just a crack, but that was enough. Outside in the yard the snow had begun to melt. A warm breeze was blowing. A chinook wind the pump fellows called it. The warm chinook wind came in through the window into the pump-factory. All the workmen laid down their tools. Many of them were Indians.

The foreman was a short, iron-jawed man. He had once made a trip as far as Duluth. Duluth was far across the blue waters of the lake in the hills of Minnesota. A wonderful thing had happened to him there.

The foreman put his finger in his mouth to moisten it and held it up in the air. He felt the warm breeze on his finger. He shook his head ruefully and smiled at the men, a little grimly perhaps.

"Well, it's a regular chinook, boys," he said.

Silently for the most part, the workmen hung up their tools. The half-completed pumps were put away in their racks. The workmen filed, some of them talking, others silent, a few muttering, to the washroom to wash up.

Outside through the window came the sound of an Indian war-whoop.

CHAPTER II

SCRIPPS O'NEIL stood outside the Mancelona High School looking up at the lighted windows. It was dark and the snow was falling. It had been falling ever since Scripps could remember. A passer-by stopped and stared at Scripps. After all, what was this man to him? He went on.

Scripps stood in the snow and stared up at the lighted windows of the High School. Inside there people were learning things. Far into the night they worked, the boys vying with the girls in their search for knowledge, this urge for the learning of things that was sweeping America. His girl, little Lousy, a girl that had cost him a cool seventy-five dollars in doctors' bills, was in there learning. Scripps was proud. It was too late for him to learn, but there, day after day and night after night, Lousy was learning. She had the stuff in her, that girl.

Scripps went on up to his house. It was not a big house, but it wasn't size that mattered to Scripps's old woman.

"Scripps," she often said when they were drinking together, "I don't want a palace. All I want is a place to keep the wind out."

Scripps had taken her at her word. Now, as he walked in the late evening through the snow and saw the lights of his own home, he felt glad that he had taken her at her word. It was better this way than if he were coming home to a palace. He, Scripps, was not the sort of chap that wanted a palace.

He opened the door of his house and went in. Something kept going through his head. He tried to get it out, but it was no good. What was it that poet chap his friend Harry Parker had met once in Detroit had written? Harry used to recite it: "Through pleasures and palaces though I may roam. When you something something something there's no place like home." He could not remember the words. Not all of them. He had written a simple tune to it and taught Lucy to sing it. That was when they first were married. Scripps might have been a composer, one of these chaps that write the stuff the Chicago Symphony Orchestra plays, if he had had a chance to go on. He would get Lucy to sing that song to-night. He would never drink again. Drinking robbed him of his ear for music. Times when he was drunk the sound of the whistles of the trains at night pulling up the Boyne Falls grade seemed more lovely than anything this chap Stravinsky had ever written. Drinking had done that. It was wrong. He would get away to Paris. Like this chap Albert Spalding that played the violin.

Scripps opened the door. He went in. "Lucy," he called, "it is I, Scripps." He would never drink again. No more nights out on the railroad. Perhaps Lucy needed a new fur coat. Perhaps, after all, she had wanted a palace instead of this place. You never knew how you were treating a woman. Perhaps, after all, this place was not keeping out the wind. Fantastic. He lit a match. "Lucy!" he called, and there was a note of dumb terror in his mouth. His friend Walt Simmons had heard just such a cry from a stallion that had once been run over by a passing autobus in the Place Vendôme in Paris. In Paris there were no geldings. All the horses were stallions. They did not breed mares. Not since the war. The war changed all that.

"Lucy!" he called, and again "Lucy!" There was no answer. The house was empty. Through the snow-filled air, as he stood there

alone in his tall leanness, in his own deserted house, there came
to Scripps's ears the distant sound of an Indian war-whoop.

CHAPTER III

SCRIPPS left Mancelona. He was through with that place. What
had a town like that to give him? There was nothing to it. You
worked all your life and then a thing like that happened. The
savings of years wiped out. Everything gone. He started to Chicago to get a job. Chicago was the place. Look at its geographical
situation, right at the end of Lake Michigan. Chicago would do
big things. Any fool could see that. He would buy land in what
is now the Loop, the big shopping and manufacturing district. He
would buy the land at a low price and then hang onto it. Let them
try and get it away from him. He knew a thing or two now.

Alone, bareheaded, the snow blowing in his hair, he walked
down the G. R. & I. railway tracks. It was the coldest night he
had ever known. He picked up a dead bird that had frozen and
fallen onto the railroad tracks and put it inside his shirt to warm it.
The bird nestled close to his warm body and pecked at his chest
gratefully. "Poor little chap," Scripps said. "You feel the cold too."

Tears came into his eyes.

"Drat that wind," Scripps said and once again faced into the
blowing snow. The wind was blowing straight down from Lake
Superior. The telegraph wires above Scripps's head sang in the
wind. Through the dark, Scripps saw a great yellow eye coming
toward him. The giant locomotive came nearer through the snow-
storm. Scripps stepped to one side of the track to let it go by.
What is it that old writing fellow Shakespeare says: "Might makes
right"? Scripps thought of that quotation as the train went past
him in the snowing darkness. First the engine passed. He saw the
fireman bending to fling great shovelfuls of coal into the open
furnace door. The engineer wore goggles. His face was lit up by

the light from the open door of the engine. He was the engineer. It was he who had his hand on the throttle. Scripps thought of the Chicago anarchists who, when they were hanged, said: "Though you throttle us to-day, still you cannot something something our souls." There was a monument where they were buried in Waldheim Cemetery, right beside the Forest Park Amusement Park, in Chicago. His father used to take Scripps out there on Sundays. The monument was all black and there was a black angel. That was when Scripps had been a little boy. He used often to ask his father: "Father, why if we come to look at the anarchists on Sunday why can't we ride on the shoot the chutes?" He had never been satisfied with his father's answer. He had been a little boy in knee pants then. His father had been a great composer. His mother was an Italian woman from the north of Italy. They are strange people, these north Italians.

Scripps stood beside the track, and the long black segments of the train clicked by him in the snow. All the cars were Pullmans. The blinds were down. Light came in thin slits from the bottom of the dark windows as the cars went by. The train did not roar by as it might have if it had been going in the other direction, because it was climbing the Boyne Falls grade. It went slower than if it had been going down. Still it went too fast for Scripps to hitch on. He thought how he had been an expert at hitching on grocery wagons when he was a young boy in knee pants.

The long black train of Pullman cars passed Scripps as he stood beside the tracks. Who were in those cars? Were they Americans, piling up money while they slept? Were they mothers? Were they fathers? Were there lovers among them? Or were they Europeans, members of a worn-out civilization world-weary from the war? Scripps wondered.

The last car passed him and the train went on up the track. Scripps watched the red light at its stern disappearing into the blackness through which the snowflakes now came softly. The bird fluttered inside his shirt. Scripps started along the ties. He wanted to get to Chicago that night, if possible, to start work in the morning. The bird fluttered again. It was not so feeble now.

Scripps put his hand on it to still its little bird flutterings. The bird was calmed. Scripps strode on up the track.

After all, he did not need to go as far as Chicago. There were other places. What if that critic fellow Henry Mencken had called Chicago the Literary Capital of America? There was Grand Rapids. Once in Grand Rapids, he could start in in the furniture business. Fortunes had been made that way. Grand Rapids furniture was famous wherever young couples walked in the evening to talk of home-making. He remembered a sign he had seen in Chicago as a little boy. His mother had pointed it out to him as together they walked barefoot through what now is probably the Loop, begging from door to door. His mother loved the bright flashing of the electric lights in the sign.

"They are like San Miniato in my native Florence," she told Scripps. "Look at them, my son," she said, "for some day your music will be played there by the Firenze Symphony Orchestra."

Scripps had often watched the sign for hours while his mother slept wrapped in an old shawl on what is now probably the Blackstone Hotel. The sign had made a great impression on him.

LET HARTMAN FEATHER YOUR NEST

it had said. It flashed in many different colors. First a pure, dazzling white. That was what Scripps loved best. Then it flashed a lovely green. Then it flashed red. One night as he lay crouched against his mother's body warmth and watched the sign flash, a policeman came up. "You'll have to move along," he said.

Ah, yes, there was big money to be made in the furniture business if you knew how to go about it. He, Scripps, knew all the wrinkles of that game. In his own mind it was settled. He would stop at Grand Rapids. The little bird fluttered, happily now.

"Ah, what a beautiful gilded cage I'll build for you, my pretty one," Scripps said exultantly. The little bird pecked him confidently. Scripps strode on in the storm. The snow was beginning to drift across the track. Borne on the wind, there came to Scripps's ears the sound of a far-off Indian war-whoop.

CHAPTER IV

WHERE was Scripps now? Walking in the night in the storm, he had become confused. He had started for Chicago after that dreadful night when he had found that his home was a home no longer. Why had Lucy left? What had become of Lousy? He, Scripps, did not know. Not that he cared. That was all behind him. There was none of that now. He was standing knee-deep in snow in front of a railway station. On the railway station was written in big letters:

PETOSKEY

There were a pile of deer shipped down by hunters from the Upper Peninsula of Michigan, lying piled the one on the other, dead and stiff and drifted half over with snow on the station platform. Scripps read the sign again. Could this be Petoskey?

A man was inside the station, tapping something back of a wicketed window. He looked out at Scripps. Could he be a telegrapher? Something told Scripps that he was.

He stepped out of the snow-drift and approached the window. Behind the window the man worked busily away at his telegrapher's key.

"Are you a telegrapher?" asked Scripps.

"Yes, sir," said the man. "I'm a telegrapher."

"How wonderful!"

The telegrapher eyed him suspiciously. After all, what was this man to him?

"Is it hard to be a telegrapher?" Scripps asked. He wanted to ask the man outright if this was Petoskey. He did not know this great northern section of America, though, and he wished to be polite.

The telegrapher looked at him curiously.

"Say," he asked, "are you a fairy?"

"No," Scripps said. "I don't know what being a fairy means."

"Well," said the telegrapher, "what do you carry a bird around for?"

"Bird?" asked Scripps. "What bird?"

"That bird that's sticking out of your shirt." Scripps was at a loss. What sort of chap was this telegrapher? What sort of men went in for telegraphy? Were they like composers? Were they like artists? Were they like writers? Were they like the advertising men who write the ads in our national weeklies? Or were they like Europeans, drawn and wasted by the war, their best years behind them? Could he tell this telegrapher the whole story? Would he understand?

"I started home," he began. "I passed the Mancelona High School——"

"I knew a girl in Mancelona," the telegrapher said. "Maybe you knew her. Ethel Enright."

It was no good going on. He would cut the story short. He would give the bare essentials. Besides, it was beastly cold. It was cold standing there on the wind-swept station platform. Something told him it was useless to go on. He looked over at the deer lying there in a pile, stiff and cold. Perhaps they, too, had been lovers. Some were bucks and some were does. The bucks had horns. That was how you could tell. With cats it is more difficult. In France they geld the cats and do not geld the horses. France was a long way off.

"My wife left me," Scripps said abruptly.

"I don't wonder if you go around with a damn bird sticking out of your shirt," the telegrapher said.

"What town is this?" Scripps asked. The single moment of spiritual communion they had had, had been dissipated. They had never really had it. But they might have. It was no use now. It was no use trying to capture what had gone. What had fled.

"Petoskey," the telegrapher replied.

"Thank you," Scripps said. He turned and walked into the silent, deserted Northern town. Luckily, he had four hundred and fifty dollars in his pocket. He had sold a story to George Horace Lorimer just before he had started out with his old woman on that drinking trip. Why had he gone at all? What was it all about, anyway?

Coming toward him down the street came two Indians. They looked at him, but their faces did not change. Their faces remained the same. They went into McCarthy's barber shop.

CHAPTER V

SCRIPPS O'NEIL stood irresolutely before the barber shop. Inside there men were being shaved. Other men, no different, were having their hair cut. Other men sat against the wall in tall chairs and smoked, awaiting their turn in the barber chairs, admiring the paintings hung on the wall, or admiring their own reflections in the long mirror. Should he, Scripps, go in there? After all, he had four hundred and fifty dollars in his pocket. He could go where he wanted. He looked, once again, irresolutely. It was an inviting prospect, the society of men, the warm room, the white jackets of the barbers skilfully snipping away with their scissors or drawing their blades diagonally through the lather that covered the face of some man who was getting a shave. They could use their tools, these barbers. Somehow, it wasn't what he wanted. He wanted something different. He wanted to eat. Besides, there was his bird to look after.

Scripps O'Neil turned his back on the barber shop and strode away up the street of the silently frozen Northern town. On his right, as he walked, the weeping birches, their branches bare of leaves, hung down to the ground, heavy with snow. To his ears came the sound of sleigh bells. Perhaps it was Christmas. In the South little children would be shooting off firecrackers and crying "Christmas Gift! Christmas Gift!" to one another. His father came from the South. He had been a soldier in the rebel army. 'Way back in Civil War days. Sherman had burned their house down on his March to the Sea. "War is hell," Sherman had said. "But you see how it is, Mrs. O'Neil. I've got to do it." He had touched a match to the white-pillared old house.

"If General O'Neil were here, you dastard!" his mother had said, speaking in her broken English, "you'd never have touched a match to that house."

Smoke curled up from the old house. The fire was mounting. The white pillars were obscured in the rising smoke-wreaths. Scripps had held close to his mother's linsey-woolsey dress.

General Sherman climbed back onto his horse and made a low bow. "Mrs. O'Neil," he said, and Scripps's mother always said there were tears in his eyes, even if he was a damned Yank. The man had a heart, sir, even if he did not follow its dictates. "Mrs. O'Neil, if the general were here, we could have it out as man to man. As it is, ma'am, war being what it is, I must burn your house."

He motioned to one of his soldiers, who ran forward and threw a bucket of kerosene on the flames. The flames rose and a great column of smoke went up in the still evening air.

"At least, General Sherman," Scripps's mother said triumphantly, "that column of smoke will warn the other loyal daughters of the Confederacy that you are coming."

Sherman bowed. "That is the risk we must take, ma'am." He clapped spurs to his horse and rode away, his long white hair floating on the wind. Neither Scripps nor his mother ever saw him again. Odd that he should think of that incident now. He looked up. Facing him was a sign:

BROWN'S BEANERY THE BEST BY TEST

He would go in and eat. This was what he wanted. He would go in and eat. That sign:

THE BEST BY TEST

Ah, these big beanery owners were wise fellows. They knew how to get the customers. No ads in *The Saturday Evening Post* for them. THE BEST BY TEST. That was the stuff. He went in.

Inside the door of the beanery Scripps O'Neil looked around him. There was a long counter. There was a clock. There was a door led into the kitchen. There were a couple of tables. There were a pile of doughnuts under a glass cover. There were signs put about on the wall advertising things one might eat. Was this, after all, Brown's Beanery?

"I wonder," Scripps asked an elderly waitress who came in through the swinging door from the kitchen, "if you could tell me if this is Brown's Beanery?"

"Yes, sir," answered the waitress. "The best by test."

"Thank you," Scripps said. He sat down at the counter. "I would like to have some beans for myself and some for my bird here."

He opened his shirt and placed the bird on the counter. The bird ruffled his feathers and shook himself. He pecked inquiringly at the catsup bottle. The elderly waitress put out a hand and stroked him. "Isn't he a manly little fellow?" she remarked. "By the way," she asked, a little shamefacedly, "what was it you ordered, sir?"

"Beans," Scripps said, "for my bird and myself."

The waitress shoved up a little wicket that led into the kitchen. Scripps had a glimpse of a warm, steam-filled room, with big pots and kettles, and many shining cans on the wall.

"A pig and the noisy ones," the waitress called in a matter-of-fact voice into the open wicket. "One for a bird!"

"On the fire!" a voice answered from the kitchen.

"How old is your bird?" the elderly waitress asked.

"I don't know," Scripps said. "I never saw him before last night. I was walking on the railroad track from Mancelona. My wife left me."

"Poor little chap," the waitress said. She poured a little catsup on her finger and the bird pecked at it gratefully.

"My wife left me," Scripps said. "We'd been out drinking on the railroad track. We used to go out evenings and watch the trains pass. I write stories. I had a story in *The Post* and two in *The Dial*. Mencken's trying to get ahold of me. I'm too wise for that sort of thing. No *politzei* for mine. They give me the *katzenjammers*."

What was he saying? He was talking wildly. This would never do. He must pull himself together.

"Scofield Thayer was my best man," he said. "I'm a Harvard man. All I want is for them to give me and my bird a square deal. No more *weltpolitik*. Take Doctor Coolidge away."

His mind was wandering. He knew what it was. He was faint with hunger. This Northern air was too sharp, too keen for him.

"I say," he said. "Could you let me have just a few of those beans. I don't like to rush things. I know when to let well enough alone."

The wicket came up, and a large plate of beans and a small plate of beans, both steaming, appeared.

"Here they are," the waitress said.

Scripps fell to on the large plate of beans. There was a little pork, too. The bird was eating happily, raising its head after each swallow to let the beans go down.

"He does that to thank God for those beans," the elderly waitress explained.

"They're mighty fine beans, too," Scripps agreed. Under the influence of the beans his head was clearing. What was this rot he had been talking about that man Henry Mencken? Was Mencken really after him? It wasn't a pretty prospect to face. He had four hundred and fifty dollars in his pocket. When that was gone he could always put an end to things. If they pressed him too far they would get a big surprise. He wasn't the man to be taken alive. Just let them try it.

After eating his beans the bird had fallen asleep. He was sleeping on one leg, the other leg tucked up into his feathers.

"When he gets tired of sleeping on that leg he will change legs and rest," the waitress remarked. "We had an old osprey at home that was like that."

"Where was your home?" Scripps asked.

"In England. In the Lake District." The waitress smiled a bit wistfully. "Wordsworth's country, you know."

Ah, these English. They travelled all over the face of the globe.

They were not content to remain in their little island. Strange Nordics, obsessed with their dream of empire.

"I was not always a waitress," the elderly waitress remarked.

"I'm sure you weren't."

"Not half," the waitress went on. "It's rather a strange story. Perhaps it would bore you?"

"Not at all," Scripps said. "You wouldn't mind if I used the story sometime?"

"Not if you find it interesting," the waitress smiled. "You wouldn't use my name, of course."

"Not if you'd rather not," Scripps said. "By the way, could I have another order of beans?"

"Best by test," the waitress smiled. Her face was lined and gray. She looks a little like that actress that died in Pittsburg. What was her name? Lenore Ulric. In "Peter Pan." That was it. They say she always went about veiled, Scripps thought. There was an interesting woman. Was it Lenore Ulric? Perhaps not. No matter.

"You really want some more beans?" asked the waitress.

"Yes," Scripps answered simply.

"Once again on the loud ones," the waitress called into the wicket. "Lay off the bird."

"On the fire," came the response.

"Please go on with your story," Scripps said kindly.

"It was the year of the Paris Exposition," she began. "I was a young girl at the time, a *jeune fille*, and I came over from England with my mother. We were going to be present at the opening of the exposition. On our way from the Gare du Nord to the hotel in the Place Vendôme where we lodged, we stopped at a coiffeur's shop and made some trifling purchase. My mother, as I recall, purchased an additional bottle of 'smelling salts,' as you call them here in America."

She smiled.

"Yes, go on. Smelling salts," Scripps said.

"We registered, as is customary, in the hotel, and were given the adjoining rooms we had reserved. My mother felt a bit done in by the trip, and we dined in our rooms. I was full of excitement about seeing the exposition on the morrow. But I was tired after the journey—we had had a rather nasty crossing—and slept soundly. In the morning I awoke and called for my mother. There was no answer, and I went into the room to waken mummy. Instead of mummy there was a French general in the bed."

"Mon Dieu!" Scripps said.

"I was terribly frightened," the waitress went on, "and rang the bell for the management. The concierge came up, and I demanded to know where my mother was.

" 'But, mademoiselle,' the concierge explained, 'we know nothing about your mother. You came here with General So-and-so'—I cannot remember the general's name."

"Call him General Joffre," Scripps suggested.

"It was a name very like that," the waitress said. "I was fearfully frightened and sent for the police, and demanded to see the guest-register. 'You'll find there that I am registered with my mother,' I said. The police came and the concierge brought up the register. 'See, madame,' he said. 'You are registered with the general with whom you came to our hotel last night.'

"I was desperate. Finally, I remembered where the coiffeur's shop was. The police sent for the coiffeur. An agent of police brought him in.

" 'I stopped at your shop with my mother.' I said to the coiffeur, 'and my mother bought a bottle of aromatic salts.'

" 'I remember mademoiselle perfectly,' the coiffeur said. 'But you were not with your mother. You were with an elderly French general. He purchased, I believe, a pair of mustache tongs. My books, at any rate, will show the purchase.'

"I was in despair. In the meantime the police had brought in the cab driver who had brought us from the gare to the hotel. He swore that I had never been with my mother. Tell me, does this story bore you?"

"Go on," said Scripps. "If you had ever been as hard up for plots as I have been!"

"Well," the waitress said. "That's all there is to the tale. I never saw my mother again. I communicated with the embassy, but they could do nothing. It was finally established by them that I had crossed the channel with my mother, but they could do nothing beyond that." Tears came into the elderly waitress's eyes. "I never saw mummy again. Never again. Not even once."

"What about the general?"

"He finally loaned me one hundred francs—not a great sum even in those days—and I came to America and became a waitress. That's all there is to the story."

"There's more than that," Scripps said. "I'd stake my life there's more than that."

"Sometimes, you know, I feel there is," the waitress said. "I feel there must be more than that. Somewhere, somehow, there must be an explanation. I don't know what brought the subject into my mind this morning."

"It was a good thing to get it off your mind," Scripps said.

"Yes," the waitress smiled, the lines in her face not quite so deep now. "I feel better now."

"Tell me," Scripps asked the waitress. "Is there any work in this town for me and my bird?"

"Honest work?" asked the waitress. "I only know of honest work."

"Yes, honest work," Scripps said.

"They do say they're hiring hands at the new pump-factory," the waitress said. Why shouldn't he work with hands? Rodin had done it. Cézanne had been a butcher. Renoir a carpenter. Picasso had worked in a cigarette-factory in his boyhood. Gilbert Stuart, who painted those famous portraits of Washington that are reproduced all over this America of ours and hang in every schoolroom—Gilbert Stuart had been a blacksmith. Then there was Emerson. Emerson had been a hod-carrier. James Russell Lowell had been, he had heard, a telegraph operator in his youth. Like that chap down at the station. Perhaps even now that telegrapher at the station was working on his "Thanatopsis" or his "To a Waterfowl." Why shouldn't he, Scripps O'Neil, work in a pump-factory?

"You'll come back again?" the waitress asked.

"If I may," Scripps said.

"And bring your bird."

"Yes," Scripps said. "The little chap's rather tired now. After all, it was a hard night for him."

"I should say it was," agreed the waitress.

Scripps went out again into the town. He felt clear-headed and ready to face life. A pump-factory would be interesting. Pumps were big things now. Fortunes were made and lost in pumps every day in New York in Wall Street. He knew of a chap who'd cleaned up a cool half-million on pumps in less than half an hour. They knew what they were about, these big Wall Street operators.

Outside on the street he looked up at the sign. BEST BY TEST, he read. They had the dope all right, he said. Was it true, though, that there had been a Negro cook? Just once, just for one moment, when the wicket went up, he thought he had caught a glimpse of something black. Perhaps the chap was only sooty from the stove.

Part II

THE STRUGGLE FOR LIFE

And here I solemnly protest I have no intention to vilify or asperse any one; for though everything is copied from the book of nature, and scarce a character or action produced which I have not taken from my own observations or experience; yet I have used the utmost care to obscure the persons by such different circumstances, degrees, and colors, that it will be impossible to guess at them with any degree of certainty; and if it ever happens otherwise, it is only where the failure characterized is so minute, that it is a foible only which the party himself may laugh at as well as any other.

HENRY FIELDING

CHAPTER VI

SCRIPPS O'NEIL was looking for employment. It would be good to work with his hands. He walked down the street away from the beanery and past McCarthy's barber shop. He did not go into the barber shop. It looked as inviting as ever, but it was employment Scripps wanted. He turned sharply around the corner of the barber shop and onto the Main Street of Petoskey. It was a handsome, broad street, lined on either side with brick and pressed-stone buildings. Scripps walked along it toward the part of town where the pump-factory stood. At the door of the pump-factory he was embarrassed. Could this really be the pump-factory? True, a stream of pumps were being carried out and set up in the snow, and workmen were throwing pails of water over them to encase them in a coating of ice that would protect them from the winter winds as well as any paint would. But were they really pumps? It might all be a trick. These pump men were clever fellows.

"I say!" Scripps beckoned to one of the workmen who was sloshing water over a new, raw-looking pump that had just been carried out and stood protestingly in the snow. "Are they pumps?"

"They will be in time," the workman said.

Scripps knew it was the factory. They weren't going to fool him on that. He walked up to the door. There was a sign on it:

KEEP OUT. THIS MEANS YOU

Can that mean me? Scripps wondered. He knocked on the door and went in.

"I'd like to speak to the manager," he said, standing quietly in the half-light.

Workmen were passing him, carrying the new raw pumps on their shoulders. They hummed snatches of songs as they passed. The handles of the pumps flopped stiffly in dumb protest. Some pumps had no handles. They perhaps, after all, are the lucky ones, Scripps thought. A little man came up to him. He was well-built, short, with wide shoulders and a grim face.

"You were asking for the manager?"

"Yes, sir."

"I'm the foreman here. What I say goes."

"Can you hire and fire?" Scripps asked.

"I can do one as easily as the other," the foreman said.

"I want a job."

"Any experience?"

"Not in pumps."

"All right," the foreman said. "We'll put you on piece-work. Here, Yogi," he called to one of the men, who was standing looking out of the window of the factory, "show this new chum where to stow his swag and how to find his way around these diggings." The foreman looked Scripps up and down. "I'm an Australian," he said. "Hope you'll like the lay here." He walked off.

The man called Yogi Johnson came over from the window. "Glad to meet you," he said. He was a chunky, well-built fellow. One of the sort you see around almost anywhere. He looked as though he had been through things.

"Your foreman's the first Australian I've ever met," Scripps said.

"Oh, he's not an Australian," Yogi said. "He was just with the Australians once during the war, and it made a big impression on him."

"Were you in the war?" Scripps asked.

"Yes," Yogi Johnson said. "I was the first man to go from Cadillac."

"It must have been quite an experience."

"It's meant a lot to me," Yogi answered. "Come on and I'll show you around the works."

Scripps followed this man, who showed him through the pump-factory. It was dark but warm inside the pump-factory. Men naked to the waist took the pumps in huge tongs as they came trundling by on an endless chain, culling out the misfits and placing the perfect pumps on another endless chain that carried them up into the cooling room. Other men, Indians for the most part, wearing only breech-clouts, broke up the misfit pumps with huge hammers and adzes and rapidly recast them into axe heads, wagon springs, trombone slides, bullet moulds, all the by-products of a big pump factory. There was nothing wasted, Yogi pointed out. A group of Indian boys, humming to themselves one of the old tribal chanties, squatted in a corner of the big forging room shaping the little fragments that were chipped from the pumps in casting, into safety razor blades.

"They work naked," Yogi said. "They're searched as they go out. Sometimes they try and conceal the razor blades and take them out with them to bootleg."

"There must be quite a loss that way," Scripps said.

"Oh, no," Yogi answered. "The inspectors get most of them."

Up-stairs, apart in a separate room, two old men were working. Yogi opened the door. One of the old men looked over his steel spectacles and frowned.

"You make a draft," he said.

"Shut the door," the other old man said, in the high, complaining voice of the very old.

"They're our two hand-workers," Yogi said. "They make all the pumps the manufactory sends out to the big international pump races. You remember our Peerless Pounder that won the pump race in Italy, where Franky Dawson was killed?"

"I read about it in the paper," Scripps answered.

"Mr. Borrow, over there in the corner, made the Peerless Pounder all himself by hand," Yogi said.

"I carved it direct from the steel with this knife." Mr. Borrow held up a short-bladed, razorlike-looking knife. "Took me eighteen months to get it right."

"The Peerless Pounder was quite a pump all right," the high-voiced little old man said. "But we're working on one now that will show its heels to any of them foreign pumps, aren't we, Henry?"

"That's Mr. Shaw," Yogi said in an undertone. "He's probably the greatest living pump-maker."

"You boys get along and leave us alone," Mr. Borrow said. He was carving away steadily, his infirm old hands shaking a little between strokes.

"Let the boys watch," Mr. Shaw said. "Where you from, young feller?"

"I've just come from Mancelona," Scripps answered. "My wife left me."

"Well, you won't have no difficulty finding another one," Mr. Shaw said. "You're a likely-looking young feller. But take my advice and take your time. A poor wife ain't much better than no wife at all."

"I wouldn't say that, Henry," Mr. Borrow remarked in his high voice. "Any wife at all's a pretty good wife the way things are going now."

"You take my advice, young feller, and go slow. Get yourself a good one this time."

"Henry knows a thing or two," Mr. Borrow said. "He knows what he's talking about there." He laughed a high, cackling laugh. Mr. Shaw, the old pump-maker, blushed.

"You boys get along and leave us get on with our pump-making," he said. "Henry and me here, we got a sight of work to do."

"I'm very glad to have met you," Scripps said.

"Come on," Yogi said. "I better get you started or the foreman will be on my tail."

He put Scripps to work collaring pistons in the piston-collaring room. There Scripps worked for almost a year. In some ways it was the happiest year of his life. In other ways it was a nightmare. A hideous nightmare. In the end he grew to like it. In other ways he hated it. Before he knew it, a year had passed. He was still collaring pistons. But what strange things had happened in that year. Often he wondered about them. As he wondered, collaring a piston now almost automatically, he listened to the laughter that came up from below, where the little Indian lads were shaping what were to be razor blades. As he listened something rose in his throat and almost choked him.

CHAPTER VII

THAT night, after his first day in the pump-factory, the first day in what was or were to become an endless succession of days of dull piston-collaring, Scripps went again to the beanery to eat. All day he had kept his bird concealed. Something told him that the pump-factory was not the place to bring his bird out in. During the day the bird had several times made him uncomfortable, but he had adjusted his clothes to it and even cut a little slit the bird could poke his beak out through in search of fresh air. Now the day's work was over. It was finished. Scripps on his way to the beanery. Scripps happy that he was working with his hands. Scripps thinking of the old pump-makers. Scripps going to the society of the friendly waitress. Who was that waitress, anyway? What was it had happened to her in Paris. He must find out more about this Paris. Yogi Johnson had been there. He would quiz Yogi. Get him to talk. Draw him out. Make him tell what he knew. He knew a trick or two about that.

Watching the sunset out over the Petoskey Harbor, the lake now frozen and great blocks of ice jutting up over the breakwater, Scripps strode down the streets of Petoskey to the beanery. He would have liked to ask Yogi Johnson to eat with him, but he didn't dare. Not yet. That would come later. All in good time. No need to rush matters with a man like Yogi. Who was Yogi, anyway? Had he really been in the war? What had the war meant to him? Was he really the first man to enlist from Cadillac? Where was Cadillac, anyway? Time would tell.

Scripps O'Neil opened the door and went into the beanery. The elderly waitress got up from the chair where she had been reading the overseas edition of *The Manchester Guardian*, and put the paper and her steel-rimmed spectacles on top of the cash register.

"Good evening," she said simply. "It's good to have *you* back."

Something stirred inside Scripps O'Neil. A feeling that he could not define came within him.

"I've been working all day long"—he looked at the elderly waitress—"for *you*," he added.

"How lovely!" she said. And then smiled shyly. "And I have been working all day long—for *you*."

Tears came into Scripps's eyes. Something stirred inside him again. He reached forward to take the elderly waitress's hand, and with quiet dignity she laid it within his own. "You are my woman," he said. Tears came into her eyes, too.

"You are my man," she said.

"Once again I say: you are my woman." Scripps pronounced the words solemnly. Something had broken inside him again. He felt he could not keep from crying.

"Let this be our wedding ceremony," the elderly waitress said. Scripps pressed her hand. "You are my woman," he said simply.

"You are my man and more than my man." She looked into his eyes. "You are all of America to me."

"Let us go," Scripps said.

"Have you your bird?" asked the waitress, laying aside her apron and folding the copy of *The Manchester Guardian Weekly*. "I'll bring *The Guardian*, if you don't mind," she said, wrapping the paper in her apron. "It's a new paper and I've not read it yet."

"I'm very fond of *The Guardian*," Scripps said. "My family have taken it ever since I can remember. My father was a great admirer of Gladstone."

"My father went to Eton with Gladstone," the elderly waitress said. "And now I am ready."

She had donned a coat and stood ready, her apron, her steel-rimmed spectacles in their worn black morocco case, her copy of *The Manchester Guardian* held in her hand.

"Have you no hat?" asked Scripps.

"No."

"Then I will buy you one," Scripps said tenderly.

"It will be your wedding gift," the elderly waitress said. Again there were tears shone in her eyes.

"And now let us go," Scripps said.

The elderly waitress came out from behind the counter, and together, hand in hand, they strode out into the night.

Inside the beanery the black cook pushed up the wicket and looked through from the kitchen. "Dey've gone off," he chuckled. "Gone off into de night. Well, well, well." He closed the wicket softly. Even he was a little impressed.

CHAPTER VIII

HALF an hour later Scripps O'Neil and the elderly waitress returned to the beanery as man and wife. The beanery looked much the same. There was the long counter, the salt cellars, the sugar containers, the catsup bottle, the Worcestershire Sauce bottle. There was the wicket that led into the kitchen. Behind the counter was the relief waitress. She was a buxom, jolly-looking girl, and she wore a white apron. At the counter, reading a Detroit paper, sat a drummer. The drummer was eating a T-bone steak and hashed-brown potatoes. Something very beautiful had happened to Scripps and the elderly waitress. Now they were hungry. They wished to eat.

The elderly waitress looking at Scripps. Scripps looking at the elderly waitress. The drummer reading his paper and occasionally putting a little catsup on his hashed-brown potatoes. The other waitress, Mandy, back of the counter in her freshly starched white apron. The frost on the windows. The warmth inside. The cold outside. Scripps's bird, rather rumpled now, sitting on the counter and preening his feathers.

"So you've come back," Mandy the waitress said. "The cook said you had gone out into the night."

The elderly waitress looked at Mandy, her eyes brightened, her voice calm and now of a deeper, richer timbre.

"We are man and wife now," she said kindly. "We have just been married. What would you like to eat for supper, Scripps, dear?"

"I don't know," Scripps said. He felt vaguely uneasy. Something was stirring within him.

"Perhaps you have eaten enough of the beans, dear Scripps," the elderly waitress, now his wife, said. The drummer looked up from his paper. Scripps noticed that it was the Detroit *News*. There was a fine paper.

"That's a fine paper you're reading," Scripps said to the drummer.

"It's a good paper, the *News*," the drummer said. "You two on your honeymoon?"

"Yes," Mrs. Scripps said; "we are man and wife now."

"Well," said the drummer, "that's a mighty fine thing to be. I'm a married man myself."

"Are you?" said Scripps. "My wife left me. It was in Mancelona."

"Don't let's talk of that any more, Scripps, dear," Mrs. Scripps said. "You've told that story so many times."

"Yes, dear," Scripps agreed. He felt vaguely mistrustful of himself. Something, somewhere was stirring inside of him. He looked at the waitress called Mandy, standing robust and vigorously lovely in her newly starched white apron. He watched her hands, healthy, calm, capable hands, doing the duties of her waitresshood.

"Try one of these T-bones with hashed-brown potatoes," the drummer suggested. "They got a nice T-bone here."

"Would you like one, dear?" Scripps asked his wife.

"I'll just take a bowl of milk and crackers," the elderly Mrs. Scripps said. "You have whatever you want, dear."

"Here's your crackers and milk, Diana," Mandy said, placing them on the counter. "Do you want a T-bone, sir?"

"Yes," Scripps said. Something stirred again within him.

"Well done or rare?"

"Rare, please."

The waitress turned and called into the wicket: "Tea for one. Let it go raw!"

"Thank you," Scripps said. He eyed the waitress Mandy. She

had a gift for the picturesque in speech, that girl. It had been that very picturesque quality in her speech that had first drawn him to his present wife. That and her strange background. England, the Lake Country. Scripps striding through the Lake Country with Wordsworth. A field of golden daffodils. The wind blowing at Windermere. Far off, perhaps, a stag at bay. Ah, that was farther north, in Scotland. They were a hardy race, those Scots, deep in their mountain fastnesses. Harry Lauder and his pipe. The Highlanders in the Great War. Why had not he, Scripps, been in the war? That was where that chap Yogi Johnson had it on him. The war would have meant much to him, Scripps. Why hadn't he been in it? Why hadn't he heard of it in time? Perhaps he was too old. Look at that old French General Joffre, though. Surely he was a younger man than that old general. General Foch praying for victory. The French troops kneeling along the Chemin des Dames, praying for victory. The Germans with their *"Gott mit uns."* What a mockery. Surely he was no older than that French General Foch. He wondered.

Mandy, the waitress, placed his T-bone steak and hashed-brown potatoes on the counter before him. As she laid the plate down, just for an instant, her hand touched his. Scripps felt a strange thrill go through him. Life was before him. He was not an old man. Why were there no wars now? Perhaps there were. Men were fighting in China, Chinamen, Chinamen killing one another. What for? Scripps wondered. What was it all about, anyway?

Mandy, the buxom waitress, leaned forward. "Say," she said, "did I ever tell you about the last words of Henry James?"

"Really, dear Mandy," Mrs. Scripps said, "you've told that story rather often."

"Let's hear it," Scripps said. "I'm very interested in Henry James." Henry James, Henry James. That chap who had gone away from his own land to live in England among Englishmen. Why had he done it? For what had he left America? Weren't his roots here? His brother William. Boston. Pragmatism. Harvard University. Old John Harvard with silver buckles on his shoes. Charley Brickley. Eddie Mahan. Where were they now?

"Well," Mandy began, "Henry James became a British subject on his death-bed. At once, as soon as the king heard Henry James had become a British subject he sent around the highest decoration in his power to bestow—the Order of Merit."

"The O.M.," the elderly Mrs. Scripps explained.

"That was it," the waitress said. "Professors Gosse and Saintsbury came with the man who brought the decoration. Henry James was lying on his death-bed, and his eyes were shut. There was a single candle on a table beside the bed. The nurse allowed them to come near the bed, and they put the ribbon of the decoration around James's neck, and the decoration lay on the sheet over Henry James's chest. Professors Gosse and Saintsbury leaned forward and smoothed the ribbon of the decoration. Henry James never opened his eyes. The nurse told them they all must go out of the room, and they all went out of the room. When they were all gone, Henry James spoke to the nurse. He never opened his eyes. 'Nurse,' Henry James said, 'put out the candle, nurse, and spare my blushes.' Those were the last words he ever spoke."

"James was quite a writer," Scripps O'Neil said. He was strangely moved by the story.

"You don't always tell it the same way, dear," Mrs. Scripps remarked to Mandy. There were tears in Mandy's eyes. "I feel very strongly about Henry James," she said.

"What was the matter with James?" asked the drummer. "Wasn't America good enough for him?"

Scripps O'Neil was thinking about Mandy, the waitress. What a background she must have, that girl! What a fund of anecdote! A chap could go far with a woman like that to help him! He stroked the little bird that sat on the lunch-counter before him. The bird pecked at his finger. Was the little bird a hawk? A falcon, perhaps, from one of the big Michigan falconries. Was it perhaps a robin? Pulling and tugging at the early worm on some green lawn somewhere? He wondered.

"What do you call your bird?" the drummer asked.

"I haven't named him yet. What would you call him?"

"Why not call him Ariel?" Mandy asked.

"Or Puck," Mrs. Scripps put in.

"What's it mean?" asked the drummer.

"It's a character out of Shakespeare," Mandy explained.

"Oh, give the bird a chance."

"What would you call him?" Scripps turned to the drummer.

"He ain't a parrot, is he?" asked the drummer. "If he was a parrot you could call him Polly."

"There's a character in 'The Beggar's Opera' called Polly," Mandy explained.

Scripps wondered. Perhaps the bird was a parrot. A parrot strayed from some comfortable home with some old maid. The untilled soil of some New England spinster.

"Better wait till you see how he turns out," the drummer advised. "You got plenty of time to name him."

This drummer had sound ideas. He, Scripps, did not even know what sex the bird was. Whether he was a boy bird or a girl bird.

"Wait till you see if he lays eggs," the drummer suggested. Scripps looked into the drummer's eyes. The fellow had voiced his own unspoken thought.

"You know a thing or two, drummer," he said.

"Well," the drummer admitted modestly, "I ain't drummed all these years for nothing."

"You're right there, pal," Scripps said.

"That's a nice bird you got there, brother," the drummer said. "You want to hang onto that bird."

Scripps knew it. Ah, these drummers know a thing or two. Going up and down over the face of this great America of ours. These drummers kept their eyes open. They were no fools.

"Listen," the drummer said. He pushed his derby hat off his brow and, leaning forward, spat into the tall brass cuspidor that stood beside his stool. "I want to tell you about a pretty beautiful thing that happened to me once in Bay City."

Mandy, the waitress, leaned forward. Mrs. Scripps leaned toward the drummer to hear better. The drummer looked apologetically at Scripps and stroked the bird with his forefinger.

"Tell you about it some other time, brother," he said. Scripps understood. From out of the kitchen, through the wicket in the hall, came a high-pitched, haunting laugh. Scripps listened. Could that be the laughter of the Negro? He wondered.

CHAPTER IX

SCRIPPS going slowly to work in the pump-factory in the mornings. Mrs. Scripps looking out of the window and watching him go up the street. Not much time for reading *The Guardian* now. Not much time for reading about English politics. Not much time for worrying about the cabinet crises over there in France. The French were a strange people. Joan of Arc. Eva le Gallienne. Clemenceau. Georges Carpentier. Sacha Guitry. Yvonne Printemps. Grock. Les Fratellinis. Gilbert Seldes. *The Dial*. *The Dial* Prize. Marianne Moore. E. E. Cummings. "The Enormous Room." *Vanity Fair*. Frank Crowninshield. What was it all about? Where was it taking her?

She had a man now. A man of her own. For her own. Could she keep him? Could she hold him for her own? She wondered.

Mrs. Scripps, formerly an elderly waitress, now the wife of Scripps O'Neil, with a good job in the pump-factory. Diana Scripps. Diana was her own name. It had been her mother's, too. Diana Scripps looking into the mirror and wondering could she hold him. It was getting to be a question. Why had he ever met Mandy? Would she have the courage to break off going to the restaurant with Scripps to eat? She couldn't do that. He would go alone. She knew that. It was no use trying to pull wool over her own eyes. He would go alone and he would talk with Mandy. Diana looked into the mirror. Could she hold him? Could she hold him? That thought never left her now.

Every night at the restaurant, she couldn't call it a beanery now —that made a lump come in her throat and made her throat feel hard and choky. Every night at the restaurant now Scripps and Mandy talked together. The girl was trying to take him away.

Him, her Scripps. Trying to take him away. Take him away. Could she, Diana, hold him?

She was no better than a slut, that Mandy. Was that the way to do? Was that the thing to do? Go after another woman's man? Come between man and wife? Break up a home? And all with these interminable literary reminiscences. These endless anecdotes. Scripps was fascinated by Mandy. Diana admitted that to herself. But she might hold him. That was all that mattered now. To hold him. To hold him. Not to let him go. Make him stay. She looked into the mirror.

Diana subscribing for *The Forum*. Diana reading *The Mentor*. Diana reading William Lyon Phelps in *Scribner's*. Diana walking through the frozen streets of the silent Northern town to the Public Library, to read *The Literary Digest* "Book Review." Diana waiting for the postman to come, bringing *The Bookman*. Diana, in the snow, waiting for the postman to brng *The Saturday Review of Literature*. Diana, bareheaded now, standing in the mounting snowdrifts, waiting for the postman to bring her the New York *Times* "Literary Section." Was it doing any good? Was it holding him?

At first it seemed to be. Diana learned editorials by John Farrar by heart. Scripps brightened. A little of the old light shining in Scripps's eyes now. Then it died. Some little mistake in the wording, some slip in her understanding of a phrase, some divergence in her attitude, made it all ring false. She would go on. She was not beaten. He was her man and she would hold him. She looked away from the window and slit open the covering of the magazine that lay on her table. It was *Harper's Magazine*. *Harper's Magazine* in a new format. *Harper's Magazine* completely changed and revised. Perhaps that would do the trick. She wondered.

CHAPTER X

SPRING was coming. Spring was in the air. (Author's Note.—This is the same day on which the story starts, back on page one.) A chinook wind was blowing. Workmen were coming home from the factory. Scripps's bird singing in its cage. Diana looking out of the open window. Diana watching for her Scripps to come up the street. Could she hold him? Could she hold him? If she couldn't hold him, would he leave her his bird? She had felt lately that she couldn't hold him. In the nights, now, when she touched Scripps he rolled away, not toward her. It was a little sign, but life was made up of little signs. She felt she couldn't hold him. As she looked out of the window, a copy of *The Century Magazine* dropped from her nerveless hand. *The Century* had a new editor. There were more woodcuts. Glenn Frank had gone to head some great university somewhere. There were more Van Dorens on the magazine. Diana felt that might turn the trick. Happily she had opened *The Century* and read all morning. Then the wind, the warm chinook wind, had started to blow, and she knew Scripps would soon be home. Men were coming down the street in increasing numbers. Was Scripps among them? She did not like to put on her spectacles to look. She wanted Scripps's first glimpse of her to be of her at her best. As she felt him drawing nearer, the confidence she had had in *The Century* grew fainter. She had so hoped that would give her the something which would hold him. She wasn't sure now.

Scripps coming down the street with a crowd of excited workmen. Men stirred by the spring. Scripps swinging his lunch-bucket. Scripps waving good-by to the workmen, who trooped one by one into what had formerly been a saloon. Scripps not looking up at the window. Scripps coming up the stairs. Scripps coming nearer. Scripps coming nearer. Scripps here.

"Good afternoon, dear Scripps," she said. "I've been reading a story by Ruth Suckow."

"Hello, Diana," Scripps answered. He set down his lunch-pail. She looked worn and old. He could afford to be polite.

"What was the story about, Diana?" he asked.

"It was about a little girl in Iowa," Diana said. She moved toward him. "It was about people on the land. It reminded me a little of my own Lake Country."

"That so?" asked Scripps. In some ways the pump-factory had hardened him. His speech had become more clipped. More like these hardy Northern workers'. But his mind was the same.

"Would you like me to read a little of it out loud?" Diana asked. "They're some lovely woodcuts."

"How about going down to the beanery?" Scripps said.

"As you wish, dear," Diana said. Then her voice broke. "I wish— oh, I wish you'd never seen that place!" She wiped away her tears. Scripps had not even seen them. "I'll bring the bird, dear," Diana said. "He hasn't been out all day."

Together they went down the street to the beanery. They did not walk hand in hand now. They walked like what are called old married people. Mrs. Scripps carried the bird-cage. The bird was happy in the warm wind. Men lurching along, drunk with the spring, passed them. Many spoke to Scripps. He was well known and well liked in the town now. Some, as they lurched by, raised their hats to Mrs. Scripps. She responded vaguely. If I can only hold him, she was thinking. If I can only hold him. As they walked along the slushy snow of the narrow sidewalk of the Northern town, something began to beat in her head. Perhaps it was the rhythm of their walking together. I can't hold him. I can't hold him. I can't hold him.

Scripps took her arm as they crossed the street. When his hand touched her arm Diana knew it was true. She would never hold him. A group of Indians passed them on the street. Were they laughing at her or was it some tribal jest? Diana didn't know. All she knew was that rhythm that beat into her brain. I can't hold him. I can't hold him.

AUTHOR'S NOTE:

For the reader, not the printer. What difference does it make to the printer? Who is the printer, anyway? Gutenberg. The Gutenberg Bible. Caxton. Twelve-point open-face Caslon. The linotype machine. The author as a little boy being sent to look for type lice. The author as a young man being sent for the key to the forms. Ah, they knew a trick or two, these printers.

(In case the reader is becoming confused, we are now up to where the story opened with Yogi Johnson and Scripps O'Neil in the pump-factory itself, with the chinook wind blowing. As you see, Scripps O'Neil has now come out of the pump-factory and is on his way to the beanery with his wife, who is afraid she cannot hold him. Personally, we don't believe she can, but the reader will see for himself. We will now leave the couple on their way to the beanery and go back and take up Yogi Johnson. We want the reader to like Yogi Johnson. The story will move a little faster from now on, in case any of the readers are tiring. We will also try and work in a number of good anecdotes. Would it be any violation of confidence if we told the reader that we get the best of these anecdotes from Mr. Ford Madox Ford? We owe him our thanks, and we hope the reader does, too. At any rate, we will now go on with Yogi Johnson. Yogi Johnson, the reader may remember, is the chap who was in the war. As the story opens, he is just coming out of the pump-factory. (See page three.)

It is very hard to write this way, beginning things backward, and the author hopes the reader will realize this and not grudge this little word of explanation. I know I would be very glad to read anything the reader ever wrote, and I hope the reader will make the same sort of allowances. If any of the readers would care to send me anything they ever wrote, for criticism or advice, I am always at the Café du Dôme any afternoon, talking about Art with Harold Stearns and Sinclair Lewis, and the reader can bring his stuff along with him, or he can send it to me care of my bank, if I have a bank. Now, if the reader is ready—and understand, I don't want to rush the reader any—we will go back to Yogi Johnson. But please remember that, while we have gone back to Yogi Johnson, Scripps O'Neil and his wife are on their way to the beanery. What will happen to them there I don't know. I only wish the reader could help me.)

Part III

MEN IN WAR AND THE DEATH OF SOCIETY

It may be likewise noted that affectation does not imply an absolute negation of those qualities which are affected; and therefore, though, when it proceeds from hypocrisy, it be nearly allied to deceit; yet when it comes from vanity only, it partakes of the nature of ostentation: for instance, the affectation of liberality in a vain man differs visibly from the same affectation in the avaricious, for though the vain man is not what he would appear, or hath not the virtue he affects, to the degree he would be thought to have it; yet it sits less awkwardly on him than on the avaricious man, who is the very reverse of what he would seem to be.

HENRY FIELDING

CHAPTER XI

YOGI JOHNSON walked out of the workmen's entrance of the pump-factory and down the street. Spring was in the air. The snow was melting, and the gutters were running with snow-water. Yogi Johnson walked down the middle of the street, keeping on the as yet unmelted ice. He turned to the left and crossed the bridge over Bear River. The ice had already melted in the river and he watched the swirling brown current. Below, beside the stream, buds on the willow brush were coming out green.

It's a real chinook wind, Yogi thought. The foreman did right to let the men go. It wouldn't be safe keeping them in a day like this. Anything might happen. The owner of the factory knew a thing or two. When the chinook blew, the thing to do was to get the men out of the factory. Then, if any of them were injured, it was not on him. He didn't get caught under the Employer's Liability Act. They knew a thing or two, these big pump-manufacturers. They were smart, all right.

Yogi was worried. There was something on his mind. It was spring, there was no doubt of that now, and he did not want a woman. He had worried about it a lot lately. There was no question about it. He did not want a woman. He couldn't explain it to himself. He had gone to the Public Library and asked for a book the night before. He looked at the librarian. He did not want her. Somehow, she meant nothing to him. At the restaurant where he had a meal ticket he looked hard at the waitress who brought him his meals. He did not want her, either. He passed a group of girls on their way home from High School. He looked carefully at all of them. He did not want a single one. Decidedly something was wrong. Was he going to pieces? Was this the end?

Well, Yogi thought, women are gone, perhaps, though I hope not; but I still have my love of horses. He was walking up the steep hill that leads up from the Bear River out onto the Charlevoix road. The road was not really so steep, but it felt steep to Yogi, his legs heavy with the spring. In front of him was a grain and feed store. A team of beautiful horses were hitched in front of the feed store. Yogi went up to them. He wanted to touch them. To reassure himself that there was something left. The nigh horse looked at him as he came near. Yogi put his hand in his pocket for a lump of sugar. He had no sugar. The horse put its ears back and showed its teeth. The other horse jerked its head away. Was this all that his love of horses had brought him? After all, perhaps there was something wrong with these horses. Perhaps they had glanders or spavin. Perhaps something had been caught in the tender frog of their hoof. Perhaps they were lovers.

Yogi walked on up the hill and turned to the left onto the Charlevoix road. He passed the last houses of the outskirts of Petoskey and came out onto the open country road. On his right was a field that stretched to Little Traverse Bay. The blue of the bay opening out into the big Lake Michigan. Across the bay the pine hills behind Harbor Springs. Beyond, where you could not see it, Cross Village, where the Indians lived. Even further beyond, the Straits of Mackinac with St. Ignace, where a strange and beautiful thing had once happened to Oscar Gardner, who worked beside Yogi in the pump-factory. Further beyond, the Soo, both Canadian and American. There the wilder spirits of Petoskey sometimes went to drink beer. They were happy then. 'Way, 'way beyond, and, in the other direction, at the foot of the lake was Chicago, where Scripps O'Neil had started for on that eventful night when his first marriage had become a marriage no longer. Near there Gary, Indiana, where were the great steel mills. Near there Hammond, Indiana. Near there Michigan City, Indiana. Further beyond, there would be Indianapolis, Indiana, where Booth Tarkington lived. He had the wrong dope, that fellow. Further down there would be Cincinnati, Ohio. Beyond that, Vicksburg, Mississippi. Beyond that, Waco, Texas. Ah! there was grand sweep to this America of ours.

Yogi walked across the road and sat down on a pile of logs, where he could look out over the lake. After all, the war was over and he was still alive.

There was a chap in that fellow Anderson's book that the librarian had given him at the library last night. Why hadn't he wanted the librarian, anyway? Could it be because he thought she might have false teeth? Could it be something else? Would a little child ever tell her? He didn't know. What was the librarian to him, anyway?

This chap in the book by Anderson. He had been a soldier, too. He had been at the front two years, Anderson said. What was his name? Fred Something. This Fred had thoughts dancing in his brain—horror. One night, in the time of the fighting, he went out on parade—no, it was patrol—in No Man's Land, and saw another man stumbling along in the darkness and shot him. The man pitched forward dead. It had been the only time Fred consciously killed a man. You don't kill men in war much, the book said. The hell you don't, Yogi thought, if you're two years in the infantry at the front. They just die. Indeed they do, Yogi thought. Anderson said the act was rather hysterical on Fred's part. He and the men with him might have made the fellow surrender. They had all got the jimjams. After it happened they all ran away together. Where the hell did they run to? Yogi wondered. Paris?

Afterward, killing this man haunted Fred. It's got to be sweet and true. That was the way the soldiers thought, Anderson said. The hell it was. This Fred was supposed to have been two years in an infantry regiment at the front.

A couple of Indians were passing along the road, grunting to themselves and to each other. Yogi called to them. The Indians came over.

"Big white chief got chew of tobacco?" asked the first Indian.

"White chief carry liquor?" the second Indian asked.

Yogi handed them a package of Peerless and his pocket flask.

"White chief heap big medicine," the Indians grunted.

"Listen," Yogi Johnson said. "I am about to address to you a few remarks about the war. A subject on which I feel very deeply." The Indians sat down on the logs. One of the Indians pointed at the sky. "Up there gitchy Manitou the Mighty," he said.

The other Indian winked at Yogi. "White chief no believe every goddam thing he hear," he grunted.

"Listen," Yogi Johnson said. And he told them about the war.

War hadn't been that way to Yogi, he told the Indians. War had been to him like football. American football. What they play at the colleges. Carlisle Indian School. Both the Indians nodded. They had been to Carlisle.

Yogi had played centre at football and war had been much the same thing, intensely unpleasant. When you played football and had the ball, you were down with your legs spread out and the ball held out in front of you on the ground; you had to listen for the signal, decode it, and make the proper pass. You had to think about it all the time. While your hands were on the ball the opposing centre stood in front of you, and when you passed the ball he brought his hand up smash into your face and grabbed you with the other hand under the chin or under your armpit, and tried to pull you forward or shove you back to make a hole he could go through and break up the play. You were supposed to charge forward so hard you banged him out of the play with your body and put you both on the ground. He had all the advantage. It was not what you would call fun. When you had the ball he had all the advantage. The only good thing was that when he had the ball you could rough-house *him*. In this way things evened up and sometimes even a certain tolerance was achieved. Football, like the war, was unpleasant; stimulating and exciting after you had attained a certain hardness, and the chief difficulty had been that of remembering the signals. Yogi was thinking about the war, not the army. He meant combat. The army was something different. You could take it and ride with it or you could buck the tiger and let it smash you. The army was a silly business, but the war was different.

Yogi was not haunted by men he had killed. He knew he had killed five men. Probably he had killed more. He didn't believe men you killed haunted you. Not if you had been two years at the front. Most of the men he had known had been excited as hell when they had first killed. The trouble was to keep them from killing too much. It was hard to get prisoners back to the people that wanted them for identification. You sent a man back with two prisoners; maybe you sent two men back with four prisoners. What happened? The men came back and said the prisoners were knocked out by the barrage. They would give the prisoner a poke in the seat of the pants with a bayonet, and when the prisoner jumped they would say, "You would run, you son of a bitch," and let their gun off in the back of his head. They wanted to be sure they had killed. Also they didn't want to go back through any damn barrage. No, sir. They learned those kind of manners from the Australians. After all, what were those Jerries? A bunch of goddam Huns. "Huns" sounded like a funny word now. All this sweetness and truth. Not if you were in there two years. In the end they would have softened. Got sorry for excesses and begun to store up good deeds against getting killed themselves. But that was the fourth phase of soldiering, the gentling down.

In a good soldier in the war it went like this: First, you were brave because you didn't think anything could hit you, because you yourself were something special, and you knew that you could never die. Then you found out different. You were really scared then, but if you were a good soldier you functioned the same as before. Then after you were wounded and not killed, with new men coming on, and going through your old processes, you hardened and became a good hard-boiled soldier. Then came the second crack, which is much worse than the first, and then you began doing good deeds, and being the boy Sir Philip Sidney, and storing up treasures in heaven. At the same time, of course, functioning always the same as before. As if it were a football game.

Nobody had any damn business to write about it, though, that didn't at least know about it from hearsay. Literature has too strong an effect on people's minds. Like this American writer Willa Cather, who wrote a book about the war where all the last part of it was taken from the action in the "Birth of a Nation," and ex-servicemen wrote to her from all over America to tell her how much they liked it.

One of the Indians was asleep. He had been chewing tobacco, and his mouth was pursed up in sleep. He was leaning on the other Indian's shoulder. The Indian who was awake pointed at the other Indian, who was asleep, and shook his head.

"Well how did you like the speech?" Yogi asked the Indian who was awake.

"White chief have heap much sound ideas," the Indian said. "White chief educated like hell."

"Thank you," Yogi said. He felt touched. Here among the simple aborigines, the only real Americans, he had found that true communion. The Indian looked at him, holding the sleeping Indian carefully that his head might not fall back upon the snow-covered logs.

"Was white chief in the war?" the Indian asked.

"I landed in France in May, 1917," Yogi began.

"I thought maybe white chief was in the war from the way he talked," the Indian said. "Him," he raised the head of his sleeping companion up so the last rays of the sunset shone on the sleeping Indian's face, "he got V. C. Me I got D. S. O. and M. C. with bar. I was major in the Fourth C. M. R.'s."

"I'm glad to meet you," Yogi said. He felt strangely humiliated. It was growing dark. There was a single line of sunset where the sky and the water met 'way out on Lake Michigan. Yogi watched the narrow line of the sunset grow darker red, thin to a mere slit, and then fade. The sun was down behind the lake. Yogi stood up from the pile of logs. The Indian stood up too. He awakened his companion, and the Indian who had been sleeping stood up and looked at Yogi Johnson.

"We go to Petoskey to join Salvation Army," the larger and more wakeful Indian said.

"White chief come too," said the smaller Indian, who had been asleep.

"I'll walk in with you," Yogi replied. Who were these Indians? What did they mean to him?

With the sun down, the slushy road was stiffening. It was freezing again. After all, maybe spring was not coming. Maybe it did not make a difference that he did not want a woman. Now that the spring was perhaps not coming there was a question about that. He would walk into town with the Indians and look for a beautiful woman and try and want her. He turned down the now frozen road. The two Indians walked by his side. They were all bound in the same direction.

CHAPTER XII

THROUGH the night down the frozen road the three walked into Petoskey. They had been silent walking along the frozen road. Their shoes broke the new-formed crusts of ice. Sometimes Yogi Johnson stepped through a thin film of ice into a pool of water. The Indians avoided the pools of water.

They came down the hill past the feed store, crossed the bridge over the Bear River, their boots ringing hollowly on the frozen planks of the bridge, and climbed the hill that led past Doctor Rumsey's house and the Home Tea-Room up to the pool-room. In front of the pool-room the two Indians stopped.

"White chief shoot pool?" the big Indian asked.

"No," Yogi Johnson said. "My right arm was crippled in the war."

"White chief have hard luck," the small Indian said. "Shoot one game Kelly pool."

"He got both arms and both legs shot off at Ypres," the big Indian said in an aside to Yogi. "Him very sensitive."

"All right," Yogi Johnson said. "I'll shoot one game."

They went into the hot, smoke-filled warmth of the pool-room. They obtained a table and took down cues from the wall. As the little Indian reached up to take down his cue Yogi noticed that he had two artificial arms. They were brown leather and were both buckled on at the elbow. On the smooth green cloth, under the bright electric lights, they played pool. At the end of an hour and a half, Yogi Johnson found that he owed the little Indian four dollars and thirty cents.

"You shoot a pretty nice stick," he remarked to the small Indian.

"Me not shoot so good since the war," the small Indian replied.

"White chief like to drink a little?" asked the larger Indian.

"Where do you get it?" asked Yogi. "I have to go to Cheboygan for mine."

"White chief come with red brothers," the big Indian said.

They left the pool-table, placed their cues in the rack on the wall, paid at the counter, and went out into the night.

Along the dark streets men were sneaking home. The frost had come and frozen everything stiff and cold. The chinook had not been a real chinook, after all. Spring had not yet come, and the men who had commenced their orgies were halted by the chill in the air that told them the chinook wind had been a fake. That foreman, Yogi thought, he'll catch hell to-morrow. Perhaps it had all been engineered by the pump-manufacturers to get the foreman out of his job. Such things were done. Through the dark of the night men were sneaking home in little groups.

The two Indians walked on either side of Yogi. They turned down a side street, and all three halted before a building that looked something like a stable. It was a stable. The two Indians opened the door and Yogi followed them inside. A ladder led upstairs to the floor above. It was dark inside the stable, but one of the Indians lit a match to show Yogi the ladder. The little Indian climbed up first, the metal hinges of his artificial limbs squeaking as he climbed. Yogi followed him, and the other Indian climbed last, lighting Yogi's way with matches. The little Indian knocked on the roof where the ladder stopped against the wall. There was an answering knock. The little Indian knocked in answer, three sharp knocks on the roof above his head. A trap-door in the roof was raised, and they climbed up through into the lighted room.

In one corner of the room there was a bar with a brass rail and tall spittoons. Behind the bar was a mirror. Easy-chairs were all around the room. There was a pool-table. Magazines on sticks hung in a line on the wall. There was a framed autographed portrait of Henry Wadsworth Longfellow on the wall draped in the American flag. Several Indians were sitting in the easy-chairs reading. A little group stood at the bar.

"Nice little club, eh?" an Indian came up and shook hands with Yogi. "I see you almost every day at the pump-factory."

He was a man who worked at one of the machines near Yogi in the factory. Another Indian came up and shook hands with Yogi. He also worked in the pump-factory.

"Rotten luck about the chinook," he said.

"Yes," Yogi said. "Just a false alarm."

"Come and have a drink," the first Indian said.

"I'm with a party," Yogi answered. Who were these Indians anyway?

"Bring them along too," the first Indian said. "Always room for one more."

Yogi looked around him. The two Indians who had brought him were gone. Where were they? Then he saw them. They were over at the pool-table. The tall refined Indian to whom Yogi was talking followed his glance. He nodded his head in understanding.

"They're woods Indians," he explained apologetically. "We're most of us town Indians here."

"Yes, of course," Yogi agreed.

"The little chap has a very good war record," the tall refined Indian remarked. "The other chap was a major too, I believe."

Yogi was guided over to the bar by the tall refined Indian. Behind the bar was the bartender. He was a Negro.

"How would some Dog's Head ale go?" asked the Indian.

"Fine," Yogi said.

"Two Dog's Heads, Bruce," the Indian remarked to the bartender. The bartender broke into a chuckle.

"What are you laughing at, Bruce?" the Indian asked.

The Negro broke into a shrill haunting laugh.

"I knowed it, Massa Red Dog," he said. "I knowed you'd ordah dat Dog's Head all the time."

"He's a merry fellow," the Indian remarked to Yogi. "I must introduce myself. Red Dog's the name."

"Johnson's the name," Yogi said. "Yogi Johnson."

"Oh, we are all quite familiar with your name, Mr. Johnson," Red Dog smiled. "I would like you to meet my friends Mr. Sitting Bull, Mr. Poisoned Buffalo, and Chief Running Skunk-Backwards."

"Sitting Bull's a name I know," Yogi remarked, shaking hands.

"Oh, I'm not one of those Sitting Bulls," Mr. Sitting Bull said.

"Chief Running Skunk-Backwards's great-grandfather once sold the entire Island of Manhattan for a few strings of wampum," Red Dog explained.

"How very interesting," Yogi said.

"That was a costly bit of wampum for our family," Chief Running Skunk-Backwards smiled ruefully.

"Chief Running Skunk-Backwards has some of that wampum. Would you like to see it?" Red Dog asked.

"Indeed, I would."

"It's really no different from any other wampum," Skunk-Backwards explained deprecatingly. He pulled a chain of wampum out of his pocket, and handed it to Yogi Johnson. Yogi looked at it curiously. What a part that string of wampum had played in this America of ours.

"Would you like to have one or two wampums for a keepsake?" Skunk-Backwards asked.

"I wouldn't like to take your wampum," Yogi demurred.

"They have no intrinsic value really," Skunk-Backwards explained, detaching one or two wampums from the string.

"Their value is really a sentimental one to Skunk-Backwards's family," Red Dog said.

"It's damned decent of you, Mr. Skunk-Backwards," Yogi said.

"It's nothing," Skunk-Backwards said. "You'd do the same for me in a moment."

"It's decent of you."

Behind the bar, Bruce, the Negro bartender, had been leaning forward and watching the wampums pass from hand to hand. His dark face shone. Sharply, without explanation, he broke into high-pitched uncontrolled laughter. The dark laughter of the Negro.

Red Dog looked at him sharply. "I say, Bruce," he spoke sharply; "your mirth is a little ill-timed."

Bruce stopped laughing and wiped his face on a towel. He rolled his eyes apologetically.

"Ah, can't help it, Massa Red Dog. When I seen Mistah Skunk-Backhouse passin' dem wampums around I jess couldn't stand it no longa. Whad he wan sell a big town like New Yawk foh dem wampums for? Wampums! Take away yoah wampums!"

"Bruce is an eccentric," Red Dog explained, "but he's a corking bartender and a good-hearted chap."

"Youah right theah, Massa Red Dog," the bartender leaned forward. "I'se got a heart of puah gold."

"He is an eccentric, though," Red Dog apologized. "The house committee are always after me to get another bartender, but I like the chap, oddly enough."

"I'm all right, boss," Bruce said. "It's just that when I see something funny I just have to laff. You know I don' mean no harm, boss."

"Right enough, Bruce," Red Dog agreed. "You are an honest chap."

Yogi Johnson looked about the room. The other Indians had gone away from the bar, and Skunk-Backwards was showing the wampum to a little group of Indians in dinner dress who had just come in. At the pool-table the two woods Indians were still playing. They had removed their coats, and the light above the pool-table glinted on the metal joints in the little woods Indian's artificial arms. He had just run the table for the eleventh consecutive time.

"That little chap would have made a pool-player if he hadn't had a bit of hard luck in the war," Red Dog remarked. "Would you like to have a look about the club?" He took the check from Bruce, signed it, and Yogi followed him into the next room.

"Our committee room," Red Dog said. On the walls were framed autographed photographs of Chief Bender, Francis Parkman, D. H. Lawrence, Chief Meyers, Stewart Edward White, Mary Austin, Jim Thorpe, General Custer, Glenn Warner, Mabel Dodge, and a full-length oil painting of Henry Wadsworth Longfellow.

Beyond the committee room was a locker room with a small plunge bath or swimming-pool. "It's really ridiculously small for a club," Red Dog said. "But it makes a comfortable little hole to pop into when the evenings are dull." He smiled. "We call it the wigwam, you know. That's a little conceit of my own."

"It's a damned nice club," Yogi said enthusiastically.

"Put you up if you like," Red Dog offered. "What's your tribe?"

"What do you mean?"

"Your tribe. What are you—Sac and Fox? Jibway? Cree, I imagine."

"Oh," said Yogi. "My parents came from Sweden."

Red Dog looked at him closely. His eyes narrowed.

"You're not having me on?"

"No. They either came from Sweden or Norway," Yogi said.

"I'd have sworn you looked a bit on the white side," Red Dog said. "Damned good thing this came out in time. There'd have been no end of scandal." He put his hand to his head and pursed his lips. "Here, you," he turned suddenly and gripped Yogi by the vest. Yogi felt the barrel of an automatic pushed hard against his stomach. "You'll go quietly through the club-room, get your coat and hat and leave as though nothing had happened. Say polite good-by to any one who happens to speak to you. And never come back. Get that, you Swede."

"Yes," said Yogi. "Put up your gun. I'm not afraid of your gun."

"Do as I say," Red Dog ordered. "As for those two pool-players that brought you here, I'll soon have them out of this."

Yogi went into the bright room, looked at the bar, where Bruce, the bartender, was regarding him, got his hat and coat, said good-night to Skunk-Backwards, who asked him why he was leaving so early, and the outside trap-door was swung up by Bruce. As Yogi started down the ladder the Negro burst out laughing. "I knowed it," he laughed. "I knowed it all de time. No Swede gwine to fool ole Bruce."

Yogi looked back and saw the laughing black face of the Negro framed in the oblong square of light that came through the raised trap-door. Once on the stable floor, Bruce looked around him. He was alone. The straw of the old stable was stiff and frozen under his feet. Where had he been? Had he been in an Indian club? What was it all about? Was this the end?

Above him a slit of light came in the roof. Then it was blocked by two black figures, there was the sound of a kick, a blow, a series of thuds, some dull, some sharp, and two human forms came crashing down the ladder. From above floated the dark, haunting sound of black Negro laughter.

The two woods Indians picked themselves up from the straw and limped toward the door. One of them, the little one, was crying. Yogi followed them out into the cold night. It was cold. The night was clear. The stars were out.

"Club no damn good," the big Indian said. "Club heap no damn good."

The little Indian was crying. Yogi, in the starlight, saw that he had lost one of his artificial arms.

"Me no play pool no more," the little Indian sobbed. He shook his one arm at the window of the club, from which a thin slit of light came. "Club heap goddam hell no good."

"Never mind," Yogi said. "I'll get you a job in the pump-factory."

"Pump-factory, hell," the big Indian said. "We all go join Salvation Army."

"Don't cry," Yogi said to the little Indian. "I'll buy you a new arm."

The little Indian went on crying. He sat down in the snowy road. "No can play pool me no care about nothing," he said.

From above them, out of the window of the club came the haunting sound of a Negro laughing.

Author's Note to the Reader

In case it may have any historical value, I am glad to state that I wrote the foregoing chapter in two hours directly on the typewriter, and then went out to lunch with John Dos Passos, whom I consider a very forceful writer, and an exceedingly pleasant fellow besides. This is what is known in the provinces as log-rolling. We lunched on rollmops, Sole Meunière, Civet de Lièvre à la Chez Cocotte, marmelade de pommes, and washed it all down, as we used to say (eh, reader?) with a bottle of Montrachet 1919, with the sole, and a bottle of Hospice de Beaune 1919 apiece with the jugged hare. Mr. Dos Passos, I believe, shared a bottle of Chambertin with me over the marmelade de pommes (Eng., apple sauce). We drank two vieux marcs, and after deciding not to go to the Café du Dôme and talk about Art we both went to our respective homes and I wrote the following chapter. I would like the reader to particularly remark the way the complicated threads of the lives of the various characters in the book are gathered together, and then held there in that memorable scene in the beanery. It was when I read this chapter aloud to him that Mr. Dos Passos exclaimed, "Hemingway, you have wrought a masterpiece."

P.S.—FROM THE AUTHOR TO THE READER

It is at this point, reader, that I am going to try and get that sweep and movement into the book that shows that the book is really a great book. I know you hope just as much as I do, reader, that I will get this sweep and movement because think what it will mean to both of us. Mr. H. G. Wells, who has been visiting at our home (we're getting along in the literary game, eh, reader?) asked us the other day if perhaps our reader, that's you, reader— just think of it, H. G. Wells talking about you right in our home. Anyway, H. G. Wells asked us if perhaps our reader would not think too much of this story was autobiographical. Please, reader, just get that idea out of your head. We have lived in Petoskey, Mich., it is true, and naturally many of the characters are drawn from life as we lived it then. But they are other people, not the author. The author only comes into the story in these little notes. It is true that before starting this story we spent twelve years studying the various Indian dialects of the North, and there is still preserved in the museum at Cross Village our translation of the New Testament into Ojibway. But you would have done the same thing in our place, reader, and I think if you think it over you will agree with us on this. Now to get back to the story. It is meant in the best spirit of friendship when I say that you have no idea, reader, what a hard chapter this is going to be to write. As a matter of fact, and I try to be frank about these things, we will not even try and write it until to-morrow.

Part IV

THE PASSING OF A GREAT RACE AND THE
MAKING AND MARRING OF AMERICANS

*But perhaps it may be objected to me, that I have
against my own rules introduced vices, and of a very
black kind, into this work. To which I shall answer:
first, that it is very difficult to pursue a series of human
actions, and keep clear from them. Secondly, that the
vices to be found here are rather the accidental consequences of some human frailty or foible, than causes
habitually existing in the mind. Thirdly, that they
are never set forth as the objects of ridicule, but de-
testation. Fourthly, that they are never the principal
figure at that time on the scene: and lastly, they never
produce the intended evil.*

HENRY FIELDING

CHAPTER XIII

YOGI JOHNSON walking down the silent street with his arm around
the little Indian's shoulder. The big Indian walking along beside
them. The cold night. The shuttered houses of the town. The
little Indian, who has lost his artificial arm. The big Indian, who
was also in the war. Yogi Johnson, who was in the war too. The
three of them walking, walking, walking. Where were they
going? Where could they go? What was there left?

Suddenly under a street light that swung on its drooping wire
above a street corner, casting its light down on the snow, the big
Indian stopped. "Walking no get us nowhere," he grunted. "Walking no good. Let white chief speak. Where we go, white chief?"

Yogi Johnson did not know. Obviously, walking was not the
solution of their problem. Walking was all right in its way.
Coxey's Army. A horde of men, seeking work, pressing on toward
Washington. Marching men, Yogi thought. Marching on and on

and where were they getting? Nowhere. Yogi knew it only too well. Nowhere. No damn where at all.

"White chief speak up," the big Indian said.

"I don't know," Yogi said. "I don't know at all." Was this what they had fought the war for? Was this what it was all about? It looked like it. Yogi standing under the street light. Yogi thinking and wondering. The two Indians in their mackinaw coats. One of the Indians with an empty sleeve. All of them wondering.

"White chief no speak?" the big Indian asked.

"No." What could Yogi say? What was there to say?

"Red brother speak?" asked the Indian.

"Speak out," Yogi said. He looked down at the snow. "One man's as good as another now."

"White chief ever go to Brown's Beanery?" asked the big Indian, looking into Yogi's face under the arc light.

"No," Yogi felt all in. Was this the end? A beanery. Well a beanery as well as any other place. But a beanery. Well, why not? These Indians knew the town. They were ex-service men. They both had splendid war records. He knew that himself. But a beanery.

"White chief come with red brothers," the tall Indian put his arm under Yogi's arm. The little Indian fell into step. "Forward to the beanery," Yogi spoke quietly. He was a white man, but he knew when he had enough. After all, the white race might not always be supreme. This Moslem revolt. Unrest in the East. Trouble in the West. Things looked black in the South. Now this condition of things in the North. Where was it taking him? Where did it all lead? Would it help him to want a woman? Would spring ever come? Was it worth while after all? He wondered.

The three of them striding along the frozen streets of Petoskey. Going somewhere now. En route. Huysmans wrote that. It would be interesting to read French. He must try it sometime. There was a street in Paris named after Huysmans. Right around the corner from where Gertrude Stein lived. Ah, there was a woman! Where were her experiments in words leading her? What was at the bottom of it? All that in Paris. Ah, Paris. How far it was to Paris now. Paris in the morning. Paris in the evening. Paris at night. Paris in the morning again. Paris at noon, perhaps. Why not? Yogi Johnson striding on. His mind never still.

All three of them striding on together. The arms of those that had arms linked through each other's arms. Red men and white men walking together. Something had brought them together. Was it the war? Was it fate? Was it accident? Or was it just chance? These questions struggled with each other in Yogi Johnson's brain. His brain was tired. He had been thinking too much lately. On still they strode. Then, abruptly, they stopped.

The little Indian looked up at the sign. It shone in the night outside the frosted windows of the beanery. BEST BY TEST.

"Makeum heap big test," the little Indian grunted.

"White man's beanery got heap fine T-bone steak," the tall Indian grunted. "Take it from red brother." The Indians stood a little uncertainly outside the door. The tall Indian turned to Yogi. "White chief got dollars?"

"Yes, I've got money," Yogi answered. He was prepared to go the route. It was no time to turn back now. "The feed's on me, boys."

"White chief nature's nobleman," the tall Indian grunted.

"White chief rough diamond," the little Indian agreed.

"You'd do the same for me," Yogi deprecated. After all, perhaps it was true. It was a chance he was taking. He had taken a chance in Paris once. Steve Brodie had taken a chance. Or so they said. Chances were taken all over the world every day. In China, Chinamen were taking chances. In Africa, Africans. In Egypt, Egyptians. In Poland, Poles. In Russia, Russians. In Ireland, Irish. In Armenia——

"Armenians no take chances," the tall Indian grunted quietly. He had voiced Yogi's unspoken doubt. They were a canny folk these red men.

"Not even in the rug game?"

"Red brother think not," the Indian said. His tones carried conviction to Yogi. Who were these Indians? There was something back of all this. They went into the beanery.

AUTHOR'S NOTE TO READER

It was at this point in the story, reader, that Mr. F. Scott Fitzgerald came to our home one afternoon, and after remaining for quite a while suddenly sat down in the fireplace and would not (or was it could not, reader?) get up and let the fire burn something else so as to keep the room warm. I know, reader, that these things sometimes do not show in a story, but, just the same, they are happening, and think what they mean to chaps like you and me in the literary game. If you should think this part of the story is not as good as it might have been remember, reader, that day in and day out all over the world things like this are happening. Need I add, reader, that I have the utmost respect for Mr. Fitzgerald, and let anybody else attack him and I would be the first to spring to his defense! And that includes you too, reader, though I hate to speak out bluntly like this, and take the risk of breaking up a friendship of the sort that ours has gotten to be.

P.S.—TO THE READER

As I read that chapter over, reader, it doesn't seem so bad. You may like it. I hope you will. And if you do like it, reader, and the rest of the book as well, will you tell your friends about it, and try and get them to buy the book just as you have done? I only get twenty cents on each book that is sold, and while twenty cents is not much nowadays still it will mount up to a lot if two or three hundred thousand copies of the book are sold. They will be, too, if every one likes the book as much as you and I do, reader. And listen, reader. I meant it when I said I would be glad to read anything you wrote. That wasn't just talk. Bring it along and we will go over it together. If you like, I'll rewrite bits of it for you. I don't mean that in any critical sort of way either. If there is anything you do not like in this book just write to Mr. Scribner's Sons at the home office. They'll change it for you. Or, if you would rather, I will change it myself. You know what I think of you, reader. And you're not angry or upset about what I said about Scott Fitzgerald either, are you? I hope not. Now I am going to write the next chapter. Mr. Fitzgerald is gone and Mr. Dos Passos had gone to England, and I think I can promise you that it will be a bully chapter. At least, it will be just as good as I can write it. We both know how good that can be, if we read the blurbs, eh, reader?

CHAPTER XIV

INSIDE the beanery. They are all inside the beanery. Some do not see the others. Each are intent on themselves. Red men are intent on red men. White men are intent on white men or on white women. There are no red women. Are there no squaws any more? What has become of the squaws? Have we lost our squaws in America? Silently, through the door which she had opened, a squaw came into the room. She was clad only in a pair of worn moccasins. On her back was a papoose. Beside her walked a husky dog.

"Don't look!" the drummer shouted to the women at the counter.

"Here! Get her out of here!" the owner of the beanery shouted. The squaw was forcibly ejected by the Negro cook. They heard her thrashing around in the snow outside. Her husky dog was barking.

"My God! What that might have led to!" Scripps O'Neil mopped his forehead with a napkin.

The Indians had watched with impassive faces. Yogi Johnson had been unable to move. The waitresses had covered their faces with napkins or whatever was handy. Mrs. Scripps had covered her eyes with *The American Mercury*. Scripps O'Neil was feeling faint and shaken. Something had stirred inside him, some vague primordial feeling, as the squaw had come into the room.

"Wonder where that squaw came from?" the drummer asked.

"Her my squaw," the little Indian said.

"Good God, man! Can't you clothe her?" Scripps O'Neil said in a dumb voice. There was a note of terror in his words.

"Her no like clothes," the little Indian explained. "Her woods Indian."

Yogi Johnson was not listening. Something had broken inside of him. Something had snapped as the squaw came into the room. He had a new feeling. A feeling he thought had been lost for ever. Lost for always. Lost. Gone permanently. He knew now it was a mistake. He was all right now. By the merest chance he had found it out. What might he not have thought if that squaw had never come into the beanery? What black thoughts he had been thinking! He had been on the verge of suicide. Self-destruction. Killing himself. Here in this beanery. What a mistake that would have been. He knew now. What a botch he might have made of life. Killing himself. Let spring come now. Let it come. It couldn't come fast enough. Let spring come. He was ready for it.

"Listen," he said to the two Indians. "I want to tell you about something that happened to me in Paris."

The two Indians leaned forward. "White chief got the floor," the tall Indian remarked.

"What I thought was a very beautiful thing happened to me in Paris," Yogi began. "You Indians know Paris? Good. Well it turned out to be the ugliest thing that ever happened to me."

The Indians grunted. They knew their Paris.

"It was the first day of my leave. I was walking along the Boulevard Malesherbes. A car passed me and a beautiful woman leaned out. She called to me and I came. She took me to a house, a mansion rather, in a distant part of Paris, and there a very beautiful thing happened to me. Afterward some one took me out a different door than I had come in by. The beautiful woman had told me that she would never, that she could never, see me again. I tried to get the number of the mansion but it was one of a block of mansions all looking the same.

"From then on all through my leave I tried to see that beautiful lady. Once I thought I saw her in the theatre. It wasn't her. Another time I caught a glimpse of what I thought was her in a passing taxi and leaped into another taxi and followed. I lost the taxi. I was desperate. Finally on the next to the last night of my leave I was so desperate and dull that I went with one of those guides that guarantee to show you all of Paris. We started out and visited various places. 'Is this all you've got?' I asked the guide.

" 'There is a real place, but it's very expensive,' the guide said. We compromised on a price finally, and the guide took me. It was in an old mansion. You looked through a slit in the wall. All around the wall were people looking through slits. There, looking through slits could be seen the uniforms of men of all the Allied countries, and many handsome South Americans in evening dress. I looked through a slit myself. For a while nothing happened. Then a beautiful woman came into the room with a young British officer. She took off her long fur coat and her hat and threw them into a chair. The officer was taking off his Sam Browne belt. I recognized her. It was the lady whom I had been with when the beautiful thing happened to me." Yogi Johnson looked at his empty plate of beans. "Since then," he said, "I have never wanted a woman. How I have suffered I cannot tell. But I've suffered, boys, I've suffered. I blamed it on the war, I blamed it on France. I blamed it on the decay of morality in general. I blamed it on the younger generation. I blamed it here, I blamed it there. Now I am cured. Here's five dollars for you, boys," his eyes were shining. "Get some more to eat. Take a trip somewhere. This is the happiest day of my life."

He stood up from his stool before the counter, shook the one Indian impulsively by the hand, rested his hand for a minute on the other Indian's shoulder, opened the door of the beanery, and strode out into the night.

The two Indians looked at one another. "White chief heap nice fella," observed the big Indian.

"Think him was in the war?" asked the little Indian.

"Me wonder," the big Indian said.

"White chief said he buy me new artificial arm," the little Indian grumbled.

"Maybe you get more than that," the big Indian said.

"Me wonder," the little Indian said. They went on eating.

At the other end of the counter of the beanery a marriage was coming to an end.

Scripps O'Neil and his wife sat side by side. Mrs. Scripps knew now. She couldn't hold him. She had tried and failed. She had lost. She knew it was a losing game. There was no holding him now. Mandy was talking again. Talking. Talking. Always talking. That interminable stream of literary gossip that was bringing her, Diana's, marriage to an end. She couldn't hold him. He was going. Going. Going away from her. Diana sitting there in misery. Scripps listening to Mandy talking. Mandy talking. Talking. Talking. The drummer, an old friend now, the drummer, sitting reading his Detroit *News*. She couldn't hold him. She couldn't hold him. She couldn't hold him.

The little Indian got up from his stool at the beanery counter, and went over to the window. The glass on the window was covered with thick rimy frost. The little Indian breathed on the frozen windowpane, rubbed the spot bare with the empty sleeve of his mackinaw coat and looked out into the night. Suddenly he turned from the window and rushed out into the night. The tall Indian watched him go, leisurely finished his meal, took a toothpick, placed it between his teeth, and then he too followed his friend out into the night.

CHAPTER XV

THEY were alone in the beanery now. Scripps and Mandy and Diana. Only the drummer was with them. He was an old friend now. But his nerves were on edge tonight. He folded his paper abruptly and started for the door.

"See you all later," he said. He went out into the night. It seemed the only thing to do. He did it.

Only three of them in the beanery now. Scripps and Mandy and Diana. Only those three. Mandy was talking. Leaning on the counter and talking. Scripps with his eyes fixed on Mandy. Diana made no pretense of listening now. She knew it was over. It was all over now. But she would make one more attempt. One more last gallant try. Perhaps she still could hold him. Perhaps it had all been just a dream. She steadied her voice and then she spoke.

"Scripps, dear," she said. Her voice shook a little. She steadied it.

"What's on your mind?" Scripps asked abruptly. Ah, there it was. That horrid clipped speech again.

"Scripps, dear, wouldn't you like to come home?" Diana's voice quavered. "There's a new *Mercury*." She had changed from the London *Mercury* to *The American Mercury* just to please Scripps. "It just came. I wish you felt like coming home, Scripps, there's a splendid thing in this *Mercury*. Do come home, Scripps, I've never asked anything of you before. Come home, Scripps! Oh, won't you come home?"

Scripps looked up. Diana's heart beat faster. Perhaps he was coming. Perhaps she was holding him. Holding him. Holding him.

"Do come, Scripps, dear," Diana said softly. "There's a wonderful editorial in it by Mencken about chiropractors."

Scripps looked away.

"Won't you come, Scripps?" Diana pleaded.

"No," Scripps said. "I don't give a damn about Mencken any more."

Diana dropped her head. "Oh, Scripps," she said. "Oh, Scripps." This was the end. She had her answer now. She had lost him. Lost him. Lost him. It was over. Finished. Done for. She sat crying silently. Mandy was talking again.

Suddenly Diana straightened up. She had one last request to make. One thing she would ask him. Only one. He might refuse her. He might not grant it. But she would ask him.

"Scripps," she said.

"What's the trouble?" Scripps turned in irritation. Perhaps, after all, he was sorry for her. He wondered.

"Can I take the bird, Scripps?" Diana's voice broke.

"Sure," said Scripps. "Why not?"

Diana picked up the bird-cage. The bird was asleep. Perched

on one leg as on that night when they had first met. What was it he was like? Ah, yes. Like an old osprey. An old, old osprey from her own Lake Country. She held the cage to her tightly.

"Thank you, Scripps," she said. "Thank you for this bird." Her voice broke. "And now I must be going."

Quietly, silently, gathering her shawl around her, clutching the cage with the sleeping bird and the copy of *The Mercury* to her breast, with only a backward glance, a last glance at him who had been her Scripps, she opened the door of the beanery, and went out into the night. Scripps did not even see her go. He was intent on what Mandy was saying. Mandy was talking again.

"That bird she just took out," Mandy was saying.

"Oh, did she take a bird out?" Scripps asked. "Go on with the story."

"You used to wonder about what sort of bird that was," Mandy went on.

"That's right," Scripps agreed.

"Well that reminds me of a story about Gosse and the Marquis of Buque," Mandy went on.

"Tell it, Mandy. Tell it," Scripps urged.

"It seems a great friend of mine, Ford, you've heard me speak of him before, was in the marquis's castle during the war. His regiment was billeted there and the marquis, one of the richest if not the richest man in England, was serving in Ford's regiment as a private. Ford was sitting in the library one evening. The library was a most extraordinary place. The walls were made of bricks of gold set into tiles or something. I forget exactly how it was."

"Go on," Scripps urged. "It doesn't matter."

"Anyhow, in the middle of the wall of the library was a stuffed flamingo in a glass case."

"They understand interior decorating, these English," Scripps said.

"Your wife was English, wasn't she?" asked Mandy.

"From the Lake Country," Scripps answered. "Go on with the story."

"Well, anyway," Mandy went on, "Ford was sitting there in the library one evening after mess when the butler came in and said: 'The Marquis of Buque's compliments and might he show the library to a group of friends with whom he has been dining?' They used to let him dine out and sometimes they let him sleep in the castle. Ford said, 'Quite,' and in came the marquis in his private's uniform followed by Sir Edmund Gosse and professor Whatsisname, I forget it for the moment, from Oxford. Gosse stopped in front of the stuffed flamingo in the glass case and said, 'What have we here, Buque?'

" 'It's a flamingo, Sir Edmund,' the marquis answered.

" 'That's not my idea of a flamingo,' Gosse remarked.

" 'No, Gosse. That's God's idea of a flamingo,' Professor Whatsisname said. I wish I could remember his name."

"Don't bother," Scripps said. His eyes were bright. He leaned forward. Something was pounding inside of him. Something he could not control. "I love you, Mandy," he said. "I love you. You are my woman." The thing was pounding away inside of him. It would not stop.

"That's all right," Mandy answered. "I've known you were my man for a long time. Would you like to hear another story? Speaking of woman."

"Go on," Scripps said. "You must never stop, Mandy. You are my woman now."

"Sure," Mandy agreed, "This story is about when Knut Hamsun was a street-car conductor in Chicago."

"Go on," Scripps said. "You are my woman now, Mandy."

He repeated the phrase to himself. My woman. My woman. You are my woman. She is my woman. It is my woman. My woman. But, somehow, he was not satisfied. Somewhere, somehow, there must be something else. Something else. My woman. The words were a little hollow now. Into his mind, though he tried to thrust it out, there came again the monstrous picture of the squaw as she had strode silently into the room. That squaw. She did not wear clothes, because she did not like them. Hardy, braving the winter nights. What might not the spring bring? Mandy was talking. Mandy talking on in the beanery. Mandy telling her stories. It grows late in the beanery. Mandy talks on. She is his woman now. He is her man. But is he her man? In Scripps's brain that vision of the squaw. The squaw that strode unannounced into the beanery. The squaw who had been thrown out into the snow. Mandy talking on. Telling literary reminiscences. Authentic incidents. They had the ring of truth. But were they enough? Scripps wondered. She was his woman. But for how long? Scripps wondered. Mandy talking on in the beanery. Scripps listening. But his mind straying away. Straying away. Straying away. Where was it straying? Out into the night. Out into the night.

CHAPTER XVI

NIGHT in Petoskey. Long past midnight. Inside the beanery a light burning. The town asleep under the Northern moon. To the North the tracks of the G. R. & I. Railroad running far into the North. Cold tracks, stretching North toward Mackinaw City and St. Ignace. Cold tracks to be walking on at this time of night.

North of the frozen little Northern town a couple walking side by side on the tracks. It is Yogi Johnson walking with the squaw. As they walk Yogi Johnson silently strips off his garments. One by one he strips off his garments, and casts them beside the track. In the end he is clad only in a worn pair of pump-maker shoes. Yogi Johnson, naked in the moonlight, walking North beside the squaw. The squaw striding along beside him. She carries the papoose on her back in his bark cradle. Yogi attempts to take the papoose from her. He would carry the papoose. The husky dog whines and licks at Yogi Johnson's ankles. No, the squaw would carry the papoose herself. On they stride. Into the North. Into the Northern night.

Behind them come two figures. Sharply etched in the moonlight. It is the two Indians. The two woods Indians. They stoop and gather up the garments Yogi Johnson has cast away. Occasionally, they grunt to one another. Striding softly along in the moonlight. Their keen eyes not missing a single cast-off garment. When the last garment has been cast off they look and see far ahead of them the two figures in the moonlight. The two Indians straighten up. They examine the garments.

"White chief snappy dresser," the tall Indian remarks, holding up an initialled shirt.

"White chief going get pretty cold," small Indian remarks. He hands a vest to the tall Indian. The tall Indian rolls all the clothing, all the cast-off garments, into a bundle, and they start back along the tracks to the town.

"Better keep clothes for white chief or sellem Salvation Army?" asks the short Indian.

"Better sellem Salvation Army," the tall Indian grunts. "White chief maybe never come back."

"White chief come back all right," grunted the little Indian.

"Better sellem Salvation Army, anway," grunts the tall Indian. "White chief need new clothes, anyhow, when spring comes."

As they walked down the tracks toward town, the air seemed to soften. The Indians walk uneasily now. Through the tamaracks and cedars beside the railway tracks a warm wind is blowing. The snow-drifts are melting now beside the tracks. Something stirs inside the two Indians. Some urge. Some strange pagan disturbance. The warm wind is blowing. The tall Indian stops, moistens his finger and holds it up in the air. The little Indian watches. "Chinook?" he asks.

"Heap chinook," the tall Indian says. They hurry on toward town. The moon is blurred now by clouds carried by the warm chinook wind that is blowing.

"Want to get in town before rush," the tall Indian grunts.

"Red brothers want be well up in line," the little Indian grunts anxiously.

"Nobody work in factory now," the tall Indian grunted.

"Better hurry."

The warm wind blows. Inside the Indians strange longings were stirring. They knew what they wanted. Spring at last was coming to the frozen little Northern town. The two Indians hurried along the track.

THE END

AUTHOR'S FINAL NOTE TO THE READER

Well, reader, how did you like it? It took me ten days to write it. Has it been worth it? There is just one place I would like to clear up. You remember back in the story where the elderly waitress, Diana, tells about how she lost her mother in Paris, and woke up to find herself with a French general in the next room? I thought perhaps you might be interested to know the real explanation of that. What actually happened was that her mother was taken violently ill with the bubonic plague in the night, and the doctor who was called diagnosed the case and warned the authorities. It was the day the great exposition was to be opened, and think what a case of bubonic plague would have done for the exposition as publicity. So the French authorities simply had the woman disappear. She died toward morning. The general who was summoned and who then got into bed in the same room where the mother had been, always seemed to us like a pretty brave man. He was one of the big stockholders in the exposition, though, I believe. Anyway, reader, as a piece of secret history it always seemed to me like an awfully good story, and I know you would rather have me explain it here than drag an explanation into the novel, where really, after all, it has no place. It is interesting to observe, though, how the French police hushed the whole matter up, and how quickly they got ahold of the coiffeur and the cab-driver. Of course, what it shows is that when you're travelling abroad alone, or even with your mother, you simply cannot be too careful. I hope it is all right about bringing this in here, but I just felt I owed it to you, reader, to give some explanation. I do not believe in these protracted good-bys any more than I do in long engagements, so I will just say a simple farewell and Godspeed, reader, and leave you now to your own devices.

THE SUN ALSO RISES

"You are all a lost generation."
—GERTRUDE STEIN *in conversation*

"One generation passeth away, and another generation cometh; but the earth abideth forever. . . . The sun also ariseth, and the sun goeth down, and hasteth to the place where he arose. . . . The wind goeth toward the south, and turneth about unto the north; it whirleth about continually, and the wind returneth again according to his circuits. . . . All the rivers run into the sea; yet the sea is not full; unto the place from whence the rivers come, thither they return again."

—ECCLESIASTES

THE SUN ALSO RISES was his first great success as a novelist. It was published in 1926 at the crest of the Twenties and at once became an emblem of a generation in the unpredictable way such things come about. All over America and in the world at large young men and women happily took uninvited guidance from it, though Hemingway viewed this development moodily. They had already been pleased with the idea that they belonged to something special called The younger generation; they were enchanted with the melancholy glamour implied in also being Lost. A certain freedom of association made them feel as worldly and debonair as Lady Brett and Jake and Robert and Mike; they suddenly seemed to know an improbable lot about bullfighting and to have lived, at least vicariously, rather lavishly in Madrid and Paris and Pamplona. That generation has weathered considerably. Other generations have sent The Sun Also Rises through its endless editions for other reasons.

The heart of the story is not a transitory matter; it is the tragedy of limited responsibility in the face of limitless temptation. The scenes have wonderful lucidity. The persons in them stand their gaffs, take their falls, win, lose and draw, show their prejudices and cowardices and valor as they truly are, not as we might wish them to be always.

Hemingway wrote and rewrote The Sun Also Rises in various parts of Spain and France between 1924 and 1926. "I knew nothing about writing a novel when I started it," he once said, "but in re-writing I learned much." Others are still learning from it as they read it for business or pleasure.

C. P.

THE SUN ALSO RISES

Book 1

CHAPTER I

ROBERT COHN was once middleweight boxing champion of
Princeton. Do not think that I am very much impressed by that
as a boxing title, but it meant a lot to Cohn. He cared nothing for
boxing, in fact he disliked it, but he learned it painfully and
thoroughly to counteract the feeling of inferiority and shyness he
had felt on being treated as a Jew at Princeton. There was a certain inner comfort in knowing he could knock down anybody who
was snooty to him, although, being very shy and a thoroughly
nice boy, he never fought except in the gym. He was Spider
Kelly's star pupil. Spider Kelly taught all his young gentlemen to
box like featherweights, no matter whether they weighed one
hundred and five or two hundred and five pounds. But it seemed
to fit Cohn. He was really very fast. He was so good that Spider
promptly overmatched him and got his nose permanently flattened.
This increased Cohn's distaste for boxing, but it gave him a certain satisfaction of some strange sort, and it certainly improved his
nose. In his last year at Princeton he read too much and took to
wearing spectacles. I never met any one of his class who remembered him. They did not even remember that he was middleweight boxing champion.

I mistrust all frank and simple people, especially when their
stories hold together, and I always had a suspicion that perhaps
Robert Cohn had never been middleweight boxing champion,
and that perhaps a horse had stepped on his face, or that maybe
his mother had been frightened or seen something, or that he had,

maybe, bumped into something as a young child, but I finally had somebody verify the story from Spider Kelly. Spider Kelly not only remembered Cohn. He had often wondered what had become of him.

Robert Cohn was a member, through his father, of one of the richest Jewish families in New York, and through his mother of one of the oldest. At the military school where he prepped for Princeton, and played a very good end on the football team, no one had made him race-conscious. No one had ever made him feel he was a Jew, and hence any different from anybody else, until he went to Princeton. He was a nice boy, a friendly boy, and very shy, and it made him bitter. He took it out in boxing, and he came out of Princeton with painful self-consciousness and the flat-tened nose, and was married by the first girl who was nice to him. He was married five years, had three children, lost most of the fifty thousand dollars his father left him, the balance of the estate having gone to his mother, hardened into a rather unattractive mould under domestic unhappiness with a rich wife; and just when he had made up his mind to leave his wife she left him and went off with a miniature-painter. As he had been thinking for months about leaving his wife and had not done it because it would be too cruel to deprive her of himself, her departure was a very healthful shock.

The divorce was arranged and Robert Cohn went out to the Coast. In California he fell among literary people and, as he still had a little of the fifty thousand left, in a short time he was back-ing a review of the Arts. The review commenced publication in Carmel, California, and finished in Provincetown, Massachusetts. By that time Cohn, who had been regarded purely as an angel, and whose name had appeared on the editorial page merely as a member of the advisory board, had become the sole editor. It was his money and he discovered he liked the authority of editing. He was sorry when the magazine became too expensive and he had to give it up.

By that time, though, he had other things to worry about. He had been taken in hand by a lady who hoped to rise with the magazine. She was very forceful, and Cohn never had a chance of not being taken in hand. Also he was sure that he loved her. When this lady saw that the magazine was not going to rise, she became a little disgusted with Cohn and decided that she might as well get what there was to get while there was still something available, so she urged that they go to Europe, where Cohn could write. They came to Europe, where the lady had been educated, and stayed three years. During these three years, the first spent in travel, the last two in Paris, Robert Cohn had two friends, Braddocks and myself. Braddocks was his literary friend. I was his tennis friend.

The lady who had him, her name was Frances, found toward the end of the second year that her looks were going, and her attitude toward Robert changed from one of careless possession and exploitation to the absolute determination that he should marry her. During this time Robert's mother had settled an allowance on him, about three hundred dollars a month. During two years and a half I do not believe that Robert Cohn looked at another woman. He was fairly happy, except that, like many people living in Europe, he would rather have been in America, and he had discovered writing. He wrote a novel, and it was not really such a bad novel as the critics later called it, although it was a very poor novel. He read many books, played bridge, played tennis, and boxed at a local gymnasium.

I first became aware of his lady's attitude toward him one night after the three of us had dined together. We had dined at l'Avenue's and afterward went to the Café de Versailles for coffee. We had several *fines* after the coffee, and I said I must be going. Cohn had been talking about the two of us going off somewhere on a weekend trip. He wanted to get out of town and get in a good walk. I suggested we fly to Strasbourg and walk up to Saint Odile, or somewhere or other in Alsace. "I know a girl in Strasbourg who can show us the town," I said.

Somebody kicked me under the table. I thought it was accidental and went on: "She's been there two years and knows everything there is to know about the town. She's a swell girl."

I was kicked again under the table and, looking, saw Frances, Robert's lady, her chin lifting and her face hardening.

"Hell," I said, "why go to Strasbourg? We could go up to Bruges, or to the Ardennes."

Cohn looked relieved. I was not kicked again. I said good-night and went out. Cohn said he wanted to buy a paper and would walk to the corner with me. "For God's sake," he said, "why did you say that about that girl in Strasbourg for? Didn't you see Frances?"

"No, why should I? If I know an American girl that lives in Strasbourg what the hell is it to Frances?"

"It doesn't make any difference. Any girl. I couldn't go, that would be all."

"Don't be silly."

"You don't know Frances. Any girl at all. Didn't you see the way she looked?"

"Oh, well," I said, "let's go to Senlis."

"Don't get sore."

"I'm not sore. Senlis is a good place and we can stay at the Grand Cerf and take a hike in the woods and come home."

"Good, that will be fine."

"Well, I'll see you to-morrow at the courts," I said.

"Good-night, Jake," he said, and started back to the café.

"You forgot to get your paper," I said.

"That's so." He walked with me up to the kiosque at the corner. "You are not sore, are you, Jake?" He turned with the paper in his hand.

"No, why should I be?"

"See you at tennis," he said. I watched him walk back to the café holding his paper. I rather liked him and evidently she led him quite a life.

CHAPTER II

THAT winter Robert Cohn went over to America with his novel, and it was accepted by a fairly good publisher. His going made an awful row I heard, and I think that was where Frances lost him, because several women were nice to him in New York, and

when he came back he was quite changed. He was more enthu-
siastic about America than ever, and he was not so simple, and he
was not so nice. The publishers had praised his novel pretty
highly and it rather went to his head. Then several women had
put themselves out to be nice to him, and his horizons had all
shifted. For four years his horizon had been absolutely limited to
his wife. For three years, or almost three years, he had never seen
beyond Frances. I am sure he had never been in love in his life.

He had married on the rebound from the rotten time he had in
college, and Frances took him on the rebound from his discovery
that he had not been everything to his first wife. He was not in
love yet but he realized that he was an attractive quantity to
women, and that the fact of a woman caring for him and wanting
to live with him was not simply a divine miracle. This changed
him so that he was not so pleasant to have around. Also, playing
for higher stakes than he could afford in some rather steep bridge
games with his New York connections, he had held cards and
won several hundred dollars. It made him rather vain of his bridge
game, and he talked several times of how a man could always
make a living at bridge if he were ever forced to.

Then there was another thing. He had been reading W. H.
Hudson. That sounds like an innocent occupation, but Cohn had
read and reread "The Purple Land." "The Purple Land" is a very
sinister book if read too late in life. It recounts splendid imaginary
amorous adventures of a perfect English gentleman in an intensely
romantic land, the scenery of which is very well described. For a
man to take it at thirty-four as a guide-book to what life holds is
about as safe as it would be for a man of the same age to enter
Wall Street direct from a French convent, equipped with a complete set of the more practical Alger books. Cohn, I believe, took
every word of "The Purple Land" as literally as though it had
been an R. G. Dun report. You understand me, he made some
reservations, but on the whole the book to him was sound. It was
all that was needed to set him off. I did not realize the extent to
which it had set him off until one day he came into my office.

"Hello, Robert," I said. "Did you come in to cheer me up?"

"Would you like to go to South America, Jake?" he asked.

"No."

"Why not?"

"I don't know. I never wanted to go. Too expensive. You can see all the South Americans you want in Paris anyway."

"They're not the real South Americans."

"They look awfully real to me."

I had a boat train to catch with a week's mail stories, and only half of them written.

"Do you know any dirt?" I asked.

"No."

"None of your exalted connections getting divorces?"

"No; listen, Jake. If I handled both our expenses, would you go to South America with me?"

"Why me?"

"You can talk Spanish. And it would be more fun with two of us."

"No," I said, "I like this town and I go to Spain in the summertime."

"All my life I've wanted to go on a trip like that," Cohn said. He sat down. "I'll be too old before I can ever do it."

"Don't be a fool," I said. "You can go anywhere you want. You've got plenty of money."

"I know. But I can't get started."

"Cheer up," I said. "All countries look just like the moving pictures."

But I felt sorry for him. He had it badly.

"I can't stand it to think my life is going so fast and I'm not really living it."

"Nobody ever lives their life all the way up except bull-fighters."

"I'm not interested in bull-fighters. That's an abnormal life. I want to go back in the country in South America. We could have a great trip."

"Did you ever think about going to British East Africa to shoot?"

"No, I wouldn't like that."

"I'd go there with you."

"No; that doesn't interest me."

"That's because you never read a book about it. Go on and read

THE SUN ALSO RISES 95

a book all full of love affairs with the beautiful shiny black princesses."

"I want to go to South America."

He had a hard, Jewish, stubborn streak.

"Come on down-stairs and have a drink."

"Aren't you working?"

"No," I said. We went down the stairs to the café on the ground floor. I had discovered that was the best way to get rid of friends. Once you had a drink all you had to say was: "Well, I've got to get back and get off some cables," and it was done. It is very important to discover graceful exits like that in the newspaper business, where it is such an important part of the ethics that you should never seem to be working. Anyway, we went down-stairs to the bar and had a whiskey and soda. Cohn looked at the bottles in bins around the wall. "This is a good place," he said.

"There's a lot of liquor," I agreed.

"Listen, Jake," he leaned forward on the bar. "Don't you ever get the feeling that all your life is going by and you're not taking advantage of it? Do you realize you've lived nearly half the time you have to live already?"

"Yes, every once in a while."

"Do you know that in about thirty-five years more we'll be dead?"

"What the hell, Robert," I said. "What the hell."

"I'm serious."

"It's one thing I don't worry about," I said.

"You ought to."

"I've had plenty to worry about one time or other. I'm through worrying."

"Well, I want to go to South America."

"Listen, Robert, going to another country doesn't make any difference. I've tried all that. You can't get away from yourself by moving from one place to another. There's nothing to that."

"But you've never been to South America."

"South America hell! If you went there the way you feel now it would be exactly the same. This is a good town. Why don't you start living your life in Paris?"

"I'm sick of Paris, and I'm sick of the Quarter."

"Stay away from the Quarter. Cruise around by yourself and see what happens to you."

"Nothing happens to me. I walked alone all one night and nothing happened except a bicycle cop stopped me and asked to see my papers."

"Wasn't the town nice at night?"

"I don't care for Paris."

So there you were. I was sorry for him, but it was not a thing you could do anything about, because right away you ran up against the two stubbornnesses: South America could fix it and he did not like Paris. He got the first idea out of a book, and I suppose the second came out of a book too.

"Well," I said, "I've got to go up-stairs and get off some cables."

"Do you really have to go?"

"Yes, I've got to get these cables off."

"Do you mind if I come up and sit around the office?"

"No, come on up."

He sat in the outer room and read the papers, and the Editor and Publisher and I worked hard for two hours. Then I sorted out the carbons, stamped on a by-line, put the stuff in a couple of big manila envelopes and rang for a boy to take them to the Gare St. Lazare. I went out into the other room and there was Robert Cohn asleep in the big chair. He was asleep with his head on his arms. I did not like to wake him up, but I wanted to lock the office and shove off. I put my hand on his shoulder. He shook his head. "I can't do it," he said, and put his head deeper into his arms. "I can't do it. Nothing will make me do it."

"Robert," I said, and shook him by the shoulder. He looked up. He smiled and blinked.

"Did I talk out loud just then?"

"Something. But it wasn't clear."

"God, what a rotten dream!"

"Did the typewriter put you to sleep?"

"Guess so. I didn't sleep all last night."

"What was the matter?"

"Talking," he said.

I could picture it. I have a rotten habit of picturing the bed-room scenes of my friends. We went out to the Café Napolitain to have an *apéritif* and watch the evening crowd on the Boulevard.

CHAPTER III

IT was a warm spring night and I sat at a table on the terrace of the Napolitain after Robert had gone, watching it get dark and the electric signs come on, and the red and green stop-and-go traffic-signal, and the crowd going by, and the horse-cabs clippety-clopping along at the edge of the solid taxi traffic, and the *poules* going by, singly and in pairs, looking for the evening meal. I watched a good-looking girl walk past the table and watched her go up the street and lost sight of her, and watched another, and then saw the first one coming back again. She went by once more and I caught her eye, and she came over and sat down at the table. The waiter came up.

"Well, what will you drink?" I asked.

"Pernod."

"That's not good for little girls."

"Little girl yourself. Dites garçon, un pernod."

"A pernod for me, too."

"What's the matter?" she asked. "Going on a party?"

"Sure. Aren't you?"

"I don't know. You never know in this town."

"Don't you like Paris?"

"No."

"Why don't you go somewhere else?"

"Isn't anywhere else."

"You're happy, all right."

"Happy, hell!"

Pernod is greenish imitation absinthe. When you add water it turns milky. It tastes like licorice and it has a good uplift, but it drops you just as far. We sat and drank it, and the girl looked sullen.

"Well," I said, "are you going to buy me a dinner?"

She grinned and I saw why she made a point of not laughing. With her mouth closed she was a rather pretty girl. I paid for the saucers and we walked out to the street. I hailed a horse-cab and the driver pulled up at the curb. Settled back in the slow, smoothly rolling *fiacre* we moved up the Avenue de l'Opéra, passed the locked doors of the shops, their windows lighted, the Avenue broad and shiny and almost deserted. The cab passed the New York *Herald* bureau with the window full of clocks.

"What are all the clocks for?" she asked.

"They show the hour all over America."

"Don't kid me."

We turned off the Avenue up the Rue des Pyramides, through the traffic of the Rue de Rivoli, and through a dark gate into the Tuileries. She cuddled against me and I put my arm around her. She looked up to be kissed. She touched me with one hand and I put her hand away.

"Never mind."

"What's the matter? You sick?"

"Yes."

"Everybody's sick. I'm sick, too."

We came out of the Tuileries into the light and crossed the Seine and then turned up the Rue des Saints Pères.

"You oughtn't to drink pernod if you're sick."

"You neither."

"It doesn't make any difference with me. It doesn't make any difference with a woman."

"What are you called?"

"Georgette. How are you called?"

"Jacob."

"That's a Flemish name."

"American too."

"You're not Flamand?"

"No, American."

"Good, I detest Flamands."

By this time we were at the restaurant. I called to the *cocher* to stop. We got out and Georgette did not like the looks of the place. "This is no great thing of a restaurant."

"No," I said. "Maybe you would rather go to Foyot's. Why don't you keep the cab and go on?"

I had picked her up because of a vague sentimental idea that it would be nice to eat with some one. It was a long time since I had dined with a *poule*, and I had forgotten how dull it could be. We went into the restaurant, passed Madame Lavigne at the desk and into a little room. Georgette cheered up a little under the food.

"It isn't bad here," she said. "It isn't chic, but the food is all right."

"Better than you eat in Liège."

"Brussels, you mean."

We had another bottle of wine and Georgette made a joke. She smiled and showed all her bad teeth, and we touched glasses. "You're not a bad type," she said. "It's a shame you're sick. We get on well. What's the matter with you, anyway?"

"I got hurt in the war," I said.

"Oh, that dirty war."

We would probably have gone on and discussed the war and agreed that it was in reality a calamity for civilization, and perhaps would have been better avoided. I was bored enough. Just then from the other room some one called: "Barnes! I say, Barnes! Jacob Barnes!"

"It's a friend calling me," I explained, and went out.

There was Braddocks at a big table with a party: Cohn, Frances Clyne, Mrs. Braddocks, several people I did not know.

"You're coming to the dance, aren't you?" Braddocks asked.

"What dance?"

"Why, the dancings. Don't you know we've revived them?" Mrs. Braddocks put in.

"You must come, Jake. We're all going," Frances said from the end of the table. She was tall and had a smile.

"Of course, he's coming," Braddocks said. "Come in and have coffee with us, Barnes."

"Right."

"And bring your friend," said Mrs. Braddocks laughing. She was a Canadian and had all their easy social graces.

"Thanks, we'll be in," I said. I went back to the small room.

"Who are your friends?" Georgette asked.

"Writers and artists."

"There are lots of those on this side of the river."

"Too many."

"I think so. Still, some of them make money."

"Oh, yes."

We finished the meal and the wine. "Come on," I said. "We're going to have coffee with the others."

Georgette opened her bag, made a few passes at her face as she looked in the little mirror, re-defined her lips with the lip-stick, and straightened her hat.

"Good," she said.

We went into the room full of people and Braddocks and the men at his table stood up.

"I wish to present my fiancée, Mademoiselle Georgette Leblanc," I said. Georgette smiled that wonderful smile, and we shook hands all round.

"Are you related to Georgette Leblanc, the singer?" Mrs. Braddocks asked.

"Connais pas," Georgette answered.

"But you have the same name," Mrs. Braddocks insisted cordially.

"No," said Georgette. "Not at all. My name is Hobin."

"But Mr. Barnes introduced you as Mademoiselle Georgette Leblanc. Surely he did," insisted Mrs. Braddocks, who in the excitement of talking French was liable to have no idea what she was saying.

"He's a fool," Georgette said.

"Oh, it was a joke, then," Mrs. Braddocks said.

"Yes," said Georgette. "To laugh at."

"Did you hear that, Henry?" Mrs. Braddocks called down the table to Braddocks. "Mr. Barnes introduced his fiancée as Mademoiselle Leblanc, and her name is actually Hobin."

"Of course, darling. Mademoiselle Hobin, I've known her for a very long time."

"Oh, Mademoiselle Hobin," Frances Clyne called, speaking French very rapidly and not seeming so proud and astonished as Mrs. Braddocks at its coming out really French. "Have you been in Paris long? Do you like it here? You love Paris, do you not?"

"Who's she?" Georgette turned to me. "Do I have to talk to her?"

She turned to Frances, sitting smiling, her hands folded, her head poised on her long neck, her lips pursed ready to start talking again.

"No, I don't like Paris. It's expensive and dirty."

"Really? I find it so extraordinarily clean. One of the cleanest cities in all Europe."

"I find it dirty."

"How strange! But perhaps you have not been here very long."

"I've been here long enough."

"But it does have nice people in it. One must grant that."

Georgette turned to me. "You have nice friends."

Frances was a little drunk and would have liked to have kept it up but the coffee came, and Lavigne with the liqueurs, and after that we all went out and started for Braddocks's dancing-club.

The dancing-club was a *bal musette* in the Rue de la Montagne Sainte Geneviève. Five nights a week the working people of the Pantheon quarter danced there. One night a week it was the dancing-club. On Monday nights it was closed. When we arrived it was quite empty, except for a policeman sitting near the door, the wife of the proprietor back of the zinc bar, and the proprietor himself. The daughter of the house came downstairs as we went in. There were long benches, and tables ran across the room, and at the far end a dancing-floor.

"I wish people would come earlier," Braddocks said. The daughter came up and wanted to know what we would drink. The proprietor got up on a high stool beside the dancing-floor and began to play the accordion. He had a string of bells around one of his ankles and beat time with his foot as he played. Every one danced. It was hot and we came off the floor perspiring.

"My God," Georgette said. "What a box to sweat in!"

"It's hot."

"Hot, my God!"

"Take off your hat."

"That's a good idea."

Some one asked Georgette to dance, and I went over to the bar. It was really very hot and the accordion music was pleasant in the hot night. I drank a beer, standing in the doorway and getting the cool breath of wind from the street. Two taxis were coming down the steep street. They both stopped in front of the Bal. A crowd of young men, some in jerseys and some in their shirt-sleeves, got out. I could see their hands and newly washed, wavy hair in the light from the door. The policeman standing by the door looked at me and smiled. They came in. As they went in, under the light I saw white hands, wavy hair, white faces, grimacing, gesturing, talking. With them was Brett. She looked very lovely and she was very much with them.

One of them saw Georgette and said: "I do declare. There is an actual harlot. I'm going to dance with her, Lett. You watch me."

The tall dark one, called Lett, said: "Don't you be rash."

The wavy blond one answered: "Don't you worry, dear." And with them was Brett.

I was very angry. Somehow they always made me angry. I know they are supposed to be amusing, and you should be tolerant, but I wanted to swing on one, any one, anything to shatter that superior, simpering composure. Instead, I walked down the street and had a beer at the bar at the next Bal. The beer was not good and I had a worse cognac to take the taste out of my mouth. When I came back to the Bal there was a crowd on the floor and Georgette was dancing with the tall blond youth, who danced big-hippily, carrying his head on one side, his eyes lifted as he danced. As soon as the music stopped another one of them asked her to dance. She had been taken up by them. I knew then that they would all dance with her. They are like that.

I sat down at a table. Cohn was sitting there. Frances was dancing. Mrs. Braddocks brought up somebody and introduced him as Robert Prentiss. He was from New York by way of Chicago, and was a rising new novelist. He had some sort of an English accent. I asked him to have a drink.

"Thanks so much," he said, "I've just had one."

"Have another."

"Thanks, I will then."

We got the daughter of the house over and each had a *fine à l'eau.*

"You're from Kansas City, they tell me," he said.

"Yes."

"Do you find Paris amusing?"

"Yes."

"Really?"

I was a little drunk. Not drunk in any positive sense but just enough to be careless.

"For God's sake," I said, "yes. Don't you?"

"Oh, how charmingly you get angry," he said. "I wish I had that faculty."

I got up and walked over toward the dancing-floor. Mrs. Braddocks followed me. "Don't be cross with Robert," she said. "He's still only a child, you know."

"I wasn't cross," I said. "I just thought perhaps I was going to throw up."

"Your fiancée is having a great success," Mrs. Braddocks looked out on the floor where Georgette was dancing in the arms of the tall, dark one, called Lett.

"Isn't she?" I said.

"Rather," said Mrs. Braddocks.

Cohn came up. "Come on, Jake," he said, "have a drink." We walked over to the bar. "What's the matter with you? You seem all worked up over something?"

"Nothing. This whole show makes me sick is all."

Brett came up to the bar.

"Hello, you chaps."

"Hello, Brett," I said. "Why aren't you tight?"

"Never going to get tight any more. I say, give a chap a brandy and soda."

She stood holding the glass and I saw Robert Cohn looking at her. He looked a great deal as his compatriot must have looked when he saw the promised land. Cohn, of course, was much younger. But he had that look of eager, deserving expectation.

Brett was damned good-looking. She wore a slipover jersey sweater and a tweed skirt, and her hair was brushed back like a boy's. She started all that. She was built with curves like the hull of a racing yacht, and you missed none of it with that wool jersey.

"It's a fine crowd you're with, Brett," I said.

"Aren't they lovely? And you, my dear. Where did you get it?"

"At the Napolitain."

"And have you had a lovely evening?"

"Oh, priceless," I said.

Brett laughed. "It's wrong of you, Jake. It's an insult to all of us. Look at Frances there, and Jo."

This for Cohn's benefit.

"It's in restraint of trade," Brett said. She laughed again.

"You're wonderfully sober," I said.

"Yes. Aren't I? And when one's with the crowd I'm with, one can drink in such safety, too."

The music started and Robert Cohn said: "Will you dance this with me, Lady Brett?"

Brett smiled at him. "I've promised to dance this with Jacob," she laughed. "You've a hell of a biblical name, Jake."

"How about the next?" asked Cohn.

"We're going," Brett said. "We've a date up at Montmartre."

Dancing, I looked over Brett's shoulder and saw Cohn, standing at the bar, still watching her.

"You've made a new one there," I said to her.

"Don't talk about it. Poor chap. I never knew it till just now."

"Oh, well," I said. "I suppose you like to add them up."

"Don't talk like a fool."

"You do."

"Oh, well. What if I do?"

"Nothing," I said. We were dancing to the accordion and some one was playing the banjo. It was hot and I felt happy. We passed close to Georgette dancing with another one of them.

"What possessed you to bring her?"

"I don't know, I just brought her."

"You're getting damned romantic."

"No, bored."

"Now?"

"No, not now."

"Let's get out of here. She's well taken care of."

"Do you want to?"

"Would I ask you if I didn't want to?"

We left the floor and I took my coat off a hanger on the wall and put it on. Brett stood by the bar. Cohn was talking to her. I stopped at the bar and asked them for an envelope. The patronne found one. I took a fifty-franc note from my pocket, put it in the envelope, sealed it, and handed it to the patronne.

"If the girl I came with asks for me, will you give her this?" I said. "If she goes out with one of those gentlemen, will you save this for me?"

"C'est entendu, Monsieur," the patronne said. "You go now? So early?"

"Yes," I said.

We started out the door. Cohn was still talking to Brett. She said good night and took my arm. "Good night, Cohn," I said. Outside in the street we looked for a taxi.

"You're going to lose your fifty francs," Brett said.

"Oh, yes."

"No taxis."

"We could walk up to the Pantheon and get one."

"Come on and we'll get a drink in the pub next door and send for one."

"You wouldn't walk across the street."

"Not if I could help it."

We went into the next bar and I sent a waiter for a taxi.

"Well," I said, "we're out away from them."

We stood against the tall zinc bar and did not talk and looked at each other. The waiter came and said the taxi was outside. Brett pressed my hand hard. I gave the waiter a franc and we went out. "Where should I tell him?" I asked.

"Oh, tell him to drive around."

I told the driver to go to the Parc Montsouris, and got in, and slammed the door. Brett was leaning back in the corner, her eyes closed. I got in and sat beside her. The cab started with a jerk.

"Oh, darling, I've been so miserable," Brett said.

CHAPTER IV

THE taxi went up the hill, passed the lighted square, then on into the dark, still climbing, then levelled out onto a dark street behind St. Etienne du Mont, went smoothly down the asphalt, passed the trees and the standing bus at the Place de la Contrescarpe, then turned onto the cobbles of the Rue Mouffetard. There were lighted bars and late open shops on each side of the street. We were sitting apart and we jolted close together going down the old street. Brett's hat was off. Her head was back. I saw her face in the lights from the open shops, then it was dark, then I saw her face clearly as we came out on the Avenue des Gobelins. The street was torn up and men were working on the car-tracks by the light of acetylene flares. Brett's face was white and the long line of her neck showed in the bright light of the flares. The street was dark again and I kissed her. Our lips were tight together and then she turned away and pressed against the corner of the seat, as far away as she could get. Her head was down.

"Don't touch me," she said. "Please don't touch me."

"What's the matter?"

"I can't stand it."

"Oh, Brett."

"You mustn't. You must know. I can't stand it, that's all. Oh, darling, please understand!"

"Don't you love me?"

"Love you? I simply turn all to jelly when you touch me."

"Isn't there anything we can do about it?"

She was sitting up now. My arm was around her and she was leaning back against me, and we were quite calm. She was looking into my eyes with that way she had of looking that made you wonder whether she really saw out of her own eyes. They would look on and on after every one else's eyes in the world would have stopped looking. She looked as though there were nothing on earth she would not look at like that, and really she was afraid of so many things.

"And there's not a damn thing we could do," I said.

"I don't know," she said. "I don't want to go through that hell again."

"We'd better keep away from each other."

"But, darling, I have to see you. It isn't all that you know."

"No, but it always gets to be."

"That's my fault. Don't we pay for all the things we do, though?"

She had been looking into my eyes all the time. Her eyes had different depths, sometimes they seemed perfectly flat. Now you could see all the way into them.

"When I think of the hell I've put chaps through. I'm paying for it all now."

"Don't talk like a fool," I said. "Besides, what happened to me is supposed to be funny. I never think about it."

"Oh, no. I'll lay you don't."

"Well, let's shut up about it."

"I laughed about it too, myself, once." She wasn't looking at me. "A friend of my brother's came home that way from Mons. It seemed like a hell of a joke. Chaps never know anything, do they?"

"No," I said. "Nobody ever knows anything."

I was pretty well through with the subject. At one time or another I had probably considered it from most of its various angles, including the one that certain injuries or imperfections are a subject of merriment while remaining quite serious for the person possessing them.

"It's funny," I said. "It's very funny. And it's a lot of fun, too, to be in love."

"Do you think so?" her eyes looked flat again.

"I don't mean fun that way. In a way it's an enjoyable feeling."

"No," she said. "I think it's hell on earth."

"It's good to see each other."

"No. I don't think it is."

"Don't you want to?"

"I have to."

We were sitting now like two strangers. On the right was the Parc Montsouris. The restaurant where they have the pool of live trout and where you can sit and look out over the park was closed and dark. The driver leaned his head around.

"Where do you want to go?" I asked. Brett turned her head away.

"Oh, go to the Select."

"Café Select," I told the driver. "Boulevard Montparnasse." We drove straight down, turning around the Lion de Belfort that guards the passing Montrouge trams. Brett looked straight ahead. On the Boulevard Raspail, with the lights of Montparnasse in sight, Brett said: "Would you mind very much if I asked you to do something?"

"Don't be silly."

"Kiss me just once more before we get there."

When the taxi stopped I got out and paid. Brett came out putting on her hat. She gave me her hand as she stepped down. Her hand was shaky. "I say, do I look too much of a mess?" She pulled her man's felt hat down and started in for the bar. Inside, against the bar and at tables, were most of the crowd who had been at the dance.

"Hello, you chaps," Brett said. "I'm going to have a drink."

"Oh, Brett! Brett!" the little Greek portrait-painter, who called himself a duke, and whom everybody called Zizi, pushed up to her. "I got something fine to tell you."

"Hello, Zizi," Brett said.

"I want you to meet a friend," Zizi said. A fat man came up.

"Count Mippipopolous, meet my friend Lady Ashley."

"How do you do?" said Brett.

"Well, does your Ladyship have a good time here in Paris?" asked Count Mippipopolous, who wore an elk's tooth on his watch-chain.

"Rather," said Brett.

"Paris is a fine town all right," said the count. "But I guess you have pretty big doings yourself over in London."

"Oh, yes," said Brett. 'Enormous."

Braddocks called to me from a table. "Barnes," he said, "have a drink. That girl of yours got in a frightful row."

"What about?"

"Something the patronne's daughter said. A corking row. She was rather splendid, you know. Showed her yellow card and demanded the patronne's daughter's too. I say it was a row."

"What finally happened?"

"Oh, some one took her home. Not a bad-looking girl. Wonderful command of the idiom. Do stay and have a drink."

"No," I said. "I must shove off. Seen Cohn?"

"He went home with Frances," Mrs. Braddock put in.

"Poor chap, he looks awfully down," Braddocks said.

"I dare say he is," said Mrs. Braddocks.

"I have to shove off," I said. "Good night."

I said good night to Brett at the bar. The count was buying champagne. "Will you take a glass of wine with us, sir?" he asked.

"No. Thanks awfully. I have to go."

"Really going?" Brett asked.

"Yes," I said. "I've got a rotten headache."

"I'll see you to-morrow?"

"Come in at the office."

"Hardly."

"Well, where will I see you?"

"Anywhere around five o'clock."

"Make it the other side of town then."

"Good. I'll be at the Crillon at five."

"Try and be there," I said.

"Don't worry," Brett said. "I've never let you down, have I?"

"Heard from Mike?"

"Letter to-day."

"Good night, sir," said the count.

I went out onto the sidewalk and walked down toward the Boulevard St. Michel, passed the tables of the Rotonde, still crowded, looked across the street at the Dome, its tables running out to the edge of the pavement. Some one waved at me from a table, I did not see who it was and went on. I wanted to get home. The Boulevard Montparnasse was deserted. Lavigne's was closed tight, and they were stacking the tables outside the Closerie des Lilas. I passed Ney's statue standing among the new-leaved chestnut-trees in the arc-light. There was a faded purple wreath leaning against the base. I stopped and read the inscription: from the Bonapartist Groups, some date; I forget. He looked very fine, Marshal Ney in his top-boots, gesturing with his sword among the green new horse-chestnut leaves. My flat was just across the street, a little way down the Boulevard St. Michel.

There was a light in the concierge's room and I knocked on the door and she gave me my mail. I wished her good night and went up-stairs. There were two letters and some papers. I looked at them under the gas-light in the dining-room. The letters were from the States. One was a bank statement. It showed a balance of $2432.60. I got out my check-book and deducted four checks drawn since the first of the month, and discovered I had a balance of $1832.60. I wrote this on the back of the statement. The other letter was a wedding announcement. Mr. and Mrs. Aloysius Kirby announce the marriage of their daughter Katherine—I knew neither the girl nor the man she was marrying. They must be circularizing the town. It was a funny name. I felt sure I could remember anybody with a name like Aloysius. It was a good Catholic name. There was a crest on the announcement. Like Zizi the Greek duke. And that count. The count was funny. Brett had a title, too. Lady Ashley. To hell with Brett. To hell with you, Lady Ashley.

I lit the lamp beside the bed, turned off the gas, and opened the wide windows. The bed was far back from the windows, and I sat with the windows open and undressed by the bed. Outside a night train, running on the street-car tracks, went by carrying vegetables to the markets. They were noisy at night when you could not sleep. Undressing, I looked at myself in the mirror of the big armoire beside the bed. That was a typically French way to furnish a room. Practical, too, I suppose. Of all the ways to be wounded. I suppose it was funny. I put on my pajamas and got into bed. I had the two bull-fight papers, and I took their wrappers off. One was orange. The other yellow. They would both have the same news, so whichever I read first would spoil the other. *Le Toril* was the better paper, so I started to read it. I read it all the way through, including the Petite Correspondance and the Cornigrams. I blew out the lamp. Perhaps I would be able to sleep.

My head started to work. The old grievance. Well, it was a rotten way to be wounded and flying on a joke front like the Italian. In the Italian hospital we were going to form a society. It had a funny name in Italian. I wonder what became of the others, the Italians. That was in the Ospedale Maggiore in Milano, Padiglione Ponte. The next building was the Padiglione Zonda. There was a statue of Ponte, or maybe it was Zonda. That was where the liaison colonel came to visit me. That was funny. That was about the first funny thing. I was all bandaged up. But they had told him about it. Then he made that wonderful speech: "You, a foreigner, an Englishman" (any foreigner was an Englishman) "have given more than your life." What a speech! I would like to have it illuminated to hang in the office. He never laughed. He was putting himself in my place, I guess. "Che mala fortuna! Che mala fortuna!"

I never used to realize it, I guess. I try and play it along and just not make trouble for people. Probably I never would have had any trouble if I hadn't run into Brett when they shipped me to England. I suppose she only wanted what she couldn't have. Well, people were that way. To hell with people. The Catholic Church had an awfully good way of handling all that. Good advice, anyway. Not to think about it. Oh, it was swell advice. Try and take it sometime. Try and take it.

I lay awake thinking and my mind jumping around. Then I couldn't keep away from it, and I started to think about Brett and all the rest of it went away. I was thinking about Brett and my mind stopped jumping around and started to go in sort of a while it was better and I lay in bed and listened to the smooth waves. Then all of a sudden I started to cry. Then after heavy trains go by and way down the street and then I went to sleep.

I woke up. There was a row going on outside. I listened and I thought I recognized a voice. I put on a dressing-gown and went to the door. The concierge was talking down-stairs. She was very angry. I heard my name and called down the stairs.

"Is that you, Monsieur Barnes?" the concierge called.

"Yes. It's me."

"There's a species of woman here who's waked the whole street up. What kind of a dirty business at this time of night! She says she must see you. I've told her you're asleep."

Then I heard Brett's voice. Half asleep I had been sure it was Georgette. I don't know why. She could not have known my address.

"Will you send her up, please?"

Brett came up the stairs. I saw she was quite drunk. "Silly thing to do," she said. "Make an awful row. I say, you weren't asleep, were you?"

"What did you think I was doing?"

"Don't know. What time is it?"

I looked at the clock. It was half-past four. "Had no idea what hour it was," Brett said. "I say, can a chap sit down? Don't be cross, darling. Just left the count. He brought me here."

"What's he like?" I was getting brandy and soda and glasses.

"Just a little," said Brett. "Don't try and make me drunk. The count? Oh, rather. He's quite one of us."

"Is he a count?"

"Here's how. I rather think so, you know. Deserves to be, anyhow. Knows hell's own amount about people. Don't know where he got it all. Owns a chain of sweetshops in the States."

She sipped at her class.

"Think he called it a chain. Something like that. Linked them

all up. Told me a little about it. Damned interesting. He's one of
us, though. Oh, quite. No doubt. One can always tell."

She took another drink.

"How do I buck on about all this? You don't mind, do you?
He's putting up for Zizi, you know."

"Is Zizi really a duke, too?"

"I shouldn't wonder. Greek, you know. Rotten painter. I rather
liked the count."

"Where did you go with him?"

"Oh, everywhere. He just brought me here now. Offered me
ten thousand dollars to go to Biarritz with him. How much is that
in pounds?"

"Around two thousand."

"Lot of money. I told him I couldn't do it. He was awfully
nice about it. Told him I knew too many people in Biarritz."

Brett laughed.

"I say, you are slow on the up-take," she said. I had only sipped
my brandy and soda. I took a long drink.

"That's better. Very funny," Brett said. "Then he wanted me to
go to Cannes with him. Told him I knew too many people in
Cannes. Monte Carlo. Told him I knew too many people in
Monte Carlo. Told him I knew too many people everywhere.
Quite true, too. So I asked him to bring me here."

She looked at me, her hand on the table, her glass raised.
"Don't look like that," she said. "Told him I was in love with
you. True, too. Don't look like that. He was damn nice about it.
Wants to drive us out to dinner to-morrow night. Like to go?"

"Why not?"

"I'd better go now."

"Why?"

"Just wanted to see you. Damned silly idea. Want to get dressed
and come down? He's got the car just up the street."

"The count?"

"Himself. And a chauffeur in livery. Going to drive me around
and have breakfast in the Bois. Hampers. Got it all at Zelli's.
Dozen bottles of Mumms. Tempt you?"

"I have to work in the morning," I said. "I'm too far behind you now to catch up and be any fun."

"Don't be an ass."

"Can't do it."

"Right. Send him a tender message?"

"Anything. Absolutely."

"Good night, darling."

"Don't be sentimental."

"You make me ill."

We kissed good night and Brett shivered. "I'd better go," she said. "Good night, darling."

"You don't have to go."

"Yes."

We kissed again on the stairs and as I called for the cordon the concierge muttered something behind her door. I went back upstairs and from the open window watched Brett walking up the street to the big limousine drawn up to the curb under the arc-light. She got in and it started off. I turned around. On the table was an empty glass and a glass half-full of brandy and soda. I took them both out to the kitchen and poured the half-full glass down the sink. I turned off the gas in the dining-room, kicked off my slippers sitting on the bed, and got into bed. This was Brett, that I had felt like crying about. Then I thought of her walking up the street and stepping into the car, as I had last seen her, and of course in a little while I felt like hell again. It is awfully easy to be hard-boiled about everything in the daytime, but at night it is another thing.

CHAPTER V

IN the morning I walked down the Boulevard to the rue Soufflot for coffee and brioche. It was a fine morning. The horse-chestnut trees in the Luxembourg gardens were in bloom. There was the pleasant early-morning feeling of a hot day. I read the papers with the coffee and then smoked a cigarette. The flower-women were coming up from the market and arringing their daily stock. Students went by going up to the law school, or down to the Sorbonne. The Boulevard was busy with trams and people going to work. I got on an S bus and rode down to the Madeleine, standing on the back platform. From the Madeleine I walked along the Boulevard des Capucines to the Opéra, and up to my office. I passed the man with the jumping frogs and the man with the boxer toys. I stepped aside to avoid walking into the thread with which his girl assistant manipulated the boxers. She was standing looking away, the thread in her folded hands. The man was urging two tourists to buy. Three more tourists had stopped and were watching. I walked on behind a man who was pushing a roller that printed the name CINZANO on the sidewalk in damp letters. All along people were going to work. It felt pleasant to be going to work. I walked across the avenue and turned in to my office.

Up-stairs in the office I read the French morning papers, smoked, and then sat at the typewriter and got off a good morning's work. At eleven o'clock I went over to the Quai d'Orsay in a taxi and went in and sat with about a dozen correspondents, while the foreign-office mouthpiece, a young Nouvelle Revue Française diplomat in horn-rimmed spectacles, talked and answered questions for half an hour. The President of the Council was in Lyons making a speech, or, rather he was on his way back. Several people asked questions to hear themselves talk and there were a couple of questions asked by news service men who wanted to know the answers. There was no news. I shared a taxi back from the Quai d'Orsay with Woolsey and Krum.

"What do you do nights, Jake?" asked Krum. "I never see you around."

"Oh, I'm over in the Quarter."

"I'm coming over some night. The Dingo. That's the great place, isn't it?"

"Yes. That, or this new dive, The Select."

"I've meant to get over," said Krum. "You know how it is, though, with a wife and kids."

"Playing any tennis?" Woolsey asked.

"Well, no," said Krum. "I can't say I've played any this year. I've tried to get away, but Sundays it's always rained, and the courts are so damned crowded."

"The Englishmen all have Saturday off," Woolsey said.

"Lucky beggars," said Krum. "Well, I'll tell you. Some day I'm not going to be working for an agency. Then I'll have plenty of time to get out in the country."

"That's the thing to do. Live out in the country and have a little car."

"I've been thinking some about getting a car next year."

I banged on the glass. The chauffeur stopped. "Here's my street," I said. "Come in and have a drink."

"Thanks, old man," Krum said. Woolsey shook his head. "I've got to file that line he got off this morning."

I put a two-franc piece in Krum's hand.

"You're crazy, Jake," he said. "This is on me."

"It's all on the office, anyway."

"Nope. I want to get it."

I waved good-by. Krum put his head out. "See you at the lunch on Wednesday."

"You bet."

I went to the office in the elevator. Robert Cohn was waiting for me. "Hello, Jake," he said. "Going out to lunch?"

"Yes. Let me see if there is anything new."

"Where will we eat?"

"Anywhere."

I was looking over my desk. "Where do you want to eat?"

"How about Wetzel's? They've got good hors d'œuvres."

In the restaurant we ordered hors d'œuvres and beer. The sommelier brought the beer, tall, beaded on the outside of the steins, and cold. There were a dozen different dishes of hors d'œuvres.

"Have any fun last night?" I asked.

"No. I don't think so."

"How's the writing going?"

"Rotten. I can't get this second book going."

"That happens to everybody."

"Oh, I'm sure of that. It gets me worried, though."

"Thought any more about going to South America?"

"I mean that."

"Well, why don't you start off?"

"Frances."

"Well," I said, "take her with you."

"She wouldn't like it. That isn't the sort of thing she likes. She likes a lot of people around."

"Tell her to go to hell."

"I can't. I've got certain obligations to her."

He shoved the sliced cucumbers away and took a pickled herring.

"What do you know about Lady Brett Ashley, Jake?"

"Her name's Lady Ashley. Brett's her own name. She's a nice girl," I said. "She's getting a divorce and she's going to marry Mike Campbell. He's over in Scotland now. Why?"

"She's a remarkably attractive woman."

"Isn't she?"

"There's a certain quality about her, a certain fineness. She seems to be absolutely fine and straight."

"She's very nice."

"I don't know how to describe the quality," Cohn said. "I suppose it's breeding."

"You sound as though you liked her pretty well."

"I do. I shouldn't wonder if I were in love with her."

"She's a drunk," I said. "She's in love with Mike Campbell, and she's going to marry him. He's going to be rich as hell some day."

"I don't believe she'll ever marry him."

"Why not?"

"I don't know. I just don't believe it. Have you known her a long time?"

"Yes," I said. "She was a V. A. D. in a hospital I was in during the war."

"She must have been just a kid then."

"She's thirty-four now."

"When did she marry Ashley?"

"During the war. Her own true love had just kicked off with the dysentery."

"You talk sort of bitter."

"Sorry. I didn't mean to. I was just trying to give you the facts."

"I don't believe she would marry anybody she didn't love."

"Well," I said. "She's done it twice."

"I don't believe it."

"Well," I said, "don't ask me a lot of fool questions if you don't like the answers."

"I didn't ask you that."

"You asked me what I knew about Brett Ashley."

"I didn't ask you to insult her."

"Oh, go to hell."

He stood up from the table his face white, and stood there white and angry behind the little plates of hors d'œuvres.

"Sit down," I said. "Don't be a fool."

"You've got to take that back."

"Oh, cut out the prep-school stuff."

"Take it back."

"Sure. Anything. I never heard of Brett Ashley. How's that?"

"No. Not that. About me going to hell."

"Oh, don't go to hell," I said. "Stick around. We're just starting lunch."

Cohn smiled again and sat down. He seemed glad to sit down. What the hell would he have done if he hadn't sat down? "You say such damned insulting things, Jake."

"I'm sorry. I've got a nasty tongue. I never mean it when I say nasty things."

"I know it," Cohn said. "You're really about the best friend I have, Jake."

God help you, I thought. "Forget what I said," I said out loud. "I'm sorry."

"It's all right. It's fine. I was just sore for a minute."

"Good. Let's get something else to eat."

After we finished the lunch we walked up to the Café de la Paix and had coffee. I could feel Cohn wanted to bring up Brett again, but I held him off it. We talked about one thing and another, and I left him to come to the office.

CHAPTER VI

AT five o'clock I was in the Hotel Crillon waiting for Brett. She was not there, so I sat down and wrote some letters. They were not very good letters but I hoped their being on Crillon stationery would help them. Brett did not turn up, so about quarter to six I went down to the bar and had a Jack Rose with George the barman. Brett had not been in the bar either, and so I looked for her upstairs on my way out, and took a taxi to the Café Select. Crossing the Seine I saw a string of barges being towed empty down the current, riding high, the bargemen at the sweeps as they came toward the bridge. The river looked nice. It was always pleasant crossing bridges in Paris.

The taxi rounded the statue of the inventor of the semaphore engaged in doing same, and turned up the Boulevard Raspail, and I sat back to let that part of the ride pass. The Boulevard Raspail always made dull riding. It was like a certain stretch on the P.L.M. between Fontainebleau and Montereau that always made me feel bored and dead and dull until it was over. I suppose it is some association of ideas that makes those dead places in a journey. There are other streets in Paris as ugly as the Boulevard Raspail. It is a street I do not mind walking down at all. But I cannot stand to ride along it. Perhaps I had read something about it once. That was the way Robert Cohn was about all of Paris. I wondered where Cohn got that incapacity to enjoy Paris. Possibly from Mencken. Mencken hates Paris, I believe. So many young men get their likes and dislikes from Mencken.

The taxi stopped in front of the Rotonde. No matter what café in Montparnasse you ask a taxi-driver to bring you to from the right bank of the river, they always take you to the Rotonde. Ten years from now it will probably be the Dome. It was near enough, anyway. I walked past the sad tables of the Rotonde to the Select. There were a few people inside at the bar, and outside, alone, sat Harvey Stone. He had a pile of saucers in front of him, and he needed a shave.

"Sit down," said Harvey, "I've been looking for you."

"What's the matter?"

"Nothing. Just looking for you."

"Been out to the races?"

"No. Not since Sunday."

"What do you hear from the States?"

"Nothing. Absolutely nothing."

"What's the matter?"

"I don't know. I'm through with them. I'm absolutely through with them."

He leaned forward and looked me in the eye.

"Do you want to know something, Jake?"

"Yes."

"I haven't had anything to eat for five days."

I figured rapidly back in my mind. It was three days ago that Harvey had won two hundred francs from me shaking poker dice in the New York Bar.

"What's the matter?"

"No money. Money hasn't come," he paused. "I tell you it's strange, Jake. When I'm like this I just want to be alone. I want to stay in my own room. I'm like a cat."

I felt in my pocket.

"Would a hundred help you any, Harvey?"

"Yes."

"Come on. Let's go and eat."

"There's no hurry. Have a drink."

"Better eat."

"No. When I get like this I don't care whether I eat or not."

We had a drink. Harvey added my saucer to his own pile.

"Do you know Mencken, Harvey?"

"Yes. Why?"

"What's he like?"

"He's all right. He says some pretty funny things. Last time I had dinner with him we talked about Hoffenheimer. 'The trouble is,' he said, 'he's a garter snapper.' That's not bad."

"That's not bad."

"He's through now," Harvey went on. "He's written about all the things he knows, and now he's on all the things he doesn't know."

"I guess he's all right," I said. "I just can't read him."

"Oh, nobody reads him now," Harvey said, "except the people that used to read the Alexander Hamilton Institute."

"Well," I said. "That was a good thing, too."

"Sure," said Harvey. So we sat and thought deeply for a while.

"Have another port?"

"All right," said Harvey.

"There comes Cohn," I said. Robert Cohn was crossing the street.

"That moron," said Harvey. Cohn came up to our table.

"Hello, you bums," he said.

"Hello, Robert," Harvey said. "I was just telling Jake here that you're a moron."

"What do you mean?"

"Tell us right off. Don't think. What would you rather do if you could do anything you wanted?"

Cohn started to consider.

"Don't think. Bring it right out."

"I don't know," Cohn said. "What's it all about, anyway?"

"I mean what would you rather do. What comes into your head first. No matter how silly it is."

"I don't know," Cohn said. "I think I'd rather play football again with what I know about handling myself, now."

"I misjudged you," Harvey said. "You're not a moron. You're only a case of arrested development."

"You're awfully funny, Harvey," Cohn said. "Some day somebody will push your face in."

Harvey Stone laughed. "You think so. They won't, though. Because it wouldn't make any difference to me. I'm not a fighter."

"It would make a difference to you if anybody did it."

"No, it wouldn't. That's where you make your big mistake. Because you're not intelligent."

"Cut it out about me."

"Sure," said Harvey. "It doesn't make any difference to me. You don't mean anything to me."

"Come on, Harvey," I said. "Have another porto."

"No," he said. "I'm going up the street and eat. See you later, Jake."

He walked out and up the street. I watched him crossing the street through the taxis, small, heavy, slowly sure of himself in the traffic.

"He always gets me sore," Cohn said. "I can't stand him."

"I like him," I said. "I'm fond of him. You don't want to get sore at him."

"I know it," Cohn said. "He just gets on my nerves."

"Write this afternoon?"

"No. I couldn't get it going. It's harder to do than my first book. I'm having a hard time handling it."

The sort of healthy conceit that he had when he returned from America early in the spring was gone. Then he had been sure of his work, only with these personal longings for adventure. Now the sureness was gone. Somehow I feel I have not shown Robert Cohn clearly. The reason is that until he fell in love with Brett, I never heard him make one remark that would, in any way, detach him from other people. He was nice to watch on the tennis-court, he had a good body, and he kept it in shape; he handled his cards well at bridge, and he had a funny sort of undergraduate quality about him. If he were in a crowd nothing he said stood out. He wore what used to be called polo shirts at school, and may be called that still, but he was not professionally youthful. I do not believe he thought about his clothes much. Externally he had been formed at Princeton. Internally he had been moulded by the two women who had trained him. He had a nice, boyish sort of cheerfulness that had never been trained out of him, and I probably have not brought it out. He loved to win at tennis. He probably loved to win as much as Lenglen, for instance. On the other hand, he was not angry at being beaten. When he fell in love with Brett his tennis game went all to pieces. People beat him who had never had a chance with him. He was very nice about it.

Anyhow, we were sitting on the terrace of the Café Select, and Harvey Stone had just crossed the street.

"Come on up to the Lilas," I said.

"I have a date."

"What time?"

"Frances is coming here at seven-fifteen."

"There she is."

Frances Clyne was coming toward us from across the street. She was a very tall girl who walked with a great deal of movement. She waved and smiled. We watched her cross the street.

"Hello," she said, "I'm so glad you're here, Jake. I've been wanting to talk to you."

"Hello, Frances," said Cohn. He smiled.

"Why, hello, Robert. Are you here?" She went on, talking rapidly. "I've had the darndest time. This one"—shaking her head at Cohn—"didn't come home for lunch."

"I wasn't supposed to."

"Oh, I know. But you didn't say anything about it to the cook. Then I had a date myself, and Paula wasn't at her office. I went to the Ritz and waited for her, and she never came, and of course I didn't have enough money to lunch at the Ritz——"

"What did you do?"

"Oh, went out, of course." She spoke in a sort of imitation joyful manner. "I always keep my appointments. No one keeps theirs, nowadays. I ought to know better. How are you, Jake, anyway?"

"Fine."

"That was a fine girl you had at the dance, and then went off with that Brett one."

"Don't you like her?" Cohn asked.

"I think she's perfectly charming. Don't you?"

Cohn said nothing.

"Look, Jake. I want to talk with you. Would you come over with me to the Dome? You'll stay here, won't you, Robert? Come on, Jake."

We crossed the Boulevard Montparnasse and sat down at a table.

A boy came up with the *Paris Times,* and I bought one and opened it.

"What's the matter, Frances?"

"Oh, nothing," she said, "except that he wants to leave me."

"How do you mean?"

"Oh, he told every one that we were going to be married, and I told my mother and every one, and now he doesn't want to do it."

"What's the matter?"

"He's decided he hasn't lived enough. I knew it would happen when he went to New York."

She looked up, very bright-eyed and trying to talk inconsequentially.

"I wouldn't marry him if he doesn't want to. Of course I wouldn't. I wouldn't marry him now for anything. But it does seem to me to be a little late now, after we've waited three years, and I've just gotten my divorce."

I said nothing.

"We were going to celebrate so, and instead we've just had scenes. It's so childish. We have dreadful scenes, and he cries and begs me to be reasonable, but he says he just can't do it."

"It's rotten luck."

"I should say it is rotten luck. I've wasted two years and a half on him now. And I don't know now if any man will ever want to marry me. Two years ago I could have married anybody I wanted, down at Cannes. All the old ones that wanted to marry somebody chic and settle down were crazy about me. Now I don't think I could get anybody."

"Sure, you could marry anybody."

"No, I don't believe it. And I'm fond of him, too. And I'd like to have children. I always thought we'd have children."

She looked at me very brightly. "I never liked children much, but I don't want to think I'll never have them. I always thought I'd have them and then like them."

"He's got children."

"Oh, yes. He's got children, and he's got money, and he's got a rich mother, and he's written a book, and nobody will publish my stuff, nobody at all. It isn't bad, either. And I haven't got any money at all. I could have had alimony, but I got the divorce the quickest way."

She looked at me again very brightly.

"It isn't right. It's my own fault and it's not, too. I ought to have known better. And when I tell him he just cries and says he can't marry. Why can't he marry? I'd be a good wife. I'm easy to get along with. I leave him alone. It doesn't do any good."

"It's a rotten shame."

"Yes, it is a rotten shame. But there's no use talking about it, is there? Come on, let's go back to the café."

"And of course there isn't anything I can do."

"No. Just don't let him know I talked to you. I know what he wants." Now for the first time she dropped her bright, terribly cheerful manner. "He wants to go back to New York alone, and be there when his book comes out so when a lot of little chickens like it. That's what he wants."

"Maybe they won't like it. I don't think he's that way. Really."

"You don't know him like I do, Jake. That's what he wants to do. I know it. I know it. That's why he doesn't want to marry. He wants to have a big triumph this fall all by himself."

"Want to go back to the café?"

"Yes. Come on."

We got up from the table—they had never brought us a drink —and started across the street toward the Select, where Cohn sat smiling at us from behind the marble-topped table.

"Well, what are you smiling at?" Frances asked him. "Feel pretty happy?"

"I was smiling at you and Jake with your secrets."

"Oh, what I've told Jake isn't any secret. Everybody will know it soon enough. I only wanted to give Jake a decent version."

"What was it? About your going to England?"

"Yes, about my going to England. Oh, Jake! I forgot to tell you. I'm going to England."

"Isn't that fine!"

"Yes, that's the way it's done in the very best families. Robert's sending me. He's going to give me two hundred pounds and then

I'm going to visit friends. Won't it be lovely? The friends don't know about it, yet."

She turned to Cohn and smiled at him. He was not smiling now.

"You were only going to give me a hundred pounds, weren't you, Robert? But I made him give me two hundred. He's really very generous. Aren't you, Robert?"

I do not know how people could say such terrible things to Robert Cohn. There are people to whom you could not say insulting things. They give you a feeling that the world would be destroyed, would actually be destroyed before your eyes, if you said certain things. But here was Cohn taking it all. Here it was, all going on right before me, and I did not even feel an impulse to try and stop it. And this was friendly joking to what went on later.

"How can you say such things, Frances?" Cohn interrupted.

"Listen to him. I'm going to England. I'm going to visit friends. Ever visit friends that didn't want you? Oh, they'll have to take me, all right. 'How do you do, my dear? Such a long time since we've seen you. And how is your dear mother?' Yes, how is my dear mother? She put all her money into French war bonds. Yes, she did. Probably the only person in the world that did. 'And what about Robert?' or else very careful talking around Robert. 'You must be most careful not to mention him, my dear. Poor Frances has had a most unfortunate experience.' Won't it be fun, Robert? Don't you think it will be fun, Jake?"

She turned to me with that terribly bright smile. It was very satisfactory to her to have an audience for this.

"And where are you going to be, Robert? It's my own fault, all right. Perfectly my own fault. When I made you get rid of your little secretary on the magazine I ought to have known you'd get rid of me the same way. Jake doesn't know about that. Should I tell him?"

"Shut up, Frances, for God's sake."

"Yes, I'll tell him. Robert had a little secretary on the magazine. Just the sweetest little thing in the world, and he thought she was wonderful, and then I came along and he thought I was pretty wonderful, too. So I made him get rid of her, and he had

brought her to Provincetown from Carmel when he moved the
magazine, and he didn't even pay her fare back to the coast. All
to please me. He thought I was pretty fine, then. Didn't you,
Robert?

"You mustn't misunderstand, Jake, it was absolutely platonic
with the secretary. Not even platonic. Nothing at all, really. It
was just that she was so nice. And he did that just to please me.
Well, I suppose that we that live by the sword shall perish by the
sword. Isn't that literary, though? You want to remember that
for your next book, Robert.

"You know Robert is going to get material for a new book.
Aren't you, Robert? That's why he's leaving me. He's decided I
don't film well. You see, he was so busy all the time that we were
living together, writing on this book, that he doesn't remember
anything about us. So now he's going out and get some new
material. Well, I hope he gets something frightfully interesting.

"Listen, Robert, dear. Let me tell you something. You won't
mind, will you? Don't have scenes with your young ladies. Try
not to. Because you can't have scenes without crying, and then
you pity yourself so much you can't remember what the other
person's said. You'll never be able to remember any conversations that way. Just try and be calm. I know it's awfully hard. But
remember, it's for literature. We all ought to make sacrifices for
literature. Look at me. I'm going to England without a protest.
All for literature. We must all help young writers. Don't you
think so, Jake? But you're not a young writer. Are you, Robert?
You're thirty-four. Still, I suppose that is young for a great writer.
Look at Hardy. Look at Anatole France. He just died a little while
ago. Robert doesn't think he's any good, though. Some of his
French friends told him. He doesn't read French very well himself. He wasn't a good writer like you are, was he, Robert? Do you
think he ever had to go and look for material? What do you suppose he said to his mistresses when he wouldn't marry them? I
wonder if he cried, too? Oh, I've just thought of something." She
put her gloved hand up to her lips. "I know the real reason why
Robert won't marry me, Jake. It's just come to me. They've sent
it to me in a vision in the Café Select. Isn't it mystic? Some day

they'll put a tablet up. Like at Lourdes. Do you want to hear, Robert? I'll tell you. It's so simple. I wonder why I never thought about it. Why, you see, Robert's always wanted to have a mistress, and if he doesn't marry me, why, then he's had one. She was his mistress for over two years. See how it is? And if he marries me, like he's always promised he would, that would be the end of all the romance. Don't you think that's bright of me to figure that out? It's true, too. Look at him and see if it's not. Where are you going, Jake?"

"I've got to go in and see Harvey Stone a minute."

Cohn looked up as I went in. His face was white. Why did he sit there? Why did he keep on taking it like that?

As I stood against the bar looking out I could see them through the window. Frances was talking on to him, smiling brightly, looking into his face each time she asked: "Isn't it so, Robert?" Or maybe she did not ask that now. Perhaps she said something else. I told the barman I did not want anything to drink and went out through the side door. As I went out the door I looked back through the two thicknesses of glass and saw them sitting there. She was still talking to him. I went down a side street to the Boulevard Raspail. A taxi came along and I got in and gave the driver the address of my flat.

CHAPTER VII

As I started up the stairs the concierge knocked on the glass of the door of her lodge, and as I stopped she came out. She had some letters and a telegram.

"Here is the post. And there was a lady here to see you."

"Did she leave a card?"

"No. She was with a gentleman. It was the one who was here last night. In the end I find she is very nice."

"Was she with a friend of mine?"

"I don't know. He was never here before. He was very large. Very, very large. She was very nice. Very, very nice. Last night she was, perhaps, a little—" She put her head on one hand and rocked it up and down. "I'll speak perfectly frankly, Monsieur Barnes. Last night I found her not so gentille. Last night I formed another idea of her. But listen to what I tell you. She is très, très gentille. She is of very good family. It is a thing you can see."

"They did not leave any word?"

"Yes. They said they would be back in an hour."

"Send them up when they come."

"Yes, Monsieur Barnes. And that lady, that lady there is some one. An eccentric, perhaps, but quelqu'une, quelqu'une!"

The concierge, before she became a concierge, had owned a drink-selling concession at the Paris race-courses. Her life-work lay in the pelouse, but she kept an eye on the people of the pesage, and she took great pride in telling me which of my guests were well brought up, which were of good family, who were sportsmen, a French word pronounced with the accent on the men. The only trouble was that people who did not fall into any of those three categories were very liable to be told there was no one home, chez Barnes. One of my friends, an extremely underfed-looking painter, who was obviously to Madame Duzinell neither well brought up, of good family, nor a sportsman, wrote me a letter asking if I could get him a pass to get by the concierge so he could come up and see me occasionally in the evenings.

I went up to the flat wondering what Brett had done to the concierge. The wire was a cable from Bill Gorton, saying he was arriving on the *France*. I put the mail on the table, went back to the bedroom, undressed and had a shower. I was rubbing down when I heard the door-bell pull. I put on a bathrobe and slippers and went to the door. It was Brett. Back of her was the count. He was holding a great bunch of roses.

"Hello, darling," said Brett. "Aren't you going to let us in?"

"Come on. I was just bathing."

"Aren't you the fortunate man. Bathing."

"Only a shower. Sit down, Count Mippipopolous. What will you drink?"

"I don't know whether you like flowers, sir," the count said, "but I took the liberty of just bringing these roses."

"Here, give them to me." Brett took them. "Get me some water in this, Jake." I filled the big earthenware jug with water in the kitchen, and Brett put the roses in it, and placed them in the centre of the dining-room table.

"I say. We have had a day."

"You don't remember anything about a date with me at the Crillon?"

"No. Did we have one? I must have been blind."

"You were quite drunk, my dear," said the count.

"Wasn't I, though? And the count's been a brick, absolutely."

"You've got hell's own drag with the concierge now."

"I ought to have. Gave her two hundred francs."

"Don't be a damned fool."

"His," she said, and nodded at the count.

"I thought we ought to give her a little something for last night. It was very late."

"He's wonderful," Brett said. "He remembers everything that's happened."

"So do you, my dear."

"Fancy," said Brett. "Who'd want to? I say, Jake, *do* we get a drink?"

"You get it while I go in and dress. You know where it is."

"Rather."

While I dressed I heard Brett put down glasses and then a siphon, and then heard them talking. I dressed slowly, sitting on the bed. I felt tired and pretty rotten. Brett came in the room, a glass in her hand, and sat on the bed.

"What's the matter, darling? Do you feel rocky?"

She kissed me coolly on the forehead.

"Oh, Brett, I love you so much."

"Darling," she said. Then: "Do you want me to send him away?"

"No. He's nice."

"I'll send him away."

"No, don't."

"Yes, I'll send him away."

"You can't just like that."

"Can't I, though? You stay here. He's mad about me, I tell you."

She was gone out of the room. I lay face down on the bed. I was having a bad time. I heard them talking but I did not listen. Brett came in and sat on the bed.

"Poor old darling." She stroked my head.

"What did you say to him?" I was lying with my face away from her. I did not want to see her.

"Sent him for champagne. He loves to go for champagne."

Then later: "Do you feel better, darling? Is the head any better?"

"It's better."

"Lie quiet. He's gone to the other side of town."

"Couldn't we live together, Brett? Couldn't we just live together?"

"I don't think so. I'd just *tromper* you with everybody. You couldn't stand it."

"I stand it now."

"That would be different. It's my fault, Jake. It's the way I'm made."

"Couldn't we go off in the country for a while?"

"It wouldn't be any good. I'll go if you like. But I couldn't live quietly in the country. Not with my own true love."

"I know."

"Isn't it rotten? There isn't any use my telling you I love you."

"You know I love you."

"Let's not talk. Talking's all bilge. I'm going away from you, and then Michael's coming back."

"Why are you going away?"

"Better for you. Better for me."

"When are you going?"

"Soon as I can."

"Where?"

"San Sebastian."

"Can't we go together?"

"No. That would be a hell of an idea after we'd just talked it out."

"We never agreed."

"Oh, you know as well as I do. Don't be obstinate, darling."

"Oh, sure," I said. "I know you're right. I'm just low, and when I'm low I talk like a fool."

I sat up, leaned over, found my shoes beside the bed and put them on. I stood up.

"Don't look like that, darling."

"How do you want me to look?"

"Oh, don't be a fool. I'm going away to-morrow."

"To-morrow?"

"Yes. Didn't I say so? I am."

"Let's have a drink, then. The count will be back."

"Yes. He should be back. You know he's extraordinary about buying champagne. It means any amount to him."

We went into the dining-room. I took up the brandy bottle and poured Brett a drink and one for myself. There was a ring at the bell-pull. I went to the door and there was the count. Behind him was the chauffeur carrying a basket of champagne.

"Where should I have him put it, sir?" asked the count.

"In the kitchen," Brett said.

"Put it in there, Henry," the count motioned. "Now go down and get the ice." He stood looking after the basket inside the kitchen door. "I think you'll find that's very good wine," he said. "I know we don't get much of a chance to judge good wine in the States now, but I got this from a friend of mine that's in the business."

"Oh, you always have some one in the trade," Brett said.

"This fellow raises the grapes. He's got thousands of acres of them."

"What's his name?" asked Brett. "Veuve Cliquot?"

"No," said the count. "Mumms. He's a baron."

"Isn't it wonderful," said Brett. "We all have titles. Why haven't you a title, Jake?"

"I assure you, sir," the count put his hand on my arm. "It never does a man any good. Most of the time it costs you money."

"Oh, I don't know. It's damned useful sometimes," Brett said.

"I've never known it to do me any good."

"You haven't used it properly. I've had hell's own amount of credit on mine."

"Do sit down, count," I said. "Let me take that stick."

The count was looking at Brett across the table under the gas-light. She was smoking a cigarette and flicking the ashes on the rug. She saw me notice it. "I say, Jake, I don't want to ruin your rugs. Can't you give a chap an ash-tray?"

I found some ash-trays and spread them around. The chauffeur came up with a bucket full of salted ice. "Put two bottles in it, Henry," the count called.

"Anything else, sir?"

"No. Wait down in the car." He turned to Brett and to me. "We'll want to ride out to the Bois for dinner?"

"If you like," Brett said. "I couldn't eat a thing."

"I always like a good meal," said the count.

"Should I bring the wine in, sir?" asked the chauffeur.

"Yes. Bring it in, Henry," said the count. He took out a heavy pigskin cigar-case and offered it to me. "Like to try a real Ameri-can cigar?"

"Thanks," I said. "I'll finish the cigarette."

He cut off the end of his cigar with a gold cutter he wore on one end of his watch-chain.

"I like a cigar to really draw," said the count. "Half the cigars you smoke don't draw."

He lit the cigar, puffed at it, looking across the table at Brett. "And when you're divorced, Lady Ashley, then you won't have a title."

"No. What a pity."

"No," said the count. "You don't need a title. You got class all over you."

"Thanks. Awfully decent of you."

"I'm not joking you," the count blew a cloud of smoke. "You got the most class of anybody I ever seen. You got it. That's all."

"Nice of you," said Brett. "Mummy would be pleased. Couldn't you write it out, and I'll send it in a letter to her."

"I'd tell her, too," said the count. "I'm not joking you. I never joke people. Joke people and you make enemies. That's what I always say."

"You're right," Brett said. "You're terribly right. I always joke people and I haven't a friend in the world. Except Jake here."

"You don't joke him."

"That's it."

"Do you, now?" asked the count. "Do you joke him?"

Brett looked at me and wrinkled up the corners of her eyes.

"No," she said. "I wouldn't joke him."

"See," said the count. "You don't joke him."

"This is a hell of a dull talk," Brett said. "How about some of that champagne?"

The count reached down and twirled the bottles in the shiny bucket. "It isn't cold, yet. You're always drinking, my dear. Why don't you just talk?"

"I've talked too ruddy much. I've talked myself all out to Jake."

"I should like to hear you really talk, my dear. When you talk to me you never finish your sentences at all."

"Leave 'em for you to finish. Let any one finish them as they like."

"It is a very interesting system," the count reached down and gave the bottles a twirl. "Still I would like to hear you talk some time."

"Isn't he a fool?" Brett asked.

"Now," the count brought up a bottle. "I think this is cool."

I brought a towel and he wiped the bottle dry and held it up. "I like to drink champagne from magnums. The wine is better but it would have been too hard to cool." He held the bottle, looking at it. I put out the glasses.

"I say. You might open it," Brett suggested.

"Yes, my dear. Now I'll open it."

It was amazing champagne.

"I say that is wine," Brett held up her glass. "We ought to toast something. 'Here's to royalty.'"

"This wine is too good for toast-drinking, my dear. You don't want to mix emotions up with a wine like that. You lose the taste."

Brett's glass was empty.

"You ought to write a book on wines, count," I said.

"Mr. Barnes," answered the count, "all I want out of wines is to enjoy them."

"Let's enjoy a little more of this," Brett pushed her glass forward. The count poured very carefully. "There, my dear. Now you enjoy that slowly, and then you can get drunk."

"Drunk? Drunk?"

"My dear, you are charming when you are drunk."

"Listen to the man."

"Mr. Barnes," the count poured my glass full. "She is the only lady I have ever known who was as charming when she was drunk as when she was sober."

"You haven't been around much, have you?"

"Yes, my dear. I have been around very much. I have been around a very great deal."

"Drink your wine," said Brett. "We've all been around. I dare say Jake here has seen as much as you have."

"My dear, I am sure Mr. Barnes has seen a lot. Don't think I don't think so, sir. I have seen a lot, too."

"Of course you have, my dear," Brett said. "I was only ragging."

"I have been in seven wars and four revolutions," the count said.

"Soldiering?" Brett asked.

"Sometimes, my dear. And I have got arrow wounds. Have you ever seen arrow wounds?"

"Let's have a look at them."

The count stood up, unbuttoned his vest, and opened his shirt. He pulled up the undershirt onto his chest and stood, his chest black, and big stomach muscles bulging under the light.

"You see them?"

Below the line where his ribs stopped were two raised white welts. "See on the back where they come out." Above the small of the back were the same two scars, raised as thick as a finger.

"I say. Those are something."

"Clean through."

The count was tucking in his shirt.

"Where did you get those?" I asked.

"In Abyssinia. When I was twenty-one years old."

"What were you doing?" asked Brett. "Were you in the army?"

"I was on a business trip, my dear."

"I told you he was one of us. Didn't I?" Brett turned to me. "I love you, count. You're a darling."

"You make me very happy, my dear. But it isn't true."

"Don't be an ass."

"You see, Mr. Barnes, it is because I have lived very much that now I can enjoy everything so well. Don't you find it like that?"

"Yes. Absolutely."

"I know," said the count. "That is the secret. You must get to know the values."

"Doesn't anything ever happen to your values?" Brett asked.

"No. Not any more."

"Never fall in love?"

"Always," said the count. "I am always in love."

"What does that do to your values?"

"That, too, has got a place in my values."

"You haven't any values. You're dead, that's all."

"No, my dear. You're not right. I'm not dead at all."

We drank three bottles of the champagne and the count left the basket in my kitchen. We dined at a restaurant in the Bois. It was a good dinner. Food had an excellent place in the count's values. So did wine. The count was in fine form during the meal. So was Brett. It was a good party.

"Where would you like to go?" asked the count after dinner. We were the only people left in the restaurant. The two waiters were standing over against the door. They wanted to go home.

"We might go up on the hill," Brett said. "Haven't we had a splendid party?"

The count was beaming. He was very happy.

"You are very nice people," he said. He was smoking a cigar again. "Why don't you get married, you two?"

"We want to lead our own lives," I said.

"We have our careers," Brett said. "Come on. Let's get out of this."

"Have another brandy," the count said.

"Get it on the hill."

"No. Have it here where it is quiet."

"You and your quiet," said Brett. "What is it men feel about quiet?"

"We like it," said the count. "Like you like noise, my dear."

"All right," said Brett. "Let's have one."

"Sommelier!" the count called.

"Yes, sir."

"What is the oldest brandy you have?"

"Eighteen eleven, sir."

"Bring us a bottle."

"I say. Don't be ostentatious. Call him off, Jake."

"Listen, my dear. I get more value for my money in old brandy than in any other antiquities."

"Got many antiquities?"

"I got a houseful."

Finally we went up to Montmartre. Inside Zelli's it was crowded, smoky, and noisy. The music hit you as you went in. Brett and I danced. It was so crowded we could barely move. The nigger drummer waved at Brett. We were caught in the jam, dancing in one place in front of him.

"Hahre you?"

"Great."

"Thaats good."

He was all teeth and lips.

"He's a great friend of mine," Brett said. "Damn good drummer."

The music stopped and we started toward the table where the count sat. Then the music started again and we danced. I looked at the count. He was sitting at the table smoking a cigar. The music stopped again.

"Let's go over."

Brett started toward the table. The music started and again we danced, tight in the crowd.

"You are a rotten dancer, Jake. Michael's the best dancer I know."

"He's splendid."

"He's got his points."

"I like him," I said. "I'm damned fond of him."

"I'm going to marry him," Brett said. "Funny. I haven't thought about him for a week."

"Don't you write him?"

"Not I. Never write letters."

"I'll bet he writes to you."

"Rather. Damned good letters, too."

"When are you going to get married?"

"How do I know? As soon as we can get the divorce. Michael's trying to get his mother to put up for it."

"Could I help you?"

"Don't be an ass. Michael's people have loads of money."

The music stopped. We walked over to the table. The count stood up.

"Very nice," he said. "You looked very, very nice."

"Don't you dance, count?" I asked.

"No. I'm too old."

"Oh, come off it," Brett said.

"My dear, I would do it if I would enjoy it. I enjoy to watch you dance."

"Splendid," Brett said. "I'll dance again for you some time. I say. What about your little friend, Zizi?"

"Let me tell you. I support that boy, but I don't want to have him around."

"He is rather hard."

"You know I think that boy's got a future. But personally I don't want him around."

"Jake's rather the same way."

"He gives me the willys."

"Well," the count shrugged his shoulders. "About his future you can't ever tell. Anyhow, his father was a great friend of my father."

"Come on. Let's dance," Brett said.

We danced. It was crowded and close.

"Oh, darling," Brett said, "I'm so miserable."

I had that feeling of going through something that has all happened before. "You were happy a minute ago."

The drummer shouted: "You can't two time——"

"It's all gone."

"What's the matter?"

"I don't know. I just feel terribly."

". . . . ." the drummer chanted. Then turned to his sticks.

"Want to go?"

I had the feeling as in a nightmare of it all being something repeated, something I had been through and that now I must go through again.

". . . . ." the drummer sang softly.

"Let's go," said Brett. "You don't mind."

". . . . ." the drummer shouted and grinned at Brett.

"All right," I said. We got out from the crowd. Brett went to the dressing-room.

"Brett wants to go," I said to the count. He nodded. "Does she? That's fine. You take the car. I'm going to stay here for a while, Mr. Barnes."

We shook hands.

"It was a wonderful time," I said. "I wish you would let me get this." I took a note out of my pocket.

"Mr. Barnes, don't be ridiculous," the count said.

Brett came over with her wrap on. She kissed the count and put her hand on his shoulder to keep him from standing up. As we went out the door I looked back and there were three girls at his table. We got into the big car. Brett gave the chauffeur the address of her hotel.

"No, don't come up," she said at the hotel. She had rung and the door was unlatched.

"Really?"

"No. Please."

"Good night, Brett," I said. "I'm sorry you feel rotten."

"Good night, Jake. Good night, darling. I won't see you again." We kissed standing at the door. She pushed me away. We kissed again. "Oh, don't!" Brett said.

She turned quickly and went into the hotel. The chauffeur drove me around to my flat. I gave him twenty francs and he touched his cap and said: "Good night, sir," and drove off. I rang

the bell. The door opened and I went up-stairs and went to
bed.

Book II

CHAPTER VIII

I DID not see Brett again until she came back from San Sebastian.
One card came from her from there. It had a picture of the
Concha, and said: "Darling. Very quiet and healthy. Love to all
the chaps. BRETT."

Nor did I see Robert Cohn again. I heard Frances had left for
England and I had a note from Cohn saying he was going out
in the country for a couple of weeks, he did not know where, but
that he wanted to hold me to the fishing-trip in Spain we had
talked about last winter. I could reach him always, he wrote,
through his bankers.

Brett was gone, I was not bothered by Cohn's troubles, I rather
enjoyed not having to play tennis, there was plenty of work to do,
I went often to the races, dined with friends, and put in some
extra time at the office getting things ahead so I could leave it in
charge of my secretary when Bill Gorton and I should shove off
to Spain the end of June. Bill Gorton arrived, put up a couple of
days at the flat and went off to Vienna. He was very cheerful and
said the States were wonderful. New York was wonderful. There
had been a grand theatrical season and a whole crop of great
young light heavyweights. Any one of them was a good prospect
to grow up, put on weight and trim Dempsey. Bill was very
happy. He had made a lot of money on his last book, and was
going to make a lot more. We had a good time while he was in
Paris, and then he went off to Vienna. He was coming back in
three weeks and we would leave for Spain to get in some fishing
and go to the fiesta at Pamplona. He wrote that Vienna was won-

THE SUN ALSO RISES

derful. Then a card from Budapest: "Jake, Budapest is wonderful."
Then I got a wire: "Back on Monday."

Monday evening he turned up at the flat. I heard his taxi stop
and went to the window and called to him; he waved and started
up-stairs carrying his bags. I met him on the stairs, and took one
of the bags.

"Well," I said, "I hear you had a wonderful trip."

"Wonderful," he said. "Budapest is absolutely wonderful."

"How about Vienna?"

"Not so good, Jake. Not so good. It seemed better than it was."

"How do you mean?" I was getting glasses and a siphon.

"Tight, Jake. I was tight."

"That's strange. Better have a drink."

Bill rubbed his forehead. "Remarkable thing," he said. "Don't
know how it happened. Suddenly it happened."

"Last long?"

"Four days, Jake. Lasted just four days."

"Where did you go?"

"Don't remember. Wrote you a post-card. Remember that perfectly."

"Do anything else?"

"Not so sure. Possible."

"Go on. Tell me about it."

"Can't remember. Tell you anything I could remember."

"Go on. Take that drink and remember."

"Might remember a little," Bill said. "Remember something
about a prize-fight. Enormous Vienna prize-fight. Had a nigger in
it. Remember the nigger perfectly."

"Go on."

"Wonderful nigger. Looked like Tiger Flowers, only four times
as big. All of a sudden everybody started to throw things. Not
me. Nigger'd just knocked local boy down. Nigger put up his
glove. Wanted to make a speech. Awful noble-looking nigger.
Started to make a speech. Then local white boy hit him. Then he
knocked white boy cold. Then everybody commenced to throw
chairs. Nigger went home with us in our car. Couldn't get his

clothes. Wore my coat. Remember the whole thing now. Big sporting evening."

"What happened?"

"Loaned the nigger some clothes and went around with him to try and get his money. Claimed nigger owed them money on account of wrecking hall. Wonder who translated? Was it me?"

"Probably it wasn't you."

"You're right. Wasn't me at all. Was another fellow. Think we called him the local Harvard man. Remember him now. Studying music."

"How'd you come out?"

"Not so good, Jake. Injustice everywhere. Promoter claimed nigger promised let local boy stay. Claimed nigger violated contract. Can't knock out Vienna boy in Vienna. 'My God, Mister Gorton,' said nigger, 'I didn't do nothing in there for forty minutes but try and let him stay. That white boy musta ruptured himself swinging at me. I never did hit him.'"

"Did you get any money?"

"No money, Jake. All we could get was nigger's clothes. Somebody took his watch, too. Splendid nigger. Big mistake to have come to Vienna. Not so good, Jake. Not so good."

"What became of the nigger?"

"Went back to Cologne. Lives there. Married. Got a family. Going to write me a letter and send me the money I loaned him. Wonderful nigger. Hope I gave him the right address."

"You probably did."

"Well, anyway, let's eat," said Bill. "Unless you want me to tell you some more travel stories."

"Go on."

"Let's eat."

We went down-stairs and out onto the Boulevard St. Michel in the warm June evening.

"Where will we go?"

"Want to eat on the island?"

"Sure."

We walked down the Boulevard. At the juncture of the Rue

Denfert-Rochereau with the Boulevard is a statue of two men in flowing robes.

"I know who they are." Bill eyed the monument. "Gentlemen who invented pharmacy. Don't try and fool me on Paris."

We went on.

"Here's a taxidermist's," Bill said. "Want to buy anything? Nice stuffed dog?"

"Come on," I said. "You're pie-eyed."

"Pretty nice stuffed dogs," Bill said. "Certainly brighten up your flat."

"Come on."

"Just one stuffed dog. I can take 'em or leave 'em alone. But listen, Jake. Just one stuffed dog."

"Come on."

"Mean everything in the world to you after you bought it. Simple exchange of values. You give them money. They give you a stuffed dog."

"We'll get one on the way back."

"All right. Have it your own way. Road to hell paved with un-bought stuffed dogs. Not my fault."

We went on.

"How'd you feel that way about dogs so sudden?"

"Always felt that way about dogs. Always been a great lover of stuffed animals."

We stopped and had a drink.

"Certainly like to drink," Bill said. "You ought to try it some-times, Jake."

"You're about a hundred and forty-four ahead of me."

"Ought not to daunt you. Never be daunted. Secret of my success. Never been daunted. Never been daunted in public."

"Where were you drinking?"

"Stopped at the Crillon. George made me a couple of Jack Roses. George's a great man. Know the secret of his success? Never been daunted."

"You'll be daunted after about three more pernods."

"Not in public. If I begin to feel daunted I'll go off by myself. I'm like a cat that way."

"When did you see Harvey Stone?"

"At the Crillon. Harvey was just a little daunted. Hadn't eaten for three days. Doesn't eat any more. Just goes off like a cat. Pretty sad."

"He's all right."

"Splendid. Wish he wouldn't keep going off like a cat, though. Makes me nervous."

"What'll we do to-night?"

"Doesn't make any difference. Only let's not get daunted. Suppose they got any hard-boiled eggs here? If they had hard-boiled eggs here we wouldn't have to go all the way down to the island to eat."

"Nix," I said. "We're going to have a regular meal."

"Just a suggestion," said Bill. "Want to start now?"

"Come on."

We started on again down the Boulevard. A horse-cab passed us. Bill looked at it.

"See that horse-cab? Going to have that horse-cab stuffed for you for Christmas. Going to give all my friends stuffed animals. I'm a nature-writer."

A taxi passed, some one in it waved, then banged for the driver to stop. The taxi backed up to the curb. In it was Brett.

"Beautiful lady," said Bill. "Going to kidnap us."

"Hullo!" Brett said. "Hullo!"

"This is Bill Gorton. Lady Ashley."

Brett smiled at Bill. "I say I'm just back. Haven't bathed even. Michael comes in to-night."

"Good. Come on and eat with us, and we'll all go to meet him."

"Must clean myself."

"Oh, rot! Come on."

"Must bathe. He doesn't get in till nine."

"Come and have a drink, then, before you bathe."

"Might do that. Now you're not talking rot."

We got in the taxi. The driver looked around.

"Stop at the nearest bistro," I said.

"We might as well go to the Closerie," Brett said. "I can't drink these rotten brandies."

"Closerie des Lilas."

Brett turned to Bill.

"Have you been in this pestilential city long?"

"Just got in to-day from Budapest."

"How was Budapest?"

"Wonderful. Budapest was wonderful."

"Ask him about Vienna."

"Vienna," said Bill, "is a strange city."

"Very much like Paris," Brett smiled at him, wrinkling the corners of her eyes.

"Exactly," Bill said. "Very much like Paris at this moment."

"You *have* a good start."

Sitting out on the terraces of the Lilas Brett ordered a whiskey and soda, I took one, too, and Bill took another pernod.

"How are you, Jake?"

"Great," I said. "I've had a good time."

Brett looked at me. "I was a fool to go away," she said. "One's an ass to leave Paris."

"Did you have a good time?"

"Oh, all right. Interesting. Not frightfully amusing."

"See anybody?"

"No, hardly anybody. I never went out."

"Didn't you swim?"

"No. Didn't do a thing."

"Sounds like Vienna," Bill said.

Brett wrinkled up the corners of her eyes at him.

"So that's the way it was in Vienna."

"It was like everything in Vienna."

Brett smiled at him again.

"You've a nice friend, Jake."

"He's all right," I said. "He's a taxidermist."

"That was in another country," Bill said. "And besides all the animals were dead."

"One more," Brett said, "and I must run. Do send the waiter for a taxi."

"There's a line of them. Right out in front."

"Good."

We had the drink and put Brett into her taxi.

"Mind you're at the Select around ten. Make him come. Michael will be there."

"We'll be there," Bill said. The taxi started and Brett waved.

"Quite a girl," Bill said. "She's damned nice. Who's Michael?"

"The man she's going to marry."

"Well, well," Bill said. "That's always just the stage I meet anybody. What'll I send them? Think they'd like a couple of stuffed race-horses?"

"We better eat."

"Is she really Lady something or other?" Bill asked in the taxi on our way down to the Ile Saint Louis.

"Oh, yes. In the stud-book and everything."

"Well, well."

We ate dinner at Madame Lecomte's restaurant on the far side of the island. It was crowded with Americans and we had to stand up and wait for a place. Some one had put it in the American Women's Club list as a quaint restaurant on the Paris quais as yet untouched by Americans, so we had to wait forty-five minutes for a table. Bill had eaten at the restaurant in 1918, and right after the armistice, and Madame Lecomte made a great fuss over seeing him.

"Doesn't get us a table, though," Bill said. "Grand woman, though."

We had a good meal, a roast chicken, new green beans, mashed potatoes, a salad, and some apple-pie and cheese.

"You've got the world here all right," Bill said to Madame Lecomte. She raised her hand. "Oh, my God!"

"You'll be rich."

"I hope so."

After the coffee and a *fine* we got the bill, chalked up the same as ever on a slate, that was doubtless one of the "quaint" features, paid it, shook hands, and went out.

"You never come here any more, Monsieur Barnes," Madame Lecomte said.

"Too many compatriots."

"Come at lunch-time. It's not crowded then."

"Good. I'll be down soon."

We walked along under the trees that grew out over the river on the Quai d'Orléans side of the island. Across the river were the broken walls of old houses that were being torn down.

"They're going to cut a street through."

"They would," Bill said.

We walked on and circled the island. The river was dark and a bateau mouche went by, all bright with lights, going fast and quiet up and out of sight under the bridge. Down the river was Notre Dame squatting against the night sky. We crossed to the left bank of the Seine by the wooden foot-bridge from the Quai de Bethune, and stopped on the bridge and looked down the river at Notre Dame. Standing on the bridge the island looked dark, the houses were high against the sky, and the trees were shadows.

"It's pretty grand," Bill said. "God, I love to get back."

We leaned on the wooden rail of the bridge and looked up the river to the lights of the big bridges. Below the water was smooth and black. It made no sound against the piles of the bridge. A man and a girl passed us. They were walking with their arms around each other.

We crossed the bridge and walked up the Rue du Cardinal Lemoine. It was steep walking, and we went all the way up to the Place Contrescarpe. The arc-light shone through the leaves of the trees in the square, and underneath the trees was an S bus ready to start. Music came out of the door of the Negre Joyeux. Through the window of the Café Aux Amateurs I saw the long zinc bar. Outside on the terrace working people were drinking. In the open kitchen of the Amateurs a girl was cooking potato-chips in oil. There was an iron pot of stew. The girl ladled some onto a plate for an old man who stood holding a bottle of red wine in one hand.

"Want to have a drink?"

"No," said Bill. "I don't need it."

We turned to the right off the Place Contrescarpe, walking along smooth narrow streets with high old houses on both sides. Some of the houses jutted out toward the street. Others were cut back. We came onto the Rue du Pot de Fer and followed it along until it brought us to the rigid north and south of the Rue Saint Jacques and then walked south, past Val de Grâce, set back behind the courtyard and the iron fence, to the Boulevard du Port Royal.

"What do you want to do?" I asked. "Go up to the café and see Brett and Mike?"

"Why not?"

We walked along Port Royal until it became Montparnasse, and then on past the Lilas, Lavigne's, and all the little cafés, Damoy's, crossed the street to the Rotonde, past its lights and tables to the Select.

Michael came toward us from the tables. He was tanned and healthy-looking.

"Hel-lo, Jake," he said. "Hel-lo! Hel-lo! How are you, old lad?"

"You look very fit, Mike."

"Oh, I am. I'm frightfully fit. I've done nothing but walk. Walk all day long. One drink a day with my mother at tea."

Bill had gone into the bar. He was standing talking with Brett, who was sitting on a high stool, her legs crossed. She had no stockings on.

"It's good to see you, Jake," Michael said. "I'm a little tight you know. Amazing, isn't it? Did you see my nose?"

There was a patch of dried blood on the bridge of his nose.

"An old lady's bags did that," Mike said. "I reached up to help her with them and they fell on me."

Brett gestured at him from the bar with her cigarette-holder and wrinkled the corners of her eyes.

"An old lady," said Mike. "Her bags *fell* on me. Let's go in and see Brett. I say, she is a piece. You *are* a lovely lady, Brett. Where did you get that hat?"

"Chap bought it for me. Don't you like it?"

"It's a dreadful hat. Do get a good hat."

"Oh, we've so much money now," Brett said. "I say, haven't you met Bill yet? You *are* a lovely host, Jake."

She turned to Mike. "This is Bill Gorton. This drunkard is Mike Campbell. Mr. Campbell is an undischarged bankrupt."

"Aren't I, though? You know I met my ex-partner yesterday in London. Chap who did me in."

"What did he say?"

"Bought me a drink. I thought I might as well take it. I say, Brett, you *are* a lovely piece. Don't you think she's beautiful?"

"Beautiful. With this nose?"

"It's a lovely nose. Go on, point it at me. Isn't she a lovely piece?"

"Couldn't we have kept the man in Scotland?"

"I say, Brett, let's turn in early."

"Don't be indecent, Michael. Remember there are ladies at this bar."

"Isn't she a lovely piece? Don't you think so, Jake?"

"There's a fight to-night," Bill said. "Like to go?"

"Fight," said Mike. "Who's fighting?"

"Ledoux and somebody."

"He's very good, Ledoux," Mike said. "I'd like to see it, rather" —he was making an effort to pull himself together—"but I can't go. I had a date with this thing here. I say, Brett, do get a new hat."

Brett pulled the felt hat down far over one eye and smiled out from under it. "You two run along to the fight. I'll have to be taking Mr. Campbell home directly."

"I'm not tight," Mike said. "Perhaps just a little. I say, Brett, you are a lovely piece."

"Go on to the fight," Brett said. "Mr. Campbell's getting difficult. What are these outbursts of affection, Michael?"

"I say, you are a lovely piece."

We said good night. "I'm sorry I can't go," Mike said. Brett laughed. I looked back from the door. Mike had one hand on the bar and was leaning toward Brett, talking. Brett was looking at him quite coolly, but the corners of her eyes were smiling.

Outside on the pavement I said: "Do you want to go to the fight?"

"Sure," said Bill. "If we don't have to walk."

"Mike was pretty excited about his girl friend," I said in the taxi.

"Well," said Bill. "You can't blame him such a hell of a lot."

CHAPTER IX

THE Ledoux-Kid Francis fight was the night of the 20th of June. It was a good fight. The morning after the fight I had a letter from Robert Cohn, written from Hendaye. He was having a very quiet time, he said, bathing, playing some golf and much bridge. Hendaye had a splendid beach, but he was anxious to start on the fishing-trip. When would I be down? If I would buy him a double-tapered line he would pay me when I came down.

That same morning I wrote Cohn from the office that Bill and I would leave Paris on the 25th unless I wired him otherwise, and would meet him at Bayonne, where we could get a bus over the mountains to Pamplona. The same evening about seven o'clock I stopped in at the Select to see Michael and Brett. They were not there, and I went over to the Dingo. They were inside sitting at the bar.

"Hello, darling." Brett put out her hand.

"Hello, Jake," Mike said. "I understand I was tight last night."

"Weren't you, though," Brett said. "Disgraceful business."

"Look," said Mike, "when do you go down to Spain? Would you mind if we came down with you?"

"It would be grand."

"You wouldn't mind, really? I've been at Pamplona, you know. Brett's mad to go. You're sure we wouldn't just be a bloody nuisance?"

"Don't talk like a fool."

"I'm a little tight, you know. I wouldn't ask you like this if I weren't. You're sure you don't mind?"

"Oh, shut up, Michael," Brett said. "How can the man say he'd mind now? I'll ask him later."

"But you don't mind, do you?"

"Don't ask that again unless you want to make me sore. Bill and I go down on the morning of the 25th."

"By the way, where is Bill?" Brett asked.

"He's out at Chantilly dining with some people."

"He's a good chap."

"Splendid chap," said Mike. "He is, you know."

"You don't remember him," Brett said.

"I do. Remember him perfectly. Look, Jake, we'll come down the night of the 25th. Brett can't get up in the morning."

"Indeed not!"

"If our money comes and you're sure you don't mind."

"It will come, all right. I'll see to that."

"Tell me what tackle to send for."

"Get two or three rods with reels, and lines, and some flies."

"I won't fish," Brett put in.

"Get two rods, then, and Bill won't have to buy one."

"Right," said Mike. "I'll send a wire to the keeper."

"Won't it be splendid," Brett said. "Spain! We *will* have fun."

"The 25th. When is that?"

"Saturday."

"We *will* have to get ready."

"I say," said Mike, "I'm going to the barber's."

"I must bathe," said Brett. "Walk up to the hotel with me, Jake. Be a good chap."

"We *have* got the loveliest hotel," Mike said. "I think it's a brothel!"

"We left our bags here at the Dingo when we got in, and they asked us at this hotel if we wanted a room for the afternoon only. Seemed frightfully pleased we were going to stay all night."

"*I* believe it's a brothel," Mike said. "And *I* should know."

"Oh, shut it and go and get your hair cut."

Mike went out. Brett and I sat on at the bar.

"Have another?"

"Might."

"I needed that," Brett said.

We walked up the Rue Delambre.

"I haven't seen you since I've been back," Brett said.

"No."

"How *are* you, Jake?"

"Fine."

Brett looked at me. "I say," she said, "is Robert Cohn going on this trip?"

"Yes. Why?"

"Don't you think it will be a bit rough on him?"

"Why should it?"

"Who did you think I went down to San Sebastian with?"

"Congratulations," I said.

We walked along.

"What did you say that for?"

"I don't know. What would you like me to say?"

We walked along and turned a corner.

"He behaved rather well, too. He gets a little dull."

"Does he?"

"I rather thought it would be good for him."

"You might take up social service."

"Don't be nasty."

"I won't."

"Didn't you really know?"

"No," I said. "I guess I didn't think about it."

"Do you think it will be too rough on him?"

"That's up to him," I said. "Tell him you're coming. He can always not come."

"I'll write him and give him a chance to pull out of it."

I did not see Brett again until the night of the 24th of June.

"Did you hear from Cohn?"

"Rather. He's keen about it."

"My God!"

"I thought it was rather odd myself."

"Says he can't wait to see me."

"Does he think you're coming alone?"

"No. I told him we were all coming down together. Michael and all."

"He's wonderful."

"Isn't he?"

They expected their money the next day. We arranged to meet at Pamplona. They would go directly to San Sebastian and take the train from there. We would all meet at the Montoya in Pamplona. If they did not turn up on Monday at the latest we would go on ahead up to Burguete in the mountains, to start fishing. There was a bus to Burguete. I wrote out an itinerary so they could follow us.

Bill and I took the morning train from the Gare d'Orsay. It was a lovely day, not too hot, and the country was beautiful from the start. We went back into the diner and had breakfast. Leaving the dining-car I asked the conductor for tickets for the first service.

"Nothing until the fifth."

"What's this?"

There were never more than two servings of lunch on that train, and always plenty of places for both of them.

"They're all reserved," the dining-car conductor said. "There will be a fifth service at three-thirty."

"This is serious," I said to Bill.

"Give him ten francs."

"Here," I said. "We want to eat in the first service."

The conductor put the ten francs in his pocket.

"Thank you," he said. "I would advise you gentlemen to get some sandwiches. All the places for the first four services were reserved at the office of the company."

"You'll go a long way, brother," Bill said to him in English. "I suppose if I'd given you five francs you would have advised us to jump off the train."

"*Comment?*"

"Go to hell!" said Bill. "Get the sandwiches made and a bottle of wine. You tell him, Jake."

"And send it up to the next car." I described where we were.

In our compartment were a man and his wife and their young son.

"I suppose you're Americans, aren't you?" the man asked. "Having a good trip?"

"Wonderful," said Bill.

15

"That's what you want to do. Travel while you're young. Mother and I always wanted to get over, but we had to wait a while."

"You could have come over ten years ago, if you'd wanted to," the wife said. "What you always said was: 'See America first!' I will say we've seen a good deal, take it one way and another."

"Say, there's plenty of Americans on this train," the husband said. "They've got seven cars of them from Dayton, Ohio. They've been on a pilgrimage to Rome, and now they're going down to Biarritz and Lourdes."

"So, that's what they are. Pilgrims. Goddam Puritans," Bill said.

"What part of the States you boys from?"

"Kansas City," I said. "He's from Chicago."

"You both going to Biarritz?"

"No. We're going fishing in Spain."

"Well, I never cared for it, myself. There's plenty that do out where I come from, though. We got some of the best fishing in the State of Montana. I've been out with the boys, but I never cared for it any."

"Mighty little fishing you did on them trips," his wife said.

He winked at us.

"You know how the ladies are. If there's a jug goes along, or a case of beer, they think it's hell and damnation."

"That's the way men are," his wife said to us. She smoothed her comfortable lap. "I voted against prohibition to please him, and because I like a little beer in the house, and then he talks that way. It's a wonder they ever find any one to marry them."

"Say," said Bill, "do you know that gang of Pilgrim Fathers have cornered the dining-car until half past three this afternoon?"

"How do you mean? They can't do a thing like that."

"You try and get seats."

"Well, mother, it looks as though we better go back and get another breakfast."

She stood up and straightened her dress.

"Will you boys keep an eye on our things? Come on, Hubert."

They all three went up to the wagon restaurant. A little while after they were gone a steward went through announcing the first service, and pilgrims, with their priests, commenced filing down the corridor. Our friend and his family did not come back. A waiter passed in the corridor with our sandwiches and the bottle of Chablis, and we called him in.

"You're going to work to-day," I said.

He nodded his head. "They start now, at ten-thirty."

"When do we eat?"

"Huh! When do I eat?"

He left two glasses for the bottle, and we paid him for the sandwiches and tipped him.

"I'll get the plates," he said, "or bring them with you."

We ate the sandwiches and drank the Chablis and watched the country out of the window. The grain was just beginning to ripen and the fields were full of poppies. The pastureland was green, and there were fine trees, and sometimes big rivers and chateaux off in the trees.

At Tours we got off and bought another bottle of wine, and when we got back in the compartment the gentleman from Montana and his wife and his son, Hubert, were sitting comfortably.

"Is there good swimming in Biarritz?" asked Hubert.

"That boy's just crazy till he can get in the water," his mother said. "It's pretty hard on youngsters travelling."

"There's good swimming," I said. "But it's dangerous when it's rough."

"Did you get a meal?" Bill asked.

"We sure did. We set right there when they started to come in, and they must have just thought we were in the party. One of the waiters said something to us in French, and then they just sent three of them back."

"They thought we were snappers, all right," the man said. "It certainly shows you the power of the Catholic Church. It's a pity you boys ain't Catholics. You could get a meal, then, all right."

"I am," I said. "That's what makes me so sore."

Finally at a quarter past four we had lunch. Bill had been rather difficult at the last. He buttonholed a priest who was coming back with one of the returning streams of pilgrims.

"When do us Protestants get a chance to eat, father?"

"I don't know anything about it. Haven't you got tickets?"

"It's enough to make a man join the Klan," Bill said. The priest looked back at him.

Inside the dining-car the waiters served the fifth successive table d'hôte meal. The waiter who served us was soaked through. His white jacket was purple under the arms.

"He must drink a lot of wine."

"Or wear purple undershirts."

"Let's ask him."

"No. He's too tired."

The train stopped for half an hour at Bordeaux and we went out through the station for a little walk. There was not time to get in to the town. Afterward we passed through the Landes and watched the sun set. There were wide fire-gaps cut through the pines, and you could look up them like avenues and see wooded hills way off. About seven-thirty we had dinner and watched the country through the open window in the diner. It was all sandy pine country full of heather. There were little clearings with houses in them, and once in a while we passed a sawmill. It got dark and we could feel the country hot and sandy and dark outside of the window, and about nine o'clock we got into Bayonne. The man and his wife and Hubert all shook hands with us. They were going on to LaNegresse to change for Biarritz.

"Well, I hope you have lots of luck," he said.

"Be careful about those bull-fights."

"Maybe we'll see you at Biarritz," Hubert said.

We got off with our bags and rod-cases and passed through the dark station and out to the lights and the line of cabs and hotel buses. There, standing with the hotel runners, was Robert Cohn. He did not see us at first. Then he started forward.

"Hello, Jake. Have a good trip?"

"Fine," I said. "This is Bill Gorton."

"How are you?"

"Come on," said Robert. "I've got a cab." He was a little near-sighted. I had never noticed it before. He was looking at Bill, trying to make him out. He was shy, too.

"We'll go up to my hotel. It's all right. It's quite nice."

We got into the cab, and the cabman put the bags up on the seat beside him and climbed up and cracked his whip, and we drove over the dark bridge and into the town.

"I'm awfully glad to meet you," Robert said to Bill. "I've heard so much about you from Jake and I've read your books. Did you get my line, Jake?"

The cab stopped in front of the hotel and we all got out and went in. It was a nice hotel, and the people at the desk were very cheerful, and we each had a good small room.

CHAPTER X

IN the morning it was bright, and they were sprinkling the streets of the town, and we all had breakfast in a café. Bayonne is a nice town. It is like a very clean Spanish town and it is on a big river. Already, so early in the morning, it was very hot on the bridge across the river. We walked out on the bridge and then took a walk through the town.

I was not at all sure Mike's rods would come from Scotland in time, so we hunted a tackle store and finally bought a rod for Bill up-stairs over a drygoods store. The man who sold the tackle was out, and we had to wait for him to come back. Finally he came in, and we bought a pretty good rod cheap, and two landing-nets.

We went out into the street again and took a look at the cathedral. Cohn made some remark about it being a very good example of something or other, I forget what. It seemed like a nice cathedral, nice and dim, like Spanish churches. Then we went up past the old fort and out to the local Syndicat d'Initiative office, where the bus was supposed to start from. There they told us the bus service did not start until the 1st of July. We found out at the tourist office what we ought to pay for a motor-car to Pamplona and hired one at a big garage just around the corner from the Municipal Theatre for four hundred francs. The car was to pick us up at the hotel in forty minutes, and we stopped at the café on the square where we had eaten breakfast, and had a beer. It was hot, but the town had a cool, fresh, early-morning smell and it was pleasant sitting in the café. A breeze started to blow, and you could feel that the air came from the sea. There were pigeons out in the square, and the houses were a yellow, sun-baked color, and I did not want to leave the café. But we had to go to the hotel to get our bags packed and pay the bill. We paid for the beers, we matched and I think Cohn paid, and went up to the hotel. It was only sixteen francs apiece for Bill and me, with ten per cent added for the service, and we had the bags sent down and waited for Robert Cohn. While we were waiting I saw a cockroach on the parquet floor that must have been at least three inches long. I pointed him out to Bill and then put my shoe on him. We agreed he must have just come in from the garden. It was really an awfully clean hotel.

Cohn came down, finally, and we all went out to the car. It was a big, closed car, with a driver in a white duster with blue collar and cuffs, and we had him put the back of the car down. He piled in the bags and we started off up the street and out of the town. We passed some lovely gardens and had a good look back at the town, and then we were out in the country, green and rolling, and the road climbing all the time. We passed lots of Basques with oxen, or cattle, hauling carts along the road, and nice farmhouses, low roofs, and all white-plastered. In the Basque country the land all looks very rich and green and the houses and villages look well-off and clean. Every village had a pelota court and on some of them kids were playing in the hot sun. There were signs on the walls of the churches saying it was forbidden to play pelota against them, and the houses in the villages had red tiled roofs, and then the road turned off and commenced to climb and we were going way up close along a hillside, with a valley below and hills stretched off back toward the sea. You couldn't see the sea. It was too far away. You could see only hills and more hills, and you knew where the sea was.

We crossed the Spanish frontier. There was a little stream and a bridge, and Spanish carabineers, with patent-leather Bonaparte hats, and short guns on their backs, on one side, and on the other

fat Frenchmen in kepis and mustaches. They only opened one
bag and took the passports in and looked at them. There was a
general store and inn on each side of the line. The chauffeur had
to go in and fill out some papers about the car and we got out
and went over to the stream to see if there were any trout. Bill
tried to talk some Spanish to one of the carabineers, but it did not
go very well. Robert Cohn asked, pointing with his finger, if there
were any trout in the stream, and the carabineer said yes, but not
many.

I asked him if he ever fished, and he said no, that he didn't
care for it.

Just then an old man with long, sunburned hair and beard,
and clothes that looked as though they were made of gunny-
sacking, came striding up to the bridge. He was carrying a long
staff, and he had a kid slung on his back, tied by the four legs,
the head hanging down.

The carabineer waved him back with his sword. The man
turned without saying anything, and started back up the white
road into Spain.

"What's the matter with the old one?" I asked.

"He hasn't got any passport."

I offered the guard a cigarette. He took it and thanked me.

"What will he do?" I asked.

The guard spat in the dust.

"Oh, he'll just wade across the stream."

"Do you have much smuggling?"

"Oh," he said, "they go through."

The chauffeur came out, folding up the papers and putting
them in the inside pocket of his coat. We all got in the car and
it started up the white dusty road into Spain. For a while the
country was much as it had been; then, climbing all the time, we
crossed the top of a Col, the road winding back and forth on
itself, and then it was really Spain. There were long brown
mountains and a few pines and far-off forests of beech-trees on
some of the mountainsides. The road went along the summit of
the Col and then dropped down, and the driver had to honk, and
slow up, and turn out to avoid running into two donkeys that

were sleeping in the road. We came down out of the mountains and through an oak forest, and there were white cattle grazing in the forest. Down below there were grassy plains and clear streams, and then we crossed a stream and went through a gloomy little village, and started to climb again. We climbed up and up and crossed another high Col and turned along it, and the road ran down to the right, and we saw a whole new range of mountains off to the south, all brown and baked-looking and furrowed in strange shapes.

After a while we came out of the mountains, and there were trees along both sides of the road, and a stream and ripe fields of grain, and the road went on, very white and straight ahead, and then lifted to a little rise, and off on the left was a hill with an old castle, with buildings close around it and a field of grain going right up to the walls and shifting in the wind. I was up in front with the driver and I turned around. Robert Cohn was asleep, but Bill looked and nodded his head. Then we crossed a wide plain, and there was a big river off on the right shining in the sun from between the line of trees, and away off you could see the plateau of Pamplona rising out of the plain, and the walls of the city, and the great brown cathedral, and the broken skyline of the other churches. In back of the plateau were the mountains, and every way you looked there were other mountains, and ahead the road stretched out white across the plain going toward Pamplona.

We came into the town on the other side of the plateau, the road slanting up steeply and dustily with shade-trees on both sides, and then levelling out through the new part of town they are building up outside the old walls. We passed the bull-ring, high and white and concrete-looking in the sun, and then came into the big square by a side street and stopped in front of the Hotel Montoya.

The driver helped us down with the bags. There was a crowd of kids watching the car, and the square was hot, and the trees were green, and the flags hung on their staffs, and it was good to get out of the sun and under the shade of the arcade that runs all the way around the square. Montoya was glad to see us, and shook hands and gave us good rooms looking out on the square, and

then we washed and cleaned up and went down-stairs in the
dining-room for lunch. The driver stayed for lunch, too, and
afterward we paid him and he started back to Bayonne.

There are two dining-rooms in the Montoya. One is up-stairs
on the second floor and looks out on the square. The other is
down one floor below the level of the square and has a door that
opens on the back street that the bulls pass along when they run
through the streets early in the morning on their way to the ring.
It is always cool in the down-stairs dining-room and we had a very
good lunch. The first meal in Spain was always a shock with the
hors d'œuvres, an egg course, two meat courses, vegetables, salad,
and dessert and fruit. You have to drink plenty of wine to get it
all down. Robert Cohn tried to say he did not want any of the
second meat course, but we would not interpret for him, and so
the waitress brought him something else as a replacement, a plate
of cold meats, I think. Cohn had been rather nervous ever since
we had met at Bayonne. He did not know whether we knew Brett
had been with him at San Sebastian, and it made him rather
awkward.

"Well," I said, "Brett and Mike ought to get in to-night."

"I'm not sure they'll come," Cohn said.

"Why not?" Bill said. "Of course they'll come."

"They're always late," I said.

"I rather think they're not coming," Robert Cohn said.

He said it with an air of superior knowledge that irritated both
of us.

"I'll bet you fifty pesetas they're here to-night," Bill said. He
always bets when he is angered, and so he usually bets foolishly.

"I'll take it," Cohn said. "Good. You remember it, Jake. Fifty
pesetas."

"I'll remember it myself," Bill said. I saw he was angry and
wanted to smooth him down.

"It's a sure thing they'll come," I said. "But maybe not to-
night."

"Want to call it off?" Cohn asked.

"No. Why should I? Make it a hundred if you like."

"All right. I'll take that."

"That's enough," I said. "Or you'll have to make a book and give me some of it."

"I'm satisfied," Cohn said. He smiled. "You'll probably win it back at bridge, anyway."

"You haven't got it yet," Bill said.

We went out to walk around under the arcade to the Café Iruña for coffee. Cohn said he was going over and get a shave.

"Say," Bill said to me, "have I got any chance on that bet?"

"You've got a rotten chance. They've never been on time any-where. If their money doesn't come it's a cinch they won't get in to-night."

"I was sorry as soon as I opened my mouth. But I had to call him. He's all right, I guess, but where does he get this inside stuff? Mike and Brett fixed it up with us about coming down here."

I saw Cohn coming over across the square.

"Here he comes."

"Well, let him not get superior and Jewish."

"The barber shop's closed," Cohn said. "It's not open till four."

We had coffee at the Iruña, sitting in comfortable wicker chairs looking out from the cool of the arcade at the big square. After a while Bill went to write some letters and Cohn went over to the barber-shop. It was still closed, so he decided to go up to the hotel and get a bath, and I sat out in front of the café and then went for a walk in the town. It was very hot, but I kept on the shady side of the streets and went through the market and had a good time seeing the town again. I went to the Ayuntamiento and found the old gentleman who subscribes for the bull-fight tickets for me every year, and he had gotten the money I sent him from Paris and renewed my subscriptions, so that was all set. He was the archivist, and all the archives of the town were in his office. That has nothing to do with the story. Anyway, his office had a green baize door and a big wooden door, and when I went out I left him sitting among the archives that covered all the walls, and I shut both the doors, and as I went out of the building into the street the porter stopped me to brush off my coat.

"You must have been in a motor-car," he said.

The back of the collar and the upper part of the shoulders
were gray with dust.

"From Bayonne."

"Well, well," he said. "I knew you were in a motor-car from
the way the dust was." So I gave him two copper coins.

At the end of the street I saw the cathedral and walked up toward it. The first time I ever saw it I thought the façade was
ugly but I liked it now. I went inside. It was dim and dark and
the pillars went high up, and there were people praying, and it
smelt of incense, and there were some wonderful big windows. I
knelt and started to pray and prayed for everybody I thought of,
Brett and Mike and Bill and Robert Cohn and myself, and all the
bull-fighters, separately for the ones I liked, and lumping all the
rest, then I prayed for myself again, and while I was praying for
myself I found I was getting sleepy, so I prayed that the bull-
fights would be good, and that it would be a fine fiesta, and that
we would get some fishing. I wondered if there was anything else
I might pray for, and I thought I would like to have some money,
so I prayed that I would make a lot of money, and then I started
to think how I would make it, and thinking of making money reminded me of the count, and I started wondering about where he
was, and regretting I hadn't seen him since that night in Montmartre, and about something funny Brett told me about him, and
as all the time I was kneeling with my forehead on the wood in
front of me, and was thinking of myself as praying, I was a little
ashamed, and regretted that I was such a rotten Catholic, but
realized there was nothing I could do about it, at least for a
while, and maybe never, but that anyway it was a grand religion,
and I only wished I felt religious and maybe I would the next
time; and then I was out in the hot sun on the steps of the
cathedral, and the forefingers and the thumb of my right hand
were still damp, and I felt them dry in the sun. The sunlight was
hot and hard, and I crossed over beside some buildings, and
walked back along side-streets to the hotel.

At dinner that night we found that Robert Cohn had taken a
bath, had had a shave and a haircut and a shampoo, and something put on his hair afterward to make it stay down. He was

nervous, and I did not try to help him any. The train was due in at nine o'clock from San Sebastian, and, if Brett and Mike were coming, they would be on it. At twenty minutes to nine we were not half through dinner. Robert Cohn got up from the table and said he would go to the station. I said I would go with him, just to devil him. Bill said he would be damned if he would leave his dinner. I said we would be right back.

We walked to the station. I was enjoying Cohn's nervousness. I hoped Brett would be on the train. At the station the train was late, and we sat on a baggage-truck and waited outside in the dark. I have never seen a man in civil life as nervous as Robert Cohn—nor as eager. I was enjoying it. It was lousy to enjoy it, but I felt lousy. Cohn had a wonderful quality of bringing out the worst in anybody.

After a while we heard the train-whistle way off below on the other side of the plateau, and then we saw the headlight coming up the hill. We went inside the station and stood with a crowd of people just back of the gates, and the train came in and stopped, and everybody started coming out through the gates.

They were not in the crowd. We waited till everybody had gone through and out of the station and gotten into buses, or taken cabs, or were walking with their friends or relatives through the dark into the town.

"I knew they wouldn't come," Robert said. We were going back to the hotel.

"I thought they might," I said.

Bill was eating fruit when we came in and finishing a bottle of wine.

"Didn't come, eh?"

"No."

"Do you mind if I give you that hundred pesetas in the morning, Cohn?" Bill asked. "I haven't changed any money here yet."

"Oh, forget about it," Robert Cohn said. "Let's bet on something else. Can you bet on bull-fights?"

"You could," Bill said, "but you don't need to."

"It would be like betting on the war," I said. "You don't need any economic interest."

"I'm very curious to see them," Robert said.

Montoya came up to our table. He had a telegram in his hand. "It's for you." He handed it to me.

It read: "Stopped night San Sebastian."

"It's from them," I said. I put it in my pocket. Ordinarily I should have handed it over.

"They've stopped over in San Sebastian," I said. "Send their regards to you."

Why I felt that impulse to devil him I do not know. Of course I do know. I was blind, unforgivingly jealous of what had happened to him. The fact that I took it as a matter of course did not alter that any. I certainly did hate him. I do not think I ever really hated him until he had that little spell of superiority at lunch—that and when he went through all that barbering. So I put the telegram in my pocket. The telegram came to me, anyway.

"Well," I said. "We ought to pull out on the noon bus for Burguete. They can follow us if they get in to-morrow night."

There were only two trains up from San Sebastian, an early morning train and the one we had just met.

"That sounds like a good idea," Cohn said.

"The sooner we get on the stream the better."

"It's all one to me when we start," Bill said. "The sooner the better."

We sat in the Iruña for a while and had coffee and then took a little walk out to the bull-ring and across the field and under the trees at the edge of the cliff and looked down at the river in the dark, and I turned in early. Bill and Cohn stayed out in the café quite late, I believe, because I was asleep when they came in.

In the morning I bought three tickets for the bus to Burguete. It was scheduled to leave at two o'clock. There was nothing earlier. I was sitting over at the Iruña reading the papers when I saw Robert Cohn coming across the square. He came up to the table and sat down in one of the wicker chairs.

"This is a comfortable café," he said. "Did you have a good night, Jake?"

"I slept like a log."

"I didn't sleep very well. Bill and I were out late, too."

"Where were you?"

"Here. And after it shut we went over to that other café. The old man there speaks German and English."

"The Café Suizo."

"That's it. He seems like a nice old fellow. I think it's a better café than this one."

"It's not so good in the daytime," I said. "Too hot. By the way, I got the bus tickets."

"I'm not going up to-day. You and Bill go on ahead."

"I've got your ticket."

"Give it to me. I'll get the money back."

"It's five pesetas."

Robert Cohn took out a silver five-peseta piece and gave it to me.

"I ought to stay," he said. "You see I'm afraid there's some sort of misunderstanding."

"Why," I said. "They may not come here for three or four days now if they start on parties at San Sebastian."

"That's just it," said Robert. "I'm afraid they expected to meet me at San Sebastian, and that's why they stopped over."

"What makes you think that?"

"Well, I wrote suggesting it to Brett."

"Why in hell didn't you stay there and meet them, then?" I started to say, but I stopped. I thought that idea would come to him by itself, but I do not believe it ever did.

He was being confidential now and it was giving him pleasure to be able to talk with the understanding that I knew there was something between him and Brett.

"Well, Bill and I will go up right after lunch," I said.

"I wish I could go. We've been looking forward to this fishing all winter." He was being sentimental about it. "But I ought to stay. I really ought. As soon as they come I'll bring them right up."

"Let's find Bill."

"I want to go over to the barber-shop."

"See you at lunch."

I found Bill up in his room. He was shaving.

"Oh, yes, he told me all about it last night," Bill said. "He's a great little confider. He said he had a date with Brett at San Sebastian."

"The lying bastard!"

"Oh, no," said Bill. "Don't get sore. Don't get sore at this stage of the trip. How did you ever happen to know this fellow, anyway?"

"Don't rub it in."

Bill looked around, half-shaved, and then went on talking into the mirror while he lathered his face.

"Didn't you send him with a letter to me in New York last winter? Thank God, I'm a travelling man. Haven't you got some more Jewish friends you could bring along?" He rubbed his chin with his thumb, looked at it, and then started scraping again.

"You've got some fine ones yourself."

"Oh, yes. I've got some darbs. But not alongside of this Robert Cohn. The funny thing is he's nice, too. I like him. But he's just so awful."

"He can be damn nice."

"I know it. That's the terrible part."

I laughed.

"Yes. Go on and laugh," said Bill. "You weren't out with him last night until two o'clock."

"Was he very bad?"

"Awful. What's all this about him and Brett, anyway? Did she ever have anything to do with him?"

He raised his chin up and pulled it from side to side.

"Sure. She went down to San Sebastian with him."

"What a damn-fool thing to do. Why did she do that?"

"She wanted to get out of town and she can't go anywhere alone. She said she thought it would be good for him."

"What bloody-fool things people do. Why didn't she go off with some of her own people? Or you?"—he slurred that over—"or me? Why not me?" He looked at his face carefully in the glass, put a big dab of lather on each cheek-bone. "It's an honest face. It's a face any woman would be safe with."

"She'd never seen it."

"She should have. All women should see it. It's a face that

ought to be thrown on every screen in the country. Every woman ought to be given a copy of this face as she leaves the altar. Mothers should tell their daughters about this face. My son"—he pointed the razor at me—"go west with this face and grow up with the country."

He ducked down to the bowl, rinsed his face with cold water, put on some alcohol, and then looked at himself carefully in the glass, pulling down his long upper lip.

"My God!" he said, "isn't it an awful face?"

He looked in the glass.

"And as for this Robert Cohn," Bill said, "he makes me sick, and he can go to hell, and I'm damn glad he's staying here so we won't have him fishing with us."

"You're damn right."

"We're going trout-fishing. We're going trout-fishing in the Irati River, and we're going to get tight now at lunch on the wine of the country, and then take a swell bus ride."

"Come on. Let's go over to the Iruña and start," I said.

CHAPTER XI

IT was baking hot in the square when we came out after lunch with our bags and the rod-case to go to Burguete. People were on top of the bus, and others were climbing up a ladder. Bill went up and Robert sat beside Bill to save a place for me, and I went back in the hotel to get a couple of bottles of wine to take with us. When I came out the bus was crowded. Men and women were sitting on all the baggage and boxes on top, and the women all had their fans going in the sun. It certainly was hot. Robert climbed down and I fitted into the place he had saved on the one wooden seat that ran across the top.

Robert Cohn stood in the shade of the arcade waiting for us to start. A Basque with a big leather wine-bag in his lap lay across the top of the bus in front of our seat, leaning back against our legs. He offered the wine-skin to Bill and to me, and when I tipped it up to drink he imitated the sound of a klaxon motor-horn so well and so suddenly that I spilled some of the wine, and everybody laughed. He apologized and made me take another drink. He made the klaxon again a little later, and it fooled me the second time. He was very good at it. The Basques liked it. The man next to Bill was talking to him in Spanish and Bill was not getting it, so he offered the man one of the bottles of wine. The man waved it away. He said it was too hot and he had drunk too much at lunch. When Bill offered the bottle the second time he took a long drink, and then the bottle went all over that part of the bus. Every one took a drink very politely, and then they made us cork it up and put it away. They all wanted us to drink from their leather wine-bottles. They were peasants going up into the hills.

Finally, after a couple more false klaxons, the bus started, and Robert Cohn waved good-by to us, and all the Basques waved good-by to him. As soon as we started out on the road outside of town it was cool. It felt nice riding high up and close under the trees. The bus went quite fast and made a good breeze, and as we went out along the road with the dust powdering the trees and down the hill, we had a fine view, back through the trees, of the town rising up from the bluff above the river. The Basque lying against my knees pointed out the view with the neck of the wine-bottle, and winked at us. He nodded his head.

"Pretty nice, eh?"

"These Basques are swell people," Bill said.

The Basque lying against my legs was tanned the color of saddle-leather. He wore a black smock like all the rest. There were wrinkles in his tanned neck. He turned around and offered his wine-bag to Bill. Bill handed him one of our bottles. The Basque wagged a forefinger at him and handed the bottle back, slapping in the cork with the palm of his hand. He shoved the wine-bag up.

"Arriba! Arriba!" he said. "Lift it up."

Bill raised the wine-skin and let the stream of wine spurt out and into his mouth, his head tipped back. When he stopped drinking and tipped the leather bottle down a few drops ran down his chin.

"No! No!" several Basques said. "Not like that." One snatched the bottle away from the owner, who was himself about to give a demonstration. He was a young fellow and he held the wine-leather bag with his hand so the stream of wine hissed into his bottle at full arms' length and raised it high up, squeezing the mouth. He held the bag out there, the wine making a flat, hard trajectory into his mouth, and he kept on swallowing smoothly and regularly.

"Hey!" the owner of the bottle shouted. "Whose wine is that?"

The drinker waggled his little finger at him and smiled at us with his eyes. Then he bit the stream off sharp, made a quick lift with the wine-bag and lowered it down to the owner. He winked at us. The owner shook the wine-skin sadly.

We passed through a town and stopped in front of the posada, and the driver took on several packages. Then we started on again, and outside the town the road commenced to mount. We were going through farming country with rocky hills that sloped down into the fields. The grain-fields went up the hillsides. Now as we went higher there was a wind blowing the grain. The road was white and dusty, and the dust rose under the wheels and hung in the air behind us. The road climbed up into the hills and left the rich grain-fields below. Now there were only patches of grain on the bare hillsides and on each side of the water-courses. We turned sharply out to the side of the road to give room to pass to a long string of six mules, following one after the other, hauling a high-hooded wagon loaded with freight. The wagon and the mules were covered with dust. Close behind was another string of mules and another wagon. This was loaded with lumber, and the arriero driving the mules leaned back and put on the thick wooden brakes as we passed. Up here the country was quite barren and the hills were rocky and hard-baked clay furrowed by the rain.

We came around a curve into a town, and on both sides opened out a sudden green valley. A stream went through the centre of the town and fields of grapes touched the houses.

The bus stopped in front of a posada and many of the passengers got down, and a lot of the baggage was unstrapped from the roof from under the big tarpaulins and lifted down. Bill and I got down and went into the posada. There was a low, dark room with saddles and harness, and hay-forks made of white wood, and clusters of canvas rope-soled shoes and hams and slabs of bacon and white garlics and long sausages hanging from the roof. It was cool and dusky, and we stood in front of a long wooden counter with two women behind it serving drinks. Behind them were shelves stacked with supplies and goods.

We each had an aguardiente and paid forty centimes for the two drinks. I gave the woman fifty centimes to make a tip, and she gave me back the copper piece, thinking I had misunderstood the price.

Two of our Basques came in and insisted on buying a drink. So they bought a drink and then we bought a drink, and then they slapped us on the back and bought another drink. Then we bought, and then we all went out into the sunlight and the heat, and climbed back on top of the bus. There was plenty of room now for every one to sit on the seat, and the Basque who had been lying on the tin roof now sat between us. The woman who had been serving drinks came out wiping her hands on her apron and talked to somebody inside the bus. Then the driver came out swinging two flat leather mail-pouches and climbed up, and everybody waving we started off.

The road left the green valley at once, and we were up in the hills again. Bill and the wine-bottle Basque were having a conversation. A man leaned over from the other side of the seat and asked in English: "You're Americans?"

"Sure."

"I been there," he said. "Forty years ago."

He was an old man, as brown as the others, with the stubble of a white beard.

"How was it?"

"What you say?"

"How was America?"

"Oh, I was in California. It was fine."

"Why did you leave?"

"What you say?"

"Why did you come back here?"

"Oh! I come back to get married. I was going to go back but my wife she don't like to travel. Where you from?"

"Kansas City."

"I been there," he said. "I been in Chicago, St. Louis, Kansas City, Denver, Los Angeles, Salt Lake City."

He named them carefully.

"How long were you over?"

"Fifteen years. Then I come back and got married."

"Have a drink?"

"All right," he said. "You can't get this in America, eh?"

"There's plenty if you can pay for it."

"What you come over here for?"

"We're going to the fiesta at Pamplona."

"You like the bull-fights?"

"Sure. Don't you?"

"Yes," he said. "I guess I like them."

Then after a little:

"Where you go now?"

"Up to Burguete to fish."

"Well," he said, "I hope you catch something."

He shook hands and turned around to the back seat again. The other Basques had been impressed. He sat back comfortably and smiled at me when I turned around to look at the country. But the effort of talking American seemed to have tired him. He did not say anything after that.

The bus climbed steadily up the road. The country was barren and rocks stuck up through the clay. There was no grass beside the road. Looking back we could see the country spread out below. Far back the fields were squares of green and brown on the hillsides. Making the horizon were the brown mountains. They were strangely shaped. As we climbed higher the horizon kept changing. As the bus ground slowly up the road we could see other mountains coming up in the south. Then the road came over the crest, flattened out, and went into a forest. It was a forest of cork oaks, and the sun came through the trees in patches, and there were cattle grazing back in the trees. We went through the forest and the road came out and turned along a rise of land, and out ahead of us was a rolling green plain, with dark mountains beyond it. These were not like the brown, heat-baked mountains we had left behind. These were wooded and there were clouds coming down from them. The green plain stretched off. It was cut by fences and the white of the road showed through the trunks of a double line of trees that crossed the plain toward the north. As we came to the edge of the rise we saw the red roofs and white houses of Burguete ahead strung out on the plain, and away off on the shoulder of the first dark mountain was the gray metal-sheathed roof of the monastery of Roncesvalles.

"There's Roncevaux," I said.

"Where?"

"Way off there where the mountain starts."

"It's cold up here," Bill said.

"It's high," I said. "It must be twelve hundred metres."

"It's awful cold," Bill said.

The bus levelled down onto the straight line of road that ran to Burguete. We passed a crossroads and crossed a bridge over a stream. The houses of Burguete were along both sides of the road. There were no side-streets. We passed the church and the school-yard, and the bus stopped. We got down and the driver handed down our bags and the rod-case. A carabineer in his cocked hat and yellow leather cross-straps came up.

"What's in there?" he pointed to the rod-case.

I opened it and showed him. He asked to see our fishing permits and I got them out. He looked at the date and then waved us on.

"Is that all right?" I asked.

"Yes. Of course."

We went up the street, past the whitewashed stone houses, families sitting in their doorways watching us, to the inn.

The fat woman who ran the inn came out from the kitchen and shook hands with us. She took off her spectacles, wiped them, and put them on again. It was cold in the inn and the wind was starting to blow outside. The woman sent a girl up-stairs with us to show the room. There were two beds, a washstand, a clothes-chest, and a big, framed steel-engraving of Nuestra Señora de Roncesvalles. The wind was blowing against the shutters. The room was on the north side of the inn. We washed, put on sweaters, and came down-stairs into the dining-room. It had a stone floor, low ceiling, and was oak-panelled. The shutters were all up and it was so cold you could see your breath.

"My God!" said Bill. "It can't be this cold to-morrow. I'm not going to wade a stream in this weather."

There was an upright piano in the far corner of the room beyond the wooden tables and Bill went over and started to play.

"I got to keep warm," he said.

I went out to find the woman and ask her how much the room and board was. She put her hands under her apron and looked away from me.

"Twelve pesetas."

"Why, we only paid that in Pamplona."

She did not say anything, just took off her glasses and wiped them on her apron.

"That's too much," I said. "We didn't pay more than that at a big hotel."

"We've put in a bathroom."

"Haven't you got anything cheaper?"

"Not in the summer. Now is the big season."

We were the only people in the inn. Well, I thought, it's only a few days.

"Is the wine included?"

"Oh, yes."

"Well," I said. "It's all right."

I went back to Bill. He blew his breath at me to show how cold it was, and went on playing. I sat at one of the tables and looked at the pictures on the wall. There was one panel of rabbits, dead, one of pheasants, also dead, and one panel of dead ducks. The panels were all dark and smoky-looking. There was a cupboard full of liqueur bottles. I looked at them all. Bill was still playing. "How about a hot rum punch?" he said. "This isn't going to keep me warm permanently."

I went out and told the woman what a rum punch was and

how to make it. In a few minutes a girl brought a stone pitcher, steaming, into the room. Bill came over from the piano and we drank the hot punch and listened to the wind.

"There isn't too much rum in that."

I went over to the cupboard and brought the rum bottle and poured a half-tumblerful into the pitcher.

"Direct action," said Bill. "It beats legislation."

The girl came in and laid the table for supper.

"It blows like hell up here," Bill said.

The girl brought in a big bowl of hot vegetable soup and the wine. We had fried trout afterward and some sort of a stew and a big bowl full of wild strawberries. We did not lose money on the wine, and the girl was shy but nice about bringing it. The old woman looked in once and counted the empty bottles.

After supper we went up-stairs and smoked and read in bed to keep warm. Once in the night I woke and heard the wind blowing. It felt good to be warm and in bed.

CHAPTER XII

WHEN I woke in the morning I went to the window and looked out. It had cleared and there were no clouds on the mountains. Outside under the window were some carts and an old diligence, the wood of the roof cracked and split by the weather. It must have been left from the days before the motor-buses. A goat hopped up on one of the carts and then to the roof of the diligence. He jerked his head at the other goats below and when I waved at him he bounded down.

Bill was still sleeping, so I dressed, put on my shoes outside in the hall, and went down-stairs. No one was stirring down-stairs, so I unbolted the door and went out. It was cool outside in the early morning and the sun had not yet dried the dew that had come when the wind died down. I hunted around in the shed behind the inn and found a sort of mattock, and went down toward the stream to try and dig some worms for bait. The stream was clear and shallow but it did not look trouty. On the grassy bank where it was damp I drove the mattock into the earth and loosened a chunk of sod. There were worms underneath. They slid out of sight as I lifted the sod and I dug carefully and got a good many. Digging at the edge of the damp ground I filled two empty tobacco-tins with worms and sifted dirt onto them. The goats watched me dig.

When I went back into the inn the woman was down in the kitchen, and I asked her to get coffee for us, and that we wanted a lunch. Bill was awake and sitting on the edge of the bed.

"I saw you out of the window," he said. "Didn't want to interrupt you. What were you doing? Burying your money?"

"You lazy bum!"

"Been working for the common good? Splendid. I want you to do that every morning."

"Come on," I said. "Get up."

"What? Get up? I never get up."

He climbed into bed and pulled the sheet up to his chin.

"Try and argue me into getting up."

I went on looking for the tackle and putting it all together in the tackle-bag.

"Aren't you interested?" Bill asked.

"I'm going down and eat."

"Eat? Why didn't you say eat? I thought you just wanted me to get up for fun. Eat? Fine. Now you're reasonable. You go out and dig some more worms and I'll be right down."

"Oh, go to hell!"

"Work for the good of all." Bill stepped into his underclothes. "Show irony and pity."

I started out of the room with the tackle-bag, the nets, and the rod-case.

"Hey! come back!"

I put my head in the door.

"Aren't you going to show a little irony and pity?"

I thumbed my nose.

"That's not irony."

As I went down-stairs I heard Bill singing, "Irony and Pity.

When you're feeling . . . Oh, Give them Irony and Give them
Pity. Oh, give them Irony. When they're feeling . . . Just a little
irony. Just a little pity . . ." He kept on singing until he came
down-stairs. The tune was: "The Bells are Ringing for Me and
my Gal." I was reading a week-old Spanish paper.

"What's all this irony and pity?"

"What? Don't you know about Irony and Pity?"

"No. Who got it up?"

"Everybody. They're mad about it in New York. It's just like
the Fratellinis used to be."

The girl came in with the coffee and buttered toast. Or, rather,
it was bread toasted and buttered.

"Ask her if she's got any jam," Bill said. "Be ironical with
her."

"Have you got any jam?"

"That's not ironical. I wish I could talk Spanish."

The coffee was good and we drank it out of big bowls. The
girl brought in a glass dish of raspberry jam.

"Thank you."

"Hey! that's not the way," Bill said. "Say something ironical.
Make some crack about Primo de Rivera."

"I could ask her what kind of a jam they think they've gotten
into in the Riff."

"Poor," said Bill. "Very poor. You can't do it. That's all. You
don't understand irony. You have no pity. Say something pitiful."

"Robert Cohn."

"Not so bad. That's better. Now why is Cohn pitiful? Be
ironic."

He took a big gulp of coffee.

"Aw, hell!" I said. "It's too early in the morning."

"There you go. And you claim you want to be a writer, too.
You're only a newspaper man. An expatriated newspaper man.
You ought to be ironical the minute you get out of bed. You ought
to wake up with your mouth full of pity."

"Go on," I said. "Who did you get this stuff from?"

"Everybody. Don't you read? Don't you ever see anybody?
You know what you are? You're an expatriate. Why don't you

live in New York? Then you'd know these things. What do you want me to do? Come over here and tell you every year?"

"Take some more coffee," I said.

"Good. Coffee is good for you. It's the caffeine in it. Caffeine, we are here. Caffeine puts a man on her horse and a woman in his grave. You know what's the trouble with you? You're an expatriate. One of the worst type. Haven't you heard that? Nobody that ever left their own country ever wrote anything worth printing. Not even in the newspapers."

He drank the coffee.

"You're an expatriate. You've lost touch with the soil. You get precious. Fake European standards have ruined you. You drink yourself to death. You become obsessed by sex. You spend all your time talking, not working. You are an expatriate, see? You hang around cafés."

"It sounds like a swell life," I said. "When do I work?"

"You don't work. One group claims women support you. Another group claims you're impotent."

"No," I said. "I just had an accident."

"Never mention that," Bill said. "That's the sort of thing that can't be spoken of. That's what you ought to work up into a mystery. Like Henry's bicycle."

He had been going splendidly, but he stopped. I was afraid he thought he had hurt me with that crack about being impotent. I wanted to start him again.

"It wasn't a bicycle," I said. "He was riding horseback."

"I heard it was a tricycle."

"Well," I said. "A plane is sort of like a tricycle. The joystick works the same way."

"But you don't pedal it."

"No," I said, "I guess you don't pedal it."

"Let's lay off that," Bill said.

"All right. I was just standing up for the tricycle."

"I think he's a good writer, too," Bill said. "And you're a hell of a good guy. Anybody ever tell you you were a good guy?"

"I'm not a good guy."

"Listen. You're a hell of a good guy, and I'm fonder of you than

anybody on earth. I couldn't tell you that in New York. It'd mean
I was a faggot. That was what the Civil War was about. Abraham
Lincoln was a faggot. He was in love with General Grant. So was
Jefferson Davis. Lincoln just freed the slaves on a bet. The Dred
Scott case was framed by the Anti-Saloon League. Sex explains
it all. The Colonel's Lady and Judy O'Grady are Lesbians under
their skin."

He stopped.

"Want to hear some more?"

"Shoot," I said.

"I don't know any more. Tell you some more at lunch."

"Old Bill," I said.

"You bum!"

We packed the lunch and two bottles of wine in the rucksack,
and Bill put it on. I carried the rod-case and the landing-nets
slung over my back. We started up the road and then went across
a meadow and found a path that crossed the fields and went
toward the woods on the slope of the first hill. We walked across
the fields on the sandy path. The fields were rolling and grassy
and the grass was short from the sheep grazing. The cattle were
up in the hills. We heard their bells in the woods.

The path crossed a stream on a foot-log. The log was surfaced
off, and there was a sapling bent across for a rail. In the flat pool
beside the stream tadpoles spotted the sand. We went up a steep
bank and across the rolling fields. Looking back we saw Burguete,
white houses and red roofs, and the white road with a truck going
along it and the dust rising.

Beyond the fields we crossed another faster-flowing stream. A
sandy road led down to the ford and beyond into the woods. The
path crossed the stream on another foot-log below the ford, and
joined the road, and we went into the woods.

It was a beech wood and the trees were very old. Their roots
bulked above the ground and the branches were twisted. We
walked on the road between the thick trunks of the old beeches
and the sunlight came through the leaves in light patches on the
grass. The trees were big, and the foliage was thick but it was not
gloomy. There was no undergrowth, only the smooth grass, very

green and fresh, and the big gray trees well spaced as though it were a park.

"This is country," Bill said.

The road went up a hill and we got into thick woods, and the road kept on climbing. Sometimes it dipped down but rose again steeply. All the time we heard the cattle in the woods. Finally, the road came out on the top of the hills. We were on the top of the height of land that was the highest part of the range of wooded hills we had seen from Burguete. There were wild strawberries growing on the sunny side of the ridge in a little clearing in the trees.

Ahead the road came out of the forest and went along the shoulder of the ridge of hills. The hills ahead were not wooded, and there were great fields of yellow gorse. Way off we saw the steep bluffs, dark with trees and jutting with gray stone, that marked the course of the Irati River.

"We have to follow this road along the ridge, cross these hills, go through the woods on the far hills, and come down to the Irati valley," I pointed out to Bill.

"That's a hell of a hike."

"It's too far to go and fish and come back the same day, comfortably."

"Comfortably. That's a nice word. We'll have to go like hell to get there and back and have any fishing at all."

It was a long walk and the country was very fine, but we were tired when we came down the steep road that led out of the wooded hills into the valley of the Rio de la Fabrica.

The road came out from the shadow of the woods into the hot sun. Ahead was a river-valley. Beyond the river was a steep hill. There was a field of buckwheat on the hill. We saw a white house under some trees on the hillside. It was very hot and we stopped under some trees beside a dam that crossed the river.

Bill put the pack against one of the trees and we jointed up the rods, put on the reels, tied on leaders, and got ready to fish.

"You're sure this thing has trout in it?" Bill asked.

"It's full of them."

"I'm going to fish a fly. You got any McGintys?"

"There's some in there."

"You going to fish bait?"

"Yeah. I'm going to fish the dam here."

"Well, I'll take the fly-book, then." He tied on a fly. "Where'd I better go? Up or down?"

"Down is the best. They're plenty up above, too."

Bill went down the bank.

"Take a worm can."

"No, I don't want one. If they won't take a fly I'll just flick it around."

Bill was down below watching the stream.

"Say," he called up against the noise of the dam. "How about putting the wine in that spring up the road?"

"All right," I shouted. Bill waved his hand and started down the stream. I found the two wine-bottles in the pack, and carried them up the road to where the water of a spring flowed out of an iron pipe. There was a board over the spring and I lifted it and, knocking the corks firmly into the bottles, lowered them down into the water. It was so cold my hand and wrist felt numbed. I put back the slab of wood, and hoped nobody would find the wine.

I got my rod that was leaning against the tree, took the bait-can and landing-net, and walked out onto the dam. It was built to provide a head of water for driving logs. The gate was up, and I sat on one of the squared timbers and watched the smooth apron of water before the river tumbled into the falls. In the white water at the foot of the dam it was deep. As I baited up, a trout shot up out of the white water into the falls and was carried down. Before I could finish baiting, another trout jumped at the falls, making the same lovely arc and disappearing into the water that was thundering down. I put on a good-sized sinker and dropped into the white water close to the edge of the timbers of the dam.

I did not feel the first trout strike. When I started to pull up I felt that I had one and brought him, fighting and bending the rod almost double, out of the boiling water at the foot of the falls, and swung him up and onto the dam. He was a good trout, and I banged his head against the timber so that he quivered out straight, and then slipped him into my bag.

While I had him on, several trout had jumped at the falls. As soon as I baited up and dropped in again I hooked another and brought him in the same way. In a little while I had six. They were all about the same size. I laid them out, side by side, all their heads pointing the same way, and looked at them. They were beautifully colored and firm and hard from the cold water. It was a hot day, so I slit them all and shucked out the insides, gills and all, and tossed them over across the river. I took the trout ashore, washed them in the cold, smoothly heavy water above the dam, and then picked some ferns and packed them all in the bag, three trout on a layer of ferns, then another layer of ferns, then three more trout, and then covered them with ferns. They looked nice in the ferns, and now the bag was bulky, and I put it in the shade of the tree.

It was very hot on the dam, so I put my worm-can in the shade with the bag, and got a book out of the pack and settled down under the tree to read until Bill should come up for lunch.

It was a little past noon and there was not much shade, but I sat against the trunk of two of the trees that grew together, and read. The book was something by A. E. W. Mason, and I was reading a wonderful story about a man who had been frozen in the Alps and then fallen into a glacier and disappeared, and his bride was going to wait twenty-four years exactly for his body to come out on the moraine, while her true love waited too, and they were still waiting when Bill came up.

"Get any?" he asked. He had his rod and his bag and his net all in one hand, and he was sweating. I hadn't heard him come up, because of the noise from the dam.

"Six. What did you get?"

Bill sat down, opened up his bag, laid a big trout on the grass. He took out three more, each one a little bigger than the last, and laid them side by side in the shade from the tree. His face was sweaty and happy.

"How are yours?"

"Smaller."

"Let's see them."

"They're packed."

"How big are they really?"

"They're all about the size of your smallest."

"You're not holding out on me?"

"I wish I were."

"Get them all on worms?"

"Yes."

"You lazy bum!"

Bill put the trout in the bag and started for the river, swinging the open bag. He was wet from the waist down and I knew he must have been wading the stream.

I walked up the road and got out the two bottles of wine. They were cold. Moisture beaded on the bottles as I walked back to the trees. I spread the lunch on a newspaper, and uncorked one of the bottles and leaned the other against a tree. Bill came up drying his hands, his bag plump with ferns.

"Let's see that bottle," he said. He pulled the cork, and tipped up the bottle and drank. "Whew! That makes my eyes ache."

"Let's try it."

The wine was icy cold and tasted faintly rusty.

"That's not such filthy wine," Bill said.

"The cold helps it," I said.

We unwrapped the little parcels of lunch.

"Chicken."

"There's hard-boiled eggs."

"Find any salt?"

"First the egg," said Bill. "Then the chicken. Even Bryan could see that."

"He's dead. I read it in the paper yesterday."

"No. Not really?"

"Yes. Bryan's dead."

Bill laid down the egg he was peeling.

"Gentlemen," he said, and unwrapped a drumstick from a piece of newspaper. "I reverse the order. For Bryan's sake. As a tribute to the Great Commoner. First the chicken; then the egg."

"Wonder what day God created the chicken?"

"Oh," said Bill, sucking the drumstick, "how should we know?

We should not question. Our stay on earth is not for long. Let us rejoice and believe and give thanks."

"Eat an egg."

Bill gestured with the drumstick in one hand and the bottle of wine in the other.

"Let us rejoice in our blessings. Let us utilize the fowls of the air. Let us utilize the product of the vine. Will you utilize a little, brother?"

"After you, brother."

Bill took a long drink.

"Utilize a little, brother," he handed me the bottle. "Let us not doubt, brother. Let us not pry into the holy mysteries of the hen-coop with simian fingers. Let us accept on faith and simply say —I want you to join with me in saying— What shall we say, brother?" He pointed the drumstick at me and went on. "Let me tell you. We will say, and I for one am proud to say—and I want you to say with me, on your knees, brother. Let no man be ashamed to kneel here in the great out-of-doors. Remember the woods were God's first temples. Let us kneel and say: 'Don't eat that, Lady—that's Mencken.'"

"Here," I said. "Utilize a little of this."

We uncorked the other bottle.

"What's the matter?" I said. "Didn't you like Bryan?"

"I loved Bryan," said Bill. "We were like brothers."

"Where did you know him?"

"He and Mencken and I all went to Holy Cross together."

"And Frankie Fritsch."

"It's a lie. Frankie Fritsch went to Fordham."

"Well," I said, "I went to Loyola with Bishop Manning."

"It's a lie," Bill said. "I went to Loyola with Bishop Manning myself."

"You're cock-eyed," I said.

"On wine?"

"Why not?"

"It's the humidity," Bill said. "They ought to take this damn humidity away."

"Have another shot."

"Is this all we've got?"

"Only the two bottles."

"Do you know what you are?" Bill looked at the bottle affectionately.

"No," I said.

"You're in the pay of the Anti-Saloon League."

"I went to Notre Dame with Wayne B. Wheeler."

"It's a lie," said Bill. "I went to Austin Business College with Wayne B. Wheeler. He was class president."

"Well," I said, "the saloon must go."

"You're right there, old classmate," Bill said. "The saloon must go, and I will take it with me."

"You're cock-eyed."

"On wine?"

"On wine."

"Well, maybe I am."

"Want to take a nap?"

"All right."

We lay with our heads in the shade and looked up into the trees.

"You asleep?"

"No," Bill said. "I was thinking."

I shut my eyes. It felt good lying on the ground.

"Say," Bill said, "what about this Brett business?"

"What about it?"

"Were you ever in love with her?"

"Sure."

"For how long?"

"Off and on for a hell of a long time."

"Oh, hell!" Bill said. "I'm sorry, fella."

"It's all right," I said. "I don't give a damn any more."

"Really?"

"Really. Only I'd a hell of a lot rather not talk about it."

"You aren't sore I asked you?"

"Why the hell should I be?"

"I'm going to sleep," Bill said. He put a newspaper over his face.

"Listen, Jake," he said, "are you really a Catholic?"

"Technically."

"What does that mean?"

"I don't know."

"All right, I'll go to sleep now," he said. "Don't keep me awake by talking so much."

I went to sleep, too. When I woke up Bill was packing the rucksack. It was late in the afternoon and the shadow from the trees was long and went out over the dam. I was stiff from sleeping on the ground.

"What did you do? Wake up?" Bill asked. "Why didn't you spend the night?" I stretched and rubbed my eyes.

"I had a lovely dream," Bill said. "I don't remember what it was about, but it was a lovely dream."

"I don't think I dreamt."

"You ought to dream," Bill said. "All our biggest business men have been dreamers. Look at Ford. Look at President Coolidge. Look at Rockefeller. Look at Jo Davidson."

I disjointed my rod and Bill's and packed them in the rod-case. I put the reels in the tackle-bag. Bill had packed the rucksack and we put one of the trout-bags in. I carried the other.

"Well," said Bill, "have we got everything?"

"The worms."

"Your worms. Put them in there."

He had the pack on his back and I put the worm-cans in one of the outside flap pockets.

"You got everything now?"

I looked around on the grass at the foot of the elm-trees.

"Yes."

We started up the road into the woods. It was a long walk home to Burguete, and it was dark when we came down across the fields to the road, and along the road between the houses of the town, their windows lighted, to the inn.

We stayed five days at Burguete and had good fishing. The nights were cold and the days were hot, and there was always a breeze even in the heat of the day. It was hot enough so that it felt good to wade in a cold stream, and the sun dried you when you came out and sat on the bank. We found a stream with a pool deep enough to swim in. In the evenings we played three-handed bridge with an Englishman named Harris, who had walked over from Saint Jean Pied de Port and was stopping at the inn for the fishing. He was very pleasant and went with us twice to the Irati River. There was no word from Robert Cohn nor from Brett and Mike.

CHAPTER XIII

ONE morning I went down to breakfast and the Englishman, Harris, was already at the table. He was reading the paper through spectacles. He looked up and smiled.

"Good morning," he said. "Letter for you. I stopped at the post and they gave it me with mine."

The letter was at my place at the table, leaning against a coffee-cup. Harris was reading the paper again. I opened the letter. It had been forwarded from Pamplona. It was dated San Sebastian, Sunday:

DEAR JAKE,

We got here Friday, Brett passed out on the train, so brought her here for 3 days rest with old friends of ours. We go to Montoya Hotel Pamplona Tuesday, arriving at I don't know what hour. Will you send a note by the bus to tell us what to do to rejoin you all on Wednesday. All our love and sorry to be late, but Brett was really done in and will be quite all right by Tues. and is practically so now. I know her so well and try to look after her but it's not so easy. Love to all the chaps,

MICHAEL.

"What day of the week is it?" I asked Harris.

"Wednesday, I think. Yes, quite. Wednesday. Wonderful how one loses track of the days up here in the mountains."

"Yes. We've been here nearly a week."

"I hope you're not thinking of leaving?"

"Yes. We'll go in on the afternoon bus, I'm afraid."

"What a rotten business. I had hoped we'd all have another go at the Irati together."

"We have to go *into* Pamplona. We're meeting people there."

"What rotten luck for me. We've had a jolly time here at Burguete."

"Come on in to Pamplona. We can play some bridge there, and there's going to be a damned fine fiesta."

"I'd like to. Awfully nice of you to ask me. I'd best stop on here, though. I've not much more time to fish."

"You want those big ones in the Irati."

"I say, I do, you know. They're enormous trout there."

"I'd like to try them once more."

"Do. Stop over another day. Be a good chap."

"We really have to get into town," I said.

"What a pity."

After breakfast Bill and I were sitting warming in the sun on a bench out in front of the inn and talking it over. I saw a girl coming up the road from the centre of the town. She stopped in front of us and took a telegram out of the leather wallet that hung against her skirt.

"Por ustedes?"

I looked at it. The address was: "Barnes, Burguete."

"Yes. It's for us."

She brought out a book for me to sign, and I gave her a couple of coppers. The telegram was in Spanish: "Vengo Jueves Cohn."

I handed it to Bill.

"What does the word Cohn mean?" he asked.

"What a lousy telegram!" I said. "He could send ten words for the same price. 'I come Thursday'. That gives you a lot of dope, doesn't it?"

"It gives you all the dope that's of interest to Cohn."

"We're going in, anyway," I said. "There's no use trying to move Brett and Mike out here and back before the fiesta. Should we answer it?"

"We might as well," said Bill. "There's no need for us to be snooty."

We walked up to the post-office and asked for a telegraph blank.

"What will we say?" Bill asked.

"'Arriving to-night.' That's enough."

We paid for the message and walked back to the inn. Harris was there and the three of us walked up to Roncesvalles. We went through the monastery.

"It's a remarkable place," Harris said, when we came out. "But you know I'm not much on those sort of places."

"Me either," Bill said.

"It's a remarkable place, though," Harris said. "I wouldn't not have seen it. I'd been intending coming up each day."

"It isn't the same as fishing, though, is it?" Bill asked. He liked Harris.

"I say not."

We were standing in front of the old chapel of the monastery.

"Isn't that a pub across the way?" Harris asked. "Or do my eyes deceive me?"

"It has the look of a pub," Bill said.

"It looks to me like a pub," I said.

"I say," said Harris, "let's utilize it." He had taken up utilizing from Bill.

We had a bottle of wine apiece. Harris would not let us pay. He talked Spanish quite well, and the innkeeper would not take our money.

"I say. You don't know what it's meant to me to have you chaps up here."

"We've had a grand time, Harris."

Harris was a little tight.

"I say. Really you don't know how much it means. I've not had much fun since the war."

"We'll fish together again, some time. Don't you forget it, Harris."

"We must. We *have* had such a jolly good time."

"How about another bottle around?"

"Jolly good idea," said Harris.

"This is mine," said Bill. "Or we don't drink it."

"I wish you'd let me pay for it. It *does* give me pleasure, you know."

"This is going to give me pleasure," Bill said.

The innkeeper brought in the fourth bottle. We had kept the same glasses. Harris lifted his glass.

"I say. You know this does utilize well."

Bill slapped him on the back.

"Good old Harris."

"I say. You know my name isn't really Harris. It's Wilson-Harris. All one name. With a hyphen, you know."

"Good old Wilson-Harris," Bill said. "We call you Harris because we're so fond of you."

"I say, Barnes. You don't know what this all means to me."

"Come on and utilize another glass," I said.

"Barnes. Really, Barnes, you can't know. That's all."

"Drink up, Harris."

We walked back down the road from Roncesvalles with Harris between us. We had lunch at the inn and Harris went with us to the bus. He gave us his card, with his address in London and his club and his business address, and as we got on the bus he handed us each an envelope. I opened mine and there were a dozen flies in it. Harris had tied them himself. He tied all his own flies.

"I say, Harris—" I began.

"No, no!" he said. He was climbing down from the bus. "They're not first-rate flies at all. I only thought if you fished them some time it might remind you of what a good time we had."

The bus started. Harris stood in front of the post-office. He waved. As we started along the road he turned and walked back toward the inn.

"Say, wasn't that Harris nice?" Bill said.

"I think he really did have a good time."

"Harris? You bet he did."

"I wish he'd come into Pamplona."

"He wanted to fish."

"Yes. You couldn't tell how English would mix with each other, anyway."

"I suppose not."

We got into Pamplona late in the afternoon and the bus stopped in front of the Hotel Montoya. Out in the plaza they were stringing electric-light wires to light the plaza for the fiesta. A few kids came up when the bus stopped, and a customs officer for the town made all the people getting down from the bus open their bundles on the sidewalk. We went into the hotel and on the stairs I met Montoya. He shook hands with us, smiling in his embarrassed way.

"Your friends are here," he said.

"Mr. Campbell?"

"Yes. Mr. Cohn and Mr. Campbell and Lady Ashley."

He smiled as though there were something I would hear about.

"When did they get in?"

"Yesterday. I've saved you the rooms you had."

"That's fine. Did you give Mr. Campbell the room on the plaza?"

"Yes. All the rooms we looked at."

"Where are our friends now?"

"I think they went to the pelota."

"And how about the bulls?"

Montoya smiled. "To-night," he said. "To-night at seven o'clock they bring in the Villar bulls, and to-morrow come the Miuras. Do you all go down?"

"Oh, yes. They've never seen a desencajonada."

Montoya put his hand on my shoulder.

"I'll see you there."

He smiled again. He always smiled as though bull-fighting were a very special secret between the two of us; a rather shocking but really very deep secret that we knew about. He always smiled as though there were something lewd about the secret to outsiders, but that it was something that we understood. It would not do to expose it to people who would not understand.

"Your friend, is he aficionado, too?" Montoya smiled at Bill.

"Yes. He came all the way from New York to see the San Fermines."

"Yes?" Montoya politely disbelieved. "But he's not aficionado like you."

He put his hand on my shoulder again embarrassedly.

"Yes," I said. "He's a real aficionado."

"But he's not aficionado like you are."

Aficion means passion. An aficionado is one who is passionate about the bull-fights. All the good bull-fighters stayed at Montoya's hotel; that is, those with aficion stayed there. The commercial bull-fighters stayed once, perhaps, and then did not come back. The good ones came each year. In Montoya's room were their photographs. The photographs were dedicated to Juanito Montoya or to his sister. The photographs of bull-fighters Montoya had really believed in were framed. Photographs of bull-fighters who had been without aficion Montoya kept in a drawer of his desk. They often had the most flattering inscriptions. But they did not mean anything. One day Montoya took them all out and dropped them in the waste-basket. He did not want them around.

We often talked about bulls and bull-fighters. I had stopped at the Montoya for several years. We never talked for very long at a time. It was simply the pleasure of discovering what we each felt. Men would come in from distant towns and before they left Pamplona stop and talk for a few minutes with Montoya about bulls. These men were aficionados. Those who were aficionados could always get rooms even when the hotel was full. Montoya introduced me to some of them. They were always very polite at first, and it amused them very much that I should be an American. Somehow it was taken for granted that an American could not have aficion. He might simulate it or confuse it with excitement, but he could not really have it. When they saw that I had aficion, and there was no password, no set questions that could bring it out, rather it was a sort of oral spiritual examination with the questions always a little on the defensive and never apparent, there was this same embarrassed putting the hand on the shoulder, or a "Buen hombre." But nearly always there was the actual touching. It seemed as though they wanted to touch you to make it certain.

Montoya could forgive anything of a bull-fighter who had

aficion. He could forgive attacks of nerves, panic, bad unexplain-
able actions, all sorts of lapses. For one who had aficion he could
forgive anything. At once he forgave me all my friends. Without
his ever saying anything they were simply a little something
shameful between us, like the spilling open of the horses in bull-
fighting.

Bill had gone up-stairs as we came in, and I found him washing
and changing in his room.

"Well," he said, "talk a lot of Spanish?"

"He was telling me about the bulls coming in tonight."

"Let's find the gang and go down."

"All right. They'll probably be at the café."

"Have you got tickets?"

"Yes. I got them for all the unloadings."

"What's it like?" He was pulling his cheek before the glass,
looking to see if there were unshaved patches under the line of
the jaw.

"It's pretty good," I said. "They let the bulls out of the cages
one at a time, and they have steers in the corral to receive them
and keep them from fighting, and the bulls tear in at the steers
and the steers run around like old maids trying to quiet them
down."

"Do they ever gore the steers?"

"Sure. Sometimes they go right after them and kill them."

"Can't the steers do anything?"

"No. They're trying to make friends."

"What do they have them in for?"

"To quiet down the bulls and keep them from breaking their
horns against the stone walls, or goring each other."

"Must be swell being a steer."

We went down the stairs and out of the door and walked across
the square toward the café Iruña. There were two lonely looking
ticket-houses standing in the square. Their windows, marked SOL,
SOL Y SOMBRA, and SOMBRA, were shut. They would not open
until the day before the fiesta.

Across the square the white wicker tables and chairs of the
Iruña extended out beyond the Arcade to the edge of the street.

I looked for Brett and Mike at the tables. There they were. Brett and Mike and Robert Cohn. Brett was wearing a Basque beret. So was Mike. Robert Cohn was bare-headed and wearing his spectacles. Brett saw us coming and waved. Her eyes crinkled up as we came up to the table.

"Hello, you chaps!" she called.

Brett was happy. Mike had a way of getting an intensity of feeling into shaking hands. Robert Cohn shook hands because we were back.

"Where the hell have you been?" I asked.

"I brought them up here," Cohn said.

"What rot," Brett said. "We'd have gotten here earlier if you hadn't come."

"You'd never have gotten here."

"What rot! You chaps are brown. Look at Bill."

"Did you get good fishing?" Mike asked. "We wanted to join you."

"It wasn't bad. We missed you."

"I wanted to come," Cohn said, "but I thought I ought to bring them."

"You bring us. What rot."

"Was it really good?" Mike asked. "Did you take many?"

"Some days we took a dozen apiece. There was an Englishman up there."

"Named Harris," Bill said. "Ever know him, Mike? He was in the war, too."

"Fortunate fellow," Mike said. "What times we had. How I wish those dear days were back."

"Don't be an ass."

"Were you in the war, Mike?" Cohn asked.

"Was I not."

"He was a very distinguished soldier," Brett said. "Tell them about the time your horse bolted down Piccadilly."

"I'll not. I've told that four times."

"You never told me," Robert Cohn said.

"I'll not tell that story. It reflects discredit on me."

"Tell them about your medals."

"I'll not. That story reflects great discredit on me."

"What story's that?"

"Brett will tell you. She tells all the stories that reflect discredit on me."

"Go on. Tell it, Brett."

"Should I?"

"I'll tell it myself."

"What medals have you got, Mike?"

"I haven't got any medals."

"You must have some."

"I suppose I've the usual medals. But I never sent in for them. One time there was this wopping big dinner and the Prince of Wales was to be there, and the cards said medals will be worn. So naturally I had no medals, and I stopped at my tailor's and he was impressed by the invitation, and I thought that's a good piece of business, and I said to him: 'You've got to fix me up with some medals.' He said: 'What medals, sir?' And I said: 'Oh, any medals. Just give me a few medals.' So he said: 'What medals *have* you, sir?' And I said: 'How should I know?' Did he think I spent all my time reading the bloody gazette? 'Just give me a good lot. Pick them out yourself.' So he got me some medals, you know, minia- ture medals, and handed me the box, and I put it in my pocket and forgot it. Well, I went to the dinner, and it was the night they'd shot Henry Wilson, so the Prince didn't come and the King didn't come, and no one wore any medals, and all these coves were busy taking off their medals, and I had mine in my pocket."

He stopped for us to laugh.

"Is that all?"

"That's all. Perhaps I didn't tell it right."

"You didn't," said Brett. "But no matter."

We were all laughing.

"Ah, yes," said Mike. "I know now. It was a damn dull dinner, and I couldn't stick it, so I left. Later on in the evening I found the box in my pocket. What's this? I said. Medals? Bloody mili- tary medals? So I cut them all off their backing—you know, they put them on a strip—and gave them all around. Gave one to each girl. Form of souvenir. They thought I was hell's own shakes of a soldier. Give away medals in a night club. Dashing fellow."

"Tell the rest," Brett said.

"Don't you think that was funny?" Mike asked. We were all laughing. "It was. I swear it was. Any rate, my tailor wrote me and wanted the medals back. Sent a man around. Kept on writing for months. Seems some chap had left them to be cleaned. Frightfully military cove. Set hell's own store by them." Mike paused. "Rotten luck for the tailor," he said.

"You don't mean it," Bill said. "I should think it would have been grand for the tailor."

"Frightfully good tailor. Never believe it to see me now," Mike said. "I used to pay him a hundred pounds a year just to keep him quiet. So he wouldn't send me any bills. Frightful blow to him when I went bankrupt. It was right after the medals. Gave his letters rather a bitter tone."

"How did you go bankrupt?" Bill asked.

"Two ways," Mike said. "Gradually and then suddenly."

"What brought it on?"

"Friends," said Mike. "I had a lot of friends. False friends. Then I had creditors, too. Probably had more creditors than anybody in England."

"Tell them about in the court," Brett said.

"I don't remember," Mike said. "I was just a little tight."

"Tight!" Brett exclaimed. "You were blind!"

"Extraordinary thing," Mike said. "Met my former partner the other day. Offered to buy me a drink."

"Tell them about your learned counsel," Brett said.

"I will not," Mike said. "My learned counsel was blind, too. I say this is a gloomy subject. Are we going down and see these bulls unloaded or not?"

"Let's go down."

We called the waiter, paid, and started to walk through the town. I started off walking with Brett, but Robert Cohn came up and joined her on the other side. The three of us walked along, past the Ayuntamiento with the banners hung from the balcony, down past the market and down past the steep street that led to the bridge across the Arga. There were many people walking to go and see the bulls, and carriages drove down the hill and across the bridge, the drivers, the horses, and the whips rising above the walking people in the street. Across the bridge we turned up a road to the corrals. We passed a wine-shop with a sign in the window: Good Wine 30 Centimes A Liter.

"That's where we'll go when funds get low," Brett said.

The woman standing in the door of the wine-shop looked at us as we passed. She called to some one in the house and three girls came to the window and stared. They were staring at Brett.

At the gate of the corrals two men took tickets from the people that went in. We went in through the gate. There were trees inside and a low, stone house. At the far end was the stone wall of the corrals, with apertures in the stone that were like loopholes running all along the face of each corral. A ladder led up to the top of the wall, and people were climbing up the ladder and spreading down to stand on the walls that separated the two corrals. As we came up the ladder, walking across the grass under the trees, we passed the big, gray painted cages with the bulls in them. There was one bull in each travelling-box. They had come by train from a bull-breeding ranch in Castile, and had been unloaded off flat-cars at the station and brought up here to be let out of their cages into the corrals. Each cage was stencilled with the name and the brand of the bull-breeder.

We climbed up and found a place on the wall looking down into the corral. The stone walls were whitewashed, and there was straw on the ground and wooden feed-boxes and water-troughs set against the wall.

"Look up there," I said.

Beyond the river rose the plateau of the town. All along the old walls and ramparts people were standing. The three lines of fortifications made three black lines of people. Above the walls there were heads in the windows of the houses. At the far end of the plateau boys had climbed into the trees.

"They must think something is going to happen," Brett said.

"They want to see the bulls."

Mike and Bill were on the other wall across the pit of the corral.

They waved to us. People who had come late were standing behind us, pressing against us when other people crowded them.

"Why don't they start?" Robert Cohn asked.

A single mule was hitched to one of the cages and dragged it up against the gate in the corral wall. The men shoved and lifted it with crowbars into position against the gate. Men were standing on the wall ready to pull up the gate of the corral and then the gate of the cage. At the other end of the corral a gate opened and two steers came in, swaying their heads and trotting, their lean flanks swinging. They stood together at the far end, their heads toward the gate where the bull would enter.

"They don't look happy," Brett said.

The men on top of the wall leaned back and pulled up the door of the corral. Then they pulled up the door of the cage.

I leaned way over the wall and tried to see into the cage. It was dark. Some one rapped on the cage with an iron bar. Inside something seemed to explode. The bull, striking into the wood from side to side with his horns, made a great noise. Then I saw a dark muzzle and the shadow of horns, and then, with a clattering on the wood in the hollow box, the bull charged and came out into the corral, skidding with his forefeet in the straw as he stopped, his head up, the great hump of muscle on his neck swollen tight, his body muscles quivering as he looked up at the crowd on the stone walls. The two steers backed away against the wall, their heads sunken, their eyes watching the bull.

The bull saw them and charged. A man shouted from behind one of the boxes and slapped his hat against the planks, and the bull, before he reached the steer, turned, gathered himself and charged where the man had been, trying to reach him behind the planks with a half-dozen quick, searching drives with the right horn.

"My God, isn't he beautiful?" Brett said. We were looking right down on him.

"Look how he knows how to use his horns," I said. 'He's got a left and a right just like a boxer."

"Not really?"

"You watch."

"It goes too fast."

"Wait. There'll be another one in a minute."

They had backed up another cage into the entrance. In the far corner a man, from behind one of the plank shelters, attracted the bull, and while the bull was facing away the gate was pulled up and a second bull came out into the corral.

He charged straight for the steers and two men ran out from behind the planks and shouted, to turn him. He did not change his direction and the men shouted: "Hah! Hah! Toro!" and waved their arms; the two steers turned sideways to take the shock, and the bull drove into one of the steers.

"Don't look," I said to Brett. She was watching, fascinated.

"Fine," I said. "If it doesn't buck you."

"I saw it," she said. "I saw him shift from his left to his right horn."

"Damn good!"

The steer was down now, his neck stretched out, his head twisted, he lay the way he had fallen. Suddenly the bull left off and made for the other steer which had been standing at the far end, his head swinging, watching it all. The steer ran awkwardly and the bull caught him, hooked him lightly in the flank, and then turned away and looked up at the crowd on the walls, his crest of muscle rising. The steer came up to him and made as though to nose at him and the bull hooked perfunctorily. The next time he nosed at the steer **and** then the two of them trotted over to the other bull.

When the next bull came out, all three, the two bulls and the steer, stood together, their heads side by side, their horns against the newcomer. In a few minutes the steer picked the new bull up, quieted him down, and made him one of the herd. When the last two bulls had been unloaded the herd were all together.

The steer who had been gored had gotten to his feet and stood against the stone wall. None of the bulls came near him, and he did not attempt to join the herd.

We climbed down from the wall with the crowd, and had a last look at the bulls through the loopholes in the wall of the corral. They were all quiet now, their heads down. We got a carriage outside and rode up to the café. Mike and Bill came in half an hour later. They had stopped on the way for several drinks.

We were sitting in the café.

"That's an extraordinary business," Brett said.

"Will those last ones fight as well as the first?" Robert Cohn asked. "They seemed to quiet down awfully fast."

"They all know each other," I said. "They're only dangerous when they're alone, or only two or three of them together."

"What do you mean, dangerous?" Bill said. "They all looked dangerous to me."

"They only want to kill when they're alone. Of course, if you went in there you'd probably detach one of them from the herd, and he'd be dangerous."

"That's too complicated," Bill said. "Don't you ever detach me from the herd, Mike."

"I say," Mike said, "they *were* fine bulls, weren't they? Did you see their horns?"

"Did I not," said Brett. "I had no idea what they were like."

"Did you see the one hit that steer?" Mike asked. "That was extraordinary."

"It's no life being a steer," Robert Cohn said.

"Don't you think so?" Mike said. "I would have thought you'd loved being a steer, Robert."

"What do you mean, Mike?"

"They lead such a quiet life. They never say anything and they're always hanging about so."

We were embarrassed. Bill laughed. Robert Cohn was angry. Mike went on talking.

"I should think you'd love it. You'd never have to say a word. Come on, Robert. Do say something. Don't just sit there."

"I said something, Mike. Don't you remember? About the steers."

"Oh, say something more. Say something funny. Can't you see we're all having a good time here?"

"Come off it, Michael. You're drunk," Brett said.

"I'm not drunk. I'm quite serious. *Is* Robert Cohn going to follow Brett around like a steer all the time?"

"Shut up, Michael. Try and show a little breeding."

"Breeding be damned. Who has any breeding, anyway, except the bulls? Aren't the bulls lovely? Don't you like them, Bill? Why don't you say something, Robert? Don't sit there looking like a bloody funeral. What if Brett did sleep with you? She's slept with lots of better people than you."

"Shut up," Cohn said. He stood up. "Shut up, Mike."

"Oh, don't stand up and act as though you were going to hit me. That won't make any difference to me. Tell me, Robert. Why do you follow Brett around like a poor bloody steer? Don't you know you're not wanted? I know when I'm not wanted. Why don't you know when you're not wanted? You came down to San Sebastian where you weren't wanted, and followed Brett around like a bloody steer. Do you think that's right?"

"Shut up. You're drunk."

"Perhaps I am drunk. Why aren't you drunk? Why don't you ever get drunk, Robert? You know you didn't have a good time at San Sebastian because none of our friends would invite you on any of the parties. You can't blame them hardly. Can you? I asked them to. They wouldn't do it. You can't blame them, now. Can you? Now, answer me. Can you blame them?"

"Go to hell, Mike."

"I can't blame them. Can you blame them? Why do you follow Brett around? Haven't you any manners? How do you think it makes *me* feel?"

"You're a splendid one to talk about manners," Brett said. "You've such lovely manners."

"Come on, Robert," Bill said.

"What do you follow her around for?"

Bill stood up and took hold of Cohn.

"Don't go," Mike said. "Robert Cohn's going to buy a drink."

Bill went off with Cohn. Cohn's face was sallow. Mike went on talking. I sat and listened for a while. Brett looked disgusted.

"I say, Michael, you might not be such a bloody ass," she interrupted. "I'm not saying he's not right, you know." She turned to me.

The emotion left Mike's voice. We were all friends together.

"I'm not so damn drunk as I sounded," he said.

"I know you're not," Brett said.

"We're none of us sober," I said.

"I didn't say anything I didn't mean."

"But you put it so badly," Brett laughed.

"He was an ass, though. He came down to San Sebastian where he damn well wasn't wanted. He hung around Brett and just *looked* at her. It made me damned well sick."

"He did behave very badly," Brett said.

"Mark you. Brett's had affairs with men before. She tells me all about everything. She gave me this chap Cohn's letters to read. I wouldn't read them."

"Damned noble of you."

"No, listen, Jake. Brett's gone off with men. But they weren't ever Jews, and they didn't come and hang about afterward."

"Damned good chaps," Brett said. "It's all rot to talk about it. Michael and I understand each other."

"She gave me Robert Cohn's letters. I wouldn't read them."

"You wouldn't read any letters, darling. You wouldn't read mine."

"I can't read letters," Mike said. "Funny, isn't it?"

"You can't read anything."

"No. You're wrong there. I read quite a bit. I read when I'm at home."

"You'll be writing next," Brett said. "Come on, Michael. Do buck up. You've got to go through with this thing now. He's here. Don't spoil the fiesta."

"Well, let him behave, then."

"He'll behave. I'll tell him."

"You tell him, Jake. Tell him either he must behave or get out."

"Yes," I said, "it would be nice for me to tell him."

"Look, Brett. Tell Jake what Robert calls you. That *is* perfect, you know."

"Oh, no. I can't."

"Go on. We're all friends. Aren't we all friends, Jake?"

"I can't tell him. It's too ridiculous."

"I'll tell him."

"You won't, Michael. Don't be an ass."

"He calls her Circe," Mike said. "He claims she turns men into swine. Damn good. I wish I were one of these literary chaps."

"He'd be good, you know," Brett said. "He writes a good letter."

"I know," I said. "He wrote me from San Sebastian."

"That was nothing," Brett said. "He can write a damned amusing letter."

"She made me write that. She was supposed to be ill."

"I damned well was, too."

"Come on," I said, "we must go in and eat."

"How should I meet Cohn?" Mike said.

"Just act as though nothing had happened."

"It's quite all right with me," Mike said. "I'm not embarrassed."

"If he says anything, just say you were tight."

"Quite. And the funny thing is I think I was tight."

"Come on," Brett said. "Are these poisonous things paid for? I must bathe before dinner."

We walked across the square. It was dark and all around the square were the lights from the cafés under the arcades. We walked across the gravel under the trees to the hotel.

They went up-stairs and I stopped to speak with Montoya.

"Well, how did you like the bulls?" he asked.

"Good. They were nice bulls."

"They're all right"—Montoya shook his head—"but they're not too good."

"What didn't you like about them?"

"I don't know. They just didn't give me the feeling that they were so good."

"I know what you mean."

"They're all right."

"Yes. They're all right."

"How did your friends like them?"

"Fine."

"Good," Montoya said.

I went up-stairs. Bill was in his room standing on the balcony looking out at the square. I stood beside him.

"Where's Cohn?"

"Up-stairs in his room."

"How does he feel?"

"Like hell, naturally. Mike was awful. He's terrible when he's tight."

"He wasn't so tight."

"The hell he wasn't. I know what we had before we came to the café."

"He sobered up afterward."

"Good. He was terrible. I don't like Cohn, God knows, and I think it was a silly trick for him to go down to San Sebastian, but nobody has any business to talk like Mike."

"How'd you like the bulls?"

"Grand. It's grand the way they bring them out."

"To-morrow come the Miuras."

"When does the fiesta start?"

"Day after to-morrow."

"We've got to keep Mike from getting so tight. That kind of stuff is terrible."

"We'd better get cleaned up for supper."

"Yes. That will be a pleasant meal."

"Won't it?"

As a matter of fact, supper was a pleasant meal. Brett wore a black, sleeveless evening dress. She looked quite beautiful. Mike acted as though nothing had happened. I had to go up and bring Robert Cohn down. He was reserved and formal, and his face was still taut and sallow, but he cheered up finally. He could not stop looking at Brett. It seemed to make him happy. It must have been pleasant for him to see her looking so lovely, and know he had been away with her and that every one knew it. They could not take that away from him. Bill was very funny. So was Michael. They were good together.

It was like certain dinners I remember from the war. There was much wine, an ignored tension, and a feeling of things coming that you could not prevent happening. Under the wine I lost

the disgusted feeling and was happy. It seemed they were all
such nice people.

CHAPTER XIV

I DO not know what time I got to bed. I remember undressing,
putting on a bathrobe, and standing out on the balcony. I knew
I was quite drunk, and when I came in I put on the light over
the head of the bed and started to read. I was reading a book
by Turgenieff. Probably I read the same two pages over several
times. It was one of the stories in "A Sportsman's Sketches." I
had read it before, but it seemed quite new. The country became
very clear and the feeling of pressure in my head seemed to
loosen. I was very drunk and I did not want to shut my eyes because the room would go round and round. If I kept on reading
that feeling would pass.

I heard Brett and Robert Cohn come up the stairs. Cohn said
good night outside the door and went on up to his room. I heard
Brett go into the room next door. Mike was already in bed. He
had come in with me an hour before. He woke as she came in,
and they talked together. I heard them laugh. I turned off the
light and tried to go to sleep. It was not necessary to read any
more. I could shut my eyes without getting the wheeling sensation. But I could not sleep. There is reason why because it is
dark you should look at things differently from when it is light.
The hell there isn't!

I figured that all out once, and for six months I never slept with
the electric light off. That was another bright idea. To hell with
women, anyway. To hell with you, Brett Ashley.

Women made such swell friends. Awfully swell. In the first
place, you had to be in love with a woman to have a basis of
friendship. I had been having Brett for a friend. I had not been
thinking about her side of it. I had been getting something for
nothing. That only delayed the presentation of the bill. The bill
always came. That was one of the swell things you could count on.

I thought I had paid for everything. Not like the woman pays and pays and pays. No idea of retribution or punishment. Just exchange of values. You gave up something and got something else. Or you worked for something. You paid some way for everything that was any good. I paid my way into enough things that I liked, so that I had a good time. Either you paid by learning about them, or by experience, or by taking chances, or by money. Enjoying living was learning to get your money's worth and knowing when you had it. You could get your money's worth. The world was a good place to buy in. It seemed like a fine philosophy. In five years, I thought, it will seem just as silly as all the other fine philosophies I've had.

Perhaps that wasn't true, though. Perhaps as you went along you did learn something. I did not care what it was all about. All I wanted to know was how to live in it. Maybe if you found out how to live in it you learned from that what it was all about.

I wished Mike would not behave so terribly to Cohn, though. Mike was a bad drunk. Brett was a good drunk. Bill was a good drunk. Cohn was never drunk. Mike was unpleasant after he passed a certain point. I liked to see him hurt Cohn. I wished he would not do it, though, because afterward it made me disgusted at myself. That was morality; things that made you disgusted afterward. No, that must be immorality. That was a large statement. What a lot of bilge I could think up at night. What rot, I could hear Brett say it. What rot! When you were with English you got into the habit of using English expressions in your thinking. The English spoken language—the upper classes, anyway—must have fewer words than the Eskimo. Of course I didn't know anything about the Eskimo. Maybe the Eskimo was a fine language. Say the Cherokee. I didn't know anything about the Cherokee, either. The English talked with inflected phrases. One phrase to mean everything. I liked them, though. I liked the way they talked. Take Harris. Still Harris was not the upper classes.

I turned on the light again and read. I read the Turgenieff. I knew that now, reading it in the oversensitized state of my mind after much too much brandy, I would remember it somewhere, and afterward it would seem as though it had really happened to me.

I would always have it. That was another good thing you paid for
and then had. Some time along toward daylight I went to sleep.

The next two days in Pamplona were quiet, and there were no
more rows. The town was getting ready for the fiesta. Workmen
put up the gate-posts that were to shut off the side streets when
the bulls were released from the corrals and came running through
the streets in the morning on their way to the ring. The workmen dug holes and fitted in the timbers, each timber numbered
for its regular place. Out on the plateau beyond the town em-
ployees of the bull-ring exercised picador horses, galloping them
stiff-legged on the hard, sun-baked fields behind the bull-ring.
The big gate of the bull-ring was open, and inside the amphitheatre was being swept. The ring was rolled and sprinkled, and
carpenters replaced weakened or cracked planks in the barrera.
Standing at the edge of the smooth rolled sand you could look
up in the empty stands and see old women sweeping out the
boxes.

Outside, the fence that led from the last street of the town to
the entrance of the bull-ring was already in place and made a
long pen; the crowd would come running down with the bulls
behind them on the morning of the day of the first bull-fight.
Out across the plain, where the horse and cattle fair would be,
some gypsies had camped under the trees. The wine and aguardiente sellers were putting up their booths. One booth advertised
ANIS DEL TORO. The cloth sign hung against the planks in the
hot sun. In the big square that was the centre of the town there
was no change yet. We sat in the white wicker chairs on the terrasse of the café and watched the motor-buses come in and unload
peasants from the country coming in to the market, and we
watched the buses fill up and start out with peasants sitting with
their saddle-bags full of the things they had bought in the town.
The tall gray motor-buses were the only life of the square except
for the pigeons and the man with a hose who sprinkled the
gravelled square and watered the streets.

In the evening was the paseo. For an hour after dinner every
one, all the good-looking girls, the officers from the garrison, all

the fashionable people of the town, walked in the street on one side of the square while the café tables filled with the regular after-dinner crowd.

During the morning I usually sat in the café and read the Madrid papers and then walked in the town or out into the country. Sometimes Bill went along. Sometimes he wrote in his room. Robert Cohn spent the mornings studying Spanish or trying to get a shave at the barber-shop. Brett and Mike never got up until noon. We all had a vermouth at the café. It was a quiet life and no one was drunk. I went to church a couple of times, once with Brett. She said she wanted to hear me go to confession, but I told her that not only was it impossible but it was not as interesting as it sounded, and, besides, it would be in a language she did not know. We met Cohn as we came out of church, and although it was obvious he had followed us, yet he was very pleasant and nice, and we all three went for a walk out to the gypsy camp, and Brett had her fortune told.

It was a good morning, there were high white clouds above the mountains. It had rained a little in the night and it was fresh and cool on the plateau, and there was a wonderful view. We all felt good and we felt healthy, and I felt quite friendly to Cohn. You could not be upset about anything on a day like that.

That was the last day before the fiesta.

CHAPTER XV

At noon of Sunday, the 6th of July, the fiesta exploded. There is no other way to describe it. People had been coming in all day from the country, but they were assimilated in the town and you did not notice them. The square was as quiet in the hot sun as on any other day. The peasants were in the outlying wine-shops. There they were drinking, getting ready for the fiesta. They had come in so recently from the plains and the hills that it was necessary that they make their shifting in values gradually. They could not start in paying café prices. They got their money's worth in the wine-shops. Money still had a definite value in hours worked and bushels of grain sold. Late in the fiesta it would not matter what they paid, nor where they bought.

Now on the day of the starting of the fiesta of San Fermin they had been in the wine-shops of the narrow streets of the town since early morning. Going down the streets in the morning on the way to mass in the cathedral, I heard them singing through the open doors of the shops. They were warming up. There were many people at the eleven o'clock mass. San Fermin is also a religious festival.

I walked down the hill from the cathedral and up the street to the café on the square. It was a little before noon. Robert Cohn and Bill were sitting at one of the tables. The marble-topped tables and the white wicker chairs were gone. They were replaced by cast-iron tables and severe folding chairs. The café was like a battleship stripped for action. To-day the waiters did not leave you alone all morning to read without asking if you wanted to order something. A waiter came up as soon as I sat down.

"What are you drinking?" I asked Bill and Robert.

"Sherry," Cohn said.

"Jerez," I said to the waiter.

Before the waiter brought the sherry the rocket that announced the fiesta went up in the square. It burst and there was a gray ball of smoke high up above the Theatre Gayarre, across on the other side of the plaza. The ball of smoke hung in the sky like a shrapnel burst, and as I watched, another rocket came up to it, trickling smoke in the bright sunlight. I saw the bright flash as it burst and another little cloud of smoke appeared. By the time the second rocket had burst there were so many people in the arcade, that had been empty a minute before, that the waiter, holding the bottle high up over his head, could hardly get through the crowd to our table. People were coming into the square from all sides, and down the street we heard the pipes and the fifes and the drums coming. They were playing the *riau-riau* music, the pipes shrill and the drums pounding, and behind them came the men and boys dancing. When the fifers stopped they all crouched down in the street, and when the reed-pipes and the fifes shrilled, and the flat, dry, hollow drums tapped it out again, they all went up in the air dancing. In the crowd you saw only the heads and shoulders of the dancers going up and down.

In the square a man, bent over, was playing on a reed-pipe, and a crowd of children were following him shouting, and pulling at his clothes. He came out of the square, the children following him, and piped them past the café and down a side street. We saw his blank pockmarked face as he went by, piping, the children close behind him shouting and pulling at him.

"He must be the village idiot," Bill said. "My God! look at that!"

Down the street came dancers. The street was solid with dancers, all men. They were all dancing in time behind their own fifers and drummers. They were a club of some sort, and all wore workmen's blue smocks, and red handkerchiefs around their necks, and carried a great banner on two poles. The banner danced up and down with them as they came down surrounded by the crowd.

"Hurray for Wine! Hurray for the Foreigners!" was painted on the banner.

"Where are the foreigners?" Robert Cohn asked.

"We're the foreigners," Bill said.

All the time rockets were going up. The café tables were all full now. The square was emptying of people and the crowd was filling the cafés.

"Where's Brett and Mike?" Bill asked.

"I'll go and get them," Cohn said.

"Bring them here."

The fiesta was really started. It kept up day and night for seven days. The dancing kept up, the drinking kept up, the noise went on. The things that happened could only have happened during a fiesta. Everything became quite unreal finally and it seemed as though nothing could have any consequences. It seemed out of place to think of consequences during the fiesta. All during the fiesta you had the feeling, even when it was quiet, that you had to shout any remark to make it heard. It was the same feeling about any action. It was a fiesta and it went on for seven days.

That afternoon was the big religious procession. San Fermin was translated from one church to another. In the procession were all the dignitaries, civil and religious. We could not see them because the crowd was too great. Ahead of the formal procession and behind it danced the *riau-riau* dancers. There was one mass of yellow shirts dancing up and down in the crowd. All we could see of the procession through the closely pressed people that crowded all the side streets and curbs were the great giants, cigar-store Indians, thirty feet high, Moors, a King and Queen, whirling and waltzing solemnly to the *riau-riau*.

They were all standing outside the chapel where San Fermin and the dignitaries had passed in, leaving a guard of soldiers, the giants, with the men who danced in them standing beside their resting frames, and the dwarfs moving with their whacking bladders through the crowd. We started inside and there was a smell of incense and people filing back into the church, but Brett was stopped just inside the door because she had no hat, so we went out again and along the street that ran back from the chapel into town. The street was lined on both sides with people keeping their place at the curb for the return of the procession. Some dancers formed a circle around Brett and started to dance. They wore big wreaths of white garlics around their necks. They took Bill and me by the arms and put us in the circle. Bill started to dance, too. They were all chanting. Brett wanted to dance but they did not want her to. They wanted her as an image to dance around. When the song ended with the sharp *riau-riau!* they rushed us into a wine-shop.

We stood at the counter. They had Brett seated on a wine-cask. It was dark in the wine-shop and full of men singing, hard-voiced singing. Back of the counter they drew the wine from casks. I put down money for the wine, but one of the men picked it up and put it back in my pocket.

"I want a leather wine-bottle," Bill said.

"There's a place down the street," I said. "I'll go get a couple."

The dancers did not want me to go out. Three of them were sitting on the high wine-cask beside Brett, teaching her to drink out of the wine-skins. They had hung a wreath of garlics around her neck. Some one insisted on giving her a glass. Somebody was teaching Bill a song. Singing it into his ear. Beating time on Bill's back.

I explained to them that I would be back. Outside in the street I went down the street looking for the shop that made leather wine-bottles. The crowd was packed on the sidewalks and many of the shops were shuttered, and I could not find it. I walked as far as the church, looking on both sides of the street. Then I asked a man and he took me by the arm and led me to it. The shutters were up but the door was open.

Inside it smelled of fresh tanned leather and hot tar. A man was stencilling completed wine-skins. They hung from the roof in bunches. He took one down, blew it up, screwed the nozzle tight, and then jumped on it.

"See! It doesn't leak."

"I want another one, too. A big one."

He took down a big one that would hold a gallon or more, from the roof. He blew it up, his cheeks puffing ahead of the wine-skin, and stood on the bota holding on to a chair.

"What are you going to do? Sell them in Bayonne?"

"No. Drink out of them."

He slapped me on the back.

"Good man. Eight pesetas for the two. The lowest price."

The man who was stencilling the new ones and tossing them into a pile stopped.

"It's true," he said. "Eight pesetas is cheap."

I paid and went out and along the street back to the wine-shop. It was darker than ever inside and very crowded. I did not see Brett and Bill, and some one said they were in the back room. At the counter the girl filled the two wine-skins for me. One held two litres. The other held five litres. Filling them both cost three pesetas sixty centimos. Some one at the counter, that I had never seen before, tried to pay for the wine, but I finally paid for it myself. The man who had wanted to pay then bought me a drink. He would not let me buy one in return, but said he would take a rinse of the mouth from the new wine-bag. He tipped the big five-litre bag up and squeezed it so the wine hissed against the back of his throat.

"All right," he said, and handed back the bag.

In the back room Brett and Bill were sitting on barrels surrounded by the dancers. Everybody had his arms on everybody else's shoulders, and they were all singing. Mike was sitting at a table with several men in their shirt-sleeves, eating from a bowl of tuna fish, chopped onions and vinegar. They were all drinking wine and mopping up the oil and vinegar with pieces of bread.

"Hello, Jake. Hello!" Mike called. "Come here. I want you to meet my friends. We're all having an hors-d'œuvre."

I was introduced to the people at the table. They supplied their names to Mike and sent for a fork for me.

"Stop eating their dinner, Michael," Brett shouted from the wine-barrels.

"I don't want to eat up your meal," I said when some one handed me a fork.

"Eat," he said. "What do you think it's here for?"

I unscrewed the nozzle of the big wine-bottle and handed it around. Every one took a drink, tipping the wine-skin at arm's length.

Outside, above the singing, we could hear the music of the procession going by.

"Isn't that the procession?" Mike asked.

"Nada," some one said. "It's nothing. Drink up. Lift the bottle."

"Where did they find you?" I asked Mike.

"Some one brought me here," Mike said. "They said you were here."

"Where's Cohn?"

"He's passed out," Brett called. "They've put him away somewhere."

"Where is he?"

"I don't know."

"How should we know," Bill said. "I think he's dead."

"He's not dead," Mike said. "I know he's not dead. He's just passed out on Anis del Mono."

As he said Anis del Mono one of the men at the table looked

up, brought out a bottle from inside his smock, and handed it to me.

"No," I said. "No, thanks!"

"Yes. Yes. Arriba! Up with the bottle!"

I took a drink. It tasted of licorice and warmed all the way. I could feel it warming in my stomach.

"Where the hell is Cohn?"

"I don't know," Mike said. "I'll ask. Where is the drunken comrade?" he asked in Spanish.

"You want to see him?"

"Yes," I said.

"Not me," said Mike. "This gent."

The Anis del Mono man wiped his mouth and stood up.

"Come on."

In a back room Robert Cohn was sleeping quietly on some wine-casks. It was almost too dark to see his face. They had covered him with a coat and another coat was folded under his head. Around his neck and on his chest was a big wreath of twisted garlics.

"Let him sleep," the man whispered. "He's all right."

Two hours later Cohn appeared. He came into the front room still with the wreath of garlics around his neck. The Spaniards shouted when he came in. Cohn wiped his eyes and grinned.

"I must have been sleeping," he said.

"Oh, not at all," Brett said.

"You were only dead," Bill said.

"Aren't we going to go and have some supper?" Cohn asked.

"Do you want to eat?"

"Yes. Why not? I'm hungry."

"Eat those garlics, Robert," Mike said. "I say. Do eat those garlics."

Cohn stood there. His sleep had made him quite all right.

"Do let's go and eat," Brett said. "I must get a bath."

"Come on," Bill said. "Let's translate Brett to the hotel."

We said good-bye to many people and shook hands with many people and went out. Outside it was dark.

"What time is it do you suppose?" Cohn asked.

"It's to-morrow," Mike said. "You've been asleep two days."

"No," said Cohn, "what time is it?"

"It's ten o'clock."

"What a lot we've drunk."

"You mean what a lot *we've* drunk. You went to sleep."

Going down the dark streets to the hotel we saw the sky-
rockets going up in the square. Down the side streets that led to
the square we saw the square solid with people, those in the
centre all dancing.

It was a big meal at the hotel. It was the first meal of the prices
being doubled for the fiesta, and there were several new courses.
After the dinner we were out in the town. I remember resolving
that I would stay up all night to watch the bulls go through the
streets at six o'clock in the morning, and being so sleepy that I
went to bed around four o'clock. The others stayed up.

My own room was locked and I could not find the key, so I
went up-stairs and slept on one of the beds in Cohn's room. The
fiesta was going on outside in the night, but I was too sleepy for
it to keep me awake. When I woke it was the sound of the rocket
exploding that announced the release of the bulls from the corrals at the edge of town. They would race through the streets and
out to the bull-ring. I had been sleeping heavily and I woke
feeling I was too late. I put on a coat of Cohn's and went out on
the balcony. Down below the narrow street was empty. All the
balconies were crowded with people. Suddenly a crowd came down
the street. They were all running, packed close together. They
passed along and up the street toward the bull-ring and behind
them came more men running faster, and then some stragglers
who were really running. Behind them was a little bare space, and
then the bulls galloping, tossing their heads up and down. It all
went out of sight around the corner. One man fell, rolled to the
gutter, and lay quiet. But the bulls went right on and did not
notice him. They were all running together.

After they went out of sight a great roar came from the bull-
ring. It kept on. Then finally the pop of the rocket that meant

the bulls had gotten through the people in the ring and into the corrals. I went back in the room and got into bed. I had been standing on the stone balcony in bare feet. I knew our crowd must have all been out at the bull-ring. Back in bed, I went to sleep.

Cohn woke me when he came in. He started to undress and went over and closed the window because the people on the balcony of the house just across the street were looking in.

"Did you see the show?" I asked.

"Yes. We were all there."

"Anybody get hurt?"

"One of the bulls got into the crowd in the ring and tossed six or eight people."

"How did Brett like it?"

"It was all so sudden there wasn't any time for it to bother anybody."

"I wish I'd been up."

"We didn't know where you were. We went to your room but it was locked."

"Where did you stay up?"

"We danced at some club."

"I got sleepy," I said.

"My gosh! I'm sleepy now," Cohn said. "Doesn't this thing ever stop?"

"Not for a week."

Bill opened the door and put his head in.

"Where were you, Jake?"

"I saw them go through from the balcony. How was it?"

"Grand."

"Where you going?"

"To sleep."

No one was up before noon. We ate at tables set out under the arcade. The town was full of people. We had to wait for a table. After lunch we went over to the Iruña. It had filled up, and as the time for the bull-fight came it got fuller, and the tables were crowded closer. There was a close, crowded hum that came every day before the bull-fight. The café did not make this same noise at any other time, no matter how crowded it was. This hum went on, and we were in it and a part of it.

I had taken six seats for all the fights. Three of them were barreras, the first row at the ring-side, and three were sobrepuertos, seats with wooden backs, half-way up the amphitheatre. Mike thought Brett had best sit high up for her first time, and Cohn wanted to sit with them. Bill and I were going to sit in the barreras, and I gave the extra ticket to a waiter to sell. Bill said something to Cohn about what to do and how to look so he would not mind the horses. Bill had seen one season of bull-fights.

"I'm not worried about how I'll stand it. I'm only afraid I may be bored," Cohn said.

"You think so?"

"Don't look at the horses, after the bull hits them," I said to Brett. "Watch the charge and see the picador try and keep the bull off, but then don't look again until the horse is dead if it's been hit."

"I'm a little nervy about it," Brett said. "I'm worried whether I'll be able to go through with it all right."

"You'll be all right. There's nothing but that horse part that will bother you, and they're only in for a few minutes with each bull. Just don't watch when it's bad."

"She'll be all right," Mike said. "I'll look after her."

"I don't think you'll be bored," Bill said.

"I'm going over to the hotel to get the glasses and the wine-skin," I said. "See you back here. Don't get cock-eyed."

"I'll come along," Bill said. Brett smiled at us.

We walked around through the arcade to avoid the heat of the square.

"That Cohn gets me," Bill said. "He's got this Jewish superiority so strong that he thinks the only emotion he'll get out of the fight will be being bored."

"We'll watch him with the glasses," I said.

"Oh, to hell with him!"

"He spends a lot of time there."

"I want him to stay there."

In the hotel on the stairs we met Montoya.

"Come on," said Montoya. "Do you want to meet Pedro Romero?"

"Fine," said Bill. "Let's go see him."

We followed Montoya up a flight and down the corridor.

"He's in room number eight," Montoya explained. "He's getting dressed for the bull-fight."

Montoya knocked on the door and opened it. It was a gloomy room with a little light coming in from the window on the narrow street. There were two beds separated by a monastic partition. The electric light was on. The boy stood very straight and unsmiling in his bull-fighting clothes. His jacket hung over the back of a chair. They were just finishing winding his sash. His black hair shone under the electric light. He wore a white linen shirt and the sword-handler finished his sash and stood up and stepped back. Pedro Romero nodded, seeming very far away and dignified when we shook hands. Montoya said something about what great aficionados we were, and that we wanted to wish him luck. Romero listened very seriously. Then he turned to me. He was the best-looking boy I have ever seen.

"You go to the bull-fight," he said in English.

"You know English," I said, feeling like an idiot.

"No," he answered, and smiled.

One of three men who had been sitting on the beds came up and asked us if we spoke French. "Would you like me to interpret for you? Is there anything you would like to ask Pedro Romero?"

We thanked him. What was there that you would like to ask? The boy was nineteen years old, alone except for his sword-handler, and the three hangers-on, and the bull-fight was to commence in twenty minutes. We wished him "Mucha suerte," shook hands, and went out. He was standing, straight and handsome and altogether by himself, alone in the room with the hangers-on as we shut the door.

"He's a fine boy, don't you think so?" Montoya asked.

"He's a good-looking kid," I said.

"He looks like a torero," Montoya said. "He has the type."

"He's a fine boy."

"We'll see how he is in the ring," Montoya said.

We found the big leather wine-bottle leaning against the wall in my room, took it and the field-glasses, locked the door, and went down-stairs.

It was a good bull-fight. Bill and I were very excited about Pedro Romero. Montoya was sitting about ten places away. After Romero had killed his first bull Montoya caught my eye and nodded his head. This was a real one. There had not been a real one for a long time. Of the other two matadors, one was very fair and the other was passable. But there was no comparison with Romero, although neither of his bulls was much.

Several times during the bull-fight I looked up at Mike and Brett and Cohn, with the glasses. They seemed to be all right. Brett did not look upset. All three were leaning forward on the concrete railing in front of them.

"Let me take the glasses," Bill said.

"Does Cohn look bored?" I asked.

"That kike!"

Outside the ring, after the bull-fight was over, you could not move in the crowd. We could not make our way through but had to be moved with the whole thing, slowly, as a glacier, back to town. We had that disturbed emotional feeling that always comes after a bull-fight, and the feeling of elation that comes after a good bull-fight. The fiesta was going on. The drums pounded and the pipe music was shrill, and everywhere the flow of the crowd was broken by patches of dancers. The dancers were in a crowd, so you did not see the intricate play of the feet. All you saw was the heads and shoulders going up and down, up and down. Finally, we got out of the crowd and made for the café. The waiter saved chairs for the others, and we each ordered an absinthe and watched the crowd in the square and the dancers.

"What do you suppose that dance is?" Bill asked.

"It's a sort of jota."

"They're not all the same," Bill said. "They dance differently to all the different tunes."

"It's swell dancing."

In front of us on a clear part of the street a company of boys were dancing. The steps were very intricate and their faces were intent and concentrated. They all looked down while they danced. Their rope-soled shoes tapped and spatted on the pavement. The toes touched. The heels touched. The balls of the feet touched. Then the music broke wildly and the step was finished and they were all dancing on up the street.

"Here come the gentry," Bill said.

They were crossing the street.

"Hello, men," I said.

"Hello, gents!" said Brett. "You saved us seats? How nice."

"I say," Mike said, "that Romero what'shisname is somebody. Am I wrong?"

"Oh, isn't he lovely," Brett said. "And those green trousers."

"Brett never took her eyes off them."

"I say, I must borrow your glasses to-morrow."

"How did it go?"

"Wonderfully! Simply perfect. I say, it is a spectacle!"

"How about the horses?"

"I couldn't help looking at them."

"She couldn't take her eyes off them," Mike said. "She's an extraordinary wench."

"They do have some rather awful things happen to them," Brett said. "I couldn't look away, though."

"Did you feel all right?"

"I didn't feel badly at all."

"Robert Cohn did," Mike put in. "You were quite green, Robert."

"The first horse did bother me," Cohn said.

"You weren't bored, were you?" asked Bill.

Cohn laughed.

"No. I wasn't bored. I wish you'd forgive me that."

"It's all right," Bill said, "so long as you weren't bored."

"He didn't look bored," Mike said. "I thought he was going to be sick."

"I never felt that bad. It was just for a minute."

"I thought he was going to be sick. You weren't bored, were you, Robert?"

"Let up on that, Mike. I said I was sorry I said it."

"He was, you know. He was positively green."

"Oh, shove it along, Michael."

"You mustn't ever get bored at your first bull-fight, Robert," Mike said. "It might make such a mess."

"Oh, shove it along, Michael," Brett said.

"He said Brett was a sadist," Mike said. "Brett's not a sadist. She's just a lovely, healthy wench."

"Are you a sadist, Brett?" I asked.

"Hope not."

"He said Brett was a sadist just because she has a good, healthy stomach."

"Won't be healthy long."

Bill got Mike started on something else than Cohn. The waiter brought the absinthe glasses.

"Did you really like it?" Bill asked Cohn.

"No, I can't say I liked it. I think it's a wonderful show."

"Gad, yes! What a spectacle!" Brett said.

"I wish they didn't have the horse part," Cohn said.

"They're not important," Bill said. "After a while you never notice anything disgusting."

"It is a bit strong just at the start," Brett said. "There's a dreadful moment for me just when the bull starts for the horse."

"The bulls were fine," Cohn said.

"They were very good," Mike said.

"I want to sit down below, next time." Brett drank from her glass of absinthe.

"She wants to see the bull-fighters close by," Mike said.

"They are something," Brett said. "That Romero lad is just a child."

"He's a damned good-looking boy," I said. "When we were up in his room I never saw a better-looking kid."

"How old do you suppose he is?"

"Nineteen or twenty."

"Just imagine it."

The bull-fight on the second day was much better than on the first. Brett sat between Mike and me at the barrera, and Bill and Cohn went up above. Romero was the whole show. I do not think Brett saw any other bull-fighter. No one else did either, except the hard-shelled technicians. It was all Romero. There were two other matadors, but they did not count. I sat beside Brett and explained to Brett what it was all about. I told her about watching the bull, not the horse, when the bulls charged the picadors, and got her to watching the picador place the point of his pic so that she saw what it was all about, so that it became more something that was going on with a definite end, and less of a spectacle with unexplained horrors. I had her watch how Romero took the bull away from a fallen horse with his cape, and how he held him with the cape and turned him, smoothly and suavely, never wasting the bull. She saw how Romero avoided every brusque movement and saved his bulls for the last when he wanted them, not winded and discomposed but smoothly worn down. She saw how close Romero always worked to the bull, and I pointed out to her the tricks the other bull-fighters used to make it look as though they were working closely. She saw why she liked Romero's cape-work and why she did not like the others.

Romero never made any contortions, always it was straight and pure and natural in line. The others twisted themselves like cork-screws, their elbows raised, and leaned against the flanks of the bull after his horns had passed, to give a faked look of danger. Afterward, all that was faked turned bad and gave an unpleasant feeling. Romero's bull-fighting gave real emotion, because he kept the absolute purity of line in his movements and always quietly and calmly let the horns pass him close each time. He did not have to emphasize their closeness. Brett saw how something that was beautiful done close to the bull was ridiculous if it were done a little way off. I told her how since the death of Joselito all the bull-fighters had been developing a technic that simulated this appearance of danger in order to give a fake emotional feeling, while the bull-fighter was really safe. Romero had the old thing, the holding of his purity of line through the maximum of exposure, while he dominated the bull by making him realize he was unattainable, while he prepared him for the killing.

"I've never seen him do an awkward thing," Brett said.

"You won't until he gets frightened," I said.

"He'll never be frightened," Mike said. "He knows too damned much."

"He knew everything when he started. The others can't ever learn what he was born with."

"And God, what looks," Brett said.

"I believe, you know, that she's falling in love with this bull-fighter chap," Mike said.

"I wouldn't be surprised."

"Be a good chap, Jake. Don't tell her anything more about him. Tell her how they beat their old mothers."

"Tell me what drunks they are."

"Oh, frightful," Mike said. "Drunk all day and spend all their time beating their poor old mothers."

"He looks that way," Brett said.

"Doesn't he?" I said.

They had hitched the mules to the dead bull and then the whips cracked, the men ran, and the mules, straining forward, their legs pushing, broke into a gallop, and the bull, one horn up, his head on its side, swept a swath smoothly across the sand and out the red gate.

"This next is the last one."

"Not really," Brett said. She leaned forward on the barrera. Romero waved his picadors to their places, then stood, his cape against his chest, looking across the ring to where the bull would come out.

After it was over we went out and were pressed tight in the crowd.

"These bull-fights are hell on one," Brett said. "I'm limp as a rag."

"Oh, you'll get a drink," Mike said.

The next day Pedro Romero did not fight. It was Miura bulls, and a very bad bull-fight. The next day there was no bull-fight scheduled. But all day and all night the fiesta kept on.

CHAPTER XVI

I𝖓 the morning it was raining. A fog had come over the mouɴ-
tains from the sea. You could not see the tops of the mountains.
The plateau was dull and gloomy, and the shapes of the trees and
the houses were changed. I walked out beyond the town to look
at the weather. The bad weather was coming over the mountains
from the sea.

The flags in the square hung wet from the white poles and the
banners were wet and hung damp against the front of the houses,
and in between the steady drizzle the rain came down and drove
every one under the arcades and made pools of water in the
square, and the streets wet and dark and deserted; yet the fiesta
kept up without any pause. It was only driven under cover.

The covered seats of the bull-ring had been crowded with
people sitting out of the rain watching the concourse of Basque
and Navarrais dancers and singers, and afterward the Val Carlos
dancers in their costumes danced down the street in the rain, the
drums sounding hollow and damp, and the chiefs of the bands
riding ahead on their big, heavy-footed horses, their costumes wet,
the horses' coats wet in the rain. The crowd was in the cafés and
the dancers came in, too, and sat, their tight-wound white legs
under the tables, shaking the water from their belled caps, and
spreading their red and purple jackets over the chairs to dry.
It was raining hard outside.

I left the crowd in the café and went over to the hotel to get
shaved for dinner. I was shaving in my room when there was a
knock on the door.

"Come in," I called.

Montoya walked in.

"How are you?" he said.

"Fine," I said.

"No bulls to-day."

"No," I said, "nothing but rain."

"Where are your friends?"

"Over at the Iruña."

Montoya smiled his embarrassed smile.

"Look," he said. "Do you know the American ambassador?"

"Yes," I said. "Everybody knows the American ambassador."

"He's here in town, now."

"Yes," I said. "Everybody's seen them."

"I've seen them, too," Montoya said. He didn't say anything. I went on shaving.

"Sit down," I said. "Let me send for a drink."

"No, I have to go."

I finished shaving and put my face down into the bowl and washed it with cold water. Montoya was standing there looking more embarrassed.

"Look," he said. "I've just had a message from them at the Grand Hotel that they want Pedro Romero and Marcial Lalanda to come over for coffee to-night after dinner."

"Well," I said, "it can't hurt Marcial any."

"Marcial has been in San Sebastian all day. He drove over in a car this morning with Marquez. I don't think they'll be back to-night."

Montoya stood embarrassed. He wanted me to say something.

"Don't give Romero the message," I said.

"You think so?"

"Absolutely."

Montoya was very pleased.

"I wanted to ask you because you were an American," he said.

"That's what I'd do."

"Look," said Montoya. "People take a boy like that. They don't know what he's worth. They don't know what he means. Any foreigner can flatter him. They start this Grand Hotel business, and in one year they're through."

"Like Algabeno," I said.

"Yes, like Algabeno."

"They're a fine lot," I said. "There's one American woman down here now that collects bull-fighters."

"I know. They only want the young ones."

"Yes," I said. "The old ones get fat."

"Or crazy like Gallo."

"Well," I said, "it's easy. All you have to do is not give him the message."

"He's such a fine boy," said Montoya. "He ought to stay with his own people. He shouldn't mix in that stuff."

"Won't you have a drink?" I asked.

"No," said Montoya, "I have to go." He went out.

I went down-stairs and out the door and took a walk around through the arcades around the square. It was still raining. I looked in at the Iruña for the gang and they were not there, so I walked on around the square and back to the hotel. They were eating dinner in the down-stairs dining-room.

They were well ahead of me and it was no use trying to catch them. Bill was buying shoe-shines for Mike. Bootblacks opened the street door and each one Bill called over and started to work on Mike.

"This is the eleventh time my boots have been polished," Mike said. "I say, Bill is an ass."

The bootblacks had evidently spread the report. Another came in.

"Limpia botas?" he said to Bill.

"No," said Bill. "For this Señor."

The bootblack knelt down beside the one at work and started on Mike's free shoe that shone already in the electric light.

"Bill's a yell of laughter," Mike said.

I was drinking red wine, and so far behind them that I felt a little uncomfortable about all this shoe-shining. I looked around the room. At the next table was Pedro Romero. He stood up when I nodded, and asked me to come over and meet a friend. His table was beside ours, almost touching. I met the friend, a Madrid bull-fight critic, a little man with a drawn face. I told Romero how much I liked his work, and he was very pleased. We talked Spanish and the critic knew a little French. I reached to our table for my wine-bottle, but the critic took my arm. Romero laughed.

"Drink here," he said in English.

He was very bashful about his English, but he was really very pleased with it, and as we went on talking he brought out words he was not sure of, and asked me about them. He was anxious to know the English for *Corrida de toros*, the exact translation. Bull-fight he was suspicious of. I explained that bull-fight in Spanish was the *lidia* of a *toro*. The Spanish word *corrida* means in English the running of bulls—the French translation is *Course de taureaux*. The critic put that in. There is no Spanish word for bull-fight.

Pedro Romero said he had learned a little English in Gibraltar. He was born in Ronda. That is not far above Gibraltar. He started bull-fighting in Malaga in the bull-fighting school there. He had only been at it three years. The bull-fight critic joked him about the number of *Malagueño* expressions he used. He was nineteen years old, he said. His older brother was with him as a banderillero, but he did not live in this hotel. He lived in a smaller hotel with the other people who worked for Romero. He asked me how many times I had seen him in the ring. I told him only three. It was really only two, but I did not want to explain after I had made the mistake.

"Where did you see me the other time? In Madrid?"

"Yes," I lied. I had read the accounts of his two appearances in Madrid in the bull-fight papers, so I was all right.

"The first or the second time?"

"The first."

"I was very bad," he said. "The second time I was better. You remember?" He turned to the critic.

He was not at all embarrassed. He talked of his work as something altogether apart from himself. There was nothing conceited or braggartly about him.

"I like it very much that you like my work," he said. "But you haven't seen it yet. To-morrow, if I get a good bull, I will try and show it to you."

When he said this he smiled, anxious that neither the bull-fight critic nor I would think he was boasting.

"I am anxious to see it," the critic said. "I would like to be convinced."

"He doesn't like my work much." Romero turned to me. He was serious.

The critic explained that he liked it very much, but that so far it had been incomplete.

"Wait till to-morrow, if a good one comes out."

"Have you seen the bulls for to-morrow?" the critic asked me.

"Yes. I saw them unloaded."

Pedro Romero leaned forward.

"What did you think of them?"

"Very nice," I said. "About twenty-six arrobas. Very short horns. Haven't you seen them?"

"Oh, yes," said Romero.

"They won't weigh twenty-six arrobas," said the critic.

"No," said Romero.

"They've got bananas for horns," the critic said.

"You call them bananas?" asked Romero. He turned to me and smiled. "*You* wouldn't call them bananas?"

"No," I said. "They're horns all right."

"They're very short," said Pedro Romero. "Very, very short. Still, they aren't bananas."

"I say, Jake," Brett called from the next table, "you *have* deserted us."

"Just temporarily," I said. "We're talking bulls."

"You *are* superior."

"Tell him that bulls have no balls," Mike shouted. He was drunk.

Romero looked at me inquiringly.

"Drunk," I said. "Borracho! Muy borracho!"

"You might introduce your friends," Brett said. She had not stopped looking at Pedro Romero. I asked them if they would like to have coffee with us. They both stood up. Romero's face was very brown. He had very nice manners.

I introduced them all around and they started to sit down, but there was not enough room, so we all moved over to the big table by the wall to have coffee. Mike ordered a bottle of Fundador and glasses for everybody. There was a lot of drunken talking.

"Tell him I think writing is lousy," Bill said. "Go on, tell him. Tell him I'm ashamed of being a writer."

Pedro Romero was sitting beside Brett and listening to her.

"Go on. Tell him!" Bill said.

Romero looked up smiling.

"This gentleman," I said, "is a writer."

Romero was impressed. "This other one, too," I said, pointing at Cohn.

"He looks like Villalta," Romero said, looking at Bill. "Rafael, doesn't he look like Villalta?"

"I can't see it," the critic said.

"Really," Romero said in Spanish. "He looks a lot like Villalta. What does the drunken one do?"

"Nothing."

"Is that why he drinks?"

"No. He's waiting to marry this lady."

"Tell him bulls have no balls!" Mike shouted, very drunk, from the other end of the table.

"What does he say?"

"He's drunk."

"Jake," Mike called. "Tell him bulls have no balls!"

"You understand?" I said.

"Yes."

I was sure he didn't, so it was all right.

"Tell him Brett wants to see him put on those green pants."

"Pipe down, Mike."

"Tell him Brett is dying to know how he can get into those pants."

"Pipe down."

During this Romero was fingering his glass and talking with Brett. Brett was talking French and he was talking Spanish and a little English, and laughing.

Bill was filling the glasses.

"Tell him Brett wants to come into——"

"Oh, pipe down, Mike, for Christ's sake!"

Romero looked up smiling. "Pipe down! I know that," he said.

Just then Montoya came into the room. He started to smile at me, then he saw Pedro Romero with a big glass of cognac in his hand, sitting laughing between me and a woman with bare shoulders, at a table full of drunks. He did not even nod.

Montoya went out of the room. Mike was on his feet proposing a toast. "Let's all drink to—" he began. "Pedro Romero," I said. Everybody stood up. Romero took it very seriously, and we touched glasses and drank it down, I rushing it a little because Mike was trying to make it clear that that was not at all what he was going to drink to. But it went off all right, and Pedro Romero shook hands with every one and he and the critic went out together.

"My God! he's a lovely boy," Brett said. "And how I would love to see him get into those clothes. He must use a shoe-horn."

"I started to tell him," Mike began. "And Jake kept interrupting me. Why do you interrupt me? Do you think you talk Spanish better than I do?"

"Oh, shut up, Mike! Nobody interrupted you."

"No, I'd like to get this settled." He turned away from me. "Do you think you amount to something, Cohn? Do you think you belong here among us? People who are out to have a good time? For God's sake don't be so noisy, Cohn!"

"Oh, cut it out, Mike," Cohn said.

"Do you think Brett wants you here? Do you think you add to the party? Why don't you say something?"

"I said all I had to say the other night, Mike."

"I'm not one of you literary chaps." Mike stood shakily and leaned against the table. "I'm not clever. But I do know when I'm not wanted. Why don't you see when you're not wanted, Cohn? Go away. Go away, for God's sake. Take that sad Jewish face away. Don't you think I'm right?"

He looked at us.

"Sure," I said. "Let's all go over to the Iruña."

"No. Don't you think I'm right? I love that woman."

"Oh, don't start that again. Do shove it along, Michael," Brett said.

"Don't you think I'm right, Jake?"

Cohn still sat at the table. His face had the sallow, yellow look it got when he was insulted, but somehow he seemed to be enjoying it. The childish, drunken heroics of it. It was his affair with a lady of title.

"Jake," Mike said. He was almost crying. "You know I'm

right. Listen, you!" He turned to Cohn: "Go away! Go away now!"

"But I won't go, Mike," said Cohn.

"Then I'll make you!" Mike started toward him around the table. Cohn stood up and took off his glasses. He stood waiting, his face sallow, his hands fairly low, proudly and firmly waiting for the assault, ready to do battle for his lady love.

I grabbed Mike. "Come on to the café," I said. "You can't hit him here in the hotel."

"Good!" said Mike. "Good idea!"

We started off. I looked back as Mike stumbled up the stairs and saw Cohn putting his glasses on again. Bill was sitting at the table pouring another glass of Fundador. Brett was sitting looking straight ahead at nothing.

Outside on the square it had stopped raining and the moon was trying to get through the clouds. There was a wind blowing. The military band was playing and the crowd was massed on the far side of the square where the fireworks specialist and his son were trying to send up fire balloons. A balloon would start up jerkily, on a great bias, and be torn by the wind or blown against the houses of the square. Some fell into the crowd. The magnesium flared and the fireworks exploded and chased about in the crowd. There was no one dancing in the square. The gravel was too wet.

Brett came out with Bill and joined us. We stood in the crowd and watched Don Manuel Orquito, the fireworks king, standing on a little platform, carefully starting the balloons with sticks, standing above the heads of the crowd to launch the balloons off into the wind. The wind brought them all down, and Don Manuel Orquito's face was sweaty in the light of his complicated fireworks that fell into the crowd and charged and chased, sputtering and cracking, between the legs of the people. The people shouted as each new luminous paper bubble careened, caught fire, and fell.

"They're razzing Don Manuel," Bill said.

"How do you know he's Don Manuel?" Brett said.

"His name's on the programme. Don Manuel Orquito, the pirotecnico of esta ciudad."

"Globos illuminados," Mike said. "A collection of globos illuminados. That's what the paper said."

The wind blew the band music away.

"I say, I wish one would go up," Brett said. "That Don Manuel chap is furious."

"He's probably worked for weeks fixing them to go off, spelling out 'Hail to San Fermin,'" Bill said.

"Globos illuminados," Mike said. "A bunch of bloody globos illuminados."

"Come on," said Brett. "We can't stand here."

"Her ladyship wants a drink," Mike said.

"How you know things," Brett said.

Inside, the café was crowded and very noisy. No one noticed us come in. We could not find a table. There was a great noise going on.

"Come on, let's get out of here," Bill said.

Outside the paseo was going in under the arcade. There were some English and Americans from Biarritz in sport clothes scattered at the tables. Some of the women stared at the people going by with lorgnons. We had acquired, at some time, a friend of Bill's from Biarritz. She was staying with another girl at the Grand Hotel. The other girl had a headache and had gone to bed.

"Here's the pub," Mike said. It was the Bar Milano, a small, tough bar where you could get food and where they danced in the back room. We all sat down at a table and ordered a bottle of Fundador. The bar was not full. There was nothing going on.

"This is a hell of a place," Bill said.

"It's too early."

"Let's take the bottle and come back later," Bill said. "I don't want to sit here on a night like this."

"Let's go and look at the English," Mike said. "I love to look at the English."

"They're awful," Bill said. "Where did they all come from?"

"They come from Biarritz," Mike said. "They come to see the last day of the quaint little Spanish fiesta."

"I'll festa them," Bill said.

"You're an extraordinarily beautiful girl." Mike turned to Bill's friend. "When did you come here?"

"Come off it, Michael."

"I say, she *is* a lovely girl. Where have I been? Where have I been looking all this while? You're a lovely thing. *Have* we met? Come along with me and Bill. We're going to festa the English."

"I'll festa them," Bill said. "What the hell are they doing at this fiesta?"

"Come on," Mike said. "Just us three. We're going to festa the bloody English. I hope you're not English? I'm Scotch. I hate the English. I'm going to festa them. Come on, Bill."

Through the window we saw them, all three arm in arm, going toward the café. Rockets were going up in the square.

"I'm going to sit here," Brett said.

"I'll stay with you," Cohn said.

"Oh, don't!" Brett said. "For God's sake, go off somewhere. Can't you see Jake and I want to talk?"

"I didn't," Cohn said. "I thought I'd sit here because I felt a little tight."

"What a hell of a reason for sitting with any one. If you're tight, go to bed. Go on to bed."

"Was I rude enough to him?" Brett asked. Cohn was gone. "My God! I'm so sick of him!"

"He doesn't add much to the gayety."

"He depresses me so."

"He's behaved very badly."

"Damned badly. He had a chance to behave so well."

"He's probably waiting just outside the door now."

"Yes. He would. You know I do know how he feels. He can't believe it didn't mean anything."

"I know."

"Nobody else would behave as badly. Oh, I'm so sick of the whole thing. And Michael. Michael's been lovely, too."

"It's been damned hard on Mike."

"Yes. But he didn't need to be a swine."

"Everybody behaves badly," I said. "Give them the proper chance."

"You wouldn't behave badly." Brett looked at me.

"I'd be as big an ass as Cohn," I said.

"Darling, don't let's talk a lot of rot."

"All right. Talk about anything you like."

"Don't be difficult. You're the only person I've got, and I feel rather awful to-night."

"You've got Mike."

"Yes, Mike. Hasn't he been pretty?"

"Well," I said, "it's been damned hard on Mike, having Cohn around and seeing him with you."

"Don't I know it, darling? Please don't make me feel any worse than I do."

Brett was nervous as I had never seen her before. She kept looking away from me and looking ahead at the wall.

"Want to go for a walk?"

"Yes. Come on."

I corked up the Fundador bottle and gave it to the bartender.

"Let's have one more drink of that," Brett said. "My nerves are rotten."

We each drank a glass of the smooth amontillado brandy.

"Come on," said Brett.

As we came out the door I saw Cohn walk out from under the arcade.

"He *was* there," Brett said.

"He can't be away from you."

"Poor devil!"

"I'm not sorry for him. I hate him, myself."

"I hate him, too," she shivered. "I hate his damned suffering."

We walked arm in arm down the side street away from the crowd and the lights of the square. The street was dark and wet, and we walked along it to the fortifications at the edge of town. We passed wine-shops with light coming out from their doors onto the black, wet street, and sudden bursts of music.

"Want to go in?"

"No."

We walked out across the wet grass and onto the stone wall of the fortifications. I spread a newspaper on the stone and Brett sat down. Across the plain it was dark, and we could see the mountains. The wind was high up and took the clouds across the moon. Below us were the dark pits of the fortifications. Behind were the trees and the shadow of the cathedral, and the town silhouetted against the moon.

"Don't feel bad," I said.

"I feel like hell," Brett said. "Don't let's talk."

We looked out at the plain. The long lines of trees were dark in the moonlight. There were the lights of a car on the road climbing the mountain. Up on the top of the mountain we saw the lights of the fort. Below to the left was the river. It was high from the rain, and black and smooth. Trees were dark along the banks. We sat and looked out. Brett stared straight ahead. Suddenly she shivered.

"It's cold."

"Want to walk back?"

"Through the park."

We climbed down. It was clouding over again. In the park it was dark under the trees.

"Do you still love me, Jake?"

"Yes," I said.

"Because I'm a goner," Brett said.

"How?"

"I'm a goner. I'm mad about the Romero boy. I'm in love with him, I think."

"I wouldn't be if I were you."

"I can't help it. I'm a goner. It's tearing me all up inside."

"Don't do it."

"I can't help it. I've never been able to help anything."

"You ought to stop it."

"How can I stop it? I can't stop things. Feel that?"

Her hand was trembling.

"I'm like that all through."

"You oughtn't to do it."

"I can't help it. I'm a goner now, anyway. Don't you see the difference?"

"No."

"I've got to do something. I've got to do something I really want to do. I've lost my self-respect."

"You don't have to do that."

"Oh, darling, don't be difficult. What do you think it's meant to have that damned Jew about, and Mike the way he's acted?"

"Sure."

"I can't just stay tight all the time."

"No."

"Oh, darling, please stay by me. Please stay by me and see me through this."

"Sure."

"I don't say it's right. It is right though for me. God knows, I've never felt such a bitch."

"What do you want me to do?"

"Come on," Brett said. "Let's go and find him."

Together we walked down the gravel path in the park in the dark, under the trees and then out from under the trees and past the gate into the street that led into town.

Pedro Romero was in the café. He was at a table with other bull-fighters and bull-fight critics. They were smoking cigars. When we came in they looked up. Romero smiled and bowed. We sat down at a table half-way down the room.

"Ask him to come over and have a drink."

"Not yet. He'll come over."

"I can't look at him."

"He's nice to look at," I said.

"I've always done just what I wanted."

"I know."

"I do feel such a bitch."

"Well," I said.

"My God!" said Brett, "the things a woman goes through."

"Yes?"

"Oh, I do feel such a bitch."

I looked across at the table. Pedro Romero smiled. He said something to the other people at his table, and stood up. He came over to our table. I stood up and we shook hands.

"Won't you have a drink?"

"You must have a drink with me," he said. He seated himself, asking Brett's permission without saying anything. He had very nice manners. But he kept on smoking his cigar. It went well with his face.

"You like cigars?" I asked.

"Oh, yes. I always smoke cigars."

It was part of his system of authority. It made him seem older. I noticed his skin. It was clear and smooth and very brown. There was a triangular scar on his cheek-bone. I saw he was watching Brett. He felt there was something between them. He must have felt it when Brett gave him her hand. He was being very careful. I think he was sure, but he did not want to make any mistake.

"You fight to-morrow?" I said.

"Yes," he said. "Algabeno was hurt to-day in Madrid. Did you hear?"

"No," I said. "Badly?"

He shook his head.

"Nothing. Here," he showed his hand. Brett reached out and spread the fingers apart.

"Oh!" he said in English, "you tell fortunes?"

"Sometimes. Do you mind?"

"No. I like it." He spread his hand flat on the table. "Tell me I live for always, and be a millionaire."

He was still very polite, but he was surer of himself. "Look," he said, "do you see any bulls in my hand?"

He laughed. His hand was very fine and the wrist was small.

"There are thousands of bulls," Brett said. She was not at all nervous now. She looked lovely.

"Good," Romero laughed. "At a thousand duros apiece," he said to me in Spanish. "Tell me some more."

"It's a good hand," Brett said. "I think he'll live a long time."

"Say it to me. Not to your friend."

"I said you'd live a long time."

"I know it," Romero said. "I'm never going to die."

I tapped with my finger-tips on the table. Romero saw it. He shook his head.

"No. Don't do that. The bulls are my best friends."

I translated to Brett.

"You kill your friends?" she asked.

"Always," he said in English, and laughed. "So they don't kill me." He looked at her across the table.

"You know English well."

"Yes," he said. "Pretty well, sometimes. But I must not let anybody know. It would be very bad, a torero who speaks English."

"Why?" asked Brett.

"It would be bad. The people would not like it. Not yet."

"Why not?"

"They would not like it. Bull-fighters are not like that."

"What are bull-fighters like?"

He laughed and tipped his hat down over his eyes and changed the angle of his cigar and the expression of his face.

"Like at the table," he said. I glanced over. He had mimicked exactly the expression of Nacional. He smiled, his face natural again. "No. I must forget English."

"Don't forget it, yet," Brett said.

"No?"

"No."

"All right."

He laughed again.

"I would like a hat like that," Brett said.

"Good. I'll get you one."

"Right. See that you do."

"I will. I'll get you one to-night."

I stood up. Romero rose, too.

"Sit down," I said. "I must go and find our friends and bring them here."

He looked at me. It was a final look to ask if it were understood. It was understood all right.

"Sit down," Brett said to him. "You must teach me Spanish."

He sat down and looked at her across the table. I went out. The hard-eyed people at the bull-fighter table watched me go. It was not pleasant. When I came back and looked in the café, twenty minutes later, Brett and Pedro Romero were gone. The coffee-glasses and our three empty cognac-glasses were on the table. A waiter came with a cloth and picked up the glasses and mopped off the table.

CHAPTER XVII

OUTSIDE the Bar Milano I found Bill and Mike and Edna. Edna was the girl's name.

"We've been thrown out," Edna said.

"By the police," said Mike. "There's some people in there that don't like me."

"I've kept them out of four fights," Edna said. "You've got to help me."

Bill's face was red.

"Come back in, Edna," he said. "Go on in there and dance with Mike."

"It's silly," Edna said. "There'll just be another row."

"Damned Biarritz swine," Bill said.

"Come on," Mike said. "After all, it's a pub. They can't occupy a whole pub."

"Good old Mike," Bill said. "Damned English swine come here and insult Mike and try and spoil the fiesta."

"They're so bloody," Mike said. "I hate the English."

"They can't insult Mike," Bill said. "Mike is a swell fellow. They can insult Mike. I won't stand it. Who cares if he is a damn bankrupt?" His voice broke.

"Who cares?" Mike said. "I don't care. Jake doesn't care. Do *you* care?"

"No," Edna said. "Are you a bankrupt?"

"Of course I am. You don't care, do you, Bill?"

Bill put his arm around Mike's shoulder.

"I wish to hell I was a bankrupt. I'd show those bastards."

"They're just English," Mike said. "It never makes any difference what the English say."

"The dirty swine," Bill said. "I'm going to clean them out."

"Bill," Edna looked at me. "Please don't go in again, Bill. They're so stupid."

"That's it," said Mike. "They're stupid. I knew that was what it was."

"They can't say things like that about Mike," Bill said.

"Do you know them?" I asked Mike.

"No. I never saw them. They say they know me."

"I won't stand it," Bill said.

"Come on. Let's go over to the Suizo," I said.

"They're a bunch of Edna's friends from Biarritz," Bill said.

"They're simply stupid," Edna said.

"One of them's Charley Blackman, from Chicago," Bill said.

"I was never in Chicago," Mike said.

Edna started to laugh and could not stop.

"Take me away from here," she said, "you bankrupts."

"What kind of a row was it?" I asked Edna. We were walking across the square to the Suizo. Bill was gone.

"I don't know what happened, but some one had the police called to keep Mike out of the back room. There were some people that had known Mike at Cannes. What's the matter with Mike?"

"Probably he owes them money," I said. "That's what people usually get bitter about."

In front of the ticket-booths out in the square there were two lines of people waiting. They were sitting on chairs or crouched on the ground with blankets and newspapers around them. They were waiting for the wickets to open in the morning to buy tickets for the bull-fight. The night was clearing and the moon was out. Some of the people in the line were sleeping.

At the Café Suizo we had just sat down and ordered Fundador when Robert Cohn came up.

"Where's Brett?" he asked.

"I don't know."

"She was with you."

"She must have gone to bed."

"She's not."

"I don't know where she is."

His face was sallow under the light. He was standing up.

"Tell me where she is."

"Sit down," I said. "I don't know where she is."

"The hell you don't!"

"You can shut your face."

"Tell me where Brett is."

"I'll not tell you a damn thing."

"You know where she is."

"If I did I wouldn't tell you."

"Oh, go to hell, Cohn," Mike called from the table. "Brett's gone off with the bull-fighter chap. They're on their honeymoon."

"You shut up."

"Oh, go to hell!" Mike said languidly.

"Is that where she is?" Cohn turned to me.

"Go to hell!"

"She was with you. Is that where she is?"

"Go to hell!"

"I'll make you tell me"—he stepped forward—"you damned pimp."

I swung at him and he ducked. I saw his face duck sideways in the light. He hit me and I sat down on the pavement. As I started to get on my feet he hit me twice. I went down backward under a table. I tried to get up and felt I did not have any legs. I felt I must get on my feet and try and hit him. Mike helped me up. Some one poured a carafe of water on my head. Mike had an arm around me, and I found I was sitting on a chair. Mike was pulling at my ears.

"I say, you were cold," Mike said.

"Where the hell were you?"

"Oh, I was around."

"You didn't want to mix in it?"

"He knocked Mike down, too," Edna said.

"He didn't knock me out," Mike said. "I just lay there."

"Does this happen every night at your fiestas?" Edna asked. "Wasn't that Mr. Cohn?"

"I'm all right," I said. "My head's a little wobbly."

There were several waiters and a crowd of people standing around.

"Vaya!" said Mike. "Get away. Go on."

The waiters moved the people away.

"It was quite a thing to watch," Edna said. "He must be a boxer."

"He is."

"I wish Bill had been here," Edna said. "I'd like to have seen Bill knocked down, too. I've always wanted to see Bill knocked down. He's so big."

"I was hoping he would knock down a waiter," Mike said, "and get arrested. I'd like to see Mr. Robert Cohn in jail."

"No," I said.

"Oh, no," said Edna. "You don't mean that."

"I do, though," Mike said. "I'm not one of these chaps likes being knocked about. I never play games, even."

Mike took a drink.

"I never liked to hunt, you know. There was always the danger of having a horse fall on you. How do you feel, Jake?"

"All right."

"You're nice," Edna said to Mike. "Are you really a bankrupt?"

"I'm a tremendous bankrupt," Mike said. "I owe money to everybody. Don't you owe any money?"

"Tons."

"I owe everybody money," Mike said. "I borrowed a hundred pesetas from Montoya to-night."

"The hell you did," I said.

"I'll pay it back," Mike said. "I always pay everything back."

"That's why you're a bankrupt, isn't it?" Edna said.

I stood up. I had heard them talking from a long way away. It all seemed like some bad play.

"I'm going over to the hotel," I said. Then I heard them talking about me.

"Is he all right?" Edna asked.

"We'd better walk with him."

"I'm all right," I said. "Don't come. I'll see you all later."

I walked away from the café. They were sitting at the table. I looked back at them and at the empty tables. There was a waiter sitting at one of the tables with his head in his hands.

Walking across the square to the hotel everything looked new and changed. I had never seen the trees before. I had never seen the flagpoles before, nor the front of the theatre. It was all different. I felt as I felt once coming home from an out-of-town football game. I was carrying a suitcase with my football things in it, and I walked up the street from the station in the town I had lived in all my life and it was all new. They were raking the lawns and burning leaves in the road, and I stopped for a long time and watched. It was all strange. Then I went on, and my feet seemed to be a long way off, and everything seemed to come from a long way off, and I could hear my feet walking a great distance away. I had been kicked in the head early in the game. It was like that crossing the square. It was like that going up the stairs in the hotel. Going up the stairs took a long time, and I had the feeling that I was carrying my suitcase. There was a light in the room. Bill came out and met me in the hall.

"Say," he said, "go up and see Cohn. He's been in a jam, and he's asking for you."

"The hell with him."

"Go on. Go on up and see him."

I did not want to climb another flight of stairs.

"What are you looking at me that way for?"

"I'm not looking at you. Go on up and see Cohn. He's in bad shape."

"You were drunk a little while ago," I said.

"I'm drunk now," Bill said. "But you go up and see Cohn. He wants to see you."

"All right," I said. It was just a matter of climbing more stairs. I went on up the stairs carrying my phantom suitcase. I walked down the hall to Cohn's room. The door was shut and I knocked.

"Who is it?"

"Barnes."

"Come in, Jake."

I opened the door and went in, and set down my suitcase. There was no light in the room. Cohn was lying, face down, on the bed in the dark.

"Hello, Jake."

"Don't call me Jake."

I stood by the door. It was just like this that I had come home. Now it was a hot bath that I needed. A deep, hot bath, to lie back in.

"Where's the bathroom?" I asked.

Cohn was crying. There he was, face down on the bed, crying. He had on a white polo shirt, the kind he'd worn at Princeton.

"I'm sorry, Jake. Please forgive me."

"Forgive you, hell."

"Please forgive me, Jake."

I did not say anything. I stood there by the door.

"I was crazy. You must see how it was."

"Oh, that's all right."

"I couldn't stand it about Brett."

"You called me a pimp."

I did not care. I wanted a hot bath. I wanted a hot bath in deep water.

"I know. Please don't remember it. I was crazy."

"That's all right."

He was crying. His voice was funny. He lay there in his white shirt on the bed in the dark. His polo shirt.

"I'm going away in the morning."

He was crying without making any noise.

"I just couldn't stand it about Brett. I've been through hell, Jake. It's been simply hell. When I met her down here Brett treated me as though I were a perfect stranger. I just couldn't stand it. We lived together at San Sebastian. I suppose you know it. I can't stand it any more."

He lay there on the bed.

"Well," I said, "I'm going to take a bath."

"You were the only friend I had, and I loved Brett so."

"Well," I said, "so long."

"I guess it isn't any use," he said. "I guess it isn't any damn use."

"What?"

"Everything. Please say you forgive me, Jake."

"Sure," I said. "It's all right."

"I felt so terribly. I've been through such hell, Jake. Now everything's gone. Everything."

"Well," I said, "so long. I've got to go."

He rolled over, sat on the edge of the bed, and then stood up.

"So long, Jake," he said. "You'll shake hands, won't you?"

"Sure. Why not?"

We shook hands. In the dark I could not see his face very well.

"Well," I said, "see you in the morning."

"I'm going away in the morning."

"Oh, yes," I said.

I went out. Cohn was standing in the door of the room.

"Are you all right, Jake?" he asked.

"Oh, yes," I said. "I'm all right."

I could not find the bathroom. After a while I found it. There was a deep stone tub. I turned on the taps and the water would not run. I sat down on the edge of the bath-tub. When I got up to go I found I had taken off my shoes. I hunted for them and found them and carried them down-stairs. I found my room and went inside and undressed and got into bed.

I woke with a headache and the noise of the bands going by in the street. I remembered I had promised to take Bill's friend Edna to see the bulls go through the street and into the ring. I dressed and went down-stairs and out into the cold early morning. People were crossing the square, hurrying toward the bull-ring. Across the square were the two lines of men in front of the ticket-booths. They were still waiting for the tickets to go on sale at seven o'clock. I hurried across the street to the café. The waiter told me that my friends had been there and gone.

"How many were they?"

"Two gentlemen and a lady."

That was all right. Bill and Mike were with Edna. She had been afraid last night they would pass out. That was why I was to be sure to take her. I drank the coffee and hurried with the other people toward the bull-ring. I was not groggy now. There was only a bad headache. Everything looked sharp and clear, and the town smelt of the early morning.

The stretch of ground from the edge of the town to the bull-ring was muddy. There was a crowd all along the fence that led to the ring, and the outside balconies and the top of the bull-ring were solid with people. I heard the rocket and I knew I could not get into the ring in time to see the bulls come in, so I shoved through the crowd to the fence. I was pushed close against the planks of the fence. Between the two fences of the runway the police were clearing the crowd along. They walked or trotted on into the bull-ring. Then people commenced to come running. A drunk slipped and fell. Two policemen grabbed him and rushed him over to the fence. The crowd were running fast now. There was a great shout from the crowd, and putting my head through between the boards I saw the bulls just coming out of the street into the long running pen. They were going fast and gaining on the crowd. Just then another drunk started out from the fence with a blouse in his hands. He wanted to do capework with the bulls. The two policemen tore out, collared him, one hit him with a club, and they dragged him against the fence and stood flat-tened out against the fence as the last of the crowd and the bulls went by. There were so many people running ahead of the bulls that the mass thickened and slowed up going through the gate into the ring, and as the bulls passed, galloping together, heavy, muddy-sided, horns swinging, one shot ahead, caught a man in the running crowd in the back and lifted him in the air. Both the man's arms were by his sides, his head went back as the horn went in, and the bull lifted him and then dropped him. The bull picked another man running in front, but the man disappeared into the crowd, and the crowd was through the gate and into the ring with the bulls behind them. The red door of the ring went shut, the crowd on the outside balconies of the bull-ring were pressing through to the inside, there was a shout, then another shout.

The man who had been gored lay face down in the trampled mud. People climbed over the fence, and I could not see the man because the crowd was so thick around him. From inside the ring came the shouts. Each shout meant a charge by some bull into the crowd. You could tell by the degree of intensity in the shout how bad a thing it was that was happening. Then the rocket went up that meant the steers had gotten the bulls out of the ring and into the corrals. I left the fence and started back toward the town.

Back in the town I went to the café to have a second coffee and some buttered toast. The waiters were sweeping out the café and mopping off the tables. One came over and took my order.

"Anything happen at the encierro?"

"I didn't see it all. One man was badly cogido."

"Where?"

"Here." I put one hand on the small of my back and the other on my chest, where it looked as though the horn must have come through. The waiter nodded his head and swept the crumbs from the table with his cloth.

"Badly cogido," he said. "All for sport. All for pleasure."

He went away and came back with the long-handled coffee and milk pots. He poured the milk and coffee. It came out of the long spouts in two streams into the big cup. The waiter nodded his head.

"Badly cogido through the back," he said. He put the pots down on the table and sat down in the chair at the table. "A big horn wound. All for fun. Just for fun. What do you think of that?"

"I don't know."

"That's it. All for fun. Fun, you understand."

"You're not an aficionado?"

"Me? What are bulls? Animals. Brute animals." He stood up and put his hand on the small of his back. "Right through the back. A cornada right through the back. For fun—you understand."

He shook his head and walked away, carrying the coffee-pots. Two men were going by in the street. The waiter shouted to them. They were grave-looking. One shook his head. "Muerto!" he called.

The waiter nodded his head. The two men went on. They were on some errand. The waiter came over to my table.

"You hear? Muerto. Dead. He's dead. With a horn through him. All for morning fun. Es muy flamenco."

"It's bad."

"Not for me," the waiter said. "No fun in that for me."

Later in the day we learned that the man who was killed was named Vicente Girones, and came from near Tafalla. The next day in the paper we read that he was twenty-eight years old, and had a farm, a wife, and two children. He had continued to come to the fiesta each year after he was married. The next day his wife came in from Tafalla to be with the body, and the day after there was a service in the chapel of San Fermin, and the coffin was carried to the railway-station by members of the dancing and drinking society of Tafalla. The drums marched ahead, and there was music on the fifes, and behind the men who carried the coffin walked the wife and two children. . . . Behind them marched all the members of the dancing and drinking societies of Pamplona, Estella, Tafalla, and Sanguesa who could stay over for the funeral. The coffin was loaded into the baggage-car of the train, and the widow and the two children rode, sitting, all three together, in an open third-class railway-carriage. The train started with a jerk, and then ran smoothly, going down grade around the edge of the plateau and out into the fields of grain that blew in the wind on the plain on the way to Tafalla.

The bull who killed Vicente Girones was named Bocanegra, was Number 118 of the bull-breeding establishment of Sanchez Taberno, and was killed by Pedro Romero as the third bull of that same afternoon. His ear was cut by popular acclamation and given to Pedro Romero, who, in turn, gave it to Brett, who wrapped it in a handkerchief belonging to myself, and left both ear and handkerchief, along with a number of Muratti cigarette-stubs, shoved far back in the drawer of the bed-table that stood beside her bed in the Hotel Montoya, in Pamplona.

Back in the hotel, the night watchman was sitting on a bench inside the door. He had been there all night and was very sleepy. He stood up as I came in. Three of the waitresses came in at the same time. They had been to the morning show at the bull-ring. They went up-stairs laughing. I followed them up-stairs and went into my room. I took off my shoes and lay down on the bed. The window was open onto the balcony and the sunlight was bright

THE SUN ALSO RISES

in the room. I did not feel sleepy. It must have been half past three o'clock when I had gone to bed and the bands had waked me at six. My jaw was sore on both sides. I felt it with my thumb and fingers. That damn Cohn. He should have hit somebody the first time he was insulted, and then gone away. He was so sure that Brett loved him. He was going to stay, and true love would conquer all. Some one knocked on the door.

"Come in."

It was Bill and Mike. They sat down on the bed.

"Some encierro," Bill said. "Some encierro."

"I say, weren't you there?" Mike asked. "Ring for some beer, Bill."

"What a morning!" Bill said. He mopped off his face. "My God! what a morning! And here's old Jake. Old Jake, the human punching-bag."

"What happened inside?"

"Good God!" Bill said, "what happened, Mike?"

"There were these bulls coming in," Mike said. "Just ahead of them was the crowd, and some chap tripped and brought the whole lot of them down."

"And the bulls all came in right over them," Bill said.

"I heard them yell."

"That was Edna," Bill said.

"Chaps kept coming out and waving their shirts."

"One bull went along the barrera and hooked everybody over."

"They took about twenty chaps to the infirmary," Mike said.

"What a morning!" Bill said. "The damn police kept arresting chaps that wanted to go and commit suicide with the bulls."

"The steers took them in, in the end," Mike said.

"It took about an hour."

"It was really about a quarter of an hour," Mike objected.

"Oh, go to hell," Bill said. "You've been in the war. It was two hours and a half for me."

"Where's that beer?" Mike asked.

"What did you do with the lovely Edna?"

"We took her home just now. She's gone to bed."

"How did she like it?"

"Fine. We told her it was just like that every morning."

"She was impressed," Mike said.

"She wanted us to go down in the ring, too," Bill said. "She likes action."

"I said it wouldn't be fair to my creditors," Mike said.

"What a morning," Bill said. "And what a night!"

"How's your jaw, Jake?" Mike asked.

"Sore," I said.

Bill laughed.

"Why didn't you hit him with a chair?"

"You can talk," Mike said. "He'd have knocked you out, too. I never saw him hit me. I rather think I saw him just before, and then quite suddenly I was sitting down in the street, and Jake was lying under a table."

"Where did he go afterward?" I asked.

"Here she is," Mike said. "Here's the beautiful lady with the beer."

The chambermaid put the tray with the beer-bottles and glasses down on the table.

"Now bring up three more bottles," Mike said.

"Where did Cohn go after he hit me?" I asked Bill.

"Don't you know about that?" Mike was opening a beer-bottle. He poured the beer into one of the glasses, holding the glass close to the bottle.

"Really?" Bill asked.

"Why he went in and found Brett and the bull-fighter chap in the bull-fighter's room, and then he massacred the poor, bloody bull-fighter."

"No."

"Yes."

"What a night!" Bill said.

"He nearly killed the poor, bloody bull-fighter. Then Cohn wanted to take Brett away. Wanted to make an honest woman of her, I imagine. Damned touching scene."

He took a long drink of the beer.

"He is an ass."

"What happened?"

"Brett gave him what for. She told him off. I think she was rather good."

"I'll bet she was," Bill said.

"Then Cohn broke down and cried, and wanted to shake hands with the bull-fighter fellow. He wanted to shake hands with Brett, too."

"I know. He shook hands with me."

"Did he? Well, they weren't having any of it. The bull-fighter fellow was rather good. He didn't say much, but he kept getting up and getting knocked down again. Cohn couldn't knock him out. It must have been damned funny."

"Where did you hear all this?"

"Brett. I saw her this morning."

"What happened finally?"

"It seems the bull-fighter fellow was sitting on the bed. He'd been knocked down about fifteen times, and he wanted to fight some more. Brett held him and wouldn't let him get up. He was weak, but Brett couldn't hold him, and he got up. Then Cohn said he wouldn't hit him again. Said he couldn't do it. Said it would be wicked. So the bull-fighter chap sort of rather staggered over to him. Cohn went back against the wall.

" 'So you won't hit me?'

" 'No,' said Cohn. 'I'd be ashamed to.'

"So the bull-fighter fellow hit him just as hard as he could in the face, and then sat down on the floor. He couldn't get up, Brett said. Cohn wanted to pick him up and carry him to the bed. He said if Cohn helped him he'd kill him, and he'd kill him anyway this morning if Cohn wasn't out of town. Cohn was crying, and Brett had told him off, and he wanted to shake hands. I've told you that before."

"Tell the rest," Bill said.

"It seems the bull-fighter chap was sitting on the floor. He was waiting to get strength enough to get up and hit Cohn again. Brett wasn't having any shaking hands, and Cohn was crying and telling her how much he loved her, and she was telling him not to be a ruddy ass. Then Cohn leaned down to shake hands with the bull-fighter fellow. No hard feelings, you know. All for forgiveness. And the bull-fighter chap hit him in the face again."

"That's quite a kid," Bill said.

"He ruined Cohn," Mike said. "You know I don't think Cohn will ever want to knock people about again."

"When did you see Brett?"

"This morning. She came in to get some things. She's looking after this Romero lad."

He poured out another bottle of beer.

"Brett's rather cut up. But she loves looking after people. That's how we came to go off together. She was looking after me."

"I know," I said.

"I'm rather drunk," Mike said. "I think I'll *stay* rather drunk. This is all awfully amusing, but it's not too pleasant. It's not too pleasant for me."

He drank off the beer.

"I gave Brett what for, you know. I said if she would go about with Jews and bull-fighters and such people, she must expect trouble." He leaned forward. "I say, Jake, do you mind if I drink that bottle of yours? She'll bring you another one."

"Please," I said. "I wasn't drinking it, anyway."

Mike started to open the bottle. "Would you mind opening it?" I pressed up the wire fastener and poured it for him.

"You know," Mike went on, "Brett was rather good. She's always rather good. I gave her a fearful hiding about Jews and bull-fighters, and all those sort of people, and do you know what she said: 'Yes. I've had such a hell of a happy life with the British aristocracy!'"

He took a drink.

"That was rather good. Ashley, chap she got the title from, was a sailor, you know. Ninth baronet. When he came home he wouldn't sleep in a bed. Always made Brett sleep on the floor. Finally, when he got really bad, he used to tell her he'd kill her. Always slept with a loaded service revolver. Brett used to take the shells out when he'd gone to sleep. She hasn't had an absolutely happy life, Brett. Damned shame, too. She enjoys things so."

He stood up. His hand was shaky.

"I'm going in the room. Try and get a little sleep."

He smiled.

"We go too long without sleep in these fiestas. I'm going to start now and get plenty of sleep. Damn bad thing not to get sleep. Makes you frightfully nervy."

"We'll see you at noon at the Iruña," Bill said.

Mike went out the door. We heard him in the next room.

He rang the bell and the chambermaid came and knocked at the door.

"Bring up half a dozen bottles of beer and a bottle of Fundador," Mike told her.

"Si, Señorito."

"I'm going to bed," Bill said. "Poor old Mike. I had a hell of a row about him last night."

"Where? At that Milano place?"

"Yes. There was a fellow there that had helped pay Brett and Mike out of Cannes, once. He was damned nasty."

"I know the story."

"I didn't. Nobody ought to have a right to say things about Mike."

"That's what makes it bad."

"They oughtn't to have any right. I wish to hell they didn't have any right. I'm going to bed."

"Was anybody killed in the ring?"

"I don't think so. Just badly hurt."

"A man was killed outside in the runway."

"Was there?" said Bill.

CHAPTER XVIII

At noon we were all at the café. It was crowded. We were eating shrimps and drinking beer. The town was crowded. Every street was full. Big motor-cars from Biarritz and San Sebastian kept driving up and parking around the square. They brought people for the bull-fight. Sight-seeing cars came up, too. There was one with twenty-five Englishwomen in it. They sat in the big, white car and looked through their glasses at the fiesta. The dancers were all quite drunk. It was the last day of the fiesta.

The fiesta was solid and unbroken, but the motor-cars and tourist-cars made little islands of onlookers. When the cars emptied, the onlookers were absorbed into the crowd. You did not see them again except as sport clothes, odd-looking at a table among the closely packed peasants in black smocks. The fiesta absorbed even the Biarritz English so that you did not see them unless you passed close to a table. All the time there was music in the street. The drums kept on pounding and the pipes were going. Inside the cafés men with their hands gripping the table, or on each other's shoulders, were singing the hard-voiced singing.

"Here comes Brett," Bill said.

I looked and saw her coming through the crowd in the square, walking, her head up, as though the fiesta were being staged in her honor, and she found it pleasant and amusing.

"Hello, you chaps!" she said. "I say, I *have* a thirst."

"Get another big beer," Bill said to the waiter.

"Shrimps?"

"Is Cohn gone?" Brett asked.

"Yes," Bill said. "He hired a car."

The beer came. Brett started to lift the glass mug and her hand shook. She saw it and smiled, and leaned forward and took a long sip.

"Good beer."

"Very good," I said. I was nervous about Mike. I did not think he had slept. He must have been drinking all the time, but he seemed to be under control.

"I heard Cohn had hurt you, Jake," Brett said.

"No. Knocked me out. That was all."

"I say, he did hurt Pedro Romero," Brett said. "He hurt him most badly."

"How is he?"

"He'll be all right. He won't go out of the room."

"Does he look badly?"

"Very. He was really hurt. I told him I wanted to pop out and see you chaps for a minute."

"Is he going to fight?"

"How's your boy friend?" Mike asked. He had not listened

"Rather. I'm going with you, if you don't mind."

to anything that Brett had said.

"Brett's got a bull-fighter," he said. "She had a Jew named Cohn, but he turned out badly."

Brett stood up.

"I am not going to listen to that sort of rot from you, Michael."

"How's your boy friend?"

"Damned well," Brett said. "Watch him this afternoon."

"Brett's got a bull-fighter," Mike said. "A beautiful, bloody bull-fighter."

"Would you mind walking over with me? I want to talk to you, Jake."

"Tell him all about your bull-fighter," Mike said. "Oh, to hell with your bull-fighter!" He tipped the table so that all the beers and the dish of shrimps went over in a crash.

"Come on," Brett said. "Let's get out of this."

In the crowd crossing the square I said: "How is it?"

"I'm not going to see him after lunch until the fight. His people come in and dress him. They're very angry about me, he says."

Brett was radiant. She was happy. The sun was out and the day was bright.

"I feel altogether changed," Brett said. "You've no idea, Jake."

"Anything you want me to do?"

"No, just go to the fight with me."

"We'll see you at lunch?"

"No. I'm eating with him."

We were standing under the arcade at the door of the hotel. They were carrying tables out and setting them up under the arcade.

"Want to take a turn out to the park?" Brett asked. "I don't want to go up yet. I fancy he's sleeping."

We walked along past the theatre and out of the square and

along through the barracks of the fair, moving with the crowd between the lines of booths. We came out on a cross-street that led to the Paseo de Sarasate. We could see the crowd walking there, all the fashionably dressed people. They were making the turn at the upper end of the park.

"Don't let's go there," Brett said. "I don't want staring at just now."

We stood in the sunlight. It was hot and good after the rain and the clouds from the sea.

"I hope the wind goes down," Brett said. "It's very bad for him."

"So do I."

"He says the bulls are all right."

"They're good."

"Is that San Fermin's?"

Brett looked at the yellow wall of the chapel.

"Yes. Where the show started on Sunday."

"Let's go in. Do you mind? I'd rather like to pray a little for him or something."

We went in through the heavy leather door that moved very lightly. It was dark inside. Many people were praying. You saw them as your eyes adjusted themselves to the half-light. We knelt at one of the long wooden benches. After a little I felt Brett stiffen beside me, and saw she was looking straight ahead.

"Come on," she whispered throatily. "Let's get out of here. Makes me damned nervous."

Outside in the hot brightness of the street Brett looked up at the tree-tops in the wind. The praying had not been much of a success.

"Don't know why I get so nervy in church," Brett said. "Never does me any good."

We walked along.

"I'm damned bad for a religious atmosphere," Brett said. "I've the wrong type of face."

"You know," Brett said, "I'm not worried about him at all. I just feel happy about him."

"Good."

"I wish the wind would drop, though."

"It's liable to go down by five o'clock."

"Let's hope."

"You might pray," I laughed.

"Never does me any good. I've never gotten anything I prayed for. Have you?"

"Oh, yes."

"Oh, rot," said Brett. "Maybe it works for some people, though. You don't look very religious, Jake."

"I'm pretty religious."

"Oh, rot," said Brett. "Don't start proselyting to-day. To-day's going to be bad enough as it is."

It was the first time I had seen her in the old happy, careless way since before she went off with Cohn. We were back again in front of the hotel. All the tables were set now, and already several were filled with people eating.

"Do look after Mike," Brett said. "Don't let him get too bad."

"Your frients haff gone up-stairs," the German maitre d'hôtel said in English. He was a continual eavesdropper. Brett turned to him:

"Thank you, so much. Have you anything else to say?"

"No, ma'am."

"Good," said Brett.

"Save us a table for three," I said to the German. He smiled his dirty little pink-and-white smile.

"Iss madam eating here?"

"No," Brett said.

"Den I think a tabul for two will be enuff."

"Don't talk to him," Brett said. "Mike must have been in bad shape," she said on the stairs. We passed Montoya on the stairs. He bowed and did not smile.

"I'll see you at the café," Brett said. "Thank you, so much, Jake."

We had stopped at the floor our rooms were on. She went straight down the hall and into Romero's room. She did not knock. She simply opened the door, went in, and closed it behind her.

I stood in front of the door of Mike's room and knocked. There was no answer. I tried the knob and it opened. Inside the room was in great disorder. All the bags were opened and clothing was strewn around. There were empty bottles beside the bed. Mike lay on the bed looking like a death mask of himself. He opened his eyes and looked at me.

"Hello, Jake," he said very slowly. "I'm getting a lit tle sleep. I've want ed a lit tle sleep for a long time."

"Let me cover you over."

"No. I'm quite warm."

"Don't go. I have n't got ten to sleep yet."

"You'll sleep, Mike. Don't worry, boy."

"Brett's got a bull-fighter," Mike said. "But her Jew has gone away."

He turned his head and looked at me.

"Damned good thing, what?"

"Yes. Now go to sleep, Mike. You ought to get some sleep."

"I'm just start ing. I'm go ing to get a lit tle sleep."

He shut his eyes. I went out of the room and turned the door to quietly. Bill was in my room reading the paper.

"See Mike?"

"Yes."

"Let's go and eat."

"I won't eat down-stairs with that German head waiter. He was damned snotty when I was getting Mike up-stairs."

"He was snotty to us, too."

"Let's go out and eat in the town."

We went down the stairs. On the stairs we passed a girl coming up with a covered tray.

"There goes Brett's lunch," Bill said.

"And the kid's," I said.

Outside on the terrace under the arcade the German head waiter came up. His red cheeks were shiny. He was being polite.

"I haff a tabul for two for you gentlemen," he said.

"Go sit at it," Bill said. We went on out across the street.

We ate at a restaurant in a side street off the square. They were all men eating in the restaurant. It was full of smoke and drinking and singing. The food was good and so was the wine. We did not talk much. Afterward we went to the café and watched

the fiesta come to the boiling-point. Brett came over soon after
lunch. She said she had looked in the room and that Mike was
asleep.

When the fiesta boiled over and toward the bull-ring we went
with the crowd. Brett sat at the ringside between Bill and me.
Directly below us was the callejon, the passageway between the
stands and the red fence of the barrera. Behind us the concrete
stands filled solidly. Out in front, beyond the red fence, the sand
of the ring was smooth-rolled and yellow. It looked a little heavy
from the rain, but it was dry in the sun and firm and smooth.
The sword-handlers and bull-ring servants came down the callejon carrying on their shoulders the wicker baskets of fighting capes
and muletas. They were bloodstained and compactly folded and
packed in the baskets. The sword-handlers opened the heavy
leather sword-cases so the red wrapped hilts of the sheaf of swords
showed as the leather case leaned against the fence. They un-
folded the dark-stained red flannel of the muletas and fixed batons
in them to spread the stuff and give the matador something to
hold. Brett watched it all. She was absorbed in the professional
details.

"He's his name stencilled on all the capes and muletas," she
said. "Why do they call them muletas?"

"I don't know."

"I wonder if they ever launder them."

"I don't think so. It might spoil the color."

"The blood must stiffen them," Bill said.

"Funny," Brett said. "How one doesn't mind the blood."

Below in the narrow passage of the callejon the sword-handlers
arranged everything. All the seats were full. Above, all the boxes
were full. There was not an empty seat except in the President's
box. When he came in the fight would start. Across the smooth
sand, in the high doorway that led into the corrals, the bull-
fighters were standing, their arms furled in their capes, talking,
waiting for the signal to march in across the arena. Brett was
watching them with the glasses.

"Here, would you like to look?"

I looked through the glasses and saw the three matadors.

Romero was in the centre, Belmonte on his left, Marcial on his right. Back of them were their people, and behind the bande-rilleros, back in the passageway and in the open space of the corral, I saw the picadors. Romero was wearing a black suit. His tricornered hat was low down over his eyes. I could not see his face clearly under the hat, but it looked badly marked. He was looking straight ahead. Marcial was smoking a cigarette guard-edly, holding it in his hand. Belmonte looked ahead, his face wan and yellow, his long wolf jaw out. He was looking at nothing. Neither he nor Romero seemed to have anything in common with the others. They were all alone. The President came in; there was handclapping above us in the grand stand, and I handed the glasses to Brett. There was applause. The music started. Brett looked through the glasses.

"Here, take them," she said.

Through the glasses I saw Belmonte speak to Romero. Marcial straightened up and dropped his cigarette, and, looking straight ahead, their heads back, their free arms swinging, the three mata-dors walked out. Behind them came all the procession, opening out, all striding in step, all the capes furled, everybody with free arms swinging, and behind rode the picadors, their pics rising like lances. Behind all came the two trains of mules and the bull-ring servants. The matadors bowed, holding their hats on, before the President's box, and then came over to the barrera below us. Pedro Romero took off his heavy gold-brocaded cape and handed it over the fence to his sword-handler. He said something to the sword-handler. Close below us we saw Romero's lips were puffed, both eyes were discolored. His face was discolored and swollen. The sword-handler took the cape, looked up at Brett, and came over to us and handed up the cape.

"Spread it out in front of you," I said.

Brett leaned forward. The cape was heavy and smoothly stiff with gold. The sword-handler looked back, shook his head, and said something. A man beside me leaned over toward Brett.

"He doesn't want you to spread it," he said. "You should fold it and keep it in your lap."

Brett folded the heavy cape.

Romero did not look up at us. He was speaking to Belmonte. Belmonte had sent his formal cape over to some friends. He looked across at them and smiled, his wolf smile that was only with the mouth. Romero leaned over the barrera and asked for the water-jug. The sword-handler brought it and Romero poured water over the percale of his fighting-cape, and then scuffed the lower folds in the sand with his slippered foot.

"What's that for?" Brett asked.

"To give it weight in the wind."

"His face looks bad," Bill said.

"He feels very badly," Brett said. "He should be in bed."

The first bull was Belmonte's. Belmonte was very good. But because he got thirty thousand pesetas and people had stayed in line all night to buy tickets to see him, the crowd demanded that he should be more than very good. Belmonte's great attraction is working close to the bull. In bull-fighting they speak of the terrain of the bull and the terrain of the bull-fighter. As long as a bull-fighter stays in his own terrain he is comparatively safe. Each time he enters into the terrain of the bull he is in great danger. Belmonte, in his best days, worked always in the terrain of the bull. This way he gave the sensation of coming tragedy. People went to the corrida to see Belmonte, to be given tragic sensations. and perhaps to see the death of Belmonte. Fifteen years ago they said if you wanted to see Belmonte you should go quickly, while he was still alive. Since then he has killed more than a thousand bulls. When he retired the legend grew up about how his bull-fighting had been, and when he came out of retirement the public were disappointed because no real man could work as close to the bulls as Belmonte was supposed to have done, not, of course, even Belmonte.

Also Belmonte imposed conditions and insisted that his bulls should not be too large, nor too dangerously armed with horns, and so the element that was necessary to give the sensation of tragedy was not there, and the public, who wanted three times as much from Belmonte, who was sick with a fistula, as Belmonte had ever been able to give, felt defrauded and cheated, and Belmonte's jaw came further out in contempt, and his face turned yellower, and he moved with greater difficulty as his pain increased, and finally the crowd were actively against him, and he was utterly contemptuous and indifferent. He had meant to have a great afternoon, and instead it was an afternoon of sneers, shouted insults, and finally a volley of cushions and pieces of bread and vegetables, thrown down at him in the plaza where he had had his greatest triumphs. His jaw only went further out. Sometimes he turned to smile that toothed, long-jawed, lipless smile when he was called something particularly insulting, and always the pain that any movement produced grew stronger and stronger, until finally his yellow face was parchment color, and after his second bull was dead and the throwing of bread and cushions was over, after he had saluted the President with the same wolf-jawed smile and contemptuous eyes, and handed his sword over the barrera to be wiped, and put back in its case, he passed through into the callejon and leaned on the barrera below us, his head on his arms, not seeing, not hearing anything, only going through his pain. When he looked up, finally, he asked for a drink of water. He swallowed a little, rinsed his mouth, spat the water, took his cape, and went back into the ring.

Because they were against Belmonte the public were for Romero. From the moment he left the barrera and went toward the bull they applauded him. Belmonte watched Romero, too, watched him always without seeming to. He paid no attention to Marcial. Marcial was the sort of thing he knew all about. He had come out of retirement to compete with Marcial, knowing it was a competition gained in advance. He had expected to compete with Marcial and the other stars of the decadence of bull-fighting, and he knew that the sincerity of his own bull-fighting would be so set off by the false æsthetics of the bull-fighters of the decadent period that he would only have to be in the ring. His return from retirement had been spoiled by Romero. Romero did always, smoothly, calmly, and beautifully, what he, Belmonte, could only bring himself to do now sometimes. The crowd felt it, even the people from Biarritz, even the American ambassador saw it, finally. It was a competition that Belmonte would not enter because it would lead only to a bad horn wound or death. Belmonte was no longer well enough. He no longer had his greatest moments in the bull-ring. He was not sure that there were any great moments. Things were not the same and now life only came in flashes. He had flashes of the old greatness with his bulls, but they were not of value because he had discounted them in advance when he had picked the bulls out for their safety, getting out of a motor and leaning on a fence, looking over at the herd on the ranch of his friend the bull-breeder. So he had two small, manageable bulls without much horns, and when he felt the greatness again coming, just a little of it through the pain that was always with him, it had been discounted and sold in advance, and it did not give him a good feeling. It was the greatness, but it did not make bull-fighting wonderful to him any more.

Pedro Romero had the greatness. He loved bull-fighting, and I think he loved the bulls, and I think he loved Brett. Everything of which he could control the locality he did in front of her all that afternoon. Never once did he look up. He made it stronger that way, and did it for himself, too, as well as for her. Because he did not look up to ask if it pleased he did it all for himself inside, and it strengthened him, and yet he did it for her, too. But he did not do it for her at any loss to himself. He gained by it all through the afternoon.

His first "quite" was directly below us. The three matadors take the bull in turn after each charge he makes at a picador. Belmonte was the first. Marcial was the second. Then came Romero. The three of them were standing at the left of the horse. The picador, his hat down over his eyes, the shaft of his pic angling sharply toward the bull, kicked in the spurs and held them and with the reins in his left hand walked the horse forward toward the bull. The bull was watching. Seemingly he watched the white horse, but really he watched the triangular steel point of the pic. Romero, watching, saw the bull start to turn his head. He did not want to charge. Romero flicked his cape so the color caught the bull's eye. The bull charged with the reflex, charged, and found not the flash of color but a white horse, and a man leaned far over the horse, shot the steel point of the long hickory shaft into the hump of muscle on the bull's shoulder, and pulled his horse sideways as he pivoted on the pic, making a wound, enforcing the iron into the bull's shoulder, making him bleed for Belmonte.

The bull did not insist under the iron. He did not really want to get at the horse. He turned and the group broke apart and Romero was taking him out with his cape. He took him out softly and smoothly, and then stopped and, standing squarely in front of the bull, offered him the cape. The bull's tail went up and he charged, and Romero moved his arms ahead of the bull, wheeling, his feet firmed. The dampened, mud-weighted cape swung open and full as a sail fills, and Romero pivoted with it just ahead of the bull. At the end of the pass they were facing each other again. Romero smiled. The bull wanted it again, and Romero's cape filled again, this time on the other side. Each time he let the bull pass so close that the man and the bull and the cape that filled and pivoted ahead of the bull were all one sharply etched mass. It was all so slow and so controlled. It was as though he were rocking the bull to sleep. He made four veronicas like that, and finished with a half-veronica that turned his back on the bull and came away toward the applause, his hand on his hip, his cape on his arm, and the bull watching his back going away.

In his own bulls he was perfect. His first bull did not see well. After the first two passes with the cape Romero knew exactly how bad the vision was impaired. He worked accordingly. It was not brilliant bull-fighting. It was only perfect bull-fighting. The crowd wanted the bull changed. They made a great row. Nothing very fine could happen with a bull that could not see the lures, but the President would not order him replaced.

"Why don't they change him?" Brett asked.

"They've paid for him. They don't want to lose their money."

"It's hardly fair to Romero."

"Watch how he handles a bull that can't see the color."

"It's the sort of thing I don't like to see."

It was not nice to watch if you cared anything about the person who was doing it. With the bull who could not see the colors of the capes, or the scarlet flannel of the muleta, Romero had to make the bull consent with his body. He had to get so close that the bull saw his body, and would start for it, and then shift the bull's charge to the flannel and finish out the pass in the classic manner. The Biarritz crowd did not like it. They thought Romero was afraid, and that was why he gave that little sidestep each time as he transferred the bull's charge from his own body to the flannel. They preferred Belmonte's imitation of himself or Marcial's imitation of Belmonte. There were three of them in the row behind us.

"What's he afraid of the bull for? The bull's so dumb he only goes after the cloth."

"He's just a young bull-fighter. He hasn't learned it yet."

"But I thought he was fine with the cape before."

"Probably he's nervous now."

Out in the centre of the ring, all alone, Romero was going on with the same thing, getting so close that the bull could see him plainly, offering the body, offering it again a little closer, the bull watching dully, then so close that the bull thought he had him, offering again and finally drawing the charge and then, just before the horns came, giving the bull the red cloth to follow with that little, almost imperceptible, jerk that so offended the critical judgment of the Biarritz bull-fight experts.

"He's going to kill now," I said to Brett. "The bull's still strong. He wouldn't wear himself out."

Out in the centre of the ring Romero profiled in front of the bull, drew the sword out from the folds of the muleta, rose on his toes, and sighted along the blade. The bull charged as Romero charged. Romero's left hand dropped the muleta over the bull's muzzle to blind him, his left shoulder went forward between the horns as the sword went in, and for just an instant he and the bull were one, Romero way out over the bull, the right arm extended high up to where the hilt of the sword had gone in between the bull's shoulders. Then the figure was broken. There was a little jolt as Romero came clear, and then he was standing, one hand up, facing the bull, his shirt ripped out from under his sleeve, the white blowing in the wind, and the bull, the red sword hilt tight between his shoulders, his head going down and his legs settling.

"There he goes," Bill said.

Romero was close enough so the bull could see him. His hand still up, he spoke to the bull. The bull gathered himself, then his head went forward and he went over slowly, then all over, suddenly, four feet in the air.

They handed the sword to Romero, and carrying it blade down, the muleta in his other hand, he walked over to in front of the President's box, bowed, straightened, and came over to the barrera and handed over the sword and muleta.

"Bad one," said the sword-handler.

"He made me sweat," said Romero. He wiped off his face. The sword-handler handed him the water-jug. Romero wiped his lips. It hurt him to drink out of the jug. He did not look up at us.

Marcial had a big day. They were still applauding him when Romero's last bull came in. It was the bull that had sprinted out and killed the man in the morning running.

During Romero's first bull his hurt face had been very noticeable. Everything he did showed it. All the concentration of the awkwardly delicate working with the bull that could not see well brought it out. The fight with Cohn had not touched his spirit but his face had been smashed and his body hurt. He was wiping all that out now. Each thing that he did with this bull wiped that out a little cleaner. It was a good bull, a big bull, and with horns, and it turned and recharged easily and surely. He was what Romero wanted in bulls.

When he had finished his work with the muleta and was ready to kill, the crowd made him go on. They did not want the bull killed yet, they did not want it to be over. Romero went on. It was like a course in bull-fighting. All the passes he linked up, all completed, all slow, templed and smooth. There were no tricks and no mystifications. There was no brusqueness. And each pass as it reached the summit gave you a sudden ache inside. The crowd did not want it ever to be finished.

The bull was squared on all four feet to be killed, and Romero killed directly below us. He killed not as he had been forced to by the last bull, but as he wanted to. He profiled directly in front of the bull, drew the sword out of the folds of the muleta and sighted along the blade. The bull watched him. Romero spoke to the bull and tapped one of his feet. The bull charged and Romero waited for the charge, the muleta held low, sighting along the blade, his feet firm. Then without taking a step forward, he became one with the bull, the sword was in high between the shoulders, the bull had followed the low-swung flannel, that disappeared as Romero lurched clear to the left, and it was over. The bull tried to go forward, his legs commenced to settle, he swung from side to side, hesitated, then went down on his knees, and Romero's older brother leaned forward behind him and drove a short knife into the bull's neck at the base of the horns. The first time he missed. He drove the knife in again, and the bull went over, twitching and rigid. Romero's brother, holding the bull's horn in one hand, the knife in the other, looked up at the President's box. Handkerchiefs were waving all over the bull-ring. The President looked down from the box and waved his handkerchief. The brother cut the notched black ear from the dead bull and trotted over with it to Romero. The bull lay heavy and black on the sand, his tongue out. Boys were running toward him from all parts of the arena, making a little circle around him. They were starting to dance around the bull.

Romero took the ear from his brother and held it up toward the President. The President bowed and Romero, running to get ahead of the crowd, came toward us. He leaned up against the barrera and gave the ear to Brett. He nodded his head and smiled. The crowd were all about him. Brett held down the cape.

"You liked it?" Romero called.

Brett did not say anything. They looked at each other and smiled. Brett had the ear in her hand.

"Don't get bloody," Romero said, and grinned. The crowd wanted him. Several boys shouted at Brett. The crowd was the boys, the dancers, and the drunks. Romero turned and tried to get through the crowd. They were all around him trying to lift him and put him on their shoulders. He fought and twisted away, and started running, in the midst of them, toward the exit. He did not want to be carried on people's shoulders. But they held him and lifted him. It was uncomfortable and his legs were spraddled and his body was very sore. They were lifting him and all running toward the gate. He had his hand on somebody's shoulder. He looked around at us apologetically. The crowd, running, went out the gate with him.

We all three went back to the hotel. Brett went upstairs. Bill and I sat in the down-stairs dining-room and ate some hard-boiled eggs and drank several bottles of beer. Belmonte came down in his street clothes with his manager and two other men. They sat at the next table and ate. Belmonte ate very little. They were leaving on the seven o'clock train for Barcelona. Belmonte wore a blue-striped shirt and a dark suit, and ate soft-boiled eggs. The others ate a big meal. Belmonte did not talk. He only answered questions.

Bill was tired after the bull-fight. So was I. We both took a bull-fight very hard. We sat and ate the eggs and I watched Belmonte and the people at his table. The men with him were tough-looking and businesslike.

"Come on over to the café," Bill said. "I want an absinthe."

It was the last day of the fiesta. Outside it was beginning to be cloudy again. The square was full of people and the fireworks experts were making up their set pieces for the night and covering them over with beech branches. Boys were watching. We passed stands of rockets with long bamboo stems. Outside the café there was a great crowd. The music and the dancing were going on. The giants and the dwarfs were passing.

"Where's Edna?" I asked Bill.

"I don't know."

We watched the beginning of the evening of the last night of the fiesta. The absinthe made everything seem better. I drank it without sugar in the dripping glass, and it was pleasantly bitter.

"I feel sorry about Cohn," Bill said. "He had an awful time."

"Oh, to hell with Cohn," I said.

"Where do you suppose he went?"

"Up to Paris."

"What do you suppose he'll do?"

"Oh, to hell with him."

"What do you suppose he'll do?"

"Pick up with his old girl, probably."

"Who was his old girl?"

"Somebody named Frances."

We had another absinthe.

"When do you go back?" I asked.

"To-morrow."

After a little while Bill said: "Well, it was a swell fiesta."

"Yes," I said; "something doing all the time."

"You wouldn't believe it. It's like a wonderful nightmare."

"Sure," I said. "I'd believe anything. Including nightmares."

"What's the matter? Feel low?"

"Low as hell."

"Have another absinthe. Here, waiter! Another absinthe for this señor."

"I feel like hell," I said.

"Drink that," said Bill. "Drink it slow."

It was beginning to get dark. The fiesta was going on. I began to feel drunk but I did not feel any better.

"How do you feel?"

"I feel like hell."

"Have another?"

"It won't do any good."

"Try it. You can't tell; maybe this is the one that gets it. Hey, waiter! Another absinthe for this señor!"

I poured the water directly into it and stirred it instead of letting it drip. Bill put in a lump of ice. I stirred the ice around with a spoon in the brownish, cloudy mixture.

"How is it?"

"Fine."

"Don't drink it fast that way. It will make you sick."

I set down the glass. I had not meant to drink it fast.

"I feel tight."

"You ought to."

"That's what you wanted, wasn't it?"

"Sure. Get tight. Get over your damn depression."

"Well, I'm tight. Is that what you want?"

"Sit down."

"I won't sit down," I said. "I'm going over to the hotel."

I was very drunk. I was drunker than I ever remembered having been. At the hotel I went up-stairs. Brett's door was open. I put my head in the room. Mike was sitting on the bed. He waved a bottle.

"Jake," he said. "Come in, Jake."

I went in and sat down. The room was unstable unless I looked at some fixed point.

"Brett, you know. She's gone off with the bull-fighter chap."

"No."

"Yes. She looked for you to say good-bye. They went on the seven o'clock train."

"Did they?"

"Bad thing to do," Mike said. "She shouldn't have done it."

"No."

"Have a drink? Wait while I ring for some beer."

"I'm drunk," I said. "I'm going in and lie down."

"Are you blind? I was blind myself."

"Yes," I said, "I'm blind."

"Well, bung-o," Mike said. "Get some sleep, old Jake."

I went out the door and into my own room and lay on the bed. The bed went sailing off and I sat up in bed and looked at the wall to make it stop. Outside in the square the fiesta was going on. It did not mean anything. Later Bill and Mike came in to get me to go down and eat with them. I pretended to be asleep.

"He's asleep. Better let him alone."

"He's blind as a tick," Mike said. They went out.

I got up and went to the balcony and looked out at the dancing in the square. The world was not wheeling any more. It was just very clear and bright, and inclined to blur at the edges. I washed, brushed my hair. I looked strange to myself in the glass, and went down-stairs to the dining-room.

"Here he is!" said Bill. "Good old Jake! I knew you wouldn't pass out."

"Hello, you old drunk," Mike said.

"I got hungry and woke up."

"Eat some soup," Bill said.

The three of us sat at the table, and it seemed as though about six people were missing.

Book III

CHAPTER XIX

In the morning it was all over. The fiesta was finished. I woke about nine o'clock, had a bath, dressed, and went down-stairs. The square was empty and there were no people on the streets. A few children were picking up rocket-sticks in the square. The cafés were just opening and the waiters were carrying out the comfortable white wicker chairs and arranging them around the marble-topped tables in the shade of the arcade. They were sweeping the streets and sprinkling them with a hose.

I sat in one of the wicker chairs and leaned back comfortably. The waiter was in no hurry to come. The white-paper announcements of the unloading of the bulls and the big schedules of special trains were still up on the pillars of the arcade. A waiter wearing a blue apron came out with a bucket of water and a cloth, and commenced to tear down the notices, pulling the paper off in strips and washing and rubbing away the paper that stuck to the stone. The fiesta was over.

I drank a coffee and after a while Bill came over. I watched him come walking across the square. He sat down at the table and ordered a coffee.

"Well," he said, "it's all over."

"Yes," I said. "When do you go?"

"I don't know. We better get a car, I think. Aren't you going back to Paris?"

"No. I can stay away another week. I think I'll go to San Sebastian."

"I want to get back."

"What's Mike going to do?"

"He's going to Saint Jean de Luz."

"Let's get a car and all go as far as Bayonne. You can get the train up from there to-night."

"Good. Let's go after lunch."

"All right. I'll get the car."

We had lunch and paid the bill. Montoya did not come near us. One of the maids brought the bill. The car was outside. The chauffeur piled and strapped the bags on top of the car and put them in beside him in the front seat and we got in. The car went out of the square, along through the side streets, out under the trees and down the hill and away from Pamplona. It did not seem like a very long ride. Mike had a bottle of Fundador. I only took a couple of drinks. We came over the mountains and out of Spain and down the white roads and through the overfoliaged, wet, green, Basque country, and finally into Bayonne. We left Bill's baggage at the station, and he bought a ticket to Paris. His train left at seven-ten. We came out of the station. The car was standing out in front.

"What shall we do about the car?" Bill asked.

"Oh, bother the car," Mike said. "Let's just keep the car with us."

"All right," Bill said. "Where shall we go?"

"Let's go to Biarritz and have a drink."

"Old Mike the spender," Bill said.

We drove in to Biarritz and left the car outside a very Ritz place. We went into the bar and sat on high stools and drank a whiskey and soda.

"That drink's mine," Mike said.

"Let's roll for it."

So we rolled poker dice out of a deep leather dice-cup. Bill was out first roll. Mike lost to me and handed the bartender a hundred-franc note. The whiskeys were twelve francs apiece. We had another round and Mike lost again. Each time he gave the bartender a good tip. In a room off the bar there was a good jazz band playing. It was a pleasant bar. We had another round. I went out on the first roll with four kings. Bill and Mike rolled. Mike won the

first roll with four jacks. Bill won the second. On the final roll
Mike had three kings and let them stay. He handed the dice-cup
to Bill. Bill rattled them and rolled, and there were three kings,
an ace, and a queen.

"It's yours, Mike," Bill said. "Old Mike, the gambler."

"I'm so sorry," Mike said. "I can't get it."

"What's the matter?"

"I've no money," Mike said. "I'm stony. I've just twenty francs.
Here, take twenty francs."

Bill's face sort of changed.

"I just had enough to pay Montoya. Damned lucky to have it,
too."

"I'll cash you a check," Bill said.

"That's damned nice of you, but you see I can't write checks."

"What are you going to do for money?"

"Oh, some will come through. I've two weeks allowance should
be here. I can live on tick at this pub in Saint Jean."

"What do you want to do about the car?" Bill asked me. "Do
you want to keep it on?"

"It doesn't make any difference. Seems sort of idiotic."

"Come on, let's have another drink," Mike said.

"Fine. This one is on me," Bill said. "Has Brett any money?"
He turned to Mike.

"I shouldn't think so. She put up most of what I gave to old
Montoya."

"She hasn't any money with her?" I asked.

"I shouldn't think so. She never has any money. She gets five
hundred quid a year and pays three hundred and fifty of it in
interest to Jews."

"I suppose they get it at the source," said Bill.

"Quite. They're not really Jews. We just call them Jews. They're
Scotsmen, I believe."

"Hasn't she any at all with her?" I asked.

"I hardly think so. She gave it all to me when she left."

"Well," Bill said, "we might as well have another drink."

"Damned good idea," Mike said. "One never gets anywhere by
discussing finances."

"No," said Bill. Bill and I rolled for the next two rounds. Bill lost and paid. We went out to the car.

"Anywhere you'd like to go, Mike?" Bill asked.

"Let's take a drive. It might do my credit good. Let's drive about a little."

"Fine. I'd like to see the coast. Let's drive down toward Hendaye."

"I haven't any credit along the coast."

"You can't ever tell," said Bill.

We drove out along the coast road. There was the green of the headlands, the white, red-roofed villas, patches of forest, and the ocean very blue with the tide out and the water curling far out along the beach. We drove through Saint Jean de Luz and passed through villages farther down the coast. Back of the rolling country we were going through we saw the mountains we had come over from Pamplona. The road went on ahead. Bill looked at his watch. It was time for us to go back. He knocked on the glass and told the driver to turn around. The driver backed the car out into the grass to turn it. In back of us were the woods, below a stretch of meadow, then the sea.

At the hotel where Mike was going to stay in Saint Jean we stopped the car and he got out. The chauffeur carried in his bags. Mike stood by the side of the car.

"Good-bye, you chaps," Mike said. "It was a damned fine fiesta."

"So long, Mike," Bill said.

"I'll see you around," I said.

"Don't worry about money," Mike said. "You can pay for the car, Jake, and I'll send you my share."

"So long, Mike."

"So long, you chaps. You've been damned nice."

We all shook hands. We waved from the car to Mike. He stood in the road watching. We got to Bayonne just before the train left. A porter carried Bill's bags in from the consigne. I went as far as the inner gate to the tracks.

"So long, fella," Bill said.

"So long, kid!"

"It was swell. I've had a swell time."

"Will you be in Paris?"

"No, I have to sail on the 17th. So long, fella!"

"So long, old kid!"

He went in through the gate to the train. The porter went ahead with the bags. I watched the train pull out. Bill was at one of the windows. The window passed, the rest of the train passed, and the tracks were empty. I went outside to the car.

"How much do we owe you?" I asked the driver. The price to Bayonne had been fixed at a hundred and fifty pesetas.

"Two hundred pesetas."

"How much more will it be if you drive me to San Sebastian on your way back?"

"Fifty pesetas."

"Don't kid me."

"Thirty-five pesetas."

"It's not worth it," I said. "Drive me to the Hotel Panier Fleuri."

At the hotel I paid the driver and gave him a tip. The car was powdered with dust. I rubbed the rod-case through the dust. It seemed the last thing that connected me with Spain and the fiesta. The driver put the car in gear and went down the street. I watched it turn off to take the road to Spain. I went into the hotel and they gave me a room. It was the same room I had slept in when Bill and Cohn and I were in Bayonne. That seemed a very long time ago. I washed, changed my shirt, and went out in the town.

At a newspaper kiosque I bought a copy of the New York *Herald* and sat in a café to read it. It felt strange to be in France again. There was a safe, suburban feeling. I wished I had gone up to Paris with Bill, except that Paris would have meant more fiesta-ing. I was through with fiestas for a while. It would be quiet in San Sebastian. The season does not open there until August. I could get a good hotel room and read and swim. There was a fine beach there. There were wonderful trees along the promenade above the beach, and there were many children sent down with their nurses before the season opened. In the evening there would be band concerts under the trees across from the Café Marinas. I could sit in the Marinas and listen.

"How does one eat inside?" I asked the waiter. Inside the café was a restaurant.

"Well. Very well. One eats very well."

"Good."

I went in and ate dinner. It was a big meal for France but it seemed very carefully apportioned after Spain. I drank a bottle of wine for company. It was a Château Margaux. It was pleasant to be drinking slowly and to be tasting the wine and to be drinking alone. A bottle of wine was good company. Afterward I had coffee. The waiter recommended a Basque liqueur called Izzarra. He brought in the bottle and poured a liqueur-glass full. He said Izzarra was made of the flowers of the Pyrenees. The veritable flowers of the Pyrenees. It looked like hair-oil and smelled like Italian *strega*. I told him to take the flowers of the Pyrenees away and bring me a *vieux marc*. The *marc* was good. I had a second *marc* after the coffee.

The waiter seemed a little offended about the flowers of the Pyrenees, so I overtipped him. That made him happy. It felt comfortable to be in a country where it is so simple to make people happy. You can never tell whether a Spanish waiter will thank you. Everything is on such a clear financial basis in France. It is the simplest country to live in. No one makes things complicated by becoming your friend for any obscure reason. If you want people to like you you have only to spend a little money. I spent a little money and the waiter liked me. He appreciated my valuable qualities. He would be glad to see me back. I would dine there again some time and he would be glad to see me, and would want me at his table. It would be a sincere liking because it would have a sound basis. I was back in France.

Next morning I tipped every one a little too much at the hotel to make more friends, and left on the morning train for San Sebastian. At the station I did not tip the porter more than I should because I did not think I would ever see him again. I only wanted a few good French friends in Bayonne to make me welcome in case I should come back there again. I knew that if they remembered me their friendship would be loyal.

At Irun we had to change trains and show passports. I hated to leave France. Life was so simple in France. I felt I was a fool to be going back into Spain. In Spain you could not tell about anything. I felt like a fool to be going back into it, but I stood in line with my passport, opened my bags for the customs, bought a ticket, went through a gate, climbed onto the train, and after forty minutes and eight tunnels I was at San Sebastian.

Even on a hot day San Sebastian has a certain early-morning quality. The trees seem as though their leaves were never quite dry. The streets feel as though they had just been sprinkled. It is always cool and shady on certain streets on the hottest day. I went to a hotel in the town where I had stopped before, and they gave me a room with a balcony that opened out above the roofs of the town. There was a green mountainside beyond the roofs.

I unpacked my bags and stacked my books on the table beside the head of the bed, put out my shaving things, hung up some clothes in the big armoire, and made up a bundle for the laundry. Then I took a shower in the bathroom and went down to lunch. Spain had not changed to summer-time, so I was early. I set my watch again. I had recovered an hour by coming to San Sebastian.

As I went into the dining-room the concierge brought me a police bulletin to fill out. I signed it and asked him for two telegraph forms, and wrote a message to the Hotel Montoya, telling them to forward all mail and telegrams for me to this address. I calculated how many days I would be in San Sebastian and then wrote out a wire to the office asking them to hold mail, but forward all wires for me to San Sebastian for six days. Then I went in and had lunch.

After lunch I went up to my room, read a while, and went to sleep. When I woke it was half past four. I found my swimming-suit, wrapped it with a comb in a towel, and went down-stairs and walked up the street to the Concha. The tide was about half-way out. The beach was smooth and firm, and the sand yellow. I went into a bathing-cabin, undressed, put on my suit, and walked across the smooth sand to the sea. The sand was warm under bare feet. There were quite a few people in the water and on the beach. Out beyond where the headlands of the Concha almost met to form the harbor there was a white line of breakers and the open sea. Although the tide was going out, there were a few slow rollers. They came in like undulations in the water, gathered weight of water, and then broke smoothly on the warm sand. I waded out. The water was cold. As a roller came I dove, swam out under water, and came to the surface with all the chill gone. I swam out to the raft, pulled myself up, and lay on the hot planks. A boy and girl were at the other end. The girl had undone the top strap of her bathing-suit and was browning her back. The boy lay face downward on the raft and talked to her. She laughed at things he said, and turned her brown back in the sun. I lay on the raft in the sun until I was dry. Then I tried several dives. I dove deep once, swimming down to the bottom. I swam with my eyes open and it was green and dark. The raft made a dark shadow. I came out of water beside the raft, pulled up, dove once more, holding it for length, and then swam ashore. I lay on the beach until I was dry, then went into the bathing-cabin, took off my suit, sloshed myself with fresh water, and rubbed dry.

I walked around the harbor under the trees to the casino, and then up one of the cool streets to the Café Marinas. There was an orchestra playing inside the café and I sat out on the terrace and enjoyed the fresh coolness in the hot day, and had a glass of lemon-juice and shaved ice and then a long whiskey and soda. I sat in front of the Marinas for a long time and read and watched the people, and listened to the music.

Later when it began to get dark, I walked around the harbor and out along the promenade, and finally back to the hotel for supper. There was a bicycle-race on, the Tour du Pays Basque, and the riders were stopping that night in San Sebastian. In the dining-room, at one side, there was a long table of bicycle-riders, eating with their trainers and managers. They were all French and Belgians, and paid close attention to their meal, but they were having a good time. At the head of the table were two good-looking French girls, with much Rue du Faubourg Montmartre chic. I could not make out whom they belonged to. They all spoke in slang at the long table and there were many private jokes and some jokes at the far end that were not repeated when the girls asked to hear them. The next morning at five o'clock the race resumed with the last lap, San Sebastian-Bilbao. The bicycle-riders drank much wine, and were burned and browned by the sun. They did not take the race seriously except among themselves. They had raced among themselves so often that it did not make much difference who won. Especially in a foreign country. The money could be arranged.

The man who had a matter of two minutes lead in the race had an attack of boils, which were very painful. He sat on the small of his back. His neck was very red and the blond hairs were sunburned. The other riders joked him about his boils. He tapped on the table with his fork.

"Listen," he said, "to-morrow my nose is so tight on the handle-bars that the only thing touches those boils is a lovely breeze."

One of the girls looked at him down the table, and he grinned and turned red. The Spaniards, they said, did not know how to pedal.

I had coffee out on the terrasse with the team manager of one of the big bicycle manufacturers. He said it had been a very pleasant race, and would have been worth watching if Bottechia had not abandoned it at Pamplona. The dust had been bad, but in Spain the roads were better than in France. Bicycle road-racing was the only sport in the world, he said. Had I ever followed the Tour de France? Only in the papers. The Tour de France was the greatest sporting event in the world. Following and organizing the road races had made him know France. Few people know France. All spring and all summer and all fall he spent on the road with bicycle road-racers. Look at the number of motor-cars now that followed the riders from town to town in a road race. It was a rich country and more *sportif* every year. It would be the most *sportif* country in the world. It was bicycle road-racing did it. That and football. He knew France. *La France Sportive*. He knew road-racing. We had a cognac. After all, though, it wasn't bad to get back to Paris. There is only one Paname. In all the world, that is. Paris is the town the most *sportif* in the world. Did I know the *Chope de Negre*? Did I not. I would see him there some

time. I certainly would. We would drink another *fine* together.
We certainly would. They started at six o'clock less a quarter in
the morning. Would I be up for the depart? I would certainly try
to. Would I like him to call me? It was very interesting. I would
leave a call at the desk. He would not mind calling me. I could
not let him take the trouble. I would leave a call at the desk. We
said good-bye until the next morning.

In the morning when I awoke the bicycle-riders and their following cars had been on the road for three hours. I had coffee
and the papers in bed and then dressed and took my bathing-suit
down to the beach. Everything was fresh and cool and damp in
the early morning. Nurses in uniform and in peasant costume
walked under the trees with children. The Spanish children were
beautiful. Some bootblacks sat together under a tree talking to a
soldier. The soldier had only one arm. The tide was in and there
was a good breeze and a surf on the beach.

I undressed in one of the bath-cabins, crossed the narrow line
of beach and went into the water. I swam out, trying to swim
through the rollers, but having to dive sometimes. Then in the
quiet water I turned and floated. Floating I saw only the sky, and
felt the drop and lift of the swells. I swam back to the surf and
coasted in, face down, on a big roller, then turned and swam,
trying to keep in the trough and not have a wave break over me.
It made me tired, swimming in the trough, and I turned and
swam out to the raft. The water was buoyant and cold. It felt as
though you could never sink. I swam slowly, it seemed like a long
swim with the high tide, and then pulled up on the raft and sat,
dripping, on the boards that were becoming hot in the sun. I
looked around at the bay, the old town, the casino, the line of
trees along the promenade, and the big hotels with their white
porches and gold-lettered names. Off on the right, almost closing
the harbor, was a green hill with a castle. The raft rocked with
the motion of the water. On the other side of the narrow gap that
led into the open sea was another high headland. I thought I
would like to swim across the bay but I was afraid of cramp.

I sat in the sun and watched the bathers on the beach. They
looked very small. After a while I stood up, gripped with my

toes on the edge of the raft as it tipped with my weight, and
dove cleanly and deeply, to come up through the lightening
water, blew the salt water out of my head, and swam slowly and
steadily in to shore.

After I was dressed and had paid for the bath-cabin, I walked
back to the hotel. The bicycle-racers had left several copies of
L'Auto around, and I gathered them up in the reading-room and
took them out and sat in an easy chair in the sun to read about and
catch up on French sporting life. While I was sitting there the
concierge came out with a blue envelope in his hand.

"A telegram for you, sir."

I poked my finger along under the fold that was fastened
down, spread it open, and read it. It had been forwarded from
Paris:

> COULD YOU COME HOTEL MONTANA MADRID
> AM RATHER IN TROUBLE BRETT.

I tipped the concierge and read the message again. A postman
was coming along the sidewalk. He turned in the hotel. He had a
big moustache and looked very military. He came out of the hotel
again. The concierge was just behind him.

"Here's another telegram for you, sir."

"Thank you," I said.

I opened it. It was forwarded from Pamplona.

> COULD YOU COME HOTEL MONTANA MADRID
> AM RATHER IN TROUBLE BRETT.

The concierge stood there waiting for another tip, probably.

"What time is there a train for Madrid?"

"It left at nine this morning. There is a slow train at eleven,
and the Sud Express at ten to-night."

"Get me a berth on the Sud Express. Do you want the money
now?"

"Just as you wish," he said. "I will have it put on the bill."

"Do that."

Well, that meant San Sebastian all shot to hell. I suppose,
vaguely, I had expected something of the sort. I saw the concierge standing in the doorway.

"Bring me a telegram form, please."

He brought it and I took out my fountain-pen and printed:

```
LADY ASHLEY HOTEL MONTANA MADRID
ARRIVING SUD EXPRESS TOMORROW LOVE
JAKE.
```

That seemed to handle it. That was it. Send a girl off with one man. Introduce her to another to go off with him. Now go and bring her back. And sign the wire with love. That was it all right. I went in to lunch.

I did not sleep much that night on the Sud Express. In the morning I had breakfast in the dining-car and watched the rock and pine country between Avila and Escorial. I saw the Escorial out of the window, gray and long and cold in the sun, and did not give a damn about it. I saw Madrid come up over the plain, a compact white sky-line on the top of a little cliff away off across the sun-hardened country.

The Norte station in Madrid is the end of the line. All trains finish there. They don't go on anywhere. Outside were cabs and taxis and a line of hotel runners. It was like a country town. I took a taxi and we climbed up through the gardens, by the empty palace and the unfinished church on the edge of the cliff, and on up until we were in the high, hot, modern town. The taxi coasted down a smooth street to the Puerta del Sol, and then through the traffic and out into the Carrera San Jeronimo. All the shops had their awnings down against the heat. The windows on the sunny side of the street were shuttered. The taxi stopped at the curb. I saw the sign HOTEL MONTANA on the second floor. The taxi-driver carried the bags in and left them by the elevator. I could not make the elevator work, so I walked up. On the second floor up was a cut brass sign: HOTEL MONTANA. I rang and no one came to the door. I rang again and a maid with a sullen face opened the door.

"Is Lady Ashley here?" I asked.

She looked at me dully.

"Is an Englishwoman here?"

She turned and called some one inside. A very fat woman came to the door. Her hair was gray and stiffly oiled in scallops around her face. She was short and commanding.

"Muy buenos," I said. "Is there an Englishwoman here? I would like to see this English lady."

"Muy buenos. Yes, there is a female English. Certainly you can see her if she wishes to see you."

"She wishes to see me."

"The chica will ask her."

"It is very hot."

"It is very hot in the summer in Madrid."

"And how cold in winter."

"Yes, it is very cold in winter."

Did I want to stay myself in person in the Hotel Montana?

Of that as yet I was undecided, but it would give me pleasure if my bags were brought up from the ground floor in order that they might not be stolen. Nothing was ever stolen in the Hotel Montana. In other fondas, yes. Not here. No. The personages of this establishment were rigidly selectioned. I was happy to hear it. Nevertheless I would welcome the upbringal of my bags.

The maid came in and said that the female English wanted to see the male English now, at once.

"Good," I said. "You see. It is as I said."

"Clearly."

I followed the maid's back down a long, dark corridor. At the end she knocked on a door.

"Hello," said Brett. "Is it you, Jake?"

"It's me."

"Come in. Come in."

I opened the door. The maid closed it after me. Brett was in bed. She had just been brushing her hair and held the brush in her hand. The room was in that disorder produced only by those who have always had servants.

"Darling!" Brett said.

I went over to the bed and put my arms around her. She kissed me, and while she kissed me I could feel she was thinking of something else. She was trembling in my arms. She felt very small.

"Darling! I've had such a hell of a time."

"Tell me about it."

"Nothing to tell. He only left yesterday. I made him go."

"Why didn't you keep him?"

"I don't know. It isn't the sort of thing one does. I don't think I hurt him any."

"You were probably damn good for him."

"He shouldn't be living with any one. I realized that right away."

"No."

"Oh, hell!" she said, "let's not talk about it. Let's never talk about it."

"All right."

"It was rather a knock his being ashamed of me. He was ashamed of me for a while, you know."

"No."

"Oh, yes. They ragged him about me at the café, I guess. He wanted me to grow my hair out. Me, with long hair. I'd look so like hell."

"It's funny."

"He said it would make me more womanly. I'd look a fright."

"What happened?"

"Oh, he got over that. He wasn't ashamed of me long."

"What was it about being in trouble?"

"I didn't know whether I could make him go, and I didn't have a sou to go away and leave him. He tried to give me a lot of money, you know. I told him I had scads of it. He knew that was a lie. I couldn't take his money, you know."

"No."

"Oh, let's not talk about it. There were some funny things, though. Do give me a cigarette."

I lit the cigarette.

"He learned his English as a waiter in Gib."

"Yes."

"He wanted to marry me, finally."

"Really?"

"Of course. I can't even marry Mike."

"Maybe he thought that would make him Lord Ashley."

"No. It wasn't that. He really wanted to marry me. So I couldn't go away from him, he said. He wanted to make it sure I could never go away from him. After I'd gotten more womanly, of course."

"You ought to feel set up."

"I do. I'm all right again. He's wiped out that damned Cohn."

"Good."

"You know I'd have lived with him if I hadn't seen it was bad for him. We got along damned well."

"Outside of your personal appearance."

"Oh, he'd have gotten used to that."

She put out the cigarette.

"I'm thirty-four, you know. I'm not going to be one of these bitches that ruins children."

"No."

"I'm not going to be that way. I feel rather good, you know. I feel rather set up."

"Good."

She looked away. I thought she was looking for another cigarette. Then I saw she was crying. I could feel her crying. Shaking and crying. She wouldn't look up. I put my arms around her.

"Don't let's ever talk about it. Please don't let's ever talk about it."

"Dear Brett."

"I'm going back to Mike." I could feel her crying as I held her close. "He's so damned nice and he's so awful. He's my sort of thing."

She would not look up. I stroked her hair. I could feel her shaking.

"I won't be one of those bitches," she said. "But, oh, Jake, please let's never talk about it."

We left the Hotel Montana. The woman who ran the hotel would not let me pay the bill. The bill had been paid.

"Oh, well. Let it go," Brett said. "It doesn't matter now."

We rode in a taxi down to the Palace Hotel, left the bags, arranged for berths on the Sud Express for the night, and went into the bar of the hotel for a cocktail. We sat on high stools at the bar while the barman shook the Martinis in a large nickelled shaker.

"It's funny what a wonderful gentility you get in the bar of a big hotel," I said.

"Barmen and jockeys are the only people who are polite any more."

"No matter how vulgar a hotel is, the bar is always nice."

"It's odd."

"Bartenders have always been fine."

"You know," Brett said, "it's quite true. He is only nineteen. Isn't it amazing?"

We touched the two glasses as they stood side by side on the bar. They were coldly beaded. Outside the curtained window was the summer heat of Madrid.

"I like an olive in a Martini," I said to the barman.

"Right you are, sir. There you are."

"Thanks."

"I should have asked, you know."

The barman went far enough up the bar so that he would not hear our conversation. Brett had sipped from the Martini as it stood, on the wood. Then she picked it up. Her hand was steady enough to lift it after that first sip.

"It's good. Isn't it a nice bar?"

"They're all nice bars."

"You know I didn't believe it at first. He was born in 1905. I was in school in Paris, then. Think of that."

"Anything you want me to think about it?"

"Don't be an ass. *Would* you buy a lady a drink?"

"We'll have two more Martinis."

"As they were before, sir?"

"They were very good." Brett smiled at him.

"Thank you, ma'am."

"Well, bung-o," Brett said.

"Bung-o!"

"You know," Brett said, "he'd only been with two women before. He never cared about anything but bull-fighting."

"He's got plenty of time."

"I don't know. He thinks it was me. Not the show in general."

"Well, it was you."

"Yes. It was me."

"I thought you weren't going to ever talk about it."

"How can I help it?"

"You'll lose it if you talk about it."

"I just talk around it. You know I feel rather damned good, Jake."

"You should."

"You know it makes one feel rather good deciding not to be a bitch."

"Yes."

"It's sort of what we have instead of God."

"Some people have God," I said. "Quite a lot."

"He never worked very well with me."

"Should we have another Martini?"

The barman shook up two more Martinis and poured them out into fresh glasses.

"Where will we have lunch?" I asked Brett. The bar was cool. You could feel the heat outside through the window.

"Here?" asked Brett.

"It's rotten here in the hotel. Do you know a place called Botin's?" I asked the barman.

"Yes, sir. Would you like to have me write out the address?"

"Thank you."

We lunched up-stairs at Botin's. It is one of the best restaurants in the world. We had roast young suckling pig and drank *rioja alta*. Brett did not eat much. She never ate much. I ate a very big meal and drank three bottles of *rioja alta*.

"How do you feel, Jake?" Brett asked. "My God! what a meal you've eaten."

"I feel fine. Do you want a dessert?"

"Lord, no."

Brett was smoking.

"You like to eat, don't you?" she said.

"Yes," I said. "I like to do a lot of things."

"What do you like to do?"

"Oh," I said, "I like to do a lot of things. Don't you want a dessert?"

"You asked me that once," Brett said.

"Yes," I said. "So I did. Let's have another bottle of *rioja alta.*"

"It's very good."

"You haven't drunk much of it," I said.

"I have. You haven't seen."

"Let's get two bottles," I said. The bottles came. I poured a little in my glass, then a glass for Brett, then filled my glass. We touched glasses.

"Bung-o!" Brett said. I drank my glass and poured out another. Brett put her hand on my arm.

"Don't get drunk, Jake," she said. "You don't have to."

"How do you know?"

"Don't," she said. "You'll be all right."

"I'm not getting drunk," I said. "I'm just drinking a little wine. I like to drink wine."

"Don't get drunk," she said. "Jake, don't get drunk."

"Want to go for a ride?" I said. "Want to ride through the town?"

"Right," Brett said. "I haven't seen Madrid. I should see Madrid."

"I'll finish this," I said.

Down-stairs we came out through the first-floor dining-room to the street. A waiter went for a taxi. It was hot and bright. Up the street was a little square with trees and grass where there were taxis parked. A taxi came up the street, the waiter hanging out at the side. I tipped him and told the driver where to drive, and got in beside Brett. The driver started up the street. I settled back. Brett moved close to me. We sat close against each other. I put my arm around her and she rested against me comfortably. It was very hot and bright, and the houses looked sharply white. We turned out onto the Gran Via.

"Oh, Jake," Brett said, "we could have had such a damned good time together."

Ahead was a mounted policeman in khaki directing traffic. He raised his baton. The car slowed suddenly pressing Brett against me.

"Yes," I said. "Isn't it pretty to think so?"

THE END

from A FAREWELL TO ARMS

BOOK THREE

THE RETREAT FROM CAPORETTO

STRESA

A FAREWELL TO ARMS is generally recognized as the best of all the novels of love and war that have been written by Americans. It is hard to think of a contemporary as the author of a classic. Yet this novel is decidedly a classic by standards of excellence we apply to works of the past. In a way it belongs to the past as well as to the present and the future, since it is about the first World War. We have long since had a second World War that has not brought us any novel to equal or surpass A Farewell to Arms. Instead we have had multitudes of books, some worthy, some not, that were clearly influenced by Hemingway's story of Catherine Barkley, the tragic and beautiful English girl of the Voluntary Aid Detachment, and Lieutenant Frederic Henry, the young American architecture student who served at the front with an ambulance unit of the Italian Army.

"This book," Hemingway said in 1948, "was written in Paris, France, Key West, Florida, Piggott, Arkansas, Kansas City, Missouri, Sheridan, Wyoming, and the first draft was finished near Big Horn in Wyoming." It was begun early in 1928, finished in the spring of 1929 and published early that autumn when leaves and stocks were falling.

Two crucial episodes from the book follow. The first is the narrative of the retreat from Caporetto. The second is the escape of Catherine Barkley and Lieutenant Henry into Switzerland from Italy.

C. P.

A FAREWELL TO ARMS

Book Three

THE RETREAT FROM CAPORETTO

XXV

Now in the fall the trees were all bare and the roads were muddy.
I rode to Gorizia from Udine on a camion. We passed other
camions on the road and I looked at the country. The mulberry trees
were bare and the fields were brown. There were wet dead leaves
on the road fom the rows of bare trees and men were working on
the road, tamping stone in the ruts from piles of crushed stone
along the side of the road between the trees. We saw the town with
a mist over it that cut off the mountains. We crossed the river and
I saw that it was running high. It had been raining in the mountains. We came into the town past the factories and then the houses
and villas and I saw that many more houses had been hit. On a
narrow street we passed a British Red Cross ambulance. The
driver wore a cap and his face was thin and very tanned. I did not
know him. I got down from the camion in the big square in front
of the Town Major's house, the driver handed down my rucksack
and I put it on and swung on the two musettes and walked to our
villa. It did not feel like a homecoming.

I walked down the damp gravel driveway looking at the villa
through the trees. The windows were all shut but the door was
open. I went in and found the major sitting at a table in the bare
room with maps and typed sheets of paper on the wall.

"Hello," he said. "How are you?" He looked older and drier.

"I'm good," I said. "How is everything?"

"It's all over," he said. "Take off your kit and sit down." I put my pack and the two musettes on the floor and my cap on the pack. I brought the other chair over from the wall and sat down by the desk.

"It's been a bad summer," the major said. "Are you strong now?"

"Yes."

"Did you ever get the decorations?"

"Yes. I got them fine. Thank you very much."

"Let's see them."

I opened my cape so he could see the two ribbons.

"Did you get the boxes with the medals?"

"No. Just the papers."

"The boxes will come later. That takes more time."

"What do you want me to do?"

"The cars are all away. There are six up north at Caporetto. You know Caporetto?"

"Yes," I said. I remembered it as a little white town with a campanile in a valley. It was a clean little town and there was a fine fountain in the square.

"They are working from there. There are many sick now. The fighting is over."

"Where are the others?"

"There are two up in the mountains and four still on the Bainsizza. The other two ambulance sections are in the Carso with the third army."

"What do you wish me to do?"

"You can go and take over the four cars on the Bainsizza if you like. Gino has been up there a long time. You haven't seen it up there, have you?"

"No."

"It was very bad. We lost three cars."

"I heard about it."

"Yes, Rinaldi wrote you."

"Where is Rinaldi?"

"He is here at the hospital. He has had a summer and fall of it."

"I believe it."

"It has been bad," the major said. "You couldn't believe how bad it's been. I've often thought you were lucky to be hit when you were."

"I know I was."

"Next year will be worse," the major said. "Perhaps they will attack now. They say they are to attack but I can't believe it. It is too late. You saw the river?"

"Yes. It's high already."

"I don't believe they will attack now that the rains have started. We will have the snow soon. What about your countrymen? Will there be other Americans besides yourself?"

"They are training an army of ten million."

"I hope we get some of them. But the French will hog them all. We'll never get any down here. All right. You stay here to-night and go out to-morrow with the little car and send Gino back. I'll send somebody with you that knows the road. Gino will tell you everything. They are shelling quite a little still but it is all over. You will want to see the Bainsizza."

"I'm glad to see it. I am glad to be back with you again, Signor Maggiore."

He smiled. "You are very good to say so. I am very tired of this war. If I was away I do not believe I would come back."

"Is it so bad?"

"Yes. It is so bad and worse. Go get cleaned up and find your friend Rinaldi."

I went out and carried my bags up the stairs. Rinaldi was not in the room but his things were there and I sat down on the bed and unwrapped my puttees and took the shoe off my right foot. Then I lay back on the bed. I was tired and my right foot hurt. It seemed silly to lie on the bed with one shoe off, so I sat up and unlaced the other shoe and dropped it on the floor, then lay back on the blanket again. The room was stuffy with the window closed but I was too tired to get up and open it. I saw my things were all in one corner of the room. Outside it was getting dark. I lay on the bed and thought about Catherine and waited for Rinaldi. I was going to try not to think about Catherine except at night before I went to sleep. But now I was tired and there was nothing to do, so I lay and thought about her. I was thinking about her when Rinaldi came in. He looked just the same. Perhaps he was a little thinner.

"Well, baby," he said. I sat up on the bed. He came over, sat down and put his arm around me. "Good old baby." He whacked me on the back and I held both his arms.

"Old baby," he said. "Let me see your knee."

"I'll have to take off my pants."

"Take off your pants, baby. We're all friends here. I want to see what kind of a job they did." I stood up, took off the breeches and pulled off the knee-brace. Rinaldi sat on the floor and bent the knee gently back and forth. He ran his finger along the scar; put his thumbs together over the kneecap and rocked the knee gently with his fingers.

"Is that all the articulation you have?"

"Yes."

"It's a crime to send you back. They ought to get complete articulation."

"It's a lot better than it was. It was stiff as a board."

Rinaldi bent it more. I watched his hands. He had fine surgeon's hands. I looked at the top of his head, his hair shiny and parted smoothly. He bent the knee too far.

"Ouch!" I said.

"You ought to have more treatment on it with the machines," Rinaldi said.

"It's better than it was."

"I see that, baby. This is something I know more about than you." He stood up and sat down on the bed. "The knee itself is a good job." He was through with the knee. "Tell me all about everything."

"There's nothing to tell," I said. "I've led a quiet life."

"You act like a married man," he said. "What's the matter with you?"

"Nothing." I said. "What's the matter with you?"

"This war is killing me," Rinaldi said, "I am very depressed by it." He folded his hands over his knee.

"Oh," I said.

"What's the matter? Can't I even have human impulses?"

"No. I can see you've been having a fine time. Tell me."

"All summer and all fall I've operated. I work all the time. I do everybody's work. All the hard ones they leave to me. By God, baby, I am becoming a lovely surgeon."

"That sounds better."

"I never think. No, by God, I don't think; I operate."

"That's right."

"But now, baby, it's all over. I don't operate now and I feel like hell. This is a terrible war, baby. You believe me when I say it. Now you cheer me up. Did you bring the phonograph records?"

"Yes."

They were wrapped in paper in a cardboard box in my rucksack. I was too tired to get them out.

"Don't you feel good yourself, baby?"

"I feel like hell."

"This war is terrible," Rinaldi said. "Come on. We'll both get drunk and be cheerful. Then we'll go get the ashes dragged. Then we'll feel fine."

"I've had the jaundice," I said, "and I can't get drunk."

"Oh, baby, how you've come back to me. You come back serious and with a liver. I tell you this war is a bad thing. Why did we make it anyway."

"We'll have a drink. I don't want to get drunk but we'll have a drink."

Rinaldi went across the room to the washstand and brought back two glasses and a bottle of cognac.

"It's Austrian cognac," he said. "Seven stars. It's all they captured on San Gabriele."

"Were you up there?"

"No. I haven't been anywhere. I've been here all the time operating. Look, baby, this is your old tooth-brushing glass. I kept it all the time to remind me of you."

"To remind you to brush your teeth."

"No. I have my own too. I kept this to remind me of you trying to brush away the Villa Rossa from your teeth in the morning, swearing and eating aspirin and cursing harlots. Every time I see that glass I think of you trying to clean your conscience with a toothbrush." He came over to the bed. "Kiss me once and tell me you're not serious."

"I never kiss you. You're an ape."

"I know, you are the fine good Anglo-Saxon boy. I know. You are the remorse boy, I know. I will wait till I see the Anglo-Saxon brushing away harlotry with a toothbrush."

"Put some cognac in the glass."

We touched glasses and drank. Rinaldi laughed at me.

"I will get you drunk and take out your liver and put you in a good Italian liver and make you a man again."

I held the glass for some more cognac. It was dark outside now. Holding the glass of cognac, I went over and opened the window. The rain had stopped falling. It was colder outside and there was a mist in the trees.

"Don't throw the cognac out the window," Rinaldi said. "If you can't drink it give it to me."

"Go something yourself," I said. I was glad to see Rinaldi again. He had spent two years teasing me and I had always liked it. We understood each other very well.

"Are you married?" he asked from the bed. I was standing against the wall by the window.

"Not yet."

"Are you in love?"

"Yes."

"With that English girl?"

"Yes."

"Poor baby. Is she good to you?"

"Of course."

"I mean is she good to you practically speaking?"

"Shut up."

"I will. You will see I am a man of extreme delicacy. Does she ——?"

"Rinin," I said. "Please shut up. If you want to be my friend, shut up."

"I don't *want* to be your friend, baby. I *am* your friend."

"Then shut up."

"All right."

I went over to the bed and sat down beside Rinaldi. He was holding his glass and looking at the floor.

"You see how it is, Rinin?"

"Oh, yes. All my life I encounter sacred subjects. But very few with you. I suppose you must have them too." He looked at the floor.

"You haven't any?"

"No."

"Not any?"

"No."

"I can say this about your mother and that about your sister?"

"And that about *your* sister," Rinaldi said swiftly. We both laughed.

"The old superman," I said.

"I am jealous maybe," Rinaldi said.

"No, you're not."

"I don't mean like that. I mean something else. Have you any married friends?"

"Yes," I said.

"I haven't," Rinaldi said. "Not if they love each other."

"Why not?"

"They don't like me."

"Why not?"

"I am the snake. I am the snake of reason."

"You're getting it mixed. The apple was reason."

"No, it was the snake." He was more cheerful.

"You are better when you don't think so deeply," I said.

"I love you, baby," he said. "You puncture me when I become a great Italian thinker. But I know many things I can't say. I know more than you."

"Yes. You do."

"But you will have a better time. Even with remorse you will have a better time."

"I don't think so."

"Oh, yes. That is true. Already I am only happy when I am working." He looked at the floor again.

"You'll get over that."

"No. I only like two other things; one is bad for my work and the other is over in half an hour or fifteen minutes. Sometimes less."

"Sometimes a good deal less."

"Perhaps I have improved, baby. You do not know. But there are only the two things and my work."

"You'll get other things."

"No. We never get anything. We are born with all we have and we never learn. We never get anything new. We all start complete. You should be glad not to be a Latin."

"There's no such thing as a Latin. That is 'Latin' thinking. You are so proud of your defects." Rinaldi looked up and laughed.

"We'll stop, baby. I am tired from thinking so much." He had looked tired when he came in. "It's nearly time to eat. I'm glad you're back. You are my best friend and my war brother."

"When do the war brothers eat?" I asked.

"Right away. We'll drink once more for your liver's sake."

"Like Saint Paul."

"You are inaccurate. That was wine and the stomach. Take a little wine for your stomach's sake."

"Whatever you have in the bottle," I said. "For any sake you mention."

"To your girl," Rinaldi said. He held out his glass.

"All right."

"I'll never say a dirty thing about her."

"Don't strain yourself."

He drank off the cognac. "I am pure," he said. "I am like you, baby. I will get an English girl too. As a matter of fact I knew your girl first but she was a little tall for me. A tall girl for a sister," he quoted.

"You have a lovely pure mind," I said.

"Haven't I? That's why they call me Rinaldo Purissimo."

"Rinaldo Sporchissimo."

"Come on, baby, we'll go down to eat while my mind is still pure."

I washed, combed my hair and we went down the stairs. Rinaldi was a little drunk. In the room where we ate, the meal was not quite ready.

"I'll go get the bottle," Rinaldi said. He went off up the stairs. I sat at the table and he came back with the bottle and poured us each a half tumbler of cognac.

"Too much," I said and held up the glass and sighted at the lamp on the table.

"Not for an empty stomach. It is a wonderful thing. It burns out the stomach completely. Nothing is worse for you."

"All right."

"Self-destruction day by day," Rinaldi said. "It ruins the stomach and makes the hand shake. Just the thing for a surgeon."

"You recommend it?"

"Heartily. I use no other. Drink it down, baby, and look forward to being sick."

I drank half the glass. In the hall I could hear the orderly calling. "Soup! Soup is ready!"

The major came in, nodded to us and sat down. He seemed very small at table.

"Is this all we are?" he asked. The orderly put the soup bowl down and he ladled out a plate full.

"We are all," Rinaldi said. "Unless the priest comes. If he knew Federico was here he would be here."

"Where is he?" I asked.

"He's at 307," the major said. He was busy with his soup. He wiped his mouth, wiping his upturned gray mustache carefully. "He will come I think. I called them and left word to tell him you were here."

"I miss the noise of the mess," I said.

"Yes, it's quiet," the major said.

"I will be noisy," said Rinaldi.

"Drink some wine, Enrico," said the major. He filled my glass. The spaghetti came in and we were all busy. We were finishing the spaghetti when the priest came in. He was the same as ever, small and brown and compact looking. I stood up and we shook hands. He put his hand on my shoulder.

"I came as soon as I heard," he said.

"Sit down," the major said. "You're late."

"Good-evening, priest," Rinaldi said, using the English word. They had taken that up from the priest-baiting captain, who spoke a little English. "Good-evening, Rinaldi," the priest said. The orderly brought him soup but he said he would start with the spaghetti.

"How are you?" he asked me.

"Fine," I said. "How have things been?"

"Drink some wine, priest," Rinaldi said. "Take a little wine for your stomach's sake. That's Saint Paul, you know."

"Yes I know," said the priest politely. Rinaldi filled his glass.

"That Saint Paul," said Rinaldi. "He's the one who makes all the trouble." The priest looked at me and smiled. I could see that the baiting did not touch him now.

"That Saint Paul," Rinaldi said. "He was a rounder and a chaser and then when he was no longer hot he said it was no good. When he was finished he made the rules for us who are still hot. Isn't it true, Federico?"

The major smiled. We were eating meat stew now.

"I never discuss a Saint after dark," I said. The priest looked up from the stew and smiled at me.

"There he is, gone over with the priest," Rinaldi said. "Where are all the good old priest-baiters? Where is Caval-canti? Where is Brundi? Where is Cesare? Do I have to bait this priest alone without support?"

"He is a good priest," said the major.

"He is a good priest," said Rinaldi. "But still a priest. I try to make the mess like the old days. I want to make Federico happy. To hell with you, priest!"

I saw the major look at him and notice that he was drunk. His thin face was white. The line of his hair was very black against the white of his forehead.

"It's all right, Rinaldo," said the priest. "It's all right."

"To hell with you," said Rinaldi. "To hell with the whole damn business." He sat back in his chair.

"He's been under a strain and he's tired," the major said to me.

He finished his meat and wiped up the gravy with a piece of bread.

"I don't give a damn," Rinaldi said to the table. "To hell with the whole business." He looked defiantly around the table, his eyes flat, his face pale.

"All right," I said. "To hell with the whole damn business."

"No, no," said Rinaldi. "You can't do it. You can't do it. I say you can't do it. You're dry and you're empty and there's nothing else. There's nothing else I tell you. Not a damned thing. I know, when I stop working."

The priest shook his head. The orderly took away the stew dish.

"What are you eating meat for?" Rinaldi turned to the priest. "Don't you know it's Friday?"

"It's Thursday," the priest said.

"It's a lie. It's Friday. You're eating the body of our Lord. It's God-meat. I know. It's dead Austrian. That's what you're eating."

"The white meat is from officers," I said, completing the old joke.

Rinaldi laughed. He filled his glass.

"Don't mind me," he said. "I'm just a little crazy."

"You ought to have a leave," the priest said.

The major shook his head at him. Rinaldi looked at the priest.

"You think I ought to have a leave?"

The major shook his head at the priest. Rinaldi was looking at the priest.

"Just as you like," the priest said. "Not if you don't want."

"To hell with you," Rinaldi said. "They try to get rid of me. Every night they try to get rid of me. I fight them off. What if I have it. Everybody has it. The whole world's got it. First," he went on, assuming the manner of a lecturer, "it's a little pimple. Then we notice a rash between the shoulders. Then we notice nothing at all. We put our faith in mercury."

"Or salvarsan," the major interrupted quietly.

"A mercurial product," Rinaldi said. He acted very elated now.

"I know something worth two of that. Good old priest," he said. "You'll never get it. Baby will get it. It's an industrial accident. It's a simple industrial accident."

The orderly brought in the sweet and coffee. The dessert was a sort of black bread pudding with hard sauce. The lamp was smoking; the black smoke going close up inside the chimney.

"Bring two candles and take away the lamp," the major said. The orderly brought two lighted candles each in a saucer, and took out the lamp blowing it out. Rinaldi was quiet now. He seemed all right. We talked and after the coffee we all went out into the hall.

"You want to talk to the priest. I have to go in the town," Rinaldi said. "Good-night, priest."

"Good-night, Rinaldo," the priest said.

"I'll see you, Fredi," Rinaldi said.

"Yes," I said. "Come in early." He made a face and went out the door. The major was standing with us. "He's very tired and overworked," he said. "He thinks too he has syphilis. I don't believe it but he may have. He is treating himself for it. Good-night. You will leave before daylight, Enrico?"

"Yes."

"Good-by then," he said. "Good luck. Peduzzi will wake you and go with you."

"Good-by, Signor Maggiore."

"Good-by. They talk about an Austrian offensive but I don't believe it. I hope not. But anyway it won't be here. Gino will tell you everything. The telephone works well now."

"I'll call regularly."

"Please do. Good-night. Don't let Rinaldi drink so much brandy."

"I'll try not to."

"Good-night, priest."

"Good-night, Signor Maggiore."

He went off into his office.

XXVI

I WENT to the door and looked out. It had stopped raining but there was a mist.

"Should we go upstairs?" I asked the priest.

"I can only stay a little while."

"Come on up."

We climbed the stairs and went into my room. I lay down on Rinaldi's bed. The priest sat on my cot that the orderly had set up. It was dark in the room.

"Well," he said, "how are you really?"

"I'm all right. I'm tired to-night."

"I'm tired too, but from no cause."

"What about the war?"

"I think it will be over soon. I don't know why, but I feel it."

"How do you feel it?"

"You know how your major is? Gentle? Many people are like that now."

"I feel that way myself," I said.

"It has been a terrible summer," said the priest. He was surer of himself now than when I had gone away. "You cannot believe how it has been. Except that you have been there and you know how it can be. Many people have realized the war this summer. Officers who I thought could never realize it realize it now."

"What will happen?" I stroked the blanket with my hand.

"I do not know but I do not think it can go on much longer."

"What will happen?"

"They will stop fighting."

"Who?"

"Both sides."

"I hope so," I said.

"You don't believe it?"

"I don't believe both sides will stop fighting at once."

"I suppose not. It is too much to expect. But when I see the changes in men I do not think it can go on."

"Who won the fighting this summer?"

"No one."

"The Austrians won," I said. "They kept them from taking San Gabriele. They've won. They won't stop fighting."

"If they feel as we feel they may stop. They have gone through the same thing."

"No one ever stopped when they were winning."

"You discourage me."

"I can only say what I think."

"Then you think it will go on and on? Nothing will ever happen?"

"I don't know. I only think the Austrians will not stop when they have won a victory. It is in defeat that we become Christian."

"The Austrians are Christians—except for the Bosnians."

"I don't mean technically Christian. I mean like Our Lord."

He said nothing.

"We are all gentler now because we are beaten. How would Our Lord have been if Peter had rescued him in the Garden?"

"He would have been just the same."

"I don't think so," I said.

"You discourage me," he said. "I believe and I pray that something will happen. I have felt it very close."

"Something may happen," I said. "But it will happen only to us. If they felt the way we do, it would be all right. But they have beaten us. They feel another way."

"Many of the soldiers have always felt this way. It is not because they were beaten."

"They were beaten to start with. They were beaten when they took them from their farms and put them in the army. That is why the peasant has wisdom, because he is defeated from the start. Put him in power and see how wise he is."

He did not say anything. He was thinking.

"Now I am depressed myself," I said. "That's why I never think about these things. I never think and yet when I begin to talk I say the things I have found out in my mind without thinking."

"I had hoped for something."

"Defeat?"

"No. Something more."

"There isn't anything more. Except victory. It may be worse."

"I hoped for a long time for victory."

"Me too."

"Now I don't know."

"It has to be one or the other."

"I don't believe in victory any more."

"I don't. But I don't believe in defeat. Though it may be better."

"What do you believe in?"

"In sleep." I said. He stood up.

"I am very sorry to have stayed so long. But I like so to talk with you."

"It is very nice to talk again. I said that about sleeping, meaning nothing."

We stood up and shook hands in the dark.

"I sleep at 307 now," he said.

"I go out on post early to-morrow."

"I'll see you when you come back."

"We'll have a walk and talk together." I walked with him to the door.

"Don't go down," he said. "It is very nice that you are back. Though not so nice for you." He put his hand on my shoulder.

"It's all right for me," I said. "Good-night."

"Good-night. Ciao!"

"Ciao!" I said. I was deadly sleepy.

XXVII

I woke when Rinaldi came in but he did not talk and I went back to sleep again. In the morning I was dressed and gone before it was light. Rinaldi did not wake when I left.

I had not seen the Bainsizza before and it was strange to go up the slope where the Austrians had been, beyond the place on the river where I had been wounded. There was a steep new road and many trucks. Beyond, the road flattened out and I saw woods and steep hills in the mist. There were woods that had been taken quickly and not smashed. Then beyond where the road was not protected by the hills it was screened by matting on the sides and over the top. The road ended in a wrecked village. The lines were up beyond. There was much artillery around. The houses were badly smashed but things were very well organized and there were signboards everywhere. We found Gino and he got us some coffee and later I went with him and met various people and saw the posts. Gino said the British cars were working further down the Bainsizza at Ravne. He had great admiration for the British. There was still a certain amount of shelling, he said, but not many wounded. There would be many sick now the rains had started. The Austrians were supposed to attack but he did not believe it. We were supposed to attack too, but they had not brought up any new troops so he thought that was off too. Food was scarce and he would be glad to get a full meal in Gorizia. What kind of supper had I had? I told him and he said that would be wonderful. He was especially impressed by the *dolce*. I did not describe it in detail, only said it was a *dolce,* and I think he believed it was something more elaborate than bread pudding.

Did I know where he was going to go? I said I didn't but that some of the other cars were at Caporetto. He hoped he would go up that way. It was a nice little place and he liked the high mountain hauling up beyond. He was a nice boy and every one seemed to like him. He said where it really had been hell was at San Gabriele and the attack beyond Lom that had gone bad. He said the Austrians had a great amount of artillery in the woods along Ternova ridge beyond and above us, and shelled the roads badly at night. There was a battery of naval guns that had gotten on his nerves. I would recognize them because of their flat trajectory. You heard the report and then the shriek commenced almost instantly. They usually fired two guns at once, one right after the other, and the fragments from the burst were enormous. He showed me one, a smoothly jagged piece of metal over a foot long. It looked like babbitting metal.

"I don't suppose they are so effective," Gino said. "But they scare me. They all sound as though they came directly for you.

There is the boom, then instantly the shriek and burst. What's the use of not being wounded if they scare you to death?"

He said there were Croats in the lines opposite us now and some Magyars. Our troops were still in the attacking positions. There was no wire to speak of and no place to fall back to if there should be an Austrian attack. There were fine positions for defense along the low mountains that came up out of the plateau but nothing had been done about organizing them for defense. What did I think about the Bainsizza anyway?

I had expected it to be flatter, more like a plateau. I had not realized it was so broken up.

"Alto piano," Gino said, "but no piano."

We went back to the cellar of the house where he lived. I said I thought a ridge that flattened out on top and had a little depth would be easier and more practical to hold than a succession of small mountains. It was no harder to attack up a mountain than on the level, I argued. "That depends on the mountains," he said. "Look at San Gabriele."

"Yes," I said, "but where they had trouble was at the top where it was flat. They got up to the top easy enough."

"Not so easy," he said.

"Yes," I said, "but that was a special case because it was a fortress rather than a mountain, anyway. The Austrians had been fortifying it for years." I meant tactically speaking in a war where there was some movement a succession of mountains were nothing to hold as a line because it was too easy to turn them. You should have possible mobility and a mountain is not very mobile. Also, people always over-shoot down hill. If the flank were turned, the best men would be left on the highest mountains. I did not believe in a war in mountains. I had thought about it a lot, I said. You pinched off one mountain and they pinched off another but when something really started every one had to get down off the mountains.

What were you going to do if you had a mountain frontier? he asked.

I had not worked that out yet, I said, and we both laughed. "But," I said, "in the old days the Austrians were always whipped in the quadrilateral around Verona. They let them come down onto the plain and whipped them there."

"Yes," said Gino. "But those were Frenchmen and you can work out military problems clearly when you are fighting in somebody else's country."

"Yes," I agreed, "when it is your own country you cannot use it so scientifically."

"The Russians did, to trap Napoleon."

"Yes, but they had plenty of country. If you tried to retreat to trap Napoleon in Italy you would find yourself in Brindisi."

"A terrible place," said Gino. "Have you ever been there?"

"Not to stay."

"I am a patriot," Gino said. "But I cannot love Brindisi or Taranto."

"Do you love the Bainsizza?" I asked.

"The soil is sacred," he said. "But I wish it grew more potatoes. You know when we came here we found fields of potatoes the Austrians had planted."

"Has the food really been short?"

"I myself have never had enough to eat but I am a big eater and I have not starved. The mess is average. The regiments in the line get pretty good food but those in support don't get so much. Something is wrong somewhere. There should be plenty of food."

"The dogfish are selling it somewhere else."

"Yes, they give the battalions in the front line as much as they can but the ones in back are very short. They have eaten all the Austrians' potatoes and chestnuts from the woods. They ought to feed them better. We are big eaters. I am sure there is plenty of food. It is very bad for the soldiers to be short of food. Have you ever noticed the difference it makes in the way you think?"

"Yes," I said. "It can't win a war but it can lose one."

"We won't talk about losing. There is enough talk about losing. What has been done this summer cannot have been done in vain."

I did not say anything. I was always embarrassed by the words sacred, glorious, and sacrifice and the expression in vain. We had heard them, sometimes standing in the rain almost out of ear-

shot, so that only the shouted words came through, and had read
them, on proclamations that were slapped up by billposters over
other proclamations, now for a long time, and I had seen nothing
sacred, and the things that were glorious had no glory and the
sacrifices were like the stockyards at Chicago if nothing was done
with the meat except to bury it. There were many words that
you could not stand to hear and finally only the names of places
had dignity. Certain numbers were the same way and certain
dates and these with the names of the places were all you could
say and have them mean anything. Abstract words such as glory,
honor, courage, or hallow were obscene beside the concrete names
of villages, the numbers of roads, the names of rivers, the numbers
of regiments and the dates. Gino was a patriot, so he said things
that separated us sometimes, but he was also a fine boy and I understood his being a patriot. He was born one. He left with Peduzzi
in the car to go back to Gorizia.

It stormed all that day. The wind drove down the rain and
everywhere there was standing water and mud. The plaster of
the broken houses was gray and wet. Late in the afternoon the
rain stopped and from out number two post I saw the bare wet
autumn country with clouds over the tops of the hills and the
straw screening over the roads wet and dripping. The sun came
out once before it went down and shone on the bare woods beyond
the ridge. There were many Austrian guns in the woods on that
ridge but only a few fired. I watched the sudden round puffs of
shrapnel smoke in the sky above a broken farmhouse near where
the line was; soft puffs with a yellow white flash in the centre.
You saw the flash, then heard the crack, then saw the smoke ball
distort and thin in the wind. There were many iron shrapnel balls
in the rubble of the houses and on the road beside the broken
house where the post was, but they did not shell near the post
that afternoon. We loaded two cars and drove down the road
that was screened with wet mats and the last of the sun came
through in the breaks between the strips of mattings. Before we
were out on the clear road behind the hill the sun was down. We
went on down the clear road and as it turned a corner into the

open and went into the square arched tunnel of matting the rain started again.

The wind rose in the night and at three o'clock in the morning with the rain coming in sheets there was a bombardment and the Croatians came over across the mountain meadows and through patches of woods and into the front line. They fought in the dark in the rain and a counter-attack of scared men from the second line drove them back. There was much shelling and many rockets in the rain and machine-gun and rifle fire all along the line. They did not come again and it was quieter and between the gusts of wind and rain we could hear the sound of a great bombardment far to the north.

The wounded were coming into the post, some were carried on stretchers, some walking and some were brought on the backs of men that came across the field. They were wet to the skin and all were scared. We filled two cars with stretcher cases as they came up from the cellar of the post and as I shut the door of the second car and fastened it I felt the rain on my face turn to snow. The flakes were coming heavy and fast in the rain.

When daylight came the storm was still blowing but the snow had stopped. It had melted as it fell on the wet ground and now it was raining again. There was another attack just after daylight but it was unsuccessful. We expected an attack all day but it did not come until the sun was going down. The bombardment started to the south below the long wooded ridge where the Austrian guns were concentrated. We expected a bombardment but it did not come. It was getting dark. Guns were firing from the field behind the village and the shells, going away, had a comfortable sound.

We heard that the attack to the south had been unsuccessful. They did not attack that night but we heard that they had broken through to the north. In the night word came that we were to prepare to retreat. The captain at the post told me this. He had it from the Brigade. A little while later he came from the telephone and said it was a lie. The Brigade had received orders that the line of the Bainsizza should be held no matter what happened. I asked about the break-through and he said that he had heard at the

Brigade that the Austrians had broken through the twenty-seventh army corps up toward Caporetto. There had been a great battle in the north all day.

"If those bastards let them through we are cooked," he said.

"It's Germans that are attacking," one of the medical officers said. The word Germans was something to be frightened of. We did not want to have anything to do with the Germans.

"There are fifteen divisions of Germans," the medical officer said. "They have broken through and we will be cut off."

"At the Brigade, they say this line is to be held. They say they have not broken through badly and that we will hold a line across the mountains from Monte Maggiore."

"Where do they hear this?"

"From the Division."

"The word that we were to retreat came from the Division."

"We work under the Army Corps," I said. "But here I work under you. Naturally when you tell me to go I will go. But get the orders straight."

"The orders are that we stay here. You clear the wounded from here to the clearing station."

"Sometimes we clear from the clearing station to the field hospitals too," I said. "Tell me, I have never seen a retreat—if there is a retreat how are all the wounded evacuated?"

"They are not. They take as many as they can and leave the rest."

"What will I take in the cars?"

"Hospital equipment."

"All right," I said.

The next night the retreat started. We heard the Germans and Austrians had broken through in the north and were coming down the mountain valleys toward Cividale and Udine. The retreat was orderly, wet and sullen. In the night, going slowly along the crowded roads we passed troops marching under the rain, guns, horses pulling wagons, mules, motor trucks, all moving away from the front. There was no more disorder than in an advance.

That night we helped empty the field hospitals that had been set up in the least ruined villages of the plateau, taking the wounded down to Plava on the river-bed: and the next day hauled all day in the rain to evacuate the hospitals and clearing station at Plava. It rained steadily and the army of the Bainsizza moved down off the plateau in the October rain and across the river where the great victories had commenced in the spring of that year. We came into Gorizia in the middle of the next day. The rain had stopped and the town was nearly empty. As we came up the street they were loading the girls from the soldiers' whorehouse into a truck. There were seven girls and they had on their hats and coats and carried small suitcases. Two of them were crying. Of the others one smiled at us and put out her tongue and fluttered it up and down. She had thick full lips and black eyes.

I stopped the car and went over and spoke to the matron. The girls from the officers' house had left early that morning, she said. Where were they going? To Conegliano, she said. The truck started. The girl with thick lips put out her tongue again at us. The matron waved. The two girls kept on crying. The others looked interestedly out at the town. I got back in the car.

"We ought to go with them," Monello said. "That would be a good trip."

"We'll have a good trip," I said.

"We'll have a hell of a trip."

"That's what I mean," I said. We came up the drive to the villa.

"I'd like to be there when some of those tough babies climb in and try and hop them."

"You think they will?"

"Sure. Everybody in the Second Army knows that matron."

We were outside the villa.

"They call her the Mother Superior," Bonello said. "The girls are new but everybody knows her. They must have brought them up just before the retreat."

"They'll have a time."

"I'll say they'll have a time. I'd like to have a crack at them for nothing. They charge too much at that house anyway. The government gyps us."

"Take the car out and have the mechanics go over it," I said.

"Change the oil and check the differential. Fill it up and then get some sleep."

"Yes, Signor Tenente."

The villa was empty. Rinaldi was gone with the hospital. The major was gone taking hospital personnel in the staff car. There was a note on the window for me to fill the cars with the material piled in the hall and to proceed to Pordenone. The mechanics were gone already. I went out back to the garage. The other two cars came in while I was there and their drivers got down. It was starting to rain again.

"I'm so —— sleepy I went to sleep three times coming here from Plava," Piani said. "What are we going to do, Tenente?"

"We'll change the oil, grease them, fill them up, then take them around in front and load up the junk they've left."

"Then do we start?"

"No, we'll sleep for three hours."

"Christ I'm glad to sleep," Bonello said. "I couldn't keep awake driving."

"How's your car, Aymo?" I asked.

"It's all right."

"Get me a monkey suit and I'll help you with the oil."

"Don't you do that, Tenente," Aymo said. "It's nothing to do. You go and pack your things."

"My things are all packed," I said. "I'll go and carry out the stuff that they left for us. Bring the cars around as soon as they're ready."

They brought the cars around to the front of the villa and we loaded them with the hospital equipment which was piled in the hallway. When it was all in, the three cars stood in line down the driveway under the trees in the rain. We went inside.

"Make a fire in the kitchen and dry your things," I said.

"I don't care about dry clothes," Piani said. "I want to sleep."

"I'm going to sleep on the major's bed," Bonello said. "I'm going to sleep where the old man corks off."

"I don't care where I sleep," Piani said.

"There are two beds in here." I opened the door.

"I never knew what was in that room," Bonello said.

"That was old fish-face's room," Piani said.

"You two sleep in there," I said. "I'll wake you."

"The Austrians will wake us if you sleep too long, Tenente," Bonello said.

"I won't oversleep," I said. "Where's Aymo?"

"He went out in the kitchen."

"Get to sleep," I said.

"I'll sleep," Piani said. "I've been asleep sitting up all day. The whole top of my head kept coming down over my eyes."

"Take your boots off," Bonello said. "That's old fish-face's bed."

"Fish-face is nothing to me." Piani lay on the bed, his muddy boots straight out, his head on his arm. I went out to the kitchen. Aymo had a fire in the stove and a kettle of water on.

"I thought I'd start some *pasta asciutta*," he said. "We'll be hungry when we wake up."

"Aren't you sleepy, Bartolomeo?"

"Not so sleepy. When the water boils I'll leave it. The fire will go down."

"You'd better get some sleep," I said. "We can eat cheese and monkey meat."

"This is better," he said. "Something hot will be good for those two anarchists. You go to sleep, Tenente."

"There's a bed in the major's room."

"You sleep there."

"No, I'm going up to my old room. Do you want a drink, Bartolomeo?"

"When we go, Tenente. Now it wouldn't do me any good."

"If you wake in three hours and I haven't called you, wake me, will you?"

"I haven't any watch, Tenente."

"There's a clock on the wall in the major's room."

"All right."

I went out then through the dining-room and the hall and up the marble stairs to the room where I had lived with Rinaldi. It was raining outside. I went to the window and looked out. It was getting dark and I saw the three cars standing in line under the trees. The trees were dripping in the rain. It was cold and the drops hung to the branches. I went back to Rinaldi's bed and lay down and let sleep take me.

We ate in the kitchen before we started. Aymo had a basin of spaghetti with onions and tinned meat chopped up in it. We sat around the table and drank two bottles of the wine that had been left in the cellar of the villa. It was dark outside and still raining. Piani sat at the table very sleepy.

"I like a retreat better than an advance," Bonello said. "On a retreat we drink barbera."

"We drink it now. To-morrow maybe we drink rain-water," Aymo said.

"To-morrow we'll be in Udine. We'll drink champagne. That's where the slackers live. Wake up, Piani! We'll drink champagne to-morrow in Udine!"

"I'm awake," Piani said. He filled his plate with the spaghetti and meat. "Couldn't you find tomato sauce, Barto?"

"There wasn't any," Aymo said.

"We'll drink champagne in Udine," Bonello said. He filled his glass with the clear red barbera.

"We may drink —— before Udine," Piani said.

"Have you eaten enough, Tenente?" Aymo asked.

"I've got plenty. Give me the bottle, Bartolomeo."

"I have a bottle apiece to take in the cars," Aymo said.

"Did you sleep at all?"

"I don't need much sleep. I slept a little."

"To-morrow we'll sleep in the king's bed," Bonello said. He was feeling very good.

"To-morrow maybe we'll sleep in ——," Piani said.

"I'll sleep with the queen," Bonello said. He looked to see how I took the joke.

"You'll sleep with ——," Piani said sleepily.

"That's treason, Tenente," Bonello said. "Isn't that treason?"

"Shut up," I said. "You get too funny with a little wine." Outside it was raining hard. I looked at my watch. It was half-past nine.

"It's time to roll," I said and stood up.

"Who are you going to ride with, Tenente?" Bonello asked.

"With Aymo. Then you come. Then Piani. We'll start out on the road for Cormons."

"I'm afraid I'll go to sleep," Piani said.

"All right. I'll ride with you. Then Bonello. Then Aymo."

"That's the best way," Piani said. "Because I'm so sleepy."

"I'll drive and you sleep awhile."

"No. I can drive just so long as I know somebody will wake me up if I go to sleep."

"I'll wake you up. Put out the lights, Barto."

"You might as well leave them," Bonello said. "We've got no more use for this place."

"I have a small locker trunk in my room," I said. "Will you help take it down, Piani?"

"We'll take it," Piani said. "Come on, Aldo." He went off into the hall with Bonello. I heard them going upstairs.

"This was a fine place," Bartolomeo Aymo said. He put two bottles of wine and half a cheese into his haversack. "There won't be a place like this again. Where will they retreat to, Tenente?"

"Beyond the Tagliamento, they say. The hospital and the sector are to be at Pordenone."

"This is a better town than Pordenone."

"I don't know Pordenone," I said. "I've just been through there."

"It's not much of a place," Aymo said.

XXVIII

As we moved out through the town it was empty in the rain and the dark except for columns of troops and guns that were going through the main street. There were many trucks too and some carts going through on other streets and converging on the main road. When we were out past the tanneries onto the main road the troops, the motor trucks, the horse-drawn carts and the guns were in one wide slow-moving column. We moved slowly but steadily in the rain, the radiator cap of our car almost against the tailboard of a truck that was loaded high, the load covered with wet canvas. Then the truck stopped. The whole column was stopped. It started again and we went a little farther, then stopped. I got out and walked ahead, going between the trucks and carts and under the wet necks of the horses. The block was farther ahead. I left the road, crossed the ditch on a footboard and walked along the field beyond the ditch. I could see the stalled column between the trees in the rain as I went forward across from it in the field. I went about a mile. The column did not move, although, on the other side beyond the stalled vehicles I could see the troops moving. I went back to the cars. This block might extend as far as Udine. Piani was asleep over the wheel. I climbed up beside him and went to sleep too. Several hours later I heard the truck ahead of us grinding into gear. I woke Piani and we started, moving a few yards, then stopping, then going on again. It was still raining.

The column stalled again in the night and did not start. I got down and went back to see Aymo and Benello. Bonello had two sergeants of engineers on the seat of his car with him. They stiffened when I came up.

"They were left to do something to a bridge," Bonello said. "They can't find their unit so I gave them a ride."

"With the Sir Lieutenant's permission."

"With permission," I said.

"The lieutenant is an American," Bonello said. "He'll give anybody a ride."

One of the sergeants smiled. The other asked Bonello if I was an Italian from North or South America.

"He's not an Italian. He's North American English."

The sergeants were polite but did not believe it. I left them and went back to Aymo. He had two girls on the seat with him and was sitting back in the corner and smoking.

"Barto, Barto," I said. He laughed.

"Talk to them, Tenente," he said. "I can't understand them. Hey!" he put his hand on the girl's thigh and squeezed it in a friendly way. The girl drew her shawl tight around her and pushed his hand away. "Hey!" he said. "Tell the Tenente your name and what you're doing here."

The girl looked at me fiercely. The other girl kept her eyes down. The girl who looked at me said something in a dialect I could not understand a word of. She was plump and dark and looked about sixteen.

"Sorella?" I asked and pointed at the other girl.

She nodded her head and smiled.

"All right," I said and patted her knee. I felt her stiffen away when I touched her. The sister never looked up. She looked perhaps a year younger. Aymo put his hand on the elder girl's thigh and she pushed it away. He laughed at her.

"Good man," he pointed at himself. "Good man," he pointed at me. "Don't you worry." The girl looked at him fiercely. The pair of them were like two wild birds.

"What does she ride with me for if she doesn't like me?" Aymo asked. "They got right up in the car the minute I motioned to them." He turned to the girl. "Don't worry," he said. "No danger of ———," using the vulgar word. "No place for ———." I could see she understood the word and that was all. Her eyes looked at him very scared. She pulled the shawl tight. "Car all full," Aymo said. "No danger ———. No place for ———." Every time he said the word the girl stiffened a little. Then sitting stiffly and looking at him she began to cry. I saw her lips working and then tears came down her plump cheeks. Her sister, not looking up, took her hand and they sat there together. The older one, who had been so fierce, began to sob.

"I guess I scared her," Aymo said. "I didn't mean to scare her."

Bartolomeo brought out his knapsack and cut off two pieces of cheese. "Here," he said. "Stop crying."

The older girl shook her head and still cried, but the younger girl took the cheese and commenced to eat. After a while the younger girl gave her sister the second piece of cheese and they both ate. The older sister still sobbed a little.

"She'll be all right after a while," Aymo said.

An idea came to him. "Virgin?" he asked the girl next to him. She nodded her head vigorously. "Virgin too?" he pointed to the sister. Both the girls nodded their heads and the elder said something in dialect.

"That's all right," Bartolomeo said. "That's all right."

Both the girls seemed cheered.

I left them sitting together with Aymo sitting back in the corner and went back to Piani's car. The column of vehicles did not move but the troops kept passing alongside. It was still raining hard and I thought some of the stops in the movement of the column might be from cars with wet wiring. More likely they were from horses or men going to sleep. Still, traffic could tie up in cities when every one was awake. It was the combination of horse and motor vehicles. They did not help each other any. The peasants' carts did not help much either. Those were a couple of fine girls with Barto. A retreat was no place for two virgins. Real virgins. Probably very religious. If there were no war we would probably all be in bed. In bed I lay me down my head. Bed and board. Stiff as a board in bed. Catherine was in bed now between two sheets, over her and under her. Which side did she sleep on? Maybe she wasn't asleep. Maybe she was lying thinking about me. Blow, blow, ye western wind. Well, it blew and it wasn't the small rain but the big rain down that rained. It rained all night. You knew it rained down that rained. Look at it. Christ, that my love were in my arms and I in my bed again. That my love Catherine. That my sweet love Catherine down might rain. Blow her again to me. Well, we were in it. Every one was caught in it and the small rain would not quiet it. "Good-night, Catherine," I said out loud. "I hope you sleep well. If it's too uncomfortable, darling, lie on the other side," I said. "I'll get you some cold water. In a little while it will be morning and then it won't be so bad. I'm sorry he makes you so uncomfortable. Try and go to sleep, sweet."

I was asleep all the time, she said. You've been talking in your sleep. Are you all right?

Are you really there?

Of course I'm here. I wouldn't go way. This doesn't make any difference between us.

You're so lovely and sweet. You wouldn't go away in the night, would you?

Of course I wouldn't go away. I'm always here. I come whenever you want me.

"———," Piani said. "They've started again."

"I was dopey," I said. I looked at my watch. It was three o'clock in the morning. I reached back behind the seat for a bottle of the barbera.

"You talked out loud," Piani said.

"I was having a dream in English," I said.

The rain was slacking and we were moving along. Before daylight we were stalled again and when it was light we were at a little rise in the ground and I saw the road of the retreat stretched out far ahead, everything stationary except for the infantry filtering through. We started to move again but seeing the rate of progress in the daylight, I knew we were going to have to get off that main road some way and go across country if we ever hoped to reach Udine.

In the night many peasants had joined the column from the roads of the country and in the column there were carts loaded with household goods; there were mirrors projecting up between mattresses, and chickens and ducks tied to carts. There was a sewing-machine on the cart ahead of us in the rain. They had saved the most valuable things. On some carts the women sat huddled from the rain and others walked beside the carts keeping as close to them as they could. There were dogs now in the column, keeping under the wagons as they moved along. The road was muddy, the ditches at the side were high with water and beyond the trees that lined the roads the fields looked too wet and too soggy to try to cross. I got down from the car and worked up the road a way, looking for a place where I could see ahead to find a side-road we could take across country. I knew there were many side-roads but did not want one that would lead to nothing. I could not remember them because we had always passed them bowling along in the car on the main road and they all looked much alike. Now I knew we must find one if we hoped to get through. No one knew where the Austrians were nor how things were going but I was certain that if the rains should stop and planes come over and get to work on that column that it would be all over. All that was needed was for a few men to leave their trucks or a few horses be killed to tie up completely the movement on the road.

The rain was not falling so heavily now and I thought it might clear. I went ahead along the edge of the road and when there was a small road that led off to the north between two fields with a hedge of trees on both sides, I thought that we had better take it and hurried back to the cars. I told Piani to turn off and went back to tell Bonello and Aymo.

"If it leads nowhere we can turn around and cut back in," I said.

"What about these?" Bonello asked. His two sergeants were beside him on the seat. They were unshaven but still military looking in the early morning.

"They'll be good to push," I said. I went back to Aymo and told him we were going to try it across country.

"What about my virgin family?" Aymo asked. The two girls were asleep.

"They won't be very useful," I said. "You ought to have some one that could push."

"They could go back in the car," Aymo said. "There's room in the car."

"All right if you want them," I said. "Pick up somebody with a wide back to push."

"Bersaglieri," Aymo smiled. "They have the widest backs. They measure them. How do you feel, Tenente?"

"Fine. How are you?"

"Fine. But very hungry."

"There ought to be something up that road and we will stop and eat."

"How's your leg, Tenente?"

"Fine," I said. Standing on the step and looking up ahead I could see Piani's car pulling out onto the little side-road and starting up it, his car showing through the hedge of bare branches. Bonello turned off and followed him and then Piani worked his way out and we followed the two ambulances ahead along the narrow road between hedges. It led to a farmhouse. We found Piani and Bonello stopped in the farmyard. The house was low and long with a trellis with a grape-vine over the door. There was a well in the yard and Piani was getting up water to fill his radiator. So much going in low gear had boiled it out. The farmhouse was deserted. I looked back down the road, the farmhouse was on a slight elevation above the plain, and we could see over the country, and saw the road, the hedges, the fields and the line of trees along the main road where the retreat was passing. The two sergeants were looking through the house. The girls were awake and looking at the court-yard, the well and the two big ambulances in front of the farm-house, with three drivers at the well. One of the sergeants came out with a clock in his hand.

"Put it back," I said. He looked at me, went in the house and came back without the clock.

"Where's your partner?" I asked.

"He's gone to the latrine." He got up on the seat of the ambulance. He was afraid we would leave him.

"What about breakfast, Tenente?" Bonello asked. "We could eat something. It wouldn't take very long."

"Do you think this road going down on the other side will lead to anything?"

"Sure."

"All right. Let's eat." Piani and Bonello went in the house.

"Come on," Aymo said to the girls. He held his hand to help them down. The older sister shook her head. They were not going into any deserted house. They looked after us.

"They are difficult," Aymo said. We went into the farmhouse together. It was large and dark, an abandoned feeling. Bonello and Piani were in the kitchen.

"There's not much to eat," Piani said. "They've cleaned it out." Bonello sliced a big cheese on the heavy kitchen table.

"Where was the cheese?"

"In the cellar. Piani found wine too and apples."

"That's a good breakfast."

Piani was taking the wooden cork out of a big wicker-covered wine jug. He tipped it and poured a copper pan full.

"It smells all right," he said. "Find some beakers, Barto."

The two sergeants came in.

"Have some cheese, sergeants," Bonello said.

"We should go," one of the sergeants said, eating his cheese and drinking a cup of wine.

"We'll go. Don't worry," Bonello said.

"An army travels on its stomach," I said.

"What?" asked the sergeant.

"It's better to eat."

"Yes. But time is precious."

"I believe the bastards have eaten already," Piani said. The sergeants looked at him. They hated the lot of us.

"You know the road?" one of them asked me.

"No," I said. They looked at each other.

"We would do best to start," the first one said.

"We are starting," I said. I drank another cup of the red wine. It tasted very good after the cheese and apple.

"Bring the cheese," I said and went out. Bonello came out carrying the great jug of wine.

"That's too big," I said. He looked at it regretfully.

"I guess it is," he said. "Give me the canteens to fill." He filled the canteens and some of the wine ran out on the stone paving of the courtyard. Then he picked up the wine jug and put it just inside the door.

"The Austrians can find it without breaking the door down," he said.

"We'll roll," I said. "Piani and I will go ahead." The two engineers were already on the seat beside Bonello. The girls were eating cheese and apples. Aymo was smoking. We started off down the narrow road. I looked back at the two cars coming and the farmhouse. It was a fine, low, solid stone house and the ironwork of the well was very good. Ahead of us the road was narrow and muddy and there was a high hedge on either side. Behind, the cars were following closely.

XXIX

At noon we were stuck in a muddy road about, as nearly as we could figure, ten kilometres from Udine. The rain had stopped during the forenoon and three times we had heard planes coming, seen them pass overhead, watched them go far to the left and heard them bombing on the main highroad. We had worked through a network of secondary roads and had taken many roads that were blind, but had always, by backing up and finding another road, gotten closer to Udine. Now, Aymo's car, in backing so that we might get out of a blind road, had gotten into the soft earth at the side and the wheels, spinning, had dug deeper and deeper until the car rested on its differential. The thing to do now was to dig out in front of the wheels, put in brush so that the chains could grip, and then push until the car was on the road. We were all down on the road around the car. The two sergeants looked at the car and examined the wheels. Then they started off down the road without a word. I went after them.

"Come on," I said. "Cut some brush."

"We have to go," one said.

"Get busy," I said, "and cut brush."

"We have to go," one said. The other said nothing. They were in a hurry to start. They would not look at me.

"I order you to come back to the car and cut brush," I said. The one sergeant turned. "We have to go on. In a little while you will be cut off. You can't order us. You're not our officer."

"I order you to cut brush," I said. They turned and started down the road.

"Halt," I said. They kept on down the muddy road, the hedge on either side. "I order you to halt," I called. They went a little faster. I opened up my holster, took the pistol, aimed at the one who had talked the most, and fired. I missed and they both started to run. I shot three times and dropped one. The other went through the hedge and was out of sight. I fired at him through the hedge as he ran across the field. The pistol clicked empty and I put in another clip. I saw it was too far to shoot at the second sergeant. He was far across the field, running, his head held low. I commenced to reload the empty clip. Bonello came up.

"Let me go finish him," he said. I handed him the pistol and he walked down to where the sergeant of engineers lay face down across the road. Bonello leaned over, put the pistol against the man's head and pulled the trigger. The pistol did not fire.

"You have to cock it," I said. He cocked it and fired twice. He took hold of the sergeant's legs and pulled him to the side of the road so he lay beside the hedge. He came back and handed me the pistol.

"The son of a bitch," he said. He looked toward the sergeant. "You see me shoot him, Tenente?"

"We've got to get the brush quickly," I said. "Did I hit the other one at all?"

"I don't think so," Aymo said. "He was too far away to hit with a pistol."

"The dirty scum," Piani said. We were all cutting twigs and branches. Everything had been taken out of the car. Bonello was digging out in front of the wheels. When we were ready Aymo started the car and put it into gear. The wheels spun round throwing brush and mud. Bonello and I pushed until we could feel our joints crack. The car would not move.

"Rock her back and forth, Barto," I said.

He drove the engine in reverse, then forward. The wheels only dug in deeper. Then the car was resting on the differential again, and the wheels spun freely in the holes they had dug. I straightened up.

"We'll try her with a rope," I said.

"I don't think it's any use, Tenente. You can't get a straight pull."

"We have to try it." I said. "She won't come out any other way."

Piani's and Bonello's cars could only move straight ahead down the narrow road. We roped both cars together and pulled. The wheels only pulled sideways against the ruts.

"It's no good," I shouted. "Stop it."

Piani and Bonello got down from their cars and came back.

Aymo got down. The girls were up the road about forty yards sitting on a stone wall.

"What do you say, Tenente?" Bonello asked.

"We'll dig out and try once more with the brush," I said. I looked down the road. It was my fault. I had led them up here. The sun was almost out from behind the clouds and the body of the sergeant lay beside the hedge.

"We'll put his coat and cape under," I said. Bonello went to get them. I cut brush and Aymo and Piani dug out in front and between the wheels. I cut the cape, then ripped it in two, and laid it under the wheel in the mud, then piled brush for the wheels to catch. We were ready to start and Aymo got up on the seat and started the car. The wheels spun and we pushed and pushed. But it wasn't any use.

"It's ———ed," I said. "Is there anything you want in the car, Barto?"

Aymo climbed up with Bonello, carrying the cheese and two bottles of wine and his cape. Bonello, sitting behind the wheel, was looking through the pockets of the sergeant's coat.

"Better throw the coat away," I said. "What about Barto's virgins?"

"They can get in the back," Piani said. "I don't think we are going far."

I opened the back door of the ambulance.

"Come on," I said. "Get in." The two girls climbed in and sat in the corner. They seemed to have taken no notice of the shooting. I looked back up the road. The sergeant lay in his dirty long-sleeved underwear. I got up with Piani and we started. We were going to try to cross the field. When the road entered the field I got down and walked ahead. If we could get across, there was a road on the other side. We could not get across. It was too soft and muddy for the cars. When they were finally and completely stalled, the wheels dug in to the hubs, we left them in the field and started on foot for Udine.

When we came back to the road which led toward the main highway I pointed down it to the two girls.

"Go down there," I said. "You'll meet people." They looked at me. I took out my pocket-book and gave them each a ten-lira note. "Go down there," I said, pointing. "Friends! Family!"

They did not understand but they held the money tightly and started down the road. They looked back as though they were afraid I might take the money back. I watched them go down the road, their shawls close around them, looking back apprehensively at us. The three drivers were laughing.

"How much will you give me to go in that direction, Tenente?" Bonello asked.

"They're better off in a bunch of people than alone if they catch them," I said.

"Give me two hundred lire and I'll walk straight back toward Austria," Bonello said.

"They'd take it away from you," Piani said.

"Maybe the war will be over," Aymo said. We were going up the road as fast as we could. The sun was trying to come through. Beside the road were mulberry trees. Through the trees I could see our two big moving-vans of cars stuck in the field. Piani looked back too.

"They'll have to build a road to get them out," he said.

"I wish to Christ we had bicycles," Bonello said.

"Do they ride bicycles in America?" Aymo asked.

"They used to."

"Here it is a great thing," Aymo said. "A bicycle is a splendid thing."

"I wish to Christ we had bicycles," Bonello said. "I'm no walker."

"Is that firing?" I asked. I thought I could hear firing a long way away.

"I don't know," Aymo said. He listened.

"I think so," I said.

"The first thing we will see will be the cavalry," Piani said.

"I don't think they've got any cavalry."

"I hope to Christ not," Bonello said. "I don't want to be stuck on a lance by any —— cavalry."

"You certainly shot that sergeant, Tenente," Piani said. We were walking fast.

"I killed him," Bonello said. "I never killed anybody in this war, and all my life I've wanted to kill a sergeant."

"You killed him on the sit all right," Piani said. "He wasn't flying very fast when you killed him."

"Never mind. That's one thing I can always remember. I killed that ——— of a sergeant."

"What will you say in confession?" Aymo asked.

"I'll say, 'Bless me, father, I killed a sergeant.'" They all laughed.

"He's an anarchist," Piani said. "He doesn't go to church."

"Piani's an anarchist too," Bonello said.

"Are you really anarchists?" I asked.

"No, Tenente. We're socialists. We come from Imola."

"Haven't you ever been there?"

"No."

"By Christ it's a fine place, Tenente. You come there after the war and we'll show you something."

"Are you all socialists?"

"Everybody."

"Is it a fine town?"

"Wonderful. You never saw a town like that."

"How did you get to be socialists?"

"We're all socialists. Everybody is a socialist. We've always been socialists."

"You come, Tenente. We'll make you a socialist too."

Ahead the road turned off to the left and there was a little hill and, beyond a stone wall, an apple orchard. As the road went uphill they ceased talking. We walked along together all going fast against time.

XXX

LATER we were on a road that led to a river. There was a long line of abandoned trucks and carts on the road leading up to the bridge. No one was in sight. The river was high and the bridge had been blown up in the centre; the stone arch was fallen into the river and the brown water was going over it. We went on up the bank looking for a place to cross. Up ahead I knew there was a railway bridge and I thought we might be able to get across there. The path was wet and muddy. We did not see any troops; only abandoned trucks and stores. Along the river bank there was nothing and no one but the wet brush and muddy ground. We went up to the bank and finally we saw the railway bridge.

"What a beautiful bridge," Aymo said. It was a long plain iron bridge across what was usually a dry river-bed.

"We'd better hurry and get across before they blow it up," I said.

"There's nobody to blow it up," Piani said. "They're all gone."

"It's probably mined," Bonello said. "You cross first, Tenente."

"Listen to the anarchist," Aymo said. "Make him go first."

"I'll go," I said. "It won't be mined to blow up with one man."

"You see," Piani said. "That is brains. Why haven't you brains, anarchist?"

"If I had brains I wouldn't be here," Bonello said.

"That's pretty good, Tenente," Aymo said.

"That's pretty good," I said. We were close to the bridge now. The sky had clouded over again and it was raining a little. The bridge looked long and solid. We climbed up the embankment.

"Come one at a time," I said and started across the bridge. I watched the ties and the rails for any trip-wires or signs of explosive but I saw nothing. Down below the gaps in the ties the river ran muddy and fast. Ahead across the wet countryside I could see Udine in the rain. Across the bridge I looked back. Just up the river was another bridge. As I watched, a yellow mud-colored motor car crossed it. The sides of the bridge were high and the body of the car, once on, was out of sight. But I saw the heads of the driver, the man on the seat with him, and the two men on the rear seat. They all wore German helmets. Then the car was over the bridge and out of sight behind the trees and the abandoned vehicles on the road. I waved to Aymo who was crossing and to the others to come on. I climbed down and crouched beside the railway embankment. Aymo came down with me.

"Did you see the car?" I asked.

"No. We were watching you."

"A German staff car crossed on the upper bridge."

"A staff car?"

"Yes."

"Holy Mary."

The others came and we all crouched in the mud behind the embankment, looking across the rails at the bridge, the line of trees, the ditch and the road.

"Do you think we're cut off then, Tenente?"

"I don't know. All I know is a German staff car went along that road."

"You don't feel funny, Tenente? You haven't got strange feelings in the head?"

"Don't be funny, Bonello."

"What about a drink?" Piani asked. "If we're cut off we might as well have a drink." He unhooked his canteen and uncorked it.

"Look! Look!" Aymo said and pointed toward the road. Along the top of the stone bridge we could see German helmets moving. They were bent forward and moved smoothly, almost supernaturally, along. As they came off the bridge we saw them. They were bicycle troops. I saw the faces of the first two. They were ruddy and healthy-looking. Their helmets came low down over their foreheads and the side of their faces. Their carbines were clipped to the frame of the bicycles. Stick bombs hung handle down from their belts. Their helmets and their gray uniforms were wet and they rode easily, looking ahead and to both sides. There were two—then four in line, then two, then almost a dozen; then another dozen—then one alone. They did not talk but we could not have heard them because of the noise from the river. They were gone out of sight up the road.

"Holy Mary," Aymo said.

"They were Germans," Piani said. "Those weren't Austrians."

"Why isn't there somebody here to stop them?" I said. "Why haven't they blown the bridge up? Why aren't there machine-guns along this embankment?"

"You tell us, Tenente," Bonello said.

I was very angry.

"The whole bloody thing is crazy. Down below they blow up a little bridge. Here they leave a bridge on the main road. Where is everybody? Don't they try and stop them at all?"

"You tell us, Tenente," Bonello said. I shut up. It was none of my business; all I had to do was to get to Pordenone with three ambulances. I had failed at that. All I had to do now was get to Pordenone. I probably could not even get to Udine. The hell I couldn't. The thing to do was to be calm and not get shot or captured.

"Didn't you have a canteen open?" I asked Piani. He handed it to me. I took a long drink. "We might as well start," I said. "There's no hurry though. Do you want to eat something?"

"This is no place to stay," Bonello said.

"All right. We'll start."

"Should we keep on this side—out of sight?"

"We'll be better off on top. They may come along this bridge too. We don't want them on top of us before we see them."

We walked along the railroad track. On both sides of us stretched the wet plain. Ahead across the plain was the hill of Udine. The roofs fell away from the castle on the hill. We could see the campanile and the clock-tower. There were many mulberry trees in the fields. Ahead I saw a place where the rails were torn up. The ties had been dug out too and thrown down the embankment.

"Down! down!" Aymo said. We dropped down beside the embankment. There was another group of bicyclists passing along the road. I looked over the edge and saw them go on.

"They saw us but they went on," Aymo said.

"We'll get killed up there, Tenente," Bonello said.

"They don't want us," I said. "They're after something else. We're in more danger if they should come on us suddenly."

"I'd rather walk here out of sight," Bonello said.

"All right. We'll walk along the tracks."

"Do you think we can get through?" Aymo asked.

"Sure. There aren't very many of them yet. We'll go through in the dark."

"What was that staff car doing?"

"Christ knows," I said. We kept on up the tracks. Bonello tired of walking in the mud of the embankment and came up with the rest of us. The railway moved south away from the highway now and we could not see what passed along the road. A short bridge over a canal was blown up but we climbed across on what was left of the span. We heard firing ahead of us.

We came up on the railway beyond the canal. It went on straight toward the town across the low fields. We could see the line of the other railway ahead of us. To the north was the main road where we had seen the cyclists; to the south there was a small branch-road across the fields with thick trees on each side. I thought we had better cut to the south and work around the town that way and across country toward Campoformio and the main road to the Tagliamento. We could avoid the main line of the retreat by keeping to the secondary roads beyond Udine. I knew there were plenty of side-roads across the plain. I started down the embankment.

"Come on," I said. We would make for the side-road and work to the south of the town. We all started down the embankment. A shot was fired at us from the side-road. The bullet went into the mud of the embankment.

"Go on back," I shouted. I started up the embankment, slipping in the mud. The drivers were ahead of me. I went up the embankment as fast as I could go. Two more shots came from the thick brush and Aymo, as he was crossing the tracks, lurched, tripped and fell face down. We pulled him down on the other side and turned him over. "His head ought to be uphill," I said. Piani moved him around. He lay in the mud on the side of the embankment, his feet pointing downhill, breathing blood irregularly. The three of us squatted over him in the rain. He was hit low in the back of the neck and the bullet had ranged upward and come out under the right eye. He died while I was stopping up the two holes. Piani laid his head down, wiped at his face, with a piece of the emergency dressing, then let it alone.

"The ———," he said.

"They weren't Germans," I said. "There can't be any Germans over there."

"Italians," Piani said, using the word as an epithet, "Italiani!" Bonello said nothing. He was sitting beside Aymo, not looking at him. Piani picked up Aymo's cap where it had rolled down the embankment and put it over his face. He took out his canteen.

"Do you want a drink?" Piani handed Bonello the canteen.

"No," Bonello said. He turned to me. "That might have happened to us any time on the railway tracks."

"No," I said. "It was because we started across the field."

Bonello shook his head. "Aymo's dead," he said. "Who's dead next, Tenente? Where do we go now?"

"Those were Italians that shot," I said. "They weren't Germans."

"I suppose if they were Germans they'd have killed all of us," Bonello said.

"We are in more danger from Italians than Germans," I said. "The rear guard are afraid of everything. The Germans know what they're after."

"You reason it out, Tenente," Bonello said.

"Where do we go now?" Piani asked.

"We better lie up some place till it's dark. If we could get south we'd be all right."

"They'd have to shoot us all to prove they were right the first time," Bonello said. "I'm not going to try them."

"We'll find a place to lie up as near to Udine as we can get and then go through when it's dark."

"Let's go then," Bonello said. We went down the north side of the embankment. I looked back. Aymo lay in the mud with the angle of the embankment. He was quite small and his arms were by his side, his puttee-wrapped legs and muddy boots together, his cap over his face. He looked very dead. It was raining. I had liked him as well as any one I ever knew. I had his papers in my pocket and would write to his family. Ahead across the fields was a farmhouse. There were trees around it and the farm buildings were built against the house. There was a balcony along the second floor held up by columns.

"We better keep a little way apart," I said. "I'll go ahead." I started toward the farmhouse. There was a path across the field.

Crossing the field, I did not know but that some one would fire on us from the trees near the farmhouse or from the farmhouse itself. I walked toward it, seeing it very clearly. The balcony of the second floor merged into the barn and there was hay coming out between the columns. The courtyard was of stone blocks and all the trees were dripping with the rain. There was a big empty two-wheeled cart, the shafts tipped high up in the rain. I came to the courtyard, crossed it, and stood under the shelter of the balcony. The door of the house was open and I went in. Bonello and Piani came in after me. It was dark inside. I went back to the kitchen. There were ashes of a fire on the big open hearth. The pots hung over the ashes, but they were empty. I looked around but I could not find anything to eat.

"We ought to lie up in the barn," I said. "Do you think you could find anything to eat, Piani, and bring it up there?"

"I'll look," Piani said.

"I'll look too," Bonello said.

"All right," I said. "I'll go up and look at the barn." I found a stone stairway that went up from the stable underneath. The stable smelt dry and pleasant in the rain. The cattle were all gone, probably driven off when they left. The barn was half full of hay. There were two windows in the roof, one was blocked with boards, the other was a narrow dormer window on the north side. There was a chute so that hay might be pitched down to the cattle. Beams crossed the opening down into the main floor where the hay-carts drove in when the hay was hauled in to be pitched up. I heard the rain on the roof and smelled the hay and, when I went down, the clean smell of dried dung in the stable. We could pry a board loose and see out of the south window down into the courtyard. The other window looked out on the field toward the north. We could get out of either window onto the roof and down, or go down the hay chute if the stairs were impractical. It was a big barn and we could hide in the hay if we heard any one. It seemed like a good place. I was sure we could have gotten through to the south if they had not fired on us. It was impossible that there were Germans there. They were coming from the north and down the road from Cividale. They could not have come through from the south. The

Italians were even more dangerous. They were frightened and firing on anything they saw. Last night on the retreat we had heard that there had been many Germans in Italian uniforms mixing with the retreat in the north. I did not believe it. That was one of those things you always heard in the war. It was one of the things the enemy always did to you. You did not know any one who went over in German uniform to confuse them. Maybe they did but it sounded difficult. I did not believe the Germans did it. I did not believe they had to. There was no need to confuse our retreat. The size of the army and the fewness of the roads did that. Nobody gave any orders, let alone Germans. Still, they would shoot us for Germans. They shot Aymo. The hay smelled good and lying in a barn in the hay took away all the years in between. We had lain in hay and talked and shot sparrows with an air-rifle when they perched in the triangle cut high up in the wall of the barn. The barn was gone now and one year they had cut the hemlock woods and there were only stumps, dried tree-tops, branches and fireweed where the woods had been. You could not go back. If you did not go forward what happened? You never got back to Milan. And if you got back to Milan what happened? I listened to the firing to the north toward Udine. I could hear machine-gun firing. There was no shelling. That was something. They must have gotten some troops along the road. I looked down in the half-light of the hay-barn and saw Piani standing on the hauling floor. He had a long sausage, a jar of something and two bottles of wine under his arm.

"Come up," I said. "There is the ladder." Then I realized that I should help him with the things and went down. I was vague in the head from lying in the hay. I had been nearly asleep.

"Where's Bonello?" I asked.

"I'll tell you," Piani said. We went up the ladder. Up on the hay we set the things down. Piani took out his knife with the corkscrew and drew the cork on a wine bottle.

"They have sealing-wax on it," he said. "It must be good." He smiled.

"Where's Bonello?" I asked.

Piani looked at me.

"He went away, Tenente," he said. "He wanted to be a prisoner."

I did not say anything.

"He was afraid we would get killed."

I held the bottle of wine and did not say anything.

"You see we don't believe in the war anyway, Tenente."

"Why didn't you go?" I asked.

"I did not want to leave you."

"Where did he go?"

"I don't know, Tenente. He went away."

"All right," I said. "Will you cut the sausage?"

Piani looked at me in the half-light.

"I cut it while we were talking," he said. We sat in the hay and ate the sausage and drank the wine. It must have been wine they had saved for a wedding. It was so old that it was losing its color.

"You look out of this window, Luigi," I said. "I'll go look out the other window."

We had each been drinking out of one of the bottles and I took my bottle with me and went over and lay flat on the hay and looked out the narrow window at the wet country. I do not know what I expected to see but I did not see anything except the fields and the bare mulberry trees and the rain falling. I drank the wine and it did not make me feel good. They had kept it too long and it had gone to pieces and lost its quality and color. I watched it get dark outside; the darkness came very quickly. It would be a black night with the rain. When it was dark there was no use watching any more, so I went over to Piani. He was lying asleep and I did not wake him but sat down beside him for a while. He was a big man and he slept heavily. After a while I woke him and we started.

That was a very strange night. I do not know what I had expected, death perhaps and shooting in the dark and running, but nothing happened. We waited, lying flat beyond the ditch along the main road while a German battalion passed, then when they were gone we crossed the road and went on to the north. We were very close to Germans twice in the rain but they did not see us. We got past the town to the north without seeing any Italians, then after a while came on the main channels of the retreat and

walked all night toward the Tagliamento. I had not realized how
gigantic the retreat was. The whole country was moving, as well
as the army. We walked all night, making better time than the
vehicles. My leg ached and I was tired but we made good time. It
seemed so silly for Bonello to have decided to be taken prisoner.
There was no danger. We had walked through two armies without
incident. If Aymo had not been killed there would never have
seemed to be any danger. No one had bothered us when we were
in plain sight along the railway. The killing came suddenly and
unreasonably. I wondered where Bonello was.

"How do you feel, Tenente?" Piani asked. We were going along
the side of a road crowded with vehicles and troops.

"Fine."

"I'm tired of this walking."

"Well, all we have to do is walk now. We don't have to worry."

"Bonello was a fool."

"He was a fool all right."

"What will you do about him, Tenente?"

"I don't know."

"Can't you just put him down as taken prisoner?"

"I don't know."

"You see if the war went on they would make bad trouble for
his family."

"The war won't go on," a soldier said. "We're going home. The
war is over."

"Everybody's going home."

"We're all going home."

"Come on, Tenente," Piani said. He wanted to get past them.

"Tenente? Who's a Tenente? *A basso gli ufficiali!* Down with
the officers!"

Piani took me by the arm. "I better call you by your name," he
said. "They might try and make trouble. They've shot some
officers." We worked up past them.

"I won't make a report that will make trouble for his family." I
went on with our conversation.

"If the war is over it makes no difference," Piani said. "But I
don't believe it's over. It's too good that it should be over."

"We'll know pretty soon," I said.

"I don't believe it's over. They all think it's over but I don't believe it."

"Viva la Pace!" a soldier shouted out. "We're going home!"

"It would be fine if we all went home," Piani said. "Wouldn't you like to go home?"

"Yes."

"We'll never go. I don't think it's over."

"Andiamo a casa!" a soldier shouted.

"They throw away their rifles," Piani said. "They take them off and drop them down while they're marching. Then they shout."

"They ought to keep their rifles."

"They think if they throw away their rifles they can't make them fight."

In the dark and the rain, making our way along the side of the road I could see that many of the troops still had their rifles. They stuck up above the capes.

"What brigade are you?" an officer called out.

"Brigata di Pace," some one shouted. "Peace Brigade!" The officer said nothing.

"What does he say? What does the officer say?"

"Down with the officer. *Viva la Pace!"*

"Come on," Piani said. We passed two British ambulances, abandoned in the block of vehicles.

"They're from Gorizia," Piani said. "I know the cars."

"They got further than we did."

"They started earlier."

"I wonder where the drivers are?"

"Up ahead probably."

"The Germans have stopped outside Udine," I said. "These people will all get across the river."

"Yes," Piani said. "That's why I think the war will go on."

"The Germans could come on," I said. "I wonder why they don't come on."

"I don't know. I don't know anything about this kind of war."

"They have to wait for their transport I suppose."

"I don't know," Piani said. Alone he was much gentler. When he was with the others he was a very rough talker.

"Are you married, Luigi?"

"You know I am married."

"Is that why you did not want to be a prisoner?"

"That is one reason. Are you married, Tenente?"

"No."

"Neither is Bonello."

"You can't tell anything by a man's being married. But I should think a married man would want to get back to his wife," I said. I would be glad to talk about wives.

"Yes."

"How are your feet?"

"They're sore enough."

Before daylight we reached the bank of the Tagliamento and followed down along the flooded river to the bridge where all the traffic was crossing.

"They ought to be able to hold at this river," Piani said. In the dark the flood looked high. The water swirled and it was wide. The wooden bridge was nearly three-quarters of a mile across, and the river, that usually ran in narrow channels in the wide stony bed far below the bridge, was close under the wooden planking. We went along the bank and then worked our way into the crowd that were crossing the bridge. Crossing slowly in the rain a few feet above the flood, pressed tight in the crowd, the box of an artillery caisson just ahead, I looked over the side and watched the river. Now that we could not go our own pace I felt very tired. There was no exhilaration in crossing the bridge. I wondered what it would be like if a plane bombed it in the daytime.

"Piani," I said.

"Here I am, Tenente." He was a little ahead in the jam. No one was talking. They were all trying to get across as soon as they could: thinking only of that. We were almost across. At the far end of the bridge there were officers and carabinieri standing on both sides flashing lights. I saw them silhouetted against the sky-line. As we came close to them I saw one of the officers point to a man in the column. A carabiniere went in after him and came out holding the man by the arm. He took him away from the road. We came almost opposite them. The officers were scrutinizing every one in the column, sometimes speaking to each other, going forward to flash a light in some one's face. They took some one else out just before we came opposite. I saw the man. He was a lieutenant-colonel. I saw the stars in the box on his sleeve as they flashed a light on him. His hair was gray and he was short and fat. The carabiniere pulled him in behind the line of officers. As we came opposite I saw one or two of them look at me. Then one pointed at me and spoke to a carabiniere. I saw the carabiniere start for me, come through the edge of the column toward me, then felt him take me by the collar.

"What's the matter with you?" I said and hit him in the face. I saw his face under the hat, upturned mustaches and blood coming down his cheek. Another one dove in toward us.

"What's the matter with you?" I said. He did not answer. He was watching a chance to grab me. I put my arm behind me to loosen my pistol.

"Don't you know you can't touch an officer?"

The other one grabbed me from behind and pulled my arm up so that it twisted in the socket. I turned with him and the other one grabbed me around the neck. I kicked his shins and got my left knee into his groin.

"Shoot him if he resists," I heard some one say.

"What's the meaning of this?" I tried to shout but my voice was ... very loud. They had me at the side of the road now.

"Shoot him if he resists," an officer said. "Take him over back."

"Who are you?"

"You'll find out."

"Who are you?"

"Battle police," another officer said.

"Why don't you ask me to step over instead of having one of these airplanes grab me?"

They did not answer. They did not have to answer. They were battle police.

"Take him back there with the others," the first officer said. "You see. He speaks Italian with an accent."

"So do you, you ———," I said.

"Take him back with the others," the first officer said. They took me down behind the line of officers below the road toward a group of people in a field by the river bank. As we walked toward them shots were fired. I saw flashes of the rifles and heard the reports. We came up to the group. There were four officers standing together, with a man in front of them with a carabiniere on each side of him. A group of men were standing guarded by carabinieri. Four other carabinieri stood near the questioning officers, leaning on their carbines. They were wide-hatted carabinieri. The two who had me shoved me in with the group waiting to be questioned. I looked at the man the officers were questioning. He was the fat gray-haired little lieutenant-colonel they had taken out of the column. The questioners had all the efficiency, coldness and command of themselves of Italians who are firing and are not being fired on.

"Your brigade?"

He told them.

"Regiment?"

He told them.

"Why are you not with your regiment?"

He told them.

"Do you not know that an officer should be with his troops?"

He did.

That was all. Another officer spoke.

"It is you and such as you that have let the barbarians onto the sacred soil of the fatherland."

"I beg your pardon," said the lieutenant-colonel.

"It is because of treachery such as yours that we have lost the fruits of victory."

"Have you ever been in a retreat?" the lieutenant-colonel asked.

"Italy should never retreat."

We stood there in the rain and listened to this. We were facing the officers and the prisoner stood in front and a little to one side of us.

"If you are going to shoot me," the lieutenant-colonel said, "please shoot me at once without further questioning. The questioning is stupid." He made the sign of the cross. The officers spoke together. One wrote something on a pad of paper.

"Abandoned his troops, ordered to be shot," he said.

Two carabinieri took the lieutenant-colonel to the river bank. He walked in the rain, an old man with his hat off, a carabiniere on either side. I did not watch them shoot him but I heard the shots. They were questioning some one else. This officer too was separated from his troops. He was not allowed to make an explanation. He cried when they read the sentence from the pad of paper, and they were questioning another when they shot him. They made a point of being intent on questioning the next man while the man who had been questioned before was being shot. In this way there was obviously nothing they could do about it. I did not know whether I should wait to be questioned or make a break now. I was obviously a German in Italian uniform. I saw how their minds worked; if they had minds and if they worked. They were all young men and they were saving their country. The second army was being re-formed beyond the Tagliamento. They were executing officers of the rank of major and above who were separated from their troops. They were also dealing summarily with German agitators in Italian uniform. They wore steel helmets. Only two of us had steel helmets. Some of the carabinieri had them. The other carabinieri wore the wide hat. Airplanes we called them. We stood in the rain and were taken out one at a time to be questioned and shot. So far they had shot every one they had questioned. The questioners had that beautiful detachment and devotion to stern justice of men dealing in death without being in any danger of it. They were questioning a full colonel of a line regiment. Three more officers had just been put in with us.

"Where was his regiment?"

I looked at the carabinieri. They were looking at the newcomers. The others were looking at the colonel. I ducked down, pushed between two men, and ran for the river, my head down. I tripped at the edge and went in with a splash. The water was very cold and I stayed under as long as I could. I could feel the current swirl me and I stayed under until I thought I could never come up. The minute I came up I took a breath and went down again. It was easy to stay under with so much clothing and my boots. When I came up the second time I saw a piece of timber ahead of me and reached it and held on with one hand. I kept my head behind it and did not even look over it. I did not want to see the bank. There were shots when I ran and shots when I came up the first time. I heard them when I was almost above water. There were no shots now. The piece of timber swung in the current and I held it with one hand. I looked at the bank. It seemed to be going by very fast. There was much wood in the stream. The water was very cold. We passed the brush of an island above the water. I held onto the timber with both hands and let it take me along. The shore was out of sight now.

XXXI

You DO not know how long you are in a river when the current moves swiftly. It seems a long time and it may be very short. The water was cold and in flood and many things passed that had been floated off the banks when the river rose. I was lucky to have a heavy timber to hold on to, and I lay in the icy water with my chin on the wood, holding as easily as I could with both hands. I was afraid of cramps and I hoped we would move toward the shore. We went down the river in a long curve. It was beginning to be light enough so I could see the bushes along the shore-line. There was a brush island ahead and the current moved toward the shore. I wondered if I should take off my boots and clothes and try to swim ashore, but decided not to. I had never thought of anything but that I would reach the shore some way, and I would be in a bad position if I landed barefoot. I had to get to Mestre some way.

I watched the shore come close, then swing away, then come closer again. We were floating more slowly. The shore was very close now. I could see twigs on the willow bush. The timber swung slowly so that the bank was behind me and I knew we were in an eddy. We went slowly around. As I saw the bank again, very close now, I tried holding with one arm and kicking and swimming the timber toward the bank with the other, but I did not bring it any closer. I was afraid we would move out of the eddy and, holding with one hand, I drew up my feet so they were against the side of the timber and shoved hard toward the bank. I could see the brush, but even with my momentum and swimming as hard as I could, the current was taking me away. I thought then I would drown because of my boots, but I thrashed and fought through the water, and when I looked up the bank was coming toward me, and I kept thrashing and swimming in a heavy-footed panic until I reached it. I hung to the willow branch and did not have strength to pull myself up but I knew I would not drown now. It had never occurred to me on the timber that I might drown. I felt hollow and sick in my stomach and chest from the effort, and I held to the branches and waited. When the sick feeling was gone I pulled into the willow bushes and rested again, my arms around some brush, holding tight with my hands to the branches. Then I crawled out, pushed on through the willows and onto the bank. It was half-daylight and I saw no one. I lay flat on the bank and heard the river and the rain.

After a while I got up and started along the bank. I knew there was no bridge across the river until Latisana. I thought I might be opposite San Vito. I began to think out what I should do. Ahead there was a ditch running into the river. I went toward it. So far I had seen no one and I sat down by some bushes along the bank of the ditch and took off my shoes and emptied them of water. I took off my coat, took my wallet with my papers and my money all wet in it out of the inside pocket and then wrung the coat out. I took off my trousers and wrung them too, then my shirt and underclothing. I slapped and rubbed myself and then dressed again. I had lost my cap.

Before I put on my coat I cut the cloth stars off my sleeves and put them in the inside pocket with my money. My money was wet but was all right. I counted it. There were three thousand and some lire. My clothes felt wet and clammy and I slapped my

arms to keep the circulation going. I had woven underwear and
I did not think I would catch cold if I kept moving. They had
taken my pistol at the road and I put the holster under my coat.
I had no cape and it was cold in the rain. I started up the bank
of the canal. It was daylight and the country was wet, low and
dismal looking. The fields were bare and wet; a long way away
I could see a campanile rising out of the plain. I came up onto a
road. Ahead I saw some troops coming down the road. I limped
along the side of the road and they passed me and paid no attention to me. They were a machine-gun detachment going up toward the river. I went on down the road.

That day I crossed the Venetian plain. It is a low level country
and under the rain it is even flatter. Toward the sea there are
salt marshes and very few roads. The roads all go along the river
mouths to the sea and to cross the country you must go along the
paths beside the canals. I was working across the country from
the north to the south and had crossed two railway lines and many
roads and finally I came out at the end of a path onto a railway
line where it ran beside a marsh. It was the main line from Venice
to Trieste, with a high solid embankment, a solid roadbed and
double track. Down the tracks a way was a flag-station and I
could see soldiers on guard. Up the line there was a bridge over
a stream that flowed into the marsh. I could see a guard too at
the bridge. Crossing the fields to the north I had seen a train pass
on this railroad, visible a long way across the flat plain, and I
thought a train might come from Portogruaro. I watched the
guards and lay down on the embankment so that I could see both
ways along the track. The guard at the bridge walked a way up
the line toward where I lay, then turned and went back toward
the bridge. I lay, and was hungry, and waited for the train. The
one I had seen was so long that the engine moved it very slowly
and I was sure I could get aboard it. After I had almost given up
hoping for one I saw a train coming. The engine, coming straight
on, grew larger slowly. I looked at the guard at the bridge. He was
walking on the near side of the bridge but on the other side of
the tracks. That would put him out of sight when the train
passed. I watched the engine come nearer. It was working hard.

I could see there were many cars. I knew there would be guards on the train, and I tried to see where they were, but, keeping out of sight, I could not. The engine was almost to where I was lying. When it came opposite, working and puffing even on the level, and I saw the engineer pass, I stood up and stepped up close to the passing cars. If the guards were watching I was a less suspicious object standing beside the track. Several closed freight-cars passed. Then I saw a low open car of the sort they call gondolas coming, covered with canvas. I stood until it had almost passed, then jumped and caught the rear hand-rods and pulled up. I crawled down between the gondola and the shelter of the high freight-car behind. I did not think any one had seen me. I was holding to the hand-rods and crouching low, my feet on the coupling. We were almost opposite the bridge. I remembered the guard. As we passed him he looked at me. He was a boy and his helmet was too big for him. I stared at him contemptuously and he looked away. He thought I had something to do with the train.

We were past. I saw him still looking uncomfortable, watching the other cars pass and I stooped to see how the canvas was fastened. It had grummets and was laced down at the edge with cord. I took out my knife, cut the cord and put my arm under. There were hard bulges under the canvas that tightened in the rain. I looked up and ahead. There was a guard on the freight-car ahead but he was looking forward. I let go of the hand-rails and ducked under the canvas. My forehead hit something that gave me a violent bump and I felt blood on my face but I crawled on in and lay flat. Then I turned around and fastened down the canvas.

I was in under the canvas with guns. They smelled cleanly of oil and grease. I lay and listened to the rain on the canvas and the clicking of the car over the rails. There was a little light came through and I lay and looked at the guns. They had their canvas jackets on. I thought they must have been sent ahead from the third army. The bump on my forehead was swollen and I stopped the bleeding by lying still and letting it coagulate, then picked away the dried blood except over the cut. It was nothing. I had no handkerchief, but feeling with my fingers I washed away where the dried blood had been, with rain-water that dripped from the canvas, and wiped it clean with the sleeve of my coat. I did not want to look conspicuous. I knew I would have to get out before they got to Mestre because they would be taking care of these guns. They had no guns to lose or forget about. I was terrifically hungry.

XXXII

LYING ON the floor of the flat-car with the guns beside me under the canvas I was wet, cold and very hungry. Finally I rolled over and lay flat on my stomach with my head on my arms. My knee was stiff, but it had been very satisfactory. Valentini had done a fine job. I had done half the retreat on foot and swum part of the Tagliamento with his knee. It was his knee all right. The other knee was mine. Doctors did things to you and then it was not your body any more. The head was mine, and the inside of the belly. It was very hungry in there. I could feel it turn over on itself. The head was mine, but not to use, not to think with; only to remember and not too much remember.

I could remember Catherine but I knew I would get crazy if I thought about her when I was not sure yet I would see her, so I would not think about her, only about her a little, only about her with the car going slowly and clickingly, and some light through the canvas and my lying with Catherine on the floor of the car. Hard as the floor of the car to lie not thinking only feeling, having been away too long, the clothes wet and the floor moving only a little each time and lonesome inside and alone with wet clothing and hard floor for a wife.

You did not love the floor of a flat-car nor guns with canvas jackets and the smell of vaselined metal or a canvas that rain leaked through, although it is very fine under a canvas and pleasant with guns; but you loved some one else whom now you knew was not even to be pretended there; you seeing now very clearly and coldly—not so coldly as clearly and emptily. You saw emptily, lying on your stomach, having been present when one army moved back and another came forward. You had lost your cars and your men as a floorwalker loses the stock of his department in a fire. There was, however, no insurance. You were out of it now. You had no more obligation. If they shot floorwalkers after a fire in the department store because they spoke with an accent they had always had, then certainly the floorwalkers would not be expected to return when the store opened again for business. They might seek other employment; if there was any other employment and the police did not get them.

Anger was washed away in the river along with any obligation. Although that ceased when the carabiniere put his hands on my collar. I would like to have had the uniform off although I did not care much about the outward forms. I had taken off the stars, but that was for convenience. It was no point of honor. I was not against them. I was through. I wished them all the luck. There were the good ones, and the brave ones, and the calm ones and the sensible ones, and they deserved it. But it was not my show any more and I wished this bloody train would get to Mestre and I would eat and stop thinking. I would have to stop.

Piani would tell them they had shot me. They went through the pockets and took the papers of the people they shot. They would not have my papers. They might call me drowned. I wondered what they would hear in the States. Dead from wounds and other causes. Good Christ I was hungry. I wondered what had become of the priest at the mess. And Rinaldi. He was probably at Pordenone. If they had not gone further back. Well, I would never see him now. I would never see any of them now. That life was over. I did not think he had syphilis. It was not a serious disease anyway if you took it in time, they said. But he would worry. I would worry too if I had it. Any one would worry.

I was not made to think. I was made to eat. My God, yes. Eat and drink and sleep with Catherine. To-night maybe. No that was impossible. But to-morrow night, and a good meal and sheets and never going away again except together. Probably have to go damned quickly. She would go. I knew she would go. When would we go? That was something to think about. It was getting dark. I lay and thought where we would go. There were many places.

STRESA

XXXV

CATHERINE went along the lake to the little hotel to see Ferguson and I sat in the bar and read the papers. There were comfortable leather chairs in the bar and I sat in one of them and read until the barman came in. The army had not stood at the Tagliamento. They were falling back to the Piave. I remembered the Piave. The railroad crossed it near San Dona going up to the front. It was deep and slow there and quite narrow. Down below there were mosquito marshes and canals. There were some lovely villas. Once, before the war, going up to Cortina D'Ampezzo I had gone along it for several hours in the hills. Up there it looked like a trout stream, flowing swiftly with shallow stretches and pools under the shadow of the rocks. The road turned off from it at Cadore. I wondered how the army that was up there would come down. The barman came in.

"Count Greffi was asking for you," he said.

"Who?"

"Count Greffi. You remember the old man who was here when you were here before."

"Is he here?"

"Yes, he's here with his niece. I told him you were here. He wants you to play billiards."

"Where is he?"

"He's taking a walk."

"How is he?"

"He's younger than ever. He drank three champagne cocktails last night before dinner."

"How's his billiard game?"

"Good. He beat me. When I told him you were here he was very pleased. There's nobody here for him to play with."

Count Greffi was ninety-four years old. He had been a contemporary of Metternich and was an old man with white hair and mustache and beautiful manners. He had been in the diplo-

matic service of both Austria and Italy and his birthday parties
were the great social event of Milan. He was living to be one hundred years old and played a smoothly fluent game of billiards that
contrasted with his own ninety-four-year-old brittleness. I had met
him when I had been at Stresa once before out of season and
while we played billiards we drank champagne. I thought it was
a splendid custom and he gave me fifteen points in a hundred and
beat me.

"Why didn't you tell me he was here?"

"I forgot it."

"Who else is here?"

"No one you know. There are only six people altogether."

"What are you doing now?"

"Nothing."

"Come on out fishing."

"I could come for an hour."

"Come on. Bring the trolling line."

The barman put on a coat and we went out. We went down
and got a boat and I rowed while the barman sat in the stern
and let out the line with a spinner and a heavy sinker on the
end to troll for lake trout. We rowed along the shore, the barman
holding the line in his hand and giving it occasional jerks forward. Stresa looked very deserted from the lake. There were the
long rows of bare trees, the big hotels and the closed villas. I
rowed across to Isola Bella and went close to the walls, where the
water deepened sharply, and you saw the rock wall slanting down
in the clear water, and then up and along to the fisherman's
island. The sun was under a cloud and the water was dark and
smooth and very cold. We did not have a strike though we saw
some circles on the water from rising fish.

I rowed up opposite the fisherman's island where there were
boats drawn up and men were mending nets.

"Should we get a drink?"

"All right."

I brought the boat up to the stone pier and the barman pulled
in the line, coiling it on the bottom of the boat and hooking the
spinner on the edge of the gunwale. I stepped out and tied the

boat. We went into a little café, sat at a bare wooden table and ordered vermouth.

"Are you tired from rowing?"

"No."

"I'll row back," he said.

"I like to row."

"Maybe if you hold the line it will change the luck."

"All right."

"Tell me how goes the war."

"Rotten."

"I don't have to go. I'm too old, like Count Greffi."

"Maybe you'll have to go yet."

"Next year they'll call my class. But I won't go."

"What will you do?"

"Get out of the country. I wouldn't go to war. I was at the war once in Abyssinia. Nix. Why do you go?"

"I don't know. I was a fool."

"Have another vermouth?"

"All right."

The barman rowed back. We trolled up the lake beyond Stresa and then down not far from shore. I held the taut line and felt the faint pulsing of the spinner revolving while I looked at the dark November water of the lake and the deserted shore. The barman rowed with long strokes and on the forward thrust of the boat the line throbbed. Once I had a strike: the line hardened suddenly and jerked back, I pulled and felt the live weight of the trout and then the line throbbed again. I had missed him.

"Did he feel big?"

"Pretty big."

"Once when I was out trolling alone I had the line in my teeth and one struck and nearly took my mouth out."

"The best way is to have it over your leg," I said. "Then you feel it and don't lose your teeth."

I put my hand in the water. It was very cold. We were almost opposite the hotel now.

"I have to go in," the barman said, "to be there for eleven o'clock. L'heure du cocktail."

"All right."

I pulled in the line and wrapped it on a stick notched at each end. The barman put the boat in a little slip in the stone wall and locked it with a chain and padlock.

"Any time you want it," he said, "I'll give you the key."

"Thanks."

We went up to the hotel and in to the bar. I did not want another drink so early in the morning so I went up to our room. The maid had just finished doing the room and Catherine was not back yet. I lay down on the bed and tried to keep from thinking.

When Catherine came back it was all right again. Ferguson was downstairs, she said. She was coming to lunch.

"I knew you wouldn't mind," Catherine said.

"No," I said.

"What's the matter, darling?"

"I don't know."

"I know. You haven't anything to do. All you have is me and I go away."

"That's true."

"I'm sorry, darling. I know it must be a dreadful feeling to have nothing at all suddenly."

"My life used to be full of everything," I said. "Now if you aren't with me I haven't a thing in the world."

"But I'll be with you. I was only gone for two hours. Isn't there anything you can do?"

"I went fishing with the barman."

"Wasn't it fun?"

"Yes."

"Don't think about me when I'm not here."

"That's the way I worked it at the front. But there was something to do then."

"Othello with his occupation gone," she teased.

"Othello was a nigger," I said. "Besides, I'm not jealous. I'm just so in love with you that there isn't anything else."

"Will you be a good boy and be nice to Ferguson?"

"I'm always nice to Ferguson unless she curses me."

"Be nice to her. Think how much we have and she hasn't anything."

"I don't think she wants what we have."

"You don't know much, darling, for such a wise boy."

"I'll be nice to her."

"I know you will. You're so sweet."

"She won't stay afterward, will she?"

"No. I'll get rid of her."

"And then we'll come up here."

"Of course. What do you think I want to do?"

We went downstairs to have lunch with Ferguson. She was very impressed by the hotel and the splendor of the dining-room. We had a good lunch with a couple of bottles of white capri. Count Greffi came into the dining-room and bowed to us. His niece, who looked a little like my grandmother, was with him. I told Catherine and Ferguson about him and Ferguson was very impressed. The hotel was very big and grand and empty but the food was good, the wine was very pleasant and finally the wine made us all feel very well. Catherine had no need to feel any better. She was very happy. Ferguson became quite cheerful. I felt very well myself. After lunch Ferguson went back to her hotel. She was going to lie down for a while after lunch she said.

Along late in the afternoon some one knocked on our door.

"Who is it?"

"The Count Greffi wishes to know if you will play billiards with him."

I looked at my watch; I had taken it off and it was under the pillow.

"Do you have to go, darling?" Catherine whispered.

"I think I'd better." The watch was a quarter-past four o'clock. Out loud I said, "Tell the Count Greffi I will be in the billiard-room at five o'clock."

At a quarter to five I kissed Catherine good-by and went into the bathroom to dress. Knotting my tie and looking in the glass I looked strange to myself in the civilian clothes. I must remember to buy some more shirts and socks.

"Will you be away a long time?" Catherine asked. She looked lovely in the bed. "Would you hand me the brush?"

I watched her brushing her hair, holding her head so the weight of her hair all came on one side. It was dark outside and the light over the head of the bed shone on her hair and on her neck and shoulders. I went over and kissed her and held her hand with the brush and her head sunk back on the pillow. I kissed her neck and shoulders. I felt faint with loving her so much.

"I don't want to go away."

"I don't want you to go away."

"I won't go then."

"Yes. Go. It's only for a little while and then you'll come back."

"We'll have dinner up here."

"Hurry and come back."

I found the Count Greffi in the billiard-room. He was practising strokes, looking very fragile under the light that came down above the billiard table. On a card table a little way beyond the light was a silver icing-bucket with the necks and corks of two champagne bottles showing above the ice. The Count Greffi straightened up when I came toward the table and walked toward me. He put out his hand, "It is such a great pleasure that you are here. You were very kind to come to play with me."

"It was very nice of you to ask me."

"Are you quite well? They told me you were wounded on the Isonzo. I hope you are well again."

"I'm very well. Have you been well?"

"Oh, I am always well. But I am getting old. I detect signs of age now."

"I can't believe it."

"Yes. Do you want to know one? It is easier for me to talk Italian. I discipline myself but I find when I am tired that it is so much easier to talk Italian. So I know I must be getting old."

"We could talk Italian. I am a little tired, too."

"Oh, but when you are tired it will be easier for you to talk English."

"American."

"Yes. American. You will please talk American. It is a delightful language."

"I hardly ever see Americans."

"You must miss them. One misses one's countrymen and especially one's countrywomen. I know that experience. Should we play or are you too tired?"

"I'm not really tired. I said that for a joke. What handicap will you give me?"

"Have you been playing very much?"

"None at all."

"You play very well. Ten points in a hundred?"

"You flatter me."

"Fifteen?"

"That would be fine but you will beat me."

"Should we play for a stake? You always wished to play for a stake."

"I think we'd better."

"All right. I will give you eighteen points and we will play for a franc a point."

He played a lovely game of billiards and with the handicap I was only four ahead at fifty. Count Greffi pushed a button on the wall to ring for the barman.

"Open one bottle please," he said. Then to me, "We will take a little stimulant." The wine was icy cold and very dry and good.

"Should we talk Italian? Would you mind very much? It is my weakness now."

We went on playing, sipping the wine between shots, speaking in Italian, but talking little, concentrated on the game. Count Greffi made his one hundredth point and with the handicap I was only at ninety-four. He smiled and patted me on the shoulder.

"Now we will drink the other bottle and you will tell me about the war." He waited for me to sit down.

"About anything else," I said.

"You don't want to talk about it? Good. What have you been reading?"

"Nothing," I said. "I'm afraid I am very dull."

"No. But you should read."

"What is there written in war-time?"

"There is 'Le Feu' by a Frenchman, Barbusse. There is 'Mr. Britling Sees Through It.'"

"No, he doesn't."

"What?"

"He doesn't see through it. Those books were at the hospital."

"Then you have been reading?"

"Yes, but nothing any good."

"I thought 'Mr. Britling' a very good study of the English middle-class soul."

"I don't know about the soul."

"Poor boy. We none of us know about the soul. Are you *Croyant?*"

"At night."

Count Greffi smiled and turned the glass with his fingers. "I had expected to become more devout as I grow older but somehow I haven't," he said. "It is a great pity."

"Would you like to live after death?" I asked and instantly felt a fool to mention death. But he did not mind the word.

"It would depend on the life. This life is very pleasant. I would like to live forever," he smiled. "I very nearly have."

We were sitting in the deep leather chairs, the champagne in the ice-bucket and our glasses on the table between us.

"If you ever live to be as old as I am you will find many things strange."

"You never seem old."

"It is the body that is old. Sometimes I am afraid I will break off a finger as one breaks a stick of chalk. And the spirit is no older and not much wiser."

"You are wise."

"No, that is the great fallacy; the wisdom of old men. They do not grow wise. They grow careful."

"Perhaps that is wisdom."

"It is a very unattractive wisdom. What do you value most?"

"Some one I love."

"With me it is the same. That is not wisdom. Do you value life?"

"Yes."

"So do I. Because it is all I have. And to give birthday parties," he laughed. "You are probably wiser than I am. You do not give birthday parties."

We both drank the wine.

"What do you think of the war really?" I asked.

"I think it is stupid."

"Who will win it?"

"Italy."

"Why?"

"They are a younger nation."

"Do younger nations always win wars?"

"They are apt to for a time."

"Then what happens?"

"They become older nations."

"You said you were not wise."

"Dear boy, that is not wisdom. That is cynicism."

"It sounds very wise to me."

"It's not particularly. I could quote you the examples on the other side. But it is not bad. Have we finished the champagne?"

"Almost."

"Should we drink some more? Then I must dress."

"Perhaps we'd better not now."

"You are sure you don't want more?"

"Yes." He stood up.

"I hope you will be very fortunate and very happy and very, very healthy."

"Thank you. And I hope you will live forever."

"Thank you. I have. And if you ever become devout pray for me if I am dead. I am asking several of my friends to do that. I had expected to become devout myself but it has not come." I thought he smiled sadly but I could not tell. He was so old and his face was very wrinkled, so that a smile used so many lines that all gradations were lost.

"I might become very devout," I said. "Anyway, I will pray for you."

"I had always expected to become devout. All my family died very devout. But somehow it does not come."

"It's too early."

"Maybe it is too late. Perhaps I have outlived my religious feeling."

"My own comes only at night."

"Then too you are in love. Do not forget that is a religious feeling."

"You believe so?"

"Of course." He took a step toward the table. "You were very kind to play."

"It was a great pleasure."

"We will walk upstairs together."

XXXVI

THAT NIGHT there was a storm and I woke to hear the rain lashing the window-panes. It was coming in the open window. Some one had knocked on the door. I went to the door very softly, not to disturb Catherine, and opened it. The barman stood there. He wore his overcoat and carried his wet hat.

"Can I speak to you, Tenente?"

"What's the matter?"

"It's a very serious matter."

I looked around. The room was dark. I saw the water on the floor from the window. "Come in," I said. I took him by the arm into the bathroom; locked the door and put on the light. I sat down on the edge of the bathtub.

"What's the matter, Emilio? Are you in trouble?"

"No. You are, Tenente."

"Yes?"

"They are going to arrest you in the morning."

"Yes?"

"I came to tell you. I was out in the town and I heard them talking in a café."

"I see."

He stood there, his coat wet, holding his wet hat and said nothing.

"Why are they going to arrest me?"

"For something about the war."

"Do you know what?"

"No. But I know that they know you were here before as an officer and now you are here out of uniform. After this retreat they arrest everybody."

I thought a minute.

"What time do they come to arrest me?"

"In the morning. I don't know the time."

"What do you say to do?"

He put his hat in the washbowl. It was very wet and had been dripping on the floor.

"If you have nothing to fear an arrest is nothing. But it is always bad to be arrested—especially now."

"I don't want to be arrested."

"Then go to Switzerland."

"How?"

"In my boat."

"There is a storm," I said.

"The storm is over. It is rough but you will be all right."

"When should we go?"

"Right away. They might come to arrest you early in the morning."

"What about our bags?"

"Get them packed. Get your lady dressed. I will take care of them."

"Where will you be?"

"I will wait here. I don't want any one to see me outside in the hall."

I opened the door, closed it, and went into the bedroom. Catherine was awake.

"What is it, darling?"

"It's all right, Cat," I said. "Would you like to get dressed right away and go in a boat to Switzerland?"

"Would you?"

"No," I said. "I'd like to go back to bed."

"What is it about?"

"The barman says they are going to arrest me in the morning."

"Is the barman crazy?"

"No."

"Then please hurry, darling, and get dressed so we can start." She sat up on the side of the bed. She was still sleepy. "Is that the barman in the bathroom?"

"Yes."

"Then I won't wash. Please look the other way, darling, and I'll be dressed in just a minute."

I saw her white back as she took off her nightgown and then I looked away because she wanted me to. She was beginning to be a little big with the child and she did not want me to see her. I dressed hearing the rain on the windows. I did not have much to put in my bag.

"There's plenty of room in my bag, Cat, if you need any."

"I'm almost packed," she said. "Darling, I'm awfully stupid, but why is the barman in the bathroom?"

"Sh—he's waiting to take our bags down."

"He's awfully nice."

"He's an old friend," I said. "I nearly sent him some pipe-tobacco once."

I looked out the open window at the dark night. I could not see the lake, only the dark and the rain but the wind was quieter.

"I'm ready, darling," Catherine said.

"All right." I went to the bathroom door. "Here are the bags, Emilio," I said. The barman took the two bags.

"You're very good to help us," Catherine said.

"That's nothing, lady," the barman said. "I'm glad to help you just so I don't get in trouble myself. Listen," he said to me. "I'll take these out the servants' stairs and to the boat. You just go out as though you were going for a walk."

"It's a lovely night for a walk," Catherine said.

"It's a bad night all right."

"I'm glad I've an umbrella," Catherine said.

We walked down the hall and down the wide thickly carpeted

stairs. At the foot of the stairs by the door the porter sat behind his desk.

He looked surprised at seeing us.

"You're not going out, sir?" he said.

"Yes," I said. "We're going to see the storm along the lake."

"Haven't you got an umbrella, sir?"

"No," I said. "This coat sheds water."

He looked at it doubtfully. "I'll get you an umbrella, sir," he said. He went away and came back with a big umbrella. "It is a little big, sir," he said. I gave him a ten-lire note. "Oh you are too good, sir. Thank you very much," he said. He held the door open and we went out into the rain. He smiled at Catherine and she smiled at him. "Don't stay out in the storm," he said. "You will get wet, sir and lady." He was only the second porter, and his English was still literally translated.

"We'll be back," I said. We walked down the path under the giant umbrella and out through the dark wet gardens to the road and across the road to the trellised pathway along the lake. The wind was blowing offshore now. It was a cold, wet November wind and I knew it was snowing in the mountains. We came along past the chained boats in the slips along the quay to where the barman's boat should be. The water was dark against the stone. The barman stepped out from beside the row of trees.

"The bags are in the boat," he said.

"I want to pay you for the boat," I said.

"How much money have you?"

"Not so much."

"You send me the money later. That will be all right."

"How much?"

"What you want."

"Tell me how much."

"If you get through send me five hundred francs. You won't mind that if you get through."

"All right."

"Here are sandwiches." He handed me a package. "Everything there was in the bar. It's all here. This is a bottle of brandy and a bottle of wine." I put them in my bag. "Let me pay you for those."

"All right, give me fifty lire."

I gave it to him. "The brandy is good," he said. "You don't need to be afraid to give it to your lady. She better get in the boat." He held the boat, it rising and falling against the stone wall and I helped Catherine in. She sat in the stern and pulled her cape around her.

"You know where to go?"

"Up the lake."

"You know how far?"

"Past Luino."

"Past Luino, Cannero, Cannobio, Tranzano. You aren't in Switzerland until you come to Brissago. You have to pass Monte Tamara."

"What time is it?" Catherine asked.

"It's only eleven o'clock," I said.

"If you row all the time you ought to be there by seven o'clock in the morning."

"Is it that far?"

"It's thirty-five kilometres."

"How should we go? In this rain we need a compass."

"No. Row to Isola Bella. Then on the other side of Isola Madre go with the wind. The wind will take you to Pallanza. You will see the lights. Then go up the shore."

"Maybe the wind will change."

"No," he said. "This wind will blow like this for three days. It comes straight down from the Mattarone. There is a can to bail with."

"Let me pay you something for the boat now."

"No, I'd rather take a chance. If you get through you pay me all you can."

"All right."

"I don't think you'll get drowned."

"That's good."

"Go with the wind up the lake."

"All right." I stepped in the boat.

"Did you leave the money for the hotel?"

"Yes. In an envelope in the room."

"All right. Good luck, Tenente."

"Good luck. We thank you many times."

"You won't thank me if you get drowned."

"What does he say?" Catherine asked.

"He says good luck."

"Good luck," Catherine said. "Thank you very much."

"Are you ready?"

"Yes."

He bent down and shoved us off. I dug at the water with the oars, then waved one hand. The barman waved back deprecatingly. I saw the lights of the hotel and rowed out, rowing straight out until they were out of sight. There was quite a sea running but we were going with the wind.

XXXVII

I ROWED in the dark keeping the wind in my face. The rain had stopped and only came occasionally in gusts. It was very dark, and the wind was cold. I could see Catherine in the stern but I could not see the water where the blades of the oars dipped. The oars were long and there were no leathers to keep them from slipping out. I pulled, raised, leaned forward, found the water, dipped and pulled, rowing as easily as I could. I did not feather the oars because the wind was with us. I knew my hands would blister and I wanted to delay it as long as I could. The boat was light and rowed easily. I pulled it along in the dark water. I could not see, and hoped we would soon come opposite Pallanza.

We never saw Pallanza. The wind was blowing up the lake and we passed the point that hides Pallanza in the dark and never saw the lights. When we finally saw some lights much further up the lake and close to the shore it was Intra. But for a long time we did not see any lights, nor did we see the shore but rowed steadily in the dark riding with the waves. Sometimes I missed the water with the oars in the dark as a wave lifted the boat. It was quite rough; but I kept on rowing, until suddenly we were close ashore against a point of rock that rose beside us; the waves striking against it, rushing high up, then falling back. I pulled hard on the right oar and backed water with the other and we went out into the lake again; the point was out of sight and we were going on up the lake.

"We're across the lake," I said to Catherine.

"Weren't we going to see Pallanza?"

"We've missed it."

"How are you, darling?"

"I'm fine."

"I could take the oars awhile."

"No, I'm fine."

"Poor Ferguson," Catherine said. "In the morning she'll come to the hotel and find we're gone."

"I'm not worrying so much about that," I said, "as about getting into the Swiss part of the lake before it's daylight and the customs guards see us."

"Is it a long way?"

"It's some thirty kilometres from here."

I rowed all night. Finally my hands were so sore I could hardly close them over the oars. We were nearly smashed up on the shore several times. I kept fairly close to the shore because I was afraid of getting lost on the lake and losing time. Sometimes we were so close we could see a row of trees and the road along the shore with the mountains behind. The rain stopped and the wind drove the clouds so that the moon shone through and looking back I could see the long dark point of Castagnola and the lake with white-caps and beyond, the moon on the high snow mountains. Then the clouds came over the moon again and the mountains and the lake were gone, but it was much lighter than it had been before and we could see the shore. I could see it too clearly and pulled out where they would not see the boat if there were customs guards along the Pallanza road. When the moon came out again we could see white villas on the shore on the slopes of the mountain and the white road where it showed through the trees. All the time I was rowing.

The lake widened and across it on the shore at the foot of the mountains on the other side we saw a few lights that should be Luino. I saw a wedgelike gap between the mountains on the other shore and I thought that must be Luino. If it was we were making good time. I pulled in the oars and lay back on the seat. I was very, very tired of rowing. My arms and shoulders and back ached and my hands were sore.

"I could hold the umbrella," Catherine said. "We could sail with that with the wind."

"Can you steer?"

"I think so."

"You take this oar and hold it under your arm close to the side of the boat and steer and I'll hold the umbrella." I went back to the stern and showed her how to hold the oar. I took the big umbrella the porter had given me and sat facing the bow and opened it. It opened with a clap. I held it on both sides, sitting astride the handle hooked over the seat. The wind was full in it and I felt the boat suck forward while I held as hard as I could to the two edges. It pulled hard. The boat was moving fast.

"We're going beautifully," Catherine said. All I could see was umbrella ribs. The umbrella strained and pulled and I felt us driving along with it. I braced my feet and held back on it, then suddenly, it buckled; I felt a rib snap on my forehead, I tried to grab the top that was bending with the wind and the whole thing buckled and went inside out and I was astride the handle of an inside-out, ripped umbrella, where I had been holding a wind-filled pulling sail. I unhooked the handle from the seat, laid the umbrella in the bow and went back to Catherine for the oar. She was laughing. She took my hand and kept on laughing.

"What's the matter?" I took the oar.

"You looked so funny holding that thing."

"I suppose so."

"Don't be cross, darling. It was awfully funny. You looked about twenty feet broad and very affectionate holding the umbrella by the edges—" she choked.

"I'll row."

"Take a rest and a drink. It's a grand night and we've come a long way."

"I have to keep the boat out of the trough of the waves."

"I'll get you a drink. Then rest a little while, darling."

I held the oars up and we sailed with them. Catherine was opening the bag. She handed me the brandy bottle. I pulled the cork with my pocket-knife and took a long drink. It was smooth and hot and the heat went all through me and I felt warmed and cheerful. "It's lovely brandy," I said. The moon was under again but I could see the shore. There seemed to be another point going out a long way ahead into the lake.

"Are you warm enough, Cat?"

"I'm splendid. I'm a little stiff."

"Bail out that water and you can put your feet down."

Then I rowed and listened to the oarlocks and the dip and scrape of the bailing tin under the stern seat.

"Would you give me the bailer?" I said. "I want a drink."

"It's awful dirty."

"That's all right. I'll rinse it."

I heard Catherine rinsing it over the side. Then she handed it to me dipped full of water. I was thirsty after the brandy and the water was icy cold, so cold it made my teeth ache. I looked toward the shore. We were closer to the long point. There were lights in the bay ahead.

"Thanks," I said and handed back the tin pail.

"You're ever so welcome," Catherine said. "There's much more if you want it."

"Don't you want to eat something?"

"No. I'll be hungry in a little while. We'll save it till then."

"All right."

What looked like a point ahead was a long high headland. I went further out in the lake to pass it. The lake was much narrower now. The moon was out again and the *guardia di finanza* could have seen our boat black on the water if they had been watching.

"How are you, Cat?" I asked.

"I'm all right. Where are we?"

"I don't think we have more than about eight miles more."

"That's a long way to row, you poor sweet. Aren't you dead?"

"No. I'm all right. My hands are sore is all."

We went on up the lake. There was a break in the mountains on the right bank, a flattening-out with a low shore line that I thought must be Cannobio. I stayed a long way out because it was from now on that we ran the most danger of meeting *guardia*. There was a high dome-capped mountain on the other shore a way ahead. I was tired. It was no great distance to row but when you were out of condition it had been a long way. I knew I had to pass that mountain and go up the lake at least five miles further before we would be in Swiss water. The moon was almost down now but before it went down the sky clouded over again and it was very dark. I stayed well out in the lake, rowing awhile, then resting and holding the oars so that the wind struck the blades.

"Let me row awhile," Catherine said.

"I don't think you ought to."

"Nonsense. It would be good for me. It would keep me from being too stiff."

"I don't think you should, Cat."

"Nonsense. Rowing in moderation is very good for the pregnant lady."

"All right, you row a little moderately. I'll go back, then you come up. Hold on to both gunwales when you come up."

I sat in the stern with my coat on and the collar turned up and watched Catherine row. She rowed very well but the oars were too long and bothered her. I opened the bag and ate a couple of sandwiches and took a drink of the brandy. It made everything much better and I took another drink.

"Tell me when you're tired," I said. Then a little later, "watch out the oar doesn't pop you in the tummy."

"If it did"—Catherine said between strokes—"life might be much simpler."

I took another drink of the brandy.

"How are you going?"

"All right."

"Tell me when you want to stop."

"All right."

I took another drink of the brandy, then took hold of the two gunwales of the boat and moved forward.

"No. I'm going beautifully."

"Go on back to the stern. I've had a grand rest."

For a while, with the brandy, I rowed easily and steadily. Then I began to catch crabs and soon I was just chopping along again with a thin brown taste of bile from having rowed too hard after the brandy.

"Give me a drink of water, will you?" I said.

"That's easy," Catherine said.

Before daylight it started to drizzle. The wind was down or we were protected by mountains that bounded the curve the lake had made. When I knew daylight was coming I settled down and rowed hard. I did not know where we were and I wanted to get into the Swiss part of the lake. When it was beginning to be daylight we were quite close to the shore. I could see the rocky shore and the trees.

"What's that?" Catherine said. I rested on the oars and listened. It was a motor boat chugging out on the lake. I pulled close up to the shore and lay quiet. The chugging came closer; then we saw the motor boat in the rain a little astern of us. There were four *guardia di finanza* in the stern, their *alpini* hats pulled down, their cape collars turned up and their carbines slung across their backs. They all looked sleepy so early in the morning. I could see the yellow on their hats and the yellow marks on their cape collars. The motor boat chugged on and out of sight in the rain.

I pulled out into the lake. If we were that close to the border I did not want to be hailed by a sentry along the road. I stayed out where I could just see the shore and rowed on for three quarters of an hour in the rain. We heard a motor boat once more but I kept quiet until the noise of the engine went way across the lake.

"I think we're in Switzerland, Cat," I said.

"Really?"

"There's no way to know until we see Swiss troops."

"Or the Swiss Navy."

"The Swiss navy's no joke for us. That last motor boat we heard was probably the Swiss navy."

"If we're in Switzerland let's have a big breakfast. They have wonderful rolls and butter and jam in Switzerland."

It was clear daylight now and a fine rain was falling. The wind was still blowing outside up the lake and we could see the tops of the white-caps going away from us and up the lake. I was sure we were in Switzerland now. There were many houses back in the trees from the shore and up the shore a way was a village with stone houses, some villas on the hills and a church. I had been looking at the road that skirted the shore for guards but did not see any. The road came quite close to the lake now and I saw a soldier coming out of a café on the road. He wore a gray-green uniform and a helmet like the Germans. He had a healthy-looking face and a little toothbrush mustache. He looked at us.

"Wave to him," I said to Catherine. She waved and the soldier smiled embarrassedly and gave a wave of his hand. I eased up rowing. We were passing the waterfront of the village.

"We must be well inside the border," I said.

"We want to be sure, darling. We don't want them to turn us back at the frontier."

"The frontier is a long way back. I think this is the customs town. I'm pretty sure it's Brissago."

"Won't there be Italians there? There are always both sides at a customs town."

"Not in war-time. I don't think they let the Italians cross the frontier."

It was a nice-looking little town. There were many fishing boats along the quay and nets were spread on racks. There was a fine November rain falling but it looked cheerful and clean even with the rain.

"Should we land then and have breakfast?"

"All right."

I pulled hard on the left oar and came in close, then straightened out when we were close to the quay and brought the boat alongside. I pulled in the oars, took hold of an iron ring, stepped up on the wet stone and was in Switzerland. I tied the boat and held my hand down to Catherine.

"Come on up, Cat. It's a grand feeling."

"What about the bags?"

"Leave them in the boat."

Catherine stepped up and we were in Switzerland together.

"What a lovely country," she said.

"Isn't it grand?"

"Let's go and have breakfast!"

"Isn't it a grand country? I love the way it feels under my shoes."

"I'm so stiff I can't feel it very well. But it feels like a splendid country. Darling, do you realize we're here and out of that bloody place?"

"I do. I really do. I've never realized anything before."

"Look at the houses. Isn't this a fine square? There's a place we can get breakfast."

"Isn't the rain fine? They never had rain like this in Italy. It's cheerful rain."

"And we're here, darling! Do you realize we're here?"

We went inside the café and sat down at a clean wooden table. We were cockeyed excited. A splendid clean-looking woman with an apron came and asked us what we wanted.

"Rolls and jam and coffee," Catherine said.

"I'm sorry, we haven't any rolls in war-time."

"Bread then."

"I can make you some toast."

"All right."

"I want some eggs fried too."

"How many eggs for the gentleman?"

"Three."

"Take four, darling."

"Four eggs."

The woman went away. I kissed Catherine and held her hand very tight. We looked at each other and at the café.

"Darling, darling, isn't it lovely?"

"It's grand," I said.

"I don't mind there not being rolls," Catherine said. "I thought about them all night. But I don't mind it. I don't mind it at all."

"I suppose pretty soon they will arrest us."

"Never mind, darling. We'll have breakfast first. You won't mind being arrested after breakfast. And then there's nothing they can do to us. We're British and American citizens in good standing."

"You have a passport, haven't you?"

"Of course. Oh let's not talk about it. Let's be happy."

"I couldn't be any happier," I said. A fat gray cat with a tail that lifted like a plume crossed the floor to our table and curved against my leg to purr each time she rubbed. I reached down and stroked her. Catherine smiled at me very happily. "Here comes the coffee," she said.

They arrested us after breakfast. We took a little walk through the village then went down to the quay to get our bags. A soldier was standing guard over the boat.

"Is this your boat?"

"Yes."

"Where do you come from?"

"Up the lake."

"Then I have to ask you to come with me."

"How about the bags?"

"You can carry the bags."

I carried the bags and Catherine walked beside me and the soldier walked along behind us to the old customs house. In the customs house a lieutenant, very thin and military, questioned us.

"What nationality are you?"

"American and British."

"Let me see your passports."

I gave him mine and Catherine got hers out of her handbag.

He examined them for a long time.

"Why do you enter Switzerland this way in a boat?"

"I am a sportsman," I said. "Rowing is my great sport. I always row when I get a chance."

"Why do you come here?"

"For the winter sport. We are tourists and we want to do the winter sport."

"This is no place for winter sport."

"We know it. We want to go where they have the winter sport."

"What have you been doing in Italy?"

"I have been studying architecture. My cousin has been studying art."

"Why do you leave there?"

"We want to do the winter sport. With the war going on you cannot study architecture."

"You will please stay where you are," the lieutenant said. He went back into the building with our passports.

"You're splendid, darling," Catherine said. "Keep on the same track. You want to do the winter sport."

"Do you know anything about art?"

"Rubens," said Catherine.

"Large and fat," I said.

"Titian," Catherine said.

"Titian-haired," I said. "How about Mantegna?"

"Don't ask hard ones," Catherine said. "I know him though—very bitter."

"Very bitter," I said. "Lots of nail holes."

"You see I'll make you a fine wife," Catherine said. "I'll be able to talk art with your customers."

"Here he comes," I said. The thin lieutenant came down the length of the customs house, holding our passports.

"I will have to send you into Locarno," he said. "You can get a carriage and a soldier will go in with you."

"All right," I said. "What about the boat?"

"The boat is confiscated. What have you in those bags?"

He went all through the two bags and held up the quarter-bottle of brandy. "Would you join me in a drink?" I asked.

"No thank you." He straightened up. "How much money have you?"

"Twenty-five hundred lire."

He was favorably impressed. "How much has your cousin?"

Catherine had a little over twelve hundred lire. The lieutenant was pleased. His attitude toward us became less haughty.

"If you are going for winter sports," he said, "Wengen is the place. My father has a very fine hotel at Wengen. It is open all the time."

"That's splendid," I said. "Could you give me the name?"

"I will write it on a card." He handed me the card very politely.

"The soldier will take you in to Locarno. He will keep your passports. I regret this but it is necessary. I have good hopes they will give you a visa or a police permit at Locarno."

He handed the two passports to the soldier and carrying the bags we started into the village to order a carriage. "Hi," the lieutenant called to the soldier. He said something in a German dialect to him. The soldier slung his rifle on his back and picked up the bags.

"It's a great country," I said to Catherine.

"It's so practical."

"Thank you very much," I said to the lieutenant. He waved his hand.

"Service!" he said. We followed our guard into the village.

We drove to Locarno in a carriage with the soldier sitting on the front seat with the driver. At Locarno we did not have a bad time. They questioned us but they were polite because we had passports and money. I do not think they believed a word of the story and I thought it was silly but it was like a law-court. You did not want something reasonable, you wanted something technical and then stuck to it without explanations. But we had passports and we would spend the money. So they gave us provisional visas. At any time this visa might be withdrawn. We were to report to the police wherever we went.

Could we go wherever we wanted? Yes. Where did we want to go?

"Where do you want to go, Cat?"

"Montreux."

"It's a very nice place," the official said. "I think you will like that place."

"Here at Locarno is a very nice place," another official said. "I am sure you would like it here very much at Locarno. Locarno is a very attractive place."

"We would like some place where there is winter sport."

"There is no winter sport at Montreux."

"I beg your pardon," the other official said. "I come from Montreux. There is very certainly winter sport on the Montreux Oberland Bernois railway. It would be false for you to deny that."

"I do not deny it. I simply said there is no winter sport at Montreux."

"I question that," the other official said. "I question that statement."

"I hold to that statement."

"I question that statement. I myself have *luge-ed* into the streets of Montreux. I have done it not once but several times. Luge-ing is certainly winter sport."

The other official turned to me.

"Is luge-ing your idea of winter sport, sir? I tell you you would be very comfortable here in Locarno. You would find the climate healthy, you would find the environs attractive. You would like it very much."

"The gentleman has expressed a wish to go to Montreux."

"What is luge-ing?" I asked.

"You see he has never even heard of luge-ing!"

That meant a great deal to the second official. He was pleased by that.

"Luge-ing," said the first official, "is tobogganing."

"I beg to differ," the other official shook his head. "I must differ again. The toboggan is very different from the luge. The toboggan is constructed in Canada of flat laths. The luge is a common sled with runners. Accuracy means something."

"Couldn't we toboggan?" I asked.

"Of course you could toboggan," the first official said. "You could toboggan very well. Excellent Canadian toboggans are sold in Montreux. Ochs Brothers sell toboggans. They import their own toboggans."

The second official turned away. "Tobogganing," he said, "requires a special *piste*. You could not toboggan into the streets of Montreux. Where are you stopping here?"

"We don't know," I said. "We just drove in from Brissago. The carriage is outside."

"You make no mistake in going to Montreux," the first official said. "You will find the climate delightful and beautiful. You will have no distance to go for winter sport."

"If you really want winter sport," the second official said, "you will go to the Engadine or to Mürren. I must protest against your being advised to go to Montreux for the winter sport."

"At Les Avants above Montreux there is excellent winter sport of every sort." The champion of Montreux glared at his colleague.

"Gentlemen," I said, "I am afraid we must go. My cousin is very tired. We will go tentatively to Montreux."

"I congratulate you," the first official shook my hand.

"I believe that you will regret leaving Locarno," the second official said. "At any rate you will report to the police at Montreux."

"There will be no unpleasantness with the police," the first official assured me. "You will find all the inhabitants extremely courteous and friendly."

"Thank you both very much," I said. "We appreciate your advice very much."

"Good-by," Catherine said. "Thank you both very much."

They bowed us to the door, the champion of Locarno a little coldly. We went down the steps and into the carriage.

"My God, darling," Catherine said. "Couldn't we have gotten away any sooner?" I gave the name of a hotel one of the officials had recommended to the driver. He picked up the reins.

"You've forgotten the army," Catherine said. The soldier was standing by the carriage. I gave him a ten-lira note. "I have no Swiss money yet," I said. He thanked me, saluted and went off. The carriage started and we drove to the hotel.

"How did you happen to pick out Montreux?" I asked Catherine. "Do you really want to go there?"

"It was the first place I could think of," she said. "It's not a bad place. We can find some place up in the mountains."

"Are you sleepy?"

"I'm asleep right now."

"We'll get a good sleep. Poor Cat, you had a long bad night."

"I had a lovely time," Catherine said. "Especially when you sailed with the umbrella."

"Can you realize we're in Switzerland?"

"No, I'm afraid I'll wake up and it won't be true."

"I am too."

"It is true, isn't it, darling? I'm not just driving down to the *stazione* in Milan to see you off."

"I hope not."

"Don't say that. It frightens me. Maybe that's where we're going."

"I'm so groggy I don't know," I said.

"Let me see your hands."

I put them out. They were both blistered raw.

"There's no hole in my side," I said.

"Don't be sacrilegious."

I felt very tired and vague in the head. The exhilaration was all gone. The carriage was going along the street.

"Poor hands," Catherine said.

"Don't touch them," I said. "By God I don't know where we are. Where are we going, driver?" The driver stopped his horse.

"To the Hotel Metropole. Don't you want to go there?"

"Yes," I said. "It's all right, Cat."

"It's all right, darling. Don't be upset. We'll get a good sleep and you won't feel groggy to-morrow."

"I get pretty groggy," I said. "It's like a comic opera to-day. Maybe I'm hungry."

"You're just tired, darling. You'll be fine." The carriage pulled up before the hotel. Some one came out to take our bags.

"I feel all right," I said. We were down on the pavement going into the hotel.

"I know you'll be all right. You're just tired. You've been up a long time."

"Anyhow we're here."

"Yes, we're really here."

We followed the boy with the bags into the hotel.

STORIES

"THE AUTHOR," Hemingway said in a 1936 note for a book of Georges Schreiber's sketches, "has made his own living since he was sixteen years old and has worked, before it was fashionable, as a day laborer, farmhand, dishwasher, waiter, sparring partner, newspaper reporter, foreign correspondent, and, since 1926, he has supported himself and his family as a writer. From 1919 to 1927 he sent stories to American magazines without being able to sell one until the Atlantic Monthly published a story called 'Fifty Grand.' During this time the Little Review published several things, but were unable to pay for them, and he was selling stories, articles, and poems to magazines published in France and in Germany. Since he was a young boy he has cared greatly for fishing and shooting. If he had not spent so much time at them, at skiing, at the bull ring, and in a boat, he might have written much more. On the other hand, he might have shot himself. He would rather read than do anything else except write, and nothing can make him so happy as having written well. He has been very lucky in his life and would like his luck to hold a little while longer."

All the stories in this section were written out of that experience and more, particularly combat experience and travel that ranges, as you will see, from New Jersey to the Veneto, from Key West to Madrid. But the experience is not necessarily his own, however easy that would make life for his biographers. As a true artist he also creates from what he has seen and despised or admired in others. "Sometimes," he says, "it comes easily and perfectly. Sometimes it is like drilling rock and then blasting it out with charges."

C. P.

A WAY YOU'LL NEVER BE

THE attack had gone across the field, been held up by machine-gun fire from the sunken road and from the group of farm houses, encountered no resistance in the town, and reached the bank of the river. Coming along the road on a bicycle, getting off to push the machine when the surface of the road became too broken, Nicholas Adams saw what had happened by the position of the dead.

They lay alone or in clumps in the high grass of the field and along the road, their pockets out, and over them were flies and around each body or group of bodies were the scattered papers.

In the grass and the grain, beside the road, and in some places scattered over the road, there was much material: a field kitchen, it must have come over when things were going well; many of the calf-skin-covered haversacks, stick bombs, helmets, rifles, sometimes one butt-up, the bayonet stuck in the dirt, they had dug quite a little at the last; stick bombs, helmets, rifles, intrenching tools, ammunition boxes, star-shell pistols, their shells scattered about, medical kits, gas masks, empty gas-mask cans, a squat, tripodded machine gun in a nest of empty shells, full belts protruding from the boxes, the water-cooling can empty and on its side, the breech block gone, the crew in odd positions, and around them, in the grass, more of the typical papers.

There were mass prayer books, group postcards showing the machine-gun unit standing in ranked and ruddy cheerfulness as in a football picture for a college annual; now they were humped and swollen in the grass; propaganda postcards showing a soldier in Austrian uniform bending a woman backward over a bed; the figures were impressionistically drawn; very attractively depicted and had nothing in common with actual rape in which the woman's skirts are pulled over her head to smother her, one comrade sometimes sitting upon the head. There were many of these inciting cards which had evidently been issued just before the offensive. Now they were scattered with the smutty postcards, photographic; the small photographs of village girls by village photographers, the occasional pictures of children, and the letters, letters, letters. There was always much paper about the dead and the débris of this attack was no exception.

These were new dead and no one had bothered with anything but their pockets. Our own dead, or what he thought of, still, as our own dead, were surprisingly few, Nick noticed. Their coats had been opened too and their pockets were out, and they showed, by their positions, the manner and the skill of the attack. The hot weather had swollen them all alike regardless of nationality.

The town had evidently been defended, at the last, from the line of the sunken road and there had been few or no Austrians to fall back into it. There were only three bodies in the street and they looked to have been killed running. The houses of the town were broken by the shelling and the street had much rubble of plaster and mortar and there were broken beams, broken tiles, and many holes, some of them yellow-edged from the mustard gas. There were many pieces of shell, and shrapnel balls were scattered in the rubble. There was no one in the town at all.

Nick Adams had seen no one since he had left Fornaci, although, riding along the road through the over-foliaged country, he had seen guns hidden under screens of mulberry leaves to the left of the road, noticing them by the heat-waves in the air above the leaves where the sun hit the metal. Now he went on through the town, surprised to find it deserted, and came out on the low road beneath the bank of the river. Leaving the town there was a bare open space where the road slanted down and he could see the placid reach of the river and the low curve of the opposite bank and the whitened, sun-baked mud where the Austrians had dug. It was all very lush and over-green since he had seen it last and becoming historical had made no change in this, the lower river.

The battalion was along the bank to the left. There was a series of holes in the top of the bank with a few men in them. Nick noticed where the machine guns were posted and the signal rockets in their racks. The men in the holes in the side of the bank were sleeping. No one challenged. He went on and as he came around a turn in the mud bank a young second lieutenant with a stubble of beard and red-rimmed, very blood-shot eyes pointed a pistol at him.

"Who are you?"

Nick told him.

"How do I know this?"

Nick showed him the tessera with photograph and identification and the seal of the third army. He took hold of it.

"I will keep this."

"You will not," Nick said. "Give me back the card and put your gun away. There. In the holster."

"How am I to know who you are?"

"The tessera tells you."

"And if the tessera is false? Give me that card."

"Don't be a fool," Nick said cheerfully. "Take me to your company commander."

"I should send you to battalion headquarters."

"All right," said Nick. "Listen, do you know the Captain Paravicini? The tall one with the small mustache who was an architect and speaks English?"

"You know him?"

"A little."

"What company does he command?"

"The second."

"He is commanding the battalion."

"Good," said Nick. He was relieved to know that Para was all right. "Let us go to the battalion."

As Nick had left the edge of the town three shrapnel had burst high and to the right over one of the wrecked houses and since then there had been no shelling. But the face of this officer looked like the face of a man during a bombardment. There was the same tightness and the voice did not sound natural. His pistol made Nick nervous.

"Put it away," he said. "There's the whole river between them and you."

"If I thought you were a spy I would shoot you now," the second lieutenant said.

"Come on," said Nick. "Let us go to the battalion." This officer made him very nervous.

The Captain Paravicini, acting major, thinner and more English-looking than ever, rose when Nick saluted from behind the table in the dugout that was battalion headquarters.

"Hello," he said. "I didn't know you. What are you doing in that uniform?"

"They've put me in it."

"I am very glad to see you, Niccolo."

"Right. You look well. How was the show?"

"We made a very fine attack. Truly. A very fine attack. I will show you. Look."

He showed on the map how the attack had gone.

"I came from Fornaci," Nick said. "I could see how it had been. It was very good."

"It was extraordinary. Altogether extraordinary. Are you attached to the regiment?"

"No. I am supposed to move around and let them see the uniform."

"How odd."

"If they see one American uniform that is supposed to make them believe others are coming."

"But how will they know it is an American uniform?"

"You will tell them."

"Oh. Yes, I see. I will send a corporal with you to show you about and you will make a tour of the lines."

"Like a bloody politician," Nick said.

"You would be much more distinguished in civilian clothes. They are what is really distinguished."

"With a homburg hat," said Nick.

"Or with a very furry fedora."

"I'm supposed to have my pockets full of cigarettes and postal cards and such things," Nick said. "I should have a musette full of chocolate. These I should distribute with a kind word and a pat on the back. But there weren't any cigarettes and postcards and no chocolate. So they said to circulate around anyway."

"I'm sure your appearance will be very heartening to the troops."

"I wish you wouldn't," Nick said. "I feel badly enough about it as it is. In principle, I would have brought you a bottle of brandy."

"In principle," Para said and smiled, for the first time, showing yellowed teeth. "Such a beautiful expression. Would you like some Grappa?"

"No, thank you," Nick said.

"It hasn't any ether in it."

"I can taste that still," Nick remembered suddenly and completely.

"You know I never knew you were drunk until you started talking coming back in the camions."

"I was stinking in every attack," Nick said.

"I can't do it," Para said. "I took it in the first show, the very first show, and it only made me very upset and then frightfully thirsty."

"You don't need it."

"You're much braver in an attack than I am."

"No," Nick said. "I know how I am and I prefer to get stinking. I'm not ashamed of it."

"I've never seen you drunk."

"No?" said Nick. "Never? Not when we rode from Mestre to Portogrande that night and I wanted to go to sleep and used the bicycle for a blanket and pulled it up under my chin?"

"That wasn't in the lines."

"Let's not talk about how I am," Nick said. "It's a subject I know too much about to want to think about it any more."

"You might as well stay here a while," Paravicini said. "You can take a nap if you like. They didn't do much to this in the bombardment. It's too hot to go out yet."

"I suppose there is no hurry."

"How are you really?"

"I'm fine. I'm perfectly all right."

"No. I mean really."

"I'm all right. I can't sleep without a light of some sort. That's all I have now."

"I said it should have been trepanned. I'm no doctor but I know that."

"Well, they thought it was better to have it absorb, and that's what I got. What's the matter? I don't seem crazy to you, do I?"

"You seem in top-hole shape."

"It's a hell of a nuisance once they've had you certified as nutty," Nick said. "No one ever has any confidence in you again."

"I would take a nap, Niccolo," Paravicini said. "This isn't battalion headquarters as we used to know it. We're just waiting to be pulled out. You oughtn't to go out in the heat now—it's silly. Use that bunk."

"I might just lie down," Nick said.

Nick lay on the bunk. He was very disappointed that he felt this way and more disappointed, even, that it was so obvious to Captain Paravicini. This was not as large a dugout as the one where that platoon of the class of 1899, just out at the front, got hysterics during the bombardment before the attack, and Para had had him walk them two at a time outside to show them nothing would happen, he wearing his own chin strap tight across his mouth to keep his lips quiet. Knowing they could not hold it when they took it. Knowing it was all a bloody balls—If he can't stop crying, break his nose to give him something else to think about. I'd shoot one but it's too late now. They'd all be worse. Break his nose. They've put it back to five-twenty. We've only got four minutes more. Break that other silly bugger's nose and kick his silly ass out of here. Do you think they'll go over? If they don't, shoot two and try to scoop the others out some way. Keep behind them, sergeant. It's no use to walk ahead and find there's nothing coming behind you. Bail them out as you go. What a bloody balls. All right. That's right. Then, looking at the watch, in that quiet tone, that valuable quiet tone, "Savoia." Making it cold, no time to get it, he couldn't find his own after the cave-in, one whole end had caved in; it was that started them; making it cold up that slope the only time he hadn't done it stinking. And after they came back the telefrica house burned, it seemed, and some of the wounded got down four days later and some did not get down, but we went up and we went back and we came down—we always came down. And there was Gaby Delys oddly enough, with feathers on; you called me baby doll a year ago tadada you said that I was rather nice to know tadada with feathers on, with feathers off, the great Gaby, and my name's Harry Pilcer, too, we used to step out of the far side of the taxis when it got steep going up the hill and he could see that hill every night when he dreamed with Sacré Cœur, blown white, like a soap bubble. Sometimes his girl was there and sometimes she was with some one else and he could not understand that, but those were the nights the river ran so much wider and stiller than it should and outside of Fossalta there was a low house painted yellow with willows all around it and a low stable and there was a canal, and he had been there a thousand times and never seen it, but there it was every night as plain as the hill, only it frightened him. That house meant more than anything and every night he had it. That was what he needed but it frightened him especially when the boat lay there quietly in the willows on the canal, but the banks weren't like this river. It was all lower, as it was at Porto-grande, where they had seen them come wallowing across the flooded ground holding the rifles high until they fell with them in the water. Who ordered that one? If it didn't get so damned mixed up he could follow it all right. That was why he noticed every-thing in such detail to keep it all straight so he would know just where he was, but suddenly it confused without reason as now, he lying in a bunk at battalion headquarters, with Para commanding a battalion and he in a bloody American uniform. He sat up and looked around; they all watching him. Para was gone out. He lay down again.

The Paris part came earlier and he was not frightened of it except when she had gone off with some one else and the fear that they might take the same driver twice. That was what frightened about that. Never about the front. He never dreamed about the front now any more but what frightened him so that he could not get rid of it was that long yellow house and the different width of the river. Now he was back here at the river, he had gone through that same town, and there was no house. Nor was the river that way. Then where did he go each night and what was the peril, and why would he wake, soaking wet, more frightened than he had ever been in a bombardment, because of a house and a long stable and a canal?

He sat up, swung his legs carefully down; they stiffened any time they were out straight for long; returned the stares of the adjutant, the signallers and the two runners by the door and put on his cloth-covered trench helmet.

"I regret the absence of the chocolate, the postal-cards and cigarettes," he said. "I am, however, wearing the uniform."

"The major is coming back at once," the adjutant said. In that army an adjutant is not a commissioned officer.

"The uniform is not very correct," Nick told them. "But it gives you the idea. There will be several millions of Americans here shortly."

"Do you think they will send Americans down here?" asked the adjutant.

"Oh, absolutely. Americans twice as large as myself, healthy, with clean hearts, sleep at night, never been wounded, never been blown up, never had their heads caved in, never been scared, don't drink, faithful to the girls they left behind them, many of them never had crabs, wonderful chaps. You'll see."

"Are you an Italian?" asked the adjutant.

"No, American. Look at the uniform. Spagnolini made it but it's not quite correct."

"A North or South American?"

"North," said Nick. He felt it coming on now. He would quiet down.

"But you speak Italian."

"Why not? Do you mind if I speak Italian? Haven't I a right to speak Italian?"

"You have Italian medals."

"Just the ribbons and the papers. The medals come later. Or you give them to people to keep and the people go away; or they are lost with your baggage. You can purchase others in Milan. It is the papers that are of importance. You must not feel badly about them. You will have some yourself if you stay at the front long enough."

"I am a veteran of the Eritrea campaign," said the adjutant stiffly. "I fought in Tripoli."

"It's quite something to have met you," Nick put out his hand.

"Those must have been trying days. I noticed the ribbons. Were you, by any chance, on the Carso?"

"I have just been called up for this war. My class was too old."

"At one time I was under the age limit," Nick said. "But now I am reformed out of the war."

"But why are you here now?"

"I am demonstrating the American uniform," Nick said. "Don't you think it is very significant? It is a little tight in the collar but soon you will see untold millions wearing this uniform swarming like locusts. The grasshopper, you know, what we call the grass-hopper in America, is really a locust. The true grasshopper is small and green and comparatively feeble. You must not, however, make a confusion with the seven-year locust or cicada which emits a peculiar sustained sound which at the moment I cannot recall. I try to recall it but I cannot. I can almost hear it and then it is quite gone. You will pardon me if I break off our conversation?"

"See if you can find the major," the adjutant said to one of the two runners. "I can see you have been wounded," he said to Nick.

"In various places," Nick said. "If you are interested in scars I can show you some very interesting ones but I would rather talk about grasshoppers. What we call grasshoppers that is; and what are, really, locusts. These insects at one time played a very impor-tant part in my life. It might interest you and you can look at the uniform while I am talking."

The adjutant made a motion with his hand to the second runner who went out.

"Fix your eyes on the uniform. Spagnolini made it, you know. You might as well look, too," Nick said to the signallers. "I really have no rank. We're under the American consul. It's perfectly all right for you to look. You can stare, if you like. I will tell you about the American locust. We always preferred one that we called the medium-brown. They last the best in the water and fish prefer them. The larger ones that fly making a noise somewhat similar to that produced by a rattlesnake rattling his rattlers, a very dry sound, have vivid colored wings, some are bright red, others yellow barred with black, but their wings go to pieces in the water and they make a very blowsy bait, while the medium-brown is a plump, compact, succulent hopper that I can recommend as far as one may well recommend something you gentlemen will probably never encounter. But I must insist that you will never gather a sufficient supply of these insects for a day's fishing by pursuing them with your hands or trying to hit them with a bat. That is sheer nonsense and a useless waste of time. I repeat, gentlemen, that you will get nowhere at it. The correct procedure, and one which should be taught all young officers at every small-arms course if I had anything to say about it, and who knows but what I will have, is the employment of a seine or net made of common mosquito netting. Two officers holding this length of netting at alternate ends, or let us say one at each end, stoop, hold the bottom extremity of the net in one hand and the top extremity in the other and run into the wind. The hoppers, flying with the wind, fly against the length of netting and are imprisoned in its folds. It is no trick at all to catch a very great quantity indeed, and no officer, in my opinion, should be without a length of mosquito netting suitable for the improvisation of one of these grasshopper seines. I hope I have made myself clear, gentlemen. Are there any questions? If there is anything in the course you do not understand please ask questions. Speak up. None? Then I would like to close on this note. In the words of that great soldier and gentleman, Sir Henry Wilson: Gentlemen, either you must govern or you must be governed. Let me repeat it. Gentlemen, there is one thing I would like to have you remember. One thing I would like you to take with you as you leave this room. Gentlemen, either you must govern—or you must be governed. That is all, gentlemen. Good-day."

He removed his cloth-covered helmet, put it on again and, stooping, went out the low entrance of the dugout. Para, accompanied by the two runners, was coming down the line of the sunken road. It was very hot in the sun and Nick removed the helmet.

"There ought to be a system for wetting these things," he said. "I shall wet this one in the river." He started up the bank.

"Niccolo," Paravicini called. "Niccolo. Where are you going?"

"I don't really have to go." Nick came down the slope, holding the helmet in his hands. "They're a damned nuisance wet or dry. Do you wear yours all the time?"

"All the time," said Para. "It's making me bald. Come inside."

Inside Para told him to sit down.

"You know they're absolutely no damned good," Nick said. "I remember when they were a comfort when we first had them, but I've seen them full of brains too many times."

"Niccolo," Para said. "I think you should go back. I think it would be better if you didn't come up to the line until you had those supplies. There's nothing here for you to do. If you move around, even with something worth giving away, the men will group and that invites shelling. I won't have it."

"I know it's silly," Nick said. "It wasn't my idea. I heard the brigade was here so I thought I would see you or some one else I knew. I could have gone to Zenzon or to San Dona. I'd like to go to San Dona to see the bridge again."

"I won't have you circulating around to no purpose," Captain Paravicini said.

"All right," said Nick. He felt it coming on again.

"You understand?"

"Of course," said Nick. He was trying to hold it in.

"Anything of that sort should be done at night."

"Naturally," said Nick. He knew he could not stop it now.

"You see, I am commanding the battalion," Para said.

"And why shouldn't you be?" Nick said. Here it came. "You can read and write, can't you?"

"Yes," said Para gently.

"The trouble is you have a damned small battalion to command. As soon as it gets to strength again they'll give you back your company. Why don't they bury the dead? I've seen them now. I don't care about seeing them again. They can bury them any time as far as I'm concerned and it would be much better for you. You'll all get bloody sick."

"Where did you leave your bicycle?"

"Inside the last house."

"Do you think it will be all right?"

"Don't worry," Nick said. "I'll go in a little while."

"Lie down a little while, Niccolo."

"All right."

He shut his eyes, and in place of the man with the beard who looked at him over the sights of the rifle, quite calmly before squeezing off, the white flash and clublike impact, on his knees, hot-sweet choking, coughing it onto the rock while they went past him, he saw a long, yellow house with a low stable and the river much wider than it was and stiller. "Christ," he said, "I might as well go."

He stood up.

"I'm going, Para," he said. "I'll ride back now in the afternoon. If any supplies have come I'll bring them down tonight. If not I'll come at night when I have something to bring."

"It is still hot to ride," Captain Paravicini said.

"You don't need to worry," Nick said. "I'm all right now for quite a while. I had one then but it was easy. They're getting much better. I can tell when I'm going to have one because I talk so much."

"I'll send a runner with you."

"I'd rather you didn't. I know the way."

"You'll be back soon?"

"Absolutely."

"Let me send——"

"No," said Nick. "As a mark of confidence."

"Well, Ciao then."

"Ciao," said Nick. He started back along the sunken road toward where he had left the bicycle. In the afternoon the road would be shady once he had passed the canal. Beyond that there were trees on both sides that had not been shelled at all. It was on that stretch that, marching, they had once passed the Terza Savoia cavalry regiment riding in the snow with their lances. The horses' breath made plumes in the cold air. No, that was somewhere else. Where was that?

"I'd better get to that damned bicycle," Nick said to himself. "I don't want to lose the way to Fornaci."

FIFTY GRAND

"How ARE you going yourself, Jack?" I asked him.

"You seen this Walcott?" he says.

"Just in the gym."

"Well," Jack says, "I'm going to need a lot of luck with that boy."

"He can't hit you, Jack," Soldier said.

"I wish to hell he couldn't."

"He couldn't hit you with a handful of bird-shot."

"Bird-shot'd be all right," Jack says. "I wouldn't mind bird-shot any."

"He looks easy to hit," I said.

"Sure," Jack says, "he ain't going to last long. He ain't going to last like you and me, Jerry. But right now he's got everything."

"You'll left-hand him to death."

"Maybe," Jack says. "Sure. I got a chance to."

"Handle him like you handled Kid Lewis."

"Kid Lewis," Jack said. "That kike!"

The three of us, Jack Brennan, Soldier Bartlett, and I were in Hanley's. There were a couple of broads sitting at the next table to us. They had been drinking.

"What do you mean, kike?" one of the broads says. "What do you mean, kike, you big Irish bum?"

"Sure," Jack says. "That's it."

"Kikes," this broad goes on. "They're always talking about kikes, these big Irishmen. What do you mean, kikes?"

"Come on. Let's get out of here."

"Kikes," this broad goes on. "Whoever saw you ever buy a drink? Your wife sews your pockets up every morning. These Irishmen and their kikes! Ted Lewis could lick you too."

"Sure," Jack says. "And you give away a lot of things free too, don't you?"

We went out. That was Jack. He could say what he wanted to when he wanted to say it.

Jack started training out at Danny Hogan's health farm over in Jersey. It was nice out there but Jack didn't like it much. He didn't like being away from his wife and the kids, and he was sore and grouchy most of the time. He liked me and we got along fine together; and he liked Hogan, but after a while Soldier Bartlett commenced to get on his nerves. A kidder gets to be an awful thing around a camp if his stuff goes sort of sour. Soldier was always kidding Jack, just sort of kidding him all the time. It wasn't very funny and it wasn't very good, and it began to get to Jack. It was sort of stuff like this. Jack would finish up with the weights and the bag and pull on the gloves.

"You want to work?" he'd say to Soldier.

"Sure. How you want me to work?" Soldier would ask. "Want me to treat you rough like Walcott? Want me to knock you down a few times?"

"That's it," Jack would say. He didn't like it any, though.

One morning we were all out on the road. We'd been out quite a way and now we were coming back. We'd go along fast for three minutes and then walk a minute, and then go fast for three minutes again. Jack wasn't ever what you would call a sprinter. He'd move around fast enough in the ring if he had to, but he wasn't any too fast on the road. All the time we were walking Soldier was kidding him. We came up the hill to the farmhouse.

"Well," says Jack, "you better go back to town, Soldier."

"What do you mean?"

"You better go back to town and stay there."

"What's the matter?"

"I'm sick of hearing you talk."

"Yes?" says Soldier.

"Yes," says Jack.

"You'll be a damn sight sicker when Walcott gets through with you."

"Sure," says Jack, "maybe I will. But I know I'm sick of you."

So Soldier went off on the train to town that same morning. I went down with him to the train. He was good and sore.

"I was just kidding him," he said. We were waiting on the platform. "He can't pull that stuff with me, Jerry."

"He's nervous and crabby," I said. "He's a good fellow, Soldier."

"The hell he is. The hell he's ever been a good fellow."

"Well," I said, "so long, Soldier."

The train had come in. He climbed up with his bag.

"So long, Jerry," he says. "You be in town before the fight?"

"I don't think so."

"See you then."

He went in and the conductor swung up and the train went out. I rode back to the farm in the cart. Jack was on the porch writing a letter to his wife. The mail had come and I got the papers and went over on the other side of the porch and sat down to read. Hogan came out the door and walked over to me.

"Did he have a jam with Soldier?"

"Not a jam," I said. "He just told him to go back to town."

"I could see it coming," Hogan said. "He never liked Soldier much."

"No. He don't like many people."

"He's a pretty cold one," Hogan said.

"Well, he's always been fine to me."

"Me too," Hogan said. "I got no kick on him. He's a cold one, though."

Hogan went in through the screen door and I sat there on the porch and read the papers. It was just starting to get fall weather and it's nice country there in Jersey, up in the hills, and after I read the paper through I sat there and looked out at the country and the road below against the woods with cars going along it, lifting the dust up. It was fine weather and pretty nice-looking country. Hogan came to the door and I said, "Say, Hogan, haven't you got anything to shoot out here?"

"No," Hogan said. "Only sparrows."

"Seen the paper?" I said to Hogan.

"What's in it?"

"Sande booted three of them in yesterday."

"I got that on the telephone last night."

"You follow them pretty close, Hogan?" I asked.

"Oh, I keep in touch with them," Hogan said.

"How about Jack?" I says. "Does he still play them?"

"Him?" said Hogan. "Can you see him doing it?"

Just then Jack came around the corner with the letter in his hand. He's wearing a sweater and an old pair of pants and boxing shoes.

"Got a stamp, Hogan?" he asks.

"Give me the letter," Hogan said. "I'll mail it for you."

"Say, Jack," I said, "didn't you used to play the ponies?"

"Sure."

"I knew you did. I knew I used to see you out at Sheepshead."

"What did you lay off them for?" Hogan asked.

"Lost money."

Jack sat down on the porch by me. He leaned back against a post. He shut his eyes in the sun.

"Want a chair?" Hogan asked.

"No," said Jack. "This is fine."

"It's a nice day," I said. "It's pretty nice out in the country."

"I'd a damn sight rather be in town with the wife."

"Well, you only got another week."

"Yes," Jack says. "That's so."

We sat there on the porch. Hogan was inside at the office.

"What do you think about the shape I'm in?" Jack asked me.

"Well, you can't tell," I said. "You got a week to get around into form."

"Don't stall me."

"Well," I said, "you're not right."

"I'm not sleeping," Jack said.

"You'll be all right in a couple of days."

"No," says Jack, "I got the insomnia."

"What's on your mind?"

"I miss the wife."

"Have her come out."

"No. I'm too old for that."

"We'll take a long walk before you turn in and get you good and tired."

"Tired!" Jack says. "I'm tired all the time."

He was that way all week. He wouldn't sleep at night and he'd get up in the morning feeling that way, you know, when you can't shut your hands.

"He's stale as poorhouse cake," Hogan said. "He's nothing."

"I never seen Walcott," I said.

"He'll kill him," said Hogan. "He'll tear him in two."

"Well," I said, "everybody's got to get it sometime."

"Not like this, though," Hogan said. "They'll think he never trained. It gives the farm a black eye."

"You hear what the reporters said about him?"

"Didn't I! They said he was awful. They said they oughtn't to let him fight."

"Well," I said, "they're always wrong, ain't they?"

"Yes," said Hogan. "But this time they're right."

"What the hell do they know about whether a man's right or not?"

"Well," said Hogan, "they're not such fools."

"All they did was pick Willard at Toledo. This Lardner he's so wise now, ask him about when he picked Willard at Toledo."

"Aw, he wasn't out," Hogan said. "He only writes the big fights."

"I don't care who they are," I said. "What the hell do they know? They can write maybe, but what the hell do they know?"

"You don't think Jack's in any shape, do you?" Hogan asked.

"No. He's through. All he needs is to have Corbett pick him to win for it to be all over."

"Well, Corbett'll pick him," Hogan says.

"Sure. He'll pick him."

That night Jack didn't sleep any either. The next morning was the last day before the fight. After breakfast we were out on the porch again.

"What do you think about, Jack, when you can't sleep?" I said.

"Oh, I worry," Jack says. "I worry about property I got up in the Bronx, I worry about property I got in Florida. I worry about the kids. I worry about the wife. Sometimes I think about fights. I think about that kike Ted Lewis and I get sore. I got some stocks and I worry about them. What the hell don't I think about?"

"Well," I said, "tomorrow night it'll all be over."

"Sure," said Jack. "That always helps a lot, don't it? That just fixes everything all up, I suppose. Sure."

He was sore all day. We didn't do any work. Jack just moved around a little to loosen up. He shadow-boxed a few rounds. He didn't even look good doing that. He skipped the rope a little while. He couldn't sweat.

"He'd be better not to do any work at all," Hogan said. We were standing watching him skip rope. "Don't he ever sweat at all any more?"

"He can't sweat."

"Do you suppose he's got the con? He never had any trouble making weight, did he?"

"No, he hasn't got any con. He just hasn't got anything inside any more."

"He ought to sweat," said Hogan.

Jack came over, skipping the rope. He was skipping up and down in front of us, forward and back, crossing his arms every third time.

"Well," he says. "What are you buzzards talking about?"

"I don't think you ought to work any more," Hogan says. "You'll be stale."

"Wouldn't that be awful?" Jack says and skips away down the floor, slapping the rope hard.

That afternoon John Collins showed up out at the farm. Jack was up in his room. John came out in a car from town. He had a couple of friends with him. The car stopped and they all got out.

"Where's Jack?" John asked me.

"Up in his room, lying down."

"Lying down?"

"Yes," I said.

"How is he?"

I looked at the two fellows that were with John.

"They're friends of his," John said.

"He's pretty bad," I said.

"What's the matter with him?"

"He don't sleep."

"Hell," said John. "That Irishman could never sleep."

"He isn't right," I said.

"Hell," John said. "He's never right. I've had him for ten years and he's never been right yet."

The fellows who were with him laughed.

"I want you to shake hands with Mr. Morgan and Mr. Steinfelt," John said. "This is Mr. Doyle. He's been training Jack."

"Glad to meet you," I said.

"Let's go up and see the boy," the fellow called Morgan said.

"Let's have a look at him," Steinfelt said.

We all went upstairs.

"Where's Hogan?" John asked.

"He's out in the barn with a couple of his customers," I said.

"He got many people out here now?" John asked.

"Just two."

"Pretty quiet, ain't it?" Morgan said.

"Yes," I said. "It's pretty quiet."

We were outside Jack's room. John knocked on the door. There wasn't any answer.

"Maybe he's asleep," I said.

"What the hell's he sleeping in the daytime for?"

John turned the handle and we all went in. Jack was lying asleep on the bed. He was face down and his face was in the pillow. Both his arms were around the pillow.

"Hey, Jack!" John said to him.

Jack's head moved a little on the pillow. "Jack!" John says, leaning over him. Jack just dug a little deeper in the pillow. John touched him on the shoulder. Jack sat up and looked at us. He hadn't shaved and he was wearing an old sweater.

"Christ! Why can't you let me sleep?" he says to John.

"Don't be sore," John says. "I didn't mean to wake you up."

"Oh no," Jack says. "Of course not."

"You know Morgan and Steinfelt," John said.

"Glad to see you," Jack says.

"How do you feel, Jack?" Morgan asks him.

"Fine," Jack says. "How the hell would I feel?"

"You look fine," Steinfelt says.

"Yes, don't I," says Jack. "Say," he says to John. "You're my manager. You get a big enough cut. Why the hell don't you come out here when the reporters was out! You want Jerry and me to talk to them?"

"I had Lew fighting in Philadelphia," John said.

"What the hell's that to me?" Jack says. "You're my manager. You get a big enough cut, don't you? You aren't making me any money in Philadelphia, are you? Why the hell aren't you out here when I ought to have you?"

"Hogan was here."

"Hogan," Jack says. "Hogan's as dumb as I am."

"Soldier Bahtlett was out here wukking with you for a while, wasn't he?" Steinfelt said to change the subject.

"Yes, he was out here," Jack says. "He was out here all right."

"Say, Jerry," John said to me. "Would you go and find Hogan and tell him we want to see him in about half an hour?"

"Sure," I said.

"Why the hell can't he stick around?" Jack says. "Stick around, Jerry."

Morgan and Steinfelt looked at each other.

"Quiet down, Jack," John said to him.

"I better go find Hogan," I said.

"All right, if you want to go," Jack says. "None of these guys are going to send you away, though."

"I'll go find Hogan," I said.

Hogan was out in the gym in the barn. He had a couple of his health-farm patients with the gloves on. They neither one wanted to hit the other, for fear the other would come back and hit him.

"That'll do," Hogan said when he saw me come in. "You can stop the slaughter. You gentlemen take a shower and Bruce will rub you down."

They climbed out through the ropes and Hogan came over to me.

"John Collins is out with a couple of friends to see Jack," I said.

"I saw them come up in the car."

"Who are the two fellows with John?"

"They're what you call wise boys," Hogan said. "Don't you know them two?"

"No," I said.

"That's Happy Steinfelt and Lew Morgan. They got a poolroom."

"I been away a long time," I said.

"Sure," said Hogan. "That Happy Steinfelt's a big operator."

"I've heard his name," I said.

"He's a pretty smooth boy," Hogan said. "They're a couple of sharpshooters."

"Well," I said. "They want to see us in half an hour."

"You mean they don't want to see us until a half an hour?"

"That's it."

"Come on in the office," Hogan said. "To hell with those sharpshooters."

After about thirty minutes or so Hogan and I went upstairs. We knocked on Jack's door. They were talking inside the room.

"Wait a minute," somebody said.

"To hell with that stuff," Hogan said. "When you want to see me I'm down in the office."

We heard the door unlock. Steinfelt opened it.

"Come on in, Hogan," he says. "We're all going to have a drink."

"Well," says Hogan. "That's something."

We went in. Jack was sitting on the bed. John and Morgan were sitting on a couple of chairs. Steinfelt was standing up.

"You're a pretty mysterious lot of boys," Hogan said.

"Hello, Danny," John says.

"Hello, Danny," Morgan says and shakes hands.

Jack doesn't say anything. He just sits there on the bed. He ain't with the others. He's all by himself. He was wearing an old blue jersey and pants and had on boxing shoes. He needed a shave. Steinfelt and Morgan were dressers. John was quite a dresser too. Jack sat there looking Irish and tough.

Steinfelt brought out a bottle and Hogan brought in some

glasses and everybody had a drink. Jack and I took one and the rest of them went on and had two or three each.

"Better save some for your ride back," Hogan said.

"Don't you worry. We got plenty," Morgan said.

Jack hadn't drunk anything since the one drink. He was standing up and looking at them. Morgan was sitting on the bed where Jack had sat.

"Have a drink, Jack," John said and handed him the glass and the bottle.

"No," Jack said, "I never liked to go to these wakes."

They all laughed. Jack didn't laugh.

They were all feeling pretty good when they left. Jack stood on the porch when they got into the car. They waved to him.

"So long," Jack said.

We had supper. Jack didn't say anything all during the meal except, "Will you pass me this?" or "Will you pass me that?" The two health-farm patients ate at the same table with us. They were pretty nice fellows. After we finished eating we went out on the porch. It was dark early.

"Like to take a walk, Jerry?" Jack asked.

"Sure," I said.

We put on our coats and started out. It was quite a way down to the main road and then we walked along the main road about a mile and a half. Cars kept going by and we would pull out to the side until they were past. Jack didn't say anything. After we had stepped out into the bushes to let a big car go by Jack said, "To hell with this walking. Come on back to Hogan's."

We went along a side road that cut up over the hill and cut across the fields back to Hogan's. We could see the lights of the house up on the hill. We came around to the front of the house and there standing in the doorway was Hogan.

"Have a good walk?" Hogan asked.

"Oh, fine," Jack said. "Listen, Hogan. Have you got any liquor?"

"Sure," says Hogan. "What's the idea?"

"Send it up to the room," Jack says. "I'm going to sleep tonight."

"You're the doctor," Hogan says.

"Come on up to the room, Jerry," Jack says.

Upstairs Jack sat on the bed with his head in his hands.

"Ain't it a life?" Jack says.

Hogan brought in a quart of liquor and two glasses.

"Want some ginger ale?"

"What do you think I want to do, get sick?"

"I just asked you," said Hogan.

"Have a drink?" said Jack.

"No, thanks," said Hogan. He went out.

"How about you, Jerry?"

"I'll have one with you," I said.

Jack poured out a couple of drinks. "Now," he said, "I want to take it slow and easy."

"Put some water in it," I said.

"Yes," Jack said. "I guess that's better."

We had a couple of drinks without saying anything. Jack started to pour me another.

"No," I said, "that's all I want."

"All right," Jack said. He poured himself out another big shot and put water in it. He was lighting up a little.

"That was a fine bunch out here this afternoon," he said. "They don't take any chances, those two."

Then a little later, "Well," he says, "they're right. What the hell's the good in taking chances?"

"Don't you want another, Jerry?" he said. "Come on, drink along with me."

"I don't need it, Jack," I said. "I feel all right."

"Just have one more," Jack said. It was softening him up.

"All right," I said.

Jack poured one for me and another big one for himself.

"You know," he said, "I like liquor pretty well. If I hadn't been boxing I would have drunk quite a lot."

"Sure," I said.

"You know," he said, "I missed a lot, boxing."

"You made plenty of money."

"Sure, that's what I'm after. You know I miss a lot, Jerry."

"How do you mean?"

"Well," he says, "like about the wife. And being away from

home so much. It don't do my girls any good. 'Who's your old man?' some of those society kids 'll say to them. 'My old man's Jack Brennan.' That don't do them any good."

"Hell," I said, "all that makes a difference is if they got dough."

"Well," says Jack, "I got the dough for them all right."

He poured out another drink. The bottle was about empty.

"Put some water in it," I said. Jack poured in some water.

"You know," he says, "you ain't got any idea how I miss the wife."

"Sure."

"You ain't got any idea. You can't have an idea what it's like."

"It ought to be better out in the country than in town."

"With me now," Jack said, "it don't make any difference where I am. You can't have an idea what it's like."

"Have another drink."

"Am I getting soused? Do I talk funny?"

"You're coming on all right."

"You can't have an idea what it's like. They ain't anybody can have an idea what it's like."

"Except the wife," I said.

"She knows," Jack said. "She knows all right. She knows. You bet she knows."

"Put some water in that," I said.

"Jerry," says Jack, "you can't have an idea what it gets to be like."

He was good and drunk. He was looking at me steady. His eyes were sort of too steady.

"You'll sleep all right," I said.

"Listen, Jerry," Jack says. "You want to make some money? Get some money down on Walcott."

"Yes?"

"Listen, Jerry," Jack put down the glass. "I'm not drunk now, see? You know what I'm betting on him? Fifty grand."

"That's a lot of dough."

"Fifty grand," Jack says, "at two to one. I'll get twenty-five thousand bucks. Get some money on him, Jerry."

"It sounds good," I said.

"How can I beat him?" Jack says. "It ain't crooked. How can I beat him? Why not make money on it?"

"Put some water in that," I said.

"I'm through after this fight," Jack says. "I'm through with it. I got to take a beating. Why shouldn't I make money on it?"

"Sure."

"I ain't slept for a week," Jack says. "All night I lay awake and worry my can off. I can't sleep, Jerry. You ain't got an idea what it's like when you can't sleep."

"Sure."

"I can't sleep. That's all. I just can't sleep. What's the use of taking care of yourself all these years when you can't sleep?"

"It's bad."

"You ain't got an idea what it's like, Jerry, when you can't sleep."

"Put some water in that," I said.

Well, about eleven o'clock Jack passes out and I put him to bed. Finally he's so he can't keep from sleeping. I helped him get his clothes off and got him into bed.

"You'll sleep all right, Jack," I said.

"Sure," Jack says, "I'll sleep now."

"Good night, Jack," I said.

"Good night, Jerry," Jack says. "You're the only friend I got."

"Oh, hell," I said.

"You're the only friend I got," Jack says, "the only friend I got."

"Go to sleep," I said.

"I'll sleep," Jack says.

Downstairs Hogan was sitting at the desk in the office reading the papers. He looked up. "Well, you get your boy friend to sleep?" he asks.

"He's off."

"It's better for him than not sleeping," Hogan said.

"Sure."

"You'd have a hell of a time explaining that to these sport writers though," Hogan said.

"Well, I'm going to bed myself," I said.

"Good night," said Hogan.

In the morning I came downstairs about eight o'clock and got some breakfast. Hogan had his two customers out in the barn doing exercises. I went out and watched them.

"One! Two! Three! Four!" Hogan was counting for them. "Hello, Jerry," he said. "Is Jack up yet?"

"No. He's still sleeping."

I went back to my room and packed up to go in to town. About nine-thirty I heard Jack getting up in the next room. When I heard him go downstairs I went down after him. Jack was sitting at the breakfast table. Hogan had come in and was standing beside the table.

"How do you feel, Jack?" I asked him.

"Not so bad."

"Sleep well?" Hogan asked.

"I slept all right," Jack said. "I got a thick tongue but I ain't got a head."

"Good," said Hogan. "That was good liquor."

"Put it on the bill," Jack says.

"What time you want to go into town?" Hogan asked.

"Before lunch," Jack says. "The eleven o'clock train."

"Sit down, Jerry," Jack said. Hogan went out.

I sat down at the table. Jack was eating a grapefruit. When he'd find a seed he'd spit it out in the spoon and dump it on the plate.

"I guess I was pretty stewed last night," he started.

"You drank some liquor."

"I guess I said a lot of fool things."

"You weren't bad."

"Where's Hogan?" he asked. He was through with the grapefruit.

"He's out in front in the office."

"What did I say about betting on the fight?" Jack asked. He was holding the spoon and sort of poking at the grapefruit with it.

The girl came in with some ham and eggs and took away the grapefruit.

"Bring me another glass of milk," Jack said to her. She went out.

"You said you had fifty grand on Walcott," I said.

"That's right," Jack said.

"That's a lot of money."

"I don't feel too good about it," Jack said.

"Something might happen."

"No," Jack said. "He wants the title bad. They'll be shooting with him all right."

"You can't ever tell."

"No. He wants the title. It's worth a lot of money to him."

"Fifty grand is a lot of money," I said.

"It's business," said Jack. "I can't win. You know I can't win anyway."

"As long as you're in there you got a chance."

"No," Jack says. "I'm all through. It's just business."

"How do you feel?"

"Pretty good," Jack said. "The sleep was what I needed."

"You might go good."

"I'll give them a good show," Jack said.

After breakfast Jack called up his wife on the long-distance. He was inside the booth telephoning.

"That's the first time he's called her up since he's out here," Hogan said.

"He writes her every day."

"Sure," Hogan says, "a letter only costs two cents."

Hogan said good-by to us and Bruce, the nigger rubber, drove us down to the train in the cart.

"Good-by, Mr. Brennan," Bruce said at the train, "I sure hope you knock his can off."

"So long," Jack said. He gave Bruce two dollars. Bruce had worked on him a lot. He looked kind of disappointed. Jack saw me looking at Bruce holding the two dollars.

"It's all in the bill," he said. "Hogan charged me for the rubbing."

On the train going into town Jack didn't talk. He sat in the corner of the seat with his ticket in his hat-band and looked out of the window. Once he turned and spoke to me.

"I told the wife I'd take a room at the Shelby tonight," he said.

"It's just around the corner from the Garden. I can go up to the house tomorrow morning."

"That's a good idea," I said. "Your wife ever see you fight, Jack?"

"No," Jack says. "She never seen me fight."

I thought he must be figuring on taking an awful beating if he doesn't want to go home afterward. In town we took a taxi up to the Shelby. A boy came out and took our bags and we went in to the desk.

"How much are the rooms?" Jack asked.

"We only have double rooms," the clerk says. "I can give you a nice double room for ten dollars."

"That's too steep."

"I can give you a double room for seven dollars."

"With a bath?"

"Certainly."

"You might as well bunk with me, Jerry," Jack says.

"Oh," I said, "I'll sleep down at my brother-in-law's."

"I don't mean for you to pay it," Jack says. "I just want to get my money's worth."

"Will you register, please?" the clerk says. He looked at the name. "Number 238, Mister Brennan."

We went up in the elevator. It was a nice big room with two beds and a door opening into a bath-room.

"This is pretty good," Jack says.

The boy who brought us up pulled up the curtains and brought in our bags. Jack didn't make any move, so I gave the boy a quarter. We washed up and Jack said we better go out and get something to eat.

We ate a lunch at Jimmy Hanley's place. Quite a lot of the boys were there. When we were about half through eating, John came in and sat down with us. Jack didn't talk much.

"How are you on the weight, Jack?" John asked him. Jack was putting away a pretty good lunch.

"I could make it with my clothes on," Jack said. He never had to worry about taking off weight. He was a natural welterweight and he'd never gotten fat. He'd lost weight out at Hogan's.

"Well, that's one thing you never had to worry about," John said.

"That's one thing," Jack says.

We went around to the Garden to weigh in after lunch. The match was made at a hundred forty-seven pounds at three o'clock. Jack stepped on the scales with a towel around him. The bar didn't move. Walcott had just weighed and was standing with a lot of people around him.

"Let's see what you weigh, Jack," Freedman, Walcott's manager, said.

"All right, weigh *him* then," Jack jerked his head toward Walcott.

"Drop the towel," Freedman said.

"What do you make it?" Jack asked the fellows who were weighing.

"One hundred and forty-three pounds," the fat man who was weighing said.

"You're down fine, Jack," Freedman says.

"Weigh *him*," Jack says.

Walcott came over. He was a blond with wide shoulders and arms like a heavyweight. He didn't have much legs. Jack stood about half a head taller than he did.

"Hello, Jack," he said. His face was plenty marked up.

"Hello," said Jack. "How you feel?"

"Good," Walcott says. He dropped the towel from around his waist and stood on the scales. He had the widest shoulders and back you ever saw.

"One hundred and forty-six pounds and twelve ounces."

Walcott stepped off and grinned at Jack.

"Well," John says to him, "Jack's spotting you about four pounds."

"More than that when I come in, kid," Walcott says. "I'm going to go and eat now."

We went back and Jack got dressed. "He's a pretty tough-looking boy," Jack says to me.

"He looks as though he'd been hit plenty of times."

"Oh, yes," Jack says. "He ain't hard to hit."

"Where are you going?" John asked when Jack was dressed.

"Back to the hotel," Jack says. "You looked after everything?"

"Yes," John says. "It's all looked after."

"I'm going to lie down a while," Jack says.

"I'll come around for you about a quarter to seven and we'll go and eat."

"All right."

Up at the hotel Jack took off his shoes and his coat and lay down for a while. I wrote a letter. I looked over a couple of times and Jack wasn't sleeping. He was lying perfectly still but every once in a while his eyes would open. Finally he sits up.

"Want to play some cribbage, Jerry?" he says.

"Sure," I said.

He went over to his suitcase and got out the cards and the cribbage board. We played cribbage and he won three dollars off me. John knocked at the door and came in.

"Want to play some cribbage, John?" Jack asked him.

John put his hat down on the table. It was all wet. His coat was wet too.

"Is it raining?" Jack asks.

"It's pouring," John says. "The taxi I had got tied up in the traffic and I got out and walked."

"Come on, play some cribbage," Jack says.

"You ought to go and eat."

"No," says Jack. "I don't want to eat yet."

So they played cribbage for about half an hour and Jack won a dollar and a half off him.

"Well, I suppose we got to go eat," Jack says. He went to the window and looked out.

"Is it still raining?"

"Yes."

"Let's eat in the hotel," John says.

"All right," Jack says, "I'll play you once more to see who pays for the meal."

After a little while Jack gets up and says, "You buy the meal, John," and we went downstairs and ate in the big dining-room.

After we ate we went upstairs and Jack played cribbage with John again and won two dollars and a half off him. Jack was feeling pretty good. John had a bag with him with all his stuff in it. Jack took off his shirt and collar and put on a jersey and a sweater, so he wouldn't catch cold when he came out, and put his ring clothes and his bathrobe in a bag.

"You all ready?" John asks him. "I'll call up and have them get a taxi."

Pretty soon the telephone rang and they said the taxi was waiting.

We rode down in the elevator and went out through the lobby, and got in a taxi and rode around to the Garden. It was raining hard but there was a lot of people outside on the streets. The Garden was sold out. As we came in on our way to the dressing-room I saw how full it was. It looked like half a mile down to the ring. It was all dark. Just the lights over the ring.

"It's a good thing, with this rain, they didn't try and pull this fight in the ball park," John said.

"They got a good crowd," Jack says.

"This is a fight that would draw a lot more than the Garden could hold."

"You can't tell about the weather," Jack says.

John came to the door of the dressing-room and poked his head in. Jack was sitting there with his bathrobe on, he had his arms folded and was looking at the floor. John had a couple of handlers with him. They looked over his shoulder. Jack stood up.

"Is he in?" he asked.

"He's just gone down," John said.

We started down. Walcott was just getting into the ring. The crowd gave him a big hand. He climbed through between the ropes and put his two fists together and smiled, and shook them at the crowd, first at one side of the ring, then at the other, and then sat down. Jack got a good hand coming down through the crowd. Jack is Irish and the Irish always get a pretty good hand. An Irishman don't draw in New York like a Jew or an Italian but they always get a good hand. Jack climbed up and bent down to go through the ropes and Walcott came over from his corner and pushed the rope down for Jack to go through. The crowd thought that was wonderful. Walcott put his hand on Jack's shoulder and they stood there just for a second.

"So you're going to be one of these popular champions," Jack says to him. "Take your goddam hand off my shoulder."

"Be yourself," Walcott says.

This is all great for the crowd. How gentlemanly the boys are before the fight. How they wish each other luck.

Solly Freedman came over to our corner while Jack is bandaging his hands and John is over in Walcott's corner. Jack puts his thumb through the slit in the bandage and then wrapped his hand nice and smooth. I taped it around the wrist and twice across the knuckles.

"Hey," Freedman says. "Where do you get all that tape?"

"Feel of it," Jack says. "It's soft, ain't it? Don't be a hick."

Freedman stands there all the time while Jack bandages the other hand, and one of the boys that's going to handle him brings the gloves and I pull them on and work them around.

"Say, Freedman," Jack asks, "what nationality is this Walcott?"

"I don't know," Solly says. "He's some sort of a Dane."

"He's a Bohemian," the lad who brought the gloves said.

The referee called them out to the center of the ring and Jack walks out. Walcott comes out smiling. They met and the referee put his arm on each of their shoulders.

"Hello, popularity," Jack says to Walcott.

"Be yourself."

"What do you call yourself 'Walcott' for?" Jack says. "Didn't you know he was a nigger?"

"Listen—" says the referee, and he gives them the same old line. Once Walcott interrupts him. He grabs Jack's arm and says, "Can I hit when he's got me like this?"

"Keep your hands off me," Jack says. "There ain't no moving-pictures of this."

They went to their corners. I lifted the bathrobe off Jack and he leaned on the ropes and flexed his knees a couple of times and scuffed his shoes in the rosin. The gong rang and Jack turned quick and went out. Walcott came toward him and they touched

gloves and as soon as Walcott dropped his hands Jack jumped
his left into his face twice. There wasn't anybody ever boxed
better than Jack. Walcott was after him, going forward all the
time with his chin on his chest. He's a hooker and he carries his
hands pretty low. All he knows is to get in there and sock. But
every time he gets in there close, Jack has the left hand in his face.
It's just as though it's automatic. Jack just raises the left hand up
and it's in Walcott's face. Three or four times Jack brings the
right over but Walcott gets it on the shoulder or high up on the
head. He's just like all these hookers. The only thing he's afraid
of is another one of the same kind. He's covered everywhere you
can hurt him. He don't care about a left-hand in his face.

After about four rounds Jack has him bleeding bad and his face
all cut up, but every time Walcott's got in close he's socked so
hard he's got two big red patches on both sides just below Jack's
ribs. Every time he gets in close, Jack ties him up, then gets one
hand loose and uppercuts him, but when Walcott gets his hands
loose he socks Jack in the body so they can hear it outside in the
street. He's a socker.

It goes along like that for three rounds more. They don't talk
any. They're working all the time. We worked over Jack plenty
too, in between the rounds. He don't look good at all but he never
does much work in the ring. He don't move around much and that
left-hand is just automatic. It's just like it was connected with
Walcott's face and Jack just had to wish it in every time. Jack is
always calm in close and he doesn't waste any juice. He knows
everything about working in close too and he's getting away with
a lot of stuff. While they were in our corner I watched him tie
Walcott up, get his right hand loose, turn it and come up with an
uppercut that got Walcott's nose with the heel of the glove. Walcott was bleeding bad and leaned his nose on Jack's shoulder so
as to give Jack some of it too, and Jack sort of lifted his shoulder
sharp and caught him against the nose, and then brought down the
right hand and did the same thing again.

Walcott was sore as hell. By the time they'd gone five rounds
he hated Jack's guts. Jack wasn't sore; that is, he wasn't any sorer
than he always was. He certainly did used to make the fellows

he fought hate boxing. That was why he hated Kid Lewis so. He never got the Kid's goat. Kid Lewis always had about three new dirty things Jack couldn't do. Jack was as safe as a church all the time he was in there, as long as he was strong. He certainly was treating Walcott rough. The funny thing was it looked as though Jack was an open classic boxer. That was because he had all that stuff too.

After the seventh round Jack says, "My left's getting heavy."

From then he started to take a beating. It didn't show at first. But instead of him running the fight it was Walcott was running it, instead of being safe all the time now he was in trouble. He couldn't keep him out with the left hand now. It looked as though it was the same as ever, only now instead of Walcott's punches just missing him they were just hitting him. He took an awful beating in the body.

"What's the round?" Jack asked.

"The eleventh."

"I can't stay," Jack says. "My legs are going bad."

Walcott had been just hitting him for a long time. It was like a baseball catcher pulls the ball and takes some of the shock off. From now on Walcott commenced to land solid. He certainly was a socking-machine. Jack was just trying to block everything now. It didn't show what an awful beating he was taking. In between the rounds I worked on his legs. The muscles would flutter under my hands all the time I was rubbing them. He was sick as hell.

"How's it go?" he asked John, turning around, his face all swollen.

"It's his fight."

"I think I can last," Jack says. "I don't want this bohunk to stop me."

It was going just the way he thought it would. He knew he couldn't beat Walcott. He wasn't strong any more. He was all right though. His money was all right and now he wanted to finish it off right to please himself. He didn't want to be knocked out.

The gong rang and we pushed him out. He went out slow.

Walcott came right out after him. Jack put the left in his face and
Walcott took it, came in under it and started working on Jack's
body. Jack tried to tie him up and it was just like trying to hold
on to a buzz-saw. Jack broke away from it and missed with the
right. Walcott clipped him with a left-hook and Jack went down.
He went down on his hands and knees and looked at us. The
referee started counting. Jack was watching us and shaking his
head. At eight John motioned to him. You couldn't hear on account of the crowd. Jack got up. The referee had been holding
Walcott back with one arm while he counted.

When Jack was on his feet Walcott started toward him.

"Watch yourself, Jimmy," I heard Solly Freedman yell to him.

Walcott came up to Jack looking at him. Jack stuck the left
hand at him. Walcott just shook his head. He backed Jack up
against the ropes, measured him and then hooked the left very
light to the side of Jack's head and socked the right into the body
as hard as he could sock, just as low as he could get it. He must
have hit him five inches below the belt. I thought the eyes would
come out of Jack's head. They stuck way out. His mouth come
open.

The referee grabbed Walcott. Jack stepped forward. If he went
down there went fifty thousand bucks. He walked as though all
his insides were going to fall out.

"It wasn't low," he said. "It was a accident."

The crowd were yelling so you couldn't hear anything.

"I'm all right," Jack says. They were right in front of us. The
referee looks at John and then he shakes his head.

"Come on, you polak son-of-a-bitch," Jack says to Walcott.

John was hanging onto the ropes. He had the towel ready to
chuck in. Jack was standing just a little way out from the ropes.
He took a step forward. I saw the sweat come out on his face like
somebody had squeezed it and a big drop went down his nose.

"Come on and fight," Jack says to Walcott.

The referee looked at John and waved Walcott on.

"Go in there, you slob," he says.

Walcott went in. He didn't know what to do either. He never
thought Jack could have stood it. Jack put the left in his face.

There was such a hell of a lot of yelling going on. They were right in front of us. Walcott hit him twice. Jack's face was the worst thing I ever saw—the look on it! He was holding himself and all his body together and it all showed on his face. All the time he was thinking and holding his body in where it was busted.

Then he started to sock. His face looked awful all the time. He started to sock with his hands low down by his side, swinging at Walcott. Walcott covered up and Jack was swinging wild at Walcott's head. Then he swung the left and it hit Walcott in the groin and the right hit Walcott right bang where he'd hit Jack. Way low below the belt. Walcott went down and grabbed himself there and rolled and twisted around.

The referee grabbed Jack and pushed him toward his corner. John jumps into the ring. There was all this yelling going on. The referee was talking with the judges and then the announcer got into the ring with the megaphone and says, "Walcott on a foul."

The referee is talking to John and he says, "What could I do? Jack wouldn't take the foul. Then when he's groggy he fouls him."

"He'd lost it anyway," John says.

Jack's sitting on the chair. I've got his gloves off and he's holding himself in down there with both hands. When he's got something supporting it his face doesn't look so bad.

"Go over and say you're sorry," John says into his ear. "It'll look good."

Jack stands up and the sweat comes out all over his face. I put the bathrobe around him and he holds himself in with one hand under the bathrobe and goes across the ring. They've picked Walcott up and they're working on him. There're a lot of people in Walcott's corner. Nobody speaks to Jack. He leans over Walcott.

"I'm sorry," Jack says. "I didn't mean to foul you."

Walcott doesn't say anything. He looks too damned sick.

"Well, you're the champion now," Jack says to him. "I hope you get a hell of a lot of fun out of it."

"Leave the kid alone," Solly Freedman says.

"Hello, Solly," Jack says. "I'm sorry I fouled your boy."

Freedman just looks at him.

Jack went to his corner walking that funny jerky way and we

got him down through the ropes and through the reporters' tables and out down the aisles. A lot of people want to slap Jack on the back. He goes out through all that mob in his bathrobe to the dressing-room. It's a popular win for Walcott. That's the way the money was bet in the Garden.

Once we got inside the dressing-room Jack lay down and shut his eyes.

"We want to get to the hotel and get a doctor," John says.

"I'm all busted inside," Jack says.

"I'm sorry as hell, Jack," John says.

"It's all right," Jack says.

He lies there with his eyes shut.

"They certainly tried a nice double-cross," John said.

"Your friends Morgan and Steinfelt," Jack said. "You got nice friends."

He lies there, his eyes are open now. His face has still got that awful drawn look.

"It's funny how fast you can think when it means that much money," Jack says.

"You're some boy, Jack," John says.

"No," Jack says. "It was nothing."

A CLEAN, WELL-LIGHTED PLACE

It was late and every one had left the café except an old man who sat in the shadow the leaves of the tree made against the electric light. In the day time the street was dusty, but at night the dew settled the dust and the old man liked to sit late because he was deaf and now at night it was quiet and he felt the difference. The two waiters inside the café knew that the old man was a little drunk, and while he was a good client they knew that if he became too drunk he would leave without paying, so they kept watch on him.

"Last week he tried to commit suicide," one waiter said.

"Why?"

"He was in despair."

"What about?"

"Nothing."

"How do you know it was nothing?"

"He has plenty of money."

They sat together at a table that was close against the wall near the door of the café and looked at the terrace where the tables were all empty except where the old man sat in the shadow of the leaves of the tree that moved slightly in the wind. A girl and a soldier went by in the street. The street light shone on the brass number on his collar. The girl wore no head covering and hurried beside him.

"The guard will pick him up," one waiter said.

"What does it matter if he gets what he's after?"

"He had better get off the street now. The guard will get him. They went by five minutes ago."

The old man sitting in the shadow rapped on his saucer with his glass. The younger waiter went over to him.

"What do you want?"

The old man looked at him. "Another brandy," he said.

"You'll be drunk," the waiter said. The old man looked at him. The waiter went away.

"He'll stay all night," he said to his colleague. "I'm sleepy now. I never get into bed before three o'clock. He should have killed himself last week."

The waiter took the brandy bottle and another saucer from the counter inside the café and marched out to the old man's table. He put down the saucer and poured the glass full of brandy.

"You should have killed yourself last week," he said to the deaf man. The old man motioned with his finger. "A little more," he said. The waiter poured on into the glass so that the brandy slopped over and ran down the stem into the top saucer of the pile. "Thank you," the old man said. The waiter took the bottle back inside the café. He sat down at the table with his colleague again.

"He's drunk now," he said.

"He's drunk every night."

"What did he want to kill himself for?"

"How should I know."

"How did he do it?"

"He hung himself with a rope."

"Who cut him down?"

"His niece."

"Why did they do it?"

"Fear for his soul."

"How much money has he got?"

"He's got plenty."

"He must be eighty years old."

"Anyway I should say he was eighty."

"I wish he would go home. I never get to bed before three o'clock. What kind of hour is that to go to bed?"

"He stays up because he likes it."

"He's lonely. I'm not lonely. I have a wife waiting in bed for me."

"He had a wife once too."

"A wife would be no good to him now."

"You can't tell. He might be better with a wife."

"His niece looks after him."

"I know. You said she cut him down."

"I wouldn't want to be that old. An old man is a nasty thing."

"Not always. This old man is clean. He drinks without spilling. Even now, drunk. Look at him."

"I don't want to look at him. I wish he would go home. He has no regard for those who must work."

The old man looked from his glass across the square, then over at the waiters.

"Another brandy," he said, pointing to his glass. The waiter who was in hurry came over.

"Finished," he said, speaking with that omission of syntax stupid people employ when talking to drunken people or foreigners. "No more tonight. Close now."

"Another," said the old man.

"No. Finished." The waiter wiped the edge of the table with a towel and shook his head.

The old man stood up, slowly counted the saucers, took a leather coin purse from his pocket and paid for the drinks, leaving half a peseta tip.

The waiter watched him go down the street, a very old man walking unsteadily but with dignity.

"Why didn't you let him stay and drink?" the unhurried waiter asked. They were putting up the shutters. "It is not half-past two."

"I want to go home to bed."

"What is an hour?"

"More to me than to him."

"An hour is the same."

"You talk like an old man yourself. He can buy a bottle and drink at home."

"It's not the same."

"No, it is not," agreed the waiter with a wife. He did not wish to be unjust. He was only in a hurry.

"And you? You have no fear of going home before your usual hour?"

"Are you trying to insult me?"

"No, hombre, only to make a joke."

"No," the waiter who was in a hurry said, rising from pulling down the metal shutters. "I have confidence. I am all confidence."

"You have youth, confidence, and a job," the older waiter said. "You have everything."

"And what do you lack?"

"Everything but work."

"You have everything I have."

"No. I have never had confidence and I am not young."

"Come on. Stop talking nonsense and lock up."

"I am of those who like to stay late at the café," the older waiter said. "With all those who do not want to go to bed. With all those who need a light for the night."

"I want to go home and into bed."

"We are of two different kinds," the older waiter said. He was now dressed to go home. "It is not only a question of youth and confidence although those things are very beautiful. Each night

I am reluctant to close up because there may be some one who needs the café."

"Hombre, there are bodegas open all night long."

"You do not understand. This is a clean and pleasant café. It is well lighted. The light is very good and also, now, there are shadows of the leaves."

"Good night," said the younger waiter.

"Good night," the other said. Turning off the electric light he continued the conversation with himself. It is the light of course but it is necessary that the place be clean and pleasant. You do not want music. Certainly you do not want music. Nor can you stand before a bar with dignity although that is all that is provided for these hours. What did he fear? It was not fear or dread. It was a nothing that he knew too well. It was all a nothing and a man was nothing too. It was only that and light was all it needed and a certain cleanness and order. Some lived in it and never felt it but he knew it all was nada y pues nada y nada y pues nada. Our nada who are in nada, nada be thy name thy kingdom nada thy will be nada in nada as it is in nada. Give us this nada our daily nada and nada us our nada as we nada our nada and nada us not into nada but deliver us from nada; pues nada. Hail nothing full of nothing, nothing is with thee. He smiled and stood before a bar with a shining steam pressure coffee machine.

"What's yours?" asked the barman.

"Nada."

"Otro loco mas," said the barman and turned away.

"A little cup," said the waiter.

The barman poured it for him.

"The light is very bright and pleasant but the bar is unpolished," the waiter said.

The barman looked at him but did not answer. It was too late at night for conversation.

"You want another copita?" the barman asked.

"No, thank you," said the waiter and went out. He disliked bars and bodegas. A clean, well-lighted café was a very different thing. Now, without thinking further, he would go home to his room.

He would lie in the bed and finally, with daylight, he would go to sleep. After all, he said to himself, it is probably only insomnia. Many must have it.

THE LIGHT OF THE WORLD

WHEN he saw us come in the door the bartender looked up and then reached over and put the glass covers on the two free-lunch bowls.

"Give me a beer," I said. He drew it, cut the top off with the spatula and then held the glass in his hand. I put the nickel on the wood and he slid the beer toward me.

"What's yours?" he said to Tom.

"Beer."

He drew that beer and cut it off and when he saw the money he pushed the beer across to Tom.

"What's the matter?" Tom asked.

The bartender didn't answer him. He just looked over our heads and said, "What's yours?" to a man who'd come in.

"Rye," the man said. The bartender put out the bottle and glass and a glass of water.

Tom reached over and took the glass off the free-lunch bowl. It was a bowl of pickled pig's feet and there was a wooden thing that worked like a scissors, with two wooden forks at the end to pick them up with.

"No," said the bartender and put the glass cover back on the bowl. Tom held the wooden scissors fork in his hand. "Put it back," said the bartender.

"You know where," said Tom.

The bartender reached a hand forward under the bar, watching us both. I put fifty cents on the wood and he straightened up.

"What was yours?" he said.

"Beer," I said, and before he drew the beer he uncovered both the bowls.

"Your goddam pig's feet stink," Tom said, and spit what he had in his mouth on the floor. The bartender didn't say anything. The man who had drunk the rye paid and went out without looking back.

"You stink yourself," the bartender said. "All you punks stink."

"He says we're punks," Tommy said to me.

"Listen," I said. "Let's get out."

"You punks clear the hell out of here," the bartender said.

"I said we were going out," I said. "It wasn't your idea."

"We'll be back," Tommy said.

"No, you won't," the bartender told him.

"Tell him how wrong he is," Tom turned to me.

"Come on," I said.

Outside it was good and dark.

"What the hell kind of place is this?" Tommy said.

"I don't know," I said. "Let's go down to the station."

We'd come in that town at one end and we were going out the other. It smelled of hides and tan bark and the big piles of sawdust. It was getting dark as we came in, and now that it was dark it was cold and the puddles of water in the road were freezing at the edges.

Down at the station there were five whores waiting for the train to come in, and six white men and four Indians. It was crowded and hot from the stove and full of stale smoke. As we came in nobody was talking and the ticket window was down.

"Shut the door, can't you?" somebody said.

I looked to see who said it. It was one of the white men. He wore stagged trousers and lumbermen's rubbers and a mackinaw shirt like the others, but he had no cap and his face was white and his hands were white and thin.

"Aren't you going to shut it?"

"Sure," I said, and shut it.

"Thank you," he said. One of the other men snickered.

"Ever interfere with a cook?" he said to me.

"No."

"You can interfere with this one," he looked at the cook. "He likes it."

The cook looked away from him holding his lips tight together.

"He puts lemon juice on his hands," the man said. "He wouldn't get them in dishwater for anything. Look how white they are."

One of the whores laughed out loud. She was the biggest whore I ever saw in my life and the biggest woman. And she had on one of those silk dresses that change colors. There were two other whores that were nearly as big but the big one must have weighed three hundred and fifty pounds. You couldn't believe she was real when you looked at her. All three had those changeable silk dresses. They sat side by side on the bench. They were huge. The other two were just ordinary looking whores, peroxide blondes.

"Look at his hands," the man said and nodded his head at the cook. The whore laughed again and shook all over.

The cook turned and said to her quickly, "You big disgusting mountain of flesh."

She just kept on laughing and shaking.

"Oh, my Christ," she said. She had a nice voice. "Oh, my sweet Christ."

The two other whores, the big ones, acted very quiet and placid as though they didn't have much sense, but they were big, nearly as big as the biggest one. They'd have both gone well over two hundred and fifty pounds. The other two were dignified.

Of the men, besides the cook and the one who talked, there were two other lumberjacks, one that listened, interested but bashful, and the other that seemed getting ready to say something, and two Swedes. Two Indians were sitting down at the end of the bench and one standing up against the wall.

The man who was getting ready to say something spoke to me very low, "Must be like getting on top of a hay mow."

I laughed and said it to Tommy.

"I swear to Christ I've never been anywhere like this," he said. "Look at the three of them." Then the cook spoke up.

"How old are you boys?"

"I'm ninety-six and he's sixty-nine," Tommy said.

"Ho! Ho! Ho!" the big whore shook with laughing. She had a really pretty voice. The other whores didn't smile.

"Oh, can't you be decent?" the cook said. "I asked just to be friendly."

"We're seventeen and nineteen," I said.

"What's the matter with you?" Tommy turned to me.

"That's all right."

"You can call me Alice," the big whore said and then she began to shake again.

"Is that your name?" Tommy asked.

"Sure," she said. "Alice. Isn't it?" she turned to the man who sat by the cook.

"Alice. That's right."

"That's the sort of name you'd have," the cook said.

"It's my real name," Alice said.

"What's the other girls' names?" Tom asked.

"Hazel and Ethel," Alice said. Hazel and Ethel smiled. They weren't very bright.

"What's your name?" I said to one of the blondes.

"Frances," she said.

"Frances what?"

"Frances Wilson. What's it to you?"

"What's yours?" I asked the other one.

"Oh, don't be fresh," she said.

"He just wants us all to be friends," the man who talked said. "Don't you want to be friends?"

"No," the peroxide one said. "Not with you."

"She's just a spitfire," the man said. "A regular little spitfire."

The one blonde looked at the other and shook her head.

"Goddamned mossbacks," she said.

Alice commenced to laugh again and to shake all over.

"There's nothing funny," the cook said. "You all laugh but there's nothing funny. You two young lads; where are you bound for?"

"Where are you going yourself?" Tom asked him.

"I want to go to Cadillac," the cook said. "Have you ever been there? My sister lives there."

"He's a sister himself," the man in the stagged trousers said.

"Can't you stop that sort of thing?" the cook asked. "Can't we speak decently?"

"Cadillac is where Steve Ketchel came from and where Ad Wolgast is from," the shy man said.

"Steve Ketchel," one of the blondes said in a high voice as though the name had pulled a trigger in her. "His own father shot and killed him. Yes, by Christ, his own father. There aren't any more men like Steve Ketchel."

"Wasn't his name Stanley Ketchel?" asked the cook.

"Oh, shut up," said the blonde. "What do you know about Steve? Stanley. He was no Stanley. Steve Ketchel was the finest and most beautiful man that ever lived. I never saw a man as clean and as white and as beautiful as Steve Ketchel. There never was a man like that. He moved just like a tiger and he was the finest, free-est, spender that ever lived."

"Did you know him?" one of the men asked.

"Did I know him? Did I know him? Did I love him? You ask me that? I knew him like you know nobody in the world and I loved him like you love God. He was the greatest, finest, whitest, most beautiful man that ever lived, Steve Ketchel, and his own father shot him down like a dog."

"Were you out on the coast with him?"

"No. I knew him before that. He was the only man I ever loved."

Every one was very respectful to the peroxide blonde, who said all this in a high stagey way, but Alice was beginning to shake again. I felt it sitting by her.

"You should have married him," the cook said.

"I wouldn't hurt his career," the peroxide blonde said. "I wouldn't be a drawback to him. A wife wasn't what he needed. Oh, my God, what a man he was."

"That was a fine way to look at it," the cook said. "Didn't Jack Johnson knock him out though?"

"It was a trick," Peroxide said. "That big dinge took him by surprise. He'd just knocked Jack Johnson down, the big black bastard. That nigger beat him by a fluke."

The ticket window went up and the three Indians went over to it.

"Steve knocked him down," Peroxide said. "He turned to smile at me."

"I thought you said you weren't on the coast," some one said.

"I went out just for that fight. Steve turned to smile at me and that black son of a bitch from hell jumped up and hit him by surprise. Steve could lick a hundred like that black bastard."

"He was a great fighter," the lumberjack said.

"I hope to God he was," Peroxide said. "I hope to God they don't have fighters like that now. He was like a god, he was. So white and clean and beautiful and smooth and fast and like a tiger or like lightning."

"I saw him in the moving pictures of the fight," Tom said. We were all very moved. Alice was shaking all over and I looked and saw she was crying. The Indians had gone outside on the platform.

"He was more than any husband could ever be," Peroxide said. "We were married in the eyes of God and I belong to him right now and always will and all of me is his. I don't care about my body. They take my body. My soul belongs to Steve Ketchel. By God, he was a man."

Everybody felt terribly. It was sad and embarrassing. Then Alice, who was still shaking, spoke. "You're a dirty liar," she said in that low voice. "You never layed Steve Ketchel in your life and you know it."

"How can you say that?" Peroxide said proudly.

"I say it because it's true," Alice said. "I'm the only one here that ever knew Steve Ketchel and I come from Mancelona and I knew him there and it's true and you know it's true and God can strike me dead if it isn't true."

"He can strike me too," Peroxide said.

"This is true, true, true, and you know it. Not just made up and I know exactly what he said to me."

"What did he say?" Peroxide asked, complacently.

Alice was crying so she could hardly speak from shaking so. "He said 'You're a lovely piece, Alice.' That's exactly what he said."

"It's a lie," Peroxide said.

"It's true," Alice said. "That's truly what he said."

"It's a lie," Peroxide said proudly.

"No, its true, true, true, to Jesus and Mary true."

"Steve couldn't have said that. It wasn't the way he talked," Peroxide said happily.

"It's true," said Alice in her nice voice. "And it doesn't make any difference to me whether you believe it or not." She wasn't crying any more and she was calm.

"It would be impossible for Steve to have said that," Peroxide declared.

"He said it," Alice said and smiled. "And I remember when he said it and I *was* a lovely piece then exactly as he said, and right now I'm a better piece than you, you dried up old hotwater bottle."

"You can't insult me," said Peroxide. "You big mountain of pus. I have my memories."

"No," Alice said in that sweet lovely voice, "you haven't got any real memories except having your tubes out and when you started C. and M. Everything else you just read in the papers. I'm clean and you know it and men like me, even though I'm big, and you know it, and I never lie and you know it."

"Leave me with my memories," Peroxide said. "With my true, wonderful memories."

Alice looked at her and then at us and her face lost that hurt look and she smiled and she had about the prettiest face I ever saw. She had a pretty face and a nice smooth skin and a lovely voice and she was nice all right and really friendly. But my God she was big. She was as big as three women. Tom saw me looking at her and he said, "Come on. Let's go."

"Good-bye," said Alice. She certainly had a nice voice.

"Good-bye," I said.

"Which way are you boys going?" asked the cook.

"The other way from you," Tom told him.

AFTER THE STORM

IT WASN'T about anything, something about making punch, and then we started fighting and I slipped and he had me down kneeling on my chest and choking me with both hands like he was trying to kill me and all the time I was trying to get the knife out of my pocket to cut him loose. Everybody was too drunk to pull him off me. He was choking me and hammering my head on the floor and I got the knife out and opened it up; and I cut the muscle right across his arm and he let go of me. He couldn't have held on if he wanted to. Then he rolled and hung onto that arm and started to cry and I said:

"What the hell you want to choke me for?"

I'd have killed him. I couldn't swallow for a week. He hurt my throat bad.

Well, I went out of there and there were plenty of them with him and some came out after me and I made a turn and was down by the docks and I met a fellow and he said somebody killed a man up the street. I said "Who killed him?" and he said "I don't know who killed him but he's dead all right," and it was dark and there was water standing in the street and no lights and windows broke and boats all up in the town and trees blown down and everything all blown and I got a skiff and went out and found my boat where I had her inside of Mango Key and she was all right only she was full of water. So I bailed her out and pumped her out and there was a moon but plenty of clouds and still plenty rough and I took it down along; and when it was daylight I was off Eastern Harbor.

Brother, that was some storm. I was the first boat out and you never saw water like that was. It was just as white as a lye barrel and coming from Eastern Harbor to Sou'west Key you couldn't recognize the shore. There was a big channel blown right out through the middle of the beach. Trees and all blown out and a channel cut through and all the water white as chalk and everything on it; branches and whole trees and dead birds, and all floating. Inside the keys were all the pelicans in the world and all kinds of birds flying. They must have gone inside there when they knew it was coming.

I lay at Sou'west Key a day and nobody came after me. I was the first boat out and I seen a spar floating and I knew there must be a wreck and I started out to look for her. I found her. She was a three-masted schooner and I could just see the stumps of her spars out of water. She was in too deep water and I didn't get anything off of her. So I went on looking for something else. I had the start on all of them and I knew I ought to get whatever there was. I went on down over the sand-bars from where I left that three-masted schooner and I didn't find anything and I went on a long way. I was way out toward the quicksands and I didn't find anything so I went on. Then when I was in sight of the Rebecca Light I saw all kinds of birds making over something and I headed over for them to see what it was and there was a cloud of birds all right.

I could see something looked like a spar up out of the water and when I got over close the birds all went up in the air and stayed all around me. The water was clear out there and there was a spar of some kind sticking out just above the water and when I come up close to it I saw it was all dark under water like a long shadow and I came right over it and there under water was a liner; just lying there all under water as big as the whole world. I drifted over her in the boat. She lay on her side and the stern was deep down. The port holes were all shut tight and I could see the glass shine in the water and the whole of her; the biggest boat I ever saw in my life laying there and I went along the whole length of her and then I went over and anchored and I had the skiff on the deck forward and I shoved it down into the water and sculled over with the birds all around me.

I had a water glass like we use sponging and my hand shook so I could hardly hold it. All the port holes were shut that you could see going along over her but way down below near the bottom something must have been open because there were pieces of things floating out all the time. You couldn't tell what they were. Just pieces. That's what the birds were after. You never saw so many birds. They were all around me; crazy yelling.

I could see everything sharp and clear. I could see her rounded over and she looked a mile long under the water. She was lying on a clear white bank of sand and the spar was a sort of foremast or some sort of tackle that slanted out of water the way she was laying on her side. Her bow wasn't very far under. I could stand on the letters of her name on her bow and my head was just out of water.

But the nearest port hole was twelve feet down. I could just reach it with the grains pole and I tried to break it with that but I couldn't. The glass was too stout. So I sculled back to the boat and got a wrench and lashed it to the end of the grains pole and I couldn't break it. There I was looking down through the glass at that liner with everything in her and I was the first one to her and I couldn't get into her. She must have had five million dollars worth in her.

It made me shaky to think how much she must have in her. Inside the port hole that was closest I could see something but I couldn't make it out through the water glass. I couldn't do any good with the grains pole and I took off my clothes and stood and took a couple of deep breaths and dove over off the stern with the wrench in my hand and swam down. I could hold on for a second to the edge of the port hole and I could see in and there was a woman inside with her hair floating all out. I could see her floating plain and I hit the glass twice with the wrench hard and I heard the noise clink in my ears but it wouldn't break and I had to come up.

I hung onto the dinghy and got my breath and then I climbed in and took a couple of breaths and dove again. I swam down and took hold of the edge of the port hole with my fingers and held it and hit the glass as hard as I could with the wrench. I could see the woman floated in the water through the glass. Her hair was tied once close to her head and it floated all out in the water. I could see the rings on one of her hands. She was right up close to the port hole and I hit the glass twice and I didn't even crack it. When I came up I thought I wouldn't make it to the top before I'd have to breathe.

I went down once more and I cracked the glass, only cracked it, and when I came up my nose was bleeding and I stood on the bow of the liner with my bare feet on the letters of her name and my head just out and rested there and then I swam over to the skiff and pulled up into it and sat there waiting for my head to stop aching and looking down in the water glass, but I bled so I had to wash out the water glass. Then I lay back in the skiff and held my hand under my nose to stop it and I lay there with my head back looking up and there was a million birds above and all around.

When I quit bleeding I took another look through the glass and then I sculled over to the boat to try and find something heavier than the wrench but I couldn't find a thing; not even a sponge hook. I went back and the water was clearer all the time and you could see everything that floated out over that white bank of sand. I looked for sharks but there weren't any. You could have seen a shark a long way away. The water was so clear and the sand white. There was a grapple for an anchor on the skiff and I cut it off and went overboard and down with it. It carried me right down and past the port hole and I grabbed and couldn't hold anything and went on down and down, sliding along the curved side of her. I had to let go of the grapple. I heard it bump once and it seemed like a year before I came up through to the top of the water. The skiff was floated away with the tide and I swam over to her with my nose bleeding in the water while I swam and I was plenty glad there weren't sharks; but I was tired.

My head felt cracked open and I lay in the skiff and rested and then I sculled back. It was getting along in the afternoon. I went down once more with the wrench and it didn't do any good. That wrench was too light. It wasn't any good diving unless you had a big hammer or something heavy enough to do good. Then I lashed the wrench to the grains pole again and I watched through the water glass and pounded on the glass and hammered until the wrench came off and I saw it in the glass, clear and sharp, go sliding down along her and then off and down to the quicksand and go in. Then I couldn't do a thing. The wrench was gone and I'd lost the grapple so I sculled back to the boat. I was too tired to get the skiff aboard and the sun was pretty low. The birds were all pulling out and leaving her and I headed for Sou'west Key towing the skiff and the birds going on ahead of me and behind me. I was plenty tired.

That night it came on to blow and it blew for a week. You couldn't get out to her. They come out from town and told me the fellow I'd had to cut was all right except for his arm and I went back to town and they put me under five hundred dollar bond. It came out all right because some of them, friends of mine, swore he was after me with an ax, but by the time we got back out to her the Greeks had blown her open and cleaned her out. They got the safe out with dynamite. Nobody ever knows how much they got. She carried gold and they got it all. They stripped her clean. I found her and I never got a nickel out of her.

It was a hell of thing all right. They say she was just outside of Havana harbor when the hurricane hit and she couldn't get in or the owners wouldn't let the captain chance coming in; they say he wanted to try; so she had to go with it and in the dark they were running with it trying to go through the gulf between Rebecca and Tortugas when she struck on the quicksands. Maybe her rudder was carried away. Maybe they weren't even steering. But anyway they couldn't have known they were quicksands and when she struck the captain must have ordered them to open up the ballast tanks so she'd lay solid. But it was quicksand she'd hit and when they opened the tank she went in stern first and then over on her beam ends. There were four hundred and fifty passengers and the crew on board of her and they must all have been aboard of her when I found her. They must have opened the tanks as soon as she struck and the minute she settled on it the quicksands took her down. Then her boilers must have burst and that must have been what made those pieces that came out. It was funny there weren't any sharks though. There wasn't a fish. I could have seen them on that clear white sand.

Plenty of fish now though; jewfish, the biggest kind. The biggest part of her's under the sand now but they live inside of her; the biggest kind of jewfish. Some weigh three to four hundred pounds. Sometime we'll go out and get some. You can see the Rebecca light from where she is. They've got a buoy on her now. She's right at the end of the quicksand right at the edge of the gulf. She only missed going through by about a hundred yards. In the dark in the storm they just missed it; raining the way it was they couldn't have seen the Rebecca. Then they're not used to that sort of thing. The captain of a liner isn't used to scudding that way. They have a course and they tell me they set some sort of a compass and it steers itself. They probably didn't know where they were when they ran with that blow but they come close to making it. Maybe they'd lost the rudder though. Anyway there wasn't another thing for them to hit till they'd get to Mexico once they were in that gulf. Must have been something though when they struck in that rain and wind and he told them to open her tanks. Nobody could have been on deck in that blow and rain. Everybody must have been below. They couldn't have lived on deck. There must have been some scenes inside all right because you know she settled fast. I saw that wrench go into the sand. The captain couldn't have known it was quicksand when she struck unless he knew these waters. He just knew it wasn't rock. He must have seen it all up in the bridge. He must have known what it was about when she settled. I wonder how fast she made it. I wonder if the mate was there with him. Do you think they stayed inside the bridge or do you think they took it outside? They never found any bodies. Not a one. Nobody floating. They float a long way with life belts too. They must have took it inside. Well, the Greeks got it all. Everything. They must have come fast all right. They picked her clean. First there was the birds, then me, then the Greeks, and even the birds got more out of her than I did.

from DEATH IN THE AFTERNOON

THE BULLFIGHT (Chapter Seven)

THE LAST CHAPTER

IF THE AMERICAN COUNCIL OF LEARNED SOCIETIES commanded the resources of the Ford Foundation it might sponsor a survey of this one author's influence on various fields of modern writing. Think, for example, of all the books about Spain and bullfighting that have had their sources in Death in the Afternoon. It has, with other Hemingway works on Spain, sent more authors and other travelers across the Pyrenees than anything since the Chanson de Roland.

The ghosts of best-sellers untimely born, untimely dead, rise from these pages. At their unfailingly foreseeable climaxes the hero always kills his final bull recibiendo, because Hemingway said in this book that killing recibiendo is the "most difficult, dangerous and emotional way to kill bulls; rarely seen in modern times. I have seen it executed completely three times in almost three hundred bullfights." Any critic of new novels who does not expect to see it three or even four times in a single season without moving from his chair is unaware of the capacities of modern novelists and the hazards of his vocation.

The book was published in 1932. " I wrote it," Hemingway said, "in Key West, the ranch near Cooke City, Montana, all one summer, Havana, Madrid, Hendaye and Key West. It took about two years. The glossary I remember I wrote at Hendaye. It was a bastard to do." No one has written in English anywhere near as good a book as this one about bullfighting—Spaniards have told me that they don't know anything better, as a matter of fact, in Spanish. The first selection here is not only about bullfighting, but also presents the implacably curious Old Lady, one of my favorite heroines. The second selection might have been called "A Farewell to Spain."

C. P.

DEATH IN THE AFTERNOON

THE BULLFIGHT

VII

At this point it is necessary that you see a bullfight. If I were to describe one it would not be the one that you would see, since the bullfighters and the bulls are all different, and if I were to explain the possible variations as I went along the chapter would be interminable. There are two sorts of guide books; those that are read before and those that are to be read after and the ones that are to be read after the fact are bound to be incomprehensible to a certain extent before; if the fact is of enough importance in itself. So with any book on mountain ski-ing, sexual intercourse, wing shooting, or any other thing which it is impossible to make come true on paper, or at least impossible to attempt to make more than one version of at a time on paper, it being always an individual experience, there comes a place in the guide book where you must say do not come back until you have ski-ed, had sexual intercourse, shot quail or grouse, or been to the bullfight so that you will know what we are talking about. So from now on it is inferred that you have been to the bullfight.

You went to the bullfight? How was it?

It was disguisting. I couldn't stand it.

All right, we will give you an honorable discharge but no refund.

How did you like it? It was terrible. How do you mean terrible? Just terrible. It was terrible, awful, horrible. Good. You get an honorable discharge, too.

How did it seem to you? I was simply bored to death. All right. You get the hell out of here.

Didn't anybody like the bullfight? Didn't anybody like the bullfight at all? No answer. Did you like it, sir? I did not. Did you like it, madame? Decidedly not.

An old lady in the back of the room: What is he saying? What is that young man asking?

Some one near her: He's asking if any one liked the bullfight.

Old lady: Oh, I thought he was asking if any of us wanted to be bullfighters.

Did you like the bullfight, madame?

Old lady: I liked it very much.

What did you like about it?

Old lady: I liked to see the bulls hit the horses.

Why did you like that?

Old lady: It seemed so sort of homey.

Madame, you are a mystic. You are not among friends here. Let us go to the Café Fornos where we can discuss these matters at leisure.

Old lady: Wherever you wish, sir, provided it is clean and wholesome.

Madame, there is no wholesomer place in the Peninsula.

Old lady: Will we see the bullfighters there?

Madame, the place is packed with them.

Old lady: Then let us be off.

Fornos is a café frequented only by people connected with the bullfights and by whores. There is smoke, hurrying of waiters, noise of glasses and you have the noisy privacy of a big café. We can discuss the fight, if you wish, and the old lady can sit and look at the bullfighters. There are bullfighters at every table and for all tastes and all the other people in the café live off bullfighters in some way or another. A shark rarely has more than four remoras or sucking fish that fasten to him or swim along with him, but a bullfighter, when he is making money, has dozens. The old lady does not care to discuss the bullfight. She liked it; she is now looking at the bullfighters and never discusses things she has enjoyed even with her most intimate friends. We talk about it because there were a number of things you say you did not understand.

When the bull came out did you notice that one of the banderilleros ran across his course trailing a cape and that the bull followed the cape driving at it with one horn? They run him that way always, at the start, to see which horn he favors. The matador, standing behind his shelter, watches the bull run by the trailing cape and notices whether he follows the zig-zagging cape on both his right and his left sides, this showing whether he sees with both eyes and which horn he prefers to hook with. He also notices whether he runs straight or if he has a tendency to cut ground toward the man as he charges. The man who went out with the cape in both hands after the bull had been run, and cited him from in front, standing still as the bull charged, and with his arms moving the cape slowly just ahead of the bull's horns, passing the bull's horns close by his body with a slow movement of the cape, seeming to keep him controlled, in the folds of the cape, bringing him past his body each time as he turned and recharged; doing this five times and then finishing off with a swirl of the cape that turned the man's back on the bull and, by cutting the bull's charge brusquely, fixed him to the spot; that man was the matador and the slow passes that he made were called veronicas and the half pass at the end a media-veronica. Those passes were designed to show the matador's skill and art with the cape, his domination of the bull and also to fix the bull in a certain spot before the entry of the horses. They are called veronicas after St. Veronica who wiped the face of Our Lord with a cloth and are so called because the saint is always represented holding the cloth by the two corners in the position the bullfighter holds the cape for the start of the veronica. The media-veronica that stops the bull at the end of the passes is a recorte. A recorte is any pass with the cape that, by causing the bull to try to turn in less than his own length, stops him brusquely or checks his rush by cutting his course and doubling him on himself.

The banderilleros are never supposed to use both hands on the cape when the bull first comes out. If they use only one hand the cape will be trailed and when they turn it at the end of a run the bull will turn easily and not sharply and brusquely. He will do this because the turn of the long cape gives him an indication of the turn to make and gives him something to follow. With the cape held in both hands the banderillero can snap it away from the bull, flop it brusquely out of his sight and stop him dead, and turn him sharply so that he twists his spinal column, lames himself, has his speed cut, not by being worn down, but by laming, and make him unfit for the rest of the fight. Only the matador is supposed to use two hands on the cape during the early part of the fight. Strictly speaking the banderilleros, who are also called peones, are never supposed to use two hands on the cape except when bringing the bull out from a position he has taken and refused to leave. But in the way bullfighting has developed, or decayed, with emphasis increasingly placed on the manner of execution of the various passes rather than their effect, the banderilleros now do much of the work of preparing the bull for killing that was formerly done by the matador; and matadors without resources or science, whose only ability is their plastic or artistic talent, have their bulls, if these offer the slightest difficulty, prepared, worn down, dominated and everything but killed by the skilled and destructive cape of an experienced banderillero.

It may seem foolish to speak of almost killing such an animal as a fighting bull with a cape. Of course you could not kill, but you can so damage the spinal column, twist the legs and lame the animal and, by abusing its bravery, force it to charge uselessly again and again, each time recorting it ferociously, that you may tire it, lame it, and deprive it of all speed and a great part of its natural forces. We speak of killing a trout with a rod. It is the effort made by the trout that kills it. A catfish arrives at the side of the boat in full possession of all its force and strength. A tarpon, a trout or a salmon will often kill himself fighting the rod and line if you hold him long enough.

It was for this reason that banderilleros were prohibited from caping the bull with both hands. The matador was supposed to do all of the preparation for killing and the killing himself. The picadors were to slow the bull, to change his tempo, and to bring down the carriage of his head. The banderilleros were supposed to run him at the start, to place the banderillas quickly and in such a position as to correct any faults of hooking if they existed, and never to do anything to destroy the strength of the bull, in order that he might come intact into the hands of the matador who was supposed, with the muleta, to correct any tendencies toward hooking to one side or the other, to place him in position for killing and to kill him from in front, making him lower his head with the red serge of the muleta and killing him with the sword, driving it in high up at the top of the angle between the two shoulder blades.

As the corrida has developed and decayed there has been less emphasis on the form of killing, which was once the whole thing, and more on the cape work, the placing of the banderillas and the work with the muleta. The cape, the banderillas and the muleta have all become ends in themselves rather than means to an end and the bullfight has both lost and gained thereby.

In the old days the bulls were usually bigger than they are now; they were fiercer, more uncertain, heavier and older. They had not been bred down to a smaller size to please the bullfighters and they were fought at the age of four and a half to five years instead of three and a half to four and a half years. Matadors often had from six to twelve years of apprenticeship as banderilleros and as novilleros before becoming formal matadors. They were mature men, knew bulls thoroughly, and faced bulls which were brought to the highest point of physical force, strength, knowledge of how to use their horns and general difficulty and danger. The whole end of the bullfight was the final sword thrust, the actual encounter between the man and the animal, what the Spanish call the moment of truth, and every move in the fight was to prepare the bull for that killing. With such bulls it was not necessary to give emotion for the man to pass the animal as deliberately close to him with the cape as was possible. The cape was used to run the bulls, to protect the picadors, and the passes that were made with it, by our modern standards, were exciting because of the size, strength, weight and fierceness of the animal and the danger the matador ran in making them rather than by the form or the slowness of their execution. It was exciting that the man should pass such a bull at all, that a man should be in the ring with and dominate such an animal furnished the emotion rather than that he should deliberately, as now, try to pass the points of the horn as mathematically close to his body as possible without moving his feet. It is the decadence of the modern bull that has made modern bullfighting possible. It is a decadent art in every way and like most decadent things it reaches its fullest flower at its rottenest point, which is the present.

It is impossible, day in and day out, to fight bulls that are really bulls, huge, strong, fierce and fast, knowing how to use their horns and old enough so that they have their full growth, with the technique that has been developed, starting with Juan Belmonte, in modern bullfighting. It is too dangerous. Belmonte invented the technique. He was a genius, who could break the rules of bullfighting and could torear, that is the only word for all the actions performed by a man with the bull, as it was known to be impossible to torear. Once he had done it all bullfighters had to do it, or attempt to do it since there is no going back in the matter of sensations. Joselito who was strong (Belmonte was weak), healthy (Belmonte was sickly), who had an athlete's body, gypsy grace and an intuitive and acquired knowledge of bulls that was never surpassed by any bullfighter; Joselito for whom everything in bullfighting was easy, who lived for bullfighting, and seemed to have been made and bred almost to the measurement of what a great bullfighter should be, had to learn Belmonte's way of working. Joselito, the heritor of all great bullfighters, probably the greatest bullfighter that ever lived, learned to torear as Belmonte did. Belmonte worked that way because of his lack of stature, his lack of strength, because of his feeble legs. He did not accept any rules made without testing whether they might be broken, and he was a genius and a great artist. The way Belmonte worked was not a heritage, nor a development; it was a revolution. Joselito learned it, and during the years of their competition, when they each had around a hundred corridas a year, he used to say, "They say that he, Belmonte, works closer to the bull. It looks as though he does. But that isn't true. I really work closer. But it is more natural so it doesn't look so close."

Anyway, the decadent, the impossible, the almost depraved, style of Belmonte was grafted and grown into the great healthy, intuitive genius of Joselito and in his competition with Juan Belmonte, bullfighting for seven years had a golden age in spite of the fact that it was in the process of being destroyed.

They bred the bulls down in size; they bred down the length of horn; they bred them for suavity in their charges as well as fierceness because Joselito and Belmonte could do finer things with these smaller, easier bulls. They could do fine enough things with any bulls that came out of the torils; they were not helpless with any of them but, with the smaller, easier bulls they were certain to do the wonderful things that the public wanted to see. The big bulls were easy for Joselito although they were difficult for Belmonte. All bulls were easy for Joselito and he had to make his own difficulties. The competition ended when Joselito was killed in the ring on May 16, 1920. Belmonte went on one more year, then retired, and bullfighting was left with the new decadent method, the almost impossible technique, the bred down bulls and, as bullfighters, only the bad ones, the hardy, tough ones who had not been able to learn the new method and so no longer pleased, and a crop of new ones, decadent, sad and sickly enough, who had the method but no knowledge of bulls, no apprenticeship, none of the male courage, faculties or genius of Joselito, and none of the beautiful unhealthy mystery of Belmonte.

Old lady: I saw nothing decadent or rotten about the spectacle we observed to-day.

Nor did I, to-day, madame, for the matadors were Nicanor Villalta, the courageous telephone pole of Aragon; Luis Fuentes Bejarano, the valorous and worthy workman, the pride of Union Labor, and Diego Mazquiaran, Fortuna, the brave butcher boy of Bilbao.

Old lady: They all seemed to me to be most valorous and manly chaps. In what way, sir, do you speak of decadence?

Madame, they are most manly chaps although Villalta's voice is a shade high sometimes, and the decadence I speak of does not apply to them but to the decay of a complete art through a magnification of certain of its aspects.

Old lady: Sir, you are hard to understand.

I will explain later, madame, but indeed decadence is a difficult word to use since it has become little more than a term of abuse applied by critics to anything they do not yet understand or which seems to differ from their moral concepts.

Old lady: I always understood it to mean that there was something rotten as there is at courts.

Madame, all our words from loose using have lost their edge but your inherent concepts are most sound.

Old lady: If you please, sir, I do not care for all this discussion of words. Are we not here to be instructed about the bulls and those who fight them?

If you so wish, but start your writer to talking of words and he will go on until you are wearied and wish he would show more skill in using them and preach less of their significance.

Old lady: Can you not stop then, sir?

Have you ever heard of the late Raymond Radiguet?

Old lady: I cannot say I have.

He was a young French writer who knew how to make his career not only with his pen but with his pencil if you follow me, madame.

Old lady: You mean?

Not exactly, but something of the sort.

Old lady: You mean he——?

Precisely. When the late Radiguet was alive he often wearied of the tenuous, rapturous and querulous society of his literary protector, Jean Cocteau, and spent the nights at an hotel near the Luxembourg Gardens with one of two sisters who were then working as models in the quarter. His protector was greatly upset and denounced this as decadence saying, bitterly, yet proudly of the late Radiguet, "Bebé est vicieuse—il aime les femmes." So you see, madame, we must be careful chucking the term decadence about since it cannot mean the same to all who read it.

Old lady: It repelled me from the first.

Then let us return to the bulls.

Old lady: Gladly, sir. But what finally happened to the late Radiguet?

He caught typhoid fever from swimming in the Seine and died of it.

Old lady: Poor chap.

Poor chap, indeed.

THE LAST CHAPTER

If I could have made this enough of a book it would have had everything in it. The Prado, looking like some big American college building, with sprinklers watering the grass early in the bright Madrid summer morning; the bare white mud hills looking across toward Carabanchel; days on the train in August with the blinds pulled down on the side against the sun and the wind blowing them; chaff blown against the car in the wind from the hard earthen threshing floors; the odor of grain and the stone windmills. It would have had the change when you leave the green country behind at Alsasua; it would have had Burgos far across the plain and eating the cheese later up in the room; it would have had the boy taking the wicker-bound jugs of wine on the train as samples; his first trip to Madrid and opening them in enthusiasm and they all got drunk including the pair of Guardia Civil and I lost the tickets and we were taken through the wicket by the two Guardia Civil (who took us out as though prisoners because there were no tickets and then saluted as they put us in the cab); Hadley, with the bull's ear wrapped in a handkerchief, the ear was very stiff and dry and the hair all wore off it and the man who cut the ear is bald now too and slicks long strips of hair over the top of his head and he was beau then. He was, all right.

It should make clear the change in the country as you come down out of the mountains and into Valencia in the dusk on the train holding a rooster for a woman who was bringing it to her sister; and it should show the wooden ring at Alciras where they dragged the dead horses out in the field and you had to pick your way over them; and the noise in the streets in Madrid after midnight, and the fair that goes on all night long, in June, and walking home on Sundays from the ring; or with Rafael in the cab. Que tal? Malo, hombre, malo; with that lift of the shoulders, or with Roberto, Don Roberto, Don Ernesto, so polite always, so gentle and such a good friend. Also the house where Rafael lived before being a republican became respectable with the mounted

445

head of the bull Gitanillo had killed and the great oil jar and always presents and the excellent cooking.

It should have the smell of burnt powder and the smoke and the flash and the noise of the traca going off through the green leaves of the trees and it should have the taste of horchata, ice-cold horchata, and the new-washed streets in the sun, and the melons and beads of cool on the outside of the pitchers of beer; the storks on the houses in Barco de Avila and wheeling in the sky and the red-mud color of the ring; and at night dancing to the pipes and the drum with lights through the green leaves and the portrait of Garibaldi framed in leaves. It should, if it were enough of a book, have the forced smile of Lagartito; it was once a real smile, and the unsuccessful matadors swimming with the cheap whores out on the Manzanares along the Pardo road; beggars can't be choosers, Luis said; playing ball on the grass by the stream where the fairy marquis came out in his car with the boxer; where we made the paellas, and walked home in the dark with the cars coming fast along the road; and with electric lights through the green leaves and the dew settling the dust, in the cool at night; cider in Bombilla and the road to Pontevedra from Santiago de Campostella with the high turn in the pines and blackberries beside the road; Algabeno the worst faker of them all; and Maera up in the room at Quintana's changing outfits with the priest the one year every one drank so much and no one was nasty. There really was such a year, but this is not enough of a book.

Make all that come true again; throw grasshoppers to the trout in the Tambre on the bridge in the evening; have the serious brown face of Felix Merino at the old Aguilar; have the brave, awkward, wall-eyed Pedro Montes dressing away from home because he had promised his mother he had stopped fighting, after Mariano, his brother, was killed at Tetuan; and Litri, like a little rabbit, his eyes winking nervously as the bull came; he was very bow-legged and brave and those three are all killed and never any mention made about the beer place on the cool side of the street underneath the Palace where he sat with his father and how it is a citroen show room now; nor about them carrying

Pedro Carreño, dead, through the streets with torches and finally into the church and put him naked on the altar.

There is nothing in this book about Francisco Gomez, Aldeano, who worked in Ohio in a steel plant and came home to be a matador and now is scarred and marked worse than any one except Freg, his eye twisted so a tear runs down his nose. Nor Gavira dead at the very instant as the bull with the same cornada that killed El Espartero. Nor does it tell about Zaragossa, at night on the bridge watching the Ebro, and the parachute jumper the next day and Rafael's cigars; nor the jota contests in the old red plush theatre and the wonderful boy and girl pairs; nor when they killed the Noy de Sucre in Barcelona, nor about any of that; nor anything about Navarra; nor about the lousy town Leon is; nor about lying with a muscle torn in a hotel on the sunny side of the street in Palencia when it was hot and you do not know what hot is when you have not been there; nor on the road where dust is deeper than the hubs between Requena and Madrid; nor when it was one hundred and twenty in the shade in Aragon and the car, with no carbon nor anything wrong, would boil the water out of the radiator in fifteen miles on a level road.

If it were more of a book it would make the last night of feria when Maera fought Alfredo David in the Café Kutz; and it should show the bootblacks. My God, you could not get in all the bootblacks; nor all the fine girls passing; nor the whores; nor all of us ourselves as we were then. Pamplona now is changed; they have built new apartment buildings out over all the sweep of plain that ran to the edge of the plateau; so now you cannot see the mountains. They tore down the old Gayarre and spoiled the square to cut a wide thoroughfare to the ring and in the old days there was Chicuelo's uncle sitting drunk in the upstairs dining room watching the dancing in the square; Chicuelo was in his room alone, and the cuadrilla in the café and around the town. I wrote a story about it called *A Lack of Passion*, but it was not good enough although when they threw the dead cats at the train and afterwards the wheels clicking and Chicuelo in the berth, alone; able to do it alone; it was fair enough.

It should, if it had Spain in it, have the tall thin boy, eight feet six inches, he advertised the Empastre show before they came to town, and that night, at the feria de ganado, the whores wouldn't have anything to do with the dwarf, he was full size except that his legs were only six inches long, and he said, "I'm a man like any man," and the whore said, "No you're not and that's the trouble." There are many dwarfs in Spain and cripples that you wouldn't believe that follow all the fairs.

In the morning there we would have breakfast and then go out to swim in the Irati at Aoiz, the water clear as light, and varying in temperature as you sunk down, cool, deep cool, cold, and the shade from the trees on the bank when the sun was hot, the ripe wheat in the wind up on the other side and sloping to the mountain. There was an old castle at the head of the valley where the river came out between two rocks; and we lay naked on the short grass in the sun and later in the shade. The wine at Aoiz was no good so then we brought our own, and neither was the ham, so the next time we brought a lunch from Quintana's. Quintana, the best aficionado and most loyal friend in Spain, and with a fine hotel with all the rooms full. Que tal Juanito? Que tal, hombre, que tal?

And why should it not have the cavalry crossing another stream at a ford, the shadow of the leaves on the horses, if it is Spain, and why not have them marching out from the machine-gun school across the clay white ground, very small so far away, and looking beyond from Quintanilla's window were the mountains. Or waking in the morning, the streets empty on Sunday, and the shouting far away and then the firing. That happens many times if you live long enough and move around.

And if you ride and if your memory is good you may ride still through the forest of the Irati with trees like drawings in a child's fairy book. They cut those down. They ran logs down the river and they killed the fish, or in Galicia they bombed and poisoned them; results the same; so in the end it's just like home except for yellow gorse on the high meadows and the thin rain. Clouds come across the mountains from the sea but when the wind is from the south Navarra is all the color of wheat except it does not grow on level plains but up and down the sides of hills and cut by roads with trees and many villages with bells, pelota courts, the smell of sheep manure and squares with standing horses.

If you could make the yellow flames of candles in the sun; that shines on steel of bayonets freshly oiled and yellow patent leather belts of those who guard the Host; or hunt in pairs through scrub oak in the mountains for the ones who fell into the trap at Deva (it was a bad long way to come from the Café Rotonde to be garrotted in a drafty room with consolation of the church at order of the state, acquitted once and held until the captain general of Burgos reversed the the finding of the court) and in the same town where Loyola got his wound that made him think, the bravest of those who were betrayed that year dove from the balcony onto the paving of the court, head first, because he had sworn they would not kill him; (his mother tried to make him promise not to take his life because she worried most about his soul but he dove well and cleanly with his hands tied while they walked with him praying); if I could make him; make a bishop; make Candido Tiebas and Toron; make clouds come fast in shadows moving over wheat and the small, careful stepping horses; the smell of olive oil; the feel of leather; rope soled shoes; the loops of twisted garlics; earthen pots; saddle bags carried across the shoulder; wine skins; the pitchforks made of natural wood (the tines were branches); the early morning smells; the cold mountain nights and long hot days of summer, with always trees and shade under the trees, then you would have a little of Navarra. But it's not in this book.

There ought to be Astorga, Lugo, Orense, Soria, Tarragona and Calatayud, the chestnut woods on the high hills, the green country and the rivers, the red dust, the small shade beside the dry rivers and the white, baked clay hills; cool walking under palms in the old city on the cliff above the sea, cool in the evening with the breeze; mosquitoes at night but in the morning the water clear and the sand white; then sitting in the heavy twilight at Miro's; vines as far as you can see, cut by the hedges and the road; the railroad and the sea with pebbly beach and tall papyrus grass. There were earthen jars for the different years of wine, twelve feet high, set side by side in a dark room; a tower on the house to climb to in the evening to see the vines, the villages and the mountains and to listen and hear how quiet it was. In front of the barn a woman held a duck whose throat she had cut and stroked him gently while a little girl held up a cup to catch the blood for making gravy. The duck seemed very contented and when they put him down (the blood all in the cup) he waddled twice and found that he was dead. We ate him later, stuffed and roasted; and many other dishes, with the wine of that year and the year before and the great year four years before that and other years that I lost track of while the long arms of a mechanical fly chaser that wound by clock work went round and round and we talked French. We all knew Spanish better.

That is Montroig, pronounced Montroych, one of many places in Spain, where there are also the streets of Santiago in the rain; seeing the town down in the cup of hills as you come home across the high country; and all the carts that roll, piled high, on smooth stone tracks along the road to Grau should be there with the temporary wooden ring in Noya, smelling of fresh cut boards; Chiquito with his girl's face, a great artist, fino muy fino, pero frio. Valencia II with his eye they sewed up wrong so that the inside of the lid showed and he could not be arrogant any more. Also the boy who missed the bull entirely when he went in to kill and missed him again the second time. If you could stay awake for the nocturnals you saw them funny.

In Madrid the comic bullfighter, beaten up twice by Rodalito stabbing him in the belly because he thought there was another beating coming. Aguero eating with his whole family in the dining room; they all looking alike in different ages. He looked like a shortstop or a quarterback, not like a matador. Cagancho eating in his room with his fingers because he could not use a fork. He could not learn it, so when he had enough money he never ate in public. Ortega engaged to Miss Espana, the ugliest and the prettiest, and who was the wittiest? Derperdicios in la Gaceta del Norte was the wittiest; the wittiest I ever read.

And up in Sidney's rooms, the ones coming to ask for work when he was fighting, the ones to borrow money, the ones for an old shirt, a suit of clothes; all bullfighters, all well known somewhere at the hour of eating, all formally polite, all out of luck; the muletas folded and piled; the capes all folded flat; swords in the embossed leather case; all in the armoire; muleta sticks are in the bottom drawer, suits hung in the trunk, cloth covered to protect the gold; my whiskey in an earthen crock; Mercédes, bring the glasses; she says he had a fever all night long and only went out an hour ago. So then he comes in. How do you feel? Great. She says you had fever. But I feel great now. What do you say, Doctor, why not eat here? She can get something and make a salad. Mercédes oh Mercédes.

Then you could walk across the town and to the café where they say you get your education learning who owed who money and who chiselled this from who and why he told him he could kiss his what and who had children by who and who married who before and after what and how long it took for this and that and what the doctor said. Who was so pleased because the bulls were delayed, being unloaded only the day of the fight, naturally weak in the legs, just two passes, poom, and it is all over, he said, and then it rained and the fight postponed a week and that was when he got it. Who wouldn't fight with who and when and why and does she, of course she does, you fool you didn't know she does? Absolutely and that's all and in no other fashion, she gobbles them alive, and all such valuable news you learn in cafés. In cafés where the boys are never wrong; in cafés where they are all brave; in cafés where the saucers pile and drinks are figured in pencil on the marble table tops among the shucked shrimps of seasons lost and feeling good because there are no other triumphs so secure and every man a success by eight o'clock if somebody can pay the score in cafés.

What else should it contain about a country you love very much? Rafael says things are very changed and he won't go to Pamplona any more. *La Libertad* I find is getting like *Le Temps*. It is no longer the paper where you could put a notice and know the pickpocket would see it now that Republicans are all respectable and Pamplona is changed, of course, but not as much as we are older. I found that if you took a drink that it got very much the same as it was always. I know things change now and I do not care. It's all been changed for me. Let it all change. We'll all be gone before it's changed too much and if no deluge comes when we are gone it still will rain in summer in the north and hawks will nest in the Cathedral at Santiago and in La Granja, where we practiced with the cape on the long gravelled paths between the shadows, it makes no difference if the fountains play or not. We never will ride back from Toledo in the dark, washing the dust out with Fundador, nor will there be that week of what happened in the night in that July in Madrid. We've seen it all go and we'll watch it go again. The great thing is to last and get your work done and see and hear and learn and understand; and write when there is something that you know; and not before; and not too damned much after. Let those who want to save the world if you can get to see it clear and as a whole. Then any part you make will represent the whole if it's made truly. The thing to do is work and learn to make it. No. It is not enough of a book, but still there were a few things to be said. There were a few practical things to be said.

from GREEN HILLS OF AFRICA

Chapter One

THIS IS the first chapter of GREEN HILLS OF AFRICA. *I wish I could have included the entire book. It is a fine account of big-game hunting, written in a prose that is as worth reading for itself as for what it describes. And all the shots are not aimed at the game of Tanganyika. A number of them found targets, when this book first appeared in 1935, much closer home. Even the ricochets were formidable. You will see why.*

There are those who have not liked what he has to say about the good gray busts on the schoolroom wall. This is a matter of opinion; mine is that there is no more stimulating talk, or truer, about American writing anywhere. As for Hemingway himself, I do not think there is any future in regarding him as a purely American writer. He will probably find his place, I imagine, closer to the habitat groups of Stendhal, Tolstoy and Flaubert.

"Unlike many novels," he said in a foreward to Green Hills of Africa, "none of the characters or incidents in this book is imaginary. Any one not finding sufficient love interest is at liberty, while reading it, to insert whatever love interest he or she may have at the time. The writer has attempted to write an absolutely true book to see whether the shape of a country and the pattern of a month's action can, if truly presented, compete with a work of the imagination." He succeeded well. So well that this book is in print, while works of the imagination whose praises you may read in the files of the Nineteen Thirties are dust for oblivion.

Notice, incidentally, how Kandisky's talk about the natives is tuned out, then tuned in again.

C. P.

GREEN HILLS OF AFRICA

CHAPTER I

WE WERE sitting in the blind that Wanderobo hunters had built of twigs and branches at the edge of the salt-lick when we heard the truck coming. At first it was far away and no one could tell what the noise was. Then it was stopped and we hoped it had been nothing or perhaps only the wind. Then it moved slowly nearer, unmistakable now, louder and louder until, agonizing in a clank of loud irregular explosions, it passed close behind us to go on up the road. The theatrical one of the two trackers stood up.

"It is finished," he said.

I put my hand to my mouth and motioned him down.

"It is finished," he said again and spread his arms wide. I had never liked him and I liked him less now.

"After," I whispered. M'Cola shook his head. I looked at his bald black skull and he turned his face a little so that I saw the thin Chinese hairs at the corners of his mouth.

"No good," he said. "*Hapana m'uzuri.*"

"Wait a little," I told him. He bent his head down again so that it would not show above the dead branches and we sat there in the dust of the hole until it was too dark to see the front sight on my rifle; but nothing more came. The theatrical tracker was impatient and restless. A little before the last of the light was gone he whispered to M'Cola that it was now too dark to shoot.

"Shut up, you," M'Cola told him. "The Bwana can shoot after you cannot see."

The other tracker, the educated one, gave another demonstration of his education by scratching his name, Abdullah, on the black skin of his leg with a sharp twig. I watched without admiration and M'Cola looked at the word without a shadow of expression on his face. After a while the tracker scratched it out.

Finally I made a last sight against what was left of the light and saw it was no use, even with the large aperture.

M'Cola was watching.

"No good," I said.

"Yes," he agreed, in Swahili. "Go to camp?"

"Yes."

We stood up and made our way out of the blind and out through the trees, walking on the sandy loam, feeling our way between trees and under branches, back to the road. A mile along the road was the car. As we came alongside, Kamau, the driver, put the lights on.

The truck had spoiled it. That afternoon we had left the car up the road and approached the salt-lick very carefully. There had been a little rain, the day before, though not enough to flood the lick, which was simply an opening in the trees with a patch of earth worn into deep circles and grooved at the edges with hollows where the animals had licked the dirt for salt, and we had seen long, heart-shaped, fresh tracks of four greater kudu bulls that had been on the salt the night before, as well as many newly pressed tracks of lesser kudu. There was also a rhino who, from the tracks and the kicked-up mound of strawy dung, came there each night. The blind had been built at close arrow-shot of the lick and sitting, leaning back, knees high, heads low, in a hollow half full of ashes and dust, watching through the dried leaves and thin branches I had seen a lesser kudu bull come out of the brush to the edge of the opening where the salt was and stand there, heavy-necked, gray, and handsome, the horns spiralled against the sun while I sighted on his chest and then refused the shot, wanting not to frighten the greater kudu that should surely come at dusk. But before we ever heard the truck the bull had heard it and run off into the trees and everything else that had been moving, in the bush on the flats, or coming down from the small hills through the trees, coming toward the salt, had halted at that exploding, clanking sound. They would come, later, in the dark; but then it would be too late.

So now, going along the sandy track of the road in the car, the lights picking out the eyes of night birds that squatted close on the sand until the bulk of the car was on them and they rose in soft panic; passing the fires of the travellers that all moved to the westward by day along this road, abandoning the famine country that was ahead of us; me sitting, the butt of my rifle on my foot, the barrel in the crook of my left arm, a flash of whiskey between my knees, pouring the whiskey into a tin cup and passing it over my shoulder in the dark for M'Cola to pour water into it from the canteen, drinking this, the first one of the day, the finest one there is, and looking at the thick bush we passed in the dark, feeling the cool wind of the night and smelling the good smell of Africa, I was altogether happy.

Then ahead we saw a big fire and as we came up and passed, I made out a truck beside the road. I told Kamau to stop and go back and as we backed into the firelight there was a short, bandy-legged man with a Tyroler hat, leather shorts, and an open shirt standing before an un-hooded engine in a crowd of natives.

"Can we help?" I asked him.

"No," he said. "Unless you are a mechanic. It has taken a dis-like to me. All engines dislike me."

"Do you think it could be the timer? It sounded as though it might be a timing knock when you went past us."

"I think it is much worse than that. It sounds to be something very bad."

"If you can get to our camp we have a mechanic."

"How far is it?"

"About twenty miles."

"In the morning I will try it. Now I am afraid to make it go farther with that noise of death inside. It is trying to die because it dislikes me. Well, I dislike it too. But if I die it would not annoy it."

"Will you have a drink?" I held out the flash. "Hemingway is my name."

"Kandisky," he said and bowed. "Hemingway is a name I have heard. Where? Where have I heard it? Oh, yes. The *dichter*. You know Hemingway the poet?"

"Where did you read him?"

"In the *Querschnitt*."

"That is me," I said, very pleased. The *Querschnitt* was a

German magazine I had written some rather obscene poems for, and published a long story in, years before I could sell anything in America.

"This is very strange," the man in the Tyroler hat said. "Tell me, what do you think of Ringelnatz?"

"He is splendid."

"So. You like Ringelnatz. Good. What do you think of Heinrich Mann?"

"He is no good."

"You believe it?"

"All I know is that I cannot read him."

"He is no good at all. I see we have things in common. What are you doing here?"

"Shooting."

"Not ivory, I hope."

"No. For kudu."

"Why should any man shoot a kudu? You, an intelligent man, a poet, to shoot kudu."

"I haven't shot any yet," I said. "But we've been hunting them hard now for ten days. We would have got one tonight if it hadn't been for your lorry."

"That poor lorry. But you should hunt for a year. At the end of that time you have shot everything and you are sorry for it. To hunt for one special animal is nonsense. Why do you do it?"

"I like to do it."

"Of course, if you *like* to do it. Tell me, what do you really think of Rilke?"

"I have read only the one thing."

"Which?"

"The Cornet."

"You liked it?"

"Yes."

"I have no patience with it. It is snobbery. Valéry, yes. I see the point of Valéry; although there is much snobbery too. Well at least you do not kill elephants."

"I'd kill a big enough one."

"How big?"

"A seventy pounder. Maybe smaller."

"I see there are things we do not agree on. But it is a pleasure to meet one of the great old *Querschnitt* group. Tell me what is Joyce like? I have not the money to buy it. Sinclair Lewis is nothing. I bought it. No. No. Tell me tomorrow. You do not mind if I am camped near? You are with friends? You have a white hunter?"

"With my wife. We would be delighted. Yes, a white hunter."

"Why is he not out with you?"

"He believes you should hunt kudu alone."

"It is better not to hunt them at all. What is he? English?"

"Yes."

"Bloody English?"

"No. Very nice. You will like him."

"You must go. I must not keep you. Perhaps I will see you tomorrow. It was very strange that we should meet."

"Yes," I said. "Have them look at the truck tomorrow. Anything we can do."

"Good night," he said. "Good trip."

"Good night," I said. We started off and I saw him walking toward the fire waving an arm at the natives. I had not asked him why he had twenty up-country natives with him, nor where he was going. Looking back, I had asked him nothing. I do not like to ask questions, and where I was brought up it was not polite. But here we had not seen a white man for two weeks, not since we had left Babati to go south, and then to run into one on this road where you met only an occasional Indian trader and the steady migration of the natives out of the famine country, to have him look like a caricature of Benchley in Tyrolean costume, to have him know your name, to call you a poet, to have read the *Querschnitt*, to be an admirer of Joachim Ringelnatz and to want to talk about Rilke, was too fantastic to deal with. So, just then, to crown this fantasy, the lights of the car showed three tall, conical mounds of something smoking in the road ahead. I motioned to Kamau to stop, and putting on the brakes we skidded just short of them. They were from two to three feet high and when I touched one it was quite warm.

"*Tembo*," M'Cola said.

It was dung from elephants that had just crossed the road, and in the cold of the evening you could see it steaming. In a little while we were in camp.

Next morning I was up and gone to another salt-lick before daylight. There was a kudu bull on the lick when we approached through the trees and he gave a loud bark, like a dog's but higher in pitch and sharply throaty, and was gone, making no noise at first, then crashing in the brush when he was well away; and we never saw him. This lick had an impossible approach. Trees grew around its open area so that it was as though the game were in the blind and you had to come to them across the open. The only way to make it would have been for one man to go alone and crawl and then it would be impossible to get any sort of a close shot through the interlacing trees until you were within twenty yards. Of course once you were inside the protecting trees, and in the blind, you were wonderfully placed, for anything that came to the salt had to come out in the open twenty-five yards from any cover. But though we stayed until eleven o'clock nothing came. We smoothed the dust of the lick carefully with our feet so that any new tracks would show when we came back again and walked the two miles to the road. Being hunted, the game had learned to come only at night and leave before daylight. One bull had stayed and our spooking him that morning would make it even more difficult now.

This was the tenth day we had been hunting greater kudu and I had not seen a mature bull yet. We had only three days more because the rains were moving north each day from Rhodesia and unless we were prepared to stay where we were through the rains we must be out as far as Handeni before they came. We had set the seventeenth of February as the last safe date to leave. Every morning now it took the heavy, wooled sky an hour or so longer to clear and you could feel the rains coming, as they moved steadily north, as surely as though you watched them on a chart.

Now it is pleasant to hunt something that you want very much over a long period of time, being outwitted, out-manœuvred, and

failing at the end of each day, but having the hunt and knowing
every time you are out that, sooner or later, your luck will change
and that you will get the chance that you are seeking. But it is
not pleasant to have a time limit by which you must get your kudu
or perhaps never get it, nor even see one. It is not the way hunting
should be. It is too much like those boys who used to be sent to
Paris with two years in which to make good as writers or painters
after which, if they had not made good, they could go home and
into their fathers' business. The way to hunt is for as long as you
live against as long as there is such and such an animal; just as
the way to paint is as long as there is you and colors and canvas,
and to write as long as you can live and there is pencil and paper
or ink or any machine to do it with, or anything you care to write
about, and you feel a fool, and you are a fool, to do it any other
way. But here we were, now, caught by time, by the season, and
by the running out of our money, so that what should have been
as much fun to do each day whether you killed or not was being
forced into that most exciting perversion of life; the necessity of
accomplishing something in less time than should truly be allowed
for its doing. So, coming in at noon, up since two hours before
daylight, with only three days left, I was starting to be nervous
about it, and there, at the table under the dining tent fly, talking
away, was Kandisky of the Tyroler pants. I had forgotten all
about him.

"Hello. Hello," he said. "No success? Nothing doing? Where
is the kudu?"

"He coughed once and went away," I said. "Hello, girl."

She smiled. She was worried too. The two of them had been
listening since daylight for a shot. Listening all the time, even
when our guest had arrived; listening while writing letters, listening while reading, listening when Kandisky came back and talked.

"You did not shoot him?"

"No. Nor see him." I saw that Pop was worried too, and a
little nervous. There had evidently been considerable talking
going on.

"Have a beer, Colonel," he said to me.

"We spooked one," I reported. "No chance of a shot. There were plenty of tracks. Nothing more came. The wind was blowing around. Ask the boys about it."

"As I was telling Colonel Phillips," Kandisky began, shifting his leather-breeched behind and crossing one heavy-calved, well-haired, bare leg over the other, "you must not stay here too long. You must realize the rains are coming. There is one stretch of twelve miles beyond here you can never get through if it rains. It is impossible."

"So he's been telling me," Pop said. "I'm a Mister, by the way. We use these military titles as nicknames. No offense if you're a Colonel yourself." Then to me, "Damn these salt-licks. If you'd leave them alone you'd get one."

"They ball it all up," I agreed. "You're so sure of a shot sooner or later on the lick."

"Hunt the hills too."

"I'll hunt them, Pop."

"What is killing a kudu, anyway?" Kandisky asked. "You should not take it so seriously. It is nothing. In a year you kill twenty."

"Best not say anything about that to the game department, though," Pop said.

"You misunderstand," Kandisky said. "I mean in a year a man could. Of course no man would wish to."

"Absolutely," Pop said. "If he lived in kudu country, he could. They're the commonest big antelope in this bush country. It's just that when you want to see them you don't."

"I kill nothing, you understand," Kandisky told us. "Why are you not more interested in the natives?"

"We are," my wife assured him.

"They are really interesting. Listen—" Kandisky said, and he spoke on to her.

"The hell of it is," I said to Pop, "when I'm in the hills I'm sure the bastards are down there on the salt. The cows are in the hills but I don't believe the bulls are with them now. Then you get there in the evening and there are the tracks. They *have* been on the lousy salt. I think they come any time."

"Probably they do."

"I'm sure we get different bulls there. They probably only come to the salt every couple of days. Some are certainly spooked because Karl shot that one. If he'd only killed it clean instead of following it through the whole damn countryside. Christ, if he'd only kill any damn thing clean. Other new ones will come in. All we have to do is to wait them out, though. Of course they can't all know about it. But he's spooked this country to hell."

"He gets so very excited," Pop said. "But he's a good lad. He made a beautiful shot on that leopard, you know. You don't want them killed any cleaner than that. Let it quiet down again."

"Sure. I don't mean anything when I curse him "

"What about staying in the blind all day?"

"The damned wind started to go round in a circle. It blew our scent every bloody direction. No bloody use to sit there broadcasting it. If the damn wind would hold. Abdullah took an ash can today."

"I saw him starting off with it."

"There wasn't a bit of wind when we stalked the salt and there was just light to shoot. He tried the wind with the ashes all the way. I went alone with Abdullah and left the others behind and we went quietly. I had on these crêpe-soled boots and it's soft cotton dirt. The bastard spooked at fifty yards."

"Did you ever see their ears?"

"Did I ever see their ears? If I can see the bastard's ears, the skinner can work on him."

"They're bastards," Pop said. "I hate this salt-lick business. They're not as smart as we think. The trouble is you're working on them where they are smart. They've been shot at there ever since there's been salt."

"That's what makes it fun," I said. "I'd be glad to do it for a month. I like to hunt sitting on my tail. No sweat. No nothing. Sit there and catch flies and feed them to the ant lions in the dust. I like it. But what about the time?"

"That's it. The bloody time."

"So," Kandisky was saying to my wife. "That is what you should see. The big ngomas. The big native dance festivals. The real ones."

"Listen," I said to Pop. "The other lick, the one I was at last night, is fool-proof except for being near that *bloody* road."

"The trackers say it is really the property of the lesser kudu. It's a long way too. It's eighty miles there and back."

"I know. But there were four *big* bull tracks. It's certain. If it wasn't for that truck last night. What about staying there tonight? Then I'd get the night and the early morning and give this lick a rest. There's a big rhino there too. Big track, anyway."

"Good," Pop said. "Shoot the damn rhino too." He hated to have anything killed except what we were after, no killing on the side, no ornamental killing, no killing to kill, only when you wanted it more than you wanted not to kill it, only when getting it was necessary to his being first in his trade, and I saw he was offering up the rhino to please me.

"I won't kill him unless he's good," I promised.

"Shoot the bastard," Pop said, making a gift of him.

"Ah, Pop," I said.

"Shoot him," said Pop. "You'll enjoy it, being by yourself. You can sell the horn if you don't want it. You've still one on your license."

"So," said Kandisky. "You have arrested a plan of campaign? You have decided on how to outwit the poor animals?"

"Yes," I said. "How is the truck?"

"That lorry is finished," the Austrian said. "In a way I am glad. It was too much of a symbol. It was all that remained of my shamba. Now everything is gone and it is much simpler."

"What is a shamba?" asked P. O. M., my wife. "I've been hearing about them for months. I'm afraid to ask about those words every one uses."

"A plantation," he said. "It's all gone except that lorry. With the lorry I carry laborers to the shamba of an Indian. It is a very rich Indian who raises sisal. I am a manager for this Indian. An Indian can make a profit from a sisal shamba."

"From anything," Pop said.

"Yes. Where we fail, where we would starve, he makes money. This Indian is very intelligent, however. He values me. I represent European organization. I come now from organizing recruitment of the natives. This takes time. It is impressive. I have been away from my family for three months. The organization is organized. You do it in a week as easily, but it is not so impressive."

"And your wife?" asked mine.

"She waits at my house, the house of the manager, with my daughter."

"Does she love you very much?" my wife asked.

"She must, or she would be gone long ago."

"How old is the daughter?"

"She is thirteen now."

"It must be very nice to have a daughter."

"You cannot know how nice it is. It is like a second wife. My wife knows now all I think, all I say, all I believe, all I can do, all that I cannot do and cannot be. I know also about my wife—completely. But now there is always someone you do not know, who does not know you, who loves you in ignorance and is strange to you both. Some one very attractive that is yours and not yours and that makes the conversation more—how shall I say? Yes, it is like—what do you call—having here with you—with the two of you—yes there— It is the Heinz Tomato Ketchup on the daily food."

"That's very good," I said.

"We have books," he said. "I cannot buy new books now but we can always talk. Ideas and conversation are very interesting. We discuss all things. Everything. We have a very interesting mental life. Formerly, with the shamba, we had the *Querschnitt*. That gave you a feeling of belonging, of being made a part of, to a very brilliant group of people. The people one would see if one saw whom one wished to see. You know all of those people? You must know them."

"Some of them," I said. "Some in Paris. Some in Berlin."

I did not wish to destroy anything this man had, and so I did not go into those brilliant people in detail.

"They're marvellous," I said, lying.

"I envy you to know them," he said. "And tell me, who is the greatest writer in America?"

"My husband," said my wife.

"No. I do not mean for you to speak from family pride. I mean who really? Certainly not Upton Sinclair. Certainly not Sinclair Lewis. Who is your Thomas Mann? Who is your Valéry?"

"We do not have great writers," I said. "Something happens to our good writers at a certain age. I can explain but it is quite long and may bore you."

"Please explain," he said. "This is what I enjoy. This is the best part of life. The life of the mind. This is not killing kudu."

"You haven't heard it yet," I said.

"Ah, but I can see it coming. You must take more beer to loosen your tongue."

"It's loose," I told him. "It's always too bloody loose. But *you* don't drink anything."

"No, I never drink. It is not good for the mind. It is unnecessary. But tell me. Please tell me."

"Well," I said, "we have had, in America, skillful writers. Poe is a skillful writer. It is skillful, marvelously constructed, and it is dead. We have had writers of rhetoric who had the good fortune to find a little, in a chronicle of another man and from voyaging, of how things, actual things, can be, whales for instance, and this knowledge is wrapped in the rhetoric like plums in a pudding. Occasionally it is there, alone, unwrapped in pudding, and it is good. This is Melville. But the people who praise it, praise it for the rhetoric which is not important. They put a mystery in which is not there."

"Yes," he said. "I see. But it is the mind working, its ability to work, which makes the rhetoric. Rhetoric is the blue sparks from the dynamo."

"Sometimes. And sometimes it is only blue sparks and what is the dynamo driving?"

"So. Go on."

"I've forgotten."

"No. Go on. Do not pretend to be stupid."

"Did you ever get up before daylight——"

"Every morning," he said. "Go on."

"All right. There were others who wrote like exiled English colonials from an England of which they were never a part to a newer England that they were making. Very good men with the small, dried, and excellent wisdom of Unitarians; men of letters; Quakers with a sense of humor."

"Who were these?"

"Emerson, Hawthorne, Whittier, and Company. All our early classics who did not know that a new classic does not bear any resemblance to the classics that have preceded it. It can steal from anything that it is better than, anything that is not a classic, all classics do that. Some writers are only born to help another writer to write one sentence. But it cannot derive from or resemble a previous classic. Also all these men were gentlemen, or wished to be. They were all very respectable. They did not use the words that people always have used in speech, the words that survive in language. Nor would you gather that they had bodies. They had minds, yes. Nice, dry, clean minds. This is all very dull, I would not state it except that you ask for it."

"Go on."

"There is one at that time that is supposed to be really good, Thoreau. I cannot tell you about it because I have not yet been able to read it. But that means nothing because I cannot read other naturalists unless they are being extremely accurate and not literary. Naturalists should all work alone and some one else should correlate their findings for them. Writers should work alone. They should see each other only after their work is done, and not too often then. Otherwise they become like writers in New York. All angleworms in a bottle, trying to derive knowledge and nourishment from their own contact and from the bottle. Sometimes the bottle is shaped art, sometimes economics, sometimes economic-religion. But once they are in the bottle they stay there. They are lonesome outside of the bottle. They do not want to be lonesome. They are afraid to be alone in their beliefs and no woman would love any of them enough so that they could kill their lonesomeness in that woman, or pool it with hers, or make something with her that makes the rest unimportant."

"But what about Thoreau?"

"You'll have to read him. Maybe I'll be able to later. I can do nearly everything later."

"Better have some more beer, Papa."

"All right."

"What about the good writers?"

"The good writers are Henry James, Stephen Crane, and Mark Twain. That's not the order they're good in. There is no order for good writers."

"Mark Twain is a humorist. The others I do not know."

"All modern American literature comes from one book by Mark Twain called *Huckleberry Finn*. If you read it you must stop where the Nigger Jim is stolen from the boys. That is the real end. The rest is just cheating. But it's the best book we've had. All American writing comes from that. There was nothing before. There has been nothing as good since."

"What about the others?"

"Crane wrote two fine stories. *The Open Boat* and *The Blue Hotel*. The last one is the best."

"And what happened to him?"

"He died. That's simple. He was dying from the start."

"But the other two?"

"They both lived to be old men but they did not get any wiser as they got older. I don't know what they really wanted. You see we make our writers into something very strange."

"I do not understand."

"We destroy them in many ways. First, economically. They make money. It is only by hazard that a writer makes money although good books always make money eventually. Then our writers when they have made some money increase their standard of living and they are caught. They have to write to keep up their establishments, their wives, and so on, and they write slop. It is slop not on purpose but because it is hurried. Because they write when there is nothing to say or no water in the well. Because they are ambitious. Then, once they have betrayed themselves, they justify it and you get more slop. Or else they read the critics. If they believe the critics when they say they are great then they must believe them when they say they are rotten and they lose confidence. At present we have two good writers who cannot write because they have lost confidence through reading critics. If they wrote, sometimes it would be good and sometimes not so good and sometimes it would

be quite bad, but the good would get out. But they have read the
critics and they must write masterpieces. The masterpieces the
critics said they wrote. They weren't masterpieces, of course. They
were just quite good books. So now they cannot write at all. The
critics have made them impotent."

"Who are these writers?"

"Their names would mean nothing to you and by now they may
have written, become frightened, and be impotent again."

"But what is it that happens to American writers? Be definite."

"I was not here in the old days so I cannot tell you about them,
but now there are various things. At a certain age the men writers
change into Old Mother Hubbard. The women writers become
Joan of Arc without the fighting. They become leaders. It doesn't
matter who they lead. If they do not have followers they invent
them. It is useless for those selected as followers to protest. They
are accused of disloyalty. Oh, hell. There are too many things
happen to them. That is one thing. The others try to save their
souls with what they write. That is an easy way out. Others are
ruined by the first money, the first praise, the first attack, the first
time they find they cannot write, or the first time they cannot do
anything else, or else they get frightened and join organizations
that do their thinking for them. Or they do not know what they
want. Henry James wanted to make money. He never did, of
course."

"And you?"

"I am interested in other things. I have a good life but I must
write because if I do not write a certain amount I do not enjoy
the rest of my life."

"And what do you want?"

"To write as well as I can and learn as I go along. At the same
time I have my life which I enjoy and which is a damned good
life."

"Hunting kudu?"

"Yes. Hunting kudu and many other things."

"What other things?"

"Plenty of other things."

"And you know what you want?"

"Yes."

"You really like to do this, what you do now, this silliness of kudu?"

"Just as much as I like to be in the Prado."

"One is not better than the other?"

"One is as necessary as the other. There are other things, too."

"Naturally. There must be. But this sort of thing means something to you, really?"

"Truly."

"And you know what you want?"

"Absolutely, and I get it all the time."

"But it takes money."

"I could always make money and besides I have been very lucky."

"Then you are happy?"

"Except when I think of other people."

"Oh, yes."

"But you do nothing for them?"

"No."

"Nothing?"

"Maybe a little."

"Do you think your writing is worth doing—as an end in itself?"

"Oh, yes."

"You are sure?"

"Very sure."

"That must be very pleasant."

"It is," I said. "It is the one altogether pleasant thing about it."

"This is getting awfully serious," my wife said.

"It's a damned serious subject."

"You see, he is really serious about something," Kandisky said. "I knew he must be serious on something besides kudu."

"The reason every one now tries to avoid it, to deny that it is important, to make it seem vain to try to do it, is because it is so difficult. Too many factors must combine to make it possible."

"What is this now?"

"The kind of writing that can be done. How far prose can be

carried if any one is serious enough and has luck. There is a fourth and fifth dimension that can be gotten."

"You believe it?"

"I know it."

"And if a writer can get this?"

"Then nothing else matters. It is more important than anything he can do. The chances are, of course, that he will fail. But there is a chance that he succeeds."

"But that is poetry you are talking about."

"No. It is much more difficult than poetry. It is a prose that has never been written. But it can be written, without tricks and without cheating. With nothing that will go bad afterwards."

"And why has it not been written?"

"Because there are too many factors. First, there must be talent, much talent. Talent such as Kipling had. Then there must be discipline. The discipline of Flaubert. Then there must be the conception of what it can be and an absolute conscience as unchanging as the standard meter in Paris, to prevent faking. Then the writer must be intelligent and disinterested and above all he must survive. Try to get all these in one person and have him come through all the influences that press on a writer. The hardest thing, because time is so short, is for him to survive and get his work done. But I would like us to have such a writer and to read what he would write. What do you say? Should we talk about something else?"

"It is interesting what you say. Naturally I do not agree with everything."

"Naturally."

"What about a gimlet?" Pop asked. "Don't you think a gimlet might help?"

"Tell me first what are the things, the actual, concrete things that harm a writer?"

I was tired of the conversation which was becoming an interview. So I would make it an interview and finish it. The necessity to put a thousand intangibles into a sentence, now, before lunch, was too bloody.

"Politics, women, drink, money, ambition. And the lack of politics, women, drink, money and ambition," I said profoundly.

"He's getting much too easy now," Pop said.

"But drink. I do not understand about that. That has always seemed silly to me. I understand it as a weakness."

"It is a way of ending a day. It has great benefits. Don't you ever want to change your ideas?"

"Let's have one," Pop said. "W'Wendi!"

Pop never drank before lunch except as a mistake and I knew he was trying to help me out.

"Let's all have a gimlet," I said.

"I never drink," Kandisky said. "I will go to the lorry and fetch some fresh butter for lunch. It is fresh from Kandoa, un-salted. Very good. Tonight we will have a special dish of Viennese dessert. My cook has learned to make it very well."

He went off and my wife said: "You were getting awfully profound. What was that about all these women?"

"What women?"

"When you were talking about women."

"The hell with them," I said. "Those are the ones you get involved with when you're drunk."

"So that's what you do."

"No."

"I don't get involved with people when I'm drunk."

"Come, come," said Pop. "We're none of us ever drunk. My God, that man can talk."

"He didn't have a chance to talk after B'wana M'Kumba started."

"I did have verbal dysentery," I said.

"What about his lorry? Can we tow it in without ruining ours?"

"I think so," Pop said. "When ours comes back from Handeni."

At lunch under the green fly of the dining tent, in the shade of a big tree, the wind blowing, the fresh butter much admired, Grant's gazelle chops, mashed potatoes, green corn, and then mixed fruit for dessert, Kandisky told us why the East Indians were taking the country over.

"You see, during the war they sent the Indian troops to fight here. To keep them out of India because they feared another mutiny. They promised the Aga Khan that because they fought in Africa, Indians could come freely to settle and for business afterwards. They cannot break that promise and now the Indians have taken the country over from the Europeans. They live on nothing and they send all the money back to India. When they have made enough to go home they leave, bringing out their poor relations to take over from them and continue to exploit the country."

Pop said nothing. He would not argue with a guest at table.

"It is the Aga Khan," Kandisky said. "You are an American. You know nothing of these combinations."

"Were you with Von Lettöw?" Pop asked him.

"From the start," Kandisky said. "Until the end."

"He was a great fighter," Pop said. "I have great admiration for him."

"You fought?" Kandisky asked.

"Yes."

"I do not care for Lettöw," Kandisky said. "He fought, yes. No one ever better. When we wanted quinine he would order it captured. All supplies the same. But afterwards he cared nothing for his men. After the war I am in Germany. I go to see about indemnification for my property. 'You are an Austrian,' they say. 'You must go through Austrian channels.' So I go to Austria. 'But why did you fight?' they ask me. 'You cannot hold us responsible. Suppose you go to fight in China. That is your own affair. We cannot do anything for you.'

" 'But I went as a patriot,' I say, very foolishly. 'I fight where I can because I am an Austrian and I know my duty.' 'Yes,' they say. 'That is very beautiful. But you cannot hold us responsible for your noble sentiments.' So they passed me from one to the other and nothing. Still I love the country very much. I have lost everything here but I have more than anyone has in Europe. To me it is always interesting. The natives and the language. I have many books of notes on them. Then too, in reality, I am a king here. It is very pleasant. Waking in the morning I extend one foot and the boy places the sock on it. When I am ready I extend the other foot and he adjusts the other sock. I step from under the mosquito bar into my drawers which are held for me. Don't you think that is very marvellous?"

"It's marvellous."

"When you come back another time we must take a safari to study the natives. And shoot nothing, or only to eat. Look, I will show you a dance and sing a song."

Crouched, elbows lifting and falling, knees humping, he shuffled around the table, singing. Undoubtedly it was very fine.

"That is only one of a thousand," he said. "Now I must go for a time. You will be sleeping."

"There's no hurry. Stay around."

"No. Surely you will be sleeping. I also. I will take the butter to keep it cool."

"We'll see you at supper," Pop said.

"Now you must sleep. Good-bye."

After he was gone, Pop said: "I wouldn't believe all that about the Aga Khan, you know."

"It sounded pretty good."

"Of course he feels badly," Pop said. "Who wouldn't. Von Lettöw was a hell of a man."

"He's very intelligent," my wife said. "He talks wonderfully about the natives. But he's bitter about American women."

"So am I," said Pop. "He's a good man. You better get some shut-eye. You'll need to start about three-thirty."

"Have them call me."

Molo raised the back of the tent, propping it with sticks, so the wind blew through and I went to sleep reading, the wind coming in cool and fresh under the heated canvas.

When I woke it was time to go. There were rain clouds in the sky and it was very hot. They had packed some tinned fruit, a five-pound piece of roast meat, bread, tea, a tea pot, and some tinned milk in a whiskey box with four bottles of beer. There was a canvas water bag and a ground cloth to use as a tent. M'Cola was taking the big gun out to the car.

"There's no hurry about getting back," Pop said. "We'll look for you when we see you."

"All right."

"We'll send the truck to haul that sportsman into Handeni. He's sending his men ahead walking."

"You're sure the truck can stand it? Don't do it because he's a friend of mine."

"Have to get him out. The truck will be in tonight."

"The Memsahib's still asleep," I said. "Maybe she can get out for a walk and shoot some guineas."

"I'm here," she said. "Don't worry about us. *Oh,* I hope you get them."

"Don't send out to look for us along the road until day after tomorrow," I said. "If there's a good chance we'll stay."

"Good luck."

"Good luck, sweet. Good-bye, Mr. J. P."

from TO HAVE AND HAVE NOT

ONE TRIP ACROSS

TO HAVE AND HAVE NOT is an American panel in Hemingway's chronicle of modern chivalry. The novel has three phases, the first of which is included here, illustrating various aspects of the lawlessness, the desperation and the squalor that shook our comparatively untouched half of a world swept elsewhere by recurring catastrophes of war. Here is Harry Morgan in the round, when he could still get by on fortitude and improvising and luck. It shows his relations with the sportsman, Johnson, who might have been a robber baron in the minor leagues, the lesser castles and encampments. The way Johnson cheated Harry Morgan is foreign to the spirit of noblesse oblige. And this phase, foreshadowing Morgan's experiences with other uprooted citizens during the years of the American depression, also shows Morgan's relations with his wife, and her kindness.

When you compare Hemingway to Goya, as it is natural to do, To Have and Have Not is a part of the Caprichos and the Disparates, like "The Light of the World," and such stories, not included here, as "An Alpine Idyll" and "The Sea Change," and "God Rest You Merry, Gentlemen." The Tauromaquia is easily identified in Death in the Afternoon and other works such as the second half of The Sun Also Rises and "The Undefeated." The Desastres de la Guerra are not far to find in Hemingway's work, since it is a true chronicle of modern times.

To Have and Have Not was written between 1933 and 1936 at Key West and in Cuba and Spain. Hemingway called the episode published here "One Trip Across."

C. P.

TO HAVE AND HAVE NOT

ONE TRIP ACROSS

I

You KNOW how it is there early in the morning in Havana with the bums still asleep against the walls of the buildings; before even the ice wagons come by with ice for the bars? Well, we came across the square from the dock to the Pearl of San Francisco Café to get coffee and there was only one beggar awake in the square and he was getting out of the fountain. But when we got inside the café and sat down, there were the three of them waiting for us.

We sat down and one of them came over.

"Well," he said.

"I can't do it," I told him. "I'd like to do it as a favor. But I told you last night I couldn't."

"You can name your own price."

"It isn't that. I can't do it. That's all."

The two others had come over and they stood there looking sad. They were nice-looking fellows all right and I would have liked to have done them the favor.

"A thousand apiece," said the one who spoke good English.

"Don't make me feel bad," I told him. "I tell you true I can't do it."

"Afterwards, when things are changed, it would mean a good deal to you."

"I know it. I'm all for you. But I can't do it."

"Why not?"

"I make my living with the boat. If I lose her I lose my living."

"With the money you buy another boat."

"Not in jail."

They must have thought I just needed to be argued into it because the one kept on.

"You would have three thousand dollars and it could mean a great deal to you later. All this will not last, you know."

"Listen," I said. "I don't care who is President here. But I don't carry anything to the States that can talk."

"You mean we would talk?" one of them who hadn't spoke said. He was angry.

"I said anything that *can* talk."

"Do you think we are lenguas largas?"

"No."

"Do you know what a lengua larga is?"

"Yes. One with a long tongue."

"Do you know what we do with them?"

"Don't be tough with me," I said. "You propositioned me. I didn't offer you anything."

"Shut up, Pancho," the one who had done the talking before said to the angry one.

"He said we would talk," Pancho said.

"Listen," I said. "I told you I didn't carry anything that *can* talk. Sacked liquor can't talk. Demijohns can't talk. There's other things that can't talk. Men can talk."

"Can Chinamen talk?" Pancho said, pretty nasty.

"They can talk but I can't understand them," I told him.

"So you won't?"

"It's just like I told you last night. I can't."

"But you won't talk?" Pancho said.

The one thing that he hadn't understood right had made him nasty. I guess it was disappointment, too. I didn't even answer him.

"You're not a lengua larga, are you?" he asked, still nasty.

"I don't think so."

"What's that? A threat?"

"Listen," I told him. "Don't be so tough so early in the morning. I'm sure you've cut plenty people's throats. I haven't even had my coffee yet."

"So you're sure I've cut people's throats?"

"No," I said. "And I don't give a damn. Can't you do business without getting angry?"

"I am angry now," he said. "I would like to kill you."

"Oh, hell," I told him. "Don't talk so much."

"Come on, Pancho," the first one said. Then, to me, "I am very sorry. I wish you would take us."

"I'm sorry, too. But I can't."

The three of them started for the door, and I watched them go. They were good-looking young fellows, wore good clothes; none of them wore hats, and they looked like they had plenty of money. They talked plenty of money, anyway, and they spoke the kind of English Cubans with money speak.

Two of them looked like brothers and the other one, Pancho, was a little taller but the same sort of looking kid. You know, slim, good clothes, and shiny hair. I didn't figure he was as mean as he talked. I figured he was plenty nervous.

As they turned out of the door to the right, I saw a closed car come across the square toward them. The first thing a pane of glass went and the bullet smashed into the row of bottles on the show-case wall to the right. I heard the gun going and, bop, bop, bop, there were bottles smashing all along the wall.

I jumped behind the bar on the left side and could see looking over the edge. The car was stopped and there were two fellows crouched down by it. One had a Thompson gun and the other had a sawed-off automatic shotgun. The one with the Thompson gun was a nigger. The other had a chauffeur's white duster on.

One of the boys was spread out on the sidewalk, face down, just outside the big window that was smashed. The other two were behind one of the Tropical beer ice wagons that was stopped in front of the Cunard bar next door. One of the ice-wagon horses was down in the harness, kicking, and the other was plunging his head off.

One of the boys shot from the rear corner of the wagon and it ricocheted off the sidewalk. The nigger with the Tommy gun got his face almost into the street and gave the back of the wagon a burst from underneath and sure enough one came down, falling toward the sidewalk with his head above the curb. He flopped there, putting his hands over his head, and the chauffeur shot at him with the shotgun while the nigger put in a fresh pan; but it was a long shot. You could see the buckshot marks all over the sidewalk like silver splatters.

The other fellow pulled the one who was hit back by the legs to behind the wagon, and I saw the nigger getting his face down on the paving to give them another burst. Then I saw old Pancho come around the corner of the wagon and step into the lee of the horse that was still up. He stepped clear of the horse, his face white as a dirty sheet, and got the chauffeur with the big Luger he had; holding it in both hands to keep it steady. He shot twice over the nigger's head, coming on, and once low.

He hit a tire on the car because I saw dust blowing in a spurt on the street as the air came out, and at ten feet the nigger shot him in the belly with the Tommy gun, with what must have been the last shot in it because I saw him throw it down, and old Pancho sat down hard and went over forwards. He was trying to come up, still holding onto the Luger, only he couldn't get his head up, when the nigger took the shotgun that was lying against the wheel of the car by the chauffeur and blew the side of his head off. Some nigger.

I took a quick one out of the first bottle I saw open and I couldn't tell you yet what it was. The whole thing made me feel pretty bad. I slipped along behind the bar and out through the kitchen in back and all the way out. I went clean around the outside of the square and never even looked over toward the crowd there was coming fast in front of the café and went in through the gate and out onto the dock and got on board.

The fellow who had her chartered was on board waiting. I told him what had happened.

"Where's Eddy?" this fellow Johnson that had us chartered asked me.

"I never saw him after the shooting started."

"Do you suppose he was hit?"

"Hell, no. I tell you the only shots that came in the café were into the show case. That was when the car was coming behind them. That was when they shot the first fellow right in front of the window. They came at an angle like this——"

"You seem awfully sure about it," he said.

"I was watching," I told him.

Then, as I looked up, I saw Eddy coming along the dock looking taller and sloppier than ever. He walked with his joints all slung wrong.

"There he is."

Eddy looked pretty bad. He never looked too good early in the morning; but he looked pretty bad now.

"Where were you?" I asked him.

"On the floor."

"Did you see it?" Johnson asked him.

"Don't talk about it, Mr. Johnson," Eddy said to him. "It makes me sick to even think about it."

"You better have a drink," Johnson told him. Then he said to me, "Well, are we going out?"

"That's up to you."

"What sort of a day will it be?"

"Just about like yesterday. Maybe better."

"Let's get out, then."

"All right, as soon as the bait comes."

We'd had this bird out three weeks fishing the stream and I hadn't seen any of his money yet except one hundred dollars he gave me to pay the consul, and clear, and get some grub, and put gas in her before we came across. I was furnishing all the tackle and he had her chartered at thirty-five dollars a day. He slept at a hotel and came aboard every morning. Eddy got me the charter so I had to carry him. I was giving him four dollars a day.

"I've got to put gas in her," I told Johnson.

"All right."

"I'll need some money for that."

"How much?"

"It's twenty-eight cents a gallon. I ought to put in forty gallons anyway. That's eleven-twenty."

He got out fifteen dollars.

"Do you want to put the rest on the beer and the ice?" I asked him.

"That's fine," he said. "Just put it down against what I owe you."

I was thinking three weeks was a long time to let him go, but if he was good for it what difference was there? He should have paid every week anyway. But I've let them run a month and got the money. It was my fault but I was glad to see it run at first. It was only the last few days he made me nervous but I didn't want to say anything for fear of getting him plugged at me. If he was good for it, the longer he went the better.

"Have a bottle of beer?" he asked me, opening the box.

"No, thanks."

Just then this nigger we had getting bait comes down the dock and I told Eddy to get ready to cast her off.

The nigger came on board with the bait and we cast off and started out of the harbor, the nigger fixing on a couple of mackerel; passing the hook through their mouth, out the gills, slitting the side and then putting the hook through the other side and out, tying the mouth shut on the wire leader and tying the hook good so it couldn't slip and so the bait would troll smooth without spinning.

He's a real black nigger, smart and gloomy, with blue voodoo beads around his neck under his shirt, and an old straw hat. What he liked to do on board was sleep and read the papers. But he put on a nice bait and he was fast.

"Can't you put on a bait like that, captain?" Johnson asked me.

"Yes, sir."

"Why do you carry a nigger to do it?"

"When the big fish run you'll see," I told him.

"What's the idea?"

"The nigger can do it faster than I can."

"Can't Eddy do it?"

"No, sir."

"It seems an unnecessary expense to me." He'd been giving the nigger a dollar a day and the nigger had been on a rumba every night. I could see him getting sleepy already.

"He's necessary," I said.

By then we had passed the smacks with their fish cars anchored in front of the Cabañas and the skiffs anchored fishing for mutton fish on the rock bottom by the Morro, and I headed her out where the gulf made a dark line. Eddy put the two big teasers out and the nigger had baits on three rods.

The stream was in almost to soundings and as we came toward the edge you could see her running nearly purple with regular whirlpools. There was a light east breeze coming up and we put up plenty of flying fish, those big ones with the black wings that look like the picture of Lindbergh crossing the Atlantic when they sail off.

Those big flying fish are the best sign there is. As far as you could see, there was that faded yellow gulf-weed in small patches that means the main stream is well in and there were birds ahead working over a school of little tuna. You could see them jumping; just little ones weighing a couple of pounds apiece.

"Put out any time you want," I told Johnson.

He put on his belt and his harness and put out the big rod with the Hardy reel with six hundred yards of thirty-six thread. I looked back and his bait was trolling nice, just bouncing along on the swell, and the two teasers were diving and jumping. We were going just about the right speed and I headed her into the stream.

"Keep the rod butt in the socket on the chair," I told him. "Then the rod won't be as heavy. Keep the drag off so you can slack to him when he hits. If one ever hits with the drag on he'll jerk you overboard."

Every day I'd have to tell him the same thing but I didn't mind that. One out of fifty parties you get know how to fish. Then when they do know, half the time they're goofy and want to use line that isn't strong enough to hold anything big.

"How does the day look?" he asked me.

"It couldn't be better," I told him. It was a pretty day all right.

I gave the nigger the wheel and told him to work along the edge of the stream to the eastward and went back to where Johnson was sitting watching his bait bouncing along.

"Want me to put out another rod?" I asked him.

"I don't think so," he said. "I want to hook, fight, and land my fish myself."

"Good," I said. "Do you want Eddy to put it out and hand it to you if one strikes so you can hook him?"

"No," he said. "I prefer to have only one rod out."

"All right."

The nigger was still taking her out and I looked and saw he had seen a patch of flying fish burst out ahead and up the stream a little. Looking back, I could see Havana looking fine in the sun and a ship just coming out of the harbor past the Morro.

"I think you're going to have a chance to fight one today, Mr. Johnson," I told him.

"It's about time," he said. "How long have we been out?"

"Three weeks today."

"That's a long time to fish."

"They're a funny fish," I told him. "They aren't here until they come. But when they come there's plenty of them. And they've always come. If they don't come now they're never coming. The moon is right. There's a good stream and we're going to have a good breeze."

"There were some small ones when we first came."

"Yes," I said. "Like I told you. The small ones thin out and stop before the big ones come."

"You party-boat captains always have the same line. Either it's too early or too late or the wind isn't right or the moon is wrong. But you take the money just the same."

"Well," I told him, "the hell of it is that it usually is too early or too late and plenty of time the wind is wrong. Then when you get a day that's perfect you're ashore without a party."

"But you think today's a good day?"

"Well," I told him, "I've had action enough for me already today. But I'd like to bet you're going to have plenty."

"I hope so," he said.

We settled down to troll. Eddy went forward and laid down. I was standing up watching for a tail to show. Every once in a while the nigger would doze off and I was watching him, too. I bet he had some nights.

"Would you mind getting me a bottle of beer, captain?" Johnson asked me.

"No, sir," I said, and I dug down in the ice to get him a cold one.

"Won't you have one?" he asked.

"No, sir," I said. "I'll wait till tonight."

I opened the bottle and was reaching it toward him when I saw this big brown buggar with a spear on him longer than your arm burst head and shoulders out of the water and smash at that mackerel. He looked as big around as a saw log.

"Slack it to him!" I yelled.

"He hasn't got it," Johnson said.

"Hold it, then."

He'd come up from deep down and missed it. I knew he'd turn and come for it again.

"Get ready to turn it loose to him the minute he grabs it."

Then I saw him coming from behind under water. You could see his fins out wide like purple wings and the purple stripes across the brown. He came on like a submarine and his top fin came out and you could see it slice the water. Then he came right behind the bait and his spear came out too, sort of wagging, clean out of water.

"Let it go into his mouth," I said. Johnson took his hand off the reel spool and it started to whiz and the old marlin turned and went down and I could see the whole length of him shine bright silver as he turned broadside and headed off fast toward shore.

"Put on a little drag," I said. "Not much."

He screwed down on the drag.

"Not too much," I said. I could see the line slant up. "Shut her down hard and sock him," I said. "You've got to sock him. He's going to jump anyway."

Johnson screwed the drag down and came back on the rod.

"Sock him!" I told him. "Stick it into him. Hit him half a dozen times."

He hit him pretty hard a couple of times more, and then the rod bent double and the reel commenced to screech and out he came, boom, in a long straight jump, shining silver in the sun and making a splash like throwing a horse off a cliff.

"Ease up on the drag," I told him.

"He's gone," said Johnson.

"The hell he is," I told him. "Ease up on the drag quick."

I could see the curve in the line and the next time he jumped he was astern and headed out to sea. Then he came out again and smashed the water white and I could see he was hooked in the side of the mouth. The stripes showed clear on him. He was a fine fish bright silver now, barred with purple, and as big around as a log.

"He's gone," Johnson said. The line was slack.

"Reel on him," I said. "He's hooked good. Put her ahead with all the machine!" I yelled to the nigger.

Then once, twice, he came out stiff as a post, the whole length of him jumping straight toward us, throwing the water high each time he landed. The line came taut and I saw he was headed inshore again and I could see he was turning.

"Now he'll make his run," I said. "If he hooks up I'll chase him. Keep your drag light. There's plenty of line."

The old marlin headed out to the nor'west like all the big ones go, and brother, did he hook up. He started jumping in those long lopes and every splash would be like a speed boat in a sea. We went after him, keeping him on the quarter once I'd made the turn. I had the wheel and I kept yelling to Johnson to keep his drag light and reel fast. All of a sudden I see his rod jerk and the line go slack. It wouldn't look slack unless you knew about it because of the pull of the belly of the line in the water. But I knew.

"He's gone," I told him. The fish was still jumping and he went on jumping until he was out of sight. He was a fine fish all right.

"I can still feel him pull," Johnson said.

"That's the weight of the line."

"I can hardly reel it. Maybe he's dead."

"Look at him," I said. "He's still jumping." You could see him out a half a mile, still throwing spouts of water.

I felt his drag. He had it screwed down tight. You couldn't pull out any line. It had to break.

"Didn't I tell you to keep your drag light?"

"But he kept taking out line."

"So what?"

"So I tightened it."

"Listen," I told him. "If you don't give them line when they hook up like that they break it. There isn't any line will hold them. When they want it you've got to give it to them. You have to keep a light drag. The market fishermen can't hold them tight when they do that even with a harpoon line. What we have to do is use the boat to chase them so they don't take it all when they make their run. After they make their run they'll sound and you can tighten up the drag and get it back."

"Then if it hadn't broken I would have caught him?"

"You'd have had a chance."

"He couldn't have kept that up, could he?"

"He can do plenty of other things. It isn't until after he's made his run that the fight starts."

"Well, let's catch one," he said.

"You have to reel that line in first," I told him.

We'd hooked that fish and lost him without waking Eddy up. Now old Eddy came back astern.

"What's the matter?" he said.

Eddy was a good man on a boat once, before he got to be a rummy, but he isn't any good now. I looked at him standing there tall and hollow-cheeked with his mouth loose and that white stuff in the corners of his eyes and his hair all faded in the sun. I knew he woke up dead for a drink.

"You'd better drink a bottle of beer," I told him. He took one out of the box and drank it.

"Well, Mr. Johnson," he said, "I guess I better finish my nap. Much obliged for the beer, sir." Some Eddy. The fish didn't make any difference to him.

Well, we hooked another one around noon and he jumped off. You could see the hook go thirty feet in the air when he threw it.

"What did I do wrong then?" Johnson asked.

"Nothing," I said. "He just threw it."

"Mr. Johnson," said Eddy, who'd waked up to have another bottle of beer—"Mr. Johnson, you're just unlucky. Now maybe you're lucky with women. Mr. Johnson, what do you say we go out tonight?" Then he went back and laid down again.

About four o'clock when we're coming back close in to shore against the stream; it going like a mill race, us with the sun at our backs; the biggest black marlin I ever saw in my life hit Johnson's bait. We'd put out a feather squid and caught four of those little tuna and the nigger put one on his hook for bait. It trolled pretty heavy but it made a big splash in the wake.

Johnson took the harness off the reel so he could put the rod across his knees because his arms got tired holding it in position all the time. Because his hands got tired holding the spool of the reel against the drag of the big bait, he screwed the drag down when I wasn't looking. I never knew he had it down. I didn't like to see him hold the rod that way but I hated to be crabbing at him all the time. Besides, with the drag off, line would go out so there wasn't any danger. But it was a sloppy way to fish.

I was at the wheel and was working the edge of the stream opposite that old cement factory where it makes deep so close in to shore and where it makes a sort of eddy where there is always lots of bait. Then I saw a splash like a depth bomb and the sword, and eye, and open lower-jaw and huge purple-black head of a black marlin. The whole top fin was up out of water looking as high as a full-rigged ship, and the whole scythe tail was out as he smashed at that tuna. The bill was as big around as a baseball bat and slanted up, and as he grabbed the bait he sliced the ocean wide open. He was solid purple-black and he had an eye as big as a soup bowl. He was huge. I bet he'd go a thousand pounds.

I yelled to Johnson to let him have line but before I could say a word, I saw Johnson rise up in the air off the chair as though he was being derricked, and him holding just for a second onto that rod and the rod bending like a bow, and then the butt caught him in the belly and the whole works went overboard.

He'd screwed the drag tight, and when the fish struck, it lifted Johnson right out of the chair and he couldn't hold it. He'd had the butt under one leg and the rod across his lap. If he'd had the harness on it would have taken him along, too.

I cut out the engine and went back to the stern. He was sitting there holding onto his belly where the rod butt had hit him.

"I guess that's enough for today," I said.

"What was it?" he said to me.

"Black marlin," I said.

"How did it happen?"

"You figure it out," I said. "The reel cost two hundred and fifty dollars. It costs more now. The rod cost me forty-five. There was a little under six hundred yards of thirty-six thread."

Just then Eddy slaps him on the back. "Mr. Johnson," he says, "you're just unlucky. You know I never saw that happen before in my life."

"Shut up, you rummy," I said to him.

"I tell you, Mr. Johnson," Eddy said, "that's the rarest occurrence I ever saw in my life."

"What would I do if I was hooked to a fish like that?" Johnson said.

"That's what you wanted to fight all by yourself," I told him. I was plenty sore.

"They're too big," Johnson said. "Why, it would just be punishment."

"Listen," I said. "A fish like that would kill you."

"They catch them."

"People who know how to fish catch them. But don't think they don't take punishment."

"I saw a picture of a girl who caught one."

"Sure," I said. "Still fishing. He swallowed the bait and they pulled his stomach out and he came to the top and died. I'm talking about trolling for them when they're hooked in the mouth."

"Well," said Johnson, "they're too big. If it isn't enjoyable, why do it?"

"That's right, Mr. Johnson," Eddy said. "If it isn't enjoyable, why do it? Listen, Mr. Johnson. You hit the nail on the head there. If it isn't enjoyable—why do it?"

I was still shaky from seeing that fish and feeling plenty sick about the tackle and I couldn't listen to them. I told the nigger to head her for the Morro. I didn't say anything to them and there they sat, Eddy in one of the chairs with a bottle of beer and Johnson with another.

"Captain," he said to me after a while, "could you make me a highball?"

I made him one without saying anything, and then I made myself a real one. I was thinking to myself that this Johnson had fished fifteen days, finally he hooks into a fish a fisherman would give a year to tie into, he loses him, he loses my heavy tackle, he makes a fool of himself and he sits there perfectly content, drinking with a rummy.

When we got into the dock and the nigger was standing there waiting, I said, "What about tomorrow?"

"I don't think so," Johnson said. "I'm about fed up with this kind of fishing."

"You want to pay off the nigger?"

"How much do I owe him?"

"A dollar. You can give him a tip if you want."

So Johnson gave the nigger a dollar and two Cuban twenty-cent pieces.

"What's this for?" the nigger asks me, showing the coins.

"A tip," I told him in Spanish. "You're through. He gives you that."

"Don't come tomorrow?"

"No."

The nigger gets his ball of twine he used for tying baits and his dark glasses, puts on his straw hat and goes without saying good-by. He was a nigger that never thought much of any of us.

"When do you want to settle up, Mr. Johnson?" I asked him.

"I'll go to the bank in the morning," Johnson said. "We can settle up in the afternoon."

"Do you know how many days there are?"

"Fifteen."

"No. There's sixteen with today and a day each way makes eighteen. Then there's the rod and reel and the line from today."

"The tackle's your risk."

"No, sir. Not when you lose it that way."

"I've paid every day for the rent of it. It's your risk."

"No, sir," I said. "If a fish broke it and it wasn't your fault, that

would be something else. You lost that whole outfit by careless-
ness."

"The fish pulled it out of my hands."

"Because you had the drag on and didn't have the rod in the
socket."

"You have no business to charge for that."

"If you hired a car and ran it off a cliff, don't you think you'd
have to pay for it?"

"Not if I was in it," Johnson said.

"That's pretty good, Mr. Johnson," Eddy said. "You see it, don't
you, cap? If he was in it he'd be killed. So he wouldn't have to
pay. That's a good one."

I didn't pay any attention to the rummy. "You owe two hundred
and ninety-five dollars for that rod and reel and line," I told
Johnson.

"Well, it's not right," he said. "But if that's the way you feel
about it why not split the difference?"

"I can't replace it for under three hundred and sixty. I'm not
charging you for the line. A fish like that could get all your line
and it not be your fault. If there was any one here but a rummy
they'd tell you how square I'm being with you. I know it seems
like a lot of money but it was a lot of money when I bought the
tackle, too. You can't fish like that without the best tackle you
can buy."

"Mr. Johnson, he says I'm a rummy. Maybe I am. But I tell
you he's right. He's right and he's reasonable," Eddy told him.

"I don't want to make any difficulties," Johnson said finally.
"I'll pay for it, even though I don't see it. That's eighteen days at
thirty-five dollars and two ninety-five extra."

"You gave me a hundred," I told him. "I'll give you a list of
what I spent and I'll deduct what grub there is left. What you
bought for provisions going over and back."

"That's reasonable," Johnson said.

"Listen, Mr. Johnson," Eddy said. "If you knew the way they
usually charge a stranger you'd know it was more than reasonable.
Do you know what it is? It's exceptional. The Cap is treating you
like you were his own mother."

"I'll go to the bank tomorrow and come down in the afternoon. Then I'll get the boat day after tomorrow."

"You can go back with us and save the boat fare."

"No," he said. "I'll save time with the boat."

"Well," I said. "What about a drink?"

"Fine," said Johnson. "No hard feelings now, are there?"

"No, sir," I told him. So the three of us sat there in the stern and drank a highball together.

The next day I worked around her all morning, changing the oil in her base and one thing and another. At noon I went uptown and ate at a Chink place where you get a good meal for forty cents, and then I bought some things to take home to my wife and our three girls. You know, perfume, a couple of fans and three of those high combs. When I finished I stopped in at Donovan's and had a beer and talked with the old man and then walked back to the San Francisco docks, stopping in at three or four places for a beer on the way. I bought Frankie a couple at the Cunard bar and I came on board feeling pretty good. When I came on board I had just forty cents left. Frankie came on board with me, and while we sat and waited for Johnson I drank a couple of cold ones out of the ice box with Frankie.

Eddy hadn't shown up all night or all day but I knew he would be around sooner or later, as soon as his credit ran out. Donovan told me he'd been in there the night before a little while with Johnson, and Eddy had been setting them up on credit. We waited and I began to wonder about Johnson not showing up. I'd left word at the dock for them to tell him to go on board and wait for me but they said he hadn't come. Still, I figured he had been out late and probably didn't get up till around noon. The banks were open until three-thirty. We saw the plane go out, and about five-thirty I was all over feeling good and was getting plenty worried.

At six o'clock I sent Frankie up to the hotel to see if Johnson was there. I still thought he might be out on a time or he might be there at the hotel feeling too bad to get up. I kept waiting and waiting until it was late. But I was getting plenty worried because he owed me eight hundred and twenty-five dollars.

Frankie was gone about a little over half an hour. When I saw him coming he was walking fast and shaking his head.

"He went on the plane," he said.

All right. There it was. The consulate was closed. I had forty cents, and, anyhow, the plane was in Miami by now. I couldn't even send a wire. Some Mr. Johnson, all right. It was my fault. I should have known better.

"Well," I said to Frankie, "we might as well have a cold one. Mr. Johnson bought them." There were three bottles of Tropical left.

Frankie felt as bad as I did. I don't know how he could but he seemed to. He just kept slapping me on the back and shaking his head.

So there it was. I was broke. I'd lost five hundred and thirty dollars of the charter, and tackle I couldn't replace for three hundred and fifty more. How some of that gang that hangs around the dock would be pleased at that, I thought. It certainly would make some conchs happy. And the day before I turned down three thousand dollars to land three aliens on the Keys. Anywhere, just to get them out of the country.

All right, what was I going to do now? I couldn't bring in a load because you have to have money to buy the booze and besides there's no money in it any more. The town is flooded with it and there's nobody to buy it. But I was damned if I was going home broke and starve a summer in that town. Besides I've got a family. The clearance was paid when we came in. You usually pay the broker in advance and he enters you and clears you. Hell, I didn't even have enough money to put in gas. It was a hell of a note, all right. Some Mr. Johnson.

"I've got to carry something, Frankie," I said. "I've got to make some money."

"I'll see," said Frankie. He hangs around the water front and does odd jobs and is pretty deaf and drinks too much every night. But you never saw a fellow more loyal nor with a better heart. I've known him since I first started to run over there. He used to help me load plenty of times. Then when I quit handling stuff and went party-boating and broke out this sword-fishing in Cuba I

used to see him a lot around the dock and around the café. He
seems dumb and he usually smiles instead of talking, but that's
because he's deaf.

"You carry anything?" Frankie asked.

"Sure," I said. "I can't choose now."

"Anything?"

"Sure."

"I'll see," Frankie said. "Where will you be?"

"I'll be at the Perla," I told him. "I have to eat."

You can get a good meal at the Perla for twenty-five cents.
Everything on the menu is a dime except soup, and that is a
nickel. I walked as far as there with Frankie, and I went in and he
went on. Before he went he shook me by the hand and clapped
me on the back again.

"Don't worry," he said. "Me Frankie; much politics. Much business. Much drinking. No money. But big friend. Don't worry."

"So long, Frankie," I said. "Don't you worry either, boy."

II

I WENT in the Perla and sat down at a table. They had a new
pane of glass in the window that had been shot up and the show-
case was all fixed up. There were a lot of gallegos drinking at the
bar, and some eating. One table was playing dominoes already. I
had black bean soup and a beef stew with boiled potatoes for
fifteen cents. A bottle of Hatuey beer brought it up to a quarter.
When I spoke to the waiter about the shooting he wouldn't say
anything. They were all plenty scared.

I finished the meal and sat back and smoked a cigaret and worried my head off. Then I saw Frankie coming in the door with
some one behind him. Yellow stuff, I thought to myself. So it's
yellow stuff.

"This is Mr. Sing," Frankie said, and smiled. He'd been pretty
fast all right and he knew it.

"How do you do?" said Mr. Sing.

Mr. Sing was about the smoothest-looking thing I'd ever seen. He was a Chink all right, but he talked like an Englishman and he was dressed in a white suit with a silk shirt and black tie and one of those hundred-and-twenty-five-dollar Panama hats.

"You will have some coffee?" he asked me.

"If you do."

"Thank you," said Mr. Sing. "We are quite alone here?"

"Except for everybody in the café," I told him.

"That is all right," Mr. Sing said. "You have a boat?"

"Thirty-eight feet," I said. "Hundred horse Kermath."

"Ah," said Mr. Sing. "I had imagined it was something bigger."

"It can carry two hundred and sixty-five cases without being loaded."

"Would you care to charter it to me?"

"On what terms?"

"You need not go. I will provide a captain and a crew."

"No," I said. "I go on her wherever she goes."

"I see," said Mr. Sing. "Would you mind leaving us?" he said to Frankie. Frankie looked as interested as ever and smiled at him.

"He's deaf," I said. "He doesn't understand much English."

"I see," said Mr. Sing. "You speak Spanish. Tell him to rejoin us later."

I motioned to Frankie with my thumb. He got up and went over to the bar.

"You don't speak Spanish?" I said.

"Oh, yes," said Mr. Sing. "Now what are the circumstances that would—that have made you consider . . ."

"I'm broke."

"I see," said Mr. Sing. "Does the boat owe any money? Can she be libeled?"

"No."

"Quite so," Mr. Sing said. "How many of my unfortunate compatriots could your boat accommodate?"

"You mean carry?"

"That's it."

"How far?"

"A day's voyage."

"I don't know," I said. "She can take a dozen if they didn't have any baggage."

"They would not have baggage."

"Where do you want to carry them?"

"I'd leave that to you," Mr. Sing said.

"You mean where to land them?"

"You would embark them for the Tortugas where a schooner would pick them up."

"Listen," I said. "There's a lighthouse at the Tortugas on Loggerhead Key with a radio that works both ways."

"Quite," said Mr. Sing. "It would certainly be very silly to land them there."

"Then what?"

"I said you would embark them for there. That is what their passage calls for."

"Yes," I said.

"You would land them wherever your best judgment dictated."

"Will the schooner come to Tortugas to get them?"

"Of course not," said Mr. Sing. "How silly."

"How much are they worth a head?"

"Fifty dollars," said Mr. Sing.

"No."

"How would seventy-five do?"

"What do you get a head?"

"Oh, that's quite beside the point. You see, there are a great many facets, or you would say angles, to my issuing the tickets. It doesn't stop there."

"Yes," I said. "And what I'm supposed to do doesn't have to be paid for, either. Eh?"

"I see your point absolutely," said Mr. Sing. "Should we say a hundred dollars apiece?"

"Listen," I said. "Do you know how long I would go to jail if they pick me up on this?"

"Ten years," said Mr. Sing. "Ten years at least. But there is no reason to go to jail, my dear captain. You run only one risk—when you load your passengers. Everything else is left to your discretion."

"And if they come back on your hands?"

"That's quite simple. I would accuse you to them of having betrayed me. I will make a partial refund and ship them out again. They realize, of course, that it is a difficult voyage."

"What about me?"

"I suppose I should send some word to the consulate."

"I see."

"Twelve hundred dollars, captain, is not to be despised at present."

"When would I get the money?"

"Two hundred when you agree and a thousand when you load."

"Suppose I went off with the two hundred?"

"I could do nothing, of course," he smiled. "But I know you wouldn't do such a thing, captain."

"Have you got the two hundred with you?"

"Of course."

"Put it under the plate." He did.

"All right," I said. "I'll clear in the morning and pull out at dark. Now, where do we load?"

"How would Bacuranao be?"

"All right. Have you got it fixed?"

"Of course."

"Now, about the loading," I said. "You show two lights, one above the other, at the point. I'll come in when I see them. You come out in a boat and load from the boat. You come yourself and you bring the money. I won't take one on board until I have it."

"No," he said; "one-half when you start to load and the other when you are finished."

"All right," I said. "That's reasonable."

"So everything is understood?"

"I guess so," I said. "There's no baggage and no arms. No guns, knives, or razors; nothing. I have to know about that."

"Captain," said Mr. Sing, "have you no trust in me? Don't you see our interests are identical?"

"You'll make sure?"

"Please do not embarrass me," he said. "Do you not see how our interests coincide?"

"All right," I told him. "What time will you be there?"

"Before midnight."

"All right," I said. "I guess that's all."

"How do you want the money?"

"In hundreds is all right."

He stood up and I watched him go out. Frankie smiled at him as he went. Mr. Sing didn't look at him. He was a smooth-looking Chink all right. Some Chink.

Frankie came over to the table. "Well?" he said.

"Where did you know Mr. Sing?"

"He ships Chinamen," Frankie said. "Big business."

"How long you know him?"

"He's here about two years," Frankie said. "Another one ship them before him. Somebody kill him."

"Somebody will kill Mr. Sing, too."

"Sure," said Frankie. "Why not? Plenty big business."

"Some business," I said.

"Big business," said Frankie. "Ship Chinamen never come back. Other Chinamen write letters say everything fine."

"Wonderful," I said.

"This kind of Chinamen no understand write. Chinamen can write all rich. Eat nothing. Live on rice. Hundred thousand Chinamen here. Only three Chinese women."

"Why?"

"Government no let."

"Hell of a situation," I said.

"You do business him?"

"Maybe."

"Good business," said Frankie. "Better than politics. Much money. Plenty big business."

"Have a bottle of beer," I told him.

"You not worry any more?"

"Hell no," I said. "Plenty big business. Much obliged."

"Good," said Frankie and patted me on the back. "Make me happier than nothing. All I want is you happy. Chinamen good business, eh?"

"Wonderful."

"Make me happy," said Frankie. I saw he was about ready to cry because he was so pleased everything was all right, so I patted him on the back. Some Frankie.

First thing in the morning I got hold of the broker and told him to clear us. He wanted the crew list and I told him nobody.

"You're going to cross alone, Captain?"

"That's right."

"What's become of your mate?"

"He's on a drunk," I told him.

"It's very dangerous to go alone."

"It's only ninety miles," I said. "Do you think having a rummy on board makes any difference?"

I ran her over to the Standard Oil dock across the harbor and filled up both the tanks. She held nearly two hundred gallons when I had her full. I hated to buy it at twenty-eight cents a gallon but I didn't know where we might go.

Ever since I'd seen the Chink and taken the money I'd been worrying about the business. I don't think I slept all night. I brought her back to the San Francisco dock, and there was Eddy waiting on the dock for me.

"Hello, Harry," he said to me and waved. I threw him the stern line and he made her fast, and then came aboard; longer, blearier, drunker than ever. I didn't say anything to him.

"What do you think about that fellow Johnson going off like that, Harry?" he asked me. "What do you know about that?"

"Get out of here," I told him. "You're poison to me."

"Brother, don't I feel as bad about it as you do?"

"Get off of her," I told him.

He just settled back in the chair and stretched his legs out. "I hear we're going across today," he said. "Well, I guess there isn't any use to stay around."

"You're not going."

"What's the matter, Harry? There's no sense to get plugged with me."

"No? Get off her."

"Oh, take it easy."

I hit him in the face and he stood up and then climbed up onto the dock.

"I wouldn't do a thing like that to you, Harry," he said.

"You're goddamn right you wouldn't," I told him. "I'm not going to carry you. That's all."

"Well, what did you have to hit me for?"

"So you'd believe it."

"What do you want me to do? Stay here and starve?"

"Starve, hell," I said. "You can get back on the ferry. You can work your way back."

"You aren't treating me square," he said.

"Who did you ever treat square, you rummy?" I told him. "You'd double-cross your own mother."

That was true, too. But I felt bad about hitting him. You know how you feel when you hit a drunk. But I wouldn't carry him the way things were now; not even if I wanted to.

He started to walk off down the dock looking longer than a day without breakfast. Then he turned and came back.

"How's to let me take a couple of dollars, Harry?"

I gave him a five-dollar bill of the Chink's.

"I always knew you were my pal. Harry, why don't you carry me?"

"You're bad luck."

"You're just plugged," he said. "Never mind, old pal. You'll be glad to see me yet."

Now he had money he went off a good deal faster but I tell you it was poison to see him walk, even. He walked just like his joints were backwards.

I went up to the Perla and met the broker and he gave me the papers and I bought him a drink. Then I had lunch and Frankie came in.

"Fellow gave me this for you," he said and handed me a rolled-up sort of tube wrapped in paper and tied with a piece of red string. It looked like a photograph when I unwrapped it and I unrolled it thinking it was maybe a picture some one around the dock had taken of the boat.

All right. It was a close-up picture of the head and chest of a dead nigger with his throat cut clear across from ear to ear and then stitched up neat and a card on his chest saying in Spanish: "This is what we do to Lenguas largas."

"Who gave it to you?" I asked Frankie.

He pointed out a Spanish boy that works around the docks who is just about gone with the con. This kid was standing at the lunch counter.

"Ask him to come over."

The kid came over. He said two young fellows gave it to him about eleven o'clock. They asked him if he knew me and he said, Yes. Then he gave it to Frankie for me. They gave him a dollar to see that I got it. They were well dressed, he said.

"Politics," Frankie said.

"Oh, yes," I said.

"They think you told the police you were meeting those boys here that morning."

"Oh, yes."

"Bad politics," Frankie said. "Good thing you go."

"Did they leave any message?" I asked the Spanish boy.

"No," he said. "Just to give you that."

"I'm going to leave now," I said to Frankie.

"Bad politics," Frankie said. "Very bad politics."

I had all the papers in a bunch that the broker had given me and I paid the bill and walked out of that café and across the square and through the gate and I was plenty glad to come through the warehouse and get out on the dock. Those kids had me spooked all right. They were just dumb enough to think I'd tipped somebody off about that other lot. Those kids were like Pancho. When they were scared they got excited, and when they got excited they wanted to kill somebody.

I got on board and warmed up the engine. Frankie stood on the dock watching. He was smiling that funny deaf smile. I went back to him.

"Listen," I said. "Don't you get in any trouble about this."

He couldn't hear me. I had to yell it at him.

"Me good politics," Frankie said. He cast her off.

III

I waved to Frankie, who'd thrown the bowline on board, and I headed her out of the slip and dropped down the channel with her. A British freighter was going out and I ran along beside her and passed her. She was loaded deep with sugar and her plates were rusty. A limey in an old blue sweater looked down at me from her stern as I went by her. I went out the harbor and past the Morro and put her on the course for Key West; due north. I left the wheel and went forward and coiled up the bowline and then came back and held her on her course, spreading Havana out astern, and then dropping it off behind us as we brought the mountains up.

I dropped the Morro out of sight after a while and then the National Hotel and finally I could just see the dome of the Capitol. There wasn't much current compared to the last day we had fished and there was only a light breeze. I saw a couple of smacks headed in toward Havana and they were coming from the westward, so I knew the current was light.

I cut the switch and killed the motor. There wasn't any sense in wasting gas. I'd let her drift. When it got dark I could always pick up the light of the Morro or, if she drifted up too far, the lights of Cojimar, and steer in and run along to Bacuranao. I figured the way the current looked she would drift the twelve miles up to Bacuranao by dark and I'd see the lights of Baracoa.

Well, I killed the engine and climbed up forward to have a look around. All there was to see was the two smacks off to the westward headed in, and way back the dome of the Capitol standing up white out of the edge of the sea. There was some gulfweed on the stream and a few birds working, but not many. I sat up there awhile on top of the house and watched, but the only fish I saw were those little brown ones that use around the gulfweed. Brother, don't let anybody tell you there isn't plenty of water between Havana and Key West. I was just on the edge of it.

After a while I went down into the cockpit again, and there was Eddy.

"What's the matter? What's the matter with the engine?"

"She broke down."

"Why haven't you got the hatch up?"

"Oh, hell!" I said.

Do you know what he'd done? He'd come back again and slipped the forward hatch and gone down into the cabin and gone to sleep. He had two quarts with him. He'd gone into the first bodega he'd seen and bought it and come aboard. When I started out he woke up and went back to sleep again. When I stopped her out in the gulf and she began to roll a little with the swell it woke him up.

"I knew you'd carry me, Harry," he said.

"Carry you to hell," I said. "You aren't even on the crew list. I've got a good mind to make you jump overboard now."

"You're an old joker, Harry," he said. "Us conchs ought to stick together when we're in trouble."

"You," I said, "with your mouth. Who's going to trust your mouth when you're hot?"

"I'm a good man, Harry. You put me to the test and see what a good man I am."

"Get me the two quarts," I told him. I was thinking of something else.

He brought them out and I took a drink from the open one and put them forward by the wheel. He stood there and I looked at him. I was sorry for him and for what I knew I'd have to do. Hell, I knew him when he was a good man.

"What's the matter with her, Harry?"

"She's all right."

"What's the matter, then? What are you looking at me like that for?"

"Brother," I told him, and I was sorry for him, "you're in plenty of trouble."

"What do you mean, Harry?"

"I don't know yet," I said. "I haven't got it all figured out yet."

We sat there awhile and I didn't feel like talking to him any more. Once I knew it, it was hard to talk to him. Then I went below and got out the pump-gun and the Winchester 30–30 that I always had below in the cabin and hung them up in their cases from the top of the house where we hung the rods usually, right over the wheel where I could reach thèm. I keep them in those full-length, clipped sheep's wool cases with the wool inside soaked in oil. That's the only way you can keep them from rusting on a boat.

I loosened up the pump and worked her a few times, and then filled her up and pumped one into the barrel. I put a shell in the chamber of the Winchester and filled up the magazine. I got out the Smith and Wesson thirty-eight special I had when I was on the police force up in Miami from under the mattress and cleaned and oiled it and filled it up and put it on my belt.

"What's the matter?" Eddy said. "What the hell's the matter?"

"Nothing," I told him.

"What's all the damn guns for?"

"I always carry them on board," I said. "To shoot birds that bother the baits or to shoot sharks, or for cruising along the keys."

"What's the matter, damn it?" said Eddy. "What's the matter?"

"Nothing," I told him. I sat there with the old thirty-eight flopping against my leg when she rolled, and I looked at him. I thought, there's no sense to do it now. I'm going to need him now.

"We're going to do a little job," I said. "In at Bacuranao. I'll tell you what to do when it's time."

I didn't want to tell him too far ahead because he would get to worrying and get so spooked he wouldn't be any use.

"You couldn't have anybody better than me, Harry," he said. "I'm the man for you. I'm with you on anything."

I looked at him, tall and bleary and shaky, and I didn't say anything.

"Listen, Harry. Would you give me just one?" he asked me. "I don't want to get the shakes."

I gave him one and we sat ánd waited for it to get dark. It was a fine sunset and there was a nice light breeze, and when the sun got pretty well down I started the engine and headed her in slow toward land.

IV

WE LAY offshore about a mile in the dark. The current had freshened up, with the sun down, and I noticed it running in. I could see the Morro light way down to the westward and the glow of Havana, and the lights opposite us were Rincōn and Baracoa. I headed her up against the current until I was past Bacuranao and nearly to Cojimar. Then I let her drift down. It was plenty dark but I could tell good where we were. I had all the lights out.

"What's it going to be, Harry?" Eddy asked me. He was beginning to be spooked again.

"What do you think?"

"I don't know," he said. "You've got me worried." He was pretty close to the shakes and when he came near me he had a breath like a buzzard.

"What time is it?"

"I'll go down and see," he said. He came back up and said it was half past nine.

"Are you hungry?" I asked him.

"No," he said. "You know I couldn't eat, Harry."

"All right," I told him. "You can have one."

After he had it I asked him how he felt. He said he felt fine.

"I'm going to give you a couple more in a little while," I told him. "I know you haven't got any *cojones* unless you've got rum and there isn't much on board. So you'd better go easy."

"Tell me what's up," said Eddy.

"Listen," I said, talking to him in the dark. "We're going to Bacuranao and pick up twelve Chinks. You take the wheel when I tell you to and do what I tell you to. We'll take the twelve Chinks on board and we'll lock them below forward. Go on forward now and fasten the hatch from the outside."

He went up and I saw him shadowed against the dark. He came back and he said, "Harry, can I have one of those now?"

"No," I said. "I want you rum-brave. I don't want you useless."

"I'm a good man, Harry. You'll see."

"You're a rummy," I said. "Listen. One Chink is going to bring those twelve out. He's going to give me some money at the start. When they're all on board he's going to give me some more money. When you see him start to hand me money the second time you put her ahead and hook her up and head her out to sea. Don't you pay any attention to what happens. You keep her going out no matter what happens. Do you understand?"

"Yes."

"If any Chink starts bursting out of the cabin or coming through the hatch, once we're out and under way, you take that pump-gun and blow them back as fast as they come out. Do you know how to use the pump-gun?"

"No. But you can show me."

"You'd never remember. Do you know how to use the Winchester?"

"Just pump the lever and shoot it."

"That's right," I said. "Only don't shoot any holes in the hull."

"You'd better give me that other drink," Eddy said.

"All right. I'll give you a little one."

I gave him a real one. I knew they wouldn't make him drunk now; not pouring them into all that fear. But each one would work for a little while. After he drank this Eddy said, just as though he was happy, "So we're going to run Chinks. Well, by God, I always said I'd run Chinamen if I was ever broke."

"But you never got broke before, eh?" I said to him. He was funny all right.

I gave him three more drinks to keep him brave before it was half past ten. It was funny watching him and it kept me from thinking about it myself. I hadn't figured on all this wait. I'd planned to leave after dark, run out, just out of the glare, and coast along to Cojimar.

At a little before eleven I saw the two lights show on the point. I waited a little while and then I took her in slow. Bacuranao is a cove where there used to be a big dock for loading sand. There is a little river that comes in when the rains open the bar across the mouth. The northers, in the winter, pile the sand up and close it. They used to go in with schooners and load guavas from the river and there used to be a town. But the hurricane took it and it is all gone now except one house that some gallegos built out of the shacks the hurricane blew down and that they use for a clubhouse on Sundays when they come out to swim and picnic from Havana. There is one other house where the delegate lives but it is back from the beach.

Each little place like that all down the coast has a government delegate, but I figured the Chink must use his own boat and have him fixed. As we came in I could smell the sea grape and that sweet smell from the brush you get off the land.

"Get up forward," I said to Eddy.

"You can't hit anything on that side," he said. "The reef's on the other side as you go in." You see, he'd been a good man once.

"Watch her," I said, and I took her in to where I know they could see us. With no surf they could hear the engine. I didn't want to wait around, not knowing whether they saw us or not, so I flashed the running lights on once, just the green and red, and turned them off. Then I turned her and headed her out and let her lay there, just outside, with the engine just ticking. There was quite a little swell that close in.

"Come on back here," I said to Eddy and I gave him a real drink.

"Do you cock it first with your thumb?" he whispered to me. He was sitting at the wheel now, and I had reached up and had both the cases open and the butts pulled out about six inches.

"That's right."

"Oh, boy," he said.

It certainly was wonderful what a drink would do to him and how quick.

We lay there and I could see a light from the delegate's house back through the brush. I saw the two lights on the point go down, and one of them moving off around the point. They must have blown the other one out.

Then, in a little while, coming out of the cove, I see a boat come

toward us with a man sculling. I could tell by the way he swung
back and forth. I knew he had a big oar. I was pretty pleased. If
they were sculling that meant one man.

They came alongside.

"Good evening, captain," said Mr. Sing.

"Come astern and put her broadside," I said to him.

He said something to the kid who was sculling but he couldn't
scull her backwards, so I took hold of the gunwale and passed her
astern. There were eight men in the boat. The six Chinks, Mr.
Sing, and the kid sculling. While I was pulling her astern I was
waiting for something to hit me on top of the head but nothing did.
I straightened up and let Mr. Sing hold onto the stern.

"Let's see what it looks like," I said.

He handed it to me and I took the roll of it up to where Eddy
was at the wheel and put on the binnacle light. I looked at it carefully. It looked all right to me and I turned off the light. Eddy was
trembling.

"Pour yourself one," I said. I saw him reach for the bottle and
tip it up.

I went back to the stern.

"All right," I said. "Let six come on board."

Mr. Sing and the Cuban that sculled were having a job holding
their boat from knocking in what little swell there was. I heard Mr.
Sing say something in Chink and all the Chinks in the boat started
to climb onto the stern.

"One at a time," I said.

He said something again, and then one after another six Chinks
came over the stern. They were all lengths and sizes.

"Show them forward," I said to Eddy.

"Right this way, gentlemen," said Eddy. By God, I knew he had
taken a big one.

"Lock the cabin," I said, when they were all in.

"Yes, sir," said Eddy.

"I will return with the others," said Mr. Sing.

"O.K.," I told him.

I pushed them clear and the boy with them started skulling off.

"Listen," I said to Eddy, "you lay off that bottle. You're brave enough now."

"O.K., chief," said Eddy.

"What's the matter with you?"

"This is what I like to do," said Eddy. "You say you just pull it backward with your thumb?"

"You lousy rummy," I told him. "Give me a drink out of that."

"All gone," said Eddy. "Sorry, chief."

"Listen. What you have to do now is watch when he hands me the money and put her ahead."

"O.K., chief," said Eddy.

I reached up and took the other bottle and got the corkscrew and drew the cork. I took a good drink and went back to the stern, putting the cork in tight and laying the bottle behind two wicker jugs full of water.

"Here comes Mr. Sing," I said to Eddy.

"Yes, sir," said Eddy.

The boat came out sculling toward us.

He brought her astern and I let them do the holding on. Mr. Sing had hold of the roller we had across the stern to slide a big fish aboard.

"Let them come aboard," I said, "one at a time."

Six more assorted Chinks came on board over the stern.

"Open up and show them forward," I told Eddy.

"Yes, sir," said Eddy.

"Lock the cabin."

"Yes, sir."

I saw he was at the wheel.

"All right, Mr. Sing," I said. "Let's see the rest of it."

He put his hand in his pocket and reached the money out toward me. I reached for it and grabbed his wrist with the money in his hand, and as he came forward on the stern I grabbed his throat with the other hand. I felt her start and then churn ahead as she hooked up and I was plenty busy with Mr. Sing but I could see the Cuban standing in the stern of the boat holding the sculling oar as we pulled away from her through all the flopping and bouncing Mr. Sing was doing. He was flopping and bouncing worse than any dolphin on a gaff.

I got his arm around behind him and came up on it but I brought it too far because I felt it go. When it went he made a funny little noise and came forward, me holding him throat and all, and bit me in the shoulder. But when I felt the arm go I dropped it. It wasn't any good to him any more and I took him by the throat with both hands, and brother, that Mr. Sing would flop just like a fish, true, his loose arm flailing. But I got him forward onto his knees and had both thumbs well in behind his talk-box, and I bent the whole thing back until she cracked. Don't think you can't hear it crack, either.

I held him quiet just a second, and then I laid him down across the stern. He lay there, face up, quiet, in his good clothes, with his feet in the cockpit; and I left him.

I picked up the money off the cockpit floor and took it up and put on the binnacle light and counted it. Then I took the wheel and told Eddy to look under the stern for some pieces of iron that I used for anchoring whenever we fished bottom-fishing on patches or rocky bottom where you wouldn't want to risk an anchor.

"I can't find anything," he said. He was scared being down there by Mr. Sing.

"Take the wheel," I said. "Keep her out."

There was a certain amount of moving around going on below but I wasn't spooked about them.

I found a couple of pieces of what I wanted, iron from the old coaling dock at Tortugas, and I took some snapper line and made a couple of good big pieces fast to Mr. Sing's ankles. Then when we were about two miles offshore I slid him over. He slid over smooth off the roller. I never even looked in his pockets. I didn't feel like fooling with him.

He'd bled a little on the stern from his nose and his mouth, and I dipped a bucket of water that nearly pulled me overboard the way we were going, and cleaned her off good with a scrub brush from under the stern.

"Slow her down," I said to Eddy.

"What if he floats up?" Eddy said.

"I dropped him in about seven hundred fathoms," I said. "He's going down all that way. That's a long way, brother. He won't float till the gas brings him up and all the time he's going with the current and baiting up fish. Hell," I said, "you don't have to worry about Mr. Sing."

"What did you have against him?" Eddy asked me.

"Nothing," I said. "He was the easiest man to do business with I ever met. I thought there must be something wrong all the time."

"What did you kill him for?"

"To keep from killing twelve other chinks," I told him.

"Harry," he said, "You've got to give me one because I can feel them coming on. It made me sick to see his head all loose like that."

So I gave him one.

"What about the Chinks?" Eddy said.

"I want to get them out as quick as I can," I told him. "Before they smell up the cabin."

"Where are you going to put them?"

"We'll run them right in to the long beach," I told him.

"Take her in now?"

"Sure," I said. "Take her in slow."

We came in slow over the reef and to where I could see the beach shine. There is plenty of water over the reef and inside it's all sandy bottom and slopes right into shore.

"Get up forward and give me the depth."

He kept sounding with a grains pole, motioning me on with the pole. He came back and motioned me to stop. I came astern on her.

"You've got about five feet."

"We've got to anchor," I said. "If anything happens so we haven't time to get her up, we can cut loose or break her off."

Eddy paid out rope and when finally she didn't drag he made her fast. She swung stern in.

"It's sandy bottom, you know," he said.

"How much water have we got at the stern?"

"Not over five feet."

"You take the rifle," I said. "And be careful."

"Let me have one," he said. He was plenty nervous.

I gave him one and took down the pump-gun. I unlocked the cabin door, opened it, and said: "Come on out."

Nothing happened.

Then one Chink put his head out and saw Eddy standing there with a rifle and ducked back.

"Come on out. Nobody's going to hurt you," I said.

Nothing doing. Only lots of talk in Chink.

"Come on out, you!" Eddy said. My God, I knew he'd had the bottle.

"Put that bottle away," I said to him, "or I'll blow you out of the boat."

"Come on out," I said to them, "or I'll shoot in at you."

I saw one of them looking at the corner of the door and he saw the beach evidently because he begins to chatter.

"Come on," I said, "or I'll shoot."

Out they came.

Now I tell you it would take a hell of a mean man to butcher a bunch of Chinks like that and I'll bet there would be plenty of trouble, too, let alone mess.

They came out and they were scared and they didn't have any guns but there were twelve of them. I walked backwards down to the stern holding the pump-gun. "Get overboard," I said. "It's not over your heads."

Nobody moved.

"Over you go."

Nobody moved.

"You yellow rat-eating aliens," Eddy said, "get overboard."

"Shut your drunken mouth," I told him.

"No swim," one Chink said.

"No need swim," I said. "No deep."

"Come on, get overboard," Eddy said.

"Come astern here," I said. "Take your gun in one hand and your grain pole in the other and show them how deep it is."

He showed them, holding up the wet pole.

"No need swim?" the one asked me.

"No."

"True?"

"Yes."

"Where we?"

"Cuba."

"You damn crook," he said and went over the side, hanging on and then letting go. His head went under but he came up and his chin was out of water. "Damn crook," he said. "Goddamn crook."

He was mad and plenty brave. He said something in Chink and the others started going into the water off the stern.

"All right," I said to Eddy. "Get the anchor up."

As we headed her out, the moon started to come up, and you could see the Chinks with just their heads out of water, walking ashore, and the shine of the beach and the brush behind.

We got out past the reef and I looked back once and saw the beach and the mountains starting to show up; then I put her on her course for Key West.

"Now you can take a sleep," I said to Eddy. "No, wait, go below and open all the ports to get the stink out and bring me the iodine."

"What's the matter?" he said when he brought it.

"I cut my finger."

"Do you want me to steer?"

"Get a sleep," I said. "I'll wake you up."

He lay down on the built-in bunk in the cockpit, over the gas tank, and in a little while he was asleep.

V

I HELD the wheel with my knee and opened up my shirt and saw where Mr. Sing bit me. It was quite a bite and I put iodine on it, and then I sat there steering and wondering whether a bite from a Chinaman was poisonous, and listened to her running nice and smooth and the water washing along her and I figured, Hell, no, that bite wasn't poisonous. A man like that Mr. Sing probably scrubbed his teeth two or three times a day. Some Mr. Sing. He certainly wasn't much of a business man. Maybe he was. Maybe he just trusted me. I tell you I couldn't figure him.

Well, now it was all simple except for Eddy. Because he's a rummy he'll talk when he gets hot. I sat there steering and I looked at him and I thought, hell, he's as well off dead as the way he is, and then I'm all clear. When I found he was on board I decided I'd have to do away with him but then when everything had come out so nice I didn't have the heart. But looking at him lying there it certainly was a temptation. But then I thought there's no sense spoiling it by doing something you'd be sorry for afterwards. Then I started to think he wasn't even on the crew list and I'd have to pay a fine for bringing him in and I didn't know how to consider him.

Well, I had plenty of time to think about it and I held her on her course and every once in a while I'd take a drink out of the bottle he'd brought on board. There wasn't much in it, and when I'd finished it, I opened up the only one I had left, and I tell you I felt pretty good steering, and it was a pretty night to cross. It had turned out a good trip all right, finally, even though it had looked plenty bad plenty of times.

When it got daylight Eddy woke up. He said he felt terrible.

"Take the wheel a minute," I told him. "I want to look around."

I went back to the stern and threw a little water on her. But she was perfectly clean. I scrubbed the brush over the side. I unloaded the guns and stowed them below. But I still kept the gun on my belt. It was fresh and nice as you want it below, no smell at all. A little water had come in through the starboard port onto one of the bunks was all; so I shut the ports. There wasn't a customhouse officer in the world could smell Chink in her now.

I saw the clearance papers in the net bag hanging up under her framed license where I'd shoved them when I came on board and I took them out to look them over. Then I went up to the cockpit.

"Listen," I said. "How did you get on the crew list?"

"I met the broker when he was leaving for the consulate and told him I was going."

"God looks after rummies," I told him and I took the thirty-eight off and stowed it down below.

I made some coffee down below and then I came up and took the wheel.

"There's coffee below," I told him.

"Brother, coffee wouldn't do me any good." You know you had to be sorry for him. He certainly looked bad.

About nine o'clock we saw the Sand Key light just about dead ahead. We'd seen tankers going up the Gulf for quite a while.

"We'll be in in a couple of hours now," I said to him. "I'm going to give you the same four dollars a day just as if Johnson had paid."

"How much did you get out of last night?" he asked me.

"Only six hundred," I told him.

I don't know whether he believed me or not.

"Don't I share in it?"

"That's your share," I told him. "What I just told you, and if you ever open your mouth about last night I'll hear of it and I'll do away with you."

"You know I'm no squealer, Harry."

"You're a rummy. But no matter how rum dumb you get, if you ever talk about that, I promise you."

"I'm a good man," he said. "You oughtn't to talk to me like that."

"They can't make it fast enough to keep you a good man," I told him. But I didn't worry about him any more because who was going to believe him? Mr. Sing wouldn't make any complaints. The Chinks weren't going to. You know the boy that sculled them out wasn't. He wouldn't want to get himself in trouble. Eddy would mouth about it sooner or later, maybe, but who believes a rummy?

Why, who could prove anything? Naturally it would have made plenty more talk when they saw his name on the crew list. That was luck for me, all right. I could have said he fell overboard, but it makes plenty talk. Plenty of luck for Eddy, too. Plenty of luck, all right.

Then we came to the edge of the stream and the water quit being blue and was light and greenish and inside I could see the stakes on the Eastern and the Western Dry Rocks and the wireless masts at Key West and the La Concha hotel up high out of all the low houses and plenty smoke from out where they're burning garbage. Sand Key light was plenty close now and you could see the boathouse and the little dock alongside the light and I knew we were only forty minutes away now and I felt good to be getting back and I had a good stake now for the summertime.

"What do you say about a drink, Eddy?" I said to him.

"Ah, Harry," he said, "I always knew you were my pal."

That night I was sitting in the living room smoking a cigar and drinking a whiskey and water and listening to Gracie Allen on the radio. The girls had gone to the show and sitting there I felt sleepy and I felt good. There was somebody at the front door and Marie, my wife, got up from where she was sitting and went to it. She came back and said, "It's that rummy, Eddie Marshall. He says he's got to see you."

"Tell him to get out before I run him out," I told her.

She came back in and sat down and looking out the window where I was sitting with my feet up I could see Eddy going along the road under the arc light with another rummy he'd picked up, the two of them swaying, and their shadows from the arc light swaying worse.

"Poor goddamned rummies," Marie said. "I pity a rummy."

"He's a lucky rummy."

"There ain't any lucky rummies," Marie said. "You know that, Harry."

"No," I said. "I guess there aren't."

from FOR WHOM THE BELL TOLLS

No man is an Iland, *intire of it selfe; every man is a peece of the* Continent, *a part of the* maine; *if a* Clod *bee washed away by the Sea,* Europe *is the lesse, as well as if a* Promontorie *were, as well as if a* Mannor *of thy* friends *or of thine* owne *were; any mans* death *diminishes me, because I am involved in* Mankinde; *And therefore never send to know for whom the* bell *tolls; it tolls for* thee.

—JOHN DONNE

SORDO'S STAND

FOR WHOM THE BELL TOLLS, a novel of the Spanish Civil War of the Nineteen Thirties that was a prelude to the World War of the Nineteen Forties, was the most popular of all his books until The Old Man and the Sea. It was published in 1940 and it seemed to sum up the lessons of the recent past and foretell the need for them in the immediate future. The stand of Sordo on the hill, republished here, was to be the story of many Resistance bands in lands that had been taken by the forces of the Axis Powers. Hemingway tried to be fair to both sides in Spain, a country where the bitterness was deepest; brothers were ranged against brothers; yet they were bound by a common heritage and faith. Outrage is balanced with outrage in this novel, honor with honor, courage with courage. Naturally, neither side was happy when the book came out. The Nationalists did not like the fact that the hero of the book, Robert Jordan, a young instructor of Spanish at the University of Montana, fought on the Loyalist side. The Loyalists were not pleased with a scene showing a brutal massacre of Nationalist civilians. Nor with remarks about "famous peasant and worker Spanish commanders who had sprung to arms from the people at the start of the war without any previous military training"—but who had somewhere learned to speak Russian.

The novel grew out of months Hemingway spent in Spain as a correspondent for American newspapers during the Civil War and years of knowing and loving Spain. It was written in Cuba and Idaho in 1939 and 1940, in the time of the Stalin-Hitler Pact, the period of the phony war, the fall of France. When it appeared, the free world was surrounded on a hill.

C. P.

FOR WHOM THE BELL TOLLS

SORDO'S STAND

XXVII

EL SORDO was making his fight on a hilltop. He did not like this hill and when he saw it he thought it had the shape of a chancre. But he had had no choice except this hill and he had picked it as far away as he could see it and galloped for it, the automatic rifle heavy on his back, the horse laboring, barrel heaving between his thighs, the sack of grenades swinging against one side, the sack of automatic rifle pans banging against the other, and Joaquín and Ignacio halting and firing, halting and firing to give him time to get the gun in place.

There had still been snow then, the snow that had ruined them, and when his horse was hit so that he wheezed in a slow, jerking, climbing stagger up the last part of the crest, splattering the snow with a bright, pulsing jet, Sordo had hauled him along by the bridle, the reins over his shoulder as he climbed. He climbed as hard as he could with the bullets spatting on the rocks, with the two sacks heavy on his shoulders, and then, holding the horse by the mane, had shot him quickly, expertly, and tenderly just where he had needed him, so that the horse pitched, head forward down to plug a gap between two rocks. He had gotten the gun to firing over the horse's back and he fired two pans, the gun clattering, the empty shells pitching into the snow, the smell of burnt hair from the burnt hide where the hot muzzle rested, him firing at what came up to the hill, forcing them to scatter for cover, while all the time there was a chill in his back from not knowing what was behind him. Once the last of the five men had reached the hilltop the chill went out of his back and he had saved the pans he had left until he would need them.

There were two more horses dead along the slope and three

more were dead here on the hilltop. He had only succeeded in stealing three horses last night and one had bolted when they tried to mount him bareback in the corral at the camp when the first shooting had started.

Of the five men who had reached the hilltop three were wounded. Sordo was wounded in the calf of his leg and in two places in his left arm. He was very thirsty, his wounds had stiffened, and one of the wounds in his left arm was very painful. He also had a bad headache and as he lay waiting for the planes to come he thought of a joke in Spanish. It was, *"Hay que tomar la muerte como si fuera aspirina,"* which means, "You will have to take death as an aspirin." But he did not make the joke aloud. He grinned somewhere inside the pain in his head and inside the nausea that came whenever he moved his arm and looked around at what there was left of his band.

The five men were spread out like the points of a five-pointed star. They had dug with their knees and hands and made mounds in front of their heads and shoulders with the dirt and piles of stones. Using this cover, they were linking the individual mounds up with stones and dirt. Joaquín, who was eighteen years old, had a steel helmet that he dug with and he passed dirt in it.

He had gotten this helmet at the blowing up of the train. It had a bullet hole through it and every one had always joked at him for keeping it. But he had hammered the jagged edges of the bullet hole smooth and driven a wooden plug into it and then cut the plug off and smoothed it even with the metal inside the helmet.

When the shooting started he had clapped this helmet on his head so hard it banged his head as though he had been hit with a casserole and, in the last lung-aching, leg-dead, mouth-dry, bullet-spatting, bullet-cracking, bullet-singing run up the final slope of the hill after his horse was killed, the helmet had seemed to weigh a great amount and to ring his bursting forehead with an iron band. But he had kept it. Now he dug with it in a steady, almost machinelike desperation. He had not yet been hit.

"It serves for something finally," Sordo said to him in his deep, throaty voice.

"Resistir y fortificar es vencer," Joaquín said, his mouth stiff with

the dryness of fear which surpassed the normal thirst of battle. It was one of the slogans of the Communist party and it meant, "Hold out and fortify, and you will win."

Sordo looked away and down the slope at where a cavalryman was sniping from behind a boulder. He was very fond of this boy and he was in no mood for slogans.

"What did you say?"

One of the men turned from the building that he was doing. This man was lying flat on his face, reaching carefully up with his hands to put a rock in place while keeping his chin flat against the ground.

Joaquín repeated the slogan in his dried-up boy's voice without checking his digging for a moment.

"What was the last word?" the man with his chin on the ground asked.

"*Vencer,*" the boy said. "Win."

"*Mierda,*" the man with his chin on the ground said.

"There is another that applies to here," Joaquín said, bringing them out as though they were talismans, "Pasionaria says it is better to die on your feet than to live on your knees."

"*Mierda* again," the man said and another man said, over his shoulder, "We're on our bellies, not our knees."

"Thou. Communist. Do you know your Pasionaria has a son thy age in Russia since the start of the movement?"

"It's a lie," Joaquín said.

"*Qué va,* it's a lie," the other said. "The dynamiter with the rare name told me. He was of thy party, too. Why should he lie?"

"It's a lie," Joaquín said. "She would not do such a thing as keep a son hidden in Russia out of the war."

"I wish I were in Russia," another of Sordo's men said. "Will not thy Pasionaria send me now from here to Russia, Communist?"

"If thou believest so much in thy Pasionaria, get her to get us off this hill," one of the men who had a bandaged thigh said.

"The fascists will do that," the man with his chin in the dirt said.

"Do not speak thus," Joaquín said to him.

"Wipe the pap of your mother's breasts off thy lips and give me a hatful of that dirt," the man with his chin on the ground said. "No one of us will see the sun go down this night."

El Sordo was thinking: It is shaped like a chancre. Or the breast of a young girl with no nipple. Or the top cone of a volcano. You have never seen a volcano, he thought. Nor will you ever see one. And this hill is like a chancre. Let the volcanos alone. It's late now for the volcanos.

He looked very carefully around the withers of the dead horse and there was a quick hammering of firing from behind a boulder well down the slope and he heard the bullets from the submachine gun thud into the horse. He crawled along behind the horse and looked out of the angle between the horse's hindquarters and the rock. There were three bodies on the slope just below him where they had fallen when the fascists had rushed the crest under cover of the automatic rifle and submachine gunfire and he and the others had broken down the attack by throwing and rolling down hand grenades. There were other bodies that he could not see on the other sides of the hill crest. There was no dead ground by which attackers could approach the summit and Sordo knew that as long as his ammunition and grenades held out and he had as many as four men they could not get him out of there unless they brought up a trench mortar. He did not know whether they had sent to La Granja for a trench mortar. Perhaps they had not, because surely, soon, the planes would come. It had been four hours since the observation plane had flown over them.

This hill is truly a chancre, Sordo thought, and we are the very pus of it. But we killed many when they made that stupidness. How could they think that they would take us thus? They have such modern armament that they lose all their sense with over-confidence. He had killed the young officer who had led the assault with a grenade that had gone bouncing and rolling down the slope as they came up it, running, bent half over. In the yellow flash and gray roar of smoke he had seen the officer dive forward to where he lay now like a heavy, broken bundle of old clothing marking the farthest point that the assault had reached. Sordo looked at this body and then, down the hill, at the others.

They are brave but stupid people, he thought. But they have

sense enough now not to attack us again until the planes come. Unless, of course, they have a mortar coming. It would be easy with a mortar. The mortar was the normal thing and he knew that they would die as soon as a mortar came up, but when he thought of the planes coming up he felt as naked on that hilltop as though all of his clothing and even his skin had been removed. There is no nakeder thing than I feel, he thought. A flayed rabbit is as well covered as a bear in comparison. But why should they bring planes? They could get us out of here with a trench mortar easily. They are proud of their planes, though, and they will probably bring them. Just as they were so proud of their automatic weapons that they made that stupidness. But undoubtedly they must have sent for a mortar, too.

One of the men fired. Then jerked the bolt and fired again, quickly.

"Save thy cartridges," Sordo said.

"One of the sons of the great whore tried to reach that boulder," the man pointed.

"Did you hit him?" Sordo asked, turning his head with difficulty.

"Nay," the man said. "The fornicator ducked back."

"Who is a whore of whores is Pilar," the man with his chin in the dirt said. "That whore knows we are dying here."

"She could do no good," Sordo said. The man had spoken on the side of his good ear and he had heard him without turning his head. "What could she do?"

"Take these sluts from the rear."

"*Qué va,*" Sordo said. "They are spread around a hillside. How would she come on them? There are a hundred and fifty of them. Maybe more now."

"But if we hold out until dark," Joaquín said.

"And if Christmas comes on Easter," the man with his chin on the ground said.

"And if thy aunt had *cojones* she would be thy uncle," another said to him. "Send for thy Pasionaria. She alone can help us."

"I do not believe that about the son," Joaquín said. "Or if he is there he is training to be an aviator or something of that sort."

"He is hidden there for safety," the man told him.

"He is studying dialectics. Thy Pasionaria has been there. So have Lister and Modesto and others. The one with the rare name told me."

"That they should go to study and return to aid us," Joaquín said.

"That they should aid us now," another man said. "That all the cruts of Russian sucking swindlers should aid us now." He fired and said, "*Me cago en tal;* I missed him again."

"Save thy cartridges and do not talk so much or thou wilt be very thirsty," Sordo said. "There is no water on this hill."

"Take this," the man said and rolling on his side he pulled a wine-skin that he wore slung from his shoulder over his head and handed it to Sordo. "Wash thy mouth out, old one. Thou must have much thirst with thy wounds."

"Let all take it," Sordo said.

"Then I will have some first," the owner said and squirted a long stream into his mouth before he handed the leather bottle around.

"Sordo, when thinkest thou the planes will come?" the man with his chin in the dirt asked.

"Any time," said Sordo. "They should have come before."

"Do you think these sons of the great whore will attack again?"

"Only if the planes do not come."

He did not think there was any need to speak about the mortar. They would know it soon enough when the mortar came.

"God knows they've enough planes with what we saw yesterday."

"Too many," Sordo said.

His head hurt very much and his arm was stiffening so that the pain of moving it was almost unbearable. He looked up at the bright, high, blue early summer sky as he raised the leather wine bottle with his good arm. He was fifty-two years old and he was sure this was the last time he would see that sky.

He was not at all afraid of dying but he was angry at being trapped on this hill which was only utilizable as a place to die. If we could have gotten clear, he thought. If we could have made them come up the long valley or if we could have broken loose across the road it would have been all right. But this chancre of a hill. We must use it as well as we can and we have used it very well so far.

If he had known how many men in history have had to use a hill to die on it would not have cheered him any for, in the moment he was passing through, men are not impressed by what has happened to other men in similar circumstances any more than a widow of one day is helped by the knowledge that other loved husbands have died. Whether one has fear of it or not, one's death is difficult to accept. Sordo had accepted it but there was no sweetness in its acceptance even at fifty-two, with three wounds and him surrounded on a hill.

He joked about it to himself but he looked at the sky and at the far mountains and he swallowed the wine and he did not want it. If one must die, he thought, and clearly one must, I can die. But I hate it.

Dying was nothing and he had no picture of it nor fear of it in his mind. But living was a field of grain blowing in the wind on the side of a hill. Living was a hawk in the sky. Living was an earthen jar of water in the dust of the threshing with the grain flailed out and the chaff blowing. Living was a horse between your legs and a carbine under one leg and a hill and a valley and a stream with trees along it and the far side of the valley and the hills beyond.

Sordo passed the wine bottle back and nodded his head in thanks. He leaned forward and patted the dead horse on the shoulder where the muzzle of the automatic rifle had burned the hide. He could still smell the burnt hair. He thought how he had held the horse there, trembling, with the fire around them, whispering and cracking, over and around them like a curtain, and had carefully shot him just at the intersection of the cross-lines between the two eyes and the ears. Then as the horse pitched down he had dropped down behind his warm, wet back to get the gun to going as they came up the hill.

"*Eras mucho caballo*," he said, meaning, "Thou wert plenty of horse."

El Sordo lay now on his good side and looked up at the sky. He was lying on a heap of empty cartridge hulls but his head was protected by the rock and his body lay in the lee of the horse. His wounds had stiffened badly and he had much pain and he felt too tired to move.

"What passes with thee, old one?" the man next to him asked.

"Nothing. I am taking a little rest."

"Sleep," the other said. "*They* will wake us when they come."

Just then some one shouted from down the slope.

"Listen, bandits!" the voice came from behind the rocks where the closest automatic rifle was placed. "Surrender now before the planes blow you to pieces."

"What is it he says?" Sordo asked.

Joaquín told him. Sordo rolled to one side and pulled himself up so that he was crouched behind the gun again.

"Maybe the planes aren't coming," he said. "Don't answer them and do not fire. Maybe we can get them to attack again."

"If we should insult them a little?" the man who had spoken to Joaquín about La Pasionaria's son in Russia asked.

"No," Sordo said. "Give me thy big pistol. Who has a big pistol?"

"Here."

"Give it to me." Crouched on his knees he took the big 9 mm. Star and fired one shot into the ground beside the dead horse, waited, then fired again four times at irregular intervals. Then he waited while he counted sixty and then fired a final shot directly into the body of the dead horse. He grinned and handed back the pistol.

"Reload it," he whispered, "and that every one should keep his mouth shut and no one shoot."

"*Bandidos!*" the voice shouted from behind the rocks.

No one spoke on the hill.

"*Bandidos!* Surrender now before we blow thee to little pieces."

"They're biting," Sordo whispered happily.

As he watched, a man showed his head over the top of the rocks. There was no shot from the hilltop and the head went down again. El Sordo waited, watching, but nothing more happened. He turned his head and looked at the others who were all watching down their sectors of the slope. As he looked at them the others shook their heads.

"Let no one move," he whispered.

"Sons of the great whore," the voice came now from behind the rocks again.

"Red swine. Mother rapers. Eaters of the milk of thy fathers."

Sordo grinned. He could just hear the bellowed insults by turning his good ear. This is better than the aspirin, he thought. How many will we get? Can they be that foolish?

The voice had stopped again and for three minutes they heard nothing and saw no movement. Then the sniper behind the boulder a hundred yards down the slope exposed himself and fired. The bullet hit a rock and richocheted with a sharp whine. Then Sordo saw a man, bent double, run from the shelter of the rocks where the automatic rifle was across the open ground to the big boulder behind which the sniper was hidden. He almost dove behind the boulder.

Sordo looked around. They signalled to him that there was no movement on the other slopes. El Sordo grinned happily and shook his head. This is ten times better than the aspirin, he thought, and he waited, as happy as only a hunter can be happy.

Below on the slope the man who had run from the pile of stones to the shelter of the boulder was speaking to the sniper.

"Do you believe it?"

"I don't know," the sniper said.

"It would be logical," the man, who was the officer in command, said. "They are surrounded. They have nothing to expect but to die."

The sniper said nothing.

"What do you think?" the officer asked.

"Nothing," the sniper said.

"Have you seen any movement since the shots?"

"None at all."

The officer looked at his wrist watch. It was ten minutes to three o'clock.

"The planes should have come an hour ago," he said. Just then another officer flopped in behind the boulder. The sniper moved over to make room for him.

"Thou, Paco," the first officer said. "How does it seem to thee?"

The second officer was breathing heavily from his sprint up and across the hillside from the automatic rifle position.

"For me it is a trick," he said.

"But if it is not? What a ridicule we make waiting here and laying siege to dead men."

"We have done something worse than ridiculous already," the second officer said. "Look at that slope."

He looked up the slope to where the dead were scattered close to the top. From where he looked the line of the hilltop showed the scattered rocks, the belly, projecting legs, shod hooves jutting out, of Sordo's horse, and the fresh dirt thrown up by the digging.

"What about the mortars?" asked the second officer.

"They should be here in an hour. If not before."

"Then wait for them. There has been enough stupidity already."

"*Bandidos!*" the first officer shouted suddenly, getting to his feet and putting his head well up above the boulder so that the crest of the hill looked much closer as he stood upright. "Red swine! Cowards!"

The second officer looked at the sniper and shook his head. The sniper looked away but his lips tightened.

The first officer stood there, his head all clear of the rock and with his hand on his pistol butt. He cursed and vilified the hilltop. Nothing happened. Then he stepped clear of the boulder and stood there looking up the hill.

"Fire, cowards, if you are alive," he shouted. "Fire on one who has no fear of any Red that ever came out of the belly of the great whore."

This last was quite a long sentence to shout and the officer's face was red and congested as he finished.

The second officer, who was a thin sunburned man with quiet eyes, a thin, long-lipped mouth and a stubble of beard over his hollow cheeks, shook his head again. It was this officer who was shouting who had ordered the first assault. The young lieutenant who

was dead up the slope had been the best friend of this other lieutenant who was named Paco Berrendo and who was listening to
the shouting of the captain, who was obviously in a state of exalta-
tion.

"Those are the swine who shot my sister and my mother," the
captain said. He had a red face and a blond, British-looking moustache and there was something wrong about his eyes. They were a
light blue and the lashes were light, too. As you looked at them
they seemed to focus slowly. Then "Reds," he shouted. "Cowards!"
and commenced cursing again.

He stood absolutely clear now and, sighting carefully, fired his
pistol at the only target that the hilltop presented: the dead horse
that had belonged to Sordo. The bullet threw up a puff of dirt
fifteen yards below the horse. The captain fired again. The bullet
hit a rock and sung off.

The captain stood there looking at the hilltop. The Lieutenant
Berrendo was looking at the body of the other lieutenant just below
the summit. The sniper was looking at the ground under his eyes.
Then he looked up at the captain.

"There is no one alive up there," the captain said. "Thou," he
said to the sniper, "go up there and see."

The sniper looked down. He said nothing.

"Don't you hear me?" the captain shouted at him.

"Yes, my captain," the sniper said, not looking at him.

"Then get up and go." The captain still had his pistol out. "Do
you hear me?"

"Yes, my captain."

"Why don't you go, then?"

"I don't want to, my captain."

"You don't *want* to?" The captain pushed the pistol against the
small of the man's back. "You don't *want* to?"

"I am afraid, my captain," the soldier said with dignity.

Lieutenant Berrendo, watching the captain's face and his odd
eyes, thought he was going to shoot the man then.

"Captain Mora," he said.

"Lieutenant Berrendo?"

"It is possible the soldier is right."

"That he is right to say he is afraid? That he is right to say he does not *want* to obey an order?"

"No. That he is right that it is a trick."

"They are all dead," the captain said. "Don't you hear me say they are all dead?"

"You mean our comrades on the slope?" Berrendo asked him. "I agree with you."

"Paco," the captain said, "don't be a fool. Do you think you are the only one who cared for Julián? I tell you the Reds are dead. Look!"

He stood up, then put both hands on top of the boulder and pulled himself up, kneeing-up awkwardly, then getting on his feet.

"Shoot," he shouted, standing on the gray granite boulder and waved both his arms. "Shoot me! Kill me!"

On the hilltop El Sordo lay behind the dead horse and grinned. What a people, he thought. He laughed, trying to hold it in because the shaking hurt his arm.

"Reds," came the shout from below. "Red canaille. Shoot me! Kill me!"

Sordo, his chest shaking, barely peeped past the horse's crupper and saw the captain on top of the boulder waving his arms. Another officer stood by the boulder. The sniper was standing at the other side. Sordo kept his eye where it was and shook his head happily.

"Shoot me," he said softly to himself. "Kill me!" Then his shoulders shook again. The laughing hurt his arm and each time he laughed his head felt as though it would burst. But the laughter shook him again like a spasm.

Captain Mora got down from the boulder.

"Now do you believe me, Paco?" he questioned Lieutenant Berrendo.

"No," said Lieutenant Berrendo.

"*Cojones!*" the captain said. "Here there is nothing but idiots and cowards."

The sniper had gotten carefully behind the boulder again and Lieutenant Berrendo was squatting beside him.

The captain, standing in the open beside the boulder, commenced to shout filth at the hilltop. There is no language so filthy as Spanish. There are words for all the vile words in English and there are other words and expressions that are used only in countries where blasphemy keeps pace with the austerity of religion. Lieutenant Berrendo was a very devout Catholic. So was the sniper. They were Carlists from Navarra and while both of them cursed and blasphemed when they were angry they regarded it as a sin which they regularly confessed.

As they crouched now behind the boulder watching the captain and listening to what he was shouting, they both disassociated themselves from him and what he was saying. They did not want to have that sort of talk on their consciences on a day in which they might die. Talking thus will not bring luck, the sniper thought. Speaking thus of the *Virgen* is bad luck. This one speaks worse than the Reds.

Julián is dead, Lieutenant Berrendo was thinking. Dead there on the slope on such a day as this is. And this foul mouth stands there bringing more ill fortune with his blasphemies.

Now the captain stopped shouting and turned to Lieutenant Berrendo. His eyes looked stranger than ever.

"Paco," he said, happily, "you and I will go up there."

"Not me."

"What?" The captain had his pistol out again.

I hate these pistol brandishers, Berrendo was thinking. They cannot give an order without jerking a gun out. They probably pull out their pistols when they go to the toilet and order the move they will make.

"I will go if you order me to. But under protest," Lieutenant Berrendo told the captain.

"Then I will go alone," the captain said. "The smell of cowardice is too strong here."

Holding his pistol in his right hand, he strode steadily up the slope. Berrendo and the sniper watched him. He was making no attempt to take any cover and he was looking straight ahead of him at the rocks, the dead horse, and the fresh-dug dirt of the hilltop.

El Sordo lay behind the horse at the corner of the rock, watching the captain come striding up the hill.

Only one, he thought. We get only one. But from his manner of speaking he is *caza mayor*. Look at him walking. Look what an animal. Look at him stride forward. This one is for me. This one I take with me on the trip. This one coming now makes the same voyage I do. Come on, Comrade Voyager. Come striding. Come right along. Come along to meet it. Come on. Keep on walking. Don't slow up. Come right along. Come as thou art coming. Don't stop and look at those. That's right. Don't even look down. Keep on coming with your eyes forward. Look, he has a moustache. What do you think of that? He runs to a moustache, the Comrade Voyager. He is a captain. Look at his sleeves. I said he was *caza mayor*. He has the face of an *Inglés*. Look. With a red face and blond hair and blue eyes. With no cap on and his moustache is yellow. With blue eyes. With pale blue eyes. With pale blue eyes with something wrong with them. With pale blue eyes that don't focus. Close enough. Too close. Yes, Comrade Voyager. Take it, Comrade Voyager.

He squeezed the trigger of the automatic rifle gently and it pounded back three times against his shoulder with the slippery jolt the recoil of a tripoded automatic weapon gives.

The captain lay on his face on the hillside. His left arm was under him. His right arm that had held the pistol was stretched forward of his head. From all down the slope they were firing on the hill crest again.

Crouched behind the boulder, thinking that now he would have to sprint across the open space under fire, Lieutenant Berrendo heard the deep hoarse voice of Sordo from the hilltop.

"*Bandidos!*" the voice came. "*Bandidos!* Shoot me! Kill me!"

On the top of the hill El Sordo lay behind the automatic rifle laughing so that his chest ached, so that he thought the top of his head would burst.

"*Bandidos,*" he shouted again happily. "Kill me, *bandidos!*" Then he shook his head happily. We have lots of company for the Voyage, he thought.

He was going to try for the other officer with the automatic rifle when he would leave the shelter of the boulder. Sooner or later he would have to leave it. Sordo knew that he could never command from there and he thought he had a very good chance to get him.

Just then the others on the hill heard the first sound of the coming of the planes.

El Sordo did not hear them. He was covering the down-slope edge of the boulder with his automatic rifle and he was thinking: when I see him he will be running already and I will miss him if I am not careful. I could shoot behind him all across that stretch. I should swing the gun with him and ahead of him. Or let him start and then get on him and ahead of him. I will try to pick him up there at the edge of the rock and swing just ahead of him. Then he felt a touch on his shoulder and he turned and saw the gray, fear-drained face of Joaquín and he looked where the boy was pointing and saw the three planes coming.

At this moment Lieutenant Berrendo broke from behind the boulder and, with his head bent and his legs plunging ran down and across the slope to the shelter of the rocks where the automatic rifle was placed.

Watching the planes, Sordo never saw him go.

"Help me to pull this out," he said to Joaquín and the boy dragged the automatic rifle clear from between the horse and the rock.

The planes were coming on steadily. They were in echelon and each second they grew larger and their noise was greater.

"Lie on your backs to fire at them," Sordo said. "Fire ahead of them as they come."

He was watching them all the time. "*Cabrones! Hijos de puta!*" he said rapidly.

"Ignacio!" he said. "Put the gun on the shoulder of the boy. Thou!" to Joaquín, "Sit there and do not move. Crouch over. More. No. More."

He lay back and sighted with the automatic rifle as the planes came on steadily.

"Thou, Ignacio, hold me the three legs of that tripod." They were dangling down the boy's back and the muzzle of the gun was shaking from the jerking of his body that Joaquín could not control as he crouched with bent head hearing the droning roar of their coming.

Lying flat on his belly and looking up into the sky watching them come, Ignacio gathered the legs of the tripod into his two hands and steadied the gun.

"Keep thy head down," he said to Joaquín. "Keep thy head forward."

"Pasionaria says 'Better to die on thy—'" Joaquín was saying to himself as the drone came nearer them. Then he shifted suddenly into "Hail Mary, full of grace, the Lord is with thee; Blessed art thou among women and Blessed is the fruit of thy womb, Jesus. Holy Mary, Mother of God, pray for us sinners now and at the hour of our death. Amen. Holy Mary, Mother of God," he started, then he remembered quickly as the roar came now unbearably and started an act of contrition racing in it, "Oh my God, I am heartily sorry for having offended thee who art worthy of all my love——"

Then there were the hammering explosions past his ears and the gun barrel hot against his shoulder. It was hammering now again and his ears were deafened by the muzzle blast. Ignacio was pulling down hard on the tripod and the barrel was burning his back. It was hammering now in the roar and he could not remember the act of contrition.

All he could remember was at the hour of our death. Amen. At the hour of our death. Amen. At the hour. At the hour. Amen. The others all were firing. Now and at the hour of our death. Amen.

Then, through the hammering of the gun, there was the whistle of the air splitting apart and then in the red black roar the earth rolled under his knees and then waved up to hit him in the face and then dirt and bits of rock were falling all over and Ignacio was lying on him and the gun was lying on him. But he was not dead because the whistle came again and the earth rolled under him with the roar. Then it came again and the earth lurched under his belly and one side of the hilltop rose into the air and then fell slowly over them where they lay.

The planes came back three times and bombed the hilltop but

no one on the hilltop knew it. Then the planes machine-gunned the hilltop and went away. As they dove on the hill for the last time with their machine guns hammering, the first plane pulled up and winged over and then each plane did the same and they moved from echelon to V-formation and went away into the sky in the direction of Segovia.

Keeping a heavy fire on the hilltop, Lieutenant Berrendo pushed a patrol up to one of the bomb craters from where they could throw grenades onto the crest. He was taking no chances of any one being alive and waiting for them in the mess that was up there and he threw four grenades into the confusion of dead horses, broken and split rocks, and torn yellow-stained explosive-stinking earth before he climbed out of the bomb crater and walked over to have a look.

No one was alive on the hilltop except the boy Joaquín, who was unconscious under the dead body of Ignacio. Joaquín was bleeding from the nose and from the ears. He had known nothing and had no feeling since he had suddenly been in the very heart of the thunder and the breath had been wrenched from his body when the one bomb struck so close and Lieutenant Berrendo made the sign of the cross and then shot him in the back of the head, as quickly and as gently, if such an abrupt movement can be gentle, as Sordo had shot the wounded horse.

Lieutenant Berrendo stood on the hilltop and looked down the slope at his own dead and then across the country seeing where they had galloped before Sordo had turned at bay here. He noticed all the dispositions that had been made of the troops and then he ordered the dead men's horses to be brought up and the bodies tied across the saddles so that they might be packed in to La Granja.

"Take that one, too," he said. "The one with his hands on the automatic rifle. That should be Sordo. He is the oldest and it was he with the gun. No. Cut the head off and wrap it in a poncho." He considered a minute. "You might as well take all the heads. And of the others below on the slope and where we first found them. Collect the rifles and pistols and pack that gun on a horse."

Then he walked down to where the lieutenant lay who had

been killed in the first assault. He looked down at him but did not touch him.

"*Qué cosa más mala es la guerra,*" he said to himself, which meant, "What a bad thing war is."

Then he made the sign of the cross again and as he walked down the hill he said five Our Fathers and five Hail Marys for the repose of the soul of his dead comrade. He did not wish to stay to see his orders being carried out.

STORIES

"THERE ARE many kinds of stories in this book," Hemingway said in a preface to a great collection, "I hope that you will find some that you like." The main block in choosing stories for this reader has been the necessity for leaving out stories that you like, stories that everybody else likes, stories that angry characters will justly denounce you for having left out of the book. If they cannot be appeased, their field may at least be reversed by the inclusion here of a fine new fable along with four stories that have been as well and widely liked as any that have been written in their day.

"The Fable of the Good Lion" was published in Holiday magazine in March, 1951, and this is the first time it has been in a book. It will not be the last time, I imagine, because it has a Venetian quality of immortality. All travelers who have returned to their homes and been asked about their impressions, and stated them, only to have their words greeted with bland irrelevancies, will be on the side of the Good Lion.

The symbols and allegories Berenson spoke about as exhalations from Hemingway's work transpire from the other stories; each reader will find what he brings to them—based usually in the grace or lack of grace, the fortitude or lack of fortitude, of chivalry. Among other qualities, one always worth noting in Hemingway's storytelling is the quality of suspense. Look, for example, how the climaxes mount on the page or two where Margot Macomber moves in for her kill, getting both men lined in her sights, until the moment when she says, for reasons of her own, "it's going to be just like the lion."

C. P.

THE SHORT HAPPY LIFE OF
FRANCIS MACOMBER

It was now lunch time and they were all sitting under the double green fly of the dining tent pretending that nothing had happened.

"Will you have lime juice or lemon squash?" Macomber asked.

"I'll have a gimlet," Robert Wilson told him.

"I'll have a gimlet too. I need something," Macomber's wife said.

"I suppose it's the thing to do," Macomber agreed. "Tell him to make three gimlets."

The mess boy had started them already, lifting the bottles out of the canvas cooling bags that sweated wet in the wind that blew through the trees that shaded the tents.

"What had I ought to give them?" Macomber asked.

"A quid would be plenty," Wilson told him. "You don't want to spoil them."

"Will the headman distribute it?"

"Absolutely."

Francis Macomber had, half an hour before, been carried to his tent from the edge of the camp in triumph on the arms and shoulders of the cook, the personal boys, the skinner and the porters. The gun-bearers had taken no part in the demonstration. When the native boys put him down at the door of his tent, he had shaken all their hands, received their congratulations, and then gone into the tent and sat on the bed until his wife came in. She did not speak to him when she came in and he left the tent at once to wash his face and hands in the portable wash basin outside and go over to the dining tent to sit in a comfortable canvas chair in the breeze and the shade.

"You've got your lion," Robert Wilson said to him, "and a damned fine one too."

Mrs. Macomber looked at Wilson quickly. She was an extremely handsome and well-kept woman of the beauty and social position which had, five years before, commanded five thousand dollars as the price of endorsing, with photographs, a beauty product which she had never used. She had been married to Francis Macomber for eleven years.

"He is a good lion, isn't he?" Macomber said. His wife looked at him now. She looked at both these men as though she had never seen them before.

One, Wilson, the white hunter, she knew she had never truly seen before. He was about middle height with sandy hair, a stubby mustache, a very red face and extremely cold blue eyes with faint white wrinkles at the corners that grooved merrily when he smiled. He smiled at her now and she looked away from his face at the way his shoulders sloped in the loose tunic he wore with the four big cartridges held in loops where the left breast pocket should have been, at his big brown hands, his old slacks, his very dirty boots and back to his red face again. She noticed where the baked red of his face stopped in a white line that marked the circle left by his Stetson hat that hung now from one of the pegs of the tent pole.

"Well, here's to the lion," Robert Wilson said. He smiled at her again and, not smiling she looked curiously at her husband.

Francis Macomber was very tall, very well built if you did not mind that length of bone, dark, his hair cropped like an oarsman, rather thin-lipped, and was considered handsome. He was dressed in the same sort of safari clothes that Wilson wore except that his were new, he was thirty-five years old, kept himself very fit, was good at court games, had a number of big-game fishing records, and had just shown himself, very publicly, to be a coward.

"Here's to the lion," he said. "I can't ever thank you for what you did."

Margaret, his wife, looked away from him and back to Wilson. "Let's not talk about the lion," she said.

Wilson looked over at her without smiling and now she smiled at him.

"It's been a very strange day," she said. "Hadn't you ought to put your hat on even under the canvas at noon? You told me that, you know."

"Might put it on," said Wilson.

"You know you have a very red face, Mr. Wilson," she told him and smiled again.

"Drink," said Wilson.

"I don't think so," she said. "Francis drinks a great deal, but his face is never red."

"It's red today," Macomber tried a joke.

"No," said Margaret. "It's mine that's red today. But Mr. Wilson's is always red."

"Must be racial," said Wilson. "I say, you wouldn't like to drop my beauty as a topic, would you?"

"I've just started on it."

"Let's chuck it," said Wilson.

"Conversation is going to be so difficult," Margaret said.

"Don't be silly, Margot," her husband said.

"No difficulty," Wilson said. "Got a damn fine lion."

Margot looked at them both and they both saw that she was going to cry. Wilson had seen it coming for a long time and he dreaded it. Macomber was past dreading it.

"I wish it hadn't happened. Oh, I wish it hadn't happened," she said and started for her tent. She made no noise of crying but they could see that her shoulders were shaking under the rose-colored, sun-proofed shirt she wore.

"Women upset," said Wilson to the tall man. "Amounts to nothing. Strain on the nerves and one thing'n another."

"No," said Macomber. "I suppose that I rate that for the rest of my life now."

"Nonsense. Let's have a spot of the giant killer," said Wilson. "Forget the whole thing. Nothing to it anyway."

"We might try," said Macomber. "I won't forget what you did for me though."

"Nothing," said Wilson. "All nonsense."

So they sat there in the shade where the camp was pitched under some wide-topped acacia trees with a boulder-strewn cliff behind them, and a stretch of grass that ran to the bank of a boulder-filled stream in front with forest beyond it, and drank their just-cool lime drinks and avoided one another's eyes while the boys set the table for lunch. Wilson could tell that the boys all knew about it now and when he saw Macomber's personal boy looking curiously at his master while he was putting dishes on the table he snapped at him in Swahili. The boy turned away with his face blank.

"What were you telling him?" Macomber asked.

"Nothing. Told him to look alive or I'd see he got about fifteen of the best."

"What's that? Lashes?"

"It's quite illegal," Wilson said. "You're supposed to fine them."

"Do you still have them whipped?"

"Oh, yes. They could raise a row if they chose to complain. But they don't. They prefer it to the fines."

"How strange!" said Macomber.

"Not strange, really," Wilson said. "Which would you rather do? Take a good birching or lose your pay?"

Then he felt embarrassed at asking it and before Macomber could answer he went on, "We all take a beating every day, you know, one way or another."

This was no better. "Good God," he thought. "I am a diplomat, aren't I?"

"Yes, we take a beating," said Macomber, still not looking at him. "I'm awfully sorry about that lion business. It doesn't have to go any further, does it? I mean no one will hear about it, will they?"

"You mean will I tell it at the Mathaiga Club?" Wilson looked at him now coldly. He had not expected this. So he's a bloody four-letter man as well as a bloody coward, he thought. I rather liked him too until today. But how is one to know about an American?

"No," said Wilson. "I'm a professional hunter. We never talk about our clients. You can be quite easy on that. It's supposed to be bad form to ask us not to talk though."

He had decided now that to break would be much easier. He would eat, then, by himself and could read a book with his meals. They would eat by themselves. He would see them through the safari on a very formal basis—what was it the French called it?

Distinguished consideration—and it would be a damn sight easier than having to go through this emotional trash. He'd insult him and make a good clean break. Then he could read a book with his meals and he'd still be drinking their whisky. That was the phrase for it when a safari went bad. You ran into another white hunter and you asked, "How is everything going?" and he answered, "Oh, I'm still drinking their whisky," and you knew everything had gone to pot.

"I'm sorry," Macomber said and looked at him with his American face that would stay adolescent until it became middle-aged, and Wilson noted his crew-cropped hair, fine eyes only faintly shifty, good nose, thin lips and handsome jaw. "I'm sorry I didn't realize that. There are lots of things I don't know."

So what could he do, Wilson thought. He was all ready to break it off quickly and neatly and here the beggar was apologizing after he had just insulted him. He made one more attempt. "Don't worry about me talking," he said. "I have a living to make. You know in Africa no woman ever misses her lion and no white man ever bolts."

"I bolted like a rabbit," Macomber said.

Now what in hell were you going to do about a man who talked like that, Wilson wondered.

Wilson looked at Macomber with his flat, blue, machine-gunner's eyes and the other smiled back at him. He had a pleasant smile if you did not notice how his eyes showed when he was hurt.

"Maybe I can fix it up on buffalo," he said. "We're after them next, aren't we?"

"In the morning if you like," Wilson told him. Perhaps he had been wrong. This was certainly the way to take it. You most certainly could not tell a damned thing about an American. He was all for Macomber again. If you could forget the morning. But, of course, you couldn't. The morning had been about as bad as they come.

"Here comes the Memsahib," he said. She was walking over from her tent looking refreshed and cheerful and quite lovely. She had a very perfect oval face, so perfect that you expected her to be stupid. But she wasn't stupid, Wilson thought, no, not stupid.

"How is the beautiful red-faced Mr. Wilson? Are you feeling better, Francis, my pearl?"

"Oh, much," said Macomber.

"I've dropped the whole thing," she said, sitting down at the table. "What importance is there to whether Francis is any good at killing lions? That's not his trade. That's Mr. Wilson's trade. Mr. Wilson is really very impressive killing anything. You do kill anything, don't you?"

"Oh, anything," said Wilson. "Simply anything." They are, he thought, the hardest in the world; the hardest, the cruelest, the most predatory and the most attractive and their men have softened or gone to pieces nervously as they have hardened. Or is it that they pick men they can handle? They can't know that much at the age they marry, he thought. He was grateful that he had gone through his education on American women before now because this was a very attractive one.

"We're going after buff in the morning," he told her.

"I'm coming," she said.

"No, you're not."

"Oh, yes, I am. Mayn't I, Francis?"

"Why not stay in camp?"

"Not for anything," she said. "I wouldn't miss something like today for anything."

When she left, Wilson was thinking, when she went off to cry, she seemed a hell of a fine woman. She seemed to understand, to realize, to be hurt for him and for herself and to know how things really stood. She is away for twenty minutes and now she is back, simply enamelled in that American female cruelty. They are the damnedest women. Really the damnedest.

"We'll put on another show for you tomorrow," Francis Macomber said.

"You're not coming," Wilson said.

"You're very mistaken," she told him. "And I want *so* to see you perform again. You were lovely this morning. That is if blowing things' heads off is lovely."

"Here's the lunch," said Wilson. "You're very merry, aren't you?"

"Why not? I didn't come out here to be dull."

"Well, it hasn't been dull," Wilson said. He could see the boulders in the river and the high bank beyond with the trees and he remembered the morning.

"Oh, no," she said. "It's been charming. And tomorrow. You don't know how I look forward to tomorrow."

"That's eland he's offering you," Wilson said.

"They're the big cowy things that jump like hares, aren't they?"

"I suppose that describes them," Wilson said.

"It's very good meat," Macomber said.

"Did you shoot it, Francis?" she asked.

"Yes."

"They're not dangerous, are they?"

"Only if they fall on you," Wilson told her.

"I'm so glad."

"Why not let up on the bitchery just a little, Margot," Macomber said, cutting the eland steak and putting some mashed potato, gravy and carrot on the down-turned fork that tined through the piece of meat.

"I suppose I could," she said, "since you put it so prettily."

"Tonight we'll have champagne for the lion," Wilson said. "It's a bit too hot at noon."

"Oh, the lion," Margot said. "I'd forgotten the lion!"

So, Robert Wilson thought to himself, she *is* giving him a ride, isn't she? Or do you suppose that's her idea of putting up a good show? How should a woman act when she discovers her husband is a bloody coward? She's damn cruel but they're all cruel. They govern, of course, and to govern one has to be cruel sometimes. Still, I've seen enough of their damn terrorism.

"Have some more eland," he said to her politely.

That afternoon, late, Wilson and Macomber went out in the motor car with the native driver and the two gun-bearers. Mrs. Macomber stayed in the camp. It was too hot to go out, she said, and she was going with them in the early morning. As they drove off Wilson saw her standing under the big tree, looking pretty rather than beautiful in her faintly rosy khaki, her dark hair drawn back off her forehead and gathered in a knot low on her neck, her face as fresh, he thought, as though she were in England. She waved to them as the car went off through the swale of high grass and curved around through the trees into the small hills of orchard bush.

In the orchard bush they found a herd of impala, and leaving the car they stalked one old ram with long, wide-spread horns and Macomber killed it with a very creditable shot that knocked the buck down at a good two hundred yards and sent the herd off bounding wildly and leaping over one another's backs in long, leg-drawn-up leaps as unbelievable and as floating as those one makes sometimes in dreams.

"That was a good shot," Wilson said. "They're a small target."

"Is it a worth-while head?" Macomber asked.

"It's excellent," Wilson told him. "You shoot like that and you'll have no trouble."

"Do you think we'll find buffalo tomorrow?"

"There's a good chance of it. They feed out early in the morning and with luck we may catch them in the open."

"I'd like to clear away that lion business," Macomber said. "It's not very pleasant to have your wife see you do something like that."

I should think it would be even more unpleasant to do it, Wilson thought, wife or no wife, or to talk about it having done it. But he said, "I wouldn't think about that any more. Any one could be upset by his first lion. That's all over."

But that night after dinner and a whisky and soda by the fire before going to bed, as Francis Macomber lay on his cot with the mosquito bar over him and listened to the night noises it was not all over. It was neither all over nor was it beginning. It was there exactly as it happened with some parts of it indelibly emphasized and he was miserably ashamed at it. But more than shame he felt cold, hollow fear in him. The fear was still there like a cold slimy hollow in all the emptiness where once his confidence had been and it made him feel sick. It was still there with him now.

It had started the night before when he had wakened and heard the lion roaring somewhere up along the river. It was a deep sound and at the end there were sort of coughing grunts that made him seem just outside the tent, and when Francis Macomber woke in the night to hear it he was afraid. He could hear his wife breathing quietly, asleep. There was no one to tell he was afraid, nor to be afraid with him, and, lying alone, he did not know the Somali proverb that says a brave man is always frightened three times by a lion; when he first sees his track, when he first hears him roar and when he first confronts him. Then while they were eating breakfast by lantern light out in the dining tent, before the sun was up, the lion roared again and Francis thought he was just at the edge of camp.

"Sounds like an old-timer," Robert Wilson said, looking up from his kippers and coffee. "Listen to him cough."

"Is he very close?"

"A mile or so up the stream."

"Will we see him?"

"We'll have a look."

"Does his roaring carry that far? It sounds as though he were right in camp."

"Carries a hell of a long way," said Robert Wilson. "It's strange the way it carries. Hope he's a shootable cat. The boys said there was a very big one about here."

"If I get a shot, where should I hit him," Macomber asked, "to stop him?"

"In the shoulders," Wilson said. "In the neck if you can make it. Shoot for bone. Break him down."

"I hope I can place it properly," Macomber said.

"You shoot very well," Wilson told him. "Take your time. Make sure of him. The first one in is the one that counts."

"What range will it be?"

"Can't tell. Lion has something to say about that. Won't shoot unless it's close enough so you can make sure."

"At under a hundred yards?" Macomber asked.

Wilson looked at him quickly.

"Hundred's about right. Might have to take him a bit under. Shouldn't chance a shot at much over that. A hundred's a decent range. You can hit him wherever you want at that. Here comes the Memsahib."

"Good morning," she said. "Are we going after that lion?"

"As soon as you deal with your breakfast," Wilson said. "How are you feeling?"

"Marvellous," she said. "I'm very excited."

"I'll just go and see that everything is ready," Wilson went off. As he left the lion roared again.

"Noisy beggar," Wilson said. "We'll put a stop to that."

"What's the matter, Francis?" his wife asked him.

"Nothing," Macomber said.

"Yes, there is," she said. "What are you upset about?"

"Nothing," he said.

"Tell me," she looked at him. "Don't you feel well?"

"It's that damned roaring," he said. "It's been going on all night, you know."

"Why didn't you wake me," she said. "I'd love to have heard it."

"I've got to kill the damned thing," Macomber said, miserably.

"Well, that's what you're out here for, isn't it?"

"Yes. But I'm nervous. Hearing the thing roar gets on my nerves."

"Well then, as Wilson said, kill him and stop his roaring."

"Yes, darling," said Francis Macomber. "It sounds easy, doesn't it?"

"You're not afraid, are you?"

"Of course not. But I'm nervous from hearing him roar all night."

"You'll kill him marvellously," she said. "I know you will. I'm awfully anxious to see it."

"Finish your breakfast and we'll be starting."

"It's not light yet," she said. "This is a ridiculous hour."

Just then the lion roared in a deep-chested moaning, suddenly guttural, ascending vibration that seemed to shake the air and ended in a sigh and a heavy, deep-chested grunt.

"He sounds almost here," Macomber's wife said.

"My God," said Macomber. "I hate that damned noise."

"It's very impressive."

"Impressive. It's frightful."

Robert Wilson came up then carrying his short, ugly, shockingly big-bored .505 Gibbs and grinning.

"Come on," he said. "Your gun-bearer has your Springfield and the big gun. Everything's in the car. Have you solids?"

"Yes."

"I'm ready," Mrs. Macomber said.

"Must make him stop that racket," Wilson said. "You get in front. The Memsahib can sit back here with me."

They climbed into the motor car and, in the gray first daylight, moved off up the river through the trees. Macomber opened the breech of his rifle and saw he had metal-cased bullets, shut the bolt and put the rifle on safety. He saw his hand was trembling. He felt in his pocket for more cartridges and moved his fingers over the cartridges in the loops of his tunic front. He turned back to where Wilson sat in the rear seat of the doorless, box-bodied motor car beside his wife, them both grinning with excitement, and Wilson leaned forward and whispered,

"See the birds dropping. Means the old boy has left his kill."

On the far bank of the stream Macomber could see, above the trees, vultures circling and plummeting down.

"Chances are he'll come to drink along here," Wilson whispered. "Before he goes to lay up. Keep an eye out."

They were driving slowly along the high bank of the stream which here cut deeply to its boulder-filled bed, and they wound in and out through big trees as they drove. Macomber was watching the opposite bank when he felt Wilson take hold of his arm. The car stopped.

"There he is," he heard the whisper. "Ahead and to the right. Get out and take him. He's a marvellous lion."

Macomber saw the lion now. He was standing almost broad-side, his great head up and turned toward them. The early morning breeze that blew toward them was just stirring his dark mane, and the lion looked huge, silhouetted on the rise of bank in the gray morning light, his shoulders heavy, his barrel of a body bulking smoothly.

"How far is he?" asked Macomber, raising his rifle.

"About seventy-five. Get out and take him."

"Why not shoot from where I am?"

"You don't shoot them from cars," he heard Wilson saying in his ear. "Get out. He's not going to stay there all day."

Macomber stepped out of the curved opening at the side of the front seat, onto the step and down onto the ground. The lion still stood looking majestically and coolly toward this object that his eyes only showed in silhouette, bulking like some super-rhino. There was no man smell carried toward him and he watched the object, moving his great head a little from side to side. Then watching the object, not afraid, but hesitating before going down the bank to drink with such a thing opposite him, he saw a man figure detach itself from it and he turned his heavy head and swung away toward the cover of the trees as he heard a cracking crash and felt the slam of a .30–06 220-grain solid bullet that bit his flank and ripped in sudden hot scalding nausea through his stomach. He trotted, heavy, big-footed, swinging wounded full-bellied, through the trees toward the tall grass and cover, and the crash came again to go past him ripping the air apart. Then it crashed again and he felt the blow as it hit his lower ribs and ripped on through, blood sudden hot and frothy in his mouth, and he galloped toward the high grass where he could crouch and not be seen and make them bring the crashing thing close enough so he could make a rush and get the man that held it.

Macomber had not thought how the lion felt as he got out of the car. He only knew his hands were shaking and as he walked away from the car it was almost impossible for him to make his legs move. They were stiff in the thighs, but he could feel the muscles fluttering. He raised the rifle, sighted on the junction of the lion's head and shoulders and pulled the trigger. Nothing happened though he pulled until he thought his finger would break. Then he knew he had the safety on and as he lowered the rifle to move the safety over he moved another frozen pace forward, and the lion seeing his silhoutte now clear of the silhouette of the car, turned and started off at a trot, and, as Macomber fired, he heard a whunk that meant that the bullet was home; but the lion kept on going. Macomber shot again and every one saw the bullet throw a spout of dirt beyond the trotting lion. He shot again, remembering to lower his aim, and they all heard the bullet hit, and the lion went into a gallop and was in the tall grass before he had the bolt pushed forward.

Macomber stood there feeling sick at his stomach, his hands that held the Springfield still cocked, shaking, and his wife and Robert Wilson were standing by him. Beside him too were the two gun-bearers chattering in Wakamba.

"I hit him," Macomber said. "I hit him twice."

"You gut-shot him and you hit him somewhere forward," Wilson said without enthusiasm. The gun-bearers looked very grave. They were silent now.

"You may have killed him," Wilson went on. "We'll have to wait a while before we go in to find out."

"What do you mean?"

"Let him get sick before we follow him up."

"Oh," said Macomber.

"He's a hell of a fine lion," Wilson said cheerfully. "He's gotten into a bad place though."

"Why is it bad?"

"Can't see him until you're on him."

"Oh," said Macomber.

"Come on," said Wilson. "The Memsahib can stay here in the car. We'll go to have a look at the blood spoor."

"Stay here, Margot," Macomber said to his wife. His mouth was very dry and it was hard for him to talk.

"Why?" she asked.

"Wilson says to."

"We're going to have a look," Wilson said. "You stay here. You can see even better from here."

"All right."

Wilson spoke in Swahili to the driver. He nodded and said, "Yes, Bwana."

Then they went down the steep bank and across the stream, climbing over and around the boulders and up the other bank, pulling up by some projecting roots, and along it until they found where the lion had been trotting when Macomber first shot. There was dark blood on the short grass that the gun-bearers pointed out with grass stems, and that ran away behind the river bank trees.

"What do we do?" asked Macomber.

"Not much choice," said Wilson. "We can't bring the car over. Bank's too steep. We'll let him stiffen up a bit and then you and I'll go in and have a look for him."

"Can't we set the grass on fire?" Macomber asked.

"Too green."

"Can't we send beaters?"

Wilson looked at him appraisingly. "Of course we can," he said. "But it's just a touch murderous. You see we know the lion's wounded. You can drive an unwounded lion—he'll move on ahead of a noise—but a wounded lion's going to charge. You can't see him until you're right on him. He'll make himself perfectly flat in cover you wouldn't think would hide a hare. You can't very well send boys in there to that sort of a show. Somebody bound to get mauled."

"What about the gun-bearers?"

"Oh, they'll go with us. It's their *shauri*. You see, they signed on for it. They don't look too happy though, do they?"

"I don't want to go in there," said Macomber. It was out before he knew he'd said it.

"Neither do I," said Wilson very cheerily. "Really no choice though." Then, as an afterthought, he glanced at Macomber and saw suddenly how he was trembling and the pitiful look on his face.

"You don't have to go in, of course," he said. "That's what I'm hired for, you know. That's why I'm so expensive."

"You mean you'd go in by yourself? Why not leave him there?"

Robert Wilson, whose entire occupation had been with the lion and the problem he presented, and who had not been thinking about Macomber except to note that he was rather windy, suddenly felt as though he had opened the wrong door in a hotel and seen something shameful.

"What do you mean?"

"Why not just leave him?"

"You mean pretend to ourselves he hasn't been hit?"

"No. Just drop it."

"It isn't done."

"Why not?"

"For one thing, he's certain to be suffering. For another, some one else might run onto him."

"I see."

"But you don't have to have anything to do with it."

"I'd like to," Macomber said. "I'm just scared, you know."

"I'll go ahead when we go in," Wilson said, "with Kongoni tracking. You keep behind me and a little to one side. Chances are we'll hear him growl. If we see him we'll both shoot. Don't worry about anything. I'll keep you backed up. As a matter of fact, you know, perhaps you'd better not go. It might be much better. Why don't you go over and join the Memsahib while I just get it over with?"

"No, I want to go."

"All right," said Wilson. "But don't go in if you don't want to. This is my *shauri* now, you know."

"I want to go," said Macomber.

They sat under a tree and smoked.

"Want to go back and speak to the Memsahib while we're waiting?" Wilson asked.

"No."

"I'll just step back and tell her to be patient."

"Good," said Macomber. He sat there, sweating under his arms, his mouth dry, his stomach hollow feeling, wanting to find courage to tell Wilson to go on and finish off the lion without him. He could not know that Wilson was furious because he had not noticed the state he was in earlier and sent him back to his wife. While he sat there Wilson came up. "I have your big gun," he said. "Take it. We've given him time, I think. Come on."

Macomber took the big gun and Wilson said:

"Keep behind me and about five yards to the right and do exactly as I tell you." Then he spoke in Swahili to the two gun-bearers who looked the picture of gloom.

"Let's go," he said.

"Could I have a drink of water?" Macomber asked. Wilson

spoke to the older gun-bearer, who wore a canteen on his belt, and the man unbuckled it, unscrewed the top and handed it to Macomber, who took it noticing how heavy it seemed and how hairy and shoddy the felt covering was in his hand. He raised it to drink and looked ahead at the high grass with the flat-topped trees behind it. A breeze was blowing toward them and the grass rippled gently in the wind. He looked at the gun-bearer and he could see the gun-bearer was suffering too with fear.

Thirty-five yards into the grass the big lion lay flattened out along the ground. His ears were back and his only movement was a slight twitching up and down of his long, black-tufted tail. He had turned at bay as soon as he had reached this cover and he was sick with the wound through his full belly, and weakening with the wound through his lungs that brought a thin foamy red to his mouth each time he breathed. His flanks were wet and hot and flies were on the little openings the solid bullets had made in his tawny hide, and his big yellow eyes, narrowed with hate, looked straight ahead, only blinking when the pain came as he breathed, and his claws dug in the soft baked earth. All of him, pain, sickness, hatred and all of his remaining strength, was tightening into an absolute concentration for a rush. He could hear the men talking and he waited, gathering all of himself into this preparation for a charge as soon as the men would come into the grass. As he heard their voices his tail stiffened to twitch up and down, and, as they came into the edge of the grass, he made a coughing grunt and charged.

Kongoni, the old gun-bearer, in the lead watching the blood spoor, Wilson watching the grass for any movement, his big gun ready, the second gun-bearer looking ahead and listening, Macomber close to Wilson, his rifle cocked, they had just moved into the grass when Macomber heard the blood-choked coughing grunt, and saw the swishing rush in the grass. The next thing he knew he was running; running wildly, in panic in the open, running toward the stream.

He heard the *ca-ra-wong!* of Wilson's big rifle, and again in a second crashing *carawong!* and turning saw the lion, horrible-looking now, with half his head seeming to be gone, crawling toward Wilson in the edge of the tall grass while the red-faced man worked the bolt on the short ugly rifle and aimed carefully as another blasting *carawong!* came from the muzzle, and the crawling, heavy, yellow bulk of the lion stiffened and the huge, mutilated head slid forward and Macomber, standing by himself in the clearing where he had run, holding a loaded rifle, while two black men and a white man looked back at him in contempt, knew the lion was dead. He came toward Wilson, his tallness all seeming a naked reproach, and Wilson looked at him and said:

"Want to take pictures?"

"No," he said.

That was all any one had said until they reached the motor car. Then Wilson had said:

"Hell of a fine lion. Boys will skin him out. We might as well stay here in the shade."

Macomber's wife had not looked at him nor he at her and he had sat by her in the back seat with Wilson sitting in the front seat. Once he had reached over and taken his wife's hand without looking at her and she had removed her hand from his. Looking across the stream to where the gun-bearers were skinning out the lion he could see that she had been able to see the whole thing. While they sat there his wife had reached forward and put her hand on Wilson's shoulder. He turned and she had leaned forward over the low seat and kissed him on the mouth.

"Oh, I say," said Wilson, going redder than his natural baked color.

"Mr. Robert Wilson," she said. "The beautiful red-faced Mr. Robert Wilson."

Then she sat down beside Macomber again and looked away across the stream to where the lion lay, with uplifted, white-muscled, tendon-marked naked forearms, and white bloating belly, as the black men fleshed away the skin. Finally the gun-bearers brought the skin over, wet and heavy, and climbed in behind with it, rolling it up before they got in, and the motor car started. No one had said anything more until they were back in camp.

That was the story of the lion. Macomber did not know how the lion had felt before he started his rush, nor during it when the

unbelievable smash of the .505 with a muzzle velocity of two
tons had hit him in the mouth, nor what kept him coming after
that, when the second ripping crash had smashed his hind
quarters and he had come crawling on toward the crashing, blasting thing that had destroyed him. Wilson knew something about
it and only expressed it by saying, "Damned fine lion," but Macomber did not know how Wilson felt about things either. He
did not know how his wife felt except that she was through with
him.

His wife had been through with him before but it never lasted.
He was very wealthy, and would be much wealthier, and he knew
she would not leave him ever now. That was one of the few things
that he really knew. He knew about that, about motor cycles—
that was earliest—about motor cars, about duck-shooting, about
fishing, trout, salmon and big-sea, about sex in books, many books,
too many books, about all court games, about dogs, not much about
horses, about hanging on to his money, about most of the other
things his world dealt in, and about his wife not leaving him. His
wife had been a great beauty and she was still a great beauty in
Africa, but she was not a great enough beauty any more at home
to be able to leave him and better herself and she knew it and he
knew it. She had missed the chance to leave him and he knew it.
If he had been better with women she would probably have
started to worry about him getting another new, beautiful wife;
but she knew too much about him to worry about him either.
Also, he had always had a great tolerance which seemed the nicest
thing about him if it were not the most sinister.

All in all they were known as a comparatively happily married
couple, one of those whose disruption is often rumored but never
occurs, and as the society columnist put it, they were adding more
than a spice of *adventure* to their much envied and ever-enduring
Romance by a *Safari* in what was known as *Darkest Africa* until
the Martin Johnsons lighted it on so many silver screens where
they were pursuing *Old Simba* the lion, the buffalo, *Tembo* the
elephant and as well collecting specimens for the Museum of
Natural History. This same columnist had reported them *on the
verge* at least three times in the past and they had been. But they

always made it up. They had a sound basis of union. Margot was too beautiful for Macomber to divorce her and Macomber had too much money for Margot ever to leave him.

It was now about three o'clock in the morning and Francis Macomber, who had been asleep a little while after he had stopped thinking about the lion, wakened and then slept again, woke suddenly, frightened in a dream of the bloody-headed lion standing over him, and listening while his heart pounded, he realized that his wife was not in the other cot in the tent. He lay awake with that knowledge for two hours.

At the end of that time his wife came into the tent, lifted her mosquito bar and crawled cozily into bed.

"Where have you been?" Macomber asked in the darkness.

"Hello," she said. "Are you awake?"

"Where have you been?"

"I just went out to get a breath of air."

"You did, like hell."

"What do you want me to say, darling?"

"Where have you been?"

"Out to get a breath of air."

"That's a new name for it. You *are* a bitch."

"Well, you're a coward."

"All right," he said. "What of it?"

"Nothing as far as I'm concerned. But please let's not talk, darling, because I'm very sleepy."

"You think that I'll take anything."

"I know you will, sweet."

"Well, I won't."

"Please, darling, let's not talk. I'm so very sleepy."

"There wasn't going to be any of that. You promised there wouldn't be."

"Well, there is now," she said sweetly.

"You said if we made this trip that there would be none of that. You promised."

"Yes, darling. That's the way I meant it to be. But the trip was spoiled yesterday. We don't have to talk about it, do we?"

"You don't wait long when you have an advantage, do you?"

"Please let's not talk. I'm so sleepy, darling."

"I'm going to talk."

"Don't mind me then, because I'm going to sleep." And she did.

At breakfast they were all three at the table before daylight and Francis Macomber found that, of all the many men that he had hated, he hated Robert Wilson the most.

"Sleep well?" Wilson asked in his throaty voice, filling a pipe.

"Did you?"

"Topping," the white hunter told him.

You bastard, thought Macomber, you insolent bastard.

So she woke him when she came in, Wilson thought, looking at them both with his flat, cold eyes. Well, why doesn't he keep his wife where she belongs? What does he think I am, a bloody plaster saint? Let him keep her where she belongs. It's his own fault.

"Do you think we'll find buffalo?" Margot asked, pushing away a dish of apricots.

"Chance of it," Wilson said and smiled at her. "Why don't you stay in camp?"

"Not for anything," she told him.

"Why not order her to stay in camp?" Wilson said to Macomber.

"You order her," said Macomber coldly.

"Let's not have any ordering, nor," turning to Macomber, "any silliness, Francis," Margot said quite pleasantly.

"Are you ready to start?" Macomber asked.

"Any time," Wilson told him. "Do you want the Memsahib to go?"

"Does it make any difference whether I do or not?"

The hell with it, thought Robert Wilson. The utter complete hell with it. So this is what it's going to be like. Well, this is what it's going to be like, then.

"Makes no difference," he said.

"You're sure you wouldn't like to stay in camp with her yourself and let me go out and hunt the buffalo?" Macomber asked.

"Can't do that," said Wilson. "Wouldn't talk rot if I were you."

"I'm not talking rot. I'm disgusted."

"Bad word, disgusted."

"Francis, will you please try to speak sensibly?" his wife said.

"I speak too damned sensibly," Macomber said. "Did you ever eat such filthy food?"

"Something wrong with the food?" asked Wilson quietly.

"No more than with everything else."

"I'd pull yourself together, laddybuck," Wilson said very quietly. "There's a boy waits at table that understands a little English."

"The hell with him."

Wilson stood up and puffing on his pipe strolled away, speaking a few words in Swahili to one of the gun-bearers who was standing waiting for him. Macomber and his wife sat on at the table. He was staring at his coffee cup.

"If you make a scene I'll leave you, darling," Margot said quietly.

"No, you won't."

"You can try it and see."

"You won't leave me."

"No," she said. "I won't leave you and you'll behave yourself."

"Behave myself? That's a way to talk. Behave myself."

"Yes. Behave yourself."

"Why don't *you* try behaving?"

"I've tried it so long. So very long."

"I hate that red-faced swine," Macomber said. "I loathe the sight of him."

"He's really *very* nice."

"Oh, *shut up,*" Macomber almost shouted. Just then the car came up and stopped in front of the dining tent and the driver and the two gun-bearers got out. Wilson walked over and looked at the husband and wife sitting there at the table.

"Going shooting?" he asked.

"Yes," said Macomber, standing up. "Yes."

"Better bring a woolly. It will be cool in the car," Wilson said.

"I'll get my leather jacket," Margot said.

"The boy has it," Wilson told her. He climbed into the front with the driver and Francis Macomber and his wife sat, not speaking, in the back seat.

Hope the silly beggar doesn't take a notion to blow the back of my head off, Wilson thought to himself. Women *are* a nuisance on safari.

The car was grinding down to cross the river at a pebbly ford in the gray daylight and then climbed, angling up the steep bank, where Wilson had ordered a way shovelled out the day before so they could reach the parklike wooded rolling country on the far side.

It was a good morning, Wilson thought. There was a heavy dew and as the wheels went through the grass and low bushes he could smell the odor of the crushed fronds. It was an odor like verbena and he liked this early morning smell of the dew, the crushed bracken and the look of the tree trunks showing black through the early morning mist, as the car made its way through the untracked, parklike country. He had put the two in the back seat out of his mind now and was thinking about buffalo. The buffalo that he was after stayed in the day-time in a thick swamp where it was impossible to get a shot, but in the night they fed out into an open stretch of country and if he could come between them and their swamp with the car, Macomber would have a good chance at them in the open. He did not want to hunt buff with Macomber in thick cover. He did not want to hunt buff or anything else with Macomber at all, but he was a professional hunter and he had hunted with some rare ones in his time. If they got buff today there would only be rhino to come and the poor man would have gone through his dangerous game and things might pick up. He'd have nothing more to do with the woman and Macomber would get over that too. He must have gone through plenty of that before by the look of things. Poor beggar. He must have a way of getting over it. Well, it was the poor sod's own bloody fault.

He, Robert Wilson, carried a double size cot on safari to accommodate any windfalls he might receive. He had hunted for a certain clientele, the international, fast, sporting set, where the women did not feel they were getting their money's worth unless they had shared that cot with the white hunter. He despised them when he was away from them although he liked some of them well enough at the time, but he made his living by them; and their standards were his standards as long as they were hiring him.

They were his standards in all except the shooting. He had his own standards about the killing and they could live up to them or get some one else to hunt them. He knew, too, that they all respected him for this. This Macomber was an odd one though. Damned if he wasn't. Now the wife. Well, the wife. Yes, the wife. Hm, the wife. Well he'd dropped all that. He looked around at them. Macomber sat grim and furious. Margot smiled at him. She looked younger today, more innocent and fresher and not so professionally beautiful. What's in her heart God knows, Wilson thought. She hadn't talked much last night. At that it was a pleasure to see her.

The motor car climbed up a slight rise and went on through the trees and then out into a grassy prairie-like opening and kept in the shelter of the trees along the edge, the driver going slowly and Wilson looking carefully out across the prairie and all along its far side. He stopped the car and studied the opening with his field glasses. Then he motioned to the driver to go on and the car moved slowly along, the driver avoiding wart-hog holes and driving around the mud castles ants had built. Then, looking across the opening, Wilson suddenly turned and said,

"By God, there they are!"

And looking where he pointed, while the car jumped forward and Wilson spoke in rapid Swahili to the driver, Macomber saw three huge, black animals looking almost cylindrical in their long heaviness, like big black tank cars, moving at a gallop across the far edge of the open prairie. They moved at a stiff-necked, stiff bodied gallop and he could see the upswept wide black horns on their heads as they galloped heads out; the heads not moving.

"They're three old bulls," Wilson said. "We'll cut them off before they get to the swamp."

The car was going a wild forty-five miles an hour across the open and as Macomber watched, the buffalo got bigger and bigger until he could see the gray, hairless, scabby look of one huge bull and how his neck was a part of his shoulders and the shiny black of his horns as he galloped a little behind the others that were strung out in that steady plunging gait; and then, the car swaying as though it had just jumped a road, they drew up close and he could see the plunging hugeness of the bull, and the dust in his sparsely haired hide, the wide boss of horn and his outstretched wide-nostrilled muzzle, and he was raising his rifle when Wilson shouted, "Not from the car, you fool!" and he had no fear, only hatred of Wilson, while the brakes clamped on and the car skidded, plowing sideways to an almost stop and Wilson was out on one side and he on the other, stumbling as his feet hit the still speeding-by of the earth, and then he was shooting at the bull as he moved away, hearing the bullets whunk into him, emptying his rifle at him as he moved steadily away, finally remembering to get his shots forward into the shoulder, and as he fumbled to re-load, he saw the bull was down. Down on his knees, his big head tossing, and seeing the other two still galloping he shot at the leader and hit him. He shot again and missed and he heard the *carawonging* roar as Wilson shot and saw the leading bull slide forward onto his nose.

"Get that other," Wilson said. "Now you're shooting!"

But the other bull was moving steadily at the same gallop and he missed, throwing a spout of dirt, and Wilson missed and the dust rose in a cloud and Wilson shouted, "Come on. He's too far!" and grabbed his arm and they were in the car again, Macomber and Wilson hanging on the sides and rocketing swayingly over the uneven ground, drawing up on the steady, plunging, heavy-necked, straight-moving gallop of the bull.

They were behind him and Macomber was filling his rifle, dropping shells onto the ground, jamming it, clearing the jam, then they were almost up with the bull when Wilson yelled "Stop," and the car skidded so that it almost swung over and Macomber fell forward onto his feet, slammed his bolt forward and fired as far forward as he could aim into the galloping, rounded black back, aimed and shot again, then again, then again, and the bullets, all of them hitting, had no effect on the buffalo that he could see. Then Wilson shot, the roar deafening him, and he could see the bull stagger. Macomber shot again, aiming carefully, and down he came, onto his knees.

"All right," Wilson said. "Nice work. That's the three."

Macomber felt a drunken elation.

"How many times did you shoot?" he asked.

"Just three," Wilson said. "You killed the first bull. The biggest one. I helped you finish the other two. Afraid they might have got into cover. You had them killed. I was just mopping up a little. You shot damn well."

"Let's go to the car," said Macomber. "I want a drink."

"Got to finish off that buff first," Wilson told him. The buffalo was on his knees and he jerked his head furiously and bellowed in pig-eyed, roaring rage as they came toward him.

"Watch he doesn't get up," Wilson said. Then, "Get a little broadside and take him in the neck just behind the ear."

Macomber aimed carefully at the center of the huge, jerking, rage-driven neck and shot. At the shot the head dropped forward.

"That does it," said Wilson. "Got the spine. They're a hell of a looking thing, aren't they?"

"Let's get the drink," said Macomber. In his life he had never felt so good.

In the car Macomber's wife sat very white faced. "You were marvellous, darling," she said to Macomber. "What a ride."

"Was it rough?" Wilson asked.

"It was frightful. I've never been more frightened in my life."

"Let's all have a drink," Macomber said.

"By all means," said Wilson. "Give it to the Memsahib." She drank the neat whisky from the flask and shuddered a little when she swallowed. She handed the flask to Macomber who handed it to Wilson.

"It was frightfully exciting," she said. "It's given me a dreadful headache. I didn't know you were allowed to shoot them from cars though."

"No one shot from cars," said Wilson coldly.

"I mean chase them from cars."

"Wouldn't ordinarily," Wilson said. "Seemed sporting enough to me though while we were doing it. Taking more chance driving that way across the plain full of holes and one thing and another than hunting on foot. Buffalo could have charged us each time we shot if he liked. Gave him every chance. Wouldn't mention it to any one though. It's illegal if that's what you mean."

"It seemed very unfair to me," Margot said, "chasing those big helpless things in a motor car."

"Did it?" said Wilson.

"What would happen if they heard about it in Nairobi?"

"I'd lose my licence for one thing. Other unpleasantnesses," Wilson said, taking a drink from the flask. "I'd be out of business."

"Really?"

"Yes, really."

"Well," said Macomber, and he smiled for the first time all day. "Now she has something on you."

"You have such a pretty way of putting things, Francis," Margot Macomber said. Wilson looked at them both. If a four-letter man marries a five-letter woman, he was thinking, what number of letters would their children be? What he said was, "We lost a gun-bearer. Did you notice it?"

"My God, no," Macomber said.

"Here he comes," Wilson said. "He's all right. He must have fallen off when we left the first bull."

Approaching them was the middle-aged gun-bearer, limping along in his knitted cap, khaki tunic, shorts and rubber sandals, gloomy-faced and disgusted looking. As he came up he called out to Wilson in Swahili and they all saw the change in the white hunter's face.

"What does he say?" asked Margot.

"He says the first bull got up and went into the bush," Wilson said with no expression in his voice.

"Oh," said Macomber blankly.

"Then it's going to be just like the lion," said Margot, full of anticipation.

"It's not going to be a damned bit like the lion," Wilson told her. "Did you want another drink, Macomber?"

"Thanks, yes," Macomber said. He expected the feeling he had had about the lion to come back but it did not. For the first time in his life he really felt wholly without fear. Instead of fear he had a feeling of definite elation.

"We'll go and have a look at the second bull," Wilson said. "I'll tell the driver to put the car in the shade."

"What are you going to do?" asked Margaret Macomber.

"Take a look at the buff," Wilson said.

"I'll come."

"Come along."

The three of them walked over to where the second buffalo bulked blackly in the open, head forward on the grass, the massive horns swung wide.

"He's a very good head," Wilson said. "That's close to a fifty-inch spread."

Macomber was looking at him with delight.

"He's hateful looking," said Margot. "Can't we go into the shade?"

"Of course," Wilson said. "Look," he said to Macomber, and pointed. "See that patch of bush?"

"Yes."

"That's where the first bull went in. The gun-bearer said when he fell off the bull was down. He was watching us helling along and the other two buff galloping. When he looked up there was the bull up and looking at him. Gun-bearer ran like hell and the bull went off slowly into that bush."

"Can we go in after him now?" asked Macomber eagerly.

Wilson looked at him appraisingly. Damned if this isn't a strange one, he thought. Yesterday he's scared sick and today he's a ruddy fire eater.

"No, we'll give him a while."

"Let's please go into the shade," Margot said. Her face was white and she looked ill.

They made their way to the car where it stood under a single, wide-spreading tree and all climbed in.

"Chances are he's dead in there," Wilson remarked. "After a little we'll have a look."

Macomber felt a wild unreasonable happiness that he had never known before.

"By God, that was a chase," he said. "I've never felt any such feeling. Wasn't it marvellous, Margot?"

"I hated it."

"Why?"

"I hated it," she said bitterly. "I loathed it."

"You know I don't think I'd ever be afraid of anything again," Macomber said to Wilson. "Something happened in me after we first saw the buff and started after him. Like a dam bursting. It was pure excitement."

"Cleans out your liver," said Wilson. "Damn funny things happen to people."

Macomber's face was shining. "You know something did happen to me," he said. "I feel absolutely different."

His wife said nothing and eyed him strangely. She was sitting far back in the seat and Macomber was sitting forward talking to Wilson who turned sideways talking over the back of the front seat.

"You know, I'd like to try another lion," Macomber said. "I'm really not afraid of them now. After all, what can they do to you?"

"That's it," said Wilson. "Worst one can do is kill you. How does it go? Shakespeare. Damned good. See if I can remember. Oh, damned good. Used to quote it to myself at one time. Let's see. 'By my troth, I care not; a man can die but once; we owe God a death and let it go which way it will he that dies this year is quit for the next.' Damned fine, eh?"

He was very embarrassed, having brought out this thing he had lived by, but he had seen men come of age before and it always moved him. It was not a matter of their twenty-first birthday.

It had taken a strange chance of hunting, a sudden precipitation into action without opportunity for worrying beforehand, to bring this about with Macomber, but regardless of how it had happened it had most certainly happened. Look at the beggar now, Wilson thought. It's that some of them stay little boys so long, Wilson thought. Sometimes all their lives. Their figures stay boyish when they're fifty. The great American boy-men. Damned strange people. But he liked this Macomber now. Damned strange fellow. Probably meant the end of cuckoldry too. Well, that would be a damned good thing. Damned good thing. Beggar had probably been afraid all his life. Don't know what started it. But over now.

Hadn't had time to be afraid with the buff. That and being angry too. Motor car too. Motor cars made it familiar. Be a damn fire eater now. He'd seen it in the war work the same way. More of a change than any loss of virginity. Fear gone like an operation. Something else grew in its place. Main thing a man had. Made him into a man. Women knew it too. No bloody fear.

From the far corner of the seat Margaret Macomber looked at the two of them. There was no change in Wilson. She saw Wilson as she had seen him the day before when she had first realized what his great talent was. But she saw the change in Francis Macomber now.

"Do you have that feeling of happiness about what's going to happen?" Macomber asked, still exploring his new wealth.

"You're not supposed to mention it," Wilson said, looking in the other's face. "Much more fashionable to say you're scared. Mind you, you'll be scared too, plenty of times."

"But you *have* a feeling of happiness about action to come?"

"Yes," said Wilson. "There's that. Doesn't do to talk too much about all this. Talk the whole thing away. No pleasure in anything if you mouth it up too much."

"You're both talking rot," said Margot. "Just because you've chased some helpless animals in a motor car you talk like heroes."

"Sorry," said Wilson. "I have been gassing too much." She's worried about it already, he thought.

"If you don't know what we're talking about why not keep out of it?" Macomber asked his wife.

"You've gotten awfully brave, awfully suddenly," his wife said contemptuously, but her contempt was not secure. She was very afraid of something.

Macomber laughed, a very natural hearty laugh. "You know I *have*," he said. "I really have."

"Isn't it sort of late?" Margot said bitterly. Because she had done the best she could for many years back and the way they were together now was no one person's fault.

"Not for me," said Macomber.

Margot said nothing but sat back in the corner of the seat.

"Do you think we've given him time enough?" Macomber asked Wilson cheerfully.

"We might have a look," Wilson said. "Have you any solids left?"

"The gun-bearer has some."

Wilson called in Swahili and the older gun-bearer, who was skinning out one of the heads, straightened up, pulled a box of solids out of his pocket and brought them over to Macomber, who filled his magazine and put the remaining shells in his pocket.

"You might as well shoot the Springfield," Wilson said. "You're used to it. We'll leave the Mannlicher in the car with the Memsahib. Your gun-bearer can carry your heavy gun. I've this damned cannon. Now let me tell you about them."

He had saved this until the last because he did not want to worry Macomber. "When a buff comes he comes with his head high and thrust straight out. The boss of the horns covers any sort of a brain shot. The only shot is straight into the nose. The only other shot is into his chest or, if you're to one side, into the neck or the shoulders. After they've been hit once they take a hell of a lot of killing. Don't try anything fancy. Take the easiest shot there is. They've finished skinning out that head now. Should we get started?"

He called to the gun-bearers, who came up wiping their hands, and the older one got into the back.

"I'll only take Kongoni," Wilson said. "The other can watch to keep the birds away."

As the car moved slowly across the open space toward the island of brushy trees that ran in a tongue of foliage along a dry water course that cut the open swale, Macomber felt his heart pounding and his mouth was dry again, but it was excitement, not fear.

"Here's where he went in," Wilson said. Then to the gun-bearer in Swahili, "Take the blood spoor."

The car was parallel to the patch of bush. Macomber, Wilson and the gun-bearer got down. Macomber, looking back, saw his wife, with the rifle by her side, looking at him. He waved to her and she did not wave back.

The brush was very thick ahead and the ground was dry. The

middle-aged gun-bearer was sweating heavily and Wilson had his hat down over his eyes and his red neck showed just ahead of Macomber. Suddenly the gun-bearer said something in Swahili to Wilson and ran forward.

"He's dead in there," Wilson said. "Good work," and he turned to grip Macomber's hand and as they shook hands, grinning at each other, the gun-bearer shouted wildly and they saw him coming out of the bush sideways, fast as a crab, and the bull coming, nose out, mouth tight closed, blood dripping, massive head straight out, coming in a charge, his little pig eyes bloodshot as he looked at them. Wilson, who was ahead was kneeling shooting, and Macomber, as he fired, unhearing his shot in the roaring of Wilson's gun, saw fragments like slate burst from the huge boss of the horns, and the head jerked, he shot again at the wide nostrils and saw the horns jolt again and fragments fly, and he did not see Wilson now and, aiming carefully, shot again with the buffalo's huge bulk almost on him and his rifle almost level with the oncoming head, nose cut, and he could see the little wicked eyes and the head started to lower and he felt a sudden white-hot, blinding flash explode inside his head and that was all he ever felt.

Wilson had ducked to one side to get in a shoulder shot. Macomber had stood solid and shot for the nose, shooting a touch high each time and hitting the heavy horns, splintering and chipping them like hitting a slate roof, and Mrs. Macomber, in the car, had shot at the buffalo with the 6.5 Mannlicher as it seemed about to gore Macomber and had hit her husband about two inches up and a little to one side of the base of his skull.

Francis Macomber lay now face down, not two yards from where the buffalo lay on his side and his wife knelt over him with Wilson beside her.

"I wouldn't turn him over," Wilson said.

The woman was crying hysterically.

"I'd get back in the car," Wilson said. "Where's the rifle?"

She shook her head, her face contorted. The gun-bearer picked up the rifle.

"Leave it as it is," said Wilson. Then, "Go get Abdulla so that he may witness the manner of the accident."

He knelt down, took a handkerchief from his pocket, and spread it over Francis Macomber's crew-cropped head where it lay. The blood sank into the dry, loose earth.

Wilson stood up and saw the buffalo on his side, his legs out, his thinly-haired belly crawling with ticks. "Hell of a good bull," his brain registered automatically. "A good fifty inches, or better. Better." He called to the driver and told him to spread a blanket over the body and stay by it. Then he walked over to the motor car where the woman sat crying in the corner.

"That was a pretty thing to do," he said in a toneless voice. "He *would* have left you too."

"Stop it," she said.

"Of course it's an accident," he said. "I know that."

"Stop it," she said.

"Don't worry," he said. "There will be a certain amount of unpleasantness but I will have some photographs taken that will be very useful at the inquest. There's the testimony of the gunbearers and the driver too. You're perfectly all right."

"Stop it," she said.

"There's a hell of a lot to be done," he said. "And I'll have to send a truck off to the lake to wireless for a plane to take the three of us into Nairobi. Why didn't you poison him? That's what they do in England."

"Stop it. Stop it. Stop it," the woman cried.

Wilson looked at her with his flat blue eyes.

"I'm through now," he said. "I was a little angry. I'd begun to like your husband."

"Oh, please stop it," she said. "Please, please stop it."

"That's better," Wilson said. "Please is much better. Now I'll stop."

THE CAPITAL OF THE WORLD

Madrid is full of boys named Paco, which is the diminutive of the name Francisco, and there is a Madrid joke about a father who came to Madrid and inserted an advertisement in the personal columns of *El Liberal* which said: PACO MEET ME AT HOTEL MONTANA NOON TUESDAY ALL IS FORGIVEN PAPA and how a squadron of Guardia Civil had to be called out to disperse the eight hundred young men who answered the advertisement. But this Paco, who waited on table at the Pension Luarca, had no father to forgive him, nor anything for the father to forgive. He had two older sisters who were chambermaids at the Luarca, who had gotten their place through coming from the same small village as a former Luarca chambermaid who had proven hardworking and honest and hence given her village and its products a good name; and these sisters had paid his way on the auto-bus to Madrid and gotten him his job as an apprentice waiter. He came from a village in a part of Extramadura where conditions were incredibly primitive, food scarce, and comforts unknown and he had worked hard ever since he could remember.

He was a well built boy with very black, rather curly hair, good teeth and a skin that his sisters envied, and he had a ready and unpuzzled smile. He was fast on his feet and did his work well and he loved his sisters, who seemed beautiful and sophisticated; he loved Madrid, which was still an unbelievable place, and he loved his work which, done under bright lights, with clean linen, the wearing of evening clothes, and abundant food in the kitchen, seemed romantically beautiful.

There were from eight to a dozen other people who lived at the Luarca and ate in the dining room but for Paco, the youngest of the three waiters who served at table, the only ones who really existed were the bull fighters.

Second-rate matadors lived at that pension because the address in the Calle San Jeronimo was good, the food was excellent and the room and board was cheap. It is necessary for a bull fighter to give the appearance, if not of prosperity, at least of respectability, since decorum and dignity rank above courage as the virtues most highly prized in Spain, and bull fighters stayed at the Luarca until their last pesetas were gone. There is no record of any bull fighter having left the Luarca for a better or more expensive hotel; second-rate bull fighters never became first rate; but the descent from the

Luarca was swift since any one could stay there who was making anything at all and a bill was never presented to a guest unasked until the woman who ran the place knew that the case was hopeless.

At this time there were three full matadors living at the Luarca as well as two very good picadors, and one excellent banderillero. The Luarca was luxury for the picadors and the banderilleros who, with their families in Seville, required lodging in Madrid during the Spring season; but they were well paid and in the fixed employ of fighters who were heavily contracted during the coming season and the three of these subalterns would probably make much more apiece than any of the three matadors. Of the three matadors one was ill and trying to conceal it; one had passed his short vogue as a novelty; and the third was a coward.

The coward had at one time, until he had received a peculiarly atrocious horn wound in the lower abdomen at the start of his first season as a full matador, been exceptionally brave and remarkably skillful and he still had many of the hearty mannerisms of his days of success. He was jovial to excess and laughed constantly with and without provocation. He had, when successful, been very addicted to practical jokes but he had given them up now. They took an assurance that he did not feel. This matador had an intelligent, very open face and he carried himself with much style.

The matador who was ill was careful never to show it and was meticulous about eating a little of all the dishes that were presented at the table. He had a great many handkerchiefs which he laundered himself in his room and, lately, he had been selling his fighting suits. He had sold one, cheaply, before Christmas and another in the first week of April. They had been very expensive suits, had always been well kept and he had one more. Before he had become ill he had been a very promising, even a sensational, fighter and, while he himself could not read, he had clippings which said that in his debut in Madrid he had been better than Belmonte. He ate alone at a small table and looked up very little.

The matador who had once been a novelty was very short and brown and very dignified. He also ate alone at a separate table and he smiled very rarely and never laughed. He came from Valladolid, where the people are extremely serious, and he was a capable matador; but his style had become old-fashioned before he had ever succeeded in endearing himself to the public through his virtues, which were courage and a calm capability, and his name on a poster would draw no one to a bull ring. His novelty had been that he was so short that he could barely see over the bull's withers, but there were other short fighters, and he had never succeeded in imposing himself on the public's fancy.

Of the picadors one was a thin, hawk-faced, gray-haired man, lightly built but with legs and arms like iron, who always wore cattle-men's boots under his trousers, drank too much every evening and gazed amorously at any woman in the pension. The other was huge, dark, brown-faced, good-looking, with black hair like an Indian and enormous hands. Both were great picadors although the first was reputed to have lost much of his ability through drink and dissipation, and the second was said to be too headstrong and quarrelsome to stay with any matador more than a single season.

The banderillero was middle-aged, gray, cat-quick in spite of his years and, sitting at the table he looked a moderately prosperous business man. His legs were still good for this season, and when they should go he was intelligent and experienced enough to keep regularly employed for a long time. The difference would be that when his speed of foot would be gone he would always be frightened where now he was assured and calm in the ring and out of it.

On this evening every one had left the dining room except the hawk-faced picador who drank too much, the birthmarked-faced auctioneer of watches at the fairs and festivals of Spain, who also drank too much, and two priests from Galicia who were sitting at a corner table and drinking if not too much certainly enough. At that time wine was included in the price of the room and board at the Luarca and the waiters had just brought fresh bottles of Valdepeñas to the tables of the auctioneer, then to the picador and, finally, to the two priests.

The three waiters stood at the end of the room. It was the rule of the house that they should all remain on duty until the diners whose tables they were responsible for should all have left, but the one who served the table of the two priests had an appointment to go to an Anarcho-Syndicalist meeting and Paco had agreed to take over his table for him.

Upstairs the matador who was ill was lying face down on his bed alone. The matador who was no longer a novelty was sitting looking out of his window preparatory to walking out to the café. The matador who was a coward had the older sister of Paco in his room with him and was trying to get her to do something which she was laughingly refusing to do. This matador was saying "Come on, little savage."

"No," said the sister. "Why should I?"

"For a favor."

"You've eaten and now you want me for dessert."

"Just once. What harm can it do?"

"Leave me alone. Leave me alone, I tell you."

"It is a very little thing to do."

"Leave me alone, I tell you."

Down in the dining room the tallest of the waiters, who was overdue at the meeting, said "Look at those black pigs drink."

"That's no way to speak," said the second waiter. "They are decent clients. They do not drink too much."

"For me it is a good way to speak," said the tall one. "There are the two curses of Spain, the bulls and the priests."

"Certainly not the individual bull and the individual priest," said the second waiter.

"Yes," said the tall waiter. "Only through the individual can you attack the class. It is necessary to kill the individual bull and the individual priest. All of them. Then there are no more."

"Save it for the meeting," said the other waiter.

"Look at the barbarity of Madrid," said the tall waiter. "It is now half-past eleven o'clock and these are still guzzling."

"They only started to eat at ten," said the other waiter. "As you know there are many dishes. That wine is cheap and these have paid for it. It is not a strong wine."

"How can there be solidarity of workers with fools like you?" asked the tall waiter.

"Look," said the second waiter who was a man of fifty. "I have worked all my life. In all that remains of my life I must work. I have no complaints against work. To work is normal."

"Yes, but the lack of work kills."

"I have always worked," said the older waiter. "Go on to the meeting. There is no necessity to stay."

"You are a good comrade," said the tall waiter. "But you lack all ideology."

"*Mejor si me falta eso que el otro,*" said the older waiter (meaning it is better to lack that than work). "Go on to the *mitin.*"

Paco had said nothing. He did not yet understand politics but it always gave him a thrill to hear the tall waiter speak of the necessity for killing the priests and the Guardia Civil. The tall waiter represented to him revolution and revolution also was romantic. He himself would like to be a good catholic, a revolutionary, and have a steady job like this, while, at the same time, being a bullfighter.

"Go on to the meeting, Ignacio," he said. "I will respond for your work."

"The two of us," said the older waiter.

"There isn't enough for one," said Paco. "Go on to the meeting."

"*Pues, me voy,*" said the tall waiter. "And thanks."

In the meantime, upstairs, the sister of Paco had gotten out of the embrace of the matador as skilfully as a wrestler breaking a hold and said, now angry, "These are the hungry people. A failed bullfighter. With your ton-load of fear. If you have so much of that, use it in the ring."

"That is the way a whore talks."

"A whore is also a woman, but I am not a whore."

"You'll be one."

"Not through you."

"Leave me," said the matador who, now, repulsed and refused, felt the nakedness of his cowardice returning.

"Leave you? What hasn't left you?" said the sister. "Don't you want me to make up the bed? I'm paid to do that."

"Leave me," said the matador, his broad good-looking face

wrinkled into a contortion that was like crying. "You whore. You dirty little whore."

"Matador," she said, shutting the door. "My matador."

Inside the room the matador sat on the bed. His face still had the contortion which, in the ring, he made into a constant smile which frightened those people in the first rows of seats who knew what they were watching. "And this," he was saying aloud. "And this. And this."

He could remember when he had been good and it had only been three years before. He could remember the weight of the heavy gold-brocaded fighting jacket on his shoulders on that hot afternoon in May when his voice had still been the same in the ring as in the café, and how he sighed along the point-dipping blade at the place in the top of the shoulders where it was dusty in the short-haired black hump of muscle above the wide, wood-knocking, splintered-tipped horns that lowered as he went in to kill, and how the sword pushed in as easy as into a mound of stiff butter with the palm of his hand pushing the pommel, his left arm crossed low, his left shoulder forward, his weight on his left leg, and then his weight wasn't on his leg. His weight was on his lower belly and as the bull raised his head the horn was out of sight in him and he swung over on it twice before they pulled him off it. So now when he went in to kill, and it was seldom, he could not look at the horns and what did any whore know about what he went through before he fought? And what had they been through that laughed at him? They were all whores and they knew what they could do with it.

Down in the dining room the picador sat looking at the priests. If there were women in the room he stared at them. If there were no women he would stare with enjoyment at a foreigner, *un inglés*, but lacking women or strangers, he now stared with enjoyment and insolence at the two priests. While he stared the birthmarked auctioneer rose and folding his napkin went out, leaving over half the wine in the last bottle he had ordered. If his accounts had been paid up at the Luarca he would have finished the bottle.

The two priests did not stare back at the picador. One of them was saying, "It is ten days since I have been here waiting to see him and all day I sit in the ante-chamber and he will not receive me."

"What is there to do?"

"Nothing. What can one do? One cannot go against authority."

"I have been here for two weeks and nothing. I wait and they will not see me."

"We are from the abandoned country. When the money runs out we can return."

"To the abandoned country. What does Madrid care about Galicia? We are a poor province."

"One understands the action of our brother Basilio."

"Still I have no real confidence in the integrity of Basilio Alvarez."

"Madrid is where one learns to understand. Madrid kills Spain."

"If they would simply see one and refuse."

"No. You must be broken and worn out by waiting."

"Well, we shall see. I can wait as well as another."

At this moment the picador got to his feet, walked over to the priests' table and stood, gray-headed and hawk-faced, staring at them and smiling.

"A torero," said one priest to the other.

"And a good one," said the picador and walked out of the dining room, gray-jacketed, trim-waisted, bow-legged, in tight breeches over his high-heeled cattleman's boots that clicked on the floor as he swaggered quite steadily, smiling to himself. He lived in a small, tight, professional world of personal efficiency, nightly alcoholic triumph, and insolence. Now he lit a cigar and tilting his hat at an angle in the hallway went out to the café.

The priests left immediately after the picador, hurriedly conscious of being the last people in the dining room, and there was no one in the room now but Paco and the middle-aged waiter. They cleared the tables and carried the bottles into the kitchen.

In the kitchen was the boy who washed the dishes. He was three years older than Paco and was very cynical and bitter.

"Take this," the middle-aged waiter said, and poured out a glass of the Valdepeñas and handed it to him.

"Why not?" the boy took the glass.

"Tu, Paco?" the older waiter asked.

"Thank you," said Paco. The three of them drank.

"I will be going," said the middle-aged waiter.

"Good night," they told him.

He went out and they were alone. Paco took a napkin one of the priests had used and standing straight, his heels planted, lowered the napkin and with head following the movement, swung his arms in the motion of a slow sweeping veronica. He turned and advancing his right foot slightly, made the second pass, gained a little terrain on the imaginary bull and made a third pass, slow, perfectly timed and suave, then gathered the napkin to his waist and swung his hips away from the bull in a media-veronica.

The dishwasher, whose name was Enrique, watched him critically and sneeringly.

"How is the bull?" he said.

"Very brave," said Paco. "Look."

Standing slim and straight he made four more perfect passes, smooth, elegant and graceful.

"And the bull?" asked Enrique standing against the sink, holding his wine glass and wearing his apron.

"Still has lots of gas," said Paco.

"You make me sick," said Enrique.

"Why?"

"Look."

Enrique removed his apron and citing the imaginary bull he sculptured four perfect, languid gypsy veronicas and ended up with a rebolera that made the apron swing in a stiff arc past the bull's nose as he walked away from him.

"Look at that," he said. "And I wash dishes."

"Why?"

"Fear," said Enrique. "*Miedo*. The same fear you would have in a ring with a bull."

"No," said Paco. "I wouldn't be afraid."

"*Leche!*" said Enrique. "Every one is afraid. But a torero can control his fear so that he can work the bull. I went in an amateur fight and I was so afraid I couldn't keep from running. Every one thought it was very funny. So would you be afraid. If it wasn't for fear every bootblack in Spain would be a bullfighter. You, a country boy, would be frightened worse than I was."

"No," said Paco.

He had done it too many times in his imagination. Too many times he had seen the horns, seen the bull's wet muzzle, the ear twitching, then the head go down and the charge, the hoofs thudding and the hot bull pass him as he swung the cape, to re-charge as he swung the cape again, then again, and again, and again, to end winding the bull around him in his great media-veronica, and walk swingingly away, with bull hairs caught in the gold ornaments of his jacket from the close passes; the bull standing hypnotized and the crowd applauding. No, he would not be afraid. Others, yes. Not he. He knew he would not be afraid. Even if he ever was afraid he knew that he could do it anyway. He had confidence. "I wouldn't be afraid," he said.

Enrique said, "*Leche,*" again.

Then he said, "If we should try it?"

"How?"

"Look," said Enrique. "You think of the bull but you do not think of the horns. The bull has such force that the horns rip like a knife, they stab like a bayonet, and they kill like a club. Look," he opened a table drawer and took out two meat knives. "I will bind these to the legs of a chair. Then I will play bull for you with the chair held before my head. The knives are the horns. If you make those passes then they mean something."

"Lend me your apron," said Paco. "We'll do it in the dining room."

"No," said Enrique, suddenly not bitter. "Don't do it, Paco."

"Yes," said Paco. "I'm not afraid."

"You will be when you see the knives come."

"We'll see," said Paco. "Give me the apron."

At this time, while Enrique was binding the two heavy-bladed razor-sharp meat knives fast to the legs of the chair with two soiled napkins holding the half of each knife, wrapping them tight and then knotting them, the two chambermaids, Paco's sisters, were on their way to the cinema to see Greta Garbo in "Anna Christie." Of the two priests, one was sitting in his underwear reading his breviary and the other was wearing a nightshirt and saying the rosary. All the bullfighters except the one who was ill had made their evening appearance at the Café Fornos, where the big, dark-haired picador was playing billiards, the short, serious matador was sitting at a crowded table before a coffee and milk, along with the middle-aged banderillero and other serious workmen.

The drinking, gray-headed picador was sitting with a glass of cazalas brandy before him staring with pleasure at a table where the matador whose courage was gone sat with another matador who had renounced the sword to become a banderillero again, and two very houseworn-looking prostitutes.

The auctioneer stood on the street corner talking with friends. The tall waiter was at the Anarcho-Syndicalist meeting waiting for an opportunity to speak. The middle-aged waiter was seated on the terrace of the Café Alvarez drinking a small beer. The woman who owned the Luarca was already asleep in her bed, where she lay on her back with the bolster between her legs; big, fat, honest, clean, easy-going, very religious and never having ceased to miss or pray daily for her husband, dead, now, twenty years. In his room, alone, the matador who was ill lay face down on his bed with his mouth against a handkerchief.

Now, in the deserted dining room, Enrique tied the last knot in the napkins that bound the knives to the chair legs and lifted the chair. He pointed the legs with the knives on them forward and held the chair over his head with the two knives pointing straight ahead, one on each side of his head.

"It's heavy," he said. "Look, Paco. It is very dangerous. Don't do it." He was sweating.

Paco stood facing him, holding the apron spread, holding a fold of it bunched in each hand, thumbs up, first finger down, spread to catch the eye of the bull.

"Charge straight," he said. "Turn like a bull. Charge as many times as you want."

"How will you know when to cut the pass?" asked Enrique. "It's better to do three and then a media."

"All right," said Paco. "But come straight. Huh, torito! Come on, little bull!"

Running with head down Enrique came toward him and Paco swung the apron just ahead of the knife blade as it passed close in front of his belly and as it went by it was, to him, the real horn, white-tipped, black, smooth, and as Enrique passed him and turned to rush again it was the hot, blood-flanked mass of the bull that thudded by, then turned like a cat and came again as he swung the cape slowly. Then the bull turned and came again and, as he watched the onrushing point, he stepped his left foot two inches too far forward and the knife did not pass, but had slipped in as easily as into a wineskin and there was a hot scalding rush above and around the sudden inner rigidity of steel and Enrique shouting. "Ay! Ay! Let me get it out! Let me get it out!" and Paco slipped forward on the chair, the apron cape still held, Enrique pulling on the chair as the knife turned in him, in him, Paco.

The knife was out now and he sat on the floor in the widening warm pool.

"Put the napkin over it. Hold it!" said Enrique. "Hold it tight. I will run for the doctor. You must hold in the hemorrhage."

"There should be a rubber cup," said Paco. He had seen that used in the ring.

"I came straight," said Enrique, crying. "All I wanted was to show the danger."

"Don't worry," said Paco, his voice sounding far away. "But bring the doctor."

In the ring they lifted you and carried you, running with you, to the operating room. If the femoral artery emptied itself before you reached there they called the priest.

"Advise one of the priests," said Paco, holding the napkin tight against his lower abdomen. He could not believe that this had happened to him.

But Enrique was running down the Carrera San Jeromino to the all-night first-aid station and Paco was alone, first sitting up, then huddled over, then slumped on the floor, until it was over, feeling his life go out of him as dirty water empties from a bathtub when the plug is drawn. He was frightened and he felt faint and he tried to say an act of contrition and he remembered how it started but before he had said, as fast as he could, "Oh, my God, I am heartily sorry for having offended Thee who art worthy of all my love and I firmly resolve . . .," he felt too faint and he was lying face down on the floor and it was over very quickly. A severed femoral artery empties itself faster than you can believe.

As the doctor from the first-aid station came up the stairs accompanied by a policeman who held on to Enrique by the arm, the two sisters of Paco were still in the moving-picture palace of the Gran Via, where they were intensely disappointed in the Garbo film, which showed the great star in miserable low surroundings when they had been accustomed to see her surrounded by great luxury and brilliance. The audience disliked the film thoroughly and were protesting by whistling and stamping their feet. All the other people from the hotel were doing almost what they had been doing when the accident happened, except that the two priests had finished their devotions and were preparing for sleep, and the gray-haired picador had moved his drink over to the table with the two houseworn prostitutes. A little later he went out of the café with one of them. It was the one for whom the matador who had lost his nerve had been buying drinks.

The boy Paco had never known about any of this nor about what all these people would be doing on the next day and on other days to come. He had no idea how they really lived nor how they ended. He did not even realize they ended. He died, as the Spanish phrase has it, full of illusions. He had not had time in his life to lose any of them, nor even, at the end, to complete an act of contrition.

He had not even had time to be disappointed in the Garbo picture which disappointed all Madrid for a week.

THE SNOWS OF KILIMANJARO

Kilimanjaro is a snow covered mountain 19,710 feet high, and it is said to be the highest mountain in Africa. Its western summit is called the Masai "Ngàje Ngài," the House of God. Close to the western summit there is the dried and frozen carcass of a leopard. No one has explained what the leopard was seeking at that altitude.

"The marvellous thing is that it's painless," he said. "That's how you know when it starts."

"Is it really?"

"Absolutely. I'm awfully sorry about the odor though. That must bother you."

"Don't! Please don't."

"Look at them," he said. "Now is it sight or is it scent that brings them like that?"

The cot the man lay on was in the wide shade of a mimosa tree and as he looked out past the shade onto the glare of the plain there were three of the big birds squatted obscenely, while in the sky a dozen more sailed, making quick-moving shadows as they passed.

"They've been there since the day the truck broke down," he said. "Today's the first time any have lit on the ground. I watched the way they sailed very carefully at first in case I ever wanted to use them in a story. That's funny now."

"I wish you wouldn't," she said.

"I'm only talking," he said. "It's much easier if I talk. But I don't want to bother you."

"You know it doesn't bother me," she said. "It's that I've gotten so very nervous not being able to do anything. I think we might make it as easy as we can until the plane comes."

"Or until the plane doesn't come."

"Please tell me what I can do. There must be something I can do."

"You can take the leg off and that might stop it, though I doubt it. Or you can shoot me. You're a good shot now. I taught you to shoot didn't I?"

"Please don't talk that way. Couldn't I read to you?"

"Read what?"

"Anything in the book bag that we haven't read."

"I can't listen to it," he said. "Talking is the easiest. We quarrel and that makes the time pass."

"I don't quarrel. I never want to quarrel. Let's not quarrel any more. No matter how nervous we get. Maybe they will be back with another truck today. Maybe the plane will come."

"I don't want to move," the man said. "There is no sense in moving now except to make it easier for you."

"That's cowardly."

"Can't you let a man die as comfortably as he can without calling him names? What's the use of slanging me?"

"You're not going to die."

"Don't be silly. I'm dying now. Ask those bastards." He looked over to where the huge, filthy birds sat, their naked heads sunk in the hunched feathers. A fourth planed down, to run quick-legged and then waddle slowly toward the others.

"They are around every camp. You never notice them. You can't die if you don't give up."

"Where did you read that? You're such a bloody fool."

"You might think about some one else."

"For Christ's sake," he said, "That's been my trade."

He lay then and was quiet for a while and looked across the heat shimmer of the plain to the edge of the bush. There were a few Tommies that showed minute and white against the yellow and, far off, he saw a herd of zebra, white against the green of the bush. This was a pleasant camp under big trees against a hill, with good water, and close by, a nearly dry water hole where sand grouse flighted in the mornings.

"Wouldn't you like me to read?" she asked. She was sitting on a canvas chair beside his cot. "There's a breeze coming up."

"No thanks."

"Maybe the truck will come."

"I don't give a damn about the truck."

"I do."

"You give a damn about so many things that I don't."

"Not so many, Harry."

"What about a drink?"

"It's supposed to be bad for you. It said in Black's to avoid all alcohol. You shouldn't drink."

"Molo!" he shouted.

"Yes Bwana."

"Bring whiskey-soda."

"Yes Bwana."

"You shouldn't," she said. "That's what I mean by giving up. It says it's bad for you. I know it's bad for you."

"No," he said. "It's good for me."

So now it was all over, he thought. So now he would never have a chance to finish it. So this was the way it ended in a bickering over a drink. Since the gangrene started in his right leg he had no pain and with the pain the horror had gone and all he felt now was a great tiredness and anger that this was the end of it. For this, that now was coming, he had very little curiosity. For years it had obsessed him; but now it meant nothing in itself. It was strange how easy being tired enough made it.

Now he would never write the things that he had saved to write until he knew enough to write them well. Well, he would not have to fail at trying to write them either. Maybe you could never write them, and that was why you put them off and delayed the starting. Well he would never know, now.

"I wish we'd never come," the woman said. She was looking at him holding the glass and biting her lip. "You never would have gotten anything like this in Paris. You always said you loved Paris. We could have stayed in Paris or gone anywhere. I'd have gone anywhere. I said I'd go anywhere you wanted. If you wanted to shoot we could have gone shooting in Hungary and been comfortable."

"Your bloody money," he said.

"That's not fair," she said. "It was always yours as much as mine. I left everything and I went wherever you wanted to go and I've done what you wanted to do. But I wish we'd never come here."

"You said you loved it."

"I did when you were all right. But now I hate it. I don't see why that had to happen to your leg. What have we done to have that happen to us?"

"I suppose what I did was to forget to put iodine on it when I first scratched it. Then I didn't pay any attention to it because I never infect. Then, later, when it got bad, it was probably using that weak carbolic solution when the other antiseptics ran out that paralzyed the minute blood vessels and started the gangrene." He looked at her, "What else?"

"I don't mean that."

"If we would have hired a good mechanic instead of a half baked kikuyu driver, he would have checked the oil and never burned out that bearing in the truck."

"I don't mean that."

"If you hadn't left your own people, your goddamned Old Westbury, Saratoga, Palm Beach people to take me on——"

"Why, I loved you. That's not fair. I love you now. I'll always love you. Don't you love me?"

"No," said the man. "I don't think so. I never have."

"Harry, what are you saying? You're out of your head."

"No. I haven't any head to go out of."

"Don't drink that," she said. "Darling, please don't drink that. We have to do everything we can."

"You do it," he said. "I'm tired."

Now in his mind he saw a railway station at Karagatch and he was standing with his pack and that was the headlight of the Simplon-Orient cutting the dark now and he was leaving Thrace then after the retreat. That was one of the things he had saved to write, with, in the morning at breakfast, looking out the window and seeing snow on the mountains in Bulgaria and Nansen's Secretary asking the old man if it were snow and the old man looking at it and saying, No, that's not snow. It's too early for snow. And the Secretary repeating to the other girls, No, you see. It's not snow and them all saying, It's not snow we were mistaken. But it was the snow all right and he sent them on into it when he evolved exchange of populations. And it was snow they tramped along in until they died that winter.

It was snow too that fell all Christmas week that year up in the Gauertal, that year they lived in the woodcutter's house with the big square porcelain stove that filled half the room, and they slept on mattresses filled with beech leaves, the time the deserter came with his feet bloody in the snow. He said the police were right behind him and they gave him woolen socks and held the gendarmes talking until the tracks had drifted over.

In Schrunz, on Christmas day, the snow was so bright it hurt your eyes when you looked out from the weinstube and saw every one coming home from church. That was where they walked up the sleigh-smoothed urine-yellowed road along the river with the steep pine hills, skis heavy on the shoulder, and where they ran that great run down the glacier above the Madlener-haus, the snow as smooth to see as cake frosting and as light as powder and he remembered the noiseless rush the speed made as you dropped down like a bird.

They were snow-bound a week in the Madlener-haus that time in the blizzard playing cards in the smoke by the lantern light and the stakes were higher all the time as Herr Lent lost more. Finally he lost it all. Everything, the skischule money and all the season's profit and then his capital. He could see him with his long nose, picking up the cards and then opening, "Sans Voir." There was always gambling then. When there was no snow you gambled and when there was too much you gambled. He thought of all the time in his life he had spent gambling.

But he had never written a line of that, nor of that cold, bright Christmas day with the mountains showing across the plain that Gardner had flown across the lines to bomb the Austrian officers' leave train, machine-gunning them as they scattered and ran. He remembered Gardner afterwards coming into the mess and starting to tell about it. And how quiet it got and then somebody saying, "You bloody murderous bastard."

Those were the same Austrians they killed then that he skied with later. No not the same. Hans, that he skied with all that year, had been in the Kaiser-Jägers and when they went hunting hares together up the little valley above the saw-mill they had talked of the fighting on Pasubio and of the attack on Pertica and Asalone and he had never written a word of that. Nor of Monte Corno, nor the Siete Commum, nor of Arsiedo.

How many winters had he lived in the Voralberg and the Arlberg? It was four and then he remembered the man who had the fox to sell when they had walked into Bludenz, that time to buy presents, and the cherry-pit taste of good kirsch, the fast-slipping rush of running powder-snow on crust, singing "Hi! Ho! said Rolly!" as you ran down the last stretch to the steep drop, taking it straight, then running the orchard in three turns and out across the ditch and onto the icy road behind the inn. Knocking your bindings loose, kicking the skis free and leaning them up against the wooden wall of the inn, the lamplight coming from the window, where inside, in the smoky, new-wine smelling warmth, they were playing the accordion.

"Where did we stay in Paris?" he asked the woman who was sitting by him in a canvas chair, now, in Africa.

"At the Crillon. You know that."

"Why do I know that?"

"That's where we always stayed."

"No. Not always."

"There and at the Pavillon Henri-Quatre in St. Germain. You said you loved it there."

"Love is a dunghill," said Harry. "And I'm the cock that gets on it to crow."

"If you have to go away," she said, "is it absolutely necessary to kill off everything you leave behind? I mean do you have to take away everything? Do you have to kill your horse, and your wife and burn your saddle and your armour?"

"Yes," he said. "Your damned money was my armour. My Swift and my Armour."

"Don't."

"All right. I'll stop that. I don't want to hurt you."

"It's a little bit late now."

"All right then. I'll go on hurting you. It's more amusing. The only thing I ever really liked to do with you I can't do now."

"No, that's not true. You liked to do many things and everything you wanted to do I did."

"Oh, for Christ sake stop bragging, will you?"

He looked at her and saw her crying.

"Listen," he said. "Do you think that it is fun to do this? I don't know why I'm doing it. It's trying to kill to keep yourself alive, I imagine. I was all right when we started talking. I didn't mean to start this, and now I'm crazy as a coot and being as cruel to you as I can be. Don't pay any attention, darling, to what I say. I love you, really. You know I love you. I've never loved any one else the way I love you."

He slipped into the familiar lie he made his bread and butter by.

"You're sweet to me."

"You bitch," he said. "You rich bitch. That's poetry. I'm full of poetry now. Rot and poetry. Rotten poetry."

"Stop it. Harry, why do you have to turn into a devil now?"

"I don't like to leave anything," the man said. "I don't like to leave things behind."

* * *

It was evening now and he had been asleep. The sun was gone behind the hill and there was a shadow all across the plain and the small animals were feeding close to camp; quick dropping heads and switching tails, he watched them keeping well out away from the bush now. The birds no longer waited on the ground. They were all perched heavily in a tree. There were many more of them. His personal boy was sitting by the bed.

"Memsahib's gone to shoot," the boy said. "Does Bwana want?"

"Nothing."

She had gone to kill a piece of meat and, knowing how he liked to watch the game, she had gone well away so she would not disturb this little pocket of the plain that he could see. She was always thoughtful, he thought. On anything she knew about, or had read, or that she had ever heard.

It was not her fault that when he went to her he was already over. How could a woman know that you meant nothing that you said; that you spoke only from habit and to be comfortable? After he no longer meant what he said, his lies were more successful with women than when he had told them the truth.

It was not so much that he lied as that there was no truth to tell. He had had his life and it was over and then he went on living it again with different people and more money, with the best of the same places, and some new ones.

You kept from thinking and it was all marvellous. You were equipped with good insides so that you did not go to pieces that way, the way most of them had, and you made an attitude that you cared nothing for the work you used to do, now that you could no longer do it. But, in yourself, you said that you would write about these people; about the very rich; that you were really not of them but a spy in their country; that you would leave it and write of it and for once it would be written by some one who knew what he was writing of. But he would never do it, because each day of not writing, of comfort, of being that which he despised, dulled his ability and softened his will to work so that, finally, he did no work at all. The people he knew now were all much more comfortable when he did not work. Africa was where he had been happiest in the good time of his life, so he had come out here to start again. They had made this safari with the minimum of comfort. There was no hardship; but there was no luxury and he had thought that he could get back into training that way. That in some way he could work the fat off his soul the way a fighter went into the mountains to work and train in order to burn it out of his body.

She had liked it. She said she loved it. She loved anything that was exciting, that involved a change of scene, where there were new people and where things were pleasant. And he had felt the illusion of returning strength of will to work. Now if this was how it ended, and he knew it was, he must not turn like some snake biting itself because its back was broken. It wasn't this woman's fault. If it had not been she it would have been another. If he lived by a lie he should try to die by it. He heard a shot beyond the hill.

She shot very well this good, this rich bitch, this kindly caretaker and destroyer of his talent. Nonsense. He had destroyed his talent himself. Why should he blame this woman because she kept him well? He had destroyed his talent by not using it, by betrayals of himself and what he believed in, by drinking so much that he blunted the edge of his perceptions, by laziness, by sloth, and by snobbery, by pride and by prejudice, by hook and by crook. What was this? A catalogue of old books? What was his talent anyway? It was a talent all right but instead of using it, he had traded on it. It was never what he had done, but always what he could do. And he had chosen to make his living with something else instead of a pen or a pencil. It was strange, too, wasn't it, that when he fell in love with another woman, that woman should always have more money than the last one? But when he no longer was in love, when he was only lying, as to this woman, now, who had the most money of all, who had all the money there was, who had had a husband and children, who had taken lovers and been dissatisfied with them, and who loved him dearly as a writer, as a man, as a companion and as a proud possession; it was strange that when he did not love her at all and was lying, that he should be able to give her more for her money than when he had really loved.

We must all be cut out for what we do, he thought. However you make your living is where your talent lies. He had sold vitality, in one form or another, all his life and when your affections are not too involved you give much better value for the money. He had found that out but he would never write that, now, either. No, he would not write that, although it was well worth writing.

Now she came in sight, walking across the open toward the camp. She was wearing jodhpurs and carrying her rifle. The two boys had a Tommie slung and they were coming along behind her. She was still a good-looking woman, he thought, and she had a pleasant body. She had a great talent and appreciation for the bed, she was not pretty, but he liked her face, she read enormously, liked to ride and shoot and, certainly, she drank too much. Her husband had died when she was still a comparatively young woman and for a while she had devoted herself to her two just-grown children, who did not need her and were embarrassed at having her about, to her stable of horses, to books, and to bottles. She liked to read in the evening before dinner and she drank Scotch and soda while she read. By dinner she was fairly drunk and after a bottle of wine at dinner she was usually drunk enough to sleep.

That was before the lovers. After she had the lovers she did not drink so much because she did not have to be drunk to sleep. But the lovers bored her. She had been married to a man who had never bored her and these people bored her very much.

Then one of her two children was killed in a plane crash and after that was over she did not want the lovers, and drink being no anæsthetic she had to make another life. Suddenly, she had been acutely frightened of being alone. But she wanted some one that she respected with her.

It had begun very simply. She liked what he wrote and she had always envied the life he led. She thought he did exactly what he wanted to. The steps by which she had acquired him and the way in which she had finally fallen in love with him were all part of a regular progression in which she had built herself a new life and he had traded away what remained of his old life.

He had traded it for security, for comfort too, there was no denying that, and for what else? He did not know. She would have bought him anything he wanted. He knew that. She was a damned nice woman too. He would as soon be in bed with her as any one; rather with her, because she was richer, because she was very pleasant and appreciative and because she never made scenes. And now this life that she had built again was coming to a term because he had not used iodine two weeks ago when a thorn had scratched his knee as they moved forward trying to photograph a herd of waterbuck standing, their heads up, peering while their nostrils searched the air, their ears spread wide to hear the first noise that would send them rushing into the bush. They had bolted, too, before he got the picture.

Here she came now.

He turned his head on the cot to look toward her. "Hello," he said.

"I shot a Tommy ram," she told him. "He'll make you good broth and I'll have them mash some potatoes with the Klim. How do you feel?"

"Much better."

"Isn't that lovely? You know I thought perhaps you would. You were sleeping when I left."

"I had a good sleep. Did you walk far?"

"No. Just around behind the hill. I made quite a good shot on the Tommy."

"You shoot marvellously, you know."

"I love it. I've loved Africa. Really. If *you're* all right it's the most fun that I've ever had. You don't know the fun it's been to shoot with you. I've loved the country."

"I love it too."

"Darling, you don't know how marvellous it is to see you feeling better. I couldn't stand it when you felt that way. You won't talk to me like that again, will you? Promise me?"

"No," he said. "I don't remember what I said."

"You don't have to destroy me. Do you? I'm only a middle-aged woman who loves you and wants to do what you want to do. I've been destroyed two or three times already. You wouldn't want to destroy me again, would you?"

"I'd like to destroy you a few times in bed," he said.

"Yes. That's the good destruction. That's the way we're made to be destroyed. The plane will be here tomorrow."

"How do you know?"

"I'm sure. It's bound to come. The boys have the wood all ready and the grass to make the smudge. I went down and looked at it again today. There's plenty of room to land and we have the smudges ready at both ends."

"What makes you think it will come tomorrow?"

"I'm sure it will. It's overdue now. Then, in town, they will fix up your leg and then we will have some good destruction. Not that dreadful talking kind."

"Should we have a drink? The sun is down."

"Do you think you should?"

"I'm having one."

"We'll have one together. *Molo, letti dui whiskey-soda!*" she called.

"You'd better put on your mosquito boots," he told her.

"I'll wait till I bathe . . ."

While it grew dark they drank and just before it was dark and there was no longer enough light to shoot, a hyena crossed the open on his way around the hill.

"That bastard crosses there every night," the man said. "Every night for two weeks."

"He's the one makes the noise at night. I don't mind it. They're a filthy animal though."

Drinking together, with no pain now except the discomfort of lying in the one position, the boys lighting a fire, its shadow jumping on the tents, he could feel the return of acquiescence in this life of pleasant surrender. She *was* very good to him. He had been cruel and unjust in the afternoon. She was a fine woman, marvellous really. And just then it occurred to him that he was going to die.

It came with a rush; not as a rush of water nor of wind; but of a sudden evil-smelling emptiness and the odd thing was that the hyena slipped lightly along the edge of it.

"What is it, Harry?" she asked him.

"Nothing," he said. "You had better move over to the other side. To windward."

"Did Molo change the dressing?"

"Yes. I'm just using the boric now."

"How do you feel?"

"A little wobbly."

"I'm going in to bathe," she said. "I'll be right out. I'll eat with you and then we'll put the cot in."

So, he said to himself, we did well to stop the quarrelling. He had never quarrelled much with this woman, while with the women that he loved he had quarrelled so much they had finally, always, with the corrosion of the quarrelling, killed what they had together. He had loved too much, demanded too much, and he wore it all out.

He thought about alone in Constantinople that time, having quarrelled in Paris before he had gone out. He had whored the whole time and then, when that was over, and he had failed to kill his loneliness, but only made it worse, he had written her, the first one, the one who left him, a letter telling her how he had never been able to kill it. . . . How when he thought he saw her outside the Regence one time it made him go all faint and sick inside, and that he would follow a woman who looked like her in some way, along the Boulevard, afraid to see it was not she, afraid to lose the feeling it gave him. How every one he had slept with had only made him miss her more. How what she had done could never matter since he knew he could not cure himself of loving her. He wrote this letter at the Club, cold sober, and mailed it to New York asking her to write him at the office in Paris. That seemed safe. And that night missing her so much it made him feel hollow sick inside, he wandered up past Taxim's, picked a girl up and took her out to supper. He had gone to a place to dance with her afterward, she danced badly, and left her for a hot Armenian slut, that swung her belly against him so it almost scalded. He took her away from a British gunner subaltern after a row. The gunner asked him outside and they fought in the street on the cobbles in the dark. He'd hit him twice, hard on the side of the jaw and when he didn't go down he knew he was in for a fight. The gunner hit him in the body, then beside his eye. He swung with his left again and landed and the gunner fell on him and grabbed his coat and tore the sleeve off and he clubbed him twice behind the ear and then smashed him with his right as he pushed him away. When the gunner went down his head hit first and he ran with the girl because they heard the M. P.'s coming. They got into a taxi and drove out to Rimmily Hissa along the Bosphorus, and around, and back in the cool night and went to bed and she felt as over-ripe as she looked but smooth, rose-

petal, syrupy, smooth-bellied, big-breasted and needed no pillow under her buttocks, and he left her before she was awake looking blousy enough in the first daylight and turned up at the Pera Palace with a black eye, carrying his coat because one sleeve was missing.

That same night he left for Anatolia and he remembered, later on that trip, riding all day through fields of the poppies that they raised for opium and how strange it made you feel, finally, and all the distances seemed wrong, to where they had made the attack with the newly arrived Constantine officers, that did not know a god-damned thing, and the artillery had fired into the troops and the British observer had cried like a child.

That was the day he'd first seen dead men wearing white ballet skirts and upturned shoes with pompons on them. The Turks had come steadily and lumpily and he had seen the skirted men running and the officers shooting into them and running then themselves and he and the British observer had run too until his lungs ached and his mouth was full of the taste of pennies and they stopped behind some rocks and there were the Turks coming as lumpily as ever. Later he had seen the things that he could never think of and later still he had seen much worse. So when he got back to Paris that time he could not talk about it or stand to have it mentioned. And there in the café as he passed was that American poet with a pile of saucers in front of him and a stupid look on his potato face talking about the Dada movement with a Roumanian who said his name was Tristan Tzara, who always wore a monocle and had a headache, and, back at the apartment with his wife that now he loved again, the quarrel all over, the madness all over, glad to be home, the office sent his mail up to the flat. So then the letter in answer to the one he'd written came in on a platter one morning and when he saw the handwriting he went cold all over and tried to slip the letter underneath another. But his wife said, "Who is that letter from, dear?" and that was the end of the beginning of that.

He remembered the good times with them all, and the quarrels. They always picked the finest places to have the quarrels. And why had they always quarrelled when he was feeling best? He

had never written any of that because, at first, he never wanted to
hurt any one and then it seemed as though there was enough to
write without it. But he had always thought that he would write
it finally. There was so much to write. He had seen the world
change; not just the events; although he had seen many of them
and had watched the people, but he had seen the subtler change
and he could remember how the people were at different times.
He had been in it and he had watched it and it was his duty to
write of it; but now he never would.

"How do you feel?" she said. She had come out from the tent
now after her bath.

"All right."

"Could you eat now?" He saw Molo behind her with the folding table and the other boy with the dishes.

"I want to write," he said.

"You ought to take some broth to keep your strength up."

"I'm going to die tonight," he said. "I don't need my strength
up."

"Don't be melodramatic, Harry, please," she said.

"Why don't you use your nose? I'm rotted half way up my thigh
now. What the hell should I fool with broth for? Molo bring
whiskey-soda."

"Please take the broth," she said gently.

"All right."

The broth was too hot. He had to hold it in the cup until it
cooled enough to take it and then he just got it down without
gagging.

"You're a fine woman," he said. "Don't pay any attention to me."

She looked at him with her well-known, well-loved face from
Spur and *Town and Country,* only a little the worse for drink,
only a little the worse for bed, but *Town and Country* never
showed those good breasts and those useful thighs and those lightly
small-of-back-caressing hands, and as he looked and saw her well
known pleasant smile, he felt death come again. This time there
was no rush. It was a puff, as of a wind that makes a candle
flicker and the flame go tall.

"They can bring my net out later and hang it from the tree and build the fire up. I'm not going in the tent tonight. It's not worth moving. It's a clear night. There won't be any rain."

So this was how you died, in whispers that you did not hear. Well, there would be no more quarrelling. He could promise that. The one experience that he had never had he was not going to spoil now. He probably would. You spoiled everything. But perhaps he wouldn't.

"You can't take dictation, can you?"

"I never learned," she told him.

"That's all right."

There wasn't time, of course, although it seemed as though it telescoped so that you might put it all into one paragraph if you could get it right.

There was a log house, chinked white with mortar, on a hill above the lake. There was a bell on a pole by the door to call the people in to meals. Behind the house were fields and behind the fields was the timber. A line of lombardy poplars ran from the house to the dock. Other poplars ran along the point. A road went up to the hills along the edge of the timber and along that road he picked blackberries. Then that log house was burned down and all the guns that had been on deer foot racks above the open fire place were burned and afterwards their barrels, with the lead melted in the magazines, and the stocks burned away, lay out on the heap of ashes that were used to make lye for the big iron soap kettles, and you asked Grandfather if you could have them to play with, and he said, no. You see they were his guns still and he never bought any others. Nor did he hunt any more. The house was rebuilt in the same place out of lumber now and painted white and from its porch you saw the poplars and the lake beyond; but there were never any more guns. The barrels of the guns that had hung on the deer feet on the wall of the log house lay out there on the heap of ashes and no one ever touched them.

In the Black Forest, after the war, we rented a trout stream and there were two ways to walk to it. One was down the valley from Triberg and around the valley road in the shade of the trees that bordered the white road, and then up a side road that went up through the hills past many small farms, with the big Schwarz-wald houses, until that road crossed the stream. That was where our fishing began.

The other way was to climb steeply up to the edge of the woods and then go across the top of the hills through the pine woods, and then out to the edge of a meadow and down across this meadow to the bridge. There were birches along the stream and it was not big, but narrow, clear and fast, with pools where it had cut under the roots of the birches. At the Hotel in Triberg the proprietor had a fine season. It was very pleasant and we were all great friends. The next year came the inflation and the money he had made the year before was not enough to buy supplies to open the hotel and he hanged himself.

You could dictate that, but you could not dictate the Place Contrescarpe where the flower sellers dyed their flowers in the street and the dye ran over the paving where the autobus started and the old men and the women, always drunk on wine and bad marc; and the children with their noses running in the cold; the smell of dirty sweat and poverty and drunkenness at the Café des Amateurs and the whores at the Bal Musette they lived above. The Concierge who entertained the trooper of the Garde Repub-licaine in her loge, his horse-hair-plumed helmet on a chair. The locataire across the hall whose husband was a bicycle racer and her joy that morning at the Crémerie when she had opened L'Auto and seen where he placed third in Paris-Tours, his first big race. She had blushed and laughed and then gone upstairs crying with the yellow sporting paper in her hand. The husband of the woman who ran the Bal Musette drove a taxi and when he, Harry, had to take an early plane the husband knocked upon the door to wake him and they each drank a glass of white wine at the zinc of the bar before they started. He knew his neighbors in that quarter then because they all were poor.

Around that Place there were two kinds; the drunkards and the sportifs. The drunkards killed their poverty that way; the sportifs took it out in exercise. They were the descendants of the Com-munards and it was no struggle for them to know their politics.

They knew who had shot their fathers, their relatives, their brothers, and their friends when the Versailles troops came in and took the town after the Commune and executed any one they could catch with calloused hands, or who wore a cap, or carried any other sign he was a working man. And in that poverty, and in that quarter across the street from a Boucherie Chevaline and a wine co-operative he had written the start of all he was to do. There never was another part of Paris that he loved like that, the sprawling trees, the old white plastered houses painted brown below, the long green of the autobus in that round square, the purple flower dye upon the paving, the sudden drop down the hill of the rue Cardinal Lemoine to the River, and the other way the narrow crowded world of the rue Mouffetard. The street that ran up toward the Pantheon and the other that he always took with the bicycle, the only asphalted street in all that quarter, smooth under the tires, with the high narrow houses and the cheap tall hotel where Paul Verlaine had died. There were only two rooms in the apartments where they lived and he had a room on the top floor of that hotel that cost him sixty francs a month where he did his writing, and from it he could see the roofs and chimney pots and all the hills of Paris.

From the apartment you could only see the wood and coal man's place. He sold wine too, bad wine. The golden horse's head outside the Boucherie Chevaline where the carcasses hung yellow gold and red in the open window, and the green painted co-operative where they bought their wine; good wine and cheap. The rest was plaster walls and the windows of the neighbors. The neighbors who, at night, when some one lay drunk in the street, moaning and groaning in that typical French ivresse that you were propaganded to believe did not exist, would open their windows and then the murmur of talk.

"Where is the policeman? When you don't want him the bugger is always there. He's sleeping with some concierge. Get the Agent." Till some one threw a bucket of water from a window and the moaning stopped. "What's that? Water. Ah, that's intelligent." And the windows shutting. Marie, his femme de menage, protesting against the eight-hour day saying, "If a husband works

until six he gets only a little drunk on the way home and does not waste too much. If he works only until five he is drunk every night and one has no money. It is the wife of the working man who suffers from this shortening of hours."

"Wouldn't you like some more broth?" the woman asked him now.

"No, thank you very much. It is awfully good."

"Try just a little."

"I would like a whiskey-soda."

"It's not good for you."

"No. It's bad for me. Cole Porter wrote the words and the music. This knowledge that you're going mad for me."

"You know I like you to drink."

"Oh yes. Only it's bad for me."

When she goes, he thought. I'll have all I want. Not all I want but all there is. Ayee he was tired. Too tired. He was going to sleep a little while. He lay still and death was not there. It must have gone around another street. It went in pairs, on bicycles, and moved absolutely silently on the pavements.

No, he had never written about Paris. Not the Paris that he cared about. But what about the rest that he had never written?

What about the ranch and the silvered gray of the sage brush, the quick, clear water in the irrigation ditches, and the heavy green of the alfalfa. The trail went up into the hills and the cattle in the summer were shy as deer. The bawling and the steady noise and slow moving mass raising a dust as you brought them down in the fall. And behind the mountains, the clear sharpness of the peak in the evening light and, riding down along the trail in the moonlight, bright across the valley. Now he remembered coming down through the timber in the dark holding the horse's tail when you could not see and all the stories that he meant to write.

About the half-wit chore boy who was left at the ranch that time and told not to let any one get any hay, and that old bastard from the Forks who had beaten the boy when he had worked for him stopping to get some feed. The boy refusing and the old man saying he would beat him again. The boy got the rifle from the kitchen and shot him when he tried to come into the barn and when they came back to the ranch he'd been dead a week, frozen in the corral, and the dogs had eaten part of him. But what was left you packed on a sled wrapped in a blanket and roped on and you got the boy to help you haul it, and the two of you took it out over the road on skis, and sixty miles down to town to turn the boy over. He having no idea that he would be arrested. Thinking he had done his duty and that you were his friend and he would be rewarded. He'd helped to haul the old man in so everybody could know how bad the old man had been and how he'd tried to steal some feed that didn't belong to him, and when the sheriff put the handcuffs on the boy he couldn't believe it. Then he'd started to cry. That was one story he had saved to write. He knew at least twenty good stories from out there and he had never written one. Why?

"You tell them why," he said.

"Why what, dear?"

"Why nothing."

She didn't drink so much, now, since she had him. But if he lived he would never write about her, he knew that now. Nor about any of them. The rich were dull and they drank too much, or they played too much backgammon. They were dull and they were repetitious. He remembered poor Julian and his romantic awe of them and how he had started a story once that began, "The very rich are different from you and me." And how some one had said to Julian, Yes, they have more money. But that was not humorous to Julian. He thought they were a special glamorous race and when he found they weren't it wrecked him just as much as any other thing that wrecked him.

He had been contemptuous of those who wrecked. You did not have to like it because you understood it. He could beat anything, he thought, because no thing could hurt him if he did not care.

All right. Now he would not care for death. One thing he had always dreaded was the pain. He could stand pain as well as any man, until it went on too long, and wore him out, but here he had something that had hurt frightfully and just when he had felt it breaking him, the pain had stopped.

He remembered long ago when Williamson, the bombing officer, had been hit by a stick bomb some one in a German patrol had thrown as he was coming in through the wire that night and, screaming, had begged every one to kill him. He was a fat man, very brave, and a good officer, although addicted to fantastic shows. But that night he was caught in the wire, with a flare lighting him up and his bowels spilled out into the wire, so when they brought him in, alive, they had to cut him loose. Shoot me, Harry. For Christ sake shoot me. They had had an argument one time about our Lord never sending you anything you could not bear and some one's theory had been that meant that at a certain time the pain passed you out automatically. But he had always remembered Williamson, that night. Nothing passed out Williamson until he gave him all his morphine tablets that he had always saved to use himself and then they did not work right away.

Still this now, that he had, was very easy; and if it was no worse as it went on there was nothing to worry about. Except that he would rather be in better company.

He thought a little about the company that he would like to have.

No, he thought, when everything you do, you do too long, and do too late, you can't expect to find the people still there. The people all are gone. The party's over and you are with your hostess now.

I'm getting as bored with dying as with everything else, he thought.

"It's a bore," he said out loud.

"What is, my dear?"

"Anything you do too bloody long."

He looked at her face between him and the fire. She was leaning back in the chair and the firelight shone on her pleasantly lined face and he could see that she was sleepy. He heard the hyena make a noise just outside the range of the fire.

"I've been writing," he said. "But I got tired."

"Do you think you will be able to sleep?"

"Pretty sure. Why don't you turn in?"

"I like to sit here with you."

"Do you feel anything strange?" he asked her.

"No. Just a little sleepy."

"I do," he said.

He had just felt death come by again.

"You know the only thing I've never lost is curiosity," he said to her.

"You've never lost anything. You're the most complete man I've ever known."

"Christ," he said. "How little a woman knows. What is that? Your intuition?"

Because, just then, death had come and rested its head on the foot of the cot and he could smell its breath.

"Never believe any of that about a scythe and a skull," he told her. "It can be two bicycle policemen as easily, or be a bird. Or it can have a wide snout like a hyena."

It had moved up on him now, but it had no shape any more. It simply occupied space.

"Tell it to go away."

It did not go away but moved a little closer.

"You've got a hell of a breath," he told it. "You stinking bastard."

It moved up closer to him still and now he could not speak to it, and when it saw he could not speak it came a little closer, and now he tried to send it away without speaking, but it moved in on him so its weight was all upon his chest, and while it crouched there and he could not move, or speak, he heard the woman say, "Bwana is asleep now. Take the cot up very gently and carry it into the tent."

He could not speak to tell her to make it go away and it crouched now, heavier, so he could not breathe. And then, while they lifted the cot, suddenly it was all right and the weight went from his chest.

It was morning and had been morning for some time and he

heard the plane. It showed very tiny and then made a wide circle and the boys ran out and lit the fires, using kerosene, and piled on grass so there were two big smudges at each end of the level place and the morning breeze blew them toward the camp and the plane circled twice more, low this time, and then glided down and levelled off and landed smoothly and, coming walking toward him, was old Compton in slacks, a tweed jacket and a brown felt hat.

"What's the matter, old cock?" Compton said.

"Bad leg," he told him. "Will you have some breakfast?"

"Thanks. I'll just have some tea. It's the Puss Moth you know. I won't be able to take the Memsahib. There's only room for one. Your lorry is on the way."

Helen had taken Compton aside and was speaking to him. Compton came back more cheery than ever.

"We'll get you right in," he said. "I'll be back for the Mem. Now I'm afraid I'll have to stop at Arusha to refuel. We'd better get going."

"What about the tea?"

"I don't really care about it you know."

The boys had picked up the cot and carried it around the green tents and down along the rock and out onto the plain and along past the smudges that were burning brightly now, the grass all consumed, and the wind fanning the fire, to the little plane. It was difficult getting him in, but once in he lay back in the leather seat, and the leg was stuck straight out to one side of the seat where Compton sat. Compton started the motor and got in. He waved to Helen and to the boys and, as the clatter moved into the old familiar roar, they swung around with Compie watching for wart-hog holes and roared, bumping, along the stretch between the fires and with the last bump rose and he saw them all standing below, waving, and the camp beside the hill, flattening now, and the plain spreading, clumps of trees, and the bush flattening, while the game trails ran now smoothly to the dry waterholes, and there was a new water that he had never known of. The zebra, small rounded backs now, and the wildebeeste, big-headed dots seeming to climb as they moved in long fingers across the plain, now scattering as the shadow came toward them, they were tiny now, and the movement had no gallop, and the plain as far as you could see, gray-yellow now and ahead old Compie's tweed back and the brown felt hat. Then they were over the first hills and the wildebeeste were trailing up them, and then they were over mountains with sudden depths of green-rising forest and the solid bamboo slopes, and then the heavy forest again, sculptured into peaks and hollows until they crossed, and hills sloped down and then another plain, hot now, and purple brown, bumpy with heat and Compie looking back to see how he was riding. Then there were other mountains dark ahead.

And then instead of going on to Arusha they turned left, he evidently figured that they had the gas, and looking down he saw a pink sifting cloud, moving over the ground, and in the air, like the first snow in a blizzard, that comes from nowhere, and he knew the locusts were coming up from the South. Then they began to climb and they were going to the East it seemed, and then it darkened and they were in a storm, the rain so thick it seemed like flying through a waterfall, and then they were out and Compie turned his head and grinned and pointed and there, ahead, all he could see, as wide as all the world, great, high, and unbelievably white in the sun, was the square top of Kilimanjaro. And then he knew that there was where he was going.

Just then the hyena stopped whimpering in the night and started to make a strange, human, almost crying sound. The woman heard it and stirred uneasily. She did not wake. In her dream she was at the house on Long Island and it was the night before her daughter's début. Somehow her father was there and he had been very rude. Then the noise the hyena made was so loud she woke and for a moment she did not know where she was and she was very afraid. Then she took the flashlight and shone it on the other cot that they had carried in after Harry had gone to sleep. She could see his bulk under the mosquito bar but somehow he had gotten his leg out and it hung down alongside the cot. The dressings had all come down and she could not look at it.

"Molo," she called, "Molo! Molo!"

Then she said, "Harry, Harry!" Then her voice rising, "Harry! Please, Oh Harry!"

There was no answer and she could not hear him breathing.

Outside the tent the hyena made the same strange noise that had awakened her. But she did not hear him for the beating of her heart.

OLD MAN AT THE BRIDGE

An old man with steel rimmed spectacles and very dusty clothes sat by the side of the road. There was a pontoon bridge across the river and carts, trucks, and men, women and children were crossing it. The mule-drawn carts staggered up the steep bank from the bridge with soldiers helping push against the spokes of the wheels. The trucks ground up and away heading out of it all and the peasants plodded along in the ankle deep dust. But the old man sat there without moving. He was too tired to go any farther.

It was my business to cross the bridge, explore the bridgehead beyond and find out to what point the enemy had advanced. I did this and returned over the bridge. There were not so many carts now and very few people on foot, but the old man was still there.

"Where do you come from?" I asked him.

"From San Carlos," he said, and smiled.

That was his native town and so it gave him pleasure to mention it and he smiled.

"I was taking care of animals," he explained.

"Oh," I said, not quite understanding.

"Yes," he said, "I stayed, you see, taking care of animals. I was the last one to leave the town of San Carlos."

He did not look like a shepherd nor a herdsman and I looked at his black dusty clothes and his gray dusty face and his steel rimmed spectacles and said, "What animals were they?"

"Various animals," he said, and shook his head. "I had to leave them."

I was watching the bridge and the African looking country of the Ebro Delta and wondering how long now it would be before we would see the enemy, and listening all the while for the first noises that would signal that ever mysterious event called contact, and the old man still sat there.

"What animals were they?" I asked.

"There were three animals altogether," he explained. "There were two goats and a cat and then there were four pairs of pigeons."

"And you had to leave them?" I asked.

"Yes. Because of the artillery. The captain told me to go because of the artillery."

"And you have no family?" I asked, watching the far end of the bridge where a few last carts were hurrying down the slope of the bank.

"No," he said, "only the animals I stated. The cat, of course, will be all right. A cat can look out for itself, but I cannot think what will become of the others."

"What politics have you?" I asked.

"I am without politics," he said. "I am seventy-six years old. I have come twelve kilometers now and I think now I can go no further."

"This is not a good place to stop," I said. "If you can make it, there are trucks up the road where it forks for Tortosa."

"I will wait a while," he said, "and then I will go. Where do the trucks go?"

"Towards Barcelona," I told him.

"I know no one in that direction," he said, "but thank you very much. Thank you again very much."

He looked at me very blankly and tiredly, then said, having to share his worry with some one, "The cat will be all right, I am sure. There is no need to be unquiet about the cat. But the others. Now what do you think about the others?"

"Why they'll probably come through it all right."

"You think so?"

"Why not," I said, watching the far bank where now there were no carts.

"But what will they do under the artillery when I was told to leave because of the artillery?"

"Did you leave the dove cage unlocked?" I asked.

"Yes."

"Then they'll fly."

"Yes, certainly they'll fly. But the others. It's better not to think about the others," he said.

"If you are rested I would go," I urged. "Get up and try to walk now."

"Thank you," he said and got to his feet, swayed from side to side and then sat down backwards in the dust.

"I was taking care of animals," he said dully, but no longer to me. "I was only taking care of animals."

There was nothing to do about him. It was Easter Sunday and the Fascists were advancing toward the Ebro. It was a gray overcast day with a low ceiling so their planes were not up. That and the fact that cats know how to look after themselves was all the good luck that old man would ever have.

THE FABLE OF THE GOOD LION

ONCE UPON a time there was a lion that lived in Africa with all the other lions. The other lions were all bad lions and every day they ate zebras and wildebeestes and every kind of antelope. Sometimes the bad lions ate people too. They ate Swahilis, Umbulus and Wandorobos and they especially liked to eat Hindu traders. All Hindu traders are very fat and delicious to a lion.

But this lion, that we love because he was so good, had wings on his back. Because he had wings on his back the other lions all made fun of him.

"Look at him with the wings on his back," they would say and then they would all roar with laughter.

"Look at what he eats," they would say because the good lion only ate pasta and scampi because he was so good.

The bad lions would roar with laughter and eat another Hindu trader and their wives would drink his blood, going lap, lap, lap with their tongues like big cats. They only stopped to growl with laughter or to roar with laughter at the good lion and to snarl at his wings. They were very bad and wicked lions indeed.

But the good lion would sit and fold his wings back and ask politely if he might have a Negroni or an Americano and he always drank that instead of the blood of Hindu traders. One day he refused to eat eight Masai cattle and only ate some tagliatelli and drank a glass of pomodoro.

This made the wicked lions very angry and one of the lionesses, who was the wickedest of them all and could never get the blood of Hindu traders off her whiskers even when she rubbed her face in the grass said, "Who are you that you think you are so much better than we are? Where do you come from, you pasta-eating lion? What are you doing here anyway?" She growled at him and they all roared without laughter.

"My father lives in a city where he stands under the clock tower and looks down on a thousand pigeons, all of whom are his subjects. When they fly they make a noise like a rushing river. There are more palaces in my father's city than in all of Africa and there are four great bronze horses that face him and they all have one foot in the air because they fear him.

"In my father's city men go on foot or in boats and no real horse would enter the city for fear of my father."

"Your father was a griffon," the wicked lioness said, licking her whiskers.

"You are a liar," one of the wicked lions said. "There is no such city."

"Pass me a piece of Hindu trader," another very wicked lion said. "This Masai cattle is too newly killed."

"You are a worthless liar and the son of a griffon," the wickedest of all the lionesses said. "And now I think I shall kill you and eat you, wings and all."

This frightened the good lion very much because he could see her yellow eyes and her tail going up and down and the blood caked on her whiskers and he smelled her breath which was very bad because she never brushed her teeth ever. Also she had old pieces of Hindu trader under her claws.

"Don't kill me," the good lion said. "My father is a noble lion and always has been respected and everything is true as I said."

Just then the wicked lioness sprang at him. But he rose into the air on his wings and circled the group of wicked lions once, with them all roaring and looking at him. He looked down and thought, "What savages these lions are."

He circled them once more to make them roar more loudly. Then he swooped low so he could look at the eyes of the wicked lioness who rose on her hind legs to try and catch him. But she missed him with her claws. "*Adios,*" he said, for he spoke beautiful Spanish, being a lion of culture. "*Au revoir,*" he called to them in his exemplary French.

They all roared and growled in African lion dialect.

Then the good lion circled higher and higher and set his course for Venice. He alighted in the Piazza and everyone was delighted to see him. He flew up for a moment and kissed his father on both cheeks and saw the horses still had their feet up and the Basilica looked more beautiful than a soap bubble. The Campanile was in place and the pigeons were going to their nests for the evening.

"How was Africa?" his father said.

"Very savage, father," the good lion replied.

"We have night lighting here now," his father said.

"So I see," the good lion answered like a dutiful son.

"It bothers my eyes a little," his father confided to him. "Where are you going now, my son?"

"To Harry's Bar," the good lion said.

"Remember me to Cipriani and tell him I will be in some day soon to see about my bill," said his father.

"Yes, father," said the good lion and he flew down lightly and walked to Harry's Bar on his own four paws.

In Cipriani's nothing was changed. All of his friends were there. But he was a little changed himself from being in Africa.

"A Negroni, Signor Barone?" asked Mr. Cipriani.

But the good lion had flown all the way from Africa and Africa had changed him.

"Do you have any Hindu trader sandwiches?" he asked Cipriani.

"No, but I can get some."

"While you are sending for them, make me a very dry Martini." He added, "With Gordon's gin."

"Very good," said Cipriani. "Very good indeed."

Now the lion looked about him at the faces of all the nice people and he knew that he was at home but that he had also traveled. He was very happy.

from ACROSS THE RIVER
AND INTO THE TREES

VENICE AND THE VENETO
Chapters Four
Five
Six

ACROSS THE RIVER AND INTO THE TREES, Hemingway's best love story since A Farewell to Arms, is a novel of many loves, particularly love for Renata, love for the true combat Army, love for Venice. It is impossible to abridge the love story of Colonel Richard Cantwell and Renata, or give the story of his love of the Army beyond the suggestions here, but I think these three chapters do show us his love of Venice and the Venetian country.

Venice is Cantwell's city: "I fought for it when I was a boy, and now that I am half a hundred years old, they know I fought for it and I am a part owner and they treat me well." The Colonel knows Venice as other men in other parts of this volume have known Paris and Madrid and loved those cities and described what they liked about them well. He is a Colonel, now; he has been a Brigadier General. The background of all those years, the foreground of the few days left to him, merge, come into focus, blur and clear again, on the road to Venice. "This country meant very much to him, more than he could or would ever tell anyone." I think that if Rembrandt's "Man in the Golden Helmet" spoke, he might speak as Colonel Cantwell speaks of places and battles he had known.

Across the River and Into the Trees stirred a curious frenzy of attacks on Hemingway when it appeared in 1950. It will be interesting for future biographers to note that while the clamor raged he was serenely writing the calm, Homeric pages of The Old Man and the Sea.

C. P.

ACROSS THE RIVER
AND INTO THE TREES

VENICE AND THE VENETO

IV

Now, on his way into Venice, keeping strictly controlled and un-
thinking his great need to be there, the big Buick cleared the last
of San Dona and came up onto the bridge over the Piave.

They crossed the bridge and were on the Italian side of the
river and he saw the old sunken road again. It was as smooth and
undistinguished now, as it was all along the river. But he could
see the old positions. And now, along each side of the straight,
flat, canal-bordered road they were making time on, were the
willows of the two canals that had contained the dead. There had
been a great killing at the last of the offensive and someone, to
clear the river bank positions and the road in the hot weather, had
ordered the dead thrown into the canals. Unfortunately, the canal
gates were still in the Austrians' hands down the river, and they
were closed.

So there was little movement to the water, and the dead had
stayed there a long time, floating and bloating face up and face
down regardless of nationality until they had attained colossal
proportions. Finally, after organization had been established, labor
troops hauled them out at night and buried them close to the
road. The Colonel looked for added greenness close to the road
but could not note any. However, there were many ducks and
geese in the canals, and men were fishing in them all along the
road.

They dug them all up anyway, the Colonel thought, and
buried them in that big *ossario* up by Nervesa.

"We fought along here when I was a kid," the Colonel told
the driver.

617

"It's a God-damn flat country to fight in," the driver said. "Did you hold that river?"

"Yes," the Colonel said. "We held it and lost it and took it back again."

"There isn't a contour here as far as you can see."

"That was the trouble," the Colonel said. "You had to use contours you couldn't see, they were so small, and ditches and houses and canal banks and hedgerows. It was like Normandy only flatter. I think it must have been something like fighting in Holland."

"That river sure doesn't look anything like the Rapido."

"It was a pretty good old river," the Colonel said. "Up above, it had plenty of water then, before all these hydro-electric projects. And it had very deep and tricky channels in the pebbles and shingle when it was shallow. There was a place called the Grave di Papadopoli where it was plenty tricky."

He knew how boring any man's war is to any other man, and he stopped talking about it. They always take it personally, he thought. No one is interested in it, abstractly, except soldiers and there are not many soldiers. You make them and the good ones are killed, and above they are always bucking for something so hard they never look or listen. They are always thinking of what they have seen and while you are talking they are thinking of what they will say and what it may lead to in their advancement or their privilege. There was no sense boring this boy, who, for all his combat infantryman badge, his Purple Heart and the other things he wore, was in no sense a soldier but only a man placed, against his will, in uniform, who had elected to remain in the army for his own ends.

"What did you do in civil life, Jackson?" he asked.

"I was partners with my brother in a garage in Rawlins, Wyoming, sir."

"Are you going back there?"

"My brother got killed in the Pacific and the guy who was running the garage was no good," the driver said. "We lost what we had put in it."

"That's bad," the Colonel said.

"You're God-damned right it's bad," the driver said and added, "sir."

The Colonel looked up the road.

He knew that if they kept on this road they would come, shortly, to the turn that he was waiting for; but he was impatient.

"Keep your eyes open and take a left hand turn on the road leading off this pike," he told the driver.

"Do you think those low roads will be good with this big car, sir?"

"We'll see," the Colonel said. "Hell, man, it hasn't rained in three weeks."

"I don't trust those side roads in this low country."

"If we get stuck, I'll haul you out with oxen."

"I was only thinking about the car, sir."

"Well, think about what I told you and turn off on the first left side road you see if it looks practicable."

"That looks like one coming up, from the hedges," the driver said.

"You're all clear behind. Pull up just ahead of it and I'll go over and have a look."

He stepped out of the car and walked across the wide, hard-surfaced road and looked at the narrow dirt road, with the swift flowing canal beside it, and the thick hedge beyond. Beyond the hedge, he saw a low red farmhouse with a big barn. The road was dry. There were not even carts ruts sunk in it. He got back into the car.

"It's a boulevard," he said. "Quit worrying."

"Yes, sir. It's your car, sir."

"I know," the Colonel said. "I'm still paying for it. Say, Jackson, do you always suffer so much any time you go off a highway onto a secondary road?"

"No, sir. But there's a lot of difference between a jeep, and a car as low hung as this. Do you know the clearance you have on your differential and your body frame on this?"

"I've got a shovel in the trunk and we've got chains. Wait till you see where we're going after we leave Venice."

"Do we go all the way in this car?"

"I don't know. I'll see."

"Think about your fenders, sir."

"We'll cut the fenders off like the Indians do in Oklahoma. She's over-fendered right now. She's got too much of everything except engine. Jackson, that's a real engine she's got. One hundred and fifty ponies."

"It certainly is, sir. It's a great pleasure to drive that big engine on the good roads. That's why I don't want anything to happen to her."

"That's very good of you, Jackson. Now just quit suffering."

"I'm not suffering, sir."

"Good," said the Colonel.

He was not, either, because just then he saw, beyond the line of close-bunched brown trees ahead, a sail moving along. It was a big red sail, raked sharply down from the peak, and it moved slowly behind the trees.

Why should it always move your heart to see a sail moving along through the country, the Colonel thought. Why does it move my heart to see the great, slow, pale oxen? It must be the gait as well as the look of them and the size and the color.

But a good fine big mule, or a string of pack mules in good condition, moves me, too. So does a coyote every time I ever see one, and a wolf, gaited like no other animal, gray and sure of himself, carrying that heavy head and with the hostile eyes.

"Ever see any wolves out around Rawlins, Jackson?"

"No, sir. Wolves were gone before my time; they poisoned them out. Plenty coyotes, though."

"Do you like coyotes?"

"I like to hear them nights."

"So do I. Better than anything, except seeing a ship sailing along through the country."

"There's a boat doing that over there, sir."

"On the Sile canal," the Colonel told him. "She's a sailing barge going to Venice. This wind is off the mountains now and she makes it along pretty good. It's liable to turn really cold tonight if this wind holds and it ought to bring in plenty ducks. Turn to your left here and we'll run along the canal. There's a good road."

"They didn't have much duck shooting where I came from. But there was plenty of it in Nebraska along the Platte."

"Do you want to shoot where we're going?"

"I don't believe so, sir. I'm not much of a shot, and I'd rather stay in that sack. It's a Sunday morning, you know."

"I know," the Colonel said. "You can stay in the sack until noon if you want."

"I brought my repellent, I ought to sleep O.K."

"I'm not sure you'll need it," the Colonel said. "Did you bring any K-rations or Ten in One? They're liable to eat Italian food, you know."

"I brought a few cans to help out and a little stuff to give away."

"That's good," the Colonel said.

He was looking ahead now to see where the canal road joined the main highway again. There he knew that he would see it on a clear day such as this was. Across the marshes, brown as those at the mouths of the Mississippi around Pilot Town are in winter, and with their reeds bent by the heavy north wind, he saw the squared tower of the church at Torcello and the high *campanile* of Burano beyond it. The sea was a slate blue and he could see the sails of twelve sailing barges running with the wind for Venice.

I'll have to wait until we cross the Dese River above Noghera to see it perfectly, he thought. It is strange to remember how we fought back there along the canal that winter to defend it and we never saw it. Then one time, I was back as far as Noghera and it was clear and cold like today, and I saw it across the water. But I never got into it. It is my city, though, because I fought for it when I was a boy, and now that I am half a hundred years old, they know I fought for it and am a part owner and they treat me well.

Do you think that's why they treat you well, he asked himself.

Maybe, he thought. Maybe they treat me well because I'm a chicken colonel on the winning side. I don't believe it, though. I hope not, anyway. It is not France, he thought.

There you fight your way into a city that you love and are very careful about breaking anything and then, if you have good sense, you are careful not to go back because you will meet some military characters who will resent your having fought your way in. *Vive la*

France et les pommes de terre frites. Liberté, Venalité, et Stupidité.
The great *clarté* of the French military thinking. They haven't had
a military thinker since du Picq. He was a poor bloody Colonel,
too. *Mangin, Maginot* and *Gamelin*. Take your choice, Gentlemen.
Three schools of thought. One; I hit them on the nose. Two; I
hide behind this thing which does not cover my left flank. Three; I
hide my head in the sand like an ostrich, confident in the greatness
of France as a military power and then take off.

Take off is putting it very cleanly and pleasantly. Sure, he
thought, whenever you over-simplify you become unjust. Remember all the fine ones in the Resistance, remember Foch both
fought and organized and remember how fine the people were.
Remember your good friends and remember your deads. Remember plenty things and your best friends again and the finest people
that you know. Don't be a bitter nor a stupid. And what has that
to do with soldiering as a trade? Cut it out, he told himself. You're
on a trip to have fun.

"Jackson," he said, "are you happy?"

"Yes, sir."

"Good. Shortly, we are coming to a view that I want you to see.
You only have to take one look at it. The entire operation will be
practically painless."

I wonder what he's riding me for now, the driver thought. Just
because he was a B.G. once he knows everything. If he was any
good as a B.G. why didn't he hold it? He's been beat up so much
he's slug-nutty.

"There's the view, Jackson," the Colonel said. "Stop her by the
side of the road and we'll take a look."

The Colonel and the driver walked over to the Venice side of
the road and looked across the lagoon that was whipped by the
strong, cold wind from the mountains that sharpened all the out-
lines of buildings so that they were geometrically clear.

"That's Torcello directly opposite us," the Colonel pointed.
"That's where the people lived that were driven off the mainland
by the Visigoths. They built that church you see there with the
square tower. There were thirty thousand people lived there once
and they built that church to honor their Lord and to worship him.

Then, after they built it, the mouth of the Sile River silted up or a big flood changed it, and all that land we came through just now got flooded and started to breed mosquitoes and malaria hit them. They all started to die, so the elders got together and decided they should pull out to a healthy place that would be defensible with boats, and where the Visigoths and the Lombards and the other bandits couldn't get at them, because these bandits had no sea-power. The Torcello boys were all great boatmen. So they took the stones of all their houses in barges, like that one we just saw, and they built Venice."

He stopped. "Am I boring you, Jackson?"

"No, sir. I had no idea who pioneered Venice."

"It was the boys from Torcello. They were very tough and they had very good taste in building. They came from a little place up the coast called Caorle. But they drew on all the people from the towns and the farms behind when the Visigoths over-ran them. It was a Torcello boy who was running arms into Alexandria, who located the body of St. Mark and smuggled it out under a load of fresh pork so the infidel customs guards wouldn't check him. This boy brought the remains of St. Mark to Venice, and he's their patron saint and they have a cathedral there to him. But by that time, they were trading so far to the east that the architecture is pretty Byzantine for my taste. They never built any better than at the start there in Torcello. That's Torcello there."

It was, indeed.

"St. Mark's square is where the pigeons are and where they have that big cathedral that looks sort of like a moving picture palace, isn't it?"

"Right, Jackson. You're on the ball. If that's the way you look at it. Now you look beyond Torcello you will see the lovely *campanile* on Burano that has damn near as much list on it as the leaning tower of Pisa. That Burano is a very over-populated little island where the women make wonderful lace, and the men make bambinis and work day-times in the glass factories in that next island you see on beyond with the other *campanile*, which is Murano. They make wonderful glass day-times for the rich of all the world, and then they come home on the little vaporetto and make bambinis. Not everyone passes every night with his wife though. They hunt ducks nights too, with big punt guns, out along the edge of the marshes on this lagoon you're looking across now. All night long on a moonlight night you hear the shots." He paused.

"Now when you look past Murano you see Venice. That's my town. There's plenty more I could show you, but I think we probably ought to roll now. But take one good look at it. This is where you can see how it all happened. But nobody ever looks at it from here."

"It's a beautiful view. Thank you, sir."

"O.K.," the Colonel said. "Let's roll."

V

But he continued to look and it was all as wonderful to him and it moved him as it had when he was eighteen years old and had seen it first, understanding nothing of it and only knowing that it was beautiful. The winter had come very cold that year and all the mountains were white beyond the plain. It was necessary for the Austrians to try to break through at the angle where the Sile River and the old bed of the Piave were the only lines of defense.

If you had the old bed of the Piave then you had the Sile to fall back on if the first line did not hold. Beyond the Sile there was nothing but bare-assed plain and a good road network into the Veneto plain and the plains of Lombardy, and the Austrians attacked again and again and again late through the winter, to try to get onto this fine road that they were rolling on now which led straight to Venice. That winter the Colonel, who was a lieutenant then, and in a foreign army, which had always made him slightly suspect afterwards in his own army, and had done his career no good, had a sore throat all winter. This sore throat was from being in the water so much. You could not get dry and it was better to get wet quickly and stay wet.

The Austrian attacks were ill-coordinated, but they were con-

stant and exasperated and you first had the heavy bombardment
which was supposed to put you out of business, and then, when it
lifted, you checked your positions and counted the people. But you
had no time to care for wounded, since you knew that the attack
was coming immediately, and then you killed the men who came
wading across the marshes, holding their rifles above the water and
coming as slow as men wade, waist deep.

If they did not lift the shelling when it started, the Colonel, then
a lieutenant, often thought, I do not know what we would be able
to do. But they always lifted it and moved it back ahead of the
attack. They went by the book.

If we had lost the old Piave and were on the Sile they would
move it back to the second and third lines; although such lines were
quite untenable, and they should have brought all their guns up
very close and whammed it in all the time they attacked and until
they breached us. But thank God, some high fool always controls
it, the Colonel thought, and they did it piecemeal.

All that winter, with a bad sore throat, he had killed men who
came, wearing the stick bombs hooked up on a harness under their
shoulders with the heavy, calf hide packs and the bucket helmets.
They were the enemy.

But he never hated them; nor could have any feeling about
them. He commanded with an old sock around his throat, which
had been dipped in turpentine, and they broke down the attacks
with rifle fire and with the machine guns which still existed, or
were usable, after the bombardment. He taught his people to shoot,
really, which is a rare ability in continental troops, and to be able
to look at the enemy when they came, and, because there was
always a dead moment when the shooting was free, they became
very good at it.

But you always had to count and count fast after the bombardment to know how many shooters you would have. He was hit
three times that winter, but they were all gift wounds; small
wounds in the flesh of the body without breaking bone, and he had
become quite confident of his personal immortality since he knew
he should have been killed in the heavy artillery bombardment
that always preceded the attacks. Finally he did get hit properly

and for good. No one of his other wounds had ever done to him what the first big one did. I suppose it is just the loss of the immortality, he thought. Well, in a way, that is quite a lot to lose.

This country meant very much to him, more than he could, or would ever tell anyone and now he sat in the car happy that in another half hour they would be in Venice. He took two mannitol hexanitrate tablets; since he had always been able to spit since 1918, he could take them dry, and asked,

"How are you doing, Jackson?"

"Fine, sir."

"Take the left outside road when we hit the fork for Mestre and we'll be able to see the boats along the canal and miss that main traffic."

"Yes, sir," the driver said. "Will you check me on the fork?"

"Of course," the Colonel said.

They were coming up on Mestre fast, and already it was like going to New York the first time you were ever there in the old days when it was shining, white and beautiful. I stole that, he thought. But that was before the smoke. We are coming into my town, he thought. Christ, what a lovely town.

They made the left turn and came along the canal where the fishing boats tied up, and the Colonel looked at them and his heart was happy because of the brown nets and the wicker fish traps and the clean, beautiful lines of the boats. It's not that they are picturesque. The hell with picturesque. They are just damned beautiful.

They passed the long line of boats in the slow canal that carried water from the Brenta, and he thought about the long stretch of the Brenta where the great villas were, with their lawns and their gardens and the plane trees and the cypresses. I'd like to be buried out there, he thought. I know the place very well. I don't believe you could fix it, though. I don't know. I know some people that might let me be buried on their place. I'll ask Alberto. He might think it was morbid, though.

For a long time he had been thinking about all the fine places he would like to be buried and what parts of the earth he would like to be a part of. The stinking, putrefying part doesn't last very long, really, he thought, and anyway you are just a sort of mulch, and even the bones will be some use finally. I'd like to be buried way out at the edge of the grounds, but in sight of the old graceful house and the tall, great trees. I don't think it would be much of a nuisance to them. I could be a part of the ground where the children play in the evenings, and in the mornings, maybe, they would still be training jumping horses and their hoofs would make the thudding on the turf, and trout would rise in the pool when there was a hatch of fly.

They were up on the causeway from Mestre to Venice now with the ugly Breda works that might have been Hammond, Indiana.

"What do they make there, sir?" Jackson asked.

"The company makes locomotives in Milan," the Colonel said. "Here they make a little of everything in the metallurgic line."

It was a miserable view of Venice now and he always disliked this causeway except that you made such good time and you could see the buoys and the channels.

"This town makes a living on its own," he said to Jackson. "She used to be the queen of the seas and the people are very tough and they give less of a good God-damn about things than almost anybody you'll ever meet. It's a tougher town than Cheyenne when you really know it, and everybody is very polite."

"I wouldn't say Cheyenne was a tough town, sir."

"Well, it's a tougher town than Caspar."

"Do you think that's a tough town, sir?"

"It's an oil town. It's a nice town."

"But I don't think it's tough, sir. Or ever was."

"O.K., Jackson. Maybe we move in different circles. Or maybe we have a differing definition for the word. But this town of Venice, with everybody being polite and having good manners, is as tough as Cooke City, Montana, on the day they have the Old Timers' Fish Fry."

"My idea of a tough town is Memphis."

"Not like Chicago, Jackson. Memphis is only tough if you are a Negro. Chicago is tough North, South, there isn't any East, and West. But nobody has any manners. But in this country, if you

ever want to know a *really* tough town where they eat wonderfully too, go to Bologna."

"I never was there."

"Well, there's the Fiat garage where we leave the car," the
Colonel said. "You can leave the key at the office. They don't steal.
I'll go in the bar while you park upstairs. They have people that
will bring the bags."

"Is it okay to leave your gun and shooting gear in the trunk, sir?"

"Sure. They don't steal here. I told you that once."

"I wanted to take the necessary precaution, sir, on your valuable
property."

"You're so damned noble that sometimes you stink," the Colonel
said. "Get the wax out of your ears and hear what I say the first
time."

"I heard you, sir," Jackson said. The Colonel looked at him
contemplatively and with the old deadliness.

He sure is a mean son of a bitch, Jackson thought, and he can
be so God-damn nice.

"Get my and your bag out and park her up there and check
your oil, your water and your tires," the Colonel said, and walked
across the oil and rubber stained cement of the entry of the bar.

VI

In the bar, sitting at the first table as he came in, there was a post-
war rich from Milan, fat and hard as only Milanese can be, sitting
with his expensive looking and extremely desirable mistress. They
were drinking *negronis*, a combination of two sweet vermouths
and seltzer water, and the Colonel wondered how much taxes the
man had escaped to buy that sleek girl in her long mink coat and
the convertible he had seen the chauffeur take up the long, winding ramp, to lock away. The pair stared at him with the bad manners of their kind and he saluted, lightly, and said to them in
Italian, "I am sorry that I am in uniform. But it is a uniform. Not a
costume."

Then he turned his back on them, without waiting to see the effect of his remark, and walked to the bar. From the bar you could watch your luggage, just as well as the two *pescecani* were watching theirs.

He is probably a Commendatore, he thought. She is a beautiful, hard piece of work. She is damned beautiful actually. I wonder what it would have been like if I had ever had the money to buy me that kind and put them into the mink? I'll settle for what I have, he thought, and they can go and hang themselves.

The bar-tender shook hands with him. This bar-tender was an Anarchist but he did not mind the Colonel being a Colonel at all. He was delighted by it and proud and loving about it as though the Anarchists had a Colonel, too, and in some ways, in the several months that they had known each other, he seemed to feel that he had invented, or at least, erected the Colonel as you might be happy about participating in the erection of a *campanile*, or even the old church at Torcello.

The bar-tender had heard the conversation, or, rather, the flat statement at the table and he was very happy.

He had already sent down, via the dumb-waiter, for a Gordon's gin and Campari and he said, "It is coming up in that hand-pulled device. How does everything go at Trieste?"

"About as you would imagine."

"I couldn't even imagine."

"Then don't strain," the Colonel said, "and you will never get piles."

"I wouldn't mind it if I was a Colonel."

"I never mind it."

"You'd be over-run like a dose of salts," the waiter said.

"Don't tell the Honorable Pacciardi," the Colonel said. He and the bar-tender had a joke about this because the Honorable Pacciardi was Minister of Defense in the Italian Republic. He was the same age as the Colonel and had fought very well in the first world war, and had also fought in Spain as a battalion Commander where the Colonel had known him when he, himself, was an observer. The seriousness with which the Honorable Pacciardi took the post of Minister of Defense of an indefensible country was a bond between the Colonel and the bar-tender. The two of them were quite practical men and the vision of the Honorable Pacciardi defending the Italian Republic stimulated their minds.

"It's sort of funny up there," the Colonel said, "and I don't mind it."

"We must mechanize the Honorable Pacciardi," the bar-tender said. "And supply him with the atomic bomb."

"I've got three of them in the back of the car," the Colonel said. "The new model, complete with handles. But we can't leave him unarmed. We must supply him with botulism and anthrax."

"We cannot fail the Honorable Pacciardi," the bartender said. "Better to live one day as a lion than a hundred years as a sheep."

"Better to die on our feet than to live on our knees," the Colonel said. "Though you better get on your belly damn fast if you want to stay alive in plenty places."

"Colonel, do not say anything subversive."

"We will strangle them with our bare hands," the Colonel said. "A million men will spring to arms overnight."

"Whose arms?" the bar-tender asked.

"All that will be attended to," the Colonel said. "It's only a phase in the Big Picture."

Just then the driver came in the door. The Colonel saw that while they had been joking, he had not watched the door and he was annoyed, always, with any lapse of vigilance or of security.

"What the hell's been keeping you, Jackson? Have a drink."

"No, thank you, sir."

You prissy jerk, the Colonel thought. But I better stop riding him, he corrected.

"We'll be going in a minute," the Colonel said. "I've been trying to learn Italian from my friend here." He turned to look at the Milan profiteers; but they were gone.

I'm getting awfully slow, he thought. Somebody will take me any day now. Maybe even the Honorable Pacciardi, he thought.

"How much do I owe you?" he asked the bar-tender shortly.

The bar-tender told him and looked at him with his wise Italian eyes, not merry now, although the lines of merriment were clearly cut where they radiated from the corners of each eye. I hope there is nothing wrong with him, the bar-tender thought. I hope to God, or anything else, there's nothing really bad.

"Good-bye, my Colonel," he said.

"*Ciao*," the Colonel said. "Jackson, we are going down the long ramp and due north from the exit to where the small launches are moored. The varnished ones. There is a porter with the two bags. It is necessary to let them carry them since they have a concession."

"Yes, sir," said Jackson.

The two of them went out the door and no one looked back at anyone.

At the *imbarcadero*, the Colonel tipped the man who had carried their two bags and then looked around for a boatman he knew.

He did not recognize the man in the launch that was first on call, but the boatman said, "Good-day, my Colonel. I'm the first."

"How much is it to the Gritti?"

"You know as well as I, my Colonel. We do not bargain. We have a fixed tariff."

"What's the tariff?"

"Three thousand five hundred."

"We could go on the vaporetto for sixty."

"And nothing prevents you going," the boatman, who was an elderly man with a red but un-choleric face, said. "They won't take you to the Gritti but they will stop at the imbarcadero past Harry's, and you can telephone for someone from the Gritti to get your bags."

And what would I buy with the God-damn three thousand five hundred lire; and this is a good old man.

"Do you want me to send that man there?" he pointed to a destroyed old man who did odd jobs and ran errands around the docks, always ready with the un-needed aid to the elbow of the ascending or descending passenger, always ready to help when no help was needed, his old felt hat held out as he bowed after the un-needed act. "He'll take you to the vaporetto. There's one in twenty minutes."

"The hell with it," the Colonel said. "Take us to the Gritti."

"*Con piacere*," the boatman said.

The Colonel and Jackson lowered themselves into the launch

which looked like a speed boat. It was radiantly varnished and lovingly kept and was powered with a marine conversion of a tiny Fiat engine that had served its allotted time in the car of a provincial doctor and had been purchased out of one of the graveyards of automobiles, those mechanical elephant cemeteries that are the one certain thing you may find in our world near any populated center, and been reconditioned and reconverted to start this new life on the canals of this city.

"How is the motor doing?" the Colonel asked. He could hear her sounding like a stricken tank or T.D., except the noises were in miniature from the lack of power.

"So-so," the boatman said. He moved his free hand in a parallel motion.

"You ought to get the smallest model Universal puts out. That's the best and lightest small marine engine I know."

"Yes," the boatman said. "There are quite a few things I should get."

"Maybe you'll have a good year."

"It's always possible. Lots of *pescecani* come down from Milano to gamble at the Lido. But nobody would ride twice in this thing on purpose. As a boat, it is fine, too. It is a well built, pleasant boat. Not beautiful as a gondola is, of course. But it needs an engine."

"I might get you a jeep engine. One that *was* condemned and you could work it over."

"Don't talk about such things," the boatman said. "Things like that don't happen. I don't want to think about it."

"You can think about it," the Colonel said. "I'm talking true."

"You mean it."

"Sure. I don't guarantee anything. I'll see what I can do. How many children have you got?"

"Six. Two male and four female."

"Hell, you mustn't have believed in the Regime. Only six."

"I *didn't* believe in the Regime."

"You don't have to give me that stuff," the Colonel said. "It would have been quite natural for you to *have* believed in it. Do you think I hold that against a man after we've won?"

They were through the dull part of the canal that runs from Piazzale Roma to Ca'Foscari, though none of it is dull, the Colonel thought.

It doesn't all have to be palaces nor churches. Certainly that isn't dull. He looked to the right, the starboard, he thought. I'm on the water. It was a long low pleasant building and there was a trattoria next to it.

I ought to live here. On retirement pay I could make it all right. No Gritti Palace. A room in a house like that and the tides and the boats going by. I could read in the mornings and walk around town before lunch and go every day to see the Tintorettos at the Accademia and to the Scuola San Rocco and eat in good cheap joints behind the market, or, maybe, the woman that ran the house would cook in the evenings.

I think it would be better to have lunch out and get some exercise walking. It's a good town to walk in. I guess the best, probably. I never walked in it that it wasn't fun. I could learn it really well, he thought, and then I'd have that.

It's a strange, tricky town and to walk from any part to any other given part of it is better than working cross-word puzzles. It's one of the few things to our credit that we never smacked it, and to *their* credit that they respected it.

Christ, I love it, he said, and I'm so happy I helped defend it when I was a punk kid, and with an insufficient command of the language and I never even saw her until that clear day in the winter when I went back to have that small wound dressed, and saw her rising from the sea. Merde, he thought, we did very well that winter up at the juncture.

I wish I could fight it again, he thought. Knowing what I know now and having what we have now. But they'd have it too and the essential problem is just the same, except who holds the air.

And all this time he had been watching the bow of the beat-up beautifully varnished, delicately brass-striped boat, with the brass all beautifully polished, cut the brown water, and seen the small traffic problems.

They went under the white bridge and under the unfinished wood bridge. Then they left the red bridge on the right and passed under the first high-flying white bridge. Then there was the black iron fret-work bridge on the canal leading into the Rio Nuovo and they passed the two stakes chained together but not touching: like us the Colonel thought. He watched the tide pull at them and he saw how the chains had worn the wood since he first had seen them. That's us, he thought. That's our monument. And how many monuments are there to us in the canals of this town?

Then they still went slowly until the great lantern that was on the right of the entrance to the Grand Canal where the engine commenced its metallic agony that produced a slight increase in speed.

Now they came down and under the Accademia between the pilings where they passed, at touching distance, a heavily loaded black, diesel boat full of cut timber, cut in chunks, to burn for firewood in the damp houses of the Sea City.

"That's beech, isn't it?" the Colonel asked the boatman.

"Beech and another wood that is cheaper that I do not recall, at this moment, the name of."

"Beech is, to an open fire, as anthracite coal is to a stove. Where do they cut that beech?"

"I'm not a man of the mountains. But I think it comes from up beyond Bassano on the other side of the Grappa. I went there to the Grappa to see where my brother was buried. It was an excursion that they made from Bassano, and we went to the big ossario. But we returned by Feltre. I could see it was a fine timber country on the other side as you came down the mountains into the valley. We came down that military road, and they were hauling lots of wood."

"In what year was your brother killed on the Grappa?"

"In nineteen-eighteen. He was a patriot and inflamed by hearing d'Annunzio talk, and he volunteered before his class was called. We never knew him very well because he went so quickly."

"How many were you in the family?"

"We were six. We lost two beyond the Isonzo, one on the Bainsizza and one on the Carso. Then we lost this brother I speak of on the Grappa and I remained."

"I'll get you the God-damned jeep complete with handles," the

Colonel said. "Now let's not be morbid and look for all the places where my friends live."

They were moving up the Grand Canal now and it was easy to see where your friends lived.

"That's the house of the Contessa Dandolo," the Colonel said.

He did not say, but thought, she is over eighty, and she is as gay as a girl and does not have any fear of dying. She dyes her hair red and it looks very well. She is a good companion and an admirable woman.

Her *palazzo* was pleasant looking, set well back from the Canal with a garden in front and a landing place of its own where many gondolas had come, in their various times, bringing hearty, cheerful, sad and disillusioned people. But most of them had been cheerful because they were going to see the Contessa Dandolo.

Now, beating up the Canal, against the cold wind off the mountains, and with the houses as clear and sharp as on a winter day, which, of course, it was, they saw the old magic of the city and its beauty. But it was conditioned, for the Colonel, by his knowing many of the people who lived in the palazzos; or if no one lived there now, knowing to what use the different places had been put.

There's Alvarito's mother's house, he thought, and did not say.

She never lives there much and stays out at the country house near Treviso where they have trees. She's tired of there not being trees in Venice. She lost a fine man and nothing really interests her now except efficiency.

But the family at one time lent the house to George Gordon, Lord Byron, and nobody sleeps now in Byron's bed nor in the other bed, two flights below, where he used to sleep with the gondolier's wife. They are not sacred, nor relics. They are just extra beds that were not used afterwards for various reasons, or possibly to respect Lord Byron who was well loved in this town, in spite of all the errors he committed. You have to be a tough boy in this town to be loved, the Colonel thought. They never cared anything for Robert Browning, nor Mrs. Robert Browning, nor for their dog. They weren't Venetians no matter how well he wrote of it. And what is a tough boy, he asked himself. You use it so loosely you should be able to define it. I suppose it is a man who will make his play and then backs it up. Or just a man who backs his play. And I'm not thinking of the theatre, he thought. Lovely as the theatre can be.

And yet, he thought, seeing now the little villa, close up against the water, ugly as a building you would see on the boat train from Havre or Cherbourg, coming into the banlieue before Paris as you came into town. It was overrun with badly administered trees, and not a place that you would live in if you could help it. There *he* lived.

They loved him for his talent, and because he was bad, and he was brave. A Jewish boy with nothing, he stormed the country with his talent, and his rhetoric. He was a more miserable character than any that I know and as mean. But the man I think of to compare him with never put the chips on the line and went to war, the Colonel thought, and Gabriele d'Annunzio (I always wondered what his real name was, he thought, because nobody is named d'Annunzio in a practical country and perhaps he was not Jewish and what difference did it make if he was or was not,) had moved through the different arms of the service as he had moved into and out of the arms of different women.

All the arms were pleasant that d'Annunzio served with and the mission was fast and easily over, except the Infantry. He remembered how d'Annunzio had lost an eye in a crash, flying as an observer, over Trieste or Pola, and how, afterwards, he had always worn a patch over it and people who did not know, for, then, no one really knew, thought it had been shot out at the Veliki or San Michele or some other bad place beyond the Carso where everyone died, or was incapacitated, that you knew. But d'Annunzio, truly, was only making heroic gestures with the other things. An Infantryman knows a strange trade, he thought; perhaps the strangest. He, Gabriele, flew, but he was not a flier. He was in the Infantry but he was not an Infantryman and it was always the same appearances.

And the Colonel remembered one time when he had stood, commanding a platoon of assault troops, while it was raining in one of the interminable winters, when the rain fell always; or at least, always when there were parades or speeches to the troops, and d'Annunzio, with his lost eye, covered by the patch, and his white face, as white as the belly of a sole, new turned over in the market, the brown side not showing, and looking thirty hours dead, was shouting, "Morire non è basta," and the Colonel, then a lieutenant, had thought, "What the muck more do they want of us?"

But he had followed the discourse and, at the end, when the Lieutenant Colonel d'Annunzio, writer and national hero, certified and true if you must have heroes, and the Colonel did not believe in heroes, asked for a moment of silence for our glorious dead, he had stood stiffly at attention. But his platoon, who had not followed the speech, there being no loud speakers then, and they being slightly out of hearing of the orator, responded, as one man, at the pause for the moment of silence for our glorious dead, with a solid and ringing "Evviva d'Annunzio."

They had been addressed before by d'Annunzio after victories, and before defeats, and they knew what they should shout if there was any pause by an orator.

The Colonel, being then a lieutenant, and loving his platoon, had joined with them and uttered, with the tone of command, "Evviva d'Annunzio," thus absolving all those who had not listened to the discourse, speech, or harangue, and attempting, in the small way a lieutenant can attempt anything, except to hold an indefensible position, or intelligently direct his own part in an attack, to share their guilt.

But now he was passing the house where the poor beat-up old boy had lived with his great, sad, and never properly loved actress, and he thought of her wonderful hands, and her so transformable face, that was not beautiful, but that gave you all love, glory, and delight and sadness; and of the way the curve of her forearm could break your heart, and he thought, Christ they are dead and I do not know where either one is buried even. But I certainly hope they had fun in that house.

"Jackson," he said, "that small villa on the left belonged to Gabriele d'Annunzio, who was a great writer."

"Yes, sir," said Jackson, "I'm glad to know about him. I never heard of him."

"I'll check you out on what he wrote if you ever want to read him," the Colonel said. "There are some fair English translations."

"Thank you, sir," said Jackson. "I'd like to read him anytime I have time. He has a nice practical looking place. What did you say the name was?"

"D'Annunzio," the Colonel said. "Writer."

He added to himself, not wishing to confuse Jackson, nor be difficult, as he had been with the man several times that day, writer, poet, national hero, phraser of the dialectic of Fascism, macabre egotist, aviator, commander, or rider, in the first of the fast torpedo attack boats, Lieutenant Colonel of Infantry without knowing how to command a company, nor a platoon properly, the great, lovely writer of *Notturno* whom we respect, and jerk.

Up ahead now there was a crossing place of gondolas at the Santa Maria del Giglio and, beyond, was the wooden dock of the Gritti.

"That's the hotel where we are stopping at, Jackson."

The Colonel indicated the three story, rose colored, small, pleasant palace abutting on the Canal. It had been a dependence of the Grand Hotel—but now it was its own hotel and a very good one. It was probably the best hotel, if you did not wish to be fawned on, or fussed over, or over-flunkied, in a city of great hotels, and the Colonel loved it.

"It looks O.K. to me, sir," Jackson said.

"It is O.K.," the Colonel said.

The motor boat came gallantly up beside the piling of the dock. Every move she makes, the Colonel thought, is a triumph of the gallantry of the aging machine. We do not have war horses now like old Traveller, or Marbot's Lysette who fought, personally, at Eylau. We have the gallantry of worn-through rods that refuse to break; the cylinder head that does not blow though it has every right to, and the rest of it.

"We're at the dock, sir," Jackson said.

"Where the hell else would we be, man. Jump out while I settle with this sportsman."

He turned to the boatman and said, "That was thirty-five hundred, wasn't it?"

"Yes, my Colonel."

"I'll not forget about the over-age jeep engine. Take this and buy your horse some oats."

The porter, who was taking the bags from Jackson, heard this and laughed.

"No veterinarian will ever fix his horse."

"She still runs," the boatman said.

"But she doesn't win any races," the porter said. "How are you, my Colonel?"

"I couldn't be better," the Colonel said. "How are all the members of the Order?"

"All members are well."

"Good," said the Colonel. "I will go in and see the Grand Master."

"He is waiting for you, my Colonel."

"Let us not keep him waiting, Jackson," the Colonel said. "You may proceed to the lobby with this gentleman and tell them to sign me in. See the sergeant gets a room," he said to the porter. "We're here for the night only."

"The Baron Alvarito was here looking for you."

"I'll find him at Harry's."

"Good, my Colonel."

"Where is the Grand Master?"

"I'll find him for you."

"Tell him I'll be in the bar."

from THE OLD MAN AND THE SEA

THE FIGHT WITH THE SHARKS

WITH THE OLD MAN AND THE SEA Hemingway received a belated Pulitzer Prize and was acclaimed as an old master. It was as if he somehow took on the age of the old fisherman, Santiago, who in this book for three days faces with valor, humor and humility the powers of darkness and unreason and the everlasting sea. There was a kind of wild logic in this recognition of Hemingway as a master and identifying him with Santiago; after all, the process had been building up a long time. Those who had begun by identifying Hemingway with the Nick Adams of the early stories had gone on to decide that he was also Jake Barnes and Lieutenant Henry and Robert Jordan and Anselmo and Sordo and every other man, no matter how different. Since Bovary was Flaubert, Hemingway would logically have to be Lady Brett Ashley and Catherine Barkley and those travelers in "Light of the World" and the Old Lady and Margot Macomber and Renata. The idea should reach its logical absurdity when he becomes the Good Lion. Perhaps he always was, at that.

The spirit that animates The Old Man and the Sea is not as new as some of those who have recognized the story as a masterpiece might think; it is in many of the early books, as all who have eyes to see and minds to read, know. And yet there is something new here, a deepening capacity for burning away words and phrases that do not count; as there always is in the work of the outstanding story-teller, the finest stylist of his time.

The Old Man and the Sea is not easy to excerpt, but I think this passage, the fight with the sharks for the great fish that means everything in the world to Santiago, is fairly taken.

THE OLD MAN AND THE SEA

[*A giant marlin on the old man's line has towed his skiff far out to sea off Cuba. Exhausted by days and nights of struggle, sleepless and famished, his back and hands burned by the line, the old man has finally outlasted his fish, brought it to the boat and killed it. The fish is too heavy for him to haul on board. He lashes it alongside, hoists a sail, and turns for home.*]

THE FIGHT WITH THE SHARKS

THEY sailed well and the old man soaked his hands in the salt water and tried to keep his head clear. There were high cumulus clouds and enough cirrus above them so that the old man knew the breeze would last all night. The old man looked at the fish constantly to make sure it was true. It was an hour before the first shark hit him.

The shark was not an accident. He had come up from deep down in the water as the dark cloud of blood had settled and dispersed in the mile deep sea. He had come up so fast and absolutely without caution that he broke the surface of the blue water and was in the sun. Then he fell back into the sea and picked up the scent and started swimming on the course the skiff and the fish had taken.

Sometimes he lost the scent. But he would pick it up again, or have just a trace of it, and he swam fast and hard on the course. He was a very big Mako shark built to swim as fast as the fastest fish in the sea and everything about him was beautiful except his jaws. His back was as blue as a sword fish's and his belly was silver and his hide was smooth and handsome. He was built as a sword fish except for his huge jaws which were tight shut now as he swam fast, just under the surface with his high dorsal fin knifing through the water without wavering. Inside the closed double lip of his jaws all of his eight rows of teeth were slanted inwards. They were not the ordinary pyramid-shaped teeth of most sharks. They were shaped like a man's fingers when they are crisped like claws. They were nearly as long as the fingers of the old man and they had razor-sharp cutting edges on both sides. This was a fish built to feed on all the fishes in the sea, that were so fast and strong and

643

well **armed** that they had no other enemy. Now he speeded up as he smelled the fresher scent and his blue dorsal fin cut the water.

When the old man saw him coming he knew that this was a shark that had no fear at all and would do exactly what he wished. He prepared the harpoon and made the rope fast while he watched the shark come on. The rope was short as it lacked what he had cut away to lash the fish.

The old man's head was clear and good now and he was full of resolution but he had little hope. It was too good to last, he thought. He took one look at the great fish as he watched the shark close in. It might as well have been a dream, he thought. I cannot keep him from hitting me but maybe I can get him. *Dentuso*, he thought. Bad luck to your mother.

The shark closed fast astern and when he hit the fish the old man saw his mouth open and his strange eyes and the clicking chop of the teeth as he drove forward in the meat just above the tail. The shark's head was out of water and his back was coming out and the old man could hear the noise of skin and flesh ripping on the big fish when he rammed the harpoon down onto the shark's head at a spot where the line between his eyes intersected with the line that ran straight back from his nose. There were no such lines. There was only the heavy sharp blue head and the big eyes and the clicking, thrusting all-swallowing jaws. But that was the location of the brain and the old man hit it. He hit it with his blood mushed hands driving a good harpoon with all his strength. He hit it without hope but with resolution and complete malignancy.

The shark swung over and the old man saw his eye was not alive and then he swung over once again, wrapping himself in two loops of the rope. The old man knew that he was dead but the shark would not accept it. Then, on his back, with his tail lashing and his jaws clicking, the shark plowed over the water as a speedboat does. The water was white where his tail beat it and three-quarters of his body was clear above the water when the rope came taut, shivered, and then snapped. The shark lay quietly for a little while on the surface and the old man watched him. Then he went down very slowly.

"He took about forty pounds," the old man said aloud. He took my harpoon too and all the rope, he thought, and now my fish bleeds again and there will be others.

He did not like to look at the fish anymore since he had been mutilated. When the fish had been hit it was as though he himself were hit.

But I killed the shark that hit my fish, he thought. And he was the biggest *dentuso* that I have ever seen. And God knows that I have seen big ones.

It was too good to last, he thought. I wish it had been a dream now and that I had never hooked the fish and was alone in bed on the newspapers.

"But man is not made for defeat," he said. "A man can be destroyed but not defeated." I am sorry that I killed the fish though, he thought. Now the bad time is coming and I do not even have the harpoon. The *dentuso* is cruel and able and strong and intelligent. But I was more intelligent than he was. Perhaps not, he thought. Perhaps I was only better armed.

"Don't think, old man," he said aloud. "Sail on this course and take it when it comes."

But I must think, he thought. Because it is all I have left. That and baseball. I wonder how the great DiMaggio would have liked the way I hit him in the brain? It was no great thing, he thought. Any man could do it. But do you think my hands were as great a handicap as the bone spurs? I cannot know. I never had anything wrong with my heel except the time the sting ray stung it when I stepped on him when swimming and paralyzed the lower leg and made the unbearable pain.

"Think about something cheerful, old man," he said. "Every minute now you are closer to home. You sail lighter for the loss of forty pounds."

He knew quite well the pattern of what could happen when he reached the inner part of the current. But there was nothing to be done now.

"Yes there is," he said aloud. "I can lash my knife to the butt of one of the oars."

So he did that with the tiller under his arm and the sheet of the sail under his foot.

"Now," he said. "I am still an old man. But I am not un-armed."

The breeze was fresh now and he sailed on well. He watched only the forward part of the fish and some of his hope returned.

It is silly not to hope, he thought. Besides I believe it is a sin. Do not think about sin, he thought. There are enough problems now without sin. Also I have no understanding of it.

I have no understanding of it and I am not sure that I believe in it. Perhaps it was a sin to kill the fish. I suppose it was even though I did it to keep me alive and feed many people. But then everything is a sin. Do not think about sin. It is much too late for that and there are people who are paid to do it. Let them think about it. You were born to be a fisherman as the fish was born to be a fish. San Pedro was a fisherman as was the father of the great DiMaggio.

But he liked to think about all things that he was involved in and since there was nothing to read and he did not have a radio, he thought much and he kept on thinking about sin. You did not kill the fish only to keep alive and to sell for food, he thought. You killed him for pride and because you are a fisherman. You loved him when he was alive and you loved him after. If you love him, it is not a sin to kill him. Or is it more?

"You think too much, old man," he said aloud.

But you enjoyed killing the *dentuso*, he thought. He lives on the live fish as you do. He is not a scavenger nor just a moving appetite as some sharks are. He is beautiful and noble and knows no fear of anything.

"I killed him in self-defense," the old man said aloud. "And I killed him well."

Besides, he thought, everything kills everything else in some way. Fishing kills me exactly as it keeps me alive. The boy keeps me alive, he thought. I must not deceive myself too much.

He leaned over the side and pulled loose a piece of the meat of the fish where the shark had cut him. He chewed it and noted its quality and its good taste. It was firm and juicy, like meat, but it was not red. There was no stringiness in it and he knew that it would bring the highest price in the market. But there was no way to keep its scent out of the water and the old man knew that a very bad time was coming.

The breeze was steady. It had backed a little further into the north-east and he knew that meant that it would not fall off. The old man looked ahead of him but he could see no sails nor could he see the hull nor the smoke of any ship. There were only the flying fish that went up from his bow sailing away to either side and the yellow patches of gulf-weed. He could not even see a bird.

He had sailed for two hours, resting in the stern and sometimes chewing a bit of the meat from the marlin, trying to rest and to be strong, when he saw the first of the two sharks.

"Ay," he said aloud. There is no translation for this word and perhaps it is just a noise such as a man might make, involuntarily, feeling the nail go through his hands and into the wood.

"Galanos," he said aloud. He had seen the second fin now coming up behind the first and had identified them as shovel-nosed sharks by the brown, triangular fin and the sweeping movements of the tail. They had the scent and were excited and in the stupidity of their great hunger they were losing and finding the scent in their excitement. But they were closing all the time.

The old man made the sheet fast and jammed the tiller. Then he took up the oar with the knife lashed to it. He lifted it as lightly as he could because his hands rebelled at the pain. Then he opened and closed them on it lightly to loosen them. He closed them firmly so they would take the pain now and would not flinch and watched the sharks come. He could see their wide, flattened, shovel-pointed heads now and their white-tipped wide pectoral fins. They were hateful sharks, bad smelling, scavengers as well as killers, and when they were hungry they would bite at an oar or the rudder of a boat. It was these sharks that would cut the turtles' legs and flippers off when the turtles were asleep on the surface, and they would hit a man in the water, if they were hungry, even if the man had no smell of fish blood nor of fish slime on him.

"*Ay*," the old man said. "*Galanos*. Come on *Galanos*."

They came. But they did not come as the Mako had come. One turned and went out of sight under the skiff and the old man could feel the skiff shake as he jerked and pulled on the fish. The other watched the old man with his slitted yellow eyes and then came in fast with his half circle of jaws wide to hit the fish where he had already been bitten. The line showed clearly on the top of his brown head and back where the brain joined the spinal cord and the old man drove the knife on the oar into the juncture, withdrew it, and drove it in again into the shark's yellow cat-like eyes. The shark let go of the fish and slid down, swallowing what he had taken as he died.

The skiff was still shaking with the destruction the other shark was doing to the fish and the old man let go the sheet so that the skiff would swing broadside and bring the shark out from under. When he saw the shark he leaned over the side and punched at him. He hit only meat and the hide was set hard and he barely got the knife in. The blow hurt not only his hands but his shoulder too. But the shark came up fast with his head out and the old man hit him squarely in the center of his flat-topped head as his nose came out of water and lay against the fish. The old man withdrew the blade and punched the shark exactly in the same spot again. He still hung to the fish with his jaws hooked and the old man stabbed him in his left eye. The shark still hung there.

"No?" the old man said and he drove the blade between the vertebrae and the brain. It was an easy shot now and he felt the cartilage sever. The old man reversed the oar and put the blade between the shark's jaw to open them. He twisted the blade and as the shark slid loose he said, "Go on, *galano*. Slide down a mile deep. Go see your friend, or maybe it's your mother."

The old man wiped the blade of his knife and laid down the oar. Then he found the sheet and the sail filled and he brought the skiff onto her course.

"They must have taken a quarter of him and of the best meat," he said aloud. "I wish it were a dream and that I had never hooked him. I'm sorry about it, fish. It makes everything wrong." He stopped and he did not want to look at the fish now. Drained of blood and awash he looked the colour of the silver backing of a mirror and his stripes still showed.

"I shouldn't have gone out so far, fish," he said. "Neither for you nor for me. I'm sorry, fish."

Now, he said to himself. Look to the lashing on the knife and see if it has been cut. Then get your hand in order because there still is more to come.

"I wish I had a stone for the knife," the old man said after he had checked the lashing on the oar butt. "I should have brought a stone." You should have brought many things, he thought. But you did not bring them, old man. Now is no time to think of what you do not have. Think of what you can do with what there is.

"You give me much good counsel," he said aloud. "I'm tired of it."

He held the tiller under his arm and soaked both his hands in the water as the skiff drove forward.

"God knows how much that last one took," he said. "But she's much lighter now." He did not want to think of the mutilated under-side of the fish. He knew that each of the jerking bumps of the shark had been meat torn away and that the fish now made a trail for all sharks as wide as a highway through the sea.

He was a fish to keep a man all winter, he thought. Don't think of that. Just rest and try to get your hands in shape to defend what is left of him. The blood smell from my hands means nothing now with all that scent in the water. Besides they do not bleed much. There is nothing cut that means anything. The bleeding may keep the left from cramping.

What can I think of now? he thought. Nothing. I must think of nothing and wait for the next ones. I wish it had really been a dream, he thought. But who knows? It might have turned out well.

The next shark that came was a single shovel-nose. He came like a pig to the trough if a pig had a mouth so wide that you could put your head in it. The old man let him hit the fish and then drove the knife on the oar down into his brain. But the shark jerked backwards as he rolled and the knife blade snapped.

The old man settled himself to steer. He did not even watch the big shark sinking slowly in the water, showing first life-size, then small, then tiny. That always fascinated the old man. But he did not even watch it now.

"I have the gaff now," he said. "But it will do no good. I have the two oars and the tiller and the short club."

Now they have beaten me, he thought. I am too old to club sharks to death. But I will try it as long as I have the oars and the short club and the tiller.

He put his hands in the water again to soak them. It was getting late in the afternoon and he saw nothing but the sea and the sky. There was more wind in the sky than there had been, and soon he hoped that he would see land.

"You're tired, old man," he said. "You're tired inside."

The sharks did not hit him again until just before sunset.

The old man saw the brown fins coming along the wide trail the fish must make in the water. They were not even quartering on the scent. They were headed straight for the skiff swimming side by side.

He jammed the tiller, made the sheet fast and reached under the stern for the club. It was an oar handle from a broken oar sawed off to about two and a half feet in length. He could only use it effectively with one hand because of the grip of the handle and he took good hold of it with his right hand, flexing his hand on it, as he watched the sharks come. They were both *galanos*.

I must let the first one get a good hold and hit him on the point of the nose or straight across the top of the head, he thought.

The two sharks closed together and as he saw the one nearest him open his jaws and sink them into the silver side of the fish, he raised the club high and brought it down heavy and slamming onto the top of the shark's broad head. He felt the rubbery solidity as the club came down. But he felt the rigidity of bone too and he struck the shark once more hard across the point of the nose as he slid down from the fish.

The other shark had been in and out and now came in again with his jaws wide. The old man could see pieces of the meat of the fish spilling white from the corner of his jaws as he bumped the fish and closed his jaws. He swung at him and hit only the head and the shark looked at him and wrenched the meat loose. The old man swung the club down on him again as he slipped away to swallow and hit only the heavy solid rubberiness.

"Come on, *galano*," the old man said. "Come in again."

The shark came in a rush and the old man hit him as he shut his jaws. He hit him solidly and from as high up as he could raise the club. This time he felt the bone at the base of the brain and he hit him again in the same place while the shark tore the meat loose sluggishly and slid down from the fish.

The old man watched for him to come again but neither shark showed. Then he saw one on the surface swimming in circles. He did not see the fin of the other.

I could not expect to kill him, he thought. I could have in my time. But I have hurt them both badly and neither one can feel very good. If I could have used a bat with two hands I could have killed the first one surely. Even now, he thought.

He did not want to look at the fish. He knew that half of him had been destroyed. The sun had gone down while he had been in the fight with the sharks.

"It will be dark soon," he said. "Then I should see the glow of Havana. If I am too far to the eastward I will see the lights of one of the new beaches."

I cannot be too far out now, he thought. I hope no one has been too worried. There is only the boy to worry, of course. But I am sure he would have confidence. Many of the older fishermen will worry. Many others too, he thought. I live in a good town.

He could not talk to the fish anymore because the fish had been ruined too badly. Then something came into his head.

"Half fish," he said. "Fish that you were. I am sorry that I went too far out. I ruined us both. But we have killed many sharks, you and I, and ruined many others. How many did you ever kill, old fish? You do not have that spear on your head for nothing."

He liked to think of the fish and what he could do to a shark if he were swimming free. I should have chopped the bill off to fight them with, he thought. But there was no hatchet and then there was no knife.

But if I had, and could have lashed it to an oar butt, what a weapon. Then we might have fought them together. What will you do now if they come in the night? What can you do?

"Fight them," he said. "I'll fight them until I die."